THE STRUDLHOF STEPS

or, Melzer and the Depth of the Years

HEIMITO VON DODERER

Translated from the German by
VINCENT KLING

Afterword by
DANIEL KEHLMANN

NEW YORK REVIEW BOOKS

New York

THIS IS A NEW YORK REVIEW BOOK
PUBLISHED BY THE NEW YORK REVIEW OF BOOKS
435 Hudson Street, New York, NY 10014
www.nyrb.com

First published in the German language in 1951 by Biederstein Verlag.
Published here by arrangement with Verlag C.H.Beck oHG, Munich.

The translation of this book was supported by the Federal Ministry of Arts,
Culture, Civil Service, and Sports of the Republic of Austria; Department of
Literature, Publishing, and Libraries.

Library of Congress Cataloging-in-Publication Data
Names: Doderer, Heimito von, 1896–1966, author. | Kling, Vincent, 1942–
  translator. | Kehlmann, Daniel, 1975– other.
Title: The Strudlhof steps: the depth of the years / by Heimito von Doderer;
  translated by Vincent Kling; introduction by Daniel Kehlmann.
Other titles: Strudlhofstiege oder Melzer und die Tiefe der Jahre. English
Description: New York: New York Review Books, [2021] | Series: New York
  Review Books classics | Translated into English from German.
Identifiers: LCCN 2020047206 (print) | LCCN 2020047207 (ebook) |
  ISBN 9781681375274 (paperback) | ISBN 9781681375281 (ebook)
Classification: LCC PT2607.O3 S713 2021 (print) | LCC PT2607.O3 (ebook) |
  DDC 833/.914—dc23
LC record available at https://lccn.loc.gov/2020047206
LC ebook record available at https://lccn.loc.gov/2020047207

ISBN 978-1-68137-527-4
Available as an electronic book; ISBN 978-1-68137-528-1

Printed in the United States of America on acid-free paper.
10 9 8 7 6 5 4 3 2 1

NEW YORK REVIEW B(
CLASSICS

THE STRUDLHOF STEPS

HEIMITO VON DODERER (1896–1966) was born into a
wealthy Austrian family, the youngest of six children. His father
was an architect and engineer; his maternal grandfather a successful
building contractor in Germany; his ancestors included the poet
Nikolaus Lenau. Doderer studied law at the University of Vienna
before enlisting in the Austro-Hungarian Army and serving as a
dragoon in World War I. Taken prisoner by the Russians, he was
sent to Siberia, and it was in prison camp that he began to write.
Only in 1920 did he make his way back to Austria, and over the
course of the next decade he published a collection of poetry and a
novel, neither of which attracted attention, and earned a doctorate
in history. In 1933, Doderer joined the Nazi Party, outlawed at the
time in Austria, but his enthusiasm for National Socialism waned
with time, and in 1940, influenced by his reading of Thomas
Aquinas, he converted to Catholicism. Called up by the Wehr-
macht in 1940, Doderer was stationed in France, where he began
work on *The Strudlhof Steps*. Denazification prevented publication
of the book until 1951, but when it did come out it proved an
unexpected best seller, making its author a literary celebrity. *The
Demons*, a sequel of sorts to *The Strudlhof Steps*, came out in 1956,
and in 1963 Doderer published *The Waterfalls of Slunj*, the first
volume of a projected four-volume work called simply *Novel 7*,
after Beethoven's Seventh Symphony. The second volume, *The
Grenzwald*, was left unfinished at the time of his death.

VINCENT KLING is a translator and scholar of German literature
who teaches at La Salle University in Philadelphia, Pennsylvania. He

has translated fiction, poetry, and criticism by Heimito von Doderer, Heimrad Bäcker, Andreas Pittler, Gert Jonke, Gerhard Fritsch, Hugo von Hofmannsthal, and Aglaja Veteranyi. He was awarded the Schlegel-Tieck Prize in 2013 for his translation of Veteranyi's *Why the Child Is Cooking in the Polenta*. He has also published several essays on the craft of literary translation.

DANIEL KEHLMANN is a novelist, playwright, and screenwriter. His most recent novel, *Tyll*, was short-listed for the 2020 International Booker Prize. He lives in New York.

IN MEMORIAM
Johannis Th. Jæger
Senatoris Viennensis
Qui Scalam Construxit
Cuius Nomen Libello
Inscribitur

ON THE STRUDLHOF STEPS IN VIENNA

When the leaves upon the steps are lying,
from the old stairs is heard an autumn sighing
of all that's gone across them in the past.
A moon in which a couple, holding fast,
embraces, lightweight shoes and heavy footfall,
the mossed urn at the middle, in the wall,
survived the years between the wars and dying.

Much is now past and gone, to our dismay,
And beauty shows the frailest power to stay.

PART ONE

WHEN MARY K.'s husband, a man named Oscar, was still alive and she was still walking around on both her beautiful legs—the right one was severed above the knee on September 21, 1925, not far from her apartment, when a streetcar ran over it—a certain Dr. Negria turned up, a young Romanian physician undergoing further training at the well-known medical school here, as a resident at the Vienna General Hospital. These kinds of Romanians and Bulgarians have been around Vienna forever, mostly in the areas close to the university and the conservatory. They were a familiar feature, with their manner of speaking, which became gradually more infused with Austrian German; the thick shocks of hair over their foreheads; their fondness for always living in the choicest residential neighborhoods, since all of these young gentlemen from Bucharest or Sofia were well-to-do or had well-to-do fathers. They remained obvious foreigners (ones to whom immense packages filled with their delicious ethnic foods were constantly being shipped)—not so deep-dyed in their foreignness as North Germans, admittedly, but a more local kind of institution, as it were, and yet Balkaneers all the same, because they never lost that characteristic intonation of their speech. Viennese ladies who were thinking of renting out a room or two in their apartment or villa were always on the lookout for a "Bulgarian or Romanian student"; they could then be sure of having their names passed along, for in the numerous cafés around the university, or around the various clinics, cohesion among compatriots was the rule.

Dr. Negria took umbrage at Mary's marriage. He could not believe, he was purely and simply incapable of believing, that Mary's marital fidelity might have a solid basis. His irritation at her fidelity knew no bounds, and that irritation manifested itself at just about the same time as his first stirrings of desire. (The author Kajetan von S. would no doubt have written here, "He desired her out of abysmal malice"— and among people of his type there might really exist such basically innocent foolishness that becomes twisted in this bizarre way.) The vexing thing about the fishhook Dr. Negria had swallowed, though, was that this irreproachable woman's fidelity was not the least bit unconscious. She was not naive enough for that; her heart had become fully aware, as early as her girlhood days—even at fourteen, her feelings had been like those of a grown woman—of various layers. She had later unfolded each of those layers and maturely smoothed them out, doing so, moreover, on that level for the attainment of which all persons are responsible who do not travel their path in life between unbroken walls of innocence, a road with no vista, like the one that led from ancient Athens to Piraeus. That said, Mary had been a virgin when she entered into marriage with her Oscar. On the other hand, her faithfulness now was not a state that remained in effect owing merely to the emergence inside her of a stable equilibrium grounded in an irrevocable decision and to a conversion, if one will, to her duties as wife and mother—as the mother of two attractive children, a girl and a boy, the girl having reddish-blond hair like her father, the boy with dark, titian-red hair like his mother.

The whole matter presented itself to Dr. Negria (not to Mary) between the baselines just sketched, and the construction he chose to put upon this existing set of circumstances conformed by and large to reality. He slid a hot griddle underneath the situation, but this piece of cookware, though completely unable to resolve the built-in standoff, at least enabled him to keep his irritation sizzling.

There is a kind of fidelity that is nothing more than a hankering for superior character traits, a quality of greed which wants to preen itself in the forefront, no matter what title deeds it may already hold. This kind of fidelity, being merely meritorious in nature, as it were—although *meritum* also has a meaning connected with a person's just deserts— forms a handy little stairstep to haughtiness, and the person possessing it gets into the habit of ascending it with pleasure, as though to a seat in a bay window from which one can look down upon the ordinary people passing by on the street below. Fidelity of this kind is not stable in its equilibrium and does not really deserve its name; it does not merit it, for the simple reason that it is merely meritorious. Even so, it is given up only with a great struggle under certain circumstances, and when these circumstances accompany the person along the road through the years as invisible walls (ones that nonetheless blinker the view), as long walls, then there's never anything more to it than that pure abstraction called *meritum*.

That's what irked Dr. Negria, and he made it his firm resolve, strongly incorporating it into his whole being without the slightest bit of critical deliberation, to achieve a breakthrough here. And he was very much a breaker-through, through and through. A man with a challenging, now-see-here, arms-akimbo temperament, an interventionist, one who was always trying to shove aside quickly whatever bothered him and who indignantly regarded anything that tried to curb him as outrageous.

It was in connection with this "interventionism" that the doctor's name would later on assume the force of a proverb or a catchphrase in a closely related group; that is how there came into being the "Negria Organization," which ended up crowning its derring-do with a campaign against the Berlin automobile dealer Helmut Biese (this is all completely out of place here, though!), overseen by Höpfner, a verse-monger or poet of advertising jingles, who was personally acquainted with Mary's Romanian admirer, by the way. But with whom was Höpfner not acquainted? He was an address book, a complete one-man business and social topography of Vienna (a trait he shared with Cavalry Captain Eulenfeld, whose official rank was Rittmeister, or master of horse). During the crucial time, Dr. Negria—from time to time knocking back a glass of slivovitz with an abrupt gesture (and racing excitedly around the room between gulps)—had uttered the following up at Höpfner's: "I can't stand to think how the spider has her ensnared in his web." The spider was Oscar, Mary's husband. Sometimes Negria would also refer to him as "Oscar the Tick."

His relationship with the K. family had started on one of the tennis courts in the Augarten, that pale park from the age of Joseph II, and then had taken a more domestic turn through the childhood illnesses of the girl and boy; Negria was on assignment in the relevant department of the Vienna General Hospital and, oddly enough, had opted to become nothing other than a pediatrician. This Romanian enjoyed the esteem and respect of his illustrious department chief, so that the great man himself had once even made a house call for Mary, to examine the children in their sickroom. From that time on, Dr. Negria had started showing up for social visits. His way of ringing the doorbell was abrupt and sharp, sounding as if someone were breaking a window or kicking a soccer ball hard from the penalty zone into the net.

Mary had been sitting by the tea table, her gaze going out into the barely rising dusk of a late-summer evening. Here she could look down along the street and then over the Danube Canal (which isn't a canal at all, but a significant channel of the river, wide and deep, its current fast), to the bank. The sound of boys playing and calling out rose from the street to the fourth floor; that noise was heard every evening, a companion through the whole summer (or at least that part of it she hadn't spent in Pörtschach or Millstatt), a sound that welcomed her back on the evening she returned from the country as something that had dependably stayed behind, belonging to this time of year and certain to last for weeks longer, since it was staying warm, if more temperately so—the best kind of weather for tennis, Oscar said, "Indian summer." Oscar will be home in half an hour. Suddenly she thinks of Lieutenant Melzer. Back then, as a young girl, she had known for certain that he was pretty stupid. It had been in Ischl, must have been the summer of 1908 or 1909; around that time there had been some political tension with Serbia. Lieutenant Melzer's eventually decamping—taking his stupidity along with him—had, in a manner of speaking, canceled out that stupidity and with it her own superiority, even though she was not at all in the dark as to the circumstances of his retreat and his disappearance into some military post or other far away in Bosnia, where there were still bears, as he was forever reporting. He was eager to go on a bear hunt himself. "If you bring me the bearskin, Herr Melzer, I'll put it on the same way you've been putting me on." Fourteen years had passed since then, incidentally. On occasion, her father had mentioned in Ischl that Melzer would have to resign his commission if he wanted to marry her. Oh yes, he could have had her then, no doubt about it. He'd been a very nice young man, very nice indeed, unfailingly cheerful and courteous at all times. He hadn't a care in the world. She would have deceived him later on, and to this day she knew that too. Because of his being so even-tempered.

There was a taxi stand at the end of the street that Mary could see from her armchair. The taxis lined up in a long row on the cross street, left and right around the corner, so that off to the left the front part of one taxi and off to the right the rear part of a different taxi were always in view. Traffic regulations back then stipulated that the first taxi in the row always had to be the one taken; and since both the head and the foot of the column were fixed by definite bounds, each car moved up a space when the front one had driven off; the returning taxis then got back in line at the end. This arrangement resulted in the slow crossing over of one or more taxis from time to time; when they'd moved up, there would always be a taxi waiting to the right, of which not much more than the rear wheels could be seen, while on the left, one would move up to the corner, but only far enough to show its front end.

In Mary's mind the unvarying movement of the taxis there at the end of the street, like beads being strung, was one of the self-evident and yet unfathomable aspects of this apartment through all the years. It was a phenomenon related on the deepest level to the dripping of water from a faucet or to the falling beads of a rosary. And because it was a considerable distance down the street to the taxi stand and the canal beyond it, the purring of the engines was totally inaudible when the windows were shut. The phenomenon was noiseless, and that constituted its essence; it was noiseless, altogether unvarying, and calm; it was monumental in its dullness and monotony, and that was what made the connection now, in Mary's wandering thoughts, between the view from her window and her recollection of Lieutenant Melzer. She did have to admit, though, that he'd had the sweetest way of laughing. Dr. Negria's ring at the bell fired some shooting stars into the picture, not so very different from the ones a man sees when he is punched in the eye. Negria seemed to be ringing with extra vigor today.

The maid opened the door, but he didn't just walk in. Instead, he launched an invasion, making a deep bow and kissing Mary's hand, already on the attack and leading the offensive; this impression stayed uppermost despite his deliberate adherence to the formalities, with proper hand-kissing and all due bowing and scraping. He looked all around the room, irately passing everything under his review, and had in a twinkling uttered a great many words soundlessly or had delivered himself of them in some fluid form. All right, then. Very well. Same old thing, I see. Still with that old Tick. Well, I'm just curious how much longer you'll be satisfied living like this. What a pointless existence anyway, missing out on life. Preconceptions are no more than a form of inertia, and inertia is a sin against life. An object with autonomous power of motion—a living being as opposed to a mere thing, that is—simply must not yield to inertia. I just don't believe you and the Tick are for real, anyway. Not one little bit! Out loud, teacup in hand, he was merely telling her that the Zerkovitz children had the chicken pox and that he had succeeded today for the first time in beating the Polish envoy (a Herr von Semski) in singles at the tennis club, even if the score was close. Apart from that, Dr. Negria looked, as Homer says of that unreliable dolt Ares, aglow with strength and health.

It's totally out of the question, of course, that the flash fire she had ignited would leave Mary herself unaffected. At the very least, she was forced to become more explicitly aware of her feminine powers, and that implied an invitation to a game, an activation of strength in free play. She wasn't the least bit afraid of Negria, for she considered him to be basically far stupider than that Lieutenant Melzer from her girlhood years.

Nor did she have any intention, not even the slightest, of turning off this high road that had already been paved, from which she was able to lower her gaze at any time down into the ravine of crushing circumstances and the waters of life, erratically coursing along, now gushing past huge boulders between which they'd been forced, now gathered in a deep, blue-green trout pool and rippling against the overhanging and hollowed-out walls of mysterious caves at its round edge. The glance downward did much good, and her contact with all that wildness—or with the small bit of it that had made its way up here and become domesticated, as it were—heightened her contentment while at the same time washing away the poison of contentment, boredom.

When Negria heard that Oscar would be coming home in half an hour, he blinked in peevish acceptance and more or less conveyed the feeling that he'd already assumed so and hadn't hoped for anything better. What could you expect from such an inane individual, after all?

Not that the inanity of any individual (any female of the species) had ever seriously hampered Dr. Negria, and so he soon opened up a new line of attack. For some time he had owned a rowboat, not built for sport and therefore wide enough for two, but a trim, elegant craft nonetheless. It lay above the city, in Nussdorf, near the branching off of the Danube Canal from the main river. Whenever Romanian or Serbian steamers with strings of barges came upriver, Negria, speaking his own language or Serbo-Croatian, knew exactly how to get them to throw him an extra line; in this way he could ride up to Greifenstein and Tulln, or even much farther, and could then just cruise back downriver in high spirits, never failing, before he untied the line, to toss a pack of Austrian cigarettes, along with many thank-yous, up onto the high deck of the boat that had taken him in tow. As time went by he came to make the acquaintance of the ships' crews and of this or that steamer captain, even on the canal, along which Negria had traveled as well, right through the heart of Vienna and all the way down to the Prater Point, as it is called, where the branch flows back into the mainstream below the city.

Along this course he would naturally have to pass very close to Mary's apartment, and so he formed the resolution of inviting her to go on a boat ride with him, before which they could have a glass of wine in Nussdorf, at one of those secluded little country taverns known as *Heurigen* that Negria seemed to know all about. He was quite aware that it was a question of hitting on a rubric for a rendezvous with her away from her home, and that was what he was aiming at first and foremost while at the same time preparing the ground further by occasionally remarking on little flaws in his comfortable bachelor apartment, which was in need of inspection by an expert eye (he also dropped casual references to some Romanian peasant embroidery and other antique pieces he'd collected in his homeland, and one time he brought an exquisite piece of this embroidery as a present for Mary).

While cruising down the canal, Negria had spotted a convenient place for tying up, and when he rowed over to the bank, there was even a ring, which allowed him to secure his boat with chain and lock. It was in the immediate vicinity of the taxi stand where the cars, crossing the street in their unvarying pattern, threaded their way through the years.

Oscar K. did come home in half an hour and was glad, in his quiet and not exactly transparent way, to find a guest present. He belonged to that type of person whose being has something concave about it, some suggestion of a curved mirror. One is always inclined to infer in such people the presence of inner focal points unless the opposite becomes evident. It's beyond doubt that anyone who keeps silent will hear and see a great deal. No one ever starts off by assuming, however, that this kind of restraint might betray nothing more than an astonishing lack of fire. It's one of those cardinal convictions held by everybody that still waters run deep; and to be sure, there's something unsettling about waters like these. Even so, people have been known to lean attentively over water no deeper than a handsbreadth only to see ordinary pebbles and nothing else at the bottom. The face of the man who was taking a seat at the tea table belongs to a rare category, examples of which are more readily found among Jewish men than among others, even though this kind of face represents the attainment of an altogether generic physiognomic possibility. It is a face that has not quite achieved cohesion, or, if one would rather, a face that is at once the display case and construction site of highly incompatible materials which had not managed to become unified in the forebears and which have now fallen into a state of crash and trash, as after an explosion. The result is that an extraordinary ugliness comes into being, a condition all the more acute for not revealing itself as bound to a splayed nose, a skewed jawline, a drooping eye, or any other single structural part, but for remaining in abeyance instead, for incorporating a little of each element, for being a cord (yes, that's exactly what it is!) hanging loose in midair, not tying disparate parts together and thus allowing the disharmony to persist. Such a face looks as if its owner were carrying a weight of atonement imposed on him for a transgression he knows nothing about.

Oscar certainly had an accurate assessment of the strengths and weaknesses of his present position, to the extent that one can speak of accuracy in the first place when dealing with the emotions, drifting and swirling like fog, that a person feels in situations like these. He thought he understood his wife, though, and better than she understood herself, at that. In this marriage, even with growing children and a period of living together going on fourteen years, the nights were still a pivot; set in place in the dark, it caused the daylight hours to rotate around it and held the cycle of the day in subjection. Here, at the inmost core of his life's condition, Oscar had observed some tremors whose aftershocks—felt in broad daylight and indeed belonging to the myriad small contingencies of daytime—struck him as necessary and self-evident. The heightened passion to which his wife had been surrendering for some time now, and its inevitable reciprocal effect on him, and then in turn back on her—resulting in the bestowal by both parties of ever more lavish tributes upon the god Eros—created a crackling aura around her, which could have been overlooked only by a totally obtuse person but never by any man whose desire was, as it were, already drawing long sparks, difficult to hide, from her wrists, her temples, her shoulders, and the hem of her skirt. She knew that, of course, and she would tone down her allure, on the one hand, by completely suppressing all flirtatious behavior and by clouding the issue a hundredfold simply through the fluidity she exuded; on the other hand and at the same time, she would be rubbing salt into an open wound with her decorum—a wound from which, acting on her very secure power of judgment, she firmly withheld any attention whatever.

Aside from that, she emphasized nothing. She did not, for example, play up for Negria's benefit the qualities that made her marital happiness remarkably complete. This little gathering at the tea table was not thrown into disorder by displays of any kind. Any such thing was at so far a remove, in fact, that the group managed to hold a pleasant conversation; by and large, Negria rather enjoyed conversing with Oscar, the "spider," the "tick," and would never have felt he was acting smarmy or two-faced when they talked. It can be said that he had a relatively high tolerance for the man, reviling him up at Höpfner's place, all right, but without the torments integral to jealousy—and by saying it, it seems to us that Mary's disparaging way of looking at the nature of that particular wound appears all but corroborated.

All these fine spiderwebs—finer even than the gossamer that once again would soon be brushing ethereally against their cheeks—were manifest and evident to the spider, the very reason being that he was a spider. But in the Augarten, on the tennis courts, under a sun suffusing the air and mingling with water vapor rising from the Danube to turn the air milky and mild—so that, with the fruit-like taste of autumn in your mouth, you could feel the passing of time almost as a thing of the senses, because it slowed down and nearly stood still—in the Augarten, even after duplicating the experiment repeatedly, Oscar achieved a result, in broad daylight and in the outside world, that unsettled him almost as much as did the tremors around the pivot in the inmost core of his life's sphere. This result had reference merely to a little routine he and his wife had worked up as a joke—or now, actually, to the absence of this routine, or even, it seemed, to the impossibility of reviving it, although it was a familiar joke they'd been playing since the time of their engagement. They had a habit—which they especially enjoyed after a game of tennis—of appearing to start a quarrel with one another, getting everyone present to react in some way (whether it was that people intervened or shrank back in dismay), and then abruptly marching off, arm in arm, tenderly and in complete happiness. It now became apparent, though, that Mary had been wanting no part of this game for quite some time.

A few remarks could be made about such a game, of course. At least the following: they were the exhibition of something self-evident, namely of the concord between a married couple.

Her children had gone to school, her husband to his office, and Mary to her bath. While she relaxed in the hot water in the tub, nonchalantly observing her body, its impact in abeyance here under the bluish water, among tiled walls and nickel-plated faucets, a knock came at the door like a shot one sees being fired but whose report one does not hear. Mary retreated from the flowing watercourse of her reveries and her quarter- or half-thoughts and told her faithful Marie, who was always looking after her, that she did not want to have breakfast here but instead at the tea table.

The living room was cozier in winter, when the large coal stove, built in the form of a fireplace, spread its glow evenly through the isinglass panes. At this time of year there was a certain palpable emptiness, though the tea table stood in the same place winter and summer. Mary had shut the window overlooking the long street down to the canal so as to keep dust from flying in and settling on the polished furniture, but the warm late-summer morning outside was leaning against the panes even so, a friendly and soft openness of all the surroundings, lightly tinged with water vapor and still milky and misty from the early morning on the canal; weather with much space, an open cavern of expectation, and in the middle of these surroundings, which diffused into muffled form the sounds of city life, Mary was now sitting over her teacup; that was the main feature of her breakfast, since the rest was measured out with great frugality. No, she was not to be numbered among those figures who, bad conscience or not, consumed mounds of whipped cream in that large café farther along the Danube Canal which has grown more familiar to the few readers of a handwritten chronicle (of which more later) prepared by Sectional Councillor Geyrenhoff.

It's clear to see that the apartment belonging to the K.s must have had the same floor plan as the Siebenscheins' right underneath. All the rooms lay along an axis—four large rooms and a small one, resulting in a view that wasn't bad at all, except for the unusually outsize bedroom (a drawing room at the Siebenscheins') and a small room of modest dimensions (Dr. S.'s study downstairs). The K.s' apartment was very large, then ("is to be regarded as very large"—this is how Senior Councillor Julius Zihal of the Central Bureau of Revenue and Tariff Computation would have expressed it in his systemized bureaucratic jargon); indeed, Dr. Siebenschein had found space for his legal office, complete with waiting room, in the apartment downstairs; and yet there was only one person more here at the K.s' (since Titi Siebenschein's wedding, that is—until then there had been four people on the lower floor as well).

The silence, polished like furniture, was now interrupted by Mary's light clattering. What she had set on display at the bottom of a serving bowl here—as if being presented on a shell, so to speak—was the circumstance of her having no plans at all for the day, which was rare for her. Furthermore, the day had even made room, yielding to her in a well-nigh calculated manner: Oscar was scheduled to have lunch with business friends in town, and the children had been invited to visit relatives at their villa in Döbling, a house with splendidly beautiful grounds, where they would eat right after school and spend the rest of the afternoon. It belonged to the owner of a large brewery. The K. children were considered well-mannered companions whom people were glad to see spending time with their own boys and girls; and both children really were a cut above average.

There remained only the boat ride with Negria. Mary as good as had an appointment with him for the early afternoon in Nussdorf. And then it would be over too late to play tennis. Oscar, for his part, had now taken to waiting on the courts only until six o'clock at the latest; he would go there on tennis days in late summer directly from the office after a short afternoon rest.

She was keeping herself free today, declining, with a smile, to look upon her arrangements with Negria as binding. He could just as well go on his ride alone; then he would inevitably tie up—or "make fast," to be correctly nautical—here at the canal and stop to see where she had been. He would just push his way into the room past Marie.

Mary laughed.

Just then the taxis started to move. One after the other they threaded across the street. The last car, whose rear wheels remained in sight, was still shaking a little, as was the first one, only its front wheels and hood visible. With that, all the soundless motion froze back into stillness.

But all the tensely waiting demonism, fragile as glass, of her slumbering surroundings did not, of course, come to Mary's consciousness under any such name. As a woman, though, she had enough depth, if not of spirit then surely of gut, to sense her state of exposure in the present, which was standing about her on all sides, upright on a tray, as it were, a small disc brightly reflecting the sun's rays while wending its way between the twin darknesses of past and future. A glance at her small gold wristwatch told her she'd been sitting here by the nearly empty teapot for an unusually long time. Nothing around her moved, and she kept still as well. By now, a good hour had passed since she'd sat down at the breakfast table and thought of Lieutenant Melzer, among other things.

Something of the brittleness of life was in her today, as an awareness and an attribute at the same time; she knew now how lightly all things leap, for she had it in her very limbs, this fragility, this Bologna-bottle quality of each good hour, which falls away and turns to dust. She wanted to touch nothing today. Behavior quite untypical for her; as a rule she was forever moving things or putting them to rights.

Which is just what she should have been doing now. She realized it when the taut silence shattered and a new situation leapt out of her with clinking and clattering. At exactly the same instant, she realized it in the way she stood up; a movement not decided by her head, but one running up her body like an ascending ripple, a totally unanticipated, arbitrary act on the part of her knees and legs, managing, with the motion still only half-complete, to take the red earthenware teapot along, the little slivers of bamboo wrapped around its handle catching the fringe of a silk shawl Mary was wearing over her shoulders, whereupon the cup too fell to the floor and the whole tray, along with the silver sugar bowl, slid and teetered on the verge of the same possibility. The muddle, calmed as a result, yielded this: cup and saucer lay on the floor, apparently unbroken; the spoon had flown far off to the side; on Mary's dress there was not a drop of the tea dregs from the pot—so the darkly steeped tea had found no opportunity to create a lasting effect here, but it still kept trying, for the pot hanging from the fringe of Mary's silk shawl was tipped in such a way that the dark liquid almost reached the edge. Mary saw all this. At the same time she heard from the entryway the sound of a key being turned in a lock from outside the apartment, and so she called out, without moving, and remaining bent as far forward as she could in order to hold her strange wrap away from herself, "Marie! Marie!" There ensued a rush to the scene, a startled look, a burst of laughter, a careful release, and finally, an outcome surely peculiar—nothing was broken, nothing was stained, nothing was damaged.

For now, however, the substance of life in Mary was not about to pay any heed whatever to a proclamation made so jestingly; it refused, even though it was a genuine proclamation that had been issued. This was the real reason why Mary didn't go for a walk in beautiful Liechtenstein Park this morning, even though she had just been thinking at the breakfast table about how she would like to, considering all the free time at her disposal. Meanwhile, she no longer wanted to risk it. Now, if this thought had entered her mind consciously and in words, she would probably have gone after all, out of a spirit of levelheaded contrariness. But it did not reach that point. She stayed at home, not from any reluctance or timorousness in her mind, but because of some restraint in her limbs.

Anyway, it was pleasant here at home. Her well-managed household surrounded her and pervaded her from all sides. It was a sensibly run house, where nothing was wasted but also where there was no economizing in the wrong places when a solid yield of comfort could be achieved with a small outlay. For instance, the five-o'clock tea table, a charming glass cart, always featured coffee and tea alike, whichever they were in the mood for, as well as butter, jam, and black and white rolls; by this time, too, Mary was able to rely on the children to be careful, so a lovely tea service remained in everyday use. People turning up unexpectedly got the feeling that special preparations had been made for their visit. Consider, too, whether these little extras don't pay off handsomely on this or that occasion. (Oscar considered such things.)

These were bright people. They lived with their minds open in every direction; therefore, they heard and saw things, and they didn't close themselves off from what they saw and heard, so there were no (as in certain other families, very different ones) knotted and tangled balls of yarn in dark and guarded corners. So Grete Siebenschein liked to stop by for a minute occasionally; she often confided in Mary and was quite open to the older woman's opinion and advice and listened to her attentively.

The obvious thing for Mary to do on this free morning was just to go and quietly take a seat at the piano. Under Grete's coaching she had been working on three Chopin études and some Schumann in the course of the past year.

So there she sits at the piano, this woman, quite lonely, really, since the morning began, and she sets the silver meditations resounding. Everything around her arranges itself, an order comes into this loneliness, and one could almost believe that this order might be capable of radiating outward, all the way into the chaotic mass of the surrounding city, or at least of subduing the nearby demons through the orphic power of music.

It is possible to give someone advice about the most basic things, but such advice can almost never be heeded. After all, if a situation has reached the point at which advice on this level is required, then usually some gear or cog has already worked loose in the mechanism, and the person caught in it gazes transfixed into this malfunctioning machinery of life, now purposefully illuminated from within. Life now seems to depend upon this machinery, rather than the other way around, which would be the normal state of things. For that reason, any advice given at this point cannot pertain to anything but the mechanism itself—only a fresh, objective approach to which could reveal its merely relative importance—and so the person giving the advice is compelled to stick to tidbits of advice, advicelets, little jogs about the little cogs, which are whirling madly because they've been shaken almost loose from the whole. A little piece of advice, a tweak. Dilatory or palliative tactics. With a great deal of variety, depending on the situation—as its finished products, and not as just one small wave from unchanging springs located at the base level. Then even the advice giver has lost a sense of direction, to say nothing of control of the steering wheel itself.

Mary hadn't had much else to offer Grete Siebenschein since the summer of 1921, meaning since the end of Grete's half-hearted engagement to little E.P. and the beginning of her relationship with René Stangeler. Mary knew the first fiancé, because Grete had brought him by once or twice; the second one she had seen—but only that—on the stairs or on the street with Grete, and taking everything she found out about him from Grete, along with what Grete's not infrequent state of near despair told her, he seemed to Mary the man perfectly suited to guarantee her young friend complete unhappiness.

Still, at the point where we are now stopping, which is in the late summer of 1923, Grete Siebenschein had already passed her twenty-ninth birthday.

No, that René, who was about the same age as Grete, did not appeal to Mary, and she had no desire to make his acquaintance—as if she were still privately hoping that this relationship would dissolve within a foreseeable time; as if she no longer wanted to function as a linchpin through the force of her personality. Enough that Stangeler had already been coming and going for some time at the Siebenscheins' and that the weight of familiarity was already starting to bear down gradually on Grete and her lover, pressing them ever closer together, as it were. No—she really didn't care for him. His eyes were somewhat aslant, and his cheekbones were in some way Magyar- or Gypsy-like. One time she had seen him down on the square in front of the train station, apparently waiting for Grete; he was lounging against the base of the street clock, legs crossed, hands in his pockets, hat pushed back on his head. Just like that, right out on the street. There was a challenge in his bearing, an air that didn't strike Mary as casual and natural, but as overemphasized. It was ludicrous, unsound, not likely to inspire much trust. Why, her own boy, at that time a youngster in the lower grades of his preparatory school, would never have lolled around like that, and this fellow was close to thirty. Besides, he was supposed to be from a good family, into the bargain. A grown man. By the time her husband was twenty-eight he'd been a breadwinner who had held down a responsible position for years. They said Stangeler was still pursuing his studies—plausibly, granted, because of his military service and his four years as a prisoner of war. But after that, he might have been expected to take up something sensible and useful without delay. Well, let people do what they do best (Mary was not at all narrow-minded in the ordinary sense!), but his behavior toward Grete should have been entirely different from the very start. Meanwhile, everything else could be left open to discussion—whether to get married now or to wait; whether to choose a practical profession or to continue with his degree program, and all the rest.

Everything was really that little E.P.'s fault.

He was the one who had brought Grete and René Stangeler together.

At least that was how it looked to Mary, for in all of her deliberations and cogitations on this subject, one point she'd never taken into account and wasn't taking into account even yet, something she'd never thought through—not with the proper emphasis, at any rate—was the altogether indisputable fact that Grete had never loved little E.P. And precisely this fact was what lay out in plain view. A blind spot for Mary. Had she loved her Oscar? Yes—no. She loved him now. It struck her that this had just come about on its own, without having been an essential prerequisite. And in the deepest part of herself she didn't see anything decisive about that, anything that could be confronted head-on or that needed to be faced up to directly. Not a predestining force, but a predestined one. A contingent entity that could be tossed into the equation over time or that would do its own tossing later, meaning that it could never serve as a point of departure for logical thought or decisive action. (This is roughly how it would sound if we were to voice what Mary carried with her on this subject as a set of totally self-evident ideas, no longer recognizing them as peculiar to herself alone.)

Nonetheless, it was just as possible to take it to mean that the inclination going by the name of love pure and simple—life's prime number, needing no factoring and accessible to none—did not exist on the part of Grete (whose feelings were entirely different) as it did that little E.P. had made a mistake, which presents itself in this light, however, as no such thing after all. Otherwise Grete would not have left him after the war to travel abroad for ages on end, no matter how pressing the need might have seemed. And that would have been because her father, Dr. Ferry Siebenschein, must be classed among the kind of people who are capable of carrying their integrity to such lengths that their families starve in the process. It had almost come to that pass in the time right after the war or, for that matter, even before 1918. His case might very well stand alone among the owners of thriving legal firms at that time in Vienna; after all, the members of this profession were the very ones who always managed, thanks to the numerous connections they inevitably forged through their activities, to obtain basic necessities, make discreet exchanges of favors, and conduct under-the-table dealings harmless in themselves, and they were able to do so, if not month by month, then at least week by week. Our good doctor,

Grete's father, proved almost monstrously untalented in all these wheel-ings and dealings, much as if he were a ram with an undeflectable preference for the path of greatest resistance. For this reason, among others, Grete loved her father very much. The mother of the Sieben-schein family, on the other hand, was always recovering from one kind of ailment only to be seized by another and different kind, which re-quired nothing in particular to be happening in her world to bring it on, since this adroit little lady was fiendishly resourceful when it came to fabricating illnesses. But should her productivity begin to ebb, the most unusual events would occur to fill in the gap: she would break or sprain some small extremity, a toe on her left foot or the ring finger of her right hand, thereby demonstrating an understanding, even in the intermissions between her big production numbers—insomnia, swell-ings, shivering fits, or simply, to use the words of Johann Nestroy, "churning with burning"—of how to keep the family spotlight trained on herself. Dr. Siebenschein's not being a physician made matters easier, allowing each new pathological episode to emerge in full vigor. It's well known that physicians act as cold as icicles toward such nui-sances, and Chief Medical Councillor Schedik, whose patient Frau Siebenschein did not become until much later, by the way—not until 1927—was accustomed, whenever he met a member of the family, to asking not, "How is Mama?" but instead, quite offhandedly, "And what is ailing Mama now?" It was possible, after all, for a completely new array of symptoms to have emerged since her last visit to his examining room just two days earlier. Schedik, who had not a few patients of this type, treated them with the greatest success on a purely psychological basis, steering almost entirely clear of any regimen of treatments or series of prescriptions, doing so without any of these individuals ever posing the question to anyone of how being treated by Chief Medical Councillor Schedik always caused them to recover so quickly, and so many times each year, from the most assorted maladies, which had set in one right after another. They considered him an extraordinary doc-tor. And indeed he was. An outstanding father-in-law, besides—sad to say, of the previously mentioned Herr Kajetan von S. One of his profes-sors at the university, who knew Dr. Schedik, had remarked to Kajetan, casually but pensively, after his divorce, "You know, Herr von S., you can get along without your wife if you really have to, but that father-in-law of yours represents an irreplaceable loss."

Not long after the First World War, our Grete (ebony black hair and classically symmetrical features) parted from the Siebenschein father, from the mother, and from her younger sister, Titi (a twig that was even then revealing the inclination of the growing tree to bend); not the least reason was to take some of the burden off the family provider, even if he didn't want any of it removed. Surely, though, her mother's periodical and pathological calendar of festal observances constituted another driving impulse, one that the retarding force of E.P. could not muster enough weight to counterbalance.

And so off Grete went to Norway. Countries that had remained neutral in the war were admitting young Austrian ladies.

She fought the good fight there, giving it her all, and as a result her personality emerged for the first time in its fuller dimensions. The unique and the differentiated in her being came to the fore, since that being was measuring itself against an unfamiliar but comparatively straightforward environment. She proved equal to the occasion, which may mean all the more considering that she had gone from a destitute and ruined country to a relatively prosperous and well-governed one. A quite general danger of becoming déclassé there in a foreign country threatened each day to deteriorate into a specific, personal state, espe-cially because Grete wasn't able to remain situated on a consistent and thoroughgoing basis inside the profession, class, and style within which she had originally come out or come up, which was as a trained musi-cian (a graduate of the conservatory in Vienna). She couldn't stick purely to teaching, though, since opportunities were not exactly offered thick and fast and the leisure to wait and choose was even less forth-coming. So Grete played dance music in a resort hotel too. Free room and board, low pay. She sat at the piano, and the ladies and gentlemen (or whatever they were) chatted and danced. In northern countries, as long as people don't drink, the surface of manners and appearance is more evenly smoothed out; the furrows and wrinkles that separate social classes are not as apparent right away to a foreigner from the south. If, in addition, if mastery of the language has not been achieved yet, or only imperfectly so, then the directional signs are missing that point to good breeding, a quality which, barely tangible though it may be, constitutes a liquid poured out on an international scale, not unlike the gravy served in the dining cars of big express trains, which after some time strikes the diner as suspiciously the same between Biarritz and Paris, Bregenz and Vienna, Manchuria and Vladivostok, such that the passenger might stumble onto the preposterous notion that it was being transmitted by a system of pneumatic tubes running alongside the tracks. The same goes for breeding. But no one who speaks only a few words of Norwegian can assay a sample in Holmenkollen. Even so, Grete was soon drawn into the social life there; they would put just anybody in her place at the piano, and that person could play just anything in just any old way (still not such a ticklish point there, at least not then). It turned out that Grete was able to produce a more direct effect by means of her own person than through her pianistic resources, which were occasionally given a real chance in a Viennese waltz, perhaps, but which were otherwise pounded away in the kinds of foxtrots and shimmies that ruled all dancing back then. Granted, she was well dressed, in a style that hadn't quite established itself there and that was intimately bound up, both in the individual details and in the total ensemble, with her native city as well. Furthermore, it forms a decisive note in the opening chord of any person's entire life if that person hails from a famous place known to everybody in the whole wide world. Paris or Vienna provide a special significance and an effortless contrasting background for attractive women; a man won't be entirely unconcerned, either, as to whether the person comes from Paris or Landes-de-Bussac, Vienna or Gross-Gerungs, Moscow or Kansk-Yeniseysk.

Grete Siebenschein was drawn into the social life, then, but not entirely without a helping hand from herself. In Oslo (which back then still hadn't been called that for very long), at the home of a dentist where she'd been giving piano lessons for some time, they'd advised her against getting involved with this job at the resort hotel; the word was that only shifty types, or con artists, as we tend to say here in Vienna, patronized the place. One of the dentist's patients, though, had presented the matter to her as a sort of oh-live-a-little change of pace. And Grete, being a young person, really wasn't afraid of anything or anybody. She was brave and honest, and not overly tormented by imagination, otherwise usually a weak point in brave people. In addition, something dwelled inside her that could be described as an impulse for research work. Whenever she was abroad—later on, as well—she would always see a great deal and make no fuss about her own likes and dislikes. Perhaps these were weak too. She adapted right away. Very soon her shoes were no longer carrying so much as a pinch of soil from her homeland. A limited imagination promotes failure of the memory, because there are no luminous and scarcely touched places back there in one's past, no votive altars of a private religion, so to speak, nor small hooks in the heart attached to lines reaching far back, such that any connection at all in the imagination, or anything that one happens to see, can exercise a gentle tug. That way is not conducive to objectivity. Grete was very objective and only occasionally sentimental; she was fully aware of the latter and, as a protection, kept open a narrow marginal gap of irony between herself and her feelings. Her temperament was akin to that of an eighteenth-century lady—she loved nothing more than *esprit*, and a measure of it was inherent in her—and so she very often actually looked like one. The clear, at times almost sharply penetrating eye, the long neck, the delicate slenderness of a woman not in the least emaciated (*fausse maigre*, the French call it): looking at her, one would not seldom be reminded of Countess Lieven, the wife of the Russian ambassador in London, known as La Maigre Lieven, the mistress for two decades of imperial chancellor Klemens von Metternich, except that the countess had been a blond. Along with all the other scholarly drivel he'd crammed into his head at the university— lashed on by a ravenous craving—René Stangeler was also a devotee of Austrian history, so of course he knew everything there was to know about La Lieven and in fact had even had to present a lengthy seminar paper on her. He carefully avoided ever telling Grete anything about this notable personality, although she certainly would have taken a lively interest. "I didn't want" (this was how he once put it to Kajetan later) "to bring this archetype of hers directly to her attention." That's understandable. He didn't exactly have it easy, either.

Now then, we said earlier, "They would put just anybody in her place at the piano" and "She was drawn into the social life." In the beginning, however, she herself did the putting (of someone else at the piano, that is), and it was not so much that she was drawn into the social life as that she herself took the initiative of entering into it. By doing so, she was deliberately performing a very characteristic action and at the same time executing one of the many counter-maneuvers against the threat of becoming déclassé, maneuvers that were a constant accompaniment to her Norwegian years (or that even dominated those years, to a great extent), just as it's necessary to continue treading water ceaselessly to remain upright in a standing position at the surface. All her life, in fact, Grete kept busy treading water in this sense, and her high-strung sensitivity toward the family of Herr Nose-in-the-Air René was explained by this trait of hers. At this juncture, in the resort hotel, though, it was only a matter of saving face for her to fit in as part of that social group (or whatever it was), and not just as the barroom "artiste," the tickleress of the ivories banished to total exile at the keyboard. Because men promptly began asking her to dance, and because she did so with complete grace, she found herself in a position to accept a second invitation following right after the first, then to turn down a third by alluding to the somewhat too much neglected piano, and finally to retreat back to the keyboard, contented and genuinely lighter in heart.

Nonetheless, these rational, evenly distributed ways and means (people like yours truly probably would have flailed away at the baby grand for five hours, banging out quicksteps without giving a damn about anybody or anything else) were, as so often with Grete, thwarted by eruptions of a totally different kind. For suddenly, in the space of just a few minutes, she had fallen head over heels in love.

Such things could befall her lightly and quickly, and the first of these adverbs must also be understood as a designation of weight; it's not that she was about to be crushed, but just that she was feeling tremendously rushed. The marginal gap stayed open nonetheless. A certain amount of reserve guaranteed. This deep-seated aspect of her makeup—we'd almost like to say "as if by virtue of her long neck she still felt herself capable of surveying the situation"—permitted Grete to go very far and still preserve undiminished the elemental authenticity of the sensations she felt. This is a pattern that would repeat itself constantly during the first two or three years of her relationship with René Stangeler, who, intimidated by Grete's individuality and enmeshed in boundless admiration, believed in a theatrically generous way that the thing to do was to shrug it off. But the stones he was purporting to swallow effortlessly lay indigestible in his psychological stomach, so to speak, and his heroic gesture came down in the end to the pettiness of paying her back in kind. How unfortunate for Grete Siebenschein, coming at the very moment when the well maintained marginal gap seemed to be trying to close—if not completely, then nearly so.

Just now, however, back at the piano, she got her first good look at someone she had already seen in passing but about whom she knew nothing except who he was, a man enjoying a sort of minor fame in Norway at the time. The Norwegians occasionally strike us as an almost Hellenic people; and even if that which has been called Nordic ugliness not seldom comes crawling out of deep old shafts, still the faces and figures of people in that country quite often, and seemingly as a matter of course, achieve a significant—to a foreigner, staggering—degree of perfection. This particular man was among the most dashing, a big name in all different sports, and rich to boot, so that in Paris and London he'd entirely smoothed off his last provincial rough edges. Grete sniffed all this out at once, and the marginal gap grew appreciably narrower, especially when she came back out from behind the piano after half an hour and danced with him—a man who had traveled widely (even in the Himalayas) and who, being the acknowledged center of the social circle there, apparently considered it a duty proper to one of his station to look after the foreigner. Moreover, with her blue-black hair she created an exotic, southern impression, though not a disconcerting one. The austere structure of her face, together with its flawlessly white skin, was closely related in many ways, beyond all contrasts in ethnic features, to a physiognomic type often encountered here.

What now ensued is a vocalization, each of whose many little trills and vibratos we're not interested in itemizing. The demigod, who conversed with Grete in French (spoken quite fluently by both parties), lost little time in taking advantage of this situation and others like it, and when the gathering had broken up, they went for a moonlight walk by themselves. The snow lay deep. Without further ado our avia-tor captain—this he had been during the World War, serving in the British army with dash and distinction—led Grete Siebenschein along a stretch of railroad track that ran just behind the hotel and was covered with a kind of wooden tunnel as a protection against snowdrifts. We may assume she was led willingly. Their conversation soon grew so animated that the little piece of jewelry she was wearing fell off un-noticed into the snow. But because he was meeting with determined and tough resistance, he put a stop to his forthright manner of speak-ing, as if cut off, and brusquely remarked that there could be only two reasons for such a decided refusal: either virginity (which she denied) or a certain physical condition prevailing at the moment (which she confirmed). This statement of his pleased Grete Siebenschein so well, however, that a complete understanding was arrived at, albeit with a slight postponement as to time. Suddenly, as he led her along the packed snow near the entrance to one of the tunnels or protective roofs—its black mouth stood like velvet in the white and star-clear night and swallowed the faintly glistening ribbons of the rails as if cutting them off—she noticed her missing jewelry. He helped her look, even though doing so seemed quite futile in the snow. But extraordinarily enough, not thirty paces from where they were and after only a few minutes, they found it lying in one place and glistening faintly on the snow cover. This sacrifice had not been accepted, then, and the ring of Poly-crates came back, as it were.

The smoking room and billiard room of the hotel had a concealed side door that opened onto the corridor almost exactly opposite Grete Siebenschein's room. In these surroundings, which were frequented almost exclusively by men, Grete's demigod could linger till all hours of the night, since there was always some drinking bout or card party in progress, and the *pjolter* served up so bountifully (we would call this a punch, but one for bears) took the clarity out of everything and threw a fog over all vigilance. Through the concealed door, across the corridor, and into her room. It may be that the captain had allowed himself other escapades of the same kind besides this one with Grete. On the third night of these carryings-on he found her up and at the table. She directed him to a chair. "Now we're going to speak plain German," she said (he was versed in this language too). So she said, "Now we're going to speak plain German," and the new resonance between them changed everything with real sovereignty, worlds away though the captain might have been from grasping the actual import of an expression in which "plain" has the meaning of "blunt" and "German" is used to mean the same thing as "germane"; perhaps he understood it to mean simply that she wanted to speak that language now. He sat down in the chair and said nothing. The room was rather cool; the heat was shut off, Grete was still completely dressed, and the wide bed, made of light birch wood, was not turned down.

"You will," continued Grete, while her neck lengthened out over the situation and the vitreous humor of her eyes appeared more transparent, "dance with me in the bar tomorrow evening and converse with me as well. Anything else is over and done with right now. I propose to keep my doors locked. The way you approach just wanting to get something started with the piano player is unfamiliar to me from Vienna and is not at all suitable. If, however, you should wish to visit me later on in Oslo—I'm going back the day after tomorrow—I have no objection."

She then gave him the telephone number of that dentist mentioned earlier. He left without saying anything, even though her whole act was really a bit too much; he might have been justified in saying something to her, looking back, for example, at the way he had reached a complete understanding with her a few days ago, near the snow tunnels, where the glittering night and the faintly shimmering rails had been swallowed by velvet, while not far away the snow had held the modest pieces of jewelry on its surface, facing the sky—a gold bracelet and pendant with a broken chain and an earring with a little screw, because Grete's ears weren't pierced. However, the captain said nothing; he left and went on to do as he'd been told. Only he never did call Grete in Oslo. She thought it possible that he might not have been able to get through, because she had forgotten to write down on the slip of paper a kind of prefix required at that time for reaching a number in Oslo. In any case, Grete was quite ready to assume that the demigod simply didn't want to be bothered with her anymore; that was what she said herself when she told Kajetan von S. (the right address!) her story. That was eight years later. Stangeler, who knew all about this part of Grete's biography and thought highly of it (!), felt that pain for her which she was not capable of feeling because of how ruthlessly she judged herself. Jealousy, too (but toward Kajetan, whom he had just come to know, and only because things like these had been told to him).

Even the most passionate of our Grete's affairs were illuminated by an incandescence of consciousness like this, and it may be amusing to note that she would often, later on, take René to task for the same kind of inner bearing, an attitude he could never genuinely have managed (lacking a sufficiently long neck) but which he, on occasion only, affected to be maintaining, so as quickly and heroically to throttle some individual instance of jealousy, and in so doing enacting a cultic ritual before the altars of Grete Siebenschein's idiosyncrasies. He who strikes and holds a pose for too long, though, will be grasped by it sooner or later, as by a handle, and will be taken at his word, though it is one he has been forever saying without really meaning. Makes no difference—he loses his balance outwardly and falls behind his word into the tumult of objects. What's more, exactly the same thing can happen to him inwardly. After all, new prosthetic limbs like these grow in both directions—outward and inward—when they've been strapped on.

As for Grete, though, we have to vindicate her to at least this extent: she was precisely the opposite of what's called a dizzy female. This, however, was exactly what seems to have induced in Herr Nose-in-the-Air René, over whose head we will see in the further course of events (to use the words of Johann Nestroy) suspiciously long ears sprouting, a state of boundless awe, and it was arising from that awe in turn that the rest of Grete's components, attractions, and weapons took on to a degree an aura of something hallowed.

Grete's long sojourn in Norway elapsed amid such constantly renewed countermaneuvers, of which we have offered a small sample here. She had short and abrupt affairs, but also some that were longer lasting. She got herself into situations that were amusing and dubious (as we've seen), but also some that were better—and boring.

Once in a while she would write to little E.P. His answers were what are called half-pound letters. Later on she even sent him some Norwegian kroner, which made quite an impressive statement in an Austrian currency that even then was beginning to fall rapidly. Coming from his background, he really wouldn't have had any need for them. But this little man, along with the rest of his family, had fallen on hard times, even though he still lived at home with his parents (Mary K. disapproved of this falling on hard times, as she did any and all brands of contrariness). Number 44 Porzellan Gasse in Vienna (it's still standing) is one half of a double structure made up of two adjacent identical buildings which together yield a symmetrical edifice—an imposing architectural style. The architect was named Miserovsky, or were there two brothers Miserovsky? Maybe they were twins; that would be most appropriate, after all. E.P.'s father—only a vague memory of that short, bald, Bohemian-looking gentleman remains—was an industrialist and owned textile mills in Smidary. (By the way, E.P. had lost both parents before his marriage, which took place in 1924, but he kept the apartment on Porzellan Gasse.) There was also a brother, but people hardly knew him in Vienna, because he kept busy in his father's mills. That is just what E.P. did not want to do. He was secretly on bad terms with them both, his father and his brother. This enmity and this family problem were a part of him, like his blue eyes, his dark, brownish skin, his hair of the same color, and perhaps as well his extreme allegiance to the emperor, republic or no.

When René Stangeler finally returned home from his prisoner-of-war camp in the summer of 1920, E.P. welcomed him back with a telegram fourteen lines long, which produced quite an impression at the country house of Stangeler's parents, to which the repatriated soldier had at once proceeded. It began with the words, "How splendid is the occasion of your return . . ." From then on, the half-pound letters to Norway always said something about René. That was how the ground was prepared.

And so things moved quickly when Grete came back in the spring of 1921. Between her arrival in Vienna and her joining forces with René Stangeler—which of course, in keeping with the disposition of little E.P., soon entailed his breaking with the new couple—only a few weeks passed. They were quite sufficient, nonetheless, for Grete Siebenschein to provide for her little ex-fiancé across the board. She secured a job for him with a large bank (the same one that was to collapse ten years later, though not through the machinations of a certain Levielle), and it was possible for her to do so because one of the directors was a friend of the Siebenschein family (Director Altschul, whom Levielle treated even more treacherously than his other victims; incidentally, his heavy-set blond wife, a good woman, was a regular patron, as was Frau Irma Siebenschein, of the same café into which Kajetan von S. was much later to drag Sectional Councillor Geyrenhoff from time to time so he could sing the praises of certain corpulent married couples, regulars there, in a manner that cried out for censorship and that was uncouth in other respects as well). Simultaneously with getting him this job—which finally made E.P. altogether independent from his family, and allowed him to continue living on Porzellan Gasse without being a burden—Grete indirectly helped the little one find his wife, too. He met her in the mortgage department of the Land Title Bank, where she worked as a shorthand typist. Her first name was Rosa, and she was later on, after marrying E.P. (as of 1924, then), called Frau Roserl. They both kept their jobs at the bank, which they would not necessarily have had to do. Come to think of it though, the factories in Smidary had gone to the brother, and the rest of the inheritance from his parents had not exactly been lucrative for E.P. either, even if it were not for the partly depressed value of the estate in the aftermath of the war. The large furnished apartment was pretty much all that was left to him.

After the break with Grete Siebenschein, E.P. never came to see Mary K. again, which seems understandable.

He and Stangeler had first spoken with each other in 1915, in a low little building at the entrance to a Slovakian village. Coming back from the drill field in the summertime, the men almost always rode past this building, almost always with a strong thirst. Nearby was a tavern sign that said BOR, SÖR, PALINKA (beer, wine, brandy), and then, farther on, there was a storage yard with a sign advertising concrete pipe and similar materials, which were also portrayed in picture form. These two advertising signs affected a man suffering from thirst in very sharply different ways; to be precise, the first one exercised an attraction, but the second, the one with the building materials—which could be seen, or else just envisioned, lying stacked out back in the blaze of the noonday sun—distinctly repelled. The men in the reserve officers' training school never stopped at this tavern; they never had occasion to, for they knew of closer and better places in the village once they dismounted. E.P. was standing by the window, because his squadron usually came marching back about a half hour earlier than the one René rode in, which was now going by at a walk. Stangeler, who was assigned to the left flank of a row of four, returned the salute and then waved from his saddle. E.P. drew his face into a little smile.

The whites of his eyes were not completely clear; in their almond-shaped pattern was a cloudiness which, oddly enough, was one of the features that added to his appeal. His small, stocky body, though sinewy and muscular, was predisposed to put on weight, and his body would have been a suitable place for it, we could say. The fat would have been appropriate, but unpleasantly so, especially around the throat and the back of the neck. E.P., had he in fact been fat, would have made actual some potential aspect of his physiognomy—not a very endearing one—that existed somewhere inside him. At that time, though, he was far too gaunt and too unhappy, forlorn, and in need of support—his feelings could be read in his eyes. His legs were somewhat too short, so that his small stature made him on horseback look more like a jockey than a future Austrian master of horse or cavalry officer; his appearance once got him into trouble, too, in spite of his eminently dashing horsemanship. There dwelt in him a droll originality as well as a very considerable charm of the same quality; in him the vanity of short men had taken the form of mordant self-irony. He was a thoroughly good man, an open book, a heart ready to share itself, but he was also not infrequently seized by wild outbursts of passion, which made him look like an enraged squirrel ready to pounce on its enemy and sink its teeth in. He once attacked Grete Siebenschein in this way and actually even tried to bite her in the neck—according to her story.

His parents' apartment on Porzellan Gasse, in most respects typical of an imposing luxury apartment of the 1880s, contained only one room that was not an impersonally well-appointed showplace like all the others, but that instead had distinct individual touches. It was

E.P.'s room; before a backdrop of conventional furnishings it pointed, as if with placards, toward the individual traces and arabesques of a highly specific life. This room, incidentally, would reverberate with a strangely hollow and lamenting sound, like an aeolian harp, whenever a streetcar would come swiftly whizzing past on the long street, which ran perfectly straight here; that was because one end of a strong transverse cable from which the transmission wires were suspended was anchored in the corner of the building right near little E.P.'s room. "Whenever I heard this sound later on, in anyone's apartment, anywhere at all," René said to Kajetan von S. in 1927, when he told him all these things, "E.P. would come back to my mind, and so would his room, with its garishly colored puppets, his books, his faintly clouded eyes, his forcefulness, his goodness, and his appeal."

This room was large, square, and mostly dark; as has already been noted, it was on the second floor, which had to be the case if the suspension equipment for the overhead streetcar wires was there.

In the entryway of this large apartment there was a telephone installed remarkably low; a person had to sit down in order to speak into it. Even so, this arrangement had been made for talking while standing up, thus for someone exceptionally short indeed, namely, E.P.'s mother—that's how tiny she was.

People seldom saw her. Every appearance by his relatives, by the way, would produce a kind of horror in E.P., which he did nothing to conceal. By those few who knew her well, the mother is remembered as a good, delicate, sad creature. It could be that the younger son hated his father because he thought his mother had been made unhappy by her husband.

Major Melzer (the former lieutenant) met E.P. and his wife in 1924, in a little restaurant where Melzer, a bachelor, also used to have dinner now and again; the place was not far from the doubled building, the Miserovsky Twins, on the same side of the street, only a little farther in toward the city. E.P. and his wife came here quite regularly on Saturday evenings, for Frau Roserl, who had to be in the mortgage department until one in the afternoon, like her husband, wanted to be exempt from her housewifely responsibilities on this one evening at the end of the week. The acquaintance was struck up with this quiet and modest married couple by the major—at that time already an official of the general director of the state tobacco administration, and likewise a resident of Porzellan Gasse—out of simple affinity, if not congeniality, and the situation was probably mutual as far as E.P. and his wife were concerned. They had once been seated at the same table when the place was crowded, and the rest just happened on its own. One is tempted to say that E.P. was in general inclined toward inclination, even before any specific object presented itself. Not long after their first meeting— some four or six weeks had passed in the meantime—E.P. asked his wife to invite the major for Sunday dinner. And this contact here in private surroundings—the large dining room with the palatial oak sideboard was still in use—worked out so well that a continuing association was established. The little man had possibly, as he imagined, found for the first time in Melzer, six years after the war and the collapse of the Hapsburg monarchy, the constituent parts, all correctly assembled, of what he had always pictured under the heading of ROYAL AND IMPERIAL OFFICER, perhaps, for that matter, without ever having encountered in external reality during the time of his own military service any full and complete counterpart to this inner image (with a single exception, that of Infantry Captain Sch., whom he in fact spoke about sometimes, by no means infrequently). In this way, then, a concept survived the demise of the thing itself and was made concrete for E.P. six years after that demise. Whenever something that dwells inside us approaches us from the outside all of a sudden, we are always highly gratified (that is true even in unpleasant cases as well, at least for a split second).

Not until a conversation that took place—or rather, that began, but would be continued at greater length sometime in the future—on August 22, 1925 (a Saturday), at the lower end of the Strudlhof Steps, did the major discover that E.P. knew René von Stangeler. (The Strudl- hof Steps in Vienna are a set of stairs connecting Boltzmann Gasse— named for the great mathematician only after the republic was founded in 1918—with Liechtenstein Strasse and making up the middle segment of Strudlhof Gasse.) It was only then that René began to arouse interest in the major's mind, we could say, and so the images of the prep-school boy and his parents' home preserved in Melzer's recollections became overlaid with some kind of connection that seemed to want to establish itself between him and the now adult (at least as years go) René. The two images infused each other at once. E.P. and Melzer did a great deal of talking about René on that evening of August 22, 1925, and that was the source from which arose a partially mistaken notion of the major's, one in which he would afterward stubbornly persist because it owed its existence to a strikingly direct impression.

Specifically, Melzer believed that René had exercised an overly dominant influence on the little man, one that had conspicuously re-mained in force after the break between the two. And *conspicuously* may be just the right word, since it lay on the surface—in expressions, turns of phrase, even outright quotations. But what E.P. had for his part left behind with Stangeler was something of a more enduring kind—his way of being. It penetrated deep into René, deeper even than the aeolian tone in the corner room when the streetcar would whiz by below. The evening-like smokiness of this little man's being, the cloud-iness of his almond-shaped eyes, which his heart seemed to have been placed directly behind, such that it could pierce the veil with a ray of extraordinary warmth. This aura of evening, so suited to evenings in winter. "I'll come around dusk," he had always said to Grete, never stating a definite time. E.P. had lived through only a single winter with Stangeler after the war, though, the winter of 1920 to 1921. Grete came home from Norway in May, and then everything was soon at an end, consisting of nothing but faits accomplis that no longer tolerated any dusk among them but that stepped out into the light of day in hex-agonal, cubic, or some other crystallized form ("crystallized race of men," says Mephistopheles at some point). These were influences, then, that went deeper than turns of phrase. The tone, the soundless aeolian one, not the audible one. The glance.

And in addition to what was overtly manifest there were other detectable remnants and vestiges—we only need to investigate! So all right, then, let's investigate.

René Stangeler had grown out of the habit of wearing suspenders since those days. Let this one example stand in for them all—surely it's trivial and handy enough. We leave traces of ourselves on one another. They don't always have to be scars from saber duels. Since those days, then, he no longer owned any (René—suspenders). There follows the not very far-fetched conclusion that E.P. possessed more chic than the other (René), more innate basic style; stronger elemental health, so to speak; and a deeper, less easily threatened sense of well-being (all his unhappiness notwithstanding). René simply imitated E.P.'s casting aside of suspenders and never wore them again himself, neither with evening dress nor with the regional outfit featuring lederhosen (even though they're an essential element of that style!); he never even owned any again, for that matter. He threw out the ones he owned at the time—that was an action with a purpose, for he meant by it to improve himself and build himself up. He threw the suspenders out. He couldn't just leave them hanging in his wardrobe, somewhere off in a corner (all this according to Kajetan von S., to whom it was told in detail).

To wean a man away from wearing suspenders is an influence, no question about it, or even an encroachment, a permanent groove in the wax disc. When Stangeler took off his suit jacket ten years later, he would find traces of E.P. on his upper body—not a scar from a saber cut (nor a scar from a bite, either), but that his suspenders were missing. That fact brought with it a whole series of changes in his dress and habits: he was more likely to remove his jacket than he had been earlier (but still never again appeared before a woman in shirtsleeves and suspenders); he began omitting a vest and from then on rarely ever wore one at all; he had his trousers made with the waist cut lower to the hip and with buckles at the sides. This is only a rough idea of what can be inferred, using simple common sense, from a man's ceasing to wear suspenders. No doubt there are also changes in the way he carries his upper body, in the way he breathes; and then there are further changes yet, some as barely discernible as hairline cracks, as grooves in the disc; some that have already dissipated along the nerve paths and become anonymous, changes in one's whole outlook on life—without suspenders.

It would have been difficult to try conveying and elucidating to Major Melzer the comparatively epoch-making nature of such an influence. He'd never worn them, after all (suspenders); he'd always worn a plain belt instead. People have to go through every experience for themselves, or else they don't understand a thing.

But to make a long story short: along with leaving aside suspenders went a kind of attitude which E.P.'s influence roused from its latent to its overt phase in René at that time.

It seems quite conceivable that René's bearing when he was lounging against the base of the street clock in front of Franz Josef Station might have been different in some way without that E.P.-esque influence. And perhaps he would have been less dislikable to Mary K. At any rate, he was already out of the habit by that time.

What do you wear to a boating party? Mary asked herself after lunch, which her faithful Marie had taken special pains to prepare for her today, since for once the menu did not need to consider the man of the house or the larger appetite of the children. Accordingly, there was less, but the selection was choice—a cup of bouillon, a morsel of freshly broiled goose liver, a sweetbread. With her coffee Mary drank a small glass of Malaga—she had just had Giesshübler with lunch—and afterward she smoked a cigarette, her only one of the day, incidentally. So now, what *do* you wear to a boating party?

She blew smoke onto the tray and laughed, and yet she couldn't help realizing that to get involved in a situation means having to devote oneself to every one of its little details as well, which demands a kind of humility, we could almost say, that was often far from the motivating force when the decision was being made to go ahead. In Mary's case, though, her sense of irony was able to remain in place above the situation in the form of an unexpected loophole, one that permitted her to withhold actual acceptance of said situation (as if she would let herself get really and truly involved in the first place) and to keep rolling it along in front of her like a ball instead—or, for those who insist on being disagreeably hairsplitting about it—to keep shoving it forward; after all, a glimpse at any summer spent in Millstatt or Pörtschach was enough to make it clear that white was required for an outing on water, just as it would never do to board a sailboat in anything but tennis shoes.

It wasn't long before Mary was standing ready in the entryway, enveloped in the supporting cloud of her spruce appearance, so to speak, in a new fleece jacket, white, over a tennis shirt, which became her excellently. Then she went down the staircase, with its relatively slender newel, circling around and around the built-in elevator, carrying herself, every hair in place and every detail perfect, through the high, echoing gateway and past the porter's lodge (this building, like so many in Vienna, dates from the Gründerzeit, or Gilded Age, as it is called, and its builder and original owner, Herr Doro Stein—a renowned owner of racing stables, by the way—had set great store by the entrance, designed for his carriage and the acoustical statement its resounding echoes would make); passing the concierge, then, who was looking out from the porter's lodge and waving, Mary stepped up to the smaller doorway set in the wide front gates, pushed it open—the automatic door catch stuck a little—and was now standing on the sidewalk, amazed, in the middle of a genuine summer day that had meantime reached peak perfection despite the waning season, and that instantly folded Mary in its embrace.

The square in front of the Bohemia Station, officially known as the Franz Josef Station, had even then grown over time to be a kind of converging place for the streetcar lines (like the Piazza del Duomo in Milan), with a myriad of trolleys coming and going here—what a hubbub of conveyances crisscrossing from every which way, brakes squealing and bells clanging, abruptly turning off onto side streets or zooming away straight ahead and across the bridge. Mary stood on the shore of this sea of traffic, in which the red and white streetcars were the most unassuming vehicles and the profusion of delivery trucks the most formidable, while threading their way through them all was the endless chain of taxis pulling up to the departure end of the rather unimpressive and old-fashioned station or moving out from behind the arrival end: Mary stood on the shore, and the summer day holding her in its embrace was not so much delighting as disconcerting her, putting her on her guard, so to speak. She stood on the edge of the sidewalk, as wide as a boulevard here, balancing there like a person hovering at the edge of a swimming pool but not really feeling the urge to take the usual headlong plunge today.

The stop at which she would need to board the streetcar for Nussdorf could only be reached in those days by crossing the square to the left on a diagonal, where a traffic island offered rest and safety. A trolley with two cars had just come around the corner, and now, ringing its bell with a quick clang-clang unmistakably directed at Mary, it pivoted on its wide red front and gathered speed as it turned into the long, straight stretch of Porzellan Gasse, where it would go whizzing past the Miserovsky Twins and produce its aeolian sound in one particular room. Little E.P. wasn't at home, though, not at that hour. He was sitting in the accounting department at the bank, totally wrapped up in deliberations about whether or not to get married. His future wife was sitting in the next room. She was wearing a dark red blouse and working at an adding machine with that measured degree of attention peculiar to all women who work in offices—not too much, holding back a bit to keep from tiring quickly, but still attentive enough to avoid errors and the resulting inconveniences, such as the obligation to do the whole job over. Down below, on Teinfalt Strasse, a horn beeped. Both E.P. and his future wife, glancing out their windows at just about the same time, became aware of the summer day that had folded Mary in its embrace when she left her building. They thought about the Vienna Woods. E.P. looked out somewhat slantwise, and the yellow in the whites of his eyes intensified the melancholy of his face.

Having already started to cross the square, Mary stepped back onto the sidewalk.

She balked inwardly, we might say. She looked out, as if at some fairly brazen piece of audacity, at the ceaseless, bewildering movement of vehicles driving and people walking that filled every inch of the broad square; she didn't want to step into it, and nobody could make her. With no debate at all—which, given a personality like Mary's, would ordinarily have brought a rebuttal in its wake at once and started a whole polemic—she slowly turned around and strolled back along the sidewalk the way she had come, walking past her own gateway; continuing across the bridge, she turned right along the canal and, pleased like someone who has found a lost or misplaced object, was filled with contentment as she made her way toward the Augarten. During no step of this entire operation would her body have needed to have its head attached; that part remained anonymous and thus was able to steer Mary along with great success.

The scent of fruit wafted toward her from the vending stands spread out all around here, as they do everywhere in Vienna about this time of year, flooding the city with peaches, pears, and grapes, so that everybody winds up feeling more or less obligated to walk around carrying a little paper bag wherever they go, whether they want to or not. Mary stopped now too, and—after tasting a little sample held out to her—bought some white pears and some muscat grapes. Walking along, Mary began to eat some of the grapes, for it was deserted here along the canal and so she wasn't self-conscious; her fingers reached gingerly into the bag. She felt superior in some way. Perhaps, on the deepest level, superior to Lieutenant Melzer, and for the first time.

Soon the park came into view, stretching roughly along a straight line in the sunlight and the calm of the wind, so a visitor might have thought it was warmer here than on the street. Palais Augarten stood in the background, flat like a stage set and somewhat blinding under the blue sky. She presently caught sight of her husband dashing up to the net on the clay surface of one of the courts. Apparently it was a hard-driving game; on the other side of the net was Herr von Semski. Mary grew irritated—without her head attached, so to speak, her irritation purely organic—but very slightly and only for a second, at Oscar, who had gone to his game all rested and unflustered after a short afternoon nap in the office, whereas she...she'd had nothing but trouble (and now she thought of the teapot dangling from her neck). What's more, he had to be playing Semski, against whom he could do nothing but lose. Negria represented a completely different class of player.

Meanwhile, Mary had reached the courts. Semski, a short man with a head somewhat too large for his height, was sweating profusely as he smashed the ball time after time hard over the net, but as good as his stroke was, including his backhand, he didn't understand how to place the ball with the same degree of skill; being a diplomat, he really should have been able to do that better. In general, Oscar was holding his own—all that practice this summer had sharpened his ability, for they'd played incessantly in Millstatt, too—and so Herr von Semski could not force his opponent down to defeat except by chipping away little by little, as it were (some time back the same strategy had worked well against Negria, incidentally). During a break, Oscar waved to his wife with his left arm raised and cried, "Mitzi, Mitzi" (that's what he called her). Mary went into the locker room to take her racket out of its press.

Embassy Councillor Semski was a Pole who spoke the Viennese German current in the high society of those days. Semski was the son of a Polish nobleman; his father had been on the staff of the diplomatic corps during the time of the empire, and the son, whose name was Stephan, had likewise entered the corps as a young man, starting out, of course, in the Foreign Ministry on Ballhaus Platz after the usual period of studying law—without a doctorate, which was how they did it then—and the usual one-year course in "international law" and other such things, which we smile to think about today. So this Semski was really a Viennese whose Polishness had gotten lost somewhere in parts unknown; he remained versed in the language, however, from periods of his childhood spent with relatives at their estates in Galicia and from later visits there. At any rate, in view of how tiny Austria had become after the collapse of the empire in 1918, Herr Stephan von Semski was better able to advance his career in the newly reestablished independent nation of Poland, which was what had induced him to opt for that country. He stayed for several years at the ministry in Warsaw and finally found a way of landing in Vienna, on Allee Gasse—now called Argentinier Strasse—in the building that houses the Polish embassy, with its wide entrance, its imposing staircase in dark wood, and its garden, not having much width along the side but running deep toward the back.

We might ask what this gentleman thought he was doing by belonging to a thoroughly middle-class club, and the question is rather awkward for the narrator, since it forces him to give a stupid answer ("Cherchez la femme"). In a word, our Semski had a bone to gnaw on here, and that's why he'd taken membership in the Augarten Tennis Club.

Semski was a bachelor. The root causes (he was no longer conscious, or at best barely conscious, of them) lay back in the time before the First World War, that is, before 1914. There'd been a scandal in connection with a Fräulein Ingrid Schmeller, whom Herr von Semski afterward hadn't been able to marry (though he'd very much wanted to), because he'd been given the boot by Herr Schmeller. I'm saying "a scandal" because something comes up in the story about a bathroom, namely the one in the Schmellers' house. During a fairly large social gathering one evening, a garden party late in the summer, a certain Fräulein Pastré came walking into this room at precisely the wrong moment (she had it all planned out), even though Asta von Stangeler—the olive-skinned youngest sister of our friend René—had posted herself as a sentry; however, she wasn't familiar enough with the layout of the Schmeller house, and besides, the arrangement of the rooms on this floor, the one above the rooms used for entertaining, was entirely different, so little Fräulein Pastré was able, at once evasively and invasively, we could say, to reach the door, which the trysting parties would not quite have dared to lock, after all.

Neither frivolous (unduly reductive) nor emotional (unduly expansive) standards and explanations are applicable here; or rather, the frivolous and the emotional are both applicable, and both at the same time. This hadn't been some adventure undertaken by a swashbuckling cavalier, but then again, perhaps that's exactly what it had been after all, when looked at objectively, and it could even be called *mesquin*. A kiss at the wrong time, nothing more. Herr von Semski paid for it, though, paid for not having been able to build his happiness on the bedrock of patience, for allowing his enthrallment to scuttle the next installment of cunning forethought required not just in the lower echelons of life but equally essential for a military commander or an artist to engage with his *daimonion*. So should Eros, a god, rest content with less punctilious observances?

Mary came out of the locker room with her racket. The game between Semski and Oscar was still in progress. Mary stood at the edge of the court, watching with irritation. At the same time, she felt that this irritation had a deeper cause than she was capable of grasping; it came gushing out of her like water out of a fountain. What's the sense of playing this way? Sports are meant to be pleasurable, whereas the veins were bulging on Oscar's forehead. Semski had to be under a great strain too, by the way; his large head was completely soaked. And so those two men went dashing about on the clay, as Homer might say in a summary formula. They came for Mary now, since she was going to play doubles.

She was in for some surprises. On the opposing side was a married couple of about her age, and for her partner she had a Frau Sandroch, ash-blond, fortyish, an ethnic German from Russia or some such place, an elegant, dissipated-looking woman who always seemed to have something dry and somehow dusty about her. This Frau Sandroch (no one had ever seen a Herr Sandroch at the club) was a far better player than any of the other three on the court. And today, furthermore, Mary's arms were made of glass, and her joints felt as if they were made of wood. Even before the game started, she wanted just suddenly to walk off the court. She was convinced that she wouldn't be able to hit even the simplest serve. It might have been better that way, too, for the match was an ordeal! Frau Sandroch played in silence, setting the pace in a casual, very nonchalant style; she played her opponent right into the ground. She excused herself and left after twenty minutes, and Oscar, who'd meanwhile been enjoying a break, came back to take her place—whereupon Mary's irritation flummoxed her completely. The path was barred that could have directed this irritation toward Frau Sandroch; after all, she'd asked right at the start to be allowed to play even though she had only a little time and would have to leave the court in the middle of the game—so she and Oscar, then, must have made arrangements for him to take her place. Mary knew all that. She also knew that Oscar would not overexert himself in this situation. And so it was, in fact. As much as possible, he left every ball to her—and she missed every one.

After Frau Sandroch left, then, the K. couple soon started falling behind, which Mary thought was unnecessary.

She began pushing herself, making a hard job of it. It didn't help much. Nor did it exactly help when, after a short time, she saw Frau Sandroch—who must have really rushed through her shower!—walking past in the background with Herr von Semski in front of some close-cropped, practically gray plots of grass that had a dry and almost dusty look, oppressed as they were by the sunlight of the advancing afternoon. Frau Sandroch was wearing a jacket that shone in brilliant electric blue, and Semski had on a summer suit with hat and walking stick. They were ambling along slowly before the open prospect; in the background could be seen just a few rows of trees and some houses in the adjoining section of the city, but quite indistinctly, only in outline. This couple struck Mary like something presenting itself, as it were (pro-menade in its literal meaning)—like a traveling stage set, a platform, a theatrical tableau. And just what might they have in mind right now? Joining forces, anyway, that much was certain. Perhaps they were going to get a bite to eat together. Mary stepped suddenly into the picture she'd made up and began walking around inside it in place of Frau Sandroch; some demand on her part was insisting that she act this way, at least today. She could have had all that.

"You've got to help me out!" she called in an aside to Oscar. "All right, Mitzi," Oscar said, smiling. It was just now his turn to serve. He started off strong and continued that way, placed the ball, ran up toward the net, and their score began to improve. But then he slacked off again, and Mary, for her part, was really all thumbs today, a bumbling extra. To all the other participants and observers, Oscar's abruptly animated game had made a surprising and perhaps even embarrassing contrast with his behavior during the rest of the set.

The K.s were beaten, of course; the other couple won handily but not headily, so to speak. Mary hurried off to the locker room at once, not thinking even remotely of playing another match today. In fact, it seemed to her at the moment that she would soon give up playing altogether at this rate. She ducked into the shower and then took a fresh sport shirt out of her locker. While she was putting her wristwatch back on—for some reason the little clasp was resisting and didn't want to snap shut—she grew seriously irritated at her husband. When she came back out, he had already changed and was standing, in his summer suit, by the benches near the courts, a briefcase under his arm and his soft, lightweight Borsalino hat pushed back on his head. Mary cast a backward glance across the park; Semski and Frau Sandroch had vanished. "Mitzi, we've been trounced, annihilated, slaughtered; we've disgraced ourselves," cried Oscar gleefully when he spotted his wife.

The way he spoke these words, he was virtually flaunting how narrow the margin of Semski's victory over him had been today, at least as Mary saw it. "It didn't have to be like that," she said, somewhat uncertain, and then, "all I need now is for you to say it's my fault." "Not at all," said the male partner from the married couple they'd played—he was an attorney who was very well known in Vienna at that time—"no one would dream of stating any such thing." "Why not? I'll state it flat out," Oscar said. "That's outrageous, and you know it," Mary cried, the charmingly pretty, slender bridge of her nose now looking as if it were being shattered by miniature bolts of lightning; "The only one who could have turned that match around was you!" "You did play below your strength, Herr K., there's no doubting that," said the lawyer soothingly, uneasy at seeing what appeared to be a marital flare-up igniting here. "I was just tired," Oscar replied offhandedly.

"But then you suddenly got your form back after all!" Mary cried out in a totally adamant tone that could not help catching the attention even of people who knew nothing at all about this match and hadn't witnessed a minute of it. "Either you play or you don't play; but to go up against weaker players and patronize them, deigning to take a few strokes here and there, and then make it so obvious..."

Herr Adler (that was the name of the attorney who had played against the K.s, along with his wife) had joined them in the meantime, and now Mary was practicing a kind of demagoguery, looking for adherents in her dispute with Oscar, even if her overt recruitment (of her own person as well, to be sure) to the ranks of the weaker players would not be demagogically very advantageous to her. Oscar K. was a sight to behold, though—he seemed to feel that today was a real red-letter day, and those disparate facial features of his achieved nothing short of unity in the smile he flashed while getting in another dig, so as to prolong the argument with his wife.

"If I'd kept taking strokes away from you, that wouldn't have been right, either."

"Of course not," she burst out, "but you might have done a better job of taking care of your own!"

"Mitzi," he said, "I didn't do a thing except follow your lead—that's what I do all the time anyway. You know that."

This heated exchange had taken Mary to a place where she did not want to go; it gushed out of her like water out of a fountain, or rather, this bickering wriggled its way out of her like pigeons and rabbits and guinea pigs out of a magician's top hat—and now those little beasties were scuttling all over the place; guinea pigs of every species had come tumbling out! But Oscar, who now took Mary's arm so affectionately and said goodbye to the group by smiling and waving backward to them at the same time, was holding out to her a large piece of wrapping paper or a cloth or a container into which every one of these accursed, swarming creatures could be made to disappear all neat and tidy, all of it a great joke. Now he was really and truly turning the match around! She was suddenly full of gratitude and allowed herself in her innermost being to sink into his sheltering arms while she walked away, leaning on him and snuggling against him. Yes, some tapering little flame inside her was leaping up past the usual boundary of their old joke; she planted a quick kiss on her husband's cheek as they walked along. Finally they both turned once again, laughing, and waved to the people standing by the courts, who waved a farewell back. Then Oscar and Mary turned off behind a row of trees and a pavilion. So they went on their way; or not, for they soon came to a standstill and embraced, here where it was secluded. They pressed closer and kissed passionately, as if each wanted to intoxicate the other. Something fits in perfectly right here and so it has to be said right now—Mary, according to her own statement, was holding two thoughts fast in her mind during this scene: the first was that she was sorry she was wearing only that white fleece jacket instead of a wrap or sweater in a bright color, something that would have seemed more stylish to her; and the second was that she was thinking back to 1910 and picturing the newly constructed Strudlhof Steps in the Alsergrund district, where her husband, whom she'd married such a short time prior, had kissed her all of a sudden on a warm evening in autumn when there was the scent of leaves on the stone stairs.

Dr. Negria, meanwhile, had become trapped inside a double-edged barricade, as an officer of the Royal and Imperial Austrian General

Staff once expressed it in regard to a similar situation. The cause was an explosion that had just taken place in the large café on Nussdorfer Platz where he was waiting for Mary. It was totally silent and totally specific, affecting Negria alone. By now either you've guessed or you haven't: a woman was sitting there, a woman who, as she sat there, looked to Negria like a gate standing open to the fulfillment of all his wishes.

Now he began to fear that this gate might be slammed shut at any moment, whether it be that the object of his rapidly awakening instinct for a breakthrough did not remain sitting alone much longer (even the appearance of a female friend would have foiled his campaign, his intervention, and it was possible, or even highly probable, that in this café she would indeed be expecting a female friend, frequented as the place was by ladies and by families), or whether it be that Mary's arrival and appearance occurred promptly at the time they'd arranged. He had fifteen minutes left.

Nothing on the face of the earth could have kept a man like Negria from swinging into action. Yes indeed, things had to be done without delay, and so they were.

Some Eros in a cheery mood, whom we might picture as rosy-cheeked and plumpish in the baroque style (almost like a Gambrinus, then, and armed, though if not with the classic bow and quiver, then perhaps with a cannon instead, albeit the proverbial one used for shooting at sparrows, that is), some celestial little rascal along these lines, appeared to be running the show here and steering everything toward the end result from the very start. To begin with, the two tables were close together, favorably situated, and screened by a corner from the rest of the spacious room; above all, though, a fluid contact had been made at once, the only kind that really counts. She was leafing through fashion magazines. Negria was leafing too. By this time Mary was a full ten minutes late, and the present soundless preliminaries had progressed to the point that Negria—making sure to be observed in the process—was able to scrawl a few lines on one of his calling cards, slip it inside a newspaper, and then exchange it for one that was lying there on the table where his new prospect was sitting, for which he received, in answer to his curt little bow, an equally formal consent (the patrons of any café in Vienna pester one another unrelentingly for the different newspapers and magazines). He watched her slowly pick up the paper after a few moments and skim the card; the mechanism would have to catch now. And it did. She looked up, squarely meeting Dr. Negria's waiting, submissive glance, and gave a scarcely noticeable nod of her head in acknowledgment.

Our pediatrician friend was no bungler, after all, and he was conservative about using the techniques he'd polished to such a high degree of smoothness through diligent practice. For example, here is what the card said:

Boris Nicolaus Negria, MD, Assisting Physician at Pediatric Clinic No. 2 ... Please, please, please, dear lady, before anything else, forgive my audacity, I really don't mean to come off that way... People keep walking past one another in life, never seeing one another ever again—right now I'm being forward enough to try preventing that for a change. If your time at the moment should happen to be as free as mine, I entreat you to grant me the privilege of taking a short walk with you outside on this beautiful late-summer day; I'll explain everything... May I wait for you outside on the square? I'm going to take a chance, anyway. With a kiss of the hand and very truly yours, Boris Negria.

Besides, he was a remarkably good-looking and elegant fellow; we mustn't forget that.

Mary could have walked in at any moment while all this was going on. Negria forgot all about her during his campaign, though, so swept up was he in his breakthrough tactics and his interventionism. Only when he was outside on the sunlit square did he start recalculating the danger (which is what it had now turned into for him) from that quarter. Mary had exceeded her time by twenty-seven minutes (how precise was the reckoning against her now!). She had to be coming on the streetcar; one had just pulled up here and let off passengers. There were at least five minutes until the next one. Moreover, Eros-Gambrinus was running the show, and he cut short the torment. Just then—while Negria was growing happily aware that he was totally in the right and, so to speak, fully covered as far as Mary was concerned (she really couldn't leave him waiting for more than half an hour; no sir, there was no such thing with him)—just then the glass door swung open with a flash and the woman of his dreams appeared and began walking toward him in a relaxed and casual manner. The streets on the other side of the square met at an acute angle, and there was Negria, lifting his hat with a flourish and greeting the young woman like an old acquaintance. But then he took good care to steer her (old boatman that he was) away from there, so they walked down to the river, toward the docking places.

E.P. and his future wife had the good luck that afternoon to be able to escape from the office early. The department head had quietly sent word around, in a friendly gesture, that the staff did not have to sit waiting till the end of the day, since they were caught up on the work they needed to get done (and his own managing director had gone off around noon, anyway). So then the employees began leaving one by one.

E.P. waited for Roserl in a bakery on Schotten Gasse; they thought they would quickly have coffee and then take a ride out to the Vienna Woods. Everything was magnificently awash in floods of sunlight pouring through the streets from heavy mists of gold in the west.

Here she came. He pressed the sight of her inside himself, as a person holds something close to the heart or presses a bandage spread with soothing ointment onto a wound. That was how he felt. On the other hand, he'd never bitten Roserl on her neck. And he'd never lost a friend on her account. He hadn't had to contend with anyone for her.

E.P. had many wounds, "pre-traumatic" ones, so to speak, and as such, integral to his whole being.

Had there been no sword to wound him, they would have opened on his body all by themselves. But of swords there were in the not-uninviting meadowlands of his life almost as many as pointed blades of grass in a meadow.

From Nussdorf they went farther upstream, toward Kahlenberger-dorf, where they would climb a steep, short path to reach the highest point and meet the disappearing sunlight again. Near the Kuchelau a very elegantly dressed couple crossed their path, evidently just coming from a *Heurige*; as though it were a kind of emblem, they were carrying wine between them in a large straw-covered bottle (those demijohns are quite rare in Vienna, or at least not customary). They were conspicuous in the way they were both holding this basket, or casket, and swinging it to and fro. Their loud laughter could be heard from far off; didn't it even look as if they might be engaging in a little tussle for the wine? At any rate, the lady and the gentleman were extremely carefree and exuberant, at a peak of enjoyment, we're tempted to say, but in a sense taking up the whole width of the empty road. Our more idyllically unruffled couple simply had to turn, as if compelled, and look back after the other two had passed; they really had no choice. Then they saw that an embarkation was in progress. The bottle of wine was just about to be stowed somewhere off to the rear when the captain, bent over the quarterdeck of his trim craft, seemed to change his mind; he rummaged around under the helmsman's bench and finally fetched two gleaming wineglasses from some compartment or other—these were for the stirrup cup, a drink for the launch, but a good part of it missed its mark and went into the water, an offering to the river god, or to Neptune, for that matter, as the Danube does eventually flow into the Black Sea.

The shadows of the mountains began cutting sharply across the sunlit swell of the river's wide stream. The boat suddenly picked up speed, propelled into the current by a few powerful strokes of the oars, and soon it was transformed into a spot of color quickly drifting away.

Negria kept to the left above Nussdorf, bearing away from the Danube Canal and keeping to the mainstream; this trip took him far away, then, from the taxi stand near Mary K.'s apartment and far away, too, from the Miserovsky Twins on Porzellan Gasse. E.P.'s room stood placid amid a stillness like that of furniture, in the deep wisdom of silent objects, and unheard went the aeolian song of the transverse cable when the streetcar whizzed by below. The nice little absurdities in every case—signs and labels all over the place, like the one on the bookcase that said BOOKCASE, the same thing on a little table, another one on the armoire (to avoid mix-ups); mounted on the wall was an emergency brake that E.P. had taken during the war from the ruins of a railroad car, and under it was a notice: PULL HANDLE IN CASE OF DANGER. PENALTY FOR MISUSE—all these nice little absurdities, including a large number of puppets, had their share in this furniture-like stillness, this silent wisdom, and they were now showing a face completely different from the one they were actually meant to. They lost all their amusing names. They stood here in the light of the waning afternoon, and all were somber at the core; true, they showed color and contour, but the edges once honed for them had dulled, the points once whetted now rounded off.

The areas around Vienna that lay along the Danube unfolded in front of the boat like a folio being opened. On the left still the silver-gray foam of the treetops in the Vienna Woods after the empty stretches of grass-covered meadow opposite Nussdorf, but also streets, houses, and factories already coming down toward the river, just as on the other bank, where the city is. A string of barges with monotonously grinding machines was going slowly upriver, and over on the right, where the Prater ends, by Kaisermühlen, many large black ships were lying along the bank.

The boat skimmed along quickly and calmly. Negria had to ply the oars only a little. His partner was sitting astern, on the helmsman's bench, leaning far back in the seat, which was like a small easy chair, without securing a life jacket or even bothering to put one on. The boat, the man, his familiarity with the river—all these instilled immediate confidence.

Below the docks, and well before the winter harbor and the Prater Point, as it is known, Negria guided his craft, without using the rudder, more and more to the right and finally over against the bank, where a convenient landing place beckoned. Some people were calling out to him (he was known here, obviously, since they were calling him "Doctor"), and then they helped his lady up onto the landing.

In this section of Vienna there has always been a special kind of small tavern that makes its living from contraband Greek wine, the cleverness of its Hungarian cook, the excellence of its fish dishes, and the hearty recommendations passed along by Serbian, Romanian, Hungarian, and Austrian sailors and mates.

So that's where she was sitting now, little Fräulein Pastré, at this point Frau Schlinger and yes, divorced again. It can safely be said of her that she did not do the right thing. What was more, she belonged to that very large group of Viennese women in whose lives Captain Eulenfeld, the Master of Horse, had been a factor, something that did nary a one of them any good, which was why Kajetan often used to call his old sidekick "Disaster of Course."

That's where she was sitting now, and she was feeling a strong urge to pour her heart out to Negria; it might have come from her tipsiness and the attraction of novel surroundings. She would have liked to tell him everything, absolutely everything, starting back when she hadn't been able to land her Semski, quite a number of years ago by now, and coming up to this very morning, when she had run into Ingrid Schmeller, now styling herself Frau von Budau, on the Graben, near the corner of Stephans Platz, by the bookstore, whereupon, as always since those bygone days, both ladies had walked past without acknowledging each other.

It was in 1910, and not, as Mary had incorrectly recalled, 1908, that Lieutenant Melzer had left Ischl and seen her for the last time, which meant it had been scarcely three months before her wedding. Through 1908, after all, the affairs of the monarchy were at such an extremely critical point in the southwest—in Vienna, marching battalions of the Royal and Imperial Fourth Infantry Regiment, the Hoch- und Deutsch-meister Regiment, were already being trained—that no officer in any company of the Twenty-Second Regiment, stationed at the fortified post near Trnovo in Bosnia, would have been granted leave to Vienna or Ischl. Fine points like this are basically matters of complete indifference to women, though. They will never take seriously, deeply seriously, the assorted imprisonments and incarcerations men lock one another into or let themselves get locked into, and will thus never accept, really accept, down deep in their hearts, any explanation based on such arguments for behavior like being late or not showing up at all.

What was happening to Lieutenant Melzer, for the first time in his life, was that he had disengaged from something and yet was still carrying it around like a rock. He was surprised, even daunted, by feeling the weight of it—certainly no feather—as he rode along the Traunsee on a beautiful summer morning and then stepped across the platform at Attnang-Puchheim to wait for the express train to Vienna. For him, this occurrence was like a disease entirely unsuspected but now suddenly attacking him, and with nothing short of savage virulence, at that. The situation in Ischl, which Melzer had drawn out and dragged out to the very last possible moment, until the very end of his leave time, had finally been decided by his simply failing to propose and his also avoiding any discussion with Mary's father, Herr Allern.

The father was probably just as glad, for it was clear that Melzer would have had to quit the service if things had turned out the other way, and then what kinds of obligations would have cropped up for the future father-in-law? To find him a job somewhere, to start with, but the boy hadn't been trained to do anything else, and he didn't seem to be exactly the brightest light, either. Herr Allern had probably been relieved to see Melzer go (and he also had breakfast with him at the café before his departure, incidentally).

Our lieutenant's lingering in Ischl had been a totally hopeless cause from the beginning, however, a campaign of watching and waiting in the face of an impossibility. His prison wall ran straight down right through the middle of himself, as it were, and it barred him from setting foot onto the terrain of his own soul, which lay before him in plain view. Opening a breach in that wall would have struck him as an act of downright self-destruction, and it is not our place, in view of his personality in those days and the ideas that occupied him, to claim the exact opposite effect, self-liberation, that is. Organically, Lieutenant Melzer's condition was grave. He may have sensed it as the cause of the weight on his spirit. No, this leave had not been one of rest and recuperation.

That was what he was thinking just as the express to Vienna came roaring in. Now there was no going back. This is how people were shifted around. By powerful forces. Now and then it would occur to Melzer that he hadn't worn a uniform in weeks. Instead, this sport suit he had on now and other nice things. In Vienna he'd check in at the Belvedere Hotel near the South Station, change clothes, and take the rest of his luggage. The train for Zagreb leaves in the evening, so there would still be time to eat at Schneider's (the restaurant in the South

Station, named after its proprietor, and genuinely renowned in Vienna at that time). Melzer found an empty second-class compartment. Pressing a gulden into the conductor's hand, he said, "See to it I'm left alone." In those days, it was still possible to ease life's burdens in many little ways through a mild form of corruption kept within proper bounds, civilized and not without dignity, we could almost say. Just now, though, there was no need for the gulden, as the train stayed half empty.

In a better novel, the thoughts of the solitary traveler during his journey to Vienna would now be imparted, purloined if need be, or reeled in gasping and spluttering from the character being presented. Such a thing is truly impossible with Melzer, though; he never had a ghost of a thought, not then, not later, not even as a major. As far as we know, the first time he ever thought anything at all came on one particular occasion, and then only at a very crucial time and very far advanced phase in his life—we will find out more about it later. Once he finally did it, he did it all the way; he didn't waste his powder with little displays of agility and ability.

After settling in, Melzer rolled himself a cigarette, holding it over the handsome old silver *tabatière* that had come to him from his late father, who had been in the service of an imperial personage for nearly two decades as an expert in equestrian matters, because he had been a cavalryman, a true master of horse. Then he opened the newspaper he had bought in Attnang-Puchheim, but since there was nothing in it, he took out of his elegant traveling case—a book. He reached for a book.

A surprising development, no doubt. It's one that Melzer over the last few days had been resorting to over and over, but only to the extent of reaching for the book—he never succeeded in getting any further, not with this one. He kept on getting stuck. Mary Allern had given it to him, some time ago now, not long after they'd met. Right at the beginning was a passage Melzer had recently stumbled over again:

My surroundings were filled with dangers wherever I was, and as far as that goes, every place, even now in the twentieth century, is a forest everywhere. We must distinguish between two kinds of dangers. The first are the ones constantly in motion, the "narrative" dangers, if we may put it that way; the forces of environment and of conditioning, of deeply ingrained laxity that robs hours from each day and is soon demanding repayment of these stolen goods, this fraudulently obtained property, as a levy and a tribute. This laxity, in turn, has some kind of connection (it carries us past the switches and the crossing places of bad conscience and past all the crowded tracks busy carrying the regularly scheduled trains of character) with the "dramatic" dangers, the ones that part the tangled vegetation like a gorilla leaping out from among the lianas in the African jungle (and at five paces away, how much is the hunter going to worry about noises that have been plaguing him for weeks, like the buzzing of mosquitoes or the rustling of snakes and lizards in the bush? He won't even hear them; they're somewhere far away now that this angry red eye is fixed on him and bloodcurdling rage is rumbling out of that furry, powerfully heaving chest) . . .

Melzer read the passage all the way through this time. He immediately related it to everything he had experienced at Ischl, and he set the image of it next to the image of those experiences and that sensation of a heavy weight inside his chest (the rock he was carrying now). One more item added itself as if it somehow just belonged—the locomotive roaring in while he stood on the platform at Attnang-Puchheim. Then it occurred to him for the first time that even at Zauner's in Ischl there had been startling developments (in addition to coffee and ice cream); outright monsters, even, but certainly no gorilla and no rustling of snakes and lizards in the bush. As we can see, Melzer was already applying something like a critical faculty to his imaginative life and its arbitrary way of making patterns, but we cannot bring ourselves to call that faculty thinking. At any rate, he suddenly wiped away everything inside himself, as a sponge erases a blackboard, dismissing it with a gesture that would have roughly the same meaning as exclaiming "Nonsense!" Melzer's gesture was merely the result of his inability to bring to completion that simple process of thought whose point it was to discover that inherent in every one of the mental images occupying him just now was a common element, even though the images might be presenting it in very different forms—a gorilla, his experience in Ischl and its burdensome aftermath, and the locomotive of an express train roaring into the station—each of these was above all an object or a phenomenon of enormously greater power than he, surpassing him in strength many times over.

He couldn't dismiss it completely, and he felt it again with fear. Like a red wall draped in purple (or was it raw flesh?), it was suddenly standing there, cruel and menacing, behind all of life, behind each and every life, and that was what it all came down to. He kept seeing this color for several moments, a red like flesh or blood, gushing forcefully and making pools and puddles. Because our lieutenant, warrior or not, felt genuine terror for a split second, he reached for his tobacco case again. And now it was over—he still didn't know what to make of these images, so he lowered his book and slept until Linz, where a couple of sausages with mustard and a stein of beer were handed up to him through the window when he called for them.

Melzer arrived in Vienna around one thirty, hailed a fiacre at the West Station, and went to eat in the center of town; while he was doing so, an old Viennese *Dienstmann*—one of those porters and messengers, a type who sported the customary white mustachios modeled on the emperor's—went with his luggage in a cab to the Belvedere Hotel near the South Station. This would be the right occasion for mentioning that our Lieutenant Melzer was none too tightfisted with his money; he enjoyed a nice income, thanks to an uncle in the beer-brewing business (*nomen est omen*), who had guaranteed it would continue as long as his nephew stayed in the military. This fondness for the service on the part of a onetime master brewer and current majority stockholder of a large-scale brewery made life easy for Melzer (who was so disrespectful, nonetheless, as to order a glass of wine with his meal). Also, the garrison at Trnovo in Bosnia was of decided benefit to his finances during leave time, since a man needed practically nothing down there.

After the hotel called Melzer on the telephone during his meal, as requested, to confirm that his luggage had arrived, he had a cup of black coffee and then walked slowly through the city to take care of a few errands that friends in Trnovo had asked him to do. His last stop was in Seidel's military bookstore on the Graben.

This was 1910, remember, a late-summer day.

It was gratifying for Melzer to have all this movement swirling around him. Had we been able to see deep inside him at that moment, behind his jacket and shirt and past his heart and kidneys, we would have discovered, I believe, that his enjoyment of the scurrying and darting and weaving on the streets of the metropolis had an unconscious tinge of "So all this is still here after all"; further, that the walking or dashing, the standing around, the rushing, or the strolling of the people here, as well as the more than lively mixture of well-maintained horse-drawn carriages and purring automobiles gave him reinforcement in his life as a whole. And really, the surroundings were eminently suited to produce that effect. Streams of sunlight lavishly coated every moving detail in gold, the blue banner of the sky fluttered high above the Graben, and by the bookstore up at the corner, St. Stephen's tower stepped onto the scene as if with the stride of a giant.

Clop-clop tapped the horses' hooves. A strong-smelling cloud of cigar smoke drifted past on the sidewalk like a greeting from tropical islands, and that cloud at once collided with another, one that caused him to glance back toward a certain someone disappearing into the crowd—Bois des Îles, wood from the islands, smoke from the islands.

He sauntered up and down the street a few times. It was getting close to three thirty. His idea about going to the Café Pucher wasn't very definite. Right here and now, though, he was given the resolve to go ahead, in a way; just by being a flâneur among all the rest of the flâneurs he was gaining a feeling of having things in common with the world around him, and he was at last rescuing himself from an isolation that not long before, in Attnang-Puchheim, had been quite intense.

Ballhaus Platz frequented the Pucher. No one belonging to the Foreign Ministry was a stranger to this relatively narrow café squeezed in on the Kohlmarkt. Melzer's connection to such circles—by no means a given through his position as a line officer in the infantry, which did not count socially for very much in the old Austria—came from his mother's side; now living a retired life in Innsbruck, Melzer's mother was the daughter of a former Royal and Imperial consul general.

The lieutenant found only a few of his acquaintances on hand at the Pucher. Sitting on red velvet benches in a large booth at the rear were Herr von Langl and Herr von Semski, as well as a Baron von Lindner, who at that same time, in 1910, took a significant step forward in his career, having been appointed that autumn to the post of district commissioner somewhere down in Carinthia. Herr von Semski was the only one of the three affiliated with Ballhaus Platz. Herr Benno von Grabmayr (the son of "Charlemagne," as they called his father, Karl, a member of the upper house) stopped by for just a few minutes later on. This Benno was not fond of sitting around in cafés, and he was in a hurry, having already changed into his golfing outfit as soon as the office closed and being on his way to the Krieau, where the golf course was; he was in the Pucher now only because he wanted to find out who was going to take a ride out to see the Stangelers at their country house the next day, Saturday.

That had become something of a custom. Everybody chattered away at once while cordially welcoming Melzer at the same time.

"Grauermann's getting engaged to Etelka Stangeler," said Grabmayr. His accent stood out somewhat from the Viennese German this group spoke. He pronounced the consonant *k* in Etelka with that true Tyrolean hardness.

"Who else from Waisenhaus Gasse is going tomorrow?" asked Semski. He was referring to the Consular Academy. As noted previously, Waisenhaus Gasse had its name changed later, in honor of a great mathematician, with the result that it sounded much less woebegone when it was no longer named for the orphanage (*Waisenhaus*) once on it. It starts on the right side of Währinger Strasse—facing Währing—goes downhill, and runs into Liechtenstein Strasse. About halfway down the street was located the institution founded by Empress Maria Theresa as the Royal and Imperial Academy for Oriental Languages, though now called the Consular Academy; it was a college at which all the students boarded, and they were supervised rather strictly. The young scholars were permitted to wear only their uniform, which was very becoming, however, and which included a sword; on the other hand, civilian clothes were prohibited, except for traveling or at sporting events, and in the first year no one was allowed out past ten o'clock.

All in all, however, it was a good life for the students in that large, handsome building, for they certainly had everything they needed—wonderful grounds, riding, and tennis. Even so, it's fair to say that they did have their share of rather unusual house customs, most of all in the autumn, when the start of the semester would bring the tyros for their first year, the "hound dogs," as they used to be called. On the very first evening after they arrived, these "hound dogs" would be subjected to a kind of test in the large salon, with everybody present, and of course each one of them without exception would fail, because a boy would either be able to answer the tough questions put to him, in which case it was a damn shame how spoiled and arrogant the kid was before he even started, or he would not, in which case the kid was simply a first-class moron. The committee of examiners was drawn from the members of the highest class, the fourth year, who were each addressed as "Your Excellency," while those who had already completed their studies and been appointed attachés were accorded the rank of "demi-god" on their occasional return visits to the academy.

For the rest, it's disheartening even to think of how much they had to learn. Aside from legal studies, especially constitutional law and commercial law, they were naturally expected to master English and French to the point of perfect fluency. The chief emphasis, however, was still placed on the Near Eastern languages, specifically Turkish, Arabic, and Persian, as absolutely mandatory, with a very extensive command representing the acceptable minimum. The prerequisite for entrance into the academy—fifteen or twenty beginners at the very most were accepted each year—was passing the comprehensive final examinations in the humanities curriculum at a preparatory school; most of the students were likely to have come from the Maria Theresa Court Academy, which people in Vienna still today refer to by its shortened name of the Theresanum.

So much for the subject of Waisenhaus Gasse ("Golden Days of Yore" would be the heading in the parlance of dotage). The students had gradually gained entrée to Herr von Stangeler's house, one bringing another on his next visit, and they showed up there during the winter very presentably decked out in green tailcoats, and at the country house during the summer in traveling clothes.

"Grauermann and Marchetti are going there tomorrow," said Herr von Langl, "that much I know for sure. Honnegger's playing in a piano quintet at my aunt's in Döbling on Sunday."

"Marchetti seems to enjoy talking with Asta," Semski noted in passing. He had a way, incidentally—he was a few years older, after all, and an official with an appointment at Ballhaus Platz—of treating the students at the Consular Academy somewhat patronizingly.

"What's wrong, Melzer?" asked Lindner quietly from across the table.

Our lieutenant had indeed become unsettled and was just at that moment struggling with some overwhelming feelings. They were all connected to the name Asta Stangeler, and they were grouping themselves around that name as if around their source and their midpoint. He'd as good as missed out on his whole leave by frittering it away. He could have been out there in the mountains, staying at that beautiful house with so many cheerful people, instead of at Zauner's in Ischl. (The single appearance Lieutenant Melzer had made at the Stangeler house always constituted a noteworthy exception—he was the one and only officer it would have been possible to encounter there, since the father harbored an invincible prejudice against this profession; everybody knew it, too, and the daughters were never allowed to invite officers to their home, although a few navy men might be tolerated, because Herr Stangeler discerned in seafaring men people "who know something about something." Melzer was once snowed in at the country place during a mountain-climbing party, and he, on the contrary, was pointed out as a "nice, alert, simple young man" and given the seal of approval.) Melzer had then started to feel something like stabs of pain as his friends talked over their plans for riding out to the Semmering area the following day, since it would be Saturday, and the feeling had finally developed a locus, an axis it could rotate on, as it were, in that one name—Asta Stangeler.

What was it that actually formed a bond between him and René's darker-skinned sister, though, just yesterday still a half-grown girl, so to speak, when it was only the winter before last that she'd been seen at dances and parties for the first time? Now she stepped before his mind's eye with greater distinctness, as part of a group sitting near the edge of a rocky cliff above the valley, with mountains looming close behind in preternaturally sharp resolution (a sign of bad weather coming), and Asta in her red and blue Styrian outfit with its many-colored shawl, laughing as only she could laugh. Melzer now remembered that he'd always done a great deal of laughing with her; it seemed to him now, in fact, that he never laughed with anyone else more heartily than he did with her. Hope instantly attached itself to this picture inside of Melzer, but what kind of hope was it? This memory dated back to a time before he'd known Mary Allern, and in fact in our lieutenant's mind it stood for that whole carefree manner of living. So his way of hoping was paradoxical, directed as it was toward the past rather than toward the future. But that's what we do for the most part anyway, isn't it?

"I'm not happy about it, but I have to go soon, you know," he said to Lindner. He still had time to hear them talking about "garden parties." During the summer just past, the Schmellers out in Grinzing had adopted this new way of entertaining for the season now in progress, when everybody in creation would fetch back up in Vienna from the spas, the mountains, and the seashore; these were summer gatherings in a garden high above the city—whose rows of lights coming up the hillsides added to the charm—where the guests had supper outdoors and danced afterward. A less formal way of socializing, without tailcoats and evening gowns, and a kind of preview of the winter season that one could enjoy in a comfortable summer suit.

"Well, why don't you come back soon, Melzer? You don't always have to use up all your leave at the same time, you know."

"And then run right off to Ischl . . ."

The glass door swung open, closed behind him, and the bath of movement in the streets received him. He hailed a fiacre on the Graben. Turning around at Stock-im-Eisen Platz, he saw the lofty cathedral standing amid the swarming crowds, and then he looked ahead, along Kärntner Strasse toward the Opera—he was going off in that direction. Off to one of those curious lands far to the south that had been parts of the old empire and whose allurements, fascinations, aromas, and even dubious odors all met right here, at this very point of intersection. Melzer's eight hired hooves went clop-clopping merrily along Favoriten

Strasse on their way to the South Station, near which was his hotel. Now he would have to change out of his sport suit; from this point on Melzer was traveling on official business and in uniform.

Dressed accordingly, he left Schneider's restaurant after his dinner and walked over to the station café.

At that time those places were beautifully kept up, relatively quiet, and more spacious than required by the amount of traffic in those days, before every little pastry cook started ceaselessly gallivanting hither and yon. It's tempting to say that inside them there still reverberated all that was meant by the opening of the Semmering rail line, even though that had been fully half a century earlier. Around the columns of dark marble hovered the traditional atmosphere of a Viennese café, the aromas of strong black coffee and cigarette smoke and that absolute absence of any cooking odor or smell of frying, since a guest could have coffee prepared and served in any of six varieties but could not order more to eat than a little ham sandwich or a couple of eggs at the very most. There were always plenty of empty tables, and everyone who came in to take a seat tried to get as far away as possible from the ones already occupied, which is in itself enough to show how the taciturn and well-nigh meditative demeanor of the patrons in a Viennese café manifests itself.

"Has the lieutenant placed his order yet?" the waiter asked, knowing full well that Melzer had just walked in; avoiding any head-on manner of address, though, was counted as one of the ceremonial prerequisites for service here.

Melzer felt tired after this day filled with activity, the more so as he'd gotten up so early that morning (and had breakfast with Herr Allern). Moreover, he'd had two mugs of pilsner beer to go with his evening meal, in view of his upcoming journey by night, to help him sleep well, that is (but even that seems disrespectful to a certain extent, as his magnanimous uncle's investments were in a different brewery, Dreher's).

It began to grow dark. A porter from the Belvedere was standing on the platform, in front of the car with the first- and second-class compartments for the Zagreb train. He handed Melzer the baggage-claim ticket and told him that he'd saved him a good seat by setting his travel bag on it; "only one other gentleman in the compartment, a major," he added. There were still twenty minutes until departure time. Melzer boarded the train, the porter opened the compartment door for him, and the lieutenant saluted when he saw a gold collar in the dim light.

"How are you, Melzer?" the major said.

"My respects, sir," Melzer answered, not able to make out who the staff officer was, not even when they stepped closer and shook hands; only when the other turned up the gas lamp, which had been all the way down on low, did his name come back to our lieutenant—it was a Major Laska, battalion commander at Banja Luka in Bosnia.

"Coming off leave, it looks like, Melzer?"

"Yes, sir."

"Listen, how about if we each give the conductor a gulden so we can be left alone and get some sleep?"

"Very good idea, sir."

Melzer was dominated by a strange twofold feeling, and while he was unbuckling his saber and putting it into the lower, narrower of the two luggage racks above the seats, he was inwardly still standing out on the platform, so to say, on this same platform where he had also at one time boarded a train for Payerbach-Reichenau to reach the Stangelers' house in the country. That was all still waiting for him out there, unfinished business, as it were, and he had grown vividly aware of it right before he stepped aboard, as he looked out through the open mouth of the terminal. Now he had an urgent desire to go back onto the platform. Just then the moving stand that sold books and newspapers went rolling past. Melzer excused himself for a moment.

"Pick up a bottle of mineral water too, all right?" Laska called after him.

The lieutenant left the car, stopped the newspaper vendor, and quickly bought five English-language detective novels (another errand for someone in Trnovo, and he'd forgotten to do it in the city!) as well as some newspapers and magazines, and finally, when the refreshment cart was being wheeled past, the mineral water and some fruit. Then he stood there with all those things in his arms and looked ahead, out of the terminal. Tomorrow afternoon that whole crowd would take off from here—Grauermann and Marchetti, Semski and Grabmayr and Edouard von Langl, the master of light piano music. There was a mild odor of railroad smoke, just as there had been back then, and in Payerbach they'd get a real whiff of fresh mountain air when they got off the train. Then they'd ride up in the landau, and maybe Asta and Etelka would meet them on the serpentine road leading to the house.

"You brought the mineral water? Good job," said the major when Melzer came back into the compartment. A wonderful aroma came at him, and Laska presently took out a long cigar case and offered Melzer a Kaiser-Virginia. "You know what?" he said in a happy mood, "I brought a bottle of Poysdorfer from Schneider's with me, chilled nice and cold. Let's have a little glass now. I hope the mineral water's cold, too." He felt the bottles, seemed satisfied, and produced from his travel bag a yellow case that held two small silver drinking cups, gold-plated on the inside.

"May I ask if the major is also coming off leave?" Melzer said, after they'd sat down by the folding table at the window.

"No, I'm not. I was just in Vienna for a few days, sort of a courier, at the ministry. Among other things, there was one item of discussion that will interest you, by the way."

"Oh, what was that? And incidentally, does this train stop in Payerbach?"

"No, I don't think so. This one here goes straight through from Gloggnitz to Semmering. But what made you think of that? Are you planning on getting out there?"

"No, I just heard people talking about it earlier."

"The express to Graz is the one that stops in Payerbach. It's standing right over there, on the next track."

"Oh," said Melzer, "the Graz express stops in Payerbach."

Pain gripped him all of a sudden. Mary would look at him so oddly. He had never really quite understood her. She was something special; she was unique. Fear of the irretrievable, of genuine loss, squeezed his chest; he could feel it like a pressure on his throat.

"Listen," said Laska, as the train began moving almost imperceptibly and glided out of the terminal, "they've just made me game warden for Bosnia, and that means your bear is guaranteed. I'm taking you to the Treskavica with me. Your old man will just have to turn you loose for a few days. I'll ask him myself. He's a friendly guy, anyway, your man Captain Zeisler. Cheers, now!"

They toasted one another.

"Many thanks and deepest respects, sir," said Melzer, "that's really great!"

A sudden sense of well-being coursed through him now, along with vague astonishment at the drastic changes in his mood throughout this day, now drawing to an end. Laska filled the cups again and in a beautiful bass voice struck up a melody from Johann Strauss's operetta *Die Fledermaus*:

> Why feel strange?
> Just arrange
> To forget what
> You can't change…
>
> Happiness,
> We profess,
> Comes when you
> Forget your stress…

He ended with "Cheers!" Melzer stared at him in boundless amazement for the briefest second. The train went gliding along, thrusting gently through the darkness, and stopped for two minutes by the empty platform in Meidling. The two gentlemen leaned back in their padded seats, the glorious local vintage tasting delicious as it went down, the blue haze floating under the hemisphere of the overhead light.

Now Melzer was traveling down to Bosnia with nothing less than passionate eagerness. However, it wasn't the prospect of a bear hunt—as much as he'd been wishing for it—that had the ability to bring about such a drastic change; instead, the atmosphere diffusing itself through the compartment seemed alone to be producing a powerful healing effect that nothing inside him was able to withstand in the long run.

Something here was lifting him up and supporting him stalwartly. Above their seats, the same saber with the same black tip was lying in the narrow luggage rack on both sides.

By the time they passed the country house, around Baden, their talk had long since worked its way down to the most minute details of their hunting plans; Laska, an old Bosnian from way back, knew his subject exhaustively. When the platforms at Payerbach went flying past a good hour later, Melzer didn't even take notice until afterward, as the train was crossing the large viaduct. They'd slid air-filled rubber pillows under their heads and stretched out to go to sleep. The hollow whooshing sound in the Semmering tunnels penetrated agreeably into the slumber enveloping them, which also had enclosed within it, as it were, something else Melzer found agreeable—his firm resolution to spend his next leave in Vienna, and a part of it in the areas around Rax and Semmering too. And what would there be to stop him, anyway?

A month later, Laska and Melzer were riding uphill along a stony path to the hunting lodge, a Catherine hut, on the Treskavica Mountain, the sky a virtually endless blue above bare and wooded hills. The lower part of the Treskavica has both at the same time; on its north slope is a dense forest of beech, while the south slope is all meadowland, and so the mountain as a whole looks something like an old man with a mighty beard but a bald head.

This was the second hunting expedition these two officers had set out on together since their journey back from Vienna. Two weeks earlier, Laska had taken the lieutenant with him on a boar hunt into Sierscha Canyon near Dobro Pole. This was completely virgin territory, still under stringent preservation in those days—in fact, the actual presence of the game warden himself, appointed by the Ministry for National Defense, was required for anyone to enter this region carrying a rifle. The major's rifle had misfired at the crucial moment of that other hunt, just as the quarry broke out from the underbrush and the black dogs were storming over a ridge with trees farther apart; the boar ran past the two huntsmen close enough for Laska to fling aside the rifle that had failed, draw his pistol, and kill a strong boar with it at scarcely ten paces. The major had practically leapt after his own pistol bullet, continuing to fire the whole time. As they later saw, three hits lodged in the boar's skull and several more in its lungs. Everything was covered with blood—bushes, grass, moss; over so great an expanse, Melzer had also had ample opportunity to use his rifle (besides, it may be that the major wanted to put his hunting skills to the test before they went after the bear—it worked out satisfactorily, in any case).

Melzer was thinking about that earlier hunt now, after they had dismounted for the day. He had gone off a short distance from the horses to a place where the stony ground was partly covered with hazel bushes. The scene of Laska killing the boar now stepped before his mind's eye—the barking crack of the pistol, the wild expression on the major's face as he leapt forward, the collapsing animal thrashing about, and the blood spattering everywhere. This image gradually spread out inside Melzer, the way a pool spreads out, and it sent little trickles off in many directions, as if seeming to seek out a dark, inexpressible connection with something else kindred but concealed. All the while, a slow, lazy, slight motion was taking place on a flat rock among the hazel, but only now did Melzer take notice and realize what it was—a hazel snake, or smooth snake, a little reptile hardly a foot long that abounds in Bosnia. Sunk deep inside himself, Melzer observed the serpentine writhing and slithering of the little body. Under other circumstances, he might have turned around and said, "Look, sir, there's a smooth snake." But the one here seemed to him to be like a movement of his own inner self, like the most secret of thoughts, ones it would be unimaginable to reveal.

Back where he was, Laska offered Melzer some cognac and chocolate. He was glad to sever the bonds of this isolation, which had lasted for some minutes, or only some seconds, but which was more of a burden than a relief to him.

Late that afternoon, when the sun was shining slantwise and making it impossible to see at any distance, they came to the lodge. Nearby was an *Alm*, or high-mountain meadow, as people would call it in Bavaria or Austria, the livestock still in the pasture for the summer. The herdsmen, notified in advance that the officers were coming, had slaughtered an ox, most of which was going to be used as bait for the bear. They had taken the best cuts of meat, though, and grilled them superbly, in the manner customary to the region, for the evening meal. Now, just after the officers' arrival, there arose the bracing smell of coffee, which Laska had doled out in generous measure among the herdsmen, along with a kilogram of sugar, some packs of cigarettes, and a bottle of slivovitz. "One hand washes the other," he said to Melzer in passing, "but now we're going to have our special treats too." With that, he unwrapped some fine Turkish pastries—*tulumba* and baklava, as well as *koravai*, fragile and flaky, in slices as large as the palm of the hand.

Before nightfall, they set out their enormous bait in the beech woods on the north slope, with the help of the herders and of both orderlies, young Bosnians who seemed to be taking special pleasure in this expedition. There was a shoulder in the mountain, in itself an almost level tract of land with a kind of trough-shaped hollow in the middle; this was where they laid out the ox. Then Laska and Melzer carefully selected their blind, checked the range of fire, and took exact bearings on the spot by several signs, doing likewise on their way back to the lodge along the path, from which they now removed all the dry wood, because it could snap, and tossed away underbrush and branches here and there so as to forestall any noise on their return by night. The herders knew exactly the main direction of the night wind here on the north slope of the Treskavica, and it favored them, blowing as it did from the bait toward the approach route. After all that, Laska and Melzer were able to lie down for a couple of hours in the lodge.

When they moved out at one o'clock, by themselves and with no dogs, the moonless night was lit only by the twinkling stars. It was so cold that their breath clouded lightly in front of their mouths; that was why Laska and Melzer were bundled up in short fur coats. Later on, when their eyes were accustomed to the darkness, it was not hard for them, walking slowly and cautiously, to find the path in the forest. About three hundred paces before they reached their blind, they could hear sounds from that direction in the silence of the night, and when the hunters reached the spot, the presence of the bear was beyond any doubt; even though they couldn't see it, they could hear it smacking its lips and chomping now and then. These sounds were often separated by long pauses. Then the bear would tug at the bait, and they would hear dragging and rustling sounds. At around three there was a real burst of noise amid which they could make out the snap of breaking bones, and soon afterward they were disappointed when they realized with certainty that the bear had torn pieces off the bait and was dragging one of them away.

Laska and Melzer sat there until it grew light enough to shoot, listening for a long time in the silence of the night to the sound moving ever farther away. For the moment, there was nothing they could do. When it had grown somewhat lighter, they looked through binoculars at the remains of the bait left behind, but they did not again go near the place where they had set out the ox. Its left hind part was almost completely missing, which in itself was enough to show that the herdsmen's reports about the bear's size were hardly exaggerated.

The two officers returned to the lodge to have breakfast.

The orderlies and the herdsmen were excited, and someone went so far as to suggest picking up the bear's trail at once, with the help of the big dogs, now out in the mountain meadow. But Laska brushed all that aside with a laugh. Not for another good hour, after a hearty and satisfying breakfast, was he to be found walking along the path with Melzer, the two alone again.

It was this outing that was to become unforgettable for Melzer, not like something you can put a name to and then just label as unforgettable; no, this image he conjured up in memory became rooted much deeper inside him, a thing enduring, dwelling within him at all times and never thrusting its way to the fore—but later it often seeped through, untold times, in a quiet and barely perceptible way, gradually spreading throughout him deep down inside, sending off trickles and flowing together with other images connected in ways that never found expression.

Admittedly, almost nothing happened outwardly. They walked along roughly the same path as they had the night before and turned off it at a bow shot's distance from the spot where they'd first waited for the bear, striking out to the right through the beech forest so as to pick up the bear's trail, the direction of which their intently listening ears had made sufficiently sure of the night before. And on this walk, without any dogs, they in fact did find the streak, distinct at first, left by the bear when he'd made off with his prey. They were even able to observe some small pieces of meat and slivers of bone that had come loose and were caught on branches in the underbrush or in the moss. As the way went on, however, these signs began to dwindle.

Their path led them across an open, flat forest floor, the dense growth receded, and they walked, as if through pillared halls, among the dull gray tree trunks. Melzer felt pleasantly fortified and warmed by his breakfast; he went along easily while still sensing every one of his muscles responding to the enjoyment of walking. There are inner states that are like being untied from the stake of one's own self and in which we govern even our bodies as never before. That was how Melzer was feeling on this reconnoitering walk, meanwhile registering everything with a special clarity and sharpness, as when the image of a garden extends into a sunny room through a newly washed windowpane.

They lost the trail as time passed and were led on more by surmises than by signs. The sun had gradually climbed high, and now it set the mighty treetops in motion, dappled the forest floor, made the air warm, and invited them to rest.

This they did on the crest, eating a second breakfast as they paused. The woods dropped off steeply ahead of them, and all the space around the tree trunks was filled with underbrush, farther back along the ridge as well as closer by, so that only this front part of the mountain ridge, which the hunters had chosen for their resting place, was left clear. Melzer felt utterly happy. Everything lay lightly on his soul, like a fragrant foam, the gentle envelopment of his consciousness at this moment completely undisturbed by any pressure, however slight, or even a twinge, however faint, of images or actualities.

He was probably not aware that Major Laska's way of living, the style of his life overall, was what was evoking and making rise within him the sense of well-being just described. Inside Melzer, that sense immediately transformed itself into a liking for the major, toward whom he simply felt gratitude for bringing him along.

Taken up with enjoying their food, the small, shiny cups from their thermos bottles filled with strong-smelling coffee, the cognac affably waiting, they felt something more than just that they were experiencing a merely sensory perception which was about to reach articulation when they heard some kind of rumbling along the crest, in the undergrowth about a hundred yards away, and they reached for their weapons. But hardly had they put their drinking cups aside and lifted their rifles than there was an absolutely tremendous jolt in the thicket, a sudden, extremely violent movement from a mass of considerable size. Right afterward, it went barreling off down the slope. Laska and Melzer jumped up, and perhaps the lieutenant might have really hoped to fire a shot, but they caught sight of the fleeing bear for only a second, as a shadow, and almost totally covered by trees.

"We'll get you yet!" Laska called after him.

At the moment when the bear had suddenly sprung up, it felt to the lieutenant as if a section of the forest floor itself had exploded into the air. The ground still seemed to be shaking even now. In his mind, this excess of power, unleashed in seconds, nay in fractions of seconds, sent the entire forest flying away, as if with a kick, from the idyllic mood he had just been savoring. He couldn't quite understand it himself, and he stared in vague wonder at the profound impression on his own soul, as at a cave that had opened unexpectedly.

After it was all over, they finished their meal in peace and then turned back. As they came near the bait in the level hollow, a swarm of vultures rose up, and they saw that the part of the skeleton left behind had been picked clean of nearly every remaining bit of meat, right down to the last little bone.

Despite everything, Melzer got his bear two days later, after they'd set out as fresh bait a goat they thought might serve the purpose. Laska had left the shot to him; the major just stood at the ready, and it was Melzer's bullet that hit home. He got the skin, and he kept possession of it for the rest of his life (years later, when he was living on Porzellan Gasse in Vienna, diagonally across from the Miserovsky Twins, he liked to lay it before the fireplace in the first of his two rooms). They and the orderlies ate the paws back at the lodge, and they gave one of the two haunches to the herdsmen.

Whenever I would think about Melzer in April of 1945, thirty-five years after that bear hunt, in my cold hotel room in Oslo (and it's something I did fairly often), I was forced to take notice that there was one period of his life during which my lieutenant never underwent—not in any way, shape, or form—the kinds of inner experiences he'd had on his journey from Attnang-Puchheim to Vienna in 1910 and, in a sense, on the Treskavica as well, even though it was a period when one might have anticipated to the extent of outright certainty that he *would* undergo such experiences, and at their most intense pitch, right off the bat, an open-and-shut case: I mean the war. From 1914 to 1918, Melzer was in on the action just about wherever there was any action to be in on—Gorlice, Col di Lana, Flitsch-Tolmein . . . names never to be forgotten! Anyone living through a war, though, acquires again and again a sense, not of himself, but of everybody else. Inside the world of legally organized terror, the harvest is not gathered into the core of the individual person but is instead redistributed throughout the collective. That's why, incidentally, there's such a special fondness for storytelling in almost all soldiers.

Now then, Melzer learned later on to tell the difference between the two basic elements of his biography, which is how he was able to fill me in, during our many talks, about never having the slightest occurrence of one of them all through the war. I've conversed with Melzer often, the first time a good twenty-five years ago, on Porzellan Gasse in Vienna, our feet on the bearskin from the Treskavica, and most recently in 1942, in Kursk, where he turned up as a lieutenant-colonel (being a former Austrian officer, he was required to report again for active duty in the German army). Though frequently having to take independent action during the First World War—what else was there to do—Melzer didn't have the slightest knack for existing independently, as he assured me. (By the way, dear reader, O reader wise of whom I fantasize, what's your opinion about taking action—I mean, is it really in our hands? Does it always indicate who we really are? Watch out, now, this is a comprehensive oral exam question with a lot riding on it; for instance, your whole approach to dramatic literature is going to have to take its direction from the answer you give now! And don't try getting around it! Every *avis au lecteur* is dubious.)

Melzer added that he stayed like that, completely unchanged, for a good many years beyond 1918 (up to a certain Saturday afternoon). As in the military, where nobody ever goes *to* any place but simply keeps reporting for duty *at* some place or other, Melzer, his military career brought to a halt by the collapse of 1918, at which time he was a major (in the little army of the new republic he wasn't able to continue serving for very long), reported for duty at the Austrian Tobacco Administration—as a civil servant, that is, and not as the proprietor of a cigar store, a post for which no officers but the totally disabled were eligible. So that was all well and good, for he continued serving his country. On Porzellan Gasse. That was where Melzer's civil service job was. It was in a large building quite near the Bohemia Station, and it housed some offices for internal-revenue administration as well. Walking past on the sidewalk, a person would be engulfed by all the waves of fragrant odors of Persia and Turkey, from Sultan Flor all the way up and down the line, since the building also contained one of the main distribution centers under the state tobacco monopoly, and the old Austrian Tobacco Administration, even though it was no longer under the domain of the emperor, really understood how to go about such things—we have to grant it that much.

Melzer didn't walk past the building very often, though, but mostly into or out of it, the former—apart from going out for his midday meal and, later on, to the café for a short while—between eight and eight thirty each morning, and the latter between four and five in the afternoon (inhuman working hours were still a thing unknown in those days). He never made his way in the opposite direction, to the corner of Althan Strasse in front of the Bohemia Station, because instead of eating his noon meal in the large restaurant located there he used to go to a wonderful little place closer to the center of the city and more in the neighborhood of the Miserovsky Twins.

Even so, Melzer frequented Bohemia Station on many a Saturday throughout the summer of 1925, and that was just one of the changes that Disaster of Course Eulenfeld brought into the major's life, though most of the adjustments hadn't been of much consequence or duration. The captain and his whole crowd, called the *troupeau*—every weekend during the summer, if the sun was shining, these good people would without fail take a trip out to one of the swimming areas along the Danube, like Kritzendorf or Greifenstein or Tulln. They would stay overnight in some little weekend cottage or other that somebody or other owned, or somehow or other otherwise had the use of.

Making the acquaintance of Captain Eulenfeld back then in Vienna seems to have been very hard to avoid; that's how it struck people, at any rate. Mary K. had that impression as well. In the course of her much later dealings with Kajetan von S., the Disaster of Course was naturally bound to turn up sooner or later, although his doings had no disastrous effect on Mary. She thought of Eulenfeld more as a kind of disease.

Melzer was right up his alley. The captain's instincts and talents, all oriented toward hedonism and probably even toward dissoluteness, found no sharp edges to bump up against in Melzer where they might have hurt themselves or broken something. In addition, there was the implied pathos of their common experience as former officers of the allied German and Austro-Hungarian armies in the First World War (well before 1914, Eulenfeld had been nursed on the mother's milk of his first drunken sprees at the breasts of the Fourteenth Hussar Regiment in Kassel; like Melzer, he had been an active officer). The Captain of Horse did not share the mistaken and warped views harbored by so many of his countrymen when it came to Austria, and so he never gave cause for offense, a thing his—by and large—good manners would have precluded anyway. Fleeing from years that had had their ups and downs, and no doubt now and then their shadier moments as well, years he had spent from 1918 on in South America, in England, and in the German civil war, he arrived in Vienna while the great turn of events of 1922 and 1923 was taking place, at first employed as the manager of a driving school, which was how he had originally come to know Melzer, who one day got it into his head that it just would not do at all for him to go on not knowing how to drive a car, and who became obsessed at the same time by the notion that now, after the collapse of his military career, he was going to have to earn his bread starting all the way at the bottom, as a newspaper vendor or maybe a taxi driver—it had just been broken to Melzer that his retention in what remained of the little Austrian army was no longer a consideration. So he learned from Eulenfeld how to drive. The captain gave up this teaching activity soon thereafter and secured himself a more comfortable berth in a Viennese agency of the Wakefield Company. Around the same time, Melzer's rather farfetched notions about having to struggle for his very existence stopped automatically with his acceptance for work in the Austrian Tobacco Administration. Not long afterward he rented those two rooms (already mentioned) on Porzellan Gasse and spread out the bearskin from the Treskavica before his fireplace; on top of that, he had come into an inheritance—no paltry sum—willed to him by his uncle, David Melzer, the military-minded master brewer, which likewise played its part in helping him consolidate his affairs.

The reasons for Melzer's friendly relations with Eulenfeld went deeper, however, at least as far as the major (now the civil service employee) was concerned, than might perhaps appear from the facts brought out so far. In Melzer's mind the captain represented a direction, toward which there existed in Melzer a certain pull or perhaps even a striving—if one can imagine such a state being almost unconscious—and at the same time, a feeling of lesser aptitude, this latter sense fairly clear to him. It could be said that the captain appeared before the outer ramparts of Melzer's being at the precise place where the defenses were weakest—and in the case of military men like these two, such comparisons will surely be admissible. When the captain (it was universal practice to call the Master of Horse simply "the captain") would tell stories about his past life with great relish, Melzer, a public servant now, would see him entering and exiting all sorts of imprisonments and prisons (and with regard to the second of these terms, I am regretfully obliged to ask that the reader take it in its literal sense this time, for Eulenfeld had caused a number of his acquaintances to end up behind bars!), would see him entering or exiting, whether into South America or the Spartacist disturbances in Berlin, and moreover, Eulenfeld would simply lock the door behind him, totally unperturbed, on the most varied kinds of situations whenever he felt like walking away. The other point that pertains to South America, and especially to Buenos Aires, is that the captain seemed to have maintained more contacts there than anywhere else. He liked to talk about that metropolis, where he had lived for a good while, and quite often he also received letters from there, which in turn interested the stamp collectors among his friends and colleagues.

Now, Eulenfeld really had started out in Vienna by selling newspapers for a few weeks, and when he wasn't doing that, he was in a hotel of the very seediest class in Mariahilf, guarding a locked trunk that held his clothes, very good ones still. They were what enabled him to march right into the lobby of the Grand Hotel after the list of guests from abroad printed in the *Neues Wiener Journal* had informed him that a grand seigneur from Germany, at one time a former boon companion of his, was staying there. This gentleman immediately set the captain up, all nice and neat, as manager of that driving school mentioned earlier; its owner was an automobile dealer who not only had Count X. to thank for one showroom already but also was hoping for another one from the same quarter. So that was the end of selling newspapers; rings, watches, and cigarette cases were soon being redeemed from the pawn shop instead. Meanwhile, Eulenfeld's patron had already established contact with the Wakefield Company, since he was now getting ready to travel to England anyway. You need a lucky break, of course. That's what is said by everybody for whom lucky breaks are a matter of course. And that was how it seemed to be with Eulenfeld.

He knew untold numbers of people in Vienna, though very few of them from the time before the war and his occasional trips to Austria; almost all of his acquaintances dated from the few short years of his continuous residence there. It was well-nigh incomprehensible. Mary K. had been quite right in saying that the captain was a kind of disease that spreads with epidemic speed. If he needed, say, an automobile, to take a quick trip to Greifenstein on the Danube with one or another of his women and stay at some weekend cottage there (which would likewise be somebody else's property), he would chat over the phone for a little while in his most engaging manner, cock his beat-up hat on his head, and be sitting at the steering wheel half an hour later, his pale leather driving gloves unbuttoned, on his way to pick up the lady outside her building by serenading her with the horn. Then they would go roaring off into the green country. His later position allowed him after a few years, by the way, to keep a little sports car of his own.

Before he owned it, he once took Melzer with him on one of these impromptu car trips (with the pale leather gloves and with a monocle, too; I nearly forgot about the monocle, and yet it was somehow an essential component of Eulenfeld's look), because it happened to come about just by chance. A vivid picture of the trip—in many ways a most vivid picture indeed—stayed with the major, an outer image of memory as well as an inner one. The car, a red four-seater, was parked on Wickenburg Gasse in Josefstadt, by the corner of Alser Strasse, near the café; in those days, this was the place where American physicians who were continuing their studies at the medical school in Vienna used to meet regularly. Naturally they knew Eulenfeld in this group, too. He was chatting with two ladies and a gentleman in front of the streamlined red vehicle; the man was one of the doctors, and he had just left the café for a minute to walk Eulenfeld to the car, which he was willing to lend him for a few hours. Eulenfeld was conversing with the American in English (the captain spoke it as fluently as he spoke German, because he'd been at Eton for a few years). The doctor was leaning against the car, no hat on, hands in his pockets. And here came Melzer walking quickly down the street. Through Eulenfeld he knew the doctor, and likewise, he thought, one of the two ladies, but not the other, who was now climbing into the narrow sports car next to the captain. That first one, however, the one he would be sitting with in the back seat, Melzer seemed to be seeing now as if for the first time in his life. She had grown to be more than strikingly pretty; she was fascinating to the highest degree. Her name, originally Pastré, was Schlinger at that time; several years later, her name wasn't Schlinger anymore, for she'd taken a second husband—no, not Dr. Negria, but a Herr Wedderkopp from Wiesbaden instead. With some kind of tiny little nod that words can hardly describe, Eulenfeld now nudged this woman, as it were, over toward the major as he turned around from the driver's seat and called out—cheerful, friendly, and agreeable (as always)—to the two of them to jump quickly into the back seat. He didn't notice, or else he just ignored, the way they said hello like people who were already acquainted. The American waved from the curb, turned away, and went back into the café. The car went roaring along Wickenburg Gasse.

Melzer sat beside this Frau Schlinger, née Pastré, who held such extraordinary appeal for him (this was the first time she'd shown up in Eulenfeld's orbit, and then just fleetingly, at least as it seemed to the major), with a totally unequivocal and strongly oppressive feeling that he'd been demoted—there really isn't any other way to put it. He'd been simply swept up and taken along, just squeezed in somewhere with a woman next to him, and then she was so appealing to him into the bargain. And there was Eulenfeld up front, hunched over the steering wheel. The captain was driving much too fast, zooming around corners, and naturally he knew all the streets wherever he went. Melzer was feeling the way any person would feel who is compelled at a moment's notice to move toward the direction of his least competence and hence of his greatest resistance—the result is a feeling reminiscent of a little toy train car that a child has set by mistake onto tracks of a different gauge. The major sat next to Frau Schlinger as if he were tied up there. A prisoner. Yet during the war he had led a company into combat, month after month, almost more times than he could count; that's what suddenly came into his mind, and at the same instant he thought he could see that this situation belonged to an entirely different area. But how so? It was very painful. Painful, too, that the dazzling blue and sonorously soaring sky of a still warm September day had unfurled over all things, a flood of light that swept everything into itself—the red car, the busy streets, the beautiful woman.

Their trip didn't last long. Frau Schlinger had only asked for a ride home. They stopped at the entryway of a building in the seventh district, Neubau. The entrance was high and narrow; to the right was a store selling typewriters and office supplies, and the green leaves of a tree could be seen back in the courtyard when they looked down the corridor. Over the store was a sign bearing the name LASKER. It was only natural for Melzer to think right away of the battalion commander at Banja Luka, later on a colonel, who had been killed in the war. At that moment he seemed to himself to be uncoupled, at a standstill, isolated like a railroad car on a siding out in the sun. Now he was by himself in the back of the car, missing his neighbor, whom he couldn't observe from the side anymore; indeed, he missed her so much that the blinding red color of the empty leather seat struck him as ferocious and offensive, so he turned his eyes away from it. And yet Melzer also felt relieved now that Frau Schlinger was gone. Sitting next to her, his frame of mind had had a distant kinship with that of an unprepared schoolboy in one of those recurring dreams we can have, now and again, all our lives and whose content is the comprehensive oral examination we have to pass to earn a diploma.

Melzer got out on Porzellan Gasse, in front of the building where he lived. It was on the captain's way in any case, for his thought was to drive straight to Kritzendorf with his current date. When they stopped and the major had climbed out and walked around to the driver's seat to say goodbye, Eulenfeld, whom it would be a mistake to number among the insensitive, couldn't help noticing the expression on his passenger's face. "Well, friend, looks to me like you're not in your most chipper mood," he said quietly, speaking low, and held on to Melzer's hand for a few seconds. The young lady sitting beside the captain was just now subjecting the building the car was standing in front of to an inspection, from top to bottom, with a vacant look. "I'm a bit tired," answered the major, "I think I'll lie down on my couch for an hour. Take care." "Good. Why don't you? Goodbye," said the dragoon captain, and he engaged the clutch. Melzer gave the lady another slight bow, and the car drove away, immediately gaining its top speed again, along the straight stretch of Porzellan Gasse in the direction of the Bohemia Station. Melzer just stayed standing there for the time being, and he could feel dropping away from his features once more the flimsy mask of the forced smile he'd held up so quickly to his face. There are certain skin creams that put a rapidly solidifying protective layer over the face after shaving; one feels a slight resistance with the first movements of the facial muscles, but then they make fine cracks which allow the layer to readjust. Until that happens, though, the man is in possession of a slow face, as it were. Melzer was feeling something like this while continuing to stand outside the building after the car had disappeared. But on the whole, his now being alone brought him great relief. He finally went up the stairs. It was a relatively new building, bright and airy. The windows of the upper stairway landings had a few panes of colored glass inset, and they were now aglow with the sunlight shining through them.

In his own rooms, the major deftly—from long practice—brewed some Turkish coffee in an embossed pot with a long spout. He used a service he'd owned as far back as his days in Bosnia—a long, slender coffee mill whose shape was designed for an Arab to carry it buckled on his saddlebag, a large, engraved copper serving tray, tiny white porcelain cups in copper holders, and a sugar bowl with a vertical half-moon atop the lid.

Then he did something unusual. When the coffee was ready, he put the tray down on the floor, next to the bearskin, filled a chibouk, and stretched out lengthwise on the skin.

Using the chibouk is the strongest method there is for savoring tobacco, in contrast to the narghile or a hookah, the Turkish water pipe, which might be considered the most healthful, because of how it draws the poison out of the tobacco smoke as it passes through the water. The chibouk, with its wide, flat bowl made of Turkish clay, has a very large surface of combustion, on the other hand, and connects to the smoker's mouth by a strong, straight cherrywood tube with an amber mouthpiece, not tapered in the slightest, so that the smoker has no way of putting it into his mouth but can only keep it on the outside, holding it against his lips instead. The chibouk has to be smoked dry, and only the very highest grades of cigarette tobacco can be used, such as the kinds that the Austrian Tobacco Administration used to offer in those days under the brand names Sultan Flor and Persichan. It goes without saying that Melzer was able to get his packages of tobacco in the freshest condition, because he was right there at the source, as it were.

Anyone who smokes the chibouk only seldomly and as described here, and always in combination with Turkish coffee correctly brewed, will find it to be a delicately narcotizing way to achieve calmness and composure, which can cross over into a state in which the Turk enjoys his kèf—this is not a complete brute slumber, but a kind of soaring twilight in which the soul hovers adrift with no hint of torpor; in fact, it is a state capable of easily setting free the creative powers, or more precisely, of cautiously bringing conscious and unconscious into proximity until a spark leaps between them.

This is how the cultivated Near Easterner will take his afternoon rest during the hottest time of day, during the hour when "great Pan slumbers," as the ancients put it. Melzer, too, tried it again today, to seek refuge in his kèf. But he didn't quite make it all the way there. A constant refrain kept coming in from outside, echoing, as it were, from sunlit Porzellan Gasse, an obstinate little triviality that kept forcing its way, over and over again, into Melzer's head. "Looks to me like you're not in your most chipper mood," the captain had said. Those words reminded Melzer very vividly and very strongly of something. But something else was standing in the way and creating interference—it was an odor, and it seemed to be coming from a completely different set of associations; Melzer sniffed around until he could smell the slight, clean scent of camphor clinging to the bearskin from its many summers of being stored in mothballs, and now cutting through the aromas of tobacco and coffee. The major sat up straight, filled his tiny coffee cup, breathed in its strong aroma, and took a small sip. From the street below there came the clattering and the clanging of a street-car driving by very fast and then whizzing past the peak of its own noise. The sun had cut a triangular section out of the top story of the building across the street and laid it gleaming on the white stucco. For the moment, Melzer was incapable of grasping how any of this was supposed to be connected with the Café Pucher—he hadn't gone there for the longest time—but right now it was the Café Pucher he was thinking about.

Then finally it came to him. Thirteen years earlier, Baron von Lindner had said roughly the same thing to him at Pucher's, or rather, had asked him roughly the same thing as what the captain had said to him half an hour ago in the car, right outside his own house, only in a different language, so to speak.

But that wasn't all. That was merely the innocuous outermost edge of what was weighing on Melzer, a man who had never learned how to think, after all, not even as a major.

For now, though, it was enough for him to *feel* while this brief, small closing of the circuit between past and present took place. And the two proved to be identical. One of those voices, whether Herr von Lindner's or the captain's, was reaching him in a prison of some kind, one which he, Melzer, had been locked inside then and still was locked now; inside a lack of independence, inside a state of being handed off from one situation to another, from the military to the tobacco administration; inside a torpor that had held him at Zauner's in Ischl, or anywhere else—it made no difference—rather than allowing him, for example, to take a ride out to the Stangelers' country house. "Asta didn't marry Marchetti any more than she did me, either, and now he's starting to get fatter than a suckling pig." And as far as the war was concerned, Melzer now began to see his independence and his responsibility as a company commander hedged in, if we will, by the general lack of independence in his life overall, during which he had never gone *to* any given place but had done nothing more than report for duty *at* this or that place instead. Even on the Treskavica. He'd been swept up and taken along behind, just like this afternoon in the automobile. This all frightened the major very much. And so he then had to suffer through a few of those moments that anyone who has truly lived is not spared—the deep fear, that is, of not having truly lived. It could be said that going through this fear means, in any event, taking an important new step in life.

In order to keep forging ahead toward the truth about Melzer's relations with Eulenfeld, it seems to us that we will now have to find some way of capturing in words the natures of these two men (always a chancy proposition when it comes to the relative indecisiveness and wishy-washiness of such people) and then of attempting to compare and contrast them. It isn't exactly their characters per se, however, with attendant psychological particulars, that call for interpretation, but rather the mechanical workings of their spirits (to the extent that this latter term can be spoken of at all), meaning the physiognomy-based predispositions which will then express themselves in the materials of character. We could say that in this respect Melzer was made up of two basic elements, one faster and one slower, but that for the present he needed to draw on only the faster one to meet life's challenges and was therefore incomplete, to a degree; for his part, Eulenfeld was made up of nothing but the faster element, and hence he presented himself to one and all, right from the start, as a finished and fully developed personality. Nonetheless, it may be possible to imagine that Melzer, over time, might be extruding that slower substance all the way out to the outer ramparts of his life so as to unite the two elements there, and in that way close and heal the slight rift that cut through his personhood. That state of being closed and healed was what he had apparently always wanted, but because he misconstrued how matters stood with him, he chose the captain as his ideal and his model of how to achieve it.

This error was compounded by a precedent from his own life—without even knowing he was doing it, Melzer was perpetually transferring to Eulenfeld his own emotions and judgments connected to the very vivid images of Major Laska he retained in his memory. To a certain extent, this was the premise on which his relationship with the captain was founded, and he accordingly had no way of anticipating any effects other than supportive and encouraging ones from that party. (The reader must have noted long ago that he always needed somebody to lean on, in any case; surely that emerged in some way with regard to Mary Allern; I'm just reminding you in passing about this general trait in Melzer's disposition.) For his part, though, Major (later Colonel) Laska—may he rest in peace—had carried both of Melzer's basic elements inside himself, albeit intermingled throughout and completely blended, without any rifts.

In the further course of his dealings with Eulenfeld, Melzer admittedly could not help growing aware, little by little, that something wasn't adding up *au fond du fond*, meaning right from his first assumptions. But the brain of our erstwhile lieutenant and bear hunter wasn't analytical. He simply felt burdened. Precisely that, however, precisely that more or less frequent sense of being burdened, was what had never once emerged in his memories of Laska, and by that token they gradually began to diverge ever more from Eulenfeld, with whom they'd long been prone to link together here and there in Melzer's mind. A few other less essential matters entered in as well. Eulenfeld was a heavy drinker, for example, and Melzer, once he started to be tugged into Eulenfeld's orbit—or rather, let's say once he became fascinated (the word is none too strong) by his style of living—practically forced himself to become one too, because there was just no other way to keep up with the captain. Besides, he liked the way Eulenfeld drank, cognac bottle wrapped in a white paper napkin on the back seat of the car, and he liked the captain's habit of smoking through a long cigarette holder when he drank; and could Melzer, that big baby, perhaps also have been hoping for a kind of loosening up if he drank, a stimulus to move him in the direction he desired? As it was, though, the young years of our friend the major had provided him with no experience whatever in the skill of mastering large quantities of alcohol on a regularly occurring basis. In the Austrian army, that degree of indulgence wasn't common to quite the same degree as it is in the German army. It didn't always do him good.

The differences now, the contrast with the images his memory held of the time when he and Laska had shared so much of their lives, were gradually becoming more distinct in his mind.

Starting from the time of the bear hunt in the autumn of 1910, we really can almost call theirs a shared life, a situation the circumstances and exigencies of duty in the service contributed to; Melzer had at one time even been ordered to Banja Luka as deputy battalion adjutant. The two hunting trips with the major, the one to Dobro Pole and the one to the Treskavica, had been only the first two in a whole series of similar ventures. And yet the bear hunt stood out for Melzer in a way that could never be surpassed, not just because of the magnificent trophy, but also inwardly, as a signpost marking the onset of a new time in his life. That was the moment at which he started to carry his severance from Mary more gracefully than before, rather like someone who has at last found the right hold for lugging a heavy suitcase. And that was exactly the moment from which point on he began to grow ever more brightly illuminated on the inside by his resolve to spend his leave time through the coming year, 1911, partly in Vienna but also partly in the country, around the Rax district, a thought which had already overtaken him, we will perhaps recall, on his journey to Trnovo, while he traveled half asleep through the Semmering Pass.

Three days after the ride in the red sports car, Melzer was reminded very vividly of that year, 1911, when he had in fact spent his summer leave the way he'd made up his mind to do the year before, during the whooshing and hollow-sounding passage through the Semmering tunnels, meaning that he'd spent a fair portion of it at the Stangelers' country house.

He ran into Editha Schlinger-Pastré unexpectedly on the Graben. It was about five o'clock. He had an errand to take care of after having finished for the day at the office.

This chance meeting would not in itself have been likely to point him back to the year in question—after all, it lay in a past quite far distant by now—and all the less so as the present was offering the loveliest of allurements in the form of her person. Two incidents greatly facilitated that glance backward, however. One of them had occurred that morning, an almost purely inner event, and the other befell Melzer on the street, in the company of Editha, a thing that made its approach from outside.

At eight o'clock, just as Melzer was setting out for his office and was walking down the hallway of his building, he saw a door, one he had never noticed before, standing open next to the concierge's apartment. From behind that door was emanating an odor—it had already reached him on the bottom stairstep—totally foreign to the stairway here, with its immaculate, whitewashed atmosphere. Decaying leaves? Mold? But there was some something heavier about it too, like rubber. Walking past, Melzer looked into this combination toolroom and storage room— that's what it was—and saw a bicycle, or maybe two bicycles, in there.

During the most routine gaps in Melzer's routine activities, this voice, or whatever it was that had addressed him, coming out of some space that had newly broken through the boundary wall holding his consciousness immured, as it were, kept persistently speaking to him all morning long; that space had certainly been there before—for a very long time, at that—but Melzer had never taken notice of it. And yet the whole thing stood its ground, blocking all efforts to remember or explain (though these were being undertaken only during gaps a few seconds long, to be sure, and so were not truly serious), the way a brick wall blocks a person's path.

When he spotted Editha on the Graben now (he caught up with her before they reached Saint Peter's), there sounded in him again here a bit of the past—but it could be named and explained this time—even though it quickly retreated, as if it were a little shadow slipping around a corner, caused by the gladness he was feeling so keenly in the present. The way she said hello to him, incidentally, might not have been downright cold, but it was rather aloof, exactly as her manner had been three days earlier in the car, despite their not having seen one another for twelve years before that; it was now 1923, after all, and that was how far in the past the garden party at the Schmellers' place in Grinzing lay, the one that had cost Herr von Semski a part of his happiness in life (at the time, of course, he thought he'd lost all of it). Melzer had been at that party, asked along somehow as one of the crowd that traveled with Asta Stangeler and hence with Ingrid Schmeller as well. That was the last occasion, at any rate, in August of 1911, on which he'd seen Editha, but that in turn had been after getting to see her almost every day for the previous two weeks, at the Stangelers', in the country, where she'd likewise been invited as a special favor to her girlfriend Ingrid Schmeller.

He walked along the Graben with Editha. Had he known that after that day he would not see her again for almost two more years, there is no question but that he would have felt a measure of pain, an empty space opening up, a loss.

But he didn't know it.

Besides, her behavior underwent a change—sudden, startling, spasmodic. After about only twenty paces she began talking to him in a very animated way, turning to face him and asking him all sorts of questions (whether he knew, for example, where Edouard von Langl was keeping himself these days, and the same about a certain Konietzki, a man who looked, as the mother of the Stangeler family always remarked, like a dethroned king of Poland—"Oh, yes, I do quite a lot of traveling abroad," she would toss in. Then she asked Melzer with obvious concern and interest about his present job and the duties involved— apparently having been filled in by the captain—and how everything was going for him now that he was "in civvies" all the time).

Still, their conversation didn't progress very far.

Right before they got to the corner of the square at Saint Stephen's, by the bookstore, they saw Ingrid von Budau, née Schmeller, walking straight toward them, arm in arm with her husband.

Melzer lifted his hat. And because they passed one another at very close range, he bowed slightly as he walked by and said, "Good afternoon." Ingrid, although this was hardly the first time he had seen her and greeted her on the street here in the city center, gave no acknowledgment of any kind, but just stared off to the right, past Melzer, as though her eyes were made of glass. Herr von Budau resorted to looking at the display in a shopwindow. Then they were gone.

The major felt somewhat taken aback and disconcerted (never mind that concerted planning was his job!), not by any means only because of the inexplicable and novel behavior of Frau von Budau; no, it was much more because those bicycles from early that morning popped into his head all of a sudden, or rather just plain barged their way in (which clearly makes no sense at all, however), and because he now imagined, after the fact, that he had actually been expecting some encounter along these lines even before it happened (and this in its turn struck him as altogether odd).

Meanwhile, they had reached Saint Stephen's Square, and there Editha let loose, not holding back in the least.

"Did you ever see such nerve? That stupid nitwit! That was the exact same spot—strange, come to think of it—where she cut me dead no more than a couple of weeks ago; all right, I admit I did the same thing to her. We never speak. Not since 1911. You remember, don't you? I'm sure you must have heard all about it from Asta Stangeler at the time."

"Yes, I did," Melzer said, "but can't we learn later on to get over these foolish little squabbles from our youth? Forgive me for saying that, but it's my honest opinion."

"Well, it's not mine," she retorted, decisively and snappishly, as they went slowly walking along, and the alternating stench and noise of the buses—which at that time used to set up a ground-shaking carousel ride around and around the cathedral, night and day—covered what they were saying so well that they had no particular need to lower their voices.

"It's not mine," Editha repeated, and continued, vehement all of a sudden, not to say almost fierce in the way she lashed out. "But don't worry, this is just between me and that dough-brained moron, that total nitwit, that decked-out organ grinder's monkey—that's what she really looks like today. But to ignore a friendly hello from a gentleman for the simple reason that he happens to be in my company, just to make sure that it could never look—oh no, perish the thought!—as if she were bidding me good day as well? That's the height of imbecilic, brazen-faced rudeness. What happens when I'm not around? This can't be the first time you've run into this Ingrid woman on the street and said hello. Does she acknowledge you then?"

"Yes," said Melzer.

"Well, there you have it!" Editha cried, turning away from him at the bus stop near the Café de l'Europe and peering out as she stood there. "Her husband, that Budau, you know, he's one of the most perfect specimens of a gibbering ninny you'll find around Vienna. Of course he's going to play along; ever the doting hubby, that imbecile. *Quant à moi, je m'embêterais à mourir avec un dandin de cette sorte.* The captain saw him playing tennis once at the Park Club and said he runs like a spavined nag."

"Herr von Budau probably didn't have much choice but to play along with his wife, as you put it," the major suggested.

"Whatever," said Editha. And with this one word, she reverted to the tone she'd begun with, when they'd met on the other side of Saint Peter's—distant and offhand, if not cold. She took a few steps over toward a bus that towered high above her as it pulled up; it was probably the one she'd been keeping an eye out for. Then she turned back to Melzer and quickly shook his hand. He looked at her, noting her whole appearance at once, but this abrupt leave-taking plunged him into something like helplessness. Only now—as if it weren't too late— did it dawn on him how beautifully she was dressed, how wonderfully becoming her dove-gray suit was, how fetchingly her little hat perched on her head. "Goodbye," she said, and climbed up the narrow stairs to the roof (these vehicles were equipped that way at the time in Vienna). She seemed to have found a seat on the other side of the bus, toward the cathedral, removed from his range of vision. The bus had pulled up and driven away with noise and stench.

Melzer stepped away from the curb and remained standing there in front of the Café de l'Europe. Strangely enough, that one sentence in French Editha had spoken so hurriedly and mixed in with everything else now seemed to him like a key to her nature, like the explanation and, in that sense, virtually the resolution of a dissonance coming from her words and grating on his ear all the while. The actual content of the sentence in French was totally insignificant ("As for myself, I'd be bored to death with a chucklehead like that"). Even so, it gave audible evidence, and in the most concise form, that Editha spoke from, as it were, a wellspring deeper inside her than Viennese German, the language which, perhaps thanks to her mood, she had gone out of her way to use just now, resorting to vulgarisms in the process but not violating its inner grammatical essence, which is just what a foreigner (and the distinction isn't necessarily geographical) would do. There are foreigners among the natives, among Parisians as among Viennese, among Genevans as among Athenians. At the moment, of course, Melzer was far from busy thinking up truisms like these. What came flying at him all of a sudden, though, flying at him like an arrow that pierces, sticks, and comes to rest with its shaft trembling, was that he could now see, as if uncovered and laid bare, the source of the appeal Editha held for him—it was this faint little hint of something foreign, this touch of the outsider looking in, somehow sweetly all thumbs; it was this language! He would have liked to hear her speaking sometime in pure standard German—would she carry over that slight, even delicate fissure there as well? Probably not. Too bad.

Look at the way, for example, she'd used the phrase "perish the thought!" right in the midst of her choice Viennese effusions, or the expression "bidding good day" instead of "saying hello," things no Viennese would ever say!

An air wafted toward Major Melzer as though from a far distant horizon of his own inner self, while at the same time this autumn day with waning sun but sky still radiant was pulling at him and sending him segmented in all directions, just as the star shape of the city went fanning out from here along the streets to the four winds, out to greenery and open country, all disconnected from here, where he stood and walked now. Out to those curious lands far to the south, too, which had once been parts of a whole as well. It was five years now since these nerve paths had been severed. Editha's sweet concoction of a doctored language oozed its way into the wound. Doctored, but not diminished in force. Likewise, a tennis ball that's been cut doesn't diminish in its tactical value through this "doctoring," but instead increases in it.

He stood adrift for a few seconds, letting his thoughts just wander. They went their own ways, unmoored from any anchor, as sometimes happens right before we fall asleep. And there was the tennis court at the Stangelers' out in the country, situated somewhat higher up than the house itself. Geyrenhoff. Ingrid Schmeller. Marchetti. The prep-school boy René. But no Editha Pastré, even though he'd been seeing her there, running all over the place, for two weeks. First and foremost—Asta. The others weren't standing against the surroundings with their feet solid on the ground; they were more like tin soldiers on a little supporting footboard cut out of the grass or the gravel.

Suddenly it occurred to him that neither of Editha's parents was originally from Vienna, but from French-speaking Switzerland instead, from Lausanne or Geneva, or some such place around there. He knew that much about her family, anyway. Now at last Melzer had come upon the real key—to everything, he thought! Still, it was less suited for opening something than for locking it. And indeed, that's what Melzer did as he started to walk away from where he'd been standing. He left it behind him and headed along Rotenturm Strasse, toward the Danube Pier.

On the twelfth of May—it was 1911, that year we've already conjured up repeatedly—at around five in the afternoon, René Stangeler, still a prep-school boy, was sitting and waiting in a parlor at the Royal and Imperial Consular Academy.

The longish, medium-sized room contained a few pieces of furniture in the Empire style. The tall, narrow window, set in a deep niche painted a glossy white with sparse ornamentation in gold, opened onto the park. The quite presentable atmosphere of this room was very much like the one prevailing in similar reception rooms around all Austrian ministries of that time. The same could be said by analogy about the doorman—a cross between tried-and-true civil servant and clean-shaven butler—who had shown René in. Half a glance from underneath the man's weary eyelids had been enough for him to size up what bin or box the young fellow there before him had come out of.

Stangeler was carrying a note in his pocket from his sister Etelka to one of the students, Stephan Grauermann (dubbed at the Consular Academy Prince Coucou out of sheer silliness).

It was very quiet here. Nothing was stirring in the wide corridors outside the door.

The boy was sitting in an elegant armchair. He had stretched out his legs and crossed them and was looking out of his slanted eyes at the tips of his tan shoes. René's facial expression was overcast, at the very least, if not altogether dark. The whole appearance of the boy (almost completely grown by now), his long legs in brown wool socks and the trousers of his gray sport suit, very stylish, made him look extremely slender, even gaunt and emaciated.

The silence came alive all of a sudden and at once took audible shape. A piano struck up nearby, on the same floor as this parlor, perhaps right in the next room. René, not moving, listened with the keenest attention, but the expression on his face did not brighten in any way; something all drawn together like a knot stayed there, even though he knew after a few bars what was being played. It was the prelude to the great piano sonata in F-sharp minor by Robert Schumann. Some seconds later he heard light footsteps echoing as they came rapidly along the outside corridor in his direction. It was this second perception that finally set his features in motion. The attentiveness he had brought to bear when listening to the piano remained in place, but obviously cutting through it now was the awareness that Grauermann was just about to step into the room; this twofold discordance caused a third entity to leap up in René, one which an onlooker would have been able to detect instantly. What had rapidly emerged out of the gap between two emotions going off in opposite directions was an irritation of no slight degree. A sharply etched furrow now appeared spontaneously between the boy's eyebrows.

It had vanished by the time Grauermann entered. The deep bell-like sounds of the prelude were still resounding from the next room. René had stood up quickly, and he took out the letter as he went toward Grauermann, who first held his hand out to René with a smile. The student's face made a smooth and youthful impression above the wine-red collar and the dark-green jacket of his uniform. "Thanks very much," he said; they sat down, and Grauermann opened the note and read it through. He nodded happily while he read.

Meanwhile, the unknown pianist next door had reached the end of the prelude and gone into the first movement, its effect on René altogether visible as Grauermann was asking him in a friendly way how he was, if his studies were going well, and other questions like that. René's divided attention, the greater part of which had by now unmistakably tipped over to the side of the piano music, caused this little chitchat to die away after it had scarcely begun, while the main theme, rhythmically punctuated and undergoing its fugal treatment next door, filled the room more and more strongly.

"What is that? I just can't place it..." asked Grauermann at last, with a nod of his head toward the next room.

"Schumann, the F-sharp minor," Stangeler said. "Etelka's working on it now," he added.

"Oh, of course!" cried Grauermann, and he slapped his forehead lightly with the flat of his hand. "If you'd like to listen, let's go next door. It's Teddy von Honnegger playing; you know him. We just have to be quiet." He stood up, and Stangeler followed him. They walked a few steps down the corridor, and Grauermann opened a tall double door painted in white enamel, exactly like the one that led into the parlor they'd just left. They made no noise at all in their movements. Stangeler looked into the room first, as it was one he'd never been in before; the green from the park came shining through three high windows, along with some rays from the evening sun, which was glowing in the white alcoves of the windows. Grauermann and René stayed near the door, now shut behind them, of the music room, and stood on the thick rug; the piano, a baby grand, was placed facing the last window on the right in such a way that the person playing had his back turned to them.

Their noiseless entrance coincided unintentionally but strikingly with the beginning of the second theme, which even by itself would send a jolt of euphony through any human being however scantily endowed with the faculty of hearing. At this point, it closed the entire situation into its compass—the gold-burnished green of the park, the solitude of the player, the impenetrable places in the heart of a very youthful individual, the equally impenetrable tensions in the relationship between Grauermann and Etelka, along with everything else, including the rapid seconds now swiftly dropping down against the slower background of time's river—the composer's upward-striving and gently cascading second movement now subsumed and tempered everything that existed here in the present moment, so that it could come streaming into this form, as it were, fill that form and take it on completely, leaving nothing at the margins or on the outside. Stangeler could not put a name to this inner state, but he could feel it very clearly and distinctly. The emotion broke through to his face this time. We might say that his face untangled its knots. To a certain extent, he saw the light (as people call it) for these few seconds. In Grauermann's features, however—he was able to observe his schoolboy friend from the side without being noticed himself—something entirely different was showing, and it was coming out of no less central a chamber of his life at that time. It was a spasm of deep-seated and, if one will, nervous pain. Looking at René's youthful physiognomy brought the strong family resemblance between him and Etelka to the forefront of his mind, as was perfectly natural to an outsider (although no one inside the family itself had ever noticed any particular resemblance between brother and sister). And now, as René's features thawed, Grauermann saw revealed in his face an undeniable and, as it were, fierce authenticity of relationship to that world—not just the world of music, or the world of the "fine arts" (as he called it), or the world of the "intelligentsia" in general (as he felt obligated to call it), in which he was constantly struggling to secure an informed foothold—rather, what he saw was a means of growing closer to life itself, although those means were not for him, since all they were ever able to effect in his case was to lead him farther away from life, imposing itself on him and turning him into a fraud the minute he came anywhere near Etelka, even though being near her was exactly what he strove for day and night. For a few seconds he was filled with repugnance as he stared at René's face, as if he were a prisoner looking at the bars of his cell window.

Granting that even then he already possessed a high degree of awareness about his own life, especially by comparison to others that same age, it still can't be asserted that Grauermann would have been at all capable of giving a name to the experience he was undergoing during those moments in the music room of the Royal and Imperial Consular Academy—not at the time, anyway. Otherwise, the moment might have been able to define him differently, been able to steer, to turn, to divert his actions. But of course that's not what happened.

Etelka Stangeler had been educated in Dresden at a boarding school led by a Fräulein Brandt, an establishment whose rolls were almost entirely filled with pupils from abroad, mainly young girls from England. Etelka returned home after several years at school very much a changed person. She brought back with her a standard of education that, to be sure, had been kept confined within the framework of instruction standard for young ladies but that was alien to her parents' home nonetheless. We can't even say it was better or worse—it was just different, and that was the main point (it's possible, too, that Etelka had in fact learned to make finer distinctions and had become somewhat more keenly attuned to nuances than was the rule in the Stangeler household). At any rate, she had gained access to a base of support lying outside her family's biases and predispositions, and she used it as an inner reference. This condition of hers lay at only a shallow depth, however, lodged no deeper than in the outer skin layer of circumstance and situation, so to speak, at which layer there was still relatively little harm done. What had far greater significance and went much deeper for Etelka, as a woman, meanwhile, was what lay on the level of style as manifested in everyday living, along with all the inner and outer niceties and proprieties that style entailed. On this level she distanced herself when she returned home—perhaps more pointedly than was necessary—from that southern penchant for letting everything slide; this was a point of emphasis for Etelka, so it was also the starting point for her disavowal of her family—an obbligato voice that unfortunately seems to accompany talented individuals. Behind it stood a forceful will, an inheritance from her father, who seems to have deposited it en bloc into Etelka's account, so to speak. It's easy to picture how the rest of it goes. It was all well and good that Herr von Stangeler never failed to make a splendid appearance, that outside the home he charmed the whole world, whether in business dealings or on social occasions; but within his family jurisdiction—at least back then, in his younger years—he would let loose with almost no restraint whatever, picking fights, bellowing, trampling things underfoot. In this respect, he and his third daughter turned out to be exactly alike, both of them real "street angels," as they say in Vienna, delightful outside the house, unbearable in many ways at home. Etelka, however, was no patriarch with a father's plenipotentiary powers and absolute, crushing authority over the finances; like the rest of the children, moreover, she had come into this world with her nerves already bad (this is one area in which the father seems to have been very lavish in spending the capital he had on deposit even while being punctiliously thrifty in all others). Whenever he would walk into the spacious dining room, sweating a little, his shoulders twitching with "nervous energy," which is what Guy de Maupassant calls it, his handsome head lowered slightly like a bull getting ready to charge any second, then Etelka's will, no less intense than her father's, would be swept aside and sent scurrying away by his forceful manner of entering the room. And when—it happened often—the aggressive opening attack would ensue, she would likely be the first to come right back with some impudent answer and then in short order switch to crying and pulling a woebegone face.

As time went by, that grew more and more to be the principal cast in which she would compose her features—at home, needless to say. There was a portrait of her dating from those years, a picture done by one of those painters who have refined ideas about their art, albeit whose paintings would not have been jarringly out of place in a photographer's studio, either (the father had commissioned portraits of all his children, one after the other, until it came to the two youngest, who had at an early age sat for pictures along similar lines). Etelka's portrait, a pastel drawing, was executed completely in the spirit of the woebegone face; it's probable that the artist, who had never met Etelka before, never got to see her in anything other than this psychological costume, and it's more than probable that she in turn went out of her way to wear it to her sittings on purpose, as opposed to reverting to her usual practice outside the home. This isolated rendering of that single facet of her total personality had been carried out with remarkable accuracy, however, with the accuracy of an illustration in a book on natural history. Once it was finished, the picture gave the impression of being somehow veiled or blurred, as if clouded over by fog or mist or cigarette smoke, from behind which screen then emerged a face full of ennui and dejection, far more ethereal than Etelka had ever been in real life, since at that time she was actually a strapping wench in the pink of health (although later in life Frau Consul Grauermann suffered from insomnia to the point of suicide and did in fact end up actually killing herself).

The outward features of Etelka Stangeler's living situation after her return to her parents' home, in particular the spatial features, were extraordinarily conducive to her new separatism vis-à-vis her family. The dark house, originally located at the tree-lined edge of the Prater, though soon to be blocked in on every side by one new street after another of the growing city—all of them pleasant, though—was four stories high; the grandmother of the family, the widow of an architect, occupied the first story until her passing. The second floor housed only company rooms and the father's office; the bedrooms were on the third floor. It will suffice to say of the fourth floor that a family of relatives, the father an architect, lived on it. Architects on top of architects, as René's father had also been an architect originally, before he began his new career as a construction engineer for the railroad. The husband of the family on the fourth floor was married to René's mother's sister and he owned the house equally with Herr von Stangeler, his brother-in-law. Quite a far-reaching consolidation of genealogy and architecture, along with an elevated (at times even stratospheric) level of self-assurance that was not without the most widespread possible consequences in the form of stiff, starchy-looking Gothic churches and gigantic Renaissance nightmares that certain sections of the city had been almost entirely uglified by. But enough of that; our aim here is to investigate the outward conditions of Etelka's living on separate terms, after all.

There were not enough bedrooms on the third floor. Etelka's father rented an apartment in the building immediately adjoining that had since been built, and he had a doorway broken through the thick fire wall, so they had several more rooms on the third floor. Three, to be exact; anyone who went to the last room (it was a breakfast room) belonging to the Stangeler house proper and opened the communicating door first saw three steps going down, as the floors of the two buildings were not level; these three steps were precisely fitted inside the door frame, which had to be sufficiently deep to fill the space of a strong, solid fire wall. Then came the three adjacent rooms, a small one first, then a moderately large one, and then another small one, all the way at the end.

Earlier, the two eldest daughters had occupied these small rooms and had used the larger one in the middle, where there was a piano, among other things, as their common living room. After the two girls had married and moved abroad, Etelka and Asta succeeded them in the two rooms, now free; as the elder, Etelka had the one at the back, which no one had to walk through, and so she lived in the very last room of the entire third floor with her back, so to speak, against the very last wall of them all (a wall that she would not infrequently be driven straight up by such a volatile father).

Now, this added-on apartment had some additional rooms besides, though—an unused kitchen, a servants' room (where two domestics employed in the Stangeler household slept), and an entryway with a separate front door for the apartment, which opened onto another staircase entirely, which one could go down and step out onto a different street, since this building was on a corner and its main entrance not on the same street as the Stangeler family's house.

No doubt our readers have already figured out where all this is leading and have for a good while now been watching the perspectives we're sketching here open up before them.

Still, those perspectives, if they were not totally obstructed, were at any rate cramped by an individual who went by the name Frau Fuček and who was the concierge in the corner building.

The rest, of course, just follows from there. Whether from the viewpoint of Etelka, of Asta, or of the two housemaids, who'd been in service here a good long time (they were all in the same boat concerning what we're about to say), it was clear that everything depended essentially on their relations with Frau Fuček, relations which by all means were cautiously maintained but nevertheless kept within tight restraints by prudence—on the other side as well (considering all the remunerative possibilities in these little arrangements); Frau Fuček had been explicitly forbidden to hand over a house key to anyone, something she would really never have had the nerve to do anyway, not even if she'd been asked outright for one (she might have made an exception here and there for the two domestics). But she was never once asked. No one wanted to be quite that open about it, and so they were all resigned to writing off that most remote and distant of escape hatches (which might have offered a way back down the wall Etelka had been driven up) as an unattainable goal after ten at night, or for that matter even earlier, because the eye of Frau Fuček ranged over the comings and goings of all and sundry through a peephole, and, as that Viennese philosopher Johann Nestroy puts it, "morals hold up until nine o'clock, but then, at quarter after, the suspect hour begins." All of this when taken together provides us with an explanation for the rather strange set of circumstances whereby Etelka Stangeler, to whose advantage the whole layout of the place seemed so well arranged, needed to make her way, when she would go out on her nocturnal jaunts back during those years, through the second floor, where her evening dress, along with a fur stole or a cape deposited there in advance, would be waiting in a huge, bowl-shaped copper urn under the sideboard in the dining room. A spiral staircase led down from the third to the second floor. Innocently dressed in everyday clothes or perhaps even wearing her nightgown as she traveled the long route from her perch at the top of that farthest wall of them all, she would walk past the entryway when everyone had gone to bed and dart down the little staircase; if she should happen to run into anybody at any point, some slight excuse, such as a book of music she'd forgotten or some such other thing she might need for her lesson the following morning, a notepad or her metronome, would easily see her through—sometimes she liked to practice on the concert grand on the second floor, because it was a better instrument and stood in a room with better acoustics than the piano in her own living room upstairs. Just before changing clothes, before putting this one last dot on the *i* of her perfect preparations by fixing her makeup and hair, she had to look one more time before she leapt, like a seasoned old chamois buck, and so she would stand in the large dining room, empty now but bright from her having turned on the chandelier, and listen once more as the seconds ticked away. Then she would rapidly complete her metamorphosis in front of the tall mirror by the pilaster arch. And now to get out of there, still listening the whole time, turning the lights out behind her. Then she was on the stairs; the house door clicked shut with almost no sound. And a key to her parents' house? She had one. Of course there was a concierge here as well, two, in fact, a married couple. But people of that sort go decline in the atmosphere of a one-family private household, where a reign of terror is not possible and the keen powers of observation needed for them to remain firmly on solid ground are no longer a matter of life and death. Measuring the Richterčeks against the Fučeks of this world was like measuring a coddled lapdog against a wolf.

As we can see, Etelka was not world-weary, even if she did present herself at home in what we might call the *façon voilée*, subdued and swathed in gloom (which of course brought on outbursts of rage from her father). At that time, her escapades by night were still entirely harmless and innocent. They led her into circles that didn't exactly have any official acquaintance or connection with her parents' world, though everything stayed pretty much inside the same box or bin; on bright moonlit nights they would take rides through the Vienna Woods or the Wachau (there was even a car crash once, and Etelka hastened to make a getaway by taxi so that she wouldn't be subpoenaed to appear as a witness in court, since one of the young fellows had almost broken his neck). She would occasionally spend half the night in some bar or boîte, though being careful to stay with her own crowd and to make sure there would be some other young women present. Asta was in on the whole thing and would faithfully wait up during Etelka's night flights. She wasn't always treated very kindly in return, by the way—markedly worse, in fact, ever since she'd made her own social debut and been through her first season of dances and parties. It even happened once that a new poppy-red dress of Asta's, which may have set off her dark-skinned beauty only too well, came back to her all ripped and stained and made totally useless by her sister. But then again, they often showed great mutual affection, and Etelka had a sweet tooth, so

Asta never failed to bring her, or to have waiting for her, a certain kind of chocolate éclair filled with marzipan from an Italian bakery in the neighborhood. After her sister's escapades, even the more exhausting ones, Asta, right before going to sleep, would pass one of these delicious bars through the crack of the door, so softly and secretly opened, whereupon a quick bite would instantly be taken out of it on the other side. That was just one of those things they did. Asta often stayed awake for hours on end when Etelka was out of the house at night. She seemed to sleep more calmly when she knew that Etelka had slipped back in safely and that again this time everything was all right.

Etelka's nocturnal expeditions had no connection whatever with Stephan Grauermann.

Their way of relating to each other was entirely different; it would have put an observer more in mind of the *façon voilée*. Grauermann was basically a healthy and sensible young fellow and, as we said before, he possessed no small degree of self-awareness for his age. He was wide-awake, a quick-witted young man. His interest in higher learning was partial evidence of that, surely, but it by no means constituted the basis for his being so alert, since it wasn't by this one means alone that he'd become so wide-awake, so sharp. Still, the general need on the part of young people to discuss everything propelled him down that track for a while, all the more so after he began to cross paths at the academy with Teddy von Honnegger, who was two years older and therefore in a more advanced class. Incidentally, Etelka was also a bit older than Stephan (whom people mostly called by his Hungarian name, Istvan or Pista, and rightly so, as his father, chief physician and department head in Pressburg, was indeed Hungarian in spite of his German name). So between these two, Etelka and Teddy—who knew each other only slightly in those days—our boy Pista got caught in a certain amount of crossfire. The ammunition was culture, which he took as his ideal, but culture in fact was not what he understood by that word, for his mind never stopped picturing it as something highly polished and best surveyed from a distance. Compared to Grauermann, though, the other two had something elemental about themselves, each in a different and individual way, but of course in a relative sense only. We could also say that their culture functioned as a gear in the overall mechanisms of their souls, such that the mechanisms would have been totally different without it; strictly speaking, then, we cannot maintain that their gears were misaligned or that they had a screw loose somewhere, however much they might have given that impression from time to time.

Honnegger, who, incidentally, was anything but what people dismissively call a nice kid, had gained an accurate idea of the life of the mind by becoming aware of the pessimism inescapably associated with it. That was just about the only thing he *had* become aware of at the time, however, and as for all the rest, he retreated into his music (thinking doesn't make for the most pleasant of lives). And yet his natural rapport with the writings of Dr. Schopenhauer (its very solid foundation unquestionably grounded in his own life) soon found its echo in Grauermann in the form of precise, comprehensive, and academically formal knowledge of said philosopher.

In Etelka, that same rapport underwent a wondrous transmogrification via discombobulation that reached the point of fruitful but ultimately frightful misunderstanding. She soaked up Schopenhauer's captivating language as dry ground soaks up rain, and this rain seemed to her to be exactly what she needed. Her powers of comprehension were quick, alert, and shot through with lightning flashes of genuine emotion; her ability was undeniably adequate for her to take in what her chosen author was saying, but the aesthetic qualities of his writing kept on brilliantly camouflaging his conclusions from her sight. Gradually, her reading became a kind of interpretation of her own moods, and as much as this might have been the wrong way of going about it, it too was genuine; for her, all of the philosopher's writings turned out to be articulations of her own manner of living. What came into being then was something like a more highly evolved and epistemologically grounded variety of the *façon voilée*. For all the absurdity and befuddlement, though, something totally authentic was set in motion inside Etelka, and this was the source of the power that these studies came, little by little, to exercise over Grauermann in a whole new way—it made no difference, either, how hard he kept trying to stage a rebellion just below the threshold of consciousness, proceeding in exactly the same way here as with music. And it was this kind of rebellion that had the power to block him from even recognizing a piano sonata, never mind that he'd heard it a dozen times before.

Strange things for a pair of lovers to be studying! I think it's entirely possible that snobbishness alone was what kept relations between them from overstepping permissible bounds, as they're called—a pretty flimsy moral foundation, one might well object, but it held. Everything about young people is permeated by a yearning for form, and they make many sacrifices to it, even the most outlandish ones, without quite knowing they're doing it. And, in this instance, their form could undoubtedly have been battered down by the, the—oh let's just say it!—vitalism so plain to see between them.

They had enough opportunities, anyway. After all, their philosophical colloquia took place by that wall up which Etelka was driven. Asta was in collusion and at her post every time. Whenever the coast was clear—such as when Stangeler père was off tramping around some mountain railroad line under construction—Pista Grauermann would make his way straight to the wall in question, but without waiting at the front door while his social call was announced; that is, he chose the route leading past the Cyclopean eye of Frau Fuček, convinced that his tracks were covered and that he wasn't attracting attention. That was where he was wrong. His uniform, mistaken for an officer's, prompted an especially keen investigation, in fact, and one winter evening, after his sixth or seventh return visit, the eye of the Fuček ranged so far as to follow him around a turn in the staircase, from landing to landing, the distance of a whole floor, her felt slippers as quiet as if they'd been a bat's wings, since she wanted to find out for sure which apartment he was slipping into, and naturally she was successful, even though, at almost the same moment, while she was making the sharp turn onto the next landing, the workings of centrifugal force caused one of her well-padded slippers to fly off and tap against the wall; when Grauermann, a boy with some experience, turned around upon hearing the noise—he'd been just about to step through the door—and peered down over the banister, he saw a gray shadow darting back downstairs and realized what was going on. A while ago, we called him an alert young man, and now he's about to prove it, so we won't look like a fool in front of the reader. What he now did, in spite of Etelka's uneasiness, was to stay in her room past the Nestroyan hour of suspicion; for that matter, he didn't leave until some time after ten o'clock, his explicit purpose, all cool and calm, being to have the concierge unlock the street door of the house, whereupon he overtipped her for her trouble, but to a moderate degree, slipping if not a gulden, then at least a crown into the outstretched prehensile claw of the Fuček. From then on, this practice was repeated at reasonable and infrequent intervals. However, Grauermann was careful after that time to avoid leaving the building too shortly before ten, for fear of causing commotion; and besides, he almost always came in the afternoon. In sum, peace was preserved.

It was a strange world that came together and mingled at Etelka's upstairs, in the "Quartier Latin," as Herr von Stangeler jokingly called the apartment given over to his two daughters who were still at home. And whoever took a closer look would begin to notice a good many behaviors that later on, in the last year of her life, it was very frightening to watch Etelka revert to, in the form of pronounced and even ir-reversibly deep-seated patterns; her dwelling behind closed curtains, the *façon voilée* even in her inner depths—no edges, no contours, no light, no shadow—all of it punctuated at times by episodes frenzied in the intensity of their attack, such as renewed nocturnal roamings with the evening dress in the copper bowl or escapades involving winter sports. That was when skiing was becoming all the rage, and Etelka was the first woman to travel with a downhill-racing team, the only woman in this prize-winning group, and one who could always keep pace with men who were considered the top-performing skiers of their time. But then it would come back—day in and day out, nothing but Turkish coffee and cigarettes, *façon voilée*.

Pista brought a Near Eastern touch. The students at the academy had that air anyway, and it was constantly being reimported to Waisen-haus Gasse whenever the attachés from Turkey, Arabia, Persia, or North Africa would come back for a visit to their alma mater. There was a path leading straight from Dr. Schopenhauer to Indian philosophy, for that matter, or at least to what Schopenhauer would have thought was Indian philosophy, in accordance with his sources, and that, as a result, Etelka and Pista likewise imagined it to be, only seventeen stories lower. A good thing that Karl Eugen Neumann's translations of the discourses of Gautama Buddha had not yet been published; who knows, but it doesn't seem as if those two would have been able to get very far with them. "And the monk rejoices," as it says every time the meditation has reached a slightly higher stage—but because he has given way to rejoicing, poor fellow, the whole thing drops all the way back to the starting point every time! It's my guess that our two monks would have done overmuch rejoicing right from the start. Pista had given Etelka a Turkish coffee service like the one Melzer owned; perhaps you still remember it. This was the way they did things on Waisenhaus Gasse; a Turkish coffee service was just part of it, as was the crescent moon with star that the academy's hockey team wore on their jerseys. Of course, hockey must have been getting to be something of a rarity at that time, for soccer had long since caught on and become popular in Vienna.

So there were many quiet and veiled times together in the Quartier Latin, and only if we were to view it from too short a distance would our pair of little snobs come to strike us as merely ridiculous. However, a glance backward from the formlessness of our own time, with all its life-driven hustle and bustle (which in reality arises from a much more radical falling away from life), shifts the perspective to an angle from which we can make a judgment. To specify, these two young people were at least making up their own lies for themselves, whereas today we can't even begin to do that anymore; we have to go out and attain this article store-bought instead, and quite naturally the goods aren't going to be anywhere nearly as fresh and pliant as if they were home-made. Seen from their vantage point, it's possible over time to mount a springboard and leap into the truth, whereas the person used to just buying readymade products has long since lost the ability to pick up the faintest scent of it with his technician's nose, now adapted to nothing but gasoline and lubricating oil.

And besides, what do we mean by a lie here, anyway? They were in love, or at least they had a strong mutual attraction (which under the most exacting scrutiny might very possibly have proven to be composed of a great many facets, like the eye of a housefly seen under the microscope—but does an analysis of a phenomenon ever make it go away?), and they had enough flair to give a nimbus, a style, an aura to their experience, to take charge, even if only slightly, of where it was going, which I still think of as a good quality compared to the short circuits, the short, shorter, and shortest links between two points of contact, which is how it is among our young people of today, who are honest and forthright all the way down to that same ground they end up trampling everything into. Shall we demand of a loving couple that their philosophy have truth content? Oh, I know, what we'd rather demand is a loving couple minus any and all philosophy. Me too. But we grow tolerant over time. Better a couple with a philosophy than no couple. Love turns everything into a mere decoration, and if we went ahead and let those people have their way, they would call in any ordinary old handyman, have him plane down the most priceless statues of all the saints to make them over into bedposts, and then feel ever so nicely edified and completely unburdened up there on the bed that would result.

For our couple here, one such decorative post was made up of a certain Omar Khayyám, a Persian poet who lived in India around the middle of the eleventh century and whose work spread beyond that region in some obscure way. His epigrammatic poems, called the Rubáiyát, were first translated into French and English, and subsequently were published in several other European languages. The edition Grauermann had given to his Etelka was exceptionally beautiful, bound in dark green leather and bearing no decoration other than a pillared Arabian arch in gold, fine lines embossed into the leather, one of those Moorish gateways that reminds one of certain leaf shapes and that can be met with everywhere in Eastern architecture (someone once gave it the very apt name of "the black-coffee style"). Each epigram stood alone, just one on each page, which seemed like the most appropriate way to lay out the quatrains, with their compression of content, because it gave them enough room to explode, so to speak, whereupon they did not just fill the thoughts of the reader but also went on to overrun the blank part of the page, as it were. These little poems acted, indeed, like the overflowing contents of a strongbox that had been crammed until bursting and now was having its lid pried off.

They worked a whole lot better than Dr. Schopenhauer. The two were alert enough readers, after all, especially Etelka.

So many strange things happen in a large city, a large, southern city under a sky that, already hot in May, sends its crackling bright blue, like a flag snapping in the wind, through the crowded and colorful streets. Omar Khayyám. Etelka smoked tiny little thin cigarettes that had a trumpet in gold stamped on them. Their brand name was Figaro. A large city like this, for all its blare and its glare, is also a place to envy for the caverns it holds inside itself, sweet-scented, well cared for, hidden away, like veiled, concealed chambers of its soul.

And the quiet coolness in the stairways. It can well be said that you didn't merely step into them from the street; instead, you retreated from the street.

Etelka was lying on a small chaise longue that Grauermann was sitting beside, on the floor, and here too stood the embossed copper tray with the coffee service from Mostar (for an Austrian of that time, this made it still a domestic product).

His face now seemed, as it so often seemed to Etelka, inexpressibly young and smooth, and that almost frightened her. It was an elegant face too, with a perfectly straight, turned-up nose from which, even at his age, two fine, sharp lines ran down to the corners of his mouth. His large gray-blue eyes beamed with decency and with a cheerful coolness that seemed able to lure Etelka into emerging from all her entanglements and into a proper measure of good humor. She leaned over, drew his head to her, and kissed his fragrant hair. Grauermann stayed leaning on her breast, his eyes closed, and he let the book in his hands drop. After a while he stood up, leaned over Etelka, and carefully brushed back her hair. She didn't much like him to do that, really, since it revealed a flaw in her beauty; her forehead, which would become visible, was high, steeply vertical, and at the same time wide (almost bovine, because of this last-named feature—and why shouldn't we say so, considering that the very father of all novelists, apparently guided by Winckelmann's "noble simplicity and quiet grandeur," compares the eyes of the goddess Hera to those of a cow?!). This forehead, which looked as if a powerful will had given it a dome shape, was decidedly too large for a woman's face; released from its covering of hair, it pressed that face together and gave it, in spite of the strong mouth and chin, an insignificant look, like a flimsy base for the steep cliff on top of it.

Against it, we could say, Grauermann's love was breaking in unceasingly querying, wearying little waves. It was her father's forehead.

Pista, however, kept on scanning this forehead for something else, namely for some kind of remote affinity with his friend Teddy von Honnegger, as though he were trying to fit them both, the girl he loved and his good friend, into the same category.

Etelka, her eyes meeting Grauermann's, smiled and then turned away slightly. She brushed her hair back over her forehead.

While she was looking up at him, it passed through her mind that she really liked him even more out in the countryside (that was where they'd first come to know one another), where he'd be wearing his baggy mountain vest and an open tennis shirt, than she did elsewhere, with him in the green jacket of his uniform, even though it became him very well. In that sunny world of short summer vacations, half-rustic but at the same time carefully groomed, in a mountain village set far back from the end of the valley and a three-hour walk from the nearest railroad station—that was where the first of her experiences connected with Grauermann were rooted, that was where, considering how little variety there was in their social life, he'd been offered to her on a silver platter, so to speak, as a singular attraction, and she'd had enough opportunities, in all the freedom of woodland and crag, to relish his romantic style of paying court. Dr. Grauermann's parents-in-law made their home out there, and Pista's maternal grandfather, who bore a name very well-known in the German publishing industry at that time, was famous—strange original that he was, his coarseness legendary—for taking solitary walks one summer after another, during which it was not exactly pleasant to meet him, because whenever he felt like it, he might throw stones at anyone who came within range. Pista had taken Etelka along, tied to the same rope, whenever he went climbing the jagged and fissured limestone crags of the Rax Alps, and these hours of concentrated effort under the brilliant blue of the sky, amid the deep silence of the steep chasms, had made up the prelude to their love, a love that then, in surroundings just like these—on a wide band of rock over some dry runnels of scree that went flowing away from one another in finger shapes—eventually came to the point of being openly declared.

For the time being, conditions were most inopportune for announcing an engagement publicly, because Etelka, much to the wrath of her father, had not long before broken off an engagement he had warmly welcomed. And at the end of this summer Grauermann would be moving into only his third year at the Consular Academy.

So the whole thing was kept secret for the time being. That was how Etelka wanted it.

Now she sat upright on the chaise longue, and Grauermann continued reading to her about the "fourfold root of the law of sufficient reason."

He'd scarcely gotten a good start when Asta's footsteps were heard in the piano room next door, followed by a faint scratching at the door of Etelka's room, a prearranged sign that the coast was clear and that there was no reason for alarm, just that Asta wanted to join them. "Come on in!" called Etelka, smiling in a somewhat distracted way, and going with Grauermann, who had stood up quickly, to the door, since nothing else was happening. Only a narrow crack was opened, noiselessly. About halfway up the door, a dark-colored, well-known object came reaching in toward Etelka, moving closer and closer, until the little tinfoil sleeve grew visible that wrapped one end of this bar of deliciousness made of chocolate and marzipan.

"Just what is this?" cried Etelka in a low voice, stepping back, her hands raised, splendidly feigning surprise and shock.

"You ought to know," Asta now said, and she opened the door all the way. Grauermann gave her a friendly hello full of genuinely warm feeling. And Etelka had meanwhile set aside her veiled, world-spurning mood and gone ahead and taken a hearty bite.

These were exactly the things Asta couldn't stand about her sister, though.

René Stangeler left the Consular Academy at quarter to six and turned left, walking a few slow steps uphill along Waisenhaus Gasse.

The boy felt totally bowled over by the impression he'd just received of a sphere of living and a manner of living that caused his own world to drop to the ground like a withered leaf and lay in the dull dust by comparison. Even leaving out of the account that at this time Stangeler couldn't so much as look at any person or thing without immediately wanting to be it and to live in the manner and the milieu proper to it—everything had the same effect on him, too, an opera or a detective movie—whatever he had just experienced fit in with his tastes the way a key fits into a lock, and it opened up a little door to the safe of his glimmering ideas.

He was not aware that it was mainly Herr von Honnegger to whom he was indebted for so profound an impression, one produced within fifteen minutes and solely because Herr Teddy was much too grown-up and long since too clever to allow his own superiority to manifest itself in front of a mere boy. (Yes, he thought of this young man in the upper prep-school grades as a boy; René's progress had been delayed, and by more than a year and a day, for he'd originally been sent off to a technical school, which did not prove to be an undeniable mistake until his second year there.)

All of it taken together was what was now bearing up and firing up René—the F-sharp minor sonata, the small waiting room, the silence in the building, the sunlight in the music salon where the three of them had sat and had even had a nice talk. The content of that talk was the most unimportant aspect of it, however. Stangeler had completely forgotten it by now, in fact. To a certain extent, he'd been forced into the conversation by the outward situation in which he'd found himself. As for the rest, everything seemed to him to have moved along easily and freely. René had a good feeling, without any of the awkwardness that would often bother him after a change of scene or after leaving a place.

For his part, Herr von Honnegger had been scrutinizing the schoolboy very attentively during their conversation while himself remaining unobserved.

He had a peculiar feeling. Something like a small meteor struck him, and now, all of a sudden, at the sight of Etelka's brother, light was shed for him on Grauermann's relationship with Etelka, whom he hardly knew. Up to this point, the whole story of Pista's engagement—and he realized it now—had been for him nothing more than a space to look into with good wishes and hold in esteem, one filled in as time went by with mere names and other vital statistics, as it were, but not containing anything concrete. However, sitting opposite René Stangeler in the music room, from which the sun was just then silently and cautiously withdrawing the last of its fingertips, he came to feel and to understand nothing less than the exact nature of the power of attraction that Etelka must be exercising over Grauermann. Teddy was deeply amazed. Until now, he had never had the experience of realizing that a woman's impact could become comprehensible through a boy.

The starting point of their conversation had been music, and it yielded a dialogue that went as follows.

Teddy: "The laws of harmony seem to be merely relative. The interval of the third, to our ears an ordinary consonance, as it were, was considered dissonant in the Middle Ages." (He was making up this dubious little tidbit of musicological wisdom on purpose to throw René off.)

René (a frown gathering on his face): "Is it your opinion that music existed before harmony, or harmony before music?"

"Music existed first, of course."

"Can you imagine grammar as an empirical science?"

Teddy hesitated, and after he'd made the mental leap, it became clear to him that it wasn't.

"No," he said. "You are correct to the extent that grammar does not merely describe the forms of a language but also indicates the concept of what language is in the first place. Let's come to an agreement in this way—before music and before language, harmony and grammar existed. But the systematized laws of harmony and of grammar came into existence after the different genres of music and the different languages."

That was how their conversation went. When Honnegger stepped into the corridor with Grauermann—they were on their way up to their rooms—he was visited by a sudden feeling of dejection concerning Pista's future. Pista himself seemed satisfied on the assumption that his future brother-in-law, whom he'd been showing off (to a degree, anyway), had made a good first impression here. "Quite an unusual character, isn't he?" Pista casually remarked while they were going up the broad staircase.

"No question about it," Honnegger said. It had struck him like an arrow whose barbs were holding fast. Unexpectedly, and by way of a strange detour, he had arrived at a concrete image of Etelka Stangeler, and he realized now, of course, that he had well-nigh disliked her from the start. Out of an insignificant facade and a photograph only half registered in his consciousness, a whole portrait, even a sculpture, now seemed to have materialized. For several days the image wouldn't leave him, and it even reached the point where he—at that time, the only concerned person among so many who were unconcerned about this matter!—shortly afterward gave utterance to a fleeting remark on the subject, specifically to Herr Stephan von Semski, in the Café Pucher, while inwardly keeping before his eye the moment when he and Grauermann had walked out of the music room, its double doors painted in white enamel.

Meanwhile, René had reached the corner of Strudlhof Gasse and remained standing there. The slanted rays of the sun were still shining wherever a surface presented itself, like a thick, dappled carpet. Here now, at the corner, the sunlight extended into the gap and over to the treetops behind it. On the right side, standing orderly and closed in, were the buildings of the university's Department of Physics and Radiology, their contents unfathomable, and they exuded a new kind of romantic air, one that proceeds chiefly from none other than the most exact of the sciences, as if their essence were being transformed during emanation into their opposite, in a way.

The direction in which René Stangeler was walking had nothing whatever to do with going home. His direction now could only have been designated as "not on the way home," in fact. The state of subjective inebriation that René now found himself in is one likely to be deemed appropriate for a youth. The actual age is of much less importance in this case, though, than might be assumed at first glance. The same state was equally prevalent in the adult members of the family, and as a basis of their everyday lives, at that. Just as René, while now walking toward the Strudlhof Steps, was expecting nothing less than the extraordinary, so too his sisters considered it a tariff due and payable to them at any time, so to speak, as well as a standard they were entitled to apply in assessing their lives; they shied away from any other. And so there was one thing that these people, so gifted in so many ways, would have found impossible to achieve—namely, to be regular, ordinary people.

Now the street ended. René stood at the head of the steps.

Stangeler had relatively little knowledge of his native city and none at all of this area here. Excursions by night, which even back then he was undertaking not infrequently, just like his sister Etelka—except that he was alone—kept leading him, again and again, no farther than to the bars and the cafés in District I, the center of the city, or to the artists' haunts along Prater Strasse, close to his family's home. The slight surprise Stangeler was now feeling at the upper end of the Strudl-hof Steps fit right in with all the rest of his romantic folderol, and it put the last dot, as it were, on the *i* of his whole mood, which was undergoing an intensification wholly out of proportion to the simplic-ity of what was giving rise to it. He was taken with the feeling that all the world's a stage and that here the curtain was just about to go up on one of life's stages, one where he was longing to play a part that would suit his taste; and while he was looking down at the stairs and the ramps, he experienced, quickly and in the deepest part of himself, a sense of treading the boards in some scene that would be able to play itself out all the way to the end here, a crucial scene, of course, an ascent and a descent with a meeting in the middle, just like an opera.

In brief, one of those scenes that we hold in memory exclusively from the theater but that actually can occur in real life as well, if only seldom; when they do, they arise altogether unexpectedly. And then only in hindsight do we recognize them for what they were.

Walking slowly down the steps, René was disposed more to ap-preciation than contemplation.

Some treetops were leaning over the edge of the slope. The stairs led gently downward, but they were surprisingly steep. There was a smell of earth here.

Liechtenstein Strasse lies at the bottom of the stairs, and Stangeler followed it to the left, where it presently runs into a wider traffic artery near a tavern called the Flight into Egypt. René was familiar with this place, of course, and at the moment that bothered him, as though a light were shining from the side into his dream, as though a draft were blowing in. He crossed Alserbach Strasse quickly and made his way along Liechtenstein Strasse, which becomes much narrower here.

This street seemed to be the boundary between two very different sections of the city, which sized up one another, like strangers, across its narrow width. More precisely, one part looked down on the other from a greater height; first, the ground on which houses had been built rises on the left, as does the whole area, and second, some shoddy-looking new buildings, four and five stories high, were situated on that left side of the street, while the right side consisted mostly of one-story houses, few much newer than a hundred years old. That part of the city is known as Lichtental, and it was the neighborhood Franz Schubert had called home; he had at one time been the organist in the parish church of Lichtental. René knew nothing about these kinds of things, though, and right now he wouldn't have cared to hear anything about them. He was an intense enough person, granted, but essentially an uncultivated one. It could be said that at the foundation of his being he was the diametrical opposite of someone who has turned out like, say, that Major Laska, subsequently Colonel Laska, who once took Lieutenant Melzer with him on the bear hunt.

Another little street, practically an alleyway, branched off to the right. Attached to one of the corner houses, Stangeler now noticed—it wasn't at any great height, on the second floor, just above the first—was a fully modeled ceramic statue, glazed in blue, depicting a unicorn.

He stayed standing there, in the narrow little side street, and was looking up at the unicorn when he heard footsteps behind him. They slowed and stopped.

René turned around and saw a girl about seventeen in a simple gray suit, with a briefcase under her arm.

He laughed right on the spot, and his laughter was a very skillful move, effortlessly establishing the connection he'd at once begun to seek. Laughing herself in turn, she looked up at the unicorn and asked, "Do you know what kind of strange animal that is?"

"A unicorn," answered Stangeler. Now he saw that she had dark red hair, which charmingly framed her temples under her flat gray hat. The temples themselves were very white and pale, but not shiny, just like her face, in which her eyes were set somewhat on a slant (not unlike René himself, but naturally that didn't enter his conscious mind).

"Was there ever really such a thing?" she asked.

"Oh yes—probably," Stangeler said, and he thought of Julius Caesar's reports about ancient Germania. "But," he added (and he was well in his stride, so that everything came out very natural and completely ingenuous), "I'd very much enjoy it if you'd let me tell you more about it—only couldn't we do it in that large café on the other side of Alserbach Strasse? I just have to have a bite to eat now. Won't you join me? They have wonderful pastries there."

After he'd stepped across the threshold that separates the boy from the young man, he'd attained something like a mechanistic security in his dealings with females, with whom, by the way, he was virtually intimate regarding the salient point. A few chances of this latter kind, remote though they might have been, had by no means escaped René's attention; right here, in this early (indeed, this very first) choice of his, he was showing the occasional inclination of all the Stangelers toward the sweet-tempered, good-natured, and, as they imagined it, intellectually inferior type, all aspects required to form a sounding board for their own self-esteem, with which seasoning they could relish this or that experience all the more, just as many people consider nutmeg or curry indispensable with certain dishes.

Our couple, meanwhile, had walked down the wide street and gone into the café, where there was no skimping on anything, because René was flush, never mind the small amount of spending money he was given. What stood him in good stead here was a forgotten bookcase, a large one, off in the corner of an entry room on the third floor of his parents' house; it was jam-packed with every novel published in the 1880s, in particular with the works of a certain Georg Ebers, books distinguished by their cloth bindings and gilt edges. Starting all the way at the back, René had been hollowing out this bookcase little by little, the way termites in Africa hollow out trees from the inside. His dealings at several secondhand book stores were pursued on a regular basis.

But now, instead of unpacking his sample case full of quaint and appealing wares and, as it were, getting his display window all arranged, he was overtaken, right here at the little marble table and as a result of the relaxed and easygoing mood of the afternoon, by something entirely different—namely, by a sovereign apathy toward that automatic mechanism which should have been operating to impress a girl. René found it flatly impossible to get himself all keyed up for the occasion, and, perhaps for the first time in his life, he was feeling indifferent as to what impression he might or might not be creating. This feeling—comparable to that of a person sitting in an easy chair only too deep and comfortable, so that it prevents him from standing up—was very distinct, and it was new to him. He welcomed it with deep joy and with the noteworthy desire to live like that all the time.

"So now, what about those cute little unicorns?" she asked, setting down her cocoa cup.

"Oh yes—unicorns," said René, looking at her and going no further.

"It seems you were just after your bite to eat and now it's too much trouble for you to talk about them," she suggested with a smile.

"No, it's not too much trouble at all," he replied with a significant degree of emphasis, as it were, looking right at her and observing her head against the background of the street, now and then full of life, behind the large pane of glass. "Well then, unicorns, or 'cute little unicorns,' as you called them so endearingly, have in all probability always existed. A century ago, anything that didn't fit inside the framework of science, which people thought had been erected once and for all, was considered sheer nonsense, merely fables and legends, but many new animals have been discovered since then, and today the belief is no longer held that there is such a thing as creatures purely and simply from the realm of legend. Everything goes back to some actuality—basilisks, dragons, and unicorns."

"Are you a student at the university?"

"Yes. The unicorn was a wild and ferocious animal that lived by itself in an impenetrable forest. But it was easy to catch."

"How did they do that?" she asked, more out of astonishment than snappishness. That latter tone didn't seem to suit her at all well and was only an exterior fortification of her true nature, artificially put forward as a rapid means of self-defense, adopted and imitated from somewhere.

"They had to have a virgin," Stangeler said, "a real one, though."

Now he felt somewhat at a loss in view of the turn the conversation was taking, though it had emerged on its own, given the topic, and he now watched that turn leading toward the area of the risqué—toward which, at any other time, it was part of his routine to move promptly—in the awareness that nothing could be done about it for the moment. It was a slight hitch. And from it he noticed, as something altogether expected, how her mouth—no pouting little pair of pursed lips, but a fairly wide mouth—twisted, going askew and mirroring the way she was wavering between her true nature and the facial expressions she'd copied from other girls her age and grown used to.

"And what did the virgin do with the unicorn?"

"All she had to do was sit down in the forest where it lived—soon it would come to her, kneel down in front of her, tame and gentle, and lay its head in her lap. Then they could tie it up and lead it away, and it would never resist."

"Oh come on now, not a word of that is true," she said by way of offering some resistance of her own, for a feeling seemed to be trying to tell her that she had unexpectedly reached the point of making contact with something completely new and enticing, and all because she'd happened to be in high spirits on the way home from the office of her employer (an attorney, for whom she'd been working as a ste-nographer for the past two years), since a very difficult case had been closed with a judgment for their side, a great deal of work had been done, and the lawyer—himself in a good mood, naturally—had praised her very highly and promised her no insubstantial raise in salary; and it was out of that good mood that she'd gone right ahead and spoken to the young fellow there in front of the Blue Unicorn, having for so long wondered what on earth kind of animal that little blue horsie could be. Now, however, not least because he passed over that open switch of their conversation without changing direction, she felt herself, tingling and drawn on by a gentle yearning, to be at the boundary of some new—to her, indeed, otherworldly—region, and a wind blew through her soul, making every novel she had ever read fly open inside her with a rustling sound.

So there they were, these two children of such different strands and climes, sitting over hot chocolate and pastries—Stangeler was drinking coffee, by the way, and smoking a cigarette, which is never looked on favorably in cafés, but the proprietor had said all right this one time because it was only shortly before closing time. Outside, the street had been lying awash for a while in a fine and even grayness through which the first lights were drifting, everything tired though still moving, worn and weary from the day. Not long before, with no actual transition, Paula Schachl had begun to speak about herself—about her boss and a major lawsuit that had just been settled (an automobile-manufacturing firm versus its lumber supplier, so an issue more or less foreign to Stangeler), about the high praise that had been directed to her that day after all her hard work, often until nine or ten at night, about an aunt with whom she lived (here in Lichtental, incidentally), and finally about some physician, a Dr. Brandeis, who was treating her in the outpatient clinic of the General Hospital, where she'd been back to see him again yesterday, a very kind man and extremely conscientious. Last winter, when she'd slipped on some ice, she had twisted her foot in a way that sprained her left ankle and did something to the ligaments.

They left the café and walked toward that old section of the city; Paula had scarcely stopped for breath while telling her life story. Now she began talking about various girlfriends and acquaintances, all of whom apparently lived right here in the neighborhood. On Sunday mornings, it seemed, there was a kind of general promenade up and down Nussdorfer Strasse, where everybody would meet up with everybody else. Now it was René who was standing at the boundary of another world, as it were, one that did not seem to lack for creature comforts, and looking into it—with longing, too, though only in passing and as if out of the corner of his eye. He had a vague sense that people's lives there were better, simpler, and for that matter, more sensible, when you got right down to it. But that was the only thing he was able to take in concretely and accurately of all that Paula was saying. For the rest, he listened as though she were singing without words, singing a lengthy song made up of a little melody with ritornelli every now and again, a song that remained the same as it stood there or stayed afloat, like certain insects that hover with a singing noise and can therefore stand in the air. That was the way this beautifully shaped song was now standing before the background of the wide street; then it soared over to where the tall, shabby buildings and the older, smaller houses faced one another across the street; then it wafted through the street with the blue unicorn at the one corner. Meanwhile, this whole scene, as it subsided between the strings of lights into an evening grown dark by now and became part of the whole mass, either motionless or crossed with movement, enclosed, far toward the rear, a lighted gateway like a gold background—the steps, the Strudlhof Steps, the stage of life ready for a dramatic performance with drums and trumpets; and it was precisely to them, or rather it was only to them, that Paula's little song had any relation in the end, as far as Stangeler was concerned.

Her soft "solo," delivered with more of a murmur and marked by that peculiar quiescence so like the sound of the English horn, proceeded in its solitary course before the gold-gleaming cavern that stood open behind it as if grounded in the powerful tutti of a full orchestra—but she wouldn't have the slightest inkling of any of this, so Stangeler thought, and that was just what seemed to him the crucial and most touching aspect of it. But René was wrong. Just as anything vague and in any way romantic held power over him, so it did over her as well, a girl in whom the pages of some agitated reading material were swirling open. Let's not discuss the level on either side, though—whether it was Puccini or a cheap romance novel, it all meant the same here. It just seems to us that René's mind was working a little harder than hers the whole time.

Now they had to go their separate ways, though. They'd already made a date. The aunt lived right around the corner.

Alone in the narrow street as if plunged into black velvet. Yearning surges out in every direction from the swelling heart. Dim light in a window here and there.

Turning the corner, Stangeler saw by the lighted clock on the wide cross street that it was twenty-five to eight. Mealtimes were observed with the most stringent punctuality at home, and woe betide anyone who came to the table even a second late. In other matters they were much less exacting, though. It really is true that civilized human beings have situated their moral center of gravity in a place that identically matches their physical one, which means they place the most weight on the very point where their weight is already sitting heaviest anyway. This could serve as a categorical explanation of indecisiveness and the resignation it leads to. The soul is present only as a kind of nebulous ring around the body, not much more than an evanescent haze that falls exclusively within the domain of the psychologists, so that what appear to be its flights and swoops could not possibly interest anybody except them.

Stangeler leapt onto a streetcar. His doing so changed everything, and as abruptly so as in a room where the light has been switched on or off. The car glided along its familiar route, the twists and turns and the more quickly traveled straight stretches of which he could anticipate in his body's reactions, as it were.

In the neighborhood where the Stangelers' house was located, the streets were quieter, indeed almost deserted, at this time of evening. He walked up the wide stairs made of red stone, past his grandmother's apartment on the first floor, and he saw the lights behind the milk-glass door of the entry as he went scurrying along the second floor; a glimpse through the peephole showed several unfamiliar overcoats hanging from the brass hooks on the green wood molding. Only now did he recall that today was the day for one of the card parties his father usually had twice a month; they were generally followed by supper for the players. He knew he now had to get ready in a hurry, which his mother's maid also immediately urged him to do the second he set foot onto the third floor. René scurried into his room and threw on a dark suit, combed and brushed his hair smooth, and dashed down the inside spiral staircase to the second floor just as the guests downstairs were solemnly making their way to the table amidst a profusion of convivial nattering and chattering.

Three gentlemen and two ladies were present as guests, old ladies, at least by René's reckoning; he considered all adults to be insurmountably different—old, somber, authoritative, and elevated high above any and all doubts, as it were. Critical insight was perhaps the weakest faculty of his mind—insofar as we can speak of any such thing as applying to him in the first place—and only in circumstances of utter desperation did he reach the point of insolence, which would then be of a strictly borrowed variety. He sat at the lower end of the table, on the narrow end right by the sideboard, where the maid was standing ready to serve, and directly opposite, separated by the length of the table, sat his father, behind whose broad-shouldered figure the room stretched on in its considerable depth. It was a second room, in fact, just as large as the dining room, just as brightly lit by an overhead chandelier of massive bronze with small iridescent pendants of Venetian milk glass hanging from its round edge. On the far wall of each room, in the exact center, was a tall mirror. Whenever Herr von Stangeler would lean to his right and speak to René's mother, or to his left, where Chief Physician Dr. Hartknoch, a man with a crown of white hair, was sitting, he could fleetingly make out his father's broad back, as well as the back of his head, in the mirror all the way at the end of the other room.

René paid almost no further attention to the upper end of the table, though. To begin with, he was hungry, and he ate each course of this wonderful meal with the greatest enjoyment, which alone was enough to claim all his energy and at the same time to keep him in the best of moods. His immediate surroundings—Asta was next to him on the left and Etelka on the right—were familiar and required nothing in the way of special caution or alertness. Not until after the fish course— it tasted exceptionally delicious to him today, and he'd been given no fewer than three helpings, since the serving maid enjoyed taking care of him—did it occur to him that he would have to find some inconspicuous way of letting Etelka know that her letter had been duly hand-delivered at the academy. For the moment, however, he had no opportunity to do so. Etelka was paying him absolutely no attention whatever—in itself a relief, actually, because she was forever picking at him during mealtimes and correcting his table manners. Instead, she now stayed facing exclusively toward the neighbor on her right the whole time. A glance at this man may prove worthwhile, not only because of his pleasing exterior but also because he occupies a place, and no inconsiderable one either, in the story of Etelka's life.

Government Councillor Guys was originally from French-speaking

Switzerland and retained Swiss citizenship while holding an Austrian passport as well. In matters of contractual negotiations and everything connected with them, the state-owned railroad company of the old monarchy employed Herr Emile Guys as a link to those places outside the country where French was spoken; the government councillor had been discharging his official duties within this sphere of activity for years and years. Even though his office was in Vienna, he would be away on a trip somewhere in France or Switzerland half the time. Inside Austria, he belonged to that group of a very select few who never traveled other than in first class on the railroad but who also never bought a ticket; all they had to do instead was reach with a quick, easy motion inside their jacket pocket and present an identifying document that fit there just so. Anybody else—Major Laska or Lieutenant Melzer, say—could have given an Austrian conductor all the bright, golden gulden that ever were and still would not have conjured up anything even remotely approaching the magical effect of instant and total deference produced by this humble identification card, complete with photograph, in its transparent celluloid holder.

His wife was a little on the quirky side, or was that just how people took her? She had a rather peculiar way of holding her head. She seldom accepted an invitation to come to the card parties at the Stangelers' (even though, as we see, several of the players brought their wives along); most of the time, she made up some excuse. Guys had two children, a bright, alert girl and an earnest, scrupulous boy of utterly astonishing ugliness who later became the kind of person who's referred to as the nicest chap in the world.

His father wasn't quite the nicest chap in the world, but just a very solid citizen, a cavalier of the old Austrian school, and he wasn't ugly, either; very much the contrary, in fact, with his dark, sharply etched Romanic head crowning a tall, slender build. The slight tinge of silver in the hair at his temples could well have been there for a good while, probably dating as far back as the not uneventful days of his youth—it's just part and parcel of that type of man and his whole style. It looked really attractive and somehow fit perfectly into that courtliness, cultivated and polished down to the minutest detail, that was so much a mark of Herr Guys.

René was suddenly seized with a feeling that it wasn't right now (wasn't in any way whatever, as far as that went) so much a matter of some signal to his sister Etelka—which she could after all have registered with the greatest discretion (a mere nod of René's head would have been enough)—to the effect that her letter had reached its destination; nor did she seem to be avoiding catching his eye or turning in his direction from any kind of apprehensiveness, for she surely must have known full well that he wouldn't pull any stupid or obvious moves. It was more that Etelka seemed to be off somewhere on a different plane, at least to a certain extent, and from that place to be warding off any information, and any cognizance of any information, that did not pertain where she was now. Stangeler was fairly clear as to what he felt was the case, even though the plane that now appeared to be at hand struck him as almost unbelievable and even preposterous; the very idea that anyone would think of latching on to a member of the . . . the upper house (and in René's mind it was to that ilk, that class of categorically mature or even old gentlemen, that the government councillor belonged, an accredited representative of the upper end of the table, even though today he just happened to be sitting close by, here at the lower end) seemed outrageous to him, all but tainted with the odor of treason and iniquity. It was to their father, after all, that the government councillor was more or less connected, and Etelka was being so bold as to perpetrate her audacity right here and now, before his very eyes.

René had once more sunk back into himself—retreating from the presence of Etelka, as it were, as from an individual not quite on the up-and-up—and was just finishing some diligent work on a piece of capon, when there followed an incursion from the upper end of the table to the lower.

Chief Physician Dr. Hartknoch, lifting his small green-stemmed glass filled with the gold of a clear wine made by a vintner in Lower Austria, declaimed:

> "*Vinum bonum et suave*
> *bonis bonum, pravis prave,*
> *cunctis sapor dulcis, ave*
> *mundana laetitia!*"

The mother of the Stangeler family looked past him in an amused way. She knew all about his little effusions in Latin; they were just part and parcel of him, and she pretty much dismissed him as a character, thereby devaluing him to some extent; but the importance of any other person at all, when juxtaposed with her husband, lay outside her powers of conception. Now the father, like so many other extroverted personalities powerful in their energy, their capacity for work, and their ability to earn money—every endeavor crowned with success— possessed in addition, even in his emotional makeup, something like a strong drive toward spatial displacement, a surging up toward others and an encroaching upon them, a way about himself, in brief, that persons of any intellectual caliber find hard to deal with and therefore avoid as a rule. Among the friends of René's father there was not to be found a single man of any genuine significance, and, as odd as it might sound when we think of little Frau von Stangeler—considering that she had become almost totally devoid of any personality of her own— it was none other than she who would least have been able to tolerate such a person and who would have found her own ways and means to get rid of him. This was how completely she had come to parallel her entire being with the unique and omnipotent role of a Zeus-like husband and father.

Among these friends of Herr von Stangeler, though, Dr. Hartknoch was in a certain sense the exception that proved the rule. As far from average as he looked was how far from it he actually was, and at the same time, just as far apart from everything that was considered the norm in this family. What's more, there was about him that scarcely definable air, that privileged position of authority, which any physician, never mind one who is recognized as outstanding, just simply seems to occupy. Dr. Hartknoch's trusting and amicable way of dealing with his two daughters, a manner he quite naturally brought to bear with the Stangeler children, whose pronouncements about life he took altogether seriously and whose opinions and problems—if that's what one wants to call them—he would discuss with them (an utter absurdity, according to the laws of the Stangeler household): all of this taken together would not exactly add up to earn him a high ranking in the mother's good graces. But because she happened to be close friends with his wife, and from the time of their girlhood, at that, she just let it pass and put up with the doctor, a man whom, deep in her heart, she wrote off as something like a mental defective. For, strange as it still might seem, she regarded it as unthinkable that anyone could be a separate entity from her husband in matters of the intellect, or that a wife could even so much as venture to take a critical stance opposed to his; and although such a thing had never, ever manifested itself or come close to expression in her presence, the very possibility alone— beyond question, quite an imminent one in this case—was enough to cause her considerable alarm.

"Now then, how was that again, Doctor?" called Judge Hunt across the table in his constantly husky voice. "My Latin's pretty rusty by now!" He was sitting between Frau von Stangeler and plump, clever Yetty Hartknoch, whose neighbor farther down was Asta, and so he was directly opposite his wife—a very decidedly Italian or southern French type, somewhat like a goat, with protruding upper incisors—as her place was between Dr. Hartknoch and Government Councillor Guys.

"Yes, what was that? Not something from the classical age?" their host asked in an offhand but not uninterested tone.

Dr. Hartknoch repeated the quatrain slowly and was just about to append a translation when Herr von Stangeler cut him short with a quick motion of his hand and said, "Just a minute, doctor. Hold on. Why don't we have our *homo gymnasiasticus sive asinus gymnasiasticus aere perennius* down there give us a translation? Let's see you do your stuff, René!" There was a certain sharpness lying behind those last words, and a good many things were gathered up and entwined in that sharpness—a tendency, perhaps, formed a priori, to intrude on René's quiet idyll of ravenousness down there at the lower end of the table; perhaps a kind of threat as to what would happen if the son were now to embarrass the father; underneath all the rest, the opportunity, seized by the forelock for reasons of sheer nerves, to launch any attack at all in any direction; and all the way up on the surface, something like the call of duty, of which pedagogical oversight was a component and which had to be exercised right now. All things considered, there had come about one of those occasions on which Herr von Stangeler—in his own way—was showing his concern for his youngest.

René had been listening intently the first time Dr. Hartknoch declaimed; things like that never got past him. Now that he was being addressed by his father, however, and the whole table had turned toward him, he felt very disturbed—that's the appropriate way to put it here, too; he was merely disturbed, but not thrown off balance in the least; disturbed roughly as he might be if several people were unexpectedly to walk into a room set aside for him alone, his very own room; in this very own room of his, though, because he was on his own turf, he was more than a match for those disturbing him. He had just finished eating and was savoring a sip of wine he'd just taken when his father spoke to him, so his mouth wasn't full and he didn't have to do all that chewing and swallowing first. That helped him out. Looking a bit morose as he half-closed his slanted eyes and took a sideways glance at the damask, the silver, the crystal on the table, he repeated the Latin text, speaking slowly and precisely, and added an impromptu translation with no hesitation:

> "Wine so mellow of bouquet,
> good to the good, the bad's dismay,
> you who sweeten sleep and rest—
> cheerfulness, be ever blest!"

"Bravo!" bellowed Judge Hunt, more loudly than the occasion required.

"Excellent!" cried Dr. Hartknoch, raising his glass and drinking to René.

By now, René's father was positively radiant with bliss and was literally smiling all over his face. But then he touched Dr. Hartknoch lightly on the arm, as if to get him to hold on a bit so that the schoolboy could be asked more questions.

"Did you already know that verse? What is it, anyway? Where is it from?"

"No, I didn't know it," said Stangeler, astonished by the effect he'd produced and unable to understand it. "But surely it can't be from the classical era."

"And why not?" cried Dr. Hartknoch.

"Because of the meter, because of the vocabulary, but above all, because of the rhymes."

"Well then, what is it, or what might it be?" his father asked. In the meantime, his tone in this question had undergone a very fundamental transformation indeed by comparison with his question just a few moments before; this one now sounded almost as though it were directed to a specialist, an expert, an authority. And Stangeler, all innocent and unsuspecting—for he had no idea that a storm was now gathering over to his right, that is, from the direction of Etelka (who felt his successes and triumphs were going on too long)—said, "I don't know. I'm hearing this poem for the first time. But it's probably medieval. It sounds to me like one of those student songs, verses by an itinerant poet, a goliardic song."

"Outstanding diagnosis!" cried Dr. Hartknoch. "You're exactly right. It's a *carmen buranum*, a goliardic song."

At this point the conversation broke up into various parts, and the upper house once again separated itself from the lower house in the ensuing babble of voices, which had been instigated at the upper end of the table mainly by Frau von Stangeler, who for her part also felt that her youngest child's showstopper had gone on quite long enough, and then some; besides, she possessed a keen sense for detecting how René had ended up essentially (albeit quite involuntarily) playing the role of an authority imparting his expertise to his own father—and such a thing went completely against the order of his mother's universe. So she simply plowed right in, talking through her son's last few sentences, and the other two ladies soon came to her aid.

Down in the lower house, however, there now came a hissing from the right; it was contemptuous, fierce, and condescending, all at the same time, spoken out of an impulse to strike a blow and cause a wound. "Here you go again! You and your conceited, stupid lying! I bet you think somebody's really going to believe you never heard that Latin poem before and never translated it into verse on the spot till this minute. People aren't that stupid. But all you ever want to do is make an impression. Just like some silly girl. Let me tell you, though—you won't get very far in life with these conceited ways of yours."

Stangeler looked at his sister, utterly dumbfounded.

"I suppose *I'm* that stupid," the government councillor remarked. Etelka had not been able to control herself, with the result that René wasn't the only one who'd heard that hissed remark. "Yes, I suppose I must be that stupid," he said again. "Something like this is simply a matter of talent, and your brother's got his share. Here's to René!"

"Oh no, I know him better than that, Herr Guys," said Etelka, but already in a more relenting voice.

"Why don't you just let him alone?" called Asta in an undertone across the table. "He's good at this Latin stuff, and it makes Daddy happy."

Guys stole an amused sidelong glance at Etelka. Right here and now he was gaining the upper hand, essential for him to have. Up to this outburst she'd been able to deadpan him with an unruffled brow, like an inscrutable Pallas Athene, but now he'd seen her under duress, struggling to be recognized, the narrow doors of her character flung open so that he could, for a brief time, see deep inside and observe its flaws.

Now, concerning these two, René (who forgot all about this episode and scarcely gave it another thought until the first time they asked him later on to be a special-delivery courier) hadn't been mistaken that evening. A very curious love affair was developing here, one of the strangest in Vienna at that time.

What attracted her to Guys? What might she have been looking for in him? A kind of security, perhaps, that no one else, and certainly not Grauermann, could have offered her, a kind of superiority based on involvement with a social plane that was of course never encountered among the young people who were regular visitors to Etelka's family home. This little affair had been going on through part of the winter, long before René's rather dull instincts had made him aware of it. Well, Etelka was twenty-four.

Every affair is played against its own backdrop, has its own milieu, as they say. Life itself is always the best director; the stage scenery is ineffably right for whatever is being enacted. If the world-shunning verses of Omar Khayyám were being read, for example, then that quiet last little room up in the Quartier Latin—we're already familiar with it—formed an indisputably well-matched setting. To the more worldly channel navigated by the relations between Etelka and Emile, however, a certain very exclusive and long-renowned wine tavern near the Augustinian Church was the proper backdrop, a place whose dark, old-world style of decoration was carried through in the highly intimate, secluded little rooms available there, the kind of private rooms called *chambres séparées*. The furnishings and the leaded-glass panes with inset coats of arms in the china-cabinet doors, items which normally would have met with Etelka Stangeler's disdain as monstrosities from the '80s (not held very high in her regard)—this whole style took on a special meaning for her here, because to a certain extent it now stood for her companion's more mature age, the older generation; in other words, for exactly what attracted her in this case, what created the stimulation for her. If we wanted to, we could perhaps find in this project or campaign of Etelka's—the first one she followed through— the key to her life as a whole and to her destruction as well. She avoided her father, but she nonetheless kept on searching for him over and over on her innermost level and striving to preempt him for herself. In the end she succeeded, too. It's beyond doubt that she was looking for a direction, a force to move her along the train tracks, an orientation. Among other things, that was the meaning behind the work she devoted to her music, at times quite resolutely— not only was Etelka preparing to become a pianist, but her singing voice was also rated by an older friend, Dame Cornelia Wett, a court singer, as having a considerable chance of success. This lady (once an internationally celebrated soprano) was totally uninterested in Etelka's efforts at the keyboard—all she wanted was that Etelka should be a singer. In the whole blend of ingredients that made up the soul of Fräulein von Stangeler, however, there was decidedly missing one particular pungent spice that imparts the ability to negotiate the steeper, narrower paths of struggle and that at the same time would have shielded her against the decay into which unused skills tend to fall. Each buried talent sends its own small pestilence up to the surface of the soul, just as the same surface will grow blind and opaque if those talents are inflated and unduly exploited.

So she was seeking a direction and an orientation. At the same time, though, she couldn't put a stop to her escapades, not ever, and it's by no means certain that she wasn't entangled with others besides Guys. Life merely looks on for a number of years while mechanisms like this are operating. But when Etelka chose to gamble away her most reliable support, the stronghold she had finally found and could live within, then the ground opened up underneath her, so to speak; everything around her started to shake, to slide away in a kind of blur, and finally to collapse, until she couldn't recognize anything anymore.

It's hard to say how long this passionate relationship with Guys went on. A year or so before World War I, that is before 1914, Grauermann was dispatched as attaché to Constantinople, armed with a wide-ranging letter of appointment from the Royal and Imperial Foreign Ministry and with a quite a pile of gold coins, for this was the form in which the old regime paid per diem travel allowances and advances. As the last daughter in the family, Etelka stayed at home for some time, well into the war years—Asta had married in the meantime—and it was only during the war that she in turn was able to get married, after Grauermann had become vice consul.

Of course, Grauermann had been granted leave from Constantinople once in a while, among other times, just before the outbreak of war, right after René had passed his Matura, his comprehensive graduation exams. It was a noteworthy time in several respects. Through its Royal and Imperial Railway Ministry, the old empire had finally made the long-anticipated announcement that it would be accepting bids for the construction of railway lines in Bosnia, and one of them, the one Herr von Stangeler had submitted to the ministry as summer was approaching (it concerned the stretch between Banja Luka and Jajce), had just been approved before any of the others. What that means, though, is that these weeks and months were a period of intense pressure for Herr von Stangeler, like being on a campaign. He spent that time in Bosnia for the most part and had only an occasional day in Vienna. At this point, then, the only people in the apartment were René, the prospective graduate, and one of the elderly maids; in the beginning of July, Etelka came in from their house in the country, naturally because of Grauermann, although some other pretext was used, for in spite of her public engagement—or rather, precisely because of her engagement—no one would have been able to grant her permission, just like that, to spend a few unchaperoned days in Vienna during the summer, with her off-duty fiancé, Grauermann. By rights, he wouldn't have been allowed to see her until he first went out to the country, where his parents were also staying at the time. But one day there Etelka was. On his temporary visits to Vienna, Herr von Stangeler didn't take his meals at home, but ate in the city instead, with colleagues and other people he needed to confer with. Seldom would he go roaring through the spacious rooms, and when he did happen to be at home, he would mainly keep to the second floor, to his large and handsome office, where the telephone would then be heard ringing; all the windows on the shady side of the house stood open because of the heat.

Etelka noticed, not without surprise, that René went off to school dressed in a tailcoat, but she thought nothing more of it until finding out from him in the afternoon that he had passed his Matura. When Grauermann, talking on the telephone with Etelka, heard this news a short time later, he seized on the occasion to celebrate with the greatest of pleasure—to that extent, a true Hungarian—and immediately extended to René a cordial invitation, along with his congratulations.

During this time, Herr von Stangeler was staying at the country house for a few days.

The three of them, pretty much loaded after their celebration, drove in a car from the Golden Woodcock in Neuwaldegg back to the Stangelers' house in Vienna, where René tiptoed in ahead of the others to make sure that the lord and master hadn't turned up sometime during the evening. But no one was there, so now, long past midnight, there was nothing more to fear. They brewed Turkish coffee and danced throughout all the third-floor rooms, laid out so generously. There were a couple of prankish little incidents, too, as when they all went into Herr von Stangeler's bedroom, where, with all the lights turned all the way up, René gave a rabble-rousing, revolutionary address that repeatedly kept culminating in the rhetorical question, "And this man calls himself democracy-minded?" The schoolboy, or actually now the graduate, was holding a wicker carpet beater in his hand and during the high points of his speech would bring it down with a whoosh onto the red silk spread that covered his father's bed. They romped and carried on for a good long while (Grauermann wouldn't have been Hungarian if he hadn't brought along at least one bottle of champagne in the back seat of the car), and it must have been half past two before René was able to get to bed. On the following morning he woke up late and, of course, in a happy frame of mind. Outside the sky was pure blue, and the sun (he could feel its heat already) was shining here and there in the wide rectangular space of the courtyard and on the yellow masonry walls of the apartment buildings all around it. Three tall ash trees, rooted deep and lined up behind one another in a garden across the way, stretched with their broad tops all the way past the second floor, into the sun's path. This spacious room lying to the rear, with a long, narrow balcony running by both windows, faced north, and so got no sunlight, which was why it was almost cool even now, in July.

It was not without a certain amount of letdown that René got up, took a cold shower, and got dressed. When he was finished, he walked in a preoccupied way into a small room right off his own. There was very little furniture there. The glass door opening onto the balcony was standing open. Above the red chimneys the blue of the sky looked vaporous and far off in the distance. The wild grapevines, wet now from their morning watering, that were growing in a row of green boxes along the railing of the balcony, as well as some leafy plants standing in large flower pots here and there, had the smell of earth and of luxuriant profusion at the same time. All of a sudden, the short and, if one will, brusque footsteps of René's father could be heard coming closer and closer through the neighboring rooms.

Herr von Stangeler was not in very easy circumstances at this time. The assassination in Sarajevo of the successor to the throne of Austria—an alarming development already a few days old, one that could have escaped the young people so completely only through their obliviousness—brought the clearly foreseeable prospect of war looming over the horizon, meaning in turn that the whole work schedule for the Bosnia project, which absolutely had to be taken in hand immediately because of the tight deadlines and the stiff penalties for not meeting them, was now very much up in the air. As if that weren't enough, his wife had put a bug in his ear out in the country about whether anybody had heard from René, whether anybody knew if he'd passed his Matura or not. (What? Matura? With all the pressure from his job right now, Herr von Stangeler had totally forgotten about it.)

The door didn't just fly open suddenly; it exploded, rather, as though excess pressure had been building up behind it.

"And just what in the hell are you doing here? What level are you on in school, anyway?"

"Well, I was on level eight."

"So then you must have to take all the exams for your Matura?"

"I took them all yesterday, and passed."

"But you didn't give your mother the news? She's sitting out there in the country and worrying! What are you, a cold-blooded animal?"

Then came the crack of a sharp slap, after which René's father took out his wallet. "Here. For you." He flung a present of fifty crowns at his son (an unusually large amount for a schoolboy in those days). "Get going!" he bellowed then. "Take off! You're heading out there today!" René turned toward the door.

As he was leaving, though, he was dismissed with a good swift kick in that part of the anatomy which Lieutenant Melzer's father had often been obliged to place under heavy requisition during his long term of service as a cavalryman.

There were two turning points in Etelka Stangeler's life. The first occurred when she was putting her right foot onto the platform as she stepped down from the train on her arrival at the main railroad station in Constantinople. Robby Fraunholzer, the consul and an older colleague of Grauermann's, was waiting there for the young couple, who, after their wedding in the spring of 1915 in Vienna (war or no war, it had been a very festive celebration), were now reporting to the post of the new husband as vice consul. Fraunholzer helped Etelka off the train. So this was where they were going to be living. And it turned out to be quite some chunk of living. Yes, it certainly did, and it started right then and there, with a man stepping up to meet Etelka who hit her like a bolt of lightning, making all the lamps and lanterns that had ever shone in her life up to now pale to the faintest of glimmers, the dullest of gleamings; that was how powerfully she was dazzled—right there in the smoky hall, between the luggage and the dry-sounding words of the foreign language (dry like a treeless landscape) in which her husband was speaking to the porter—by the flash of a fascination such as she had never felt before.

The second turning point came about ten years later, during the late summer of 1925, at the one decent hotel in the Alpine village in Lower Austria where Etelka's father had his property. Incidentally, it happened on the occasion of a party of sorts, which was what the situation developed into—through Fraunholzer's arrival, to some degree. Anyway, it was the point at which Fraunholzer came to despair of Etelka. And once he had taken this step in earnest there was virtually no chance of his going back on it.

That was the time when Major Melzer, who happened to be present, felt passing over him in a general way the shadow of a premonition that wasn't merely dispiriting but that somehow also had the chill of gloom about it, a premonition to the effect "that there were still a good many rough downward paths to come here"; and it was through this fairly strange way of expressing himself that he would refer, in many later conversations, to the point at issue.

All of this was very far distant in Constantinople in March of 1915. It was a time of the most profound astonishment for Etelka, by which we are saying a time of gentle beginnings, an early time with a rising motion in all the delicate little capillaries of life, a first breath of spring with all the dazed captivation, with all the deeply shy bemusement that hedges people in, as though they were encompassed all around by a concave mirror whose ever-shifting reflections end up always bringing into view, again and again, nothing other than their own image, whereupon it is always marveled at, as if they were catching sight of it for the very first time.

When she would go walking with her two greyhounds along the Pera side of the Boulevard Kassim Pasha, composing her face, which always seemed rather wide (the eyes being set far apart spoke for mental alertness), and appearing so secure and elegant, she looked far more self-aware and self-contained than she actually was. White looked absolutely wonderful on her, by the way. And so her turn soon came for attractive pea jackets—the very kind we once noticed Frau Mary

K. wearing. Etelka loved having enormous buttons on hers. Sometimes she was capable of looking quite haughty on the boulevard already mentioned or on the Rue de Pera.

But these were trivialities.

And the trivialities grew fewer and farther between. Like no other city, this one used to have strange islands of quiet, spaces that faded, paled, and passed away as the grass of a newer age grew over them. It wasn't only the parks in the area around the English embassy or the theater—where there actually was a cemetery, after all—that were for the most part quiet; no, the city also had some totally isolated areas, isolated like those miniature ponds in Dalmatia they call "sea eyes," which can catch only the empty blue of the sky in the treeless limestone prairies. There were spots and small patches here, windowless walls half crumbled, fountains, passageways, which in falling into ruins had also by that token drifted somewhere far away from the river of passing time.

Etelka's state of astonishment peaked in places like these, and she—she who such a very short time before had been at the center of a family whirlwind, like any other woman whose wedding was about to take place—was now suddenly standing amid surroundings that seemed like a backdrop expressly designed to be a foil to her new situation, fully enveloped in them, a feeling in her heart growing constantly more clear until she now knew that it was love, nothing more and nothing less, and that there would be no haggling anything out of life at bargain prices.

Confronted so unexpectedly with reality, and for the first time, at that, a faster maturing spread out inside her, a state comparable to a warm and powerful October sun easily dissipating the thickest fog. With contours emerging into sharp focus as they were, Etelka was in no great rush to rebel against the circumstances that were hedging her in and making demands on her, for a deep instinct proper to her kind of inner breeding was able to let her know that even when she had chosen an altogether wrong direction—and that's just what she now had to recognize her marriage to be!—one thing was owed to it so that it could be a direction in the first place, and that was to remain committed to it, at least as committed as she could be. And because everything had come into being so completely beyond her ken and fate had made all its arrangements so high over her head, as it were—and let's not examine whether what it consisted of was true or false at this point—it seemed to Etelka that all the different provisos and particulars of her situation were in no way of her own making (a tenet that people like her, with such maniacally strong wills, are usually very happy to put their credence in!) but instead had been handed down more or less as decrees and were thus to be accepted, followed, and lived out with no criticism.

This was how she reached—though without making her way along any moral path (whether we understand it in its conventional or its religious form)—a point at which her marriage could be preserved intact, as far as it was up to her, simply because she acknowledged a certain amount of commitment as a self-evident and necessary mode of manifesting this union she'd gone ahead and contracted (never mind what she might think about it now); it was a line to be held to and to be measured by at the same time. However large the share of apprehension, of emphasis on the value of social position, and even of satisfaction at having escaped in a way so very convenient to herself from the home she'd been raised in—however large the share these factors might have had in governing Etelka's behavior, they were still far from making up the whole, and they weren't its foundation, either.

So her love stayed undeclared for more than three years, but, like a light shining underwater, it gave a crystalline character to everything about her life and primed with heightened vivacity the numerous social occasions that brought Etelka and Fraunholzer together. One could say that until Constantinople, Etelka Stangeler never experienced and enjoyed what it meant to be young, with life nowhere stuck in a rut or sealed off, but everywhere to be seen as a translucent ichor full of currents, glimmers, gleamings unfathomably deep and inexplicably radiant. Etelka's youth burst out, as spring does here, around the Sea of Marmara. If up till now—say, at her boarding school in Dresden and then in the constricting and intimidating atmosphere under her parents' roof—she had truly had no way of even imagining what it meant to be free and unburdened, she came to know what that was like here, which was exactly what kept her from using her freedom now in any way that might cause it to short-circuit, something she had never had the least hesitation about trying to weasel out of her state of *durance vile* at home.

Her life in Constantinople went on for three years, that is until the collapse of the old Danube monarchy at the end of the First World War. The year 1919 found Etelka, along with husband and child and "old family retainer" (a loyal Hungarian serving maid), back in Vienna at her parents' home, though not for very long. Outward conditions and circumstances had cleared up enough for Grauermann to know that for the time being he would be kept on and would be able to continue in government service, the government in question being the Royal Hungarian one. After the restoration of orderly conditions in Hungary, he was assigned to the consulate general in Vienna, and so his little family moved into the mansion on Bank Gasse where the consulate now had its quarters. On the top floor, in cozy but spacious rooms with low ceilings—a baroque structure always has the height of the uppermost rooms very considerably reduced—was where Grauermann had been assigned his attractive and stately official residence. Etelka owned many old pieces of furniture dating from the very time when this building had been built, and so it was quite by coincidence that their new home achieved unity of form.

The ensuing years were the high point of her life. What had remained a potentiality in Constantinople turned into an actuality here.

Perhaps we should say the "public high point," but this expression has an aftertaste of success story and careerism about it, and that's exactly what it wasn't. Rather, it was one government official's little rowboat, rescued and skillfully steered away from the flotsam left by the sinking wreckage of a great power, but now fastened to a part of the wreck floating merrily along on its own. After all, it wasn't only his Hungarian homeland but really the dual monarchy as a whole that had raised Consul Grauermann, trained him and nurtured him. A merely outward high point—by all means, because in the story of a love affair the most exalted passage isn't necessarily the one that mounts a door on hinges so that it can be thrown open and clear the way for a look into connecting rooms, all brightly lit and seeming for a time to transform all of existence into a kind of colossal candy store sent from heaven on high.

Even so, there were some unutterably beautiful spring days in Vienna in 1920.

Grauermann often found himself in Budapest for fairly long periods. His official duties took him there, and he would later on use them as an excuse, too, one behind which he was actively engaged in working out his future, since Consul Grauermann was very quick to come to the realization that his diplomatic career was doing nothing but spinning its wheels and that the present Hungarian state—a strange cross between a prematurely whelped republic and a doddering old monarchy—could hold few prospects for its officials. That was how matters were bound to present themselves, anyway, to a sensible man like Grauermann in those days. So he spent those years setting up, with thoroughness and persistence, his transition to private industry, which he completed in 1923, as an officially retired consul of the Hungarian monarchy, a status that didn't exactly disadvantage him in his new situation, either. When this change came about, the Grauermanns moved into their beautiful apartment on the Fasor in Budapest—this street had been called Vilma királynö út since the war, incidentally—which was Etelka's last dwelling, the last room looking along that flight of rooms which was her life, and at quite a far remove from that small chamber where the melancholy verses of Omar Khayyám had once been delved into.

Fraunholzer was a good ten years older than Etelka; in 1909 or 1910, as soon as he'd been posted to Constantinople as consul, he had married a Fräulein Küffer. She came from the same Viennese family of brewery owners that we mentioned in passing a good while ago as being friends with Mary K.; perhaps we will remember that in the years after the First World War Mary's children would go out to Döbling to spend time with the younger generation of Küffers and that the Küffer family welcomed these friendly relations, as the two K. children, the boy as well as the girl, were brighter than average and were excel-

lently educated and well behaved. Three children came from Fraunholzer's marriage. In the years after the war, an external change took place
in Consul Fraunholzer (to say nothing of anything internal or of the
changes in his marital relations). He grew considerably stockier, as
indeed he had to, for he had survived an acute case of pneumonia in
1919, after which he was strongly urged to gain weight. His becoming
stockier, which most certainly did not mean an unattractive embon-
point, was of great advantage to his looks, though, for the simple
reason that he'd been too thin until then. It was René Stangeler—ever
the schoolboy, even if he was then well on his way to earning his
PhD—who came up with a nickname for Fraunholzer that stuck with
the subsequent consul general and that perfectly described his exterior—Pompeius. Fraunholzer, whom René got to know at his parents'
country house after the war, really did look in those days like some
ancient Roman dressed up in clothes from our own time, the compact-
ness of his head testifying to vigor—not lacking a touch of the aristo-
cratic in its contours, especially when seen from the side—his curly
dark hair, broad shoulders, and sturdy figure. In any event, his voice
was almost always a little husky, but that too seemed to fit somehow,
or else everyone had just grown completely used to it. Herr von Stangeler thought very highly of Fraunholzer and would often sit in his study
conversing with him for hours on end. Now this heading was the one
under which most people placed Fraunholzer's relations with the Grauermanns, but whether Herr von Stangeler was one of them must remain
an open question for now, much though his nostrils flared at times as
if sniffing something out, would in all these instances proclaim that
the true essence of human relationships and connections practically
never stayed hidden from him. However that was, the subsequent
consul general in Belgrade had for a long time now been firmly and
manifestly anchored in the minds of most as Grauermann's older sponsor and mentor. And no sooner had Grauermann come to Constantinople in the capacity of consular attaché than Fraunholzer in fact did
begin taking good care of him right away, and he did so without having previously known him more than very slightly; they had never
studied together at the academy in Vienna, as there was a twelve-year
difference in age between them. Teddy von Honnegger was the only

student enrolled in Grauermann's time who had any connection with Fraunholzer, and it was a very close one at that. It hadn't begun at the academy, either, but originated much farther back; they had been friends since Honnegger's years at the gymnasium, when the general-consul-to-be was nearing the end of his time at the academy. Such a thing was quite rare, comparatively speaking, and what seems even more striking about it is that a rapport based on complete mutuality of respect marked it from the very first, even from the older partner to the one so much younger. Teddy's father, a highly placed official in the Foreign Ministry, always looked happily upon the friendship between his son and that bright Robert. Fraunholzer must have taken great pleasure in seeing how early our Grauermann's abundant measure of practical intelligence was coming to fruition in Constantinople, and, as far as all "official interactions" were concerned (if we may use that almost repellently attractive expression!), the younger man's having been so efficiently briefed from the outset by someone so very alert could only have worked significantly to his advantage, in particular regarding "interpersonal interactions," which is the most important (indeed, the only important) consideration in a government agency, consisting as it does—however lofty a name it might bear—of human beings, and sometimes of inhuman beings as well.

Even so, and even though everything was beginning to slide down the slippery slope leading to total chaos, these days of spring in 1920 were indescribably beautiful for Etelka and Fraunholzer; as a result of the illness he'd suffered, which he was yet to recover from completely, he was able to be in Vienna only for brief stretches at a time, because he was staying in the Austrian Alps, in Gmunden, where his wife and the children were also living, their needs being easier to meet in Upper Austria than in the large city, given the vagaries of food distribution then.

We've been forgetting for some time now to mention even in passing that Etelka had given birth to a child in Constantinople, a healthy and good-looking little boy. He resembled his mother to the closest possible degree and his father virtually not at all, which gave Fraunholzer all the more reason to love him with deep affection and, by using all the connections at his disposal, to procure for the toddler whatever it was possible—or even impossible—to get from Upper Austria and from Hungary.

So Etelka had a little boy by Grauermann.

We can see how all parties involved were doing their share to complicate yet further matters that were already somewhat askew, or, if the truth were told, had by now fallen into complete disarray.

Even so and even though: there was an invulnerable air about these days, and that quality stayed constant throughout the whole spring. They even felt safe (Fraunholzer's highly visible role of sponsor and mentor to the young married couple made it easier for them to plan and contrive), and nothing whatever happened, not ever, to give them a scare or make them feel their footsteps were being dogged. They rode along Ring Strasse in an open fiacre; all her life, Etelka had loved riding in an open fiacre no matter what. The outer world, scattering into innumerable reflections of light, into darting shadows of leaves and dappled patches of sun under the trees left and right, this outer world, under a ceaseless barrage by ever new glass panes of light that would come tumbling down and shatter into innumerable tinkling shards—with all its delights, ones to which names could be put, this outer world still did not seep all the way into and suffuse the deepest part of Etelka's being, for there, hidden far from any light and wrapped in the pale dove gray of her life's most secret chambers, was where the substantial displacement occurred, very diffidently and almost marginally, that was the hallmark of those days; and in her memory, right up to her last hour, it was linked to Robert's strong face, alert in a masculine way under his light gray hat, and to his broad shoulders, strong but yet unburdened, leaning back against the rear seat of the carriage. Here, for the first time, something went out of her that was like a fiend grown impotent, though earlier possessed of the power to scourge her, as it were, whenever she had dealings with others, the result of which was that she had, in a manner of speaking, never so much merely approached another person as she had downright assaulted anyone and everyone while madly flailing the tattered banner of her own self-worth. All she wanted now, however, was simply to devote herself, by absorbing it ever more deeply, to this image of silent, masculine self-assurance, of modesty with no need for declaration, and she did so free of all anxiety about being pressured, hurt, humiliated, or broken, free from even the remotest twinges of the fear (which always felt the same) that a hand was about to grab her by the neck. That most intense of all her agonies, her father, went out of her and then reappeared as a thing transformed when it rose anew over the horizon of her life in an unexpected quarter; with that, she was able to take occupancy of a space in her life that had up to then remained standing vacant—anguish for her—as if some evil shadow had always frightened her away from the place. What, compared to a deliverance like this, did the breadth of the gardens opening out near the Burgtheater count for? What, compared to it, were the brilliant beams flashing forth here and there in sudden gleams of white, like new stars coming into being, by the focused glint of sun rays reflected in the windows of houses or vehicles? What, compared to it, were the spume-like expanses of lilac along the outer Burg Platz, where they were now turning? All these were overtones and nothing more, sweet-smelling little splinters of the one great bliss in which Etelka was riding along on wheels turning gently behind the snorting and prancing horses, through the Burg Tor on the way into the center of the city, where life on the sidewalks, fast-paced and apparently feeling so good about itself, made its way closer to their carriage, and where the quality of light grew much more intriguing, since a quiet, shady street would pleasantly insinuate itself once in a while, like a dove-gray trapezoid amidst all the abundance, to the left or the right, and would divide it.

On one of those days, Etelka arrived back at her home in the Hungarian mansion on Bank Gasse around noon, walking right through the broad entrance hall past the concierge, who greeted her, and doing the same in her apartment upstairs, giving just a slight nod of her head and a faint smile as she went past—or more that she drifted or floated past—her faithful Ziska, who had a bit of a puzzled look in watching the mistress walk by, as she was hoping to fill her in just then on a few household matters, an item about the little boy and another one about the noon meal. But Etelka had already vanished into the drawing room. There something forced her to come to a stop and to remain half stand-

ing and half sitting on the wide arm of an easy chair, her glance fixed
on a large, flat tray of embossed brass, now gleaming like bright gold;
nearly a meter in diameter, it sat on a low, sturdy Turkish taboret, and
the coffee service, always kept out and ready, was sparkling in the
sunlight. The windows were left open here, but in this fairly secluded
part of the city the vaguely grinding noise in the distance entered much
diluted. (Could that have been because of the great reserves of solitude
and quiet and interior absorption stored up on nearby Minoriten Platz,
with its Church of the Friars Minor, the Minoritenkirche, cushioned
and softened as if by a pillow?) Etelka was looking at the radiant brass
disc, which lay in the path of a sunbeam, but she was in reality looking
or feeling right through the metal, beyond it, and into her own inner
self. It was as though something molten were flowing through her now.
And in this flow she caught a glimpse of a possibility she'd previously
never so much as imagined—the possibility of just letting go, in some
way, of everything that had ever weighed her down and spurred her on
at the same time, but a way of letting go without painful sacrifices and
with no trace at all of being jostled off her path or forced to turn a
corner, so to speak. It offered itself as a single step up to a higher level
easily reached, a step, too, that would allow her to keep the specific,
altogether personal coloration of her life clinging to the soles of her
shoes, as it were, and to take it with her up there, without having to
give it up in any way, as for instance through one of those sharply
pointed either-or configurations hostile to life, caught, say, between
the concepts of altruism and egoism, or whatever other names these
pedagogical javelins so often hurled at her might have been going by.

Life, until now always pulling in opposite directions at once as it
straddled contradictions, now seemed to Etelka to be flowing into one
stream, into a single river with a greater power to loosen things. Etelka
didn't ask herself why, just now of all times, her glance still riveted on
the gleaming brass tray, she thought of her room at that boarding school
in Dresden—of her room and of a rather disturbing situation she had
once happened to find herself in there. Just then someone had knocked,
and in had walked Fräulein Brandt, the headmistress, though not
exactly in that capacity at the moment; her facial expression brought
with it into the room a whole new and different relationship to her

pupil, one that seemed already a fait accompli and entirely a matter of course, which made it easy for Etelka to tell this older friend of hers what she had just discovered about herself and what condition had announced its onset. Fräulein Brandt smiled and took Etelka by the hand, the girl feeling as if inwardly violated by this new flowing inside of her and this secret of her own body, revealed so suddenly and in such silence. And that was how it was again today, except that it wasn't her body. How many things were trying to wash away and depart from her in this liberating river! She sank down into the easy chair and buried her face between her hands on its wide and thickly cushioned arm.

During this time, somewhere between 1921 and 1922 (the happiest years in her life), there gradually emerged for Etelka a new focal point and resting place in her relations with the court singer Dame Cornelia Wett. Etelka once took Consul Fraunholzer to see her. Such a thing had become possible initially because of a state of affairs that, strictly speaking, was mostly negative, at least as Dame Cornelia must have seen it; she had long since given up on Etelka as a future singer (even before the war, for that matter, confronted as she had been with the thread of Etelka's whole life, which was sometimes, thanks to those escapades of hers, glaringly exposed to the light and hopelessly tangled, and at other times, thanks to her periodic *façons voilées*, cast back into the deepest darkness until it almost completely disappeared, like rivers coursing through limestone caverns). And so all professional expectations dropped away as far as the court singer was concerned, while the same happened on Etelka's side with regard to the nagging from her conscience and the embarrassment that had often caused her to avoid Cornelia Wett for long periods of time. On the initiative of Frau Consul Grauermann, relations between them now assumed a much more trusting form. First she asked Cornelia to read Fraunholzer's letters, which, for safety's sake, he then began sending to the court singer's address, where they were kept, an ever-growing treasure, in a large jewelry box. Finally she ended up bringing the consul himself to Cornelia and introducing him to her. There was some degree of astonishment connected with their meeting, for these two personalities, both strong and fundamentally not at all dissimilar, struck up the liveliest understanding from the first moment—literally from the very second Fraunholzer had set foot inside Dame Cornelia's bright, sunlit studio, on a May morning around eleven o'clock. She was sitting on a sofa, like a lion with a blond mane, sizing up with her angled eyes the man coming in through the door. No sooner had they been introduced than they started talking back and forth, like two men, about politics, and then, quite exhaustively, about business conditions in the Balkan countries (for which Fraunholzer was just then preparing to set off), and after that, about stocks and bonds. It almost reached the point where Etelka felt excluded, but from some category where it didn't hurt. Owing to the topics discussed, the style of this conversation was only too reminiscent of the talks between Fraunholzer and Etelka's husband, except that with those two, the former totally outshone the latter, a situation Pista kept on causing, over and over, by his reticent bearing, since he always wanted to listen and learn something from Fraunholzer, whereas these two now, Cornelia and Robby, flooded one another with light; each seemed to be putting the other into the lime-light, in fact, and with no self-consciousness at all.

Still it did hurt a little, but in a way that arose from somewhere other than the soft spots in the emotions. This theatrical display of sharp-wittedness somehow came close to bordering on vulgarity (in Etelka's mind), and perhaps this was her way of quickly trying, as she stood unobserved in the shadows, to devalue it, for it disclosed, as if in the innermost chamber of her life—though only through a tiny crack, only for a flash, and half blurred by a kind of dove-gray veil that her intuitions could not altogether penetrate—its most deep-seated weakness.

Cornelia Wett's apartment was located in a section of the city with a fairly high elevation. The streetcar went uphill to get there, but it ran fast and in a straight line. Cornelia's rooms had sunlight and wide vistas, not a narrowly constricted view. It was a new building.

All these elements combined inside Etelka to make a picture of this place, her love's high-lying citadel, one that swam in light, as it were;

it was the utter antithesis of the dark home she'd grown up in, which had always oppressed her in the depths of her memory. Even in Pera or Galata. Even up on the tower there, no matter the grandeur of the panorama unfolding. It was the same in the trolley that went up to it through a tunnel and in a straight line. Down below, near the station, on the square joining the Rue Yéni Djami with the Grande Rue de Galata, is a Turkish café with several rooms set one behind the other, so that a guest would go farther and farther inside, and not in a regular pattern, since the rooms did not lie along an axis (as she remembered it, anyway). Here, for a single, solitary time, she had been truly alone with Fraunholzer. Because Pista came late. They waited for him and forgot about it. (Every affair is played against its own backdrop, has its own milieu; the stage scenery is unutterably right for what is being played.) Now, in this memory, everything was colored like mother-of-pearl, and was fragrant, too, though clouded and milky (from the sea?), fragrant like the rose water one used to be able to buy in Constantinople; it came in tall, very slender bottles that looked like glass wands trimmed with gold.

PART TWO

HAVEN'T we strayed away from 1911 (getting considerably ahead of ourselves, into the bargain!), specifically from May of 1911, the point at which our gymnasiast, René Stangeler, sixteen at the time, was just making the acquaintance of Fräulein Paula Schachl? This semester of his schooling, like all the others, drew toward the usual close, and with no particular jolts, bumps, or worries as far as the individual academic subjects or the danger of possibly failing any of them were concerned. This was a stretch of time when everything went well for René; he was enjoying a smooth ride, free of bumps, and his report card fell into a respectable enough middle range—like most of his report cards, incidentally.

And so now, since the start of his summer vacation, he could be found out at his parents' house in the country, and time—always with the same isolating rock walls over the one end of the valley and always with the same confining mountains toward the lower-lying plain—had advanced beyond the middle of August.

Many locations were still partly surrounded in René's mind by a childlike sense of the whole world as a cavern; they still showed dimensions and details that would later be sealed off from the more casual glance, coming from outside only, of someone much too mature not to have outgrown all that, just like headlights that flatten whatever they sweep over so briefly, the hollows and the recesses, the mass and the contours of any solid locality, say a village or a small town through which the car is driving at night. Now, however, a good many deep grottoes of boyish captivation by green-glimmering light still opened up in the young woods amid certain groves and smaller trees. Or the dry solitude and silence of an attic room, turned away from all of summer's breadth, and yet suffused with summer all the same, a room where old utensils and tools were stored, along with many other objects that by having lain where they were for so many years had gone from being old to being new again and were thus so thoroughly intriguing when unearthed. There was a workroom in the basement too, its presence and its odors dominant, right next to the cellars and the broad curves of the cut-stone archways, underneath which the large cider press stood and atop of which the wide wooden porches of the house rested. There was the area around the dark well house, out of which ran a line for the drinking water. And there was a pond or marshy area located by the stream higher up, an artificial pool dug among the trees of the timber forest, mighty as ships' masts, where the water gathered so that it could build up enough pressure to reach the upper stories of the house—here, the walls of that bygone world-cavern were still almost entirely solid and undissolved all around; here they still worked the spell of their enchantment from a time when these few square meters of pond had had shores and coastlines plied with ships, when the water here, hardly a meter deep, had nonetheless been deep enough to cover whatever sea monster or serpent went slithering along the bottom with all the room it needed, with all the darkness it wanted, and with all the terror with which the imagination could invest the deep sea.

And so René's topography expanded quite capaciously and in quite a detailed way during the summer of 1911, and this external knowledge of places was just as much internal, the boundary between the two domains not very definitely fixed. A ravine, for example, behind a steep, hilly pine forest near the boundary of the family property, cut and hollowed out over many years, many spring seasons, by a stream that was mostly just a trickle during the summer—this ravine had its existence inside of René, independent of its external reality, which he was somewhat familiar with at that time. There—inwardly—it led to a region not at all agreeable to our schoolboy, where it smelled like toads, ugly crawling worms, slimy mud, and clammy, coiled things. Knowing that something like this dwelt inside him was a hardship, and it set up barriers to the outside, oddly enough, since it allowed others to be superior, more animated, whereas he himself had something to hide. Didn't this state of affairs, all by itself, make him feel a pressure coming from older people, to whose edicts, after all, he was forced to live in subjugation, a pressure that to some degree wasn't being exerted at all but that he himself was bringing on even so? From the general direction of his father, of course, among others. He was trying to conceal and to avoid a great deal—in fact, everything; his constant and exclusive object was to keep from bringing anything down on himself. But he was bringing it anyway.

This ravine was formed on the right side by a drop-off of earth and splinters of slate—above it lay open fields that sloped down toward the valley, but at their edge was a stand of trees and brushwood growing densely and shutting out any sense of an open landscape here. On the left were the needle-smooth hillsides of the pine forest. The stream ran down steeply and leveled off, though only a little, somewhat higher up, forming a small pond with marsh marigolds that shone bright yellow when the sun struck them. Otherwise, and especially farther down, everything here lay in the shadows of deciduous trees and pine trees growing in the same place, the deciduous trees on the right and the pines spreading their branches from the left over the ravine and the stream. René was making his way up from below, walking in the streambed. That was a habit he had gotten into so as not to muddy the water. Once, a good many years before, he, along with Asta, had discovered a crab. The children took great enjoyment in clambering up and down the steep drop-off; in the process, a good deal of earth, sand, and gravel would come loose and roll down. One time, they buried the flow of the stream this way on purpose, deeply and completely, so that they could dig down to it through a ditch they made. The next day, a crab was sitting at the bottom of the hole, where water was seeping in. It had probably fallen in while foraging by night. Ever since then, René had stayed in the habit of keeping an eye out now and then, even though he was seldom rewarded with success. As of one particular day, however, he had ceased and desisted from his habit of feeling underneath the rocks; he had seen a large maple leaf floating on the surface of a comparatively deep pool formed by the stream. He moved it aside, and under it was sitting an unusually strong specimen, almost as long as his hand, of the stone crayfish known in scientific nomenclature as *Astacus torrentium*, which in those days it was still possible to come across here and there in the mountain streams around that area. When skillfully grasped by the cephalothorax and held up to the light, though, the handsome find presented a sight that prompted René to drop it back into the water at once. The animal had been feeding. Its prey, an exceptionally large earthworm, almost like a blindworm, was tightly wrapped around the powerful claws; it was still alive and was trying to escape its destruction by twisting and turning. René was immediately gripped by the thought that if he kept reaching his hand under rocks he would catch hold of something like that. Since that time, he no longer investigated cavernous, hollow places, and he didn't catch sight of any more crabs. And yet a kind of personal habit (or was it a compulsion?) could still make him climb up through the ravine from below by following the course of the stream.

Now he was standing with his legs spread below the small swampy meadow, where the streambed was still steep.

A trembling went through the marsh marigolds in the swamp, then a quivering or shaking of their yellow speckles. At the same time there was a rustling sound on the right, from the wall that bordered the small open spot gleaming green in the sunlight.

René took up a stance now exactly like that of a primitive hunter, a Bushman or some other kind of native. He didn't move a muscle but instead froze in the half-bent position he'd just then assumed; he laid his ears back, as it were, and scanned the territory. And he certainly did get to see quite a sight.

Something gray was creeping and gliding on the dirt slope, and from there over to the edge of the swampy place—while even now it was emerging on the other side. By then, René had spotted the head of the snake, which was the largest one he had ever encountered out in nature. It moved somehow through and past the green spot, and soon it was hanging slantwise across the streambed like a garland, up where the terrain became steep and stony again. On the other side, clods of dirt were still rolling down to the foot of the embankment, from which the end of the snake's tail was just sliding away. The head, with its wide yellow jaws, had meanwhile been feeling its way uphill along the forest floor for some time.

René knew what species this snake belonged to, of course, and how harmless it was; one clap of his hands would have made it go darting off in a flash, like the crack of a whip. Then again, it would have been possible for him to catch it, given his skill and experience in such matters, and that's just what he'd always done, too, as if automatically, like some foregone conclusion, whenever he came across nonpoisonous serpents. But he had never seen such a huge specimen of *Tropidonotus natrix* before. It must have measured a good two meters in length. On quick reflection, he suspected (and not without reason, as any naturalist could confirm) that a grass snake developed to this size would have been able to wrap far more effective coils around his arms than the ones ordinary specimens would occasionally attempt). This snake that he knew so very well—its habits and habitats, its method of propagation, its movements in water and by land—was now, in its immensity, a stranger to him once more, a creature new and hitherto unknown.

Because René didn't make a move, that dragon of a *Tropidonotus* went slithering leisurely along its way toward a trench cut deep into the side of the ravine, where a little creek flowed into the stream.

René felt every one of the snake's motions as if he himself were the one executing them, only turned inward, to the inside of him, as it were: encountering an obstacle—a branch or a rock—when crawling, the head hesitating while the long body remained in motion, bunching strongly in tighter coils behind it; the suddenly resumed forward slithering of the neck, now stretched out from the resulting cluster, which was resolving, flex by flex, into ever shallower curves; the continuous writhing and weaving of the gray body, which might have been well over three fingers thick at its widest part. Only now, as the snake went creeping past closer to him, was its full powerfulness apparent to René.

And he felt love for it.

Secret sharer of his solitude here in the ravine.

Child of the deep and mighty forests, indeterminable but surely very great in age.

There could perhaps have been even more powerful specimens in the wilderness, in the clefts and ravines of the valleys to the side, sealed off as they were by fallen and decayed trees; for who could set limits to their growth once the snakes had attained a size that placed them beyond any danger from members of their own species and thus just kept on increasing, abundantly nourished by frogs, dormice, and field mice, everywhere in full supply there? Who could set limits, considering reptilian life spans, which could extend into the indeterminable? There was a good chance that this *tropidonotus* had a hundred and more sloughings of its skin behind it.

But while such little tidbits from the realm of natural history went running through his mind at the moment he was standing there in a truly downcast and indeed almost woebegone mood as he looked at the snake, there emerged more and more clearly, and with growing luminosity, in front of the gloomy background of his soul—or behind its gloomy foreground—the familiar image of forests large and deep. It fanned out; the forests unfolded and presented views from several perspectives, always leading inward until they reached a bright green glow that suffused them far to the rear when the sun went down. Every point of approach ended in the same place there, no matter whether it had skimmed along rows of tall trees, like the sounding board above the strings of a gigantic harp; whether it was presented with the green bed of a woodland meadow seen through the trees or presented with an invitation from bushes and undergrowth to come and rest in an enclosed spot, like a room in the forest; or again if it began with the edges of an open path, casually guiding the eye as they widened out and bracketed a high mountaintop in the distance; yet even here, while receding to the side, the forest offered hints of the gleaming emerald it contained. There were rocks in the woods too. Some lay on the ground, separate pieces of mountain debris, while others stood upright, though not reaching as high as the treetops, which sheltered them; they belonged to the forest still and were overgrown by its moss. Yet others jutted out over the woods. From their peaks or their platforms it was possible to look out over the trees, over the forest, the living, warm, and wavelike foam of forests in summer. Rooted in them, however, a rock could only serve their indwelling *genius*. When climbing, stepping around the corner of a rock ledge, surmounting the ridge while carefully testing each new grip on the subalpine stone, René had never quite given up anticipating that he might suddenly encounter the true denizen, the undisputed king of the forest world, might see it sunning its head, covered with green scales and topped by a comb, a horn, or even a small crown, its cold, inscrutable reptilian glance lost somewhere in the depths or fixed motionless in the distance beyond the treetops.

Even though René still wanted to keep his eyes on the slithering and gliding movements of the snake's body, he now had to turn his head left, toward that small side trench. And so he did, but hesitantly. He would have been happiest leaving this place at once and making plenty of noise as he went. But an opportunity for observation as rare as this one was what held him here, although more in name only, so to speak, than because of any outright enjoyment. Whatever it was that stole over him and crept up on him here—the mountain forest glowing in the back of his thoughts the whole time—was accompanied by the deepest uneasiness. And all of a sudden it hit him, as though plummeting vertically into him, and as though it had been the remotest of all possibilities—that here, for the first time, he was feeling repugnance when looking at a snake. Perhaps because it was so large. But there the repugnance was, and he knew now—knew with pain, as with the sweet sorrow of parting—that it would never go away again. (He was standing between two phases of his life, exactly the way he was physically standing, right here and now, legs straddling the bed of the stream, still very much the little boy and long since the skittish adolescent.) The part about it that was serious, however, the part being strongly emphasized, as he sensed it, lay outside the range of his emergent conscious thinking; rather, it lay in the twisting, coiling, balking, and struggling body of the snake itself, which right now was bringing these emergent thoughts into outward form and illustrating them so consummately for him.

It was gone. It had flitted around a bend and vanished in a deep thicket of huge coltsfoot leaves.

There he stood, all the while motionless, his hands down at his sides and smudged with resin and the tiny little stones that stuck to it. The resin was from tree trunks he'd held on to when walking down the woodland slopes, unusually steep and slick with pine needles, and the stones from climbing up through the lowest part of the ravine the stream was in, which gradually dropped away. The climb had made him hot, but now he felt the coolness of the shady ravine, and something like goose bumps came creeping over him.

There he stood astride the streambed, in his short leather pants, his hair falling over his forehead.

Suddenly René shook himself and bounded out of the ravine with a few leaps.

The terrain leveled off somewhat and merged into a preserve area that stood on a gentle incline and had young spruce trees planted in rows. Here the morning sun was coming down with full force and the spotless blue of the sky was standing high above the line of treetops. René felt himself being suffused by the warm sunlight, absorbed into it. To the rear, at the upper end of the preserve, a narrow path ran right along the slope, under some leafy trees, and among these trees and thickets and the inviting shelters they formed at the edge of the open area was another of René's special homing places—a geometrical space in which inner and outer topography coincided, one could say, each gaining thereby in concreteness and luminosity. He looked over in that direction. Ever since he'd read Virgil's eclogues in school, this place had been connected with them in his mind. Amaryllis. The name tasted like ripe fruit. Something inside René bumped against something else, something didn't mesh quite exactly with something else, and a gentle pain stretched across the gap; and as though it were this pain that had just now been tapped and it were giving off a sound like a tambourine, his ear caught the echo of a tennis ball being hit by a racket. A sunny, carefree sound in which there resonated an overtone from the gut strings stretched in the frame. Now again. Back and forth. Voices, laughter.

The release (*le déclic*, as the French say—what a wonderful word!) brought him something else, and it had nothing to do with tennis.

Something else, a whole different world somewhere else, one in which a person would have to be completely at home, not coming back from trying to catch snakes or having resin stuck to his hands. Now Virgil, there among the thickets in the tranquil silence, with warm summer softly humming all through the air, was also turning him away, separated from him as if by a membrane that stretched but wouldn't burst.

Then he saw them once more—the steps. Coming through the quiet street below, one would start to hear the plashing of the fountain. Left and right the stairs pirouetted up to the first landing. And then ramp upon ramp, stage upon stage. The overarching trees luxuriant in leafage.

What possibilities! A stage entrance from above. Everything mere background, like that of a portrait. And against this particular background hovered the face of Paula.

Town at the height of summer.

The building called the Blue Unicorn.

The Strudlhof Steps.

The Schmellers' garden party in Döbling was set for Tuesday, the twenty-second. Etelka and Asta had permission to travel to Vienna for the occasion. Nothing would suffice but that René must go as well, so he'd begun making his own little special arrangements. His private tutor (or "house teacher," as they used to say) wasn't able to spend the second half of the summer out here in the country this year but was in Vienna instead for some reason or other, taking a cram course for the second level of government law boards—or so he claimed, anyway. (René never really believed anything anybody said, but instead was of the opinion, held in all innocence, that people everywhere lied on the average at least as much as his own family did, a figure surely inflated.) This tutor was of course hand in glove with René about everything. In addition to that, he enjoyed the favorable estimation of Herr von Stangeler because he was such a hard worker, because he did such an outstanding job as the sole support of his mother, and more of the same. And so, on René's initiative, a recommendation was tendered to the effect that it would be advantageous for our prep-school boy to go to Vienna for a few days, or maybe even a week, sometime during the second half of the summer, so that he could polish his skills in this or that academic subject before the new school year began. He corresponded with Paula Schachl via box number through general delivery so that none of her letters would accidentally be delivered here, to the country house, along with the rest of the Stangeler family's mail. It was all arranged that he would meet her on the day after the garden party, that is, on the twenty-third. At that café and bakery on Alserbach Strasse. Where else?

This whole plan had met with no resistance from a higher quarter.

So he'd be able to travel with his sisters.

Then, too, the girls would have—in addition to the servant Lina, assigned and dispatched as their maid—René at their disposal, more or less as a male protector.

He'd protect them all right.

René was a melancholy young chap. He was lacking ease of manner, was missing out on the sheer pleasure that should have been part of his affairs and arrangements. He was missing as well the pleasure he should have taken in lying about everything. He only told lies because he couldn't imagine doing things any other way and because of course nothing ever worked out without them.

There were several tall old larch trees standing spaced far apart, and another stream, a bigger one. Farther along, up past the tennis court, was the reservoir, that artificial pool.

He walked up to the small sheet of water and looked down, but not with a searching eye. His glance didn't penetrate below the surface and down to the muddy bottom. He saw the blue sky and the treetops reflected. Breaking off a reed and chewing on it, he sat down on a sand pile next to the pond. Now he was no longer hearing the sounds and the voices coming from the tennis court. Those had become totally absorbed into his downcast and yet strangely ambivalent frame of mind.

What was not absorbed was a blinding white patch that now came moving along the line of shrubs on the narrow pathway leading down from the tennis court to the pond. Herr von Geyrenhoff stepped onto the dam, not quite a meter wide, from the middle of which the weak overflow of water trickled, and started to walk along it, René saluting him by waving and calling "Hello." René had stood up, in fact. Geyrenhoff laughed, shook hands with him, and kept right on walking, going a little way farther, into the woods (which was the reason he'd left the immediate vicinity of the tennis court). When he came back, he stopped and talked with René, who'd sat back down on the sand pile and had tossed the reed away.

René was now completely bowled over by this man, Geyrenhoff.

Here was yet another world of its own, and this one seemed to be really worth the effort to reach, a world of complete stability on the highest, most obvious, and most natural level. It surged out toward him, it called him; indeed, it issued him a summons, but could René follow and enter it from the state he was in right now? He could sense the extraordinary vigor emanating from this young man standing before him in such a relaxed attitude, his hands in the pockets of his loose, cream-colored pants with a narrow belt of dull antelope hide that made such a contrast to his white shirt. Mainly, he detected an odor; it was the full-bodied, crisp, and somehow comforting odor of *eau de lavande*. Behind it all, though, René could feel, as through what one might call an instinct, directed with remarkable accuracy toward the essence of the matter, an unruffled self-confidence, the free and easy way of standing up for oneself that marks a well-ordered person-ality, one that has truly earned the right to this—to being like this, that is—and earned ease of manner as a further reward.

Faced with so clarion a call, however, and with so leaden a torpor in not being able to follow it, there arose in René a kind of panic, which compelled him first and foremost to take immediate cover, to throw up a barrier whose outer side would somehow get placarded over with all the right slogans, but behind which his pain—of no slight amount—kept burrowing deeper, and his concealed anxiety—of no slight amount—kept rising.

As a result, he tried to compose himself into the form he saw stand-ing there before him and asked in an offhand and knowledgeable manner, like a person very much in the know, if the doubles match with Etelka and Grabmayr was over yet and how it had turned out.

Here is the right place to offer a few critical comments about Herr von Geyrenhoff (who, at the time we're speaking of, and according to his own statement, gave hardly any reply at all to René's question). Geyrenhoff, in those days a member of the executive committee in the Royal and Imperial Finance Ministry, would later on take an early retirement, with the rank of sectional councillor, after the republic had come into being; people said it was because he had gained possession of a significant fortune invested in England and of course sequestered there for the duration of the 1914 war. Somewhere around 1927, though, His Majesty's Government in the United Kingdom had released all assets of this kind, and they had been very nicely augmented through their mandatory conversion into English war loans! Geyrenhoff, whom the aftermath of war had largely robbed of the rest of his inheritance, had good reason to be thankful to the English government in this regard. After his retirement, this Herr von Geyrenhoff turned to a peculiar way of occupying his time. He started work on a kind of chronicle extending over many years. He wasn't the sole author, incidentally; supposedly the writer Kajetan von S. and a whole group of other people were also contributors (this was the same Kajetan von S. who later on made—or maybe would have just made—that ill-bred remark about Frau Mary K. and Dr. Negria which we quoted right at the outset of our story). Whatever Geyrenhoff thought he was after with his chronicle or miscellany, or whatever it was, is something we can't explore here. Kajetan von S., for his part, found a way, years later, of using the thing for his own purposes, as came to light with time. It was through him that the author of these pages was able to gain access to the enormous and neatly written book and even to copy some things out at one point. This tome contained all sorts of different entries; among others was an exact account of what led up to the collapse of the Austrian Lumber Bank, as it was called, in the year 1926, a result of speculation in the French franc; it also contained very detailed information about any number of people, including quite a lot, in fact a great deal, about René von Stangeler. Even the meeting at the pond in August of 1911 was described here:

We played tennis on a Sunday morning in August; the valley down into which we had a view—the tennis court lay high above the house—was on brilliant display in the sunlight, the sky new and bright blue, part of a day that was just beginning and still all spotless; up at this altitude, moisture from the dew was sparkling on leaves and grass, and below us was the wide roof of the house, where a trail of pure blue smoke went drifting up from one of the chimneys through the mild breeze, like a festive banner unfurled to celebrate the imminent joys of the midday table. From the court came the keyed-up and yet rich, cushioned *thock! thock!* of balls and rackets, along with all the small interruptions a game will bring; that sound was somehow related to the summer air, fresh but very warm even this early, and it gave the spaciousness of that air a keener tang every time it reechoed. Etelka Stangeler and Grete Hartknoch were paired against Herr von Grabmayr and Editha Pastré-Meriot, and then Grabmayr, inexhaustible in stamina and strength, had squared off against

Semski after none too long a break, which meant that the most exciting game of the morning was underway now, for Semski had always been considered the undisputed champion in our group. There was a fair crowd sitting near the sidelines, on the benches for spectators and referees. Both benches were full, and several more people were standing and walking around behind. Here and now, though, I can't single out any of them in my memory except for Grauermann, who was then a student at the Consular Academy. He was coming from the left, walking across the green grass, wearing white trousers, while holding something trim and light-colored—a racket in its press—and unscrewing it as he went. I walked away, off to the right, urged by a sudden need, and perhaps also in answer to a desire to be by myself for a little while. So it would seem, then, that the match between Semski and Grabmayr, pretty far advanced by now, must not have been of any great interest to me, and maybe that went for the game of tennis as a whole. There is one crystal-clear image, though, that I can still see—Grauermann coming from the left as I was walking away to the right, both of us dressed for tennis; in the distance, above us, and above the court and the people gathered on the benches, lay the timber forest, shrouded in the sunlight and not clearly visible, nearby though it was. A small path led among some fruit trees and some bushes, and as the path dipped, I could see the stream; the water made a trickling sound when it fell over the wall that dammed up a pond used to supply a water line to the house. Sitting on a sand pile right next to it was René, who was often on hand and would go in search of our tennis balls whenever they flew off somewhere near the court. Just then, however, I had a feeling as if I were stepping through an invisible wall here and entering an entirely different realm, as if a door had now slammed shut behind me and split me off from the gathering I had just left. The bed of the stream was worn deep, and the woods followed the ravine, curving around as far as the pond. René didn't notice me. The position he was sitting in couldn't have been comfortable; he looked as though absentmindedness had caused him to just freeze, as it were, in whatever posture he'd happened to assume. He was looking off to the side and chewing on a reed; his face was somber, or at least somewhat unhappy, and his rather squinty eyes looked as if they were even more narrowed than usual. Suddenly I was able to fathom this summer day much more deeply; suddenly I comprehended where I was and what kinds of lives the people I was in the midst of led. It was as though I were sinking into the ground and becoming like the network of roots under the grass, while the bright figures from the tennis court stood high above me—and on foot mounts, like toy people—on the terrain immediately surrounding them. This pond under tall fir trees and, beyond it, the stream flowing in the ravine with its steep wooded slopes, seemed to me like the shadowy netherworld from which all things emerge and in which they all must come to an end. René's face struck me as unattractive, and I became clearly conscious of how brutality and gentleness were converging there with a strangely glutinous apathy, all at the same time. Even so, he was looking out of his own face in a strained way, like a man peering over a wall as he chins it. He was completely separated from the tennis court and from everything else there as well. And yet, while in this ugly state and mood, his whole family was contained inside him, like a curiously reversed case of paternity. I started across the wall of the dam, which is about two meters wide, and then he noticed me; that was when the whole thing came to a stop, and fakery took over the minute he looked up and saw me. Like all the Stangelers, he contracted when touched, as a sea anemone does, in a cramp that wouldn't loosen, and he presented the picture of himself that he thought he absolutely had to present (it's a certainty that no one in their family was ever touched by a genuine doubt on this heading; for all of them it was an automatic element of their certitude, so to say), and strained every nerve making the effort to climb into this picture and its frame from the back, as it were, so as to instill into—or better yet, impose upon—himself and the person he was talking to the conviction that this picture was what he really was. At the same time I could feel that he envied me (how I just came strolling along from the tennis court, all casual and carefree, in my light clothes, and fresh from my bath—my turn to play hadn't even come yet). His way of envying me wasn't the slightest bit malicious, though; it seemed more that the mood he was in predisposed him to look upon everyone else as a model, at least in regard to the external carapace, in regard to the mold in which the other person was cast, which immediately appeared to him as worth striving for and which perhaps he might have considered it possible to strive for in the first place; ravenous for structure (he's still like that today, it turns out) and yet unwilling to travel the long detour needed to get to it, which for him, of all people, would necessarily be a very long detour indeed. Yes, all these insights were fully present to me in those moments there by the dam above the Stangelers' house, and I'm explaining it in exhaustive detail now rather than conveying it to the mind of anyone reading this record (in case there should ever be such a person) with just a single little flick of the wrist, an effect my skill is inadequate to bring about. In a businesslike tone he asked me straight off some question having to do with the tennis game—if the doubles match with Etelka and Grabmayr was over by now, and what the result was—but I gave hardly any answer, because his question was coming strictly out of the frame, so to speak (he'd never bothered learning to play tennis, either, by the way), and it fit in with the way he was trying to hold his body, which was not one bit freer or more natural. Then I noted with surprise that he was sniffing the air and whiffing all around me; he ended that by saying in a very simple way—indeed in a whole different tone from the one he'd just been using—"You smell nice." His face looked really attractive then. Now, that was extremely to my liking; to some extent I began forging deeper hopes for him inside myself, could feel a surge of easier-breathing hope for him coming over me, and I liked him really a lot now. I told him what kind of shaving lotion I used (it's the same lavender water I still buy today, produced by a very old establishment in Vienna) and decided on the spot to have a large bottle of it sent to him, which I did, that very next Monday morning, on my way to the ministry; I had just stepped out of the South Station when I remembered. I only stayed at the villa over Saturday and Sunday that time, like most of the others; a weekly roster drawn up from every ministry, academic institution, and conservatory imaginable, a group of people with nothing at all unifying them and in that sense perfectly in keeping with the nature of this family.

That's all well and good. What Geyrenhoff has to say about the Stangelers, including René, is pertinent, but only on a general level. In no way did he instinctively sense the boy's particular situation, which was that our young friend was struggling—struggling in a more or less distinct form of his own, at that—toward a goal he wasn't too numb to feel, either. But now, the question is, how shall we describe it? Was it the unity and integrity of his personhood, meaning the process of becoming a person and attendantly for the first time (we'll go ahead and risk saying it) truly becoming a human being, which is what a young troglodyte would have yearned for as he looked out from his gloomy cave, where all his talents and abilities must surely have been shackled in heavy chains? And is that all? Isn't there more underneath? If so, then we must attempt to bring it out into the light so that we can identify it as the goal Stangeler had set for himself. Wasn't he essentially agonizing over ways to force disparate phenomena, circumstances, or internal and external spaces having no basis for comparison onto some common ground so they could be subjected after all to the magical power of comparison, the one power able to master objects through the ordering thread of memory, which would otherwise come apart all over again every time it's drawn on? Memory, then, remembrance— that's what it was about for René, and it didn't matter how young he was! As if on cue, a certain someone now appeared at the other side of the dam, likewise coming from the tennis court (he'd been sent to find Herr von Geyrenhoff and bring him back, because our future chronicler was scheduled to play a singles match soon), a certain someone who was likewise taken up with memory and remembrance and other such items and would go worming and wiggling around inside himself, even if only on occasion.

But before we bring on Lieutenant Melzer for his brief cameo, let's be even briefer—but let's get it over with!—as we cast one more sidelong glance at Geyrenhoff. It's all very neat and tidy when he writes, "I walked away, off to the right, urged by a sudden need, and perhaps also in answer to a desire to be by myself for a little while." Nothing wrong with that, every word correct but still not entirely true—the "sudden urge" and the "desire to be by myself for a little while." Very precise. But Geyrenhoff is always putting everything up on a higher plane of intellection. Then, too, he's very well-bred. Not as ill-bred as someone like that Kajetan, anyway.

When Geyrenhoff left, Melzer sat down next to René on the sand pile.

Just at that moment it occurred to René—or rather it hit him, and hard—that he hadn't told Geyrenhoff anything about his having encountered that large snake; in retrospect, he now noted his own conduct with astonishment, as something in itself new and strange.

Then he recounted the whole episode to Melzer.

"Yellow cheeks?" his listener asked. "Are you sure that's what you observed? You are? Then that's what it was, all right. A grass snake can grow that large—very rarely, but it does happen. You were smart not to try to catch it, René."

"Why?" René asked eagerly.

"Because you wouldn't have gotten rid of it so easily. The really large ones, like the one you're talking about, always wrap themselves around their captor, and they're strong. That's what happened to me once. In Neulengbach. You might not have been able to get free, not by yourself. Then you would have had to go home with it coiled around you, and can't you just picture the screaming from the girls in the kitchen! Everybody would have come running—think of the uproar—they would have brought in the groundskeeper, and the poor animal might have ended up getting hurt. And let's not even mention your father."

Melzer smelled like sunshine.

He was deeply tanned, especially on his arms, which his shirt left mostly bare.

His trousers were pure white, too, not cream colored like Geyrenhoff's, cut very wide, almost like a sailor's bell-bottoms, and his belt was made of white leather. René took notice of everything about him.

"You know, Herr Melzer," he said, "as I was watching the snake there in the ravine—I just thought of this right now—it was very peculiar..."

"What was peculiar?" the lieutenant asked.

"It was as if I were watching myself."

"And?" said Melzer, totally unembarrassed.

"I mean the strain and the grace at the same time—the stopping short, the hesitating, the twisting. Like myself on the inside, the deepest, inmost part of me, my most secret thoughts, as they say."

Melzer stared straight ahead, looking out over the pond.

And suddenly, as if it were rising from the surface of the water, there was the Treskavica landscape, with its bare south slope, and the ride with Major Laska up to the cabin the day before they went bear hunting for the first time. They'd stopped for a rest and dismounted; the major had just offered him a piece of chocolate or some cognac, or whatever it was; and then Melzer had looked inside a hazelnut bush and seen a little snake, a hazel snake, moving in coils. "René!" he called suddenly, turning to face Stangeler and clasping him on the shoulder, "that's right! I know what you mean! Just think! Exactly like yourself—I was once watching a snake that same way, too, a small one, though ..."

"Like the convolutions of one's own brain," said Stangeler.

A tremendous outcry now went up from the tennis court.

"Three cheers for Grabmayr! Three cheers for Grabmayr! Three cheers for Benno!"

They got up quickly and walked single file as they crossed the dam wall and went up the path.

"Where's Melzer?" someone called.

Grabmayr was swaying above people's heads, all covered with sweat, and laughing with his whole thin, tanned face. They were carrying him past the referee's bench beyond the embankment.

"He beat Semski," everyone was yelling.

A *Fluder*, or "millrace," is what Lower Austrians call the capacious trough that directs water to an overshot mill wheel. Into the system for regulating the mountain torrent a sluice gate is set here and there to let the water flow off into the millstream (in the main watercourse, meanwhile, only a thin little trickle ripples along from that point); as the ground keeps dropping steadily, the millstream changes somewhere into the millrace, which now separates from the ground and serves as an aqueduct, reaching out on taller and taller wooden trestles until it is positioned above the wheel; at that point there is a narrow opening at the bottom of the millrace, in the center, whose shape is that of an angled spout nearly as long as an arm and whose function is to bring the water in all its concentrated force up close to the wheel buckets and let it stream in. At the end of every millrace, past the wheel, is an overflow where the excess water plunges down from a good height, like a waterfall, into a trench, through which, its work done, the stream returns to the main watercourse.

And it's all made of wood. From local trees. Here in the forest valley the planks for the millrace were cut at the lumberyard by a saw that makes a rapid panting sound—one could imagine it as being out of breath all day long, if that panting weren't so regular—and this lumber saw is powered by the same kind of millrace and wheel as the mill here, for which reason people in the area also call it a sawmill, though the word doesn't really make sense when you think about it.

And it's all full of moss. The outer side of the millrace is largely covered with it, and it hangs in wet, dripping beards from the trestles. The wheel casing, a kind of shed inside of which is a terrific roaring and a furious turning—wherever a plank is missing, the heavy spokes can be seen slowly rising and disappearing—over time, this wheel casing has become thickly furred with it and is malachite green. The trench in which the wheel turns is lined with cut stones on the sides, and these walls too are overgrown with moss. The trench has white pebbles on the bottom. When the mill is operating, the water discharged by the wheel comes out from under the casing in little waves whose force of displacement shows they've done the job. Beyond the wheel, where the overflow plummets down from the end of the millrace into the trench on its return to the streambed, the hollowing pressure of the water has created a wider and deeper spot, but it's no more than a small, foaming basin, for the waters around here would not have come down from the high mountains until just a short time before—clear, cold, rushing, more muscular than corpulent, as it were—and here are to be found none of those well-nigh stagnant ponds that back up all the way to the wheel trench so that the wide, heavy buckets are almost submerged again underneath, if it isn't the case to begin with that the wheel runs undershot overall; none of those millponds as there are in flatter areas, deep, motionless, taken over by plant life, inhabited by animal life, as if purposely made to swamp and flood everything.

The mill doesn't run all the time. There are only a few days and weeks out of the year when it does, but then not seldom at night, too. It doesn't clatter, either. That's just something made up by fellows who take joy in singing all those folk songs about clattering mills; those boys are a type I for one would hate to hang around with, and the more songs they know, the farther away I want to be. The mill doesn't clatter. It rumbles, thumps, and vibrates. The door stands half open. Now and then the miller can be seen walking through the lower mill room. And yes, he is indeed covered with white dust, so that part is true, isn't just poetic "nattering"—to use an expression Germans favor—the way it is with the clattering, and to this extent, then, the requirements of the songful types for apt imagery in their lyrics could be satisfied very nicely. What's more, the miller has to do more to make a living than just be a miller; he's a small-scale landlord who lives in a cottage thereabouts and does work for all the farmers in the district during those days and weeks. Hence we see something that doesn't quite add up about his tastes (which doesn't mean anything's "wrong with" him in any way); something just doesn't quite add up about the miller's tastes—about roaming, to be specific. There could never have been even a question of any such thing, at least not with this one—so forget about Schubert's *Die schöne Müllerin* and its first line, "Das Wandern ist des Müllers Lust" (Roaming is the miller's joy)!—because this miller walks all crooked; his left leg is shorter, so he hobbles. Besides, his name is Klettler, meaning Burrman, and burrs cling. They also stick fast to one another. Life never allows us to arrange it according to our wishes, however, like a neat and tidy little game where we can square everything away—no, all of a sudden there's a wide gap again, as for example between concepts and what we mean by them (a situation that makes us uneasy) or between people and their names. Here, then, were two people who invited mockery of their name late in life. The Burrmans did stick together for forty-seven years, but then Frau Burrman ran off from her husband in the forty-eighth, close to her seventieth birthday, explaining—for naturally she was questioned by anybody and everybody—in a simple and dignified way that for forty-seven years now he'd beaten her on an average of twice a week and that she'd had quite enough. She wanted to pass her old age in peace and quiet. So that was how the burrs came to separate.

The water flows on always. They don't close the gate in the flood-control system when the mill isn't in operation; instead, they lower a movable dam located a few meters past the branching-off point and open an overflow toward the stream at the same time, though only in springtime, when the water is at its highest. The whole contraption is very old and full of leaks, and the ground is uneven with rocks and pebbles, so the millstream and the millrace have water all the time. If they had none at all, and if the trough could be dried out by the sun, then it would become even leakier than it already is. In any case, it now releases just single threads that drop from the beards of moss.

The mill stands fixed; the water flows.

The flowing water makes the garden of the adjoining inn pleasantly cool in the summer. The garden has chestnut trees, too. Covered over here, the trench conducting the water from the mill back to the stream runs right underneath the garden. The inn is old, with thick walls and deep cellars. It lies not far from the foot of the mountain on whose slope the Stangelers have their country house. When there isn't any more room up there, some of their guests stay here, rather than at the pretentious but bad hotel at the end of the valley, so they're a little higher up, at a place where for the longest time the one concession to chic or trendiness apparently consisted of a placard bearing the puzzling inscription RESORT ROOM over the taps where the farmers congregated. Now that was just plain silly. But the aroma of good cooking coming from the clean, roomy kitchen wasn't silly; the beer was as fresh as the *Salzstangeln*, those long, crisp, salt-covered rolls; the wine was perfectly cellared; the fragrance of coffee wafting through the house, and especially through the glass-enclosed porch, morning and afternoon, gave the human touch. And the rooms were very cozy—low-ceilinged but spacious, with deep, heavy beds and eiderdown comforters, clean throughout and permeated with the smell of the old house, a patina floating through the very air, so to speak. The candlesticks on the night tables could probably have been used to beat a strong man to death.

The murmuring of the water could be heard in all the rooms looking onto the garden. One of those who heard the uninterrupted, resonant, dull rushing through his open window was Geyrenhoff. It was still hot outside; this Sunday had been a day of heavy August heat. Even now, at ten in the evening, no real coolness to speak of came up from the garden. Geyrenhoff was lying in bed without covers, in his blue-and-white striped pajamas, and was reading a strange book by the writer Emil Lucka titled *Death and Life.* He didn't like it, because he himself could so definitely have been the hero, which is usually a reason for our appreciating a book more. It perturbed Herr von Geyrenhoff, though. He had made his goodbyes up at the house a little sooner after dinner than the others, giving as a reason that he had to report to the ministry at nine the next morning. There was a comfortable express train scheduled for that very purpose. Herr von Stangeler, who generally lumped together people in the same mold as Geyrenhoff by calling them "ministerial apprentice lads," had just smiled, because when building projects were underway on the railroad, the construction engineers had to be up at four o'clock. Geyrenhoff knew that, because it was mentioned from time to time in the Stangeler household. He let the book drop and his head sink back; he lay flat on his back, and felt the sound of the flowing water as if it were pouring over him. This was a good place; he liked being here. It had grown quiet down in the garden. Geyrenhoff reached for his traveling kit, unscrewed the nickel top from a flask, sprinkled lavender water in his hand and rubbed it on his throat and his temples. Then he lit a cigarette and began thinking. Not the least bit sleepy, tennis or not. He didn't get too far with his thinking, though, because just then someone knocked at the door.

"Georgie-Porgie," said Marchetti, "we thought we'd all have some coffee. Can we come into your room, or do you want to go to sleep?"

"Sleep isn't what I need, but coffee sounds good."

"Bring us a liter of Mór wine," said Baron Buschmann (who was called the "Red Field Ant," and he really did look like one!) in the corridor, to a chambermaid, and he walked in behind Marchetti. Then came Grabmayr, who stated right away that he didn't want wine, or coffee either, for he was planning to go to the Rax Alps at four in the morning and be back in time for breakfast; it wasn't too soon to start getting in shape for ski season. "Good for you," said Herr von Langl. "Hello, Georgie-Porgie. Has anybody ordered Mór yet?" Behind Langl came a Herr von Lindner—later a district commissioner—and Lieutenant Melzer. Wine and coffee came soon after. At once Buschmann picked up the book, which was lying on the bed. He sat down beside Geyrenhoff. "Where's Semski staying, anyway?" asked Langl. "I have no idea; I think he wound up at the hotel." "No, he's in the village." "No, he's not, he's at the inn farther down. He and Konietzki couldn't get rooms here." "I'm going to go change into pajamas too." And so they all went away, one after another, and came back in their nightclothes.

Melzer, however, was thinking of taking the same tack as Grabmayr, on the topic of sleep, that is. He and Asta had plans the following day; they were going hiking, and there was a particular rock they wanted to climb. This last part Melzer had dreamed up for one reason only—to get rid of Editha Pastré, whom they would have to take along; she'd never have the nerve to go climbing, though. Well, they had to take somebody. The obvious thought had suggested itself to Melzer, which was to propose René as a companion for Editha. After all, it was only to be expected that Asta would clue her younger brother in on appropriate instructions, considering how close their relationship was. The most suitable couple of all for this little confederacy would have been Ingrid Schmeller and Semski. But of course it looked better if the girl's brother came along. And Ingrid, who was staying up at the house to be near Asta, just wasn't one for long hikes. She had a kind of invertebrate or clinging-vine style of softness about her; either she would grow tired fifteen minutes after they started, or she would get a pebble in her shoe and her feet would hurt. Day in and day out she sat in the garden, with Semski for the most part, to all appearances aimless and undecided, low-spirited and bored, and it was impossible for Asta to get anything out of her about what she wanted or didn't want, about whether she was going to tell him "yes" finally, and if not, why not. The talks between Asta and Ingrid went on and on, and always wound up exactly the same at the end as at the beginning; Asta often had the feeling when they were talking that she was trying to knead a mass of dough. Ingrid didn't play tennis. When Semski was on the court, she would sit on one of the benches and keep her large, watery eyes fixed on him with such spellbound attention that the rest couldn't help noticing. The quickest of all to notice was Editha Pastré, whose concealed attacks of rage soon went beyond all bounds. What's more, she was staying up at the house also, for two weeks. And Semski was always up there.

Finally, cooler air began coming into the room, and they closed the windows. This gathering looked odd enough in blue, green, and purple pajamas, like one of those meetings arranged in secret by children who were told to put the lights out and should have been under their blankets long before. People were sitting on both sides of the bed, while Geyrenhoff himself continued his conversation à deux with Buschmann. Herr von Langl was stretched out on a huge old leather sofa with an animal skin draped over the back.

Then they all stopped talking. The only person making a sound was Marchetti, who was leaning against the footboard, with his back to Lindner, and stirring his coffee.

The one other sound came from the stream. Now that the windows were shut, it sounded as though its murmuring had moved off to a great distance.

Geyrenhoff's talk with Buschmann resumed, and through the quiet it came presented on a silver platter, as it were.

"What can I tell you, Bushie? This Dr. Pfungen turns my stomach. He's a high-class necrophiliac."

"And who is Dr. Pfungen?" asked Marchetti, sitting up, his coffee cup in his hand.

"A character from this book." Buschmann pointed and tapped the knuckle of his index finger on the yellow cover, which had a strange pattern of red hearts all over it. "But maybe all of us are just high-class necrophiliacs."

"*Nekros* means 'the dead one,' and *philein* means 'to love' or 'to have friendly feelings toward,'" observed Herr von Lindner.

"Yes, and that's what we are!" Buschmann replied vehemently.

(Geyrenhoff admired Bushie in his own way. The Red Field Ant's hopes for Etelka Stangeler, nursed in secret, had been categorically dashed some time before; her engagement to Pista was as good as official. Still, the little baron managed to keep his chin up and his head above water; that head even did some thinking now and then as well, none other than poor Dr. Otto Weininger being in this instance the one who had to stand and deliver, metaphorically speaking, like Omar Khayyám for the engaged couple).

"Dead ones or loving ones?" Marchetti asked without turning around.

"Ones who love what is dead," Bushie immediately countered. "We're on familiar terms with what is dead. It's what's living that confuses us."

"Ain't we high-class or what," Langl called over from the sofa in a breezy tone whose lack of embarrassment had something that seemed to strip the others naked. "There was one thing in that book by Lucka— the one lying on Georgie's bed—that I liked very much: we don't find out until somewhere in the middle, and then just in an offhand sort of way, what the main character's name is. His name appears just that one single time. The effect's a very neat one, elegant and tasteful. Writers generally dish up the most freakish names, don't they? And incidentally, it's a pleasure to observe how carefully Bushie and Georgie-Porgie have done their reading. They really have Dr. Pfungen down. Talk about 'gentle readers'—tractable and attentive. Just like myself. So ain't I classy too?"

The expression on Buschmann's face betrayed impatience while Langl's words, nasty in some vague way, kept on. He didn't like the man—the deep furrows running from his nostrils down to the corners of his mouth; his eyeglasses; his crude way of mixing choice, cultivated language from the time of Maria Theresa with pointedly vulgar words and expressions from Viennese dialect; his soft, slender hands; the basically flashy kind of talent he exhibited at the keyboard, like the tacky routine of a barroom pianist, who can just plop his paws down anywhere and skip all day from one banality improvised by ear to another, purposely concocting the most farfetched and elaborate bridge passages without ever making a mistake or interrupting the incessant patter being delivered off to the side, for the benefit of any man or woman who might happen to be standing near him at the piano.

"If this is the level of class, we'll all be déclassé by tomorrow," Buschmann said calmly, collecting himself, and took a cigar case made of crocodile skin from the pocket of his pajama jacket. "Today I had an experience that shows what I mean. We were standing outside the house in the dark and had just said our goodbyes—"

"With Editha glowing in the dark because Slopski" (which is what he called Semski) "talked with her for a good while," said Langl.

"Not thinking what he was doing, either, I bet," Marchetti added.

"Maybe not thinking, but fearing. Both of them are afraid of Editha, you know. Slopski and Ingrid. Why exactly isn't easy to say. Behind those drowsy-looking eyelids of hers, Ingrid of course kind of half knows what's going on with Editha. But she herself doesn't know what she wants to do. And Editha doesn't know what she ought to do. And Herr Schmeller, Ingrid's father, knows only what he'd like to do—I mean with Editha—but of course he wouldn't dream of making the slightest move, even though, or actually precisely because, he of course thinks the sun rises and sets on her—"

"So what was going on outside the house, Bushie?" asked Geyrenhoff, rather brusquely interrupting Langl's boorish comments.

"Outside the house," Buschmann continued, but slackening, to a degree, not to say already slackened, relaxed, because he'd accommodated himself to the interruption by taking a Britannica cigar out of his case, snipping it with fingernail clippers from Geyrenhoff's traveling kit, putting it into a cardboard holder, and lighting it—"outside the house was the warm night." He stopped and kept silent, as though still feeling now its intense releasing power. This was how he was getting ready for what he wanted to say. "We said goodbye to Semski and Grauermann one more time. Etelka had come outside. Pista said to her, 'What I'd most like to do is take my sweater and mackintosh and sleep somewhere outdoors tonight.'"

"You can be sure he's in bed, though," Lindner said slowly and precisely, as if making an irrefutable determination.

"He did say 'I'd most like to' and not 'I'm going to.'" He didn't do the very thing he would have liked to do most. He disciplined himself, conquered himself." Marchetti, with his pointy nose and toothbrush mustache, had again spoken without turning around.

"Cut the stupid cross talk!" cried Geyrenhoff, who had really lost his patience now. "I'd like to finally hear what Bushie's trying to say."

"It's as good as certain that Pista's asleep in his own bed," said Buschmann, pacifically weaving the thread of the interruption into his own fabric, which he now took up again. "Did you notice? *Sweater* and *mackintosh*, English words in German. The day before yesterday I was talking with a man just back from a three-year trip around the world. Guess what his summary was—'Stay home; nowhere is it as beautiful and nowhere can you live nearly as comfortably as here in Vienna.' And what was his most striking impression? 'The whole world's gone English. That's easy to say if you've just more or less heard about it,' was his thought, 'but you have to see for yourself. Yes, the world is English!'"

"But high-class necrophiliacs know that," said Lindner.

"They do indeed, but they've 'just more or less heard about it.' They still don't really know what they mean when they say *English*. I'm not talking about the derivation and the supposed literal meaning of the word; you know the story of Pope Gregory the Great and the young boys from Britain whose milk-white skin and blond hair made them seem like angels to him, so that when he was told they were Angles, he answered, *'Non sunt Angli, sed angeli,'* and people held this in their minds and began referring to Britain as *Angel-land*, which soon elides into *England*. The story isn't quite as pointed for the English themselves as it is for us, incidentally, since it happens that the identical form of the English words *angelic* and *English* is contained in our one German adjective *englisch*. But I'm digressing, friends, and I really wanted to get at something else. If you ask anybody how this great English empire came into being in the first place and how it got to be what it is, he'll spill out a big bucketful of textbook knowledge about the geographic insularity that forced the English out onto the sea; about the limited involvement of the medieval Holy Roman Empire during the age when new continents were being discovered, because the Hanseatic League had outlived its usefulness and had never had the experience of unified, self-contained central power; and so on. Perhaps in addition he would know and say something about the seagoing heritage of the Normans in the makeup of the English and about the noteworthy fact that several of their colonies—no, all of them, on second thought—owe their founding to the daring enterprise of individuals acting on their own initiative, with the government itself lagging far behind and not catching up until much later, as it were. Then he'll end by speaking about force and deviousness, about the rather ruthless qualities needed to bring about affairs of great moment. And yet it's my contention that all these pieces of the puzzle, or any others you can think of, don't begin to yield a true picture of what we mean when we say *English*; in fact, they don't even hint at it."

"All right, but what of all this?" asked Lindner shortly.

"It's a matter of fascination, and that never gets mentioned with all the rest. The world isn't English because of England's geographical position as an island or because the North German Hanseatic League wasn't able to exploit its great potentialities or because of the Norman heritage that still runs in English veins, but because England became an object of fascination for the whole world, to the point where the English hold the globe in their hands. They didn't fascinate the world in just one isolated discipline, the way the Italians and the Germans did through their music or the French through their literature, but in the most general way imaginable, which is to say, through their manner of living. This isn't some attempt on my part, by the way, to deny those textbook explanations usually cited as the reasons for England's attaining power and greatness. Those might well have been leading causes. But the power and greatness are as consolidated and deeply embedded in the present status of the world as they are through the fascination the English exercise, and that's a force I'm simply unable to conceive of as being a mere consequence of all those amply well-known and oft-reiterated material particulars. It seems independent of all that. At least I'll contend that that's how it functions today. The idea represented by a single human being or by a society made up of human beings— which is to say, by a nation—has become visible and concrete when its style of living begins to fascinate others. This is how the world started down the road—not just as seen outwardly, measured by spheres of influence, but much more so inwardly—toward becoming English. And that's what many people are, from breakfast to five-o'clock tea."

"Benno, for example," said Langl, stretching out on the old sofa. "You can smell it."

Grabmayr laughed, his short pipe between his teeth. When he laughed, he always looked a bit like a Tyrolean goblin or troll.

"No," Bushie replied, "Benno's not a good example of what I'm saying. He has a sister over in England, as well as other relatives, and has been there a lot himself. He picked up all his mannerisms and habits directly. That stuff smells good, by the way; I really like it." He sniffed at the thick blue cloud drifting over from Grabmayr. "Capstan brand by W. D. & H. O. Wills, medium-strong cure, isn't it? But I'll stick with my Britannica; note the brand name, too, although a cigar is as un-English as anything could be."

He took a puff at the cardboard holder and blew a mouthful of smoke toward the full-bodied, honey-sweet, mature aroma of the Capstan.

"Two worlds cutting into each other," he said, while blowing smoke, and then he mixed the two clouds together by waving his open hand. "That whole assortment of indefinite but at the same time strong concepts that immediately come to mind when we even think the word *English* today is a sign that the idea known as England has become concrete, is an actuality. So much so that many people who were never in England in their lives and who have nothing whatever to do with England nonetheless have that English sense of comfort inside the clothes they wear, have the shoulders of their jackets padded the way the English do, affect a casual and yet firm way of buckling their belts that's somehow English, and even feel their very bodies to be English when they've stepped out of the bath and put on their underwear. We've all heard '*Le style, c'est l'homme.*' But it would be even more accurate to say, '*Le style, c'est la nation.*' Where you don't have the first, you can't have the second. And wherever a person feels the way I've described, and feels happy about it, is where that person has attained to that English unity of content and form; there is where England is, with all the fascination it has to offer, and it makes no difference whether the person has ever given England a moment's thought. As far back as the first half of the last century, Nestroy was making fun of Anglomania, which means that it must already have existed. And now today look how much it's grown, how much more it encompasses than those merely physical items I mentioned, especially when you see how many German words are English—the English *governess* we had when we were small; the *trainer* in the *sporting club*; how we go *fox hunting*; how we keep score by counting in English when we play *tennis*; look at Benno's *Capstan* and Pista's *sweater* and *mackintosh*. All these are ultimately outward manifestations of the phenomenon."

"Robert, I think you'll have to admit that these are things high-class necrophiliacs don't know after all," said Geyrenhoff to Lindner.

"One would have to smash every word to pieces or break it apart to escape from this state of affairs," Buschmann continued, "and that's hard to do, because under the pressure of centuries words grow hard and then smooth and rounded from use. On those rare occasions when you can really pin one of them down and hold it fast, the rough crystalline surfaces along the break reveal places where our thinking can take root and adhere."

This was the point at which Melzer and Grabmayr jumped ship or set themselves diplomatically ashore—they went to get some sleep, if later than they'd planned. Perhaps a different topic of conversation would have kept them there longer. The degree of a person's fatigue stands in inverse proportion to the person's genuine interest. (As far as Melzer is concerned, however, he didn't have a clue back then as to what his interests were.)

"So that's what *English* means to me," Buschmann added by way of summarizing, after Melzer and Grabmayr had left. "How long that *Englishness* has existed, I don't know. It hadn't yet come into being during the Elizabethan era, at least not that I can see. Very soon after we start to work our way back in time, the names we now use for different national groups begin losing the concrete and actual meaning they hold for us today. What substitutes for that living meaning is just some term out of a history book, and that holds no interest for me. Possibly the English haven't been English in today's sense for any very long time. But that current sense is the only one that can influence our course of action."

"This is all very engrossing as a theory, you know, but I'm finding it hard to imagine how any of it could lead to practical conclusions," observed Marchetti.

"All we need to do is keep pursuing this line of thought—without necrophilia, though—and the conclusions will follow on their own. When I arrived yesterday and stepped down from the wagon in front of the post office, I saw Herr von W., the son of the former justice minister, standing there. We said hello. He had just come out of the tobacco store. He takes a package of Herzegovinian cut out of his pocket, along with a silver case that can hold exactly that amount. He opens the package, stuffs the tobacco into his handsome *tabatière*, rolls himself a cigarette while we're talking, and asks me how my father's doing. Well, the way he was standing there in his loden suit and a hat decorated with a 'shaving brush,' made clear to me once again something that everybody knows anyway—though self-evident things are just the ones that most need to break down and dissolve, over and over, to the point of dying and rising anew; otherwise even the self-evident will someday be incomprehensible—it occurred to me once more that the single most outstanding achievement (overlooking all the single, isolated areas) with which we Austrians can credit ourselves is of the most general nature that could ever be imagined, which is to say, our manner of living. To that extent we resemble the English—as far as form goes—even though we're altogether un-English, don't you think? However, that formal analogy should act as a piece of practical direction for us. As it is, Austria hasn't had any real policy at all toward England since 1710, let alone a policy of friendly relations."

"If anything, our policy is exactly the opposite today," noted Marchetti.

"And I maintain we're going to pay a heavy price for it," said Buschmann. "It flies in the face of crucial affinities that get all papered over by those bucketfuls of conventional wisdom, which is necrophilic. Here's another example—the Germans are trying to find some way of building rapport with the Turks, and it's proving unnatural and hopeless, but not because there isn't the slightest ethnic kinship, and not because the Turks are Asians and Mohammedans, which would be necrophilic thinking. No, it's for no other reason than that the Germans have brought into the world that most appalling caricature and vicious mockery of the Turkish national beverage, that nauseating swill they call *Káffe*, a grave apostasy for anyone who drinks real coffee (and doesn't mispronounce the word). Accordingly, there is no way further developments in German-Turkish relations can turn out favorably. They're on the wrong path."

Marchetti began laughing out loud. "Now listen here, Otto," he cried, "that's really taking it to an extreme! You truly think foreign policy should be conducted according to views like these?"

"Yes, I do," said Buschmann, "and I assure you I'm totally serious. That concreteness I've been talking about is at the very top of my list. Whatever leads away from it leads into the realm of death. And it feels to me as though that's where we're indeed being led."

"What you just said is entirely possible," said Marchetti, not laughing this time.

"Well, then, there you have it," was how Geyrenhoff now closed the subject. He had sat upright and taken a large, square bottle from the drawer of the massive night table; now he carefully poured cognac out of it and into tiny silver cups that were kept stacked inside one another in a leather case.

The departure of Grabmayr and Melzer had opened an awkward gap that had come to everyone's awareness during the last part of this conversation. Whenever somebody leaves a room where others stay behind, the situation changes in every case. People don't like to start talking right away about those who have left. Here, though, it was as if a small flat stone had been lifted up and laid aside; quite a variety of different creatures could be seen creeping and crawling. They were all silent for a while, and they could hear the murmuring of the water again. Then it was—of course—Edouard von Langl who started.

"Well, who's getting engaged to whom up there?"

"We're talking about two couples," said Lindner.

Geyrenhoff declined comment. He looked over at Buschmann, whose face, drawn tight with exertion, gave no sign.

"Asta—" said Lindner; nothing more.

"And Semski," the baron filled in. The general burst of laughter didn't seem to make much impression on him. "What are you talking about!" the others yelled at him. "She says he looks like a potato shriveling up in the cellar!" "And his head looks like a badly packed knapsack!"

"And yet that's where the real truth is," persisted Buschmann. "Poor old Melzer doesn't have a ghost of a chance. If Asta wants . . ."

"No, that's definitely wrong," said Geyrenhoff. "The part about Melzer is probably right, poor guy. But Semski is signed, sealed, and delivered. And Asta's helping out—with Ingrid—any way she can."

"How edifying," said Langl. "She doesn't have any choice, if you ask me. Editha Pastré's about ready to declare open warfare on her some-time soon too."

"Does anybody here know the Pastrés?" Lindner asked.

Nobody spoke up. Then Geyrenhoff said, "I went to see them three or four times last year."

"Whom did you know to get an invitation?"

"I knew them as a boy, through my mother, who went to school in Geneva. She made friends there with a Fräulein Meriot, who later on became Frau Pastré, Editha's mother."

"And where do the Pastrés come from?"

"Oh, they're from Geneva. The father's a native Genevan. He started some kind of iron foundry here in Vienna, out in Semmering, I think, and he's made it big. The Pastrés have a *jour fixe*, you know."

"And you're not paying one bit of attention to Editha out here?"

"No, why should I?"

"Well, she's very pretty, in the first place; you can't deny that. You could say she's the prettiest girl here, in fact, just plain *hors concours*. And in the second place she's probably very well-off, judging by what you've told us."

"So with all that she'd be the one to marry—necrophilically think-ing," said Geyrenhoff. "There must be reasons, though, why no one anywhere is making a move in that direction. Have you ever heard of any man falling in love with Editha? No. Doesn't that tell you some-thing? Every girl has her admirers; she's the only one who doesn't. Practically a wallflower—with looks and money."

"But you know," Langl remarked in passing, "Herr Schmeller is not to be totally sneered at."

"What's with you and your Herr Schmeller, Edouard? Please!" cried Geyrenhoff. "It's getting disgusting! I'm bowing out of the garden party, incidentally. As for Editha, she's still under glass, as it were, or as if molded in glass. Break it, and you'll see a total bitch rise up from the shards of an innocence that's merely physical. Then she'll develop

an enormous power of attraction, you can be sure of that! But her appeal to men won't take hold as long as she's still a young girl, which is
what she is today. She doesn't have that sweetness, that dewy quality,
'the darling buds of May,' and it's simply because her character is basically bad. People can feel it, too. If she doesn't somehow manage through
some kind of lucky happenstance to go from her situation now straight
down the aisle into a genuinely good marriage, and pretty soon at that,
then the first lowlife who comes along will open up a Pandora's box,
by force if he has to. On top of that, the girl's washouts up to now, or
better yet the vacuum surrounding her, have really sparked her hankering for a man and predisposed her to do something stupid."

"Pandora's box—textbook example," said Langl.

"In their own way, the parents do everything they can for Editha,"
continued Geyrenhoff (this time, no one had reacted to Langl's little
side comment). "She made her debut and went to her first dances at
the same time as Asta Stangeler, and in the same carnival season the
Pastrés gave a ball at their own home, with over eighty people—"

"Sit-down supper or buffet?" Lindner interrupted.

"Sit-down," said Geyrenhoff, "à la Stangeler."

"The things that happen in dear old Vienna that nobody ever hears
about! I should have left my visiting card last November."

"You can make good next season; they're on Gusshaus Strasse.
Anyway, the behavior of the parents—with their *jours*, and in every
other respect—has been completely normal from the start, in spite of
the disaster that burst over their heads two years ago."

"That whole business with the other daughter?" Langl asked, turning onto his side on the sofa, to face the room.

"What other daughter?" Marchetti perked up; for the first time
changing position from having his back to Lindner and Buschmann,
he was now sitting diagonally on the edge of the bed and looking at
Geyrenhoff.

"Editha had a twin sister," Geyrenhoff went on. "She ran away from
home, simply absconded. And not a word has been heard from her since."

"A twin!" cried Langl. "Get outta here! For real? I had absolutely
no idea. I once heard just sort of in passing that there was supposed to
be a sister, but I thought she had died."

"She may be dead; in fact she probably is—I don't know," said Geyrenhoff. "But there was a twin sister, all right."

"Did you know her?"

"Certainly. From the time I was a boy."

"And did she and Editha look alike?"

"Alike isn't the word. It was exactly the same person, times two."

"What a horrible thought," said Buschmann. "A person having to exist twice in order to exist at all! Two of Editha Pastré—thanks but no thanks! Now that I think of it, there was a Pastré who went to the Luithlen Lyceum with my sister. Of course I don't know which one it was. Maybe both."

"Probably," said Geyrenhoff. "I for one was always totally unable to tell them apart. You know how sisters will sometimes dress alike. Well, they did that, too. I don't know if even their parents could tell them apart all the time. Possibly their mother—maybe. But not the father. He came right out and admitted that he often got them confused."

"Still, there has to have been a significant difference between them," said Lindner.

"How so?" asked Geyrenhoff.

"Very simple—one ran away and the other stayed home."

This observation could hardly be refuted, and it damped the natural volubility of the conversation for a while, as smoke blown back will cover a hearth flame. Geyrenhoff was the first to try explaining.

"The significant difference in the end result may be rooted here in very minute circumstances weighing only a milligram but tipping the scales one way or the other—images and thoughts that get linked to form a chain. Maybe the other one stopped to look in the window of an overseas travel agency and saw a model of one of those big passenger steamships. There might have been something she especially liked about it—the sheen of the varnish or models of a few crew members placed near the forward stem to give an idea of the ship's size by comparison. They might have shown a beach with palm trees as the backdrop for the ship. And that same afternoon she might have smelled nutmeg and cinnamon in a store. Or she happened to see a sharp-looking navy lieutenant standing outside the Grand Hotel."

"Good enough," said Lindner, who grew somewhat pedantic as he got involved in the topic. "But now comes a further question. Twins are always bonded very closely. Why didn't they run away together?"

"Because only the one really had the experience of those little images and ideas that tipped the scales."

"But at least she would have taken the other sister into her confidence."

"And who knows whether she did or didn't? As you can imagine, they tried squeezing it out of Editha, interrogating and grilling her until she nearly fainted; even some police detectives were in on it. They got absolutely nowhere."

"If there had indeed subsisted some collusion or conspiracy between the sisters relative to the arrangements of the one for fleeing," said Lindner, now using unalloyed bureaucratic language, "it would have been bound to facilitate considerably the execution of the plan. Is her disappearance traceable directly back to the parents' home in Vienna?"

"That's exactly how it didn't happen. The parents were at a spa in Bad Wildungen at the time—that's in the Waldeck region, not far from Kassel, I think—because of gallbladder trouble. The girls were supposed to join them when school was over, and they'd been given permission to stop on the way for a few days in Munich to see the sights. It was in Munich that Editha's sister went missing."

"Then you can't really say she ran away from home as such," Marchetti noted.

"Strictly speaking, you're right," said Geyrenhoff, "but that's how most people said it when they spread the word. And in light of conditions in the Pastré household, such a thing would be quite easy to understand."

"What were those conditions like?"

"Enough to make anybody run away. The Pastrés are one of the few Calvinist families in Vienna. Of course they knew what they needed to do socially, and they adapted. But *intra muros* they kept a very tight leash on the girls, who'd been born and raised in our atmosphere, after all, so they were Vienna girls like any others. Herr Pastré now—how should I describe him? I always had the feeling that he'd look most in character wearing a brown frock coat and a pigtail. Somehow he looks as if he'd stepped out of a painting by Jean-Baptiste Greuze. *A Father's*

Curse. He never went further than just barely tolerating social life in his own house, shall we say. And she—the mother—has these deep-set eyes, with something burning in them, like a fanatic. Both of them have gallbladder trouble."

"I believe I'd better think again about leaving my visiting card," said Lindner.

"She's still a beautiful woman," Geyrenhoff continued, "Frau Pastré-Meriot. Somehow or other she carries about herself the air of a martyr, standing with one foot in the realm of death, so to speak; in a way I find hard to describe, it oppresses me greatly whenever I'm talking with her. It could just be my imagination, though; after all, she may have more than her share of somberness, yet she's still completely youthful in outward appearance. Lots of people go to Wildungen, if they can afford it, who would have to be called healthy in every other aspect."

"If they're all that strict, I'm surprised they let the girls travel alone," said Marchetti.

"Oh but they didn't, not at all. The governess declared under questioning that the twins had worked some kind of deception on her in Munich. They probably took advantage of their being identical. That's supposed to have allowed the runaway a huge head start. Anyway, that's more or less the story as far as I remember it. And incidentally, I don't know if they ever had any leads to follow at the time. Of course, there definitely weren't any later on."

"A truly total resemblance like that could have many interesting implications," observed Langl, slowly and thoughtfully. "I can just imagine."

"And I can just imagine, too—what you must be imagining, that is," Marchetti said. "It's a good thing he doesn't have a twin brother. Two of Edouard von Langl? No way! Talk about 'grief made more grievous'!"

"They say the Pastré girls made the most of their identical looks to play all sorts of tricks in school, and on their father, too," said Geyrenhoff. "It's a natural thing to do, really."

"That kind of paired existence as a twin would drive me to despair," cried Buschmann; "a whole life as doppelgänger to another person! Could that be why she ran away?"

"Most certainly not," said Langl. "And by the way, that doesn't have anything whatever to do with a doppelgänger. Having a twin brother would seem to me something almost purely physical or biological by comparison. A doppelgänger, however—that's the most evil part of us, the part buried deepest, the part that's most uncontrolled, and we've lost all power over it. It's broken loose. It's become an entity of its own. It goes around doing things in our name that we *could* do but never would."

"How about Edouard here? Look at all he knows," Marchetti said in reaction. "Do you have one?"

"One what?"

"A doppelgänger, I mean."

"Yes," said Langl. "But I never have any trouble telling us apart. He doesn't know how to play the piano, thank God."

A scrambling is heard in the forest, which normally is at noiseless rest in its own steady humming. Every sound can be heard far away, every noise—a woodpecker tapping, two squirrels wrangling up in the branches. The light from the sky sifts down through the tips of the trees, the silence descends in oppressive masses, the forest is silent toward the ground, the branches of the large pines droop low all around the tree. Here they start only a short distance above the ground. It isn't a place where farmers come to chop off branches far up the trunk to strew as bedding for the cattle, so the trees aren't "trimmed up tidy," or *geschnatzelt*, to use the term common in a good many parts of Lower Austria. These are deserted forests ranging over broad tracts of land, rising over many hillsides, climbing high over mountain peaks, sometimes tilting like a steep roof, sometimes as level as a parquet floor from the layers of pine needles pressed into the ground by the snow. The hand of a nobleman and his love of hunting protect these woods and their wild-life.

A scrambling is heard, because four people are attempting to climb a gigantic table rock in the forest, on the flat top of which is enough room for a small fort, a citadel, or a solid dwelling. Two of them (Asta and Melzer) are making rapid progress; the other two (Editha and

René Stangeler) are still far below. Our young friend has to keep boost-
ing her onward and upward, helping her, placing her feet as he stands
below her, pointing the next handhold out to her. She's stretching and
sprawling in every which direction. Melzer notices. It makes him feel
bad. He slackens, and Asta gets a few meters ahead of him. She evidently
didn't tell that damn kid brother to make use of Editha's fearfulness
as an excuse for keeping her down below with him. Besides, something
could easily happen. This very spot is pretty precarious for about fifty
meters going toward the valley side. It's bare and treeless. Here and
there the rocks are full of tricky crevices. Melzer was clinging to a rock
face as he eased his way around a corner.

Meanwhile, Editha has given up. She says feebly and quietly, "René,
I have to go back down. Hold me." "All right," he says. He's had all he
can take too. Not so much of climbing and helping her. No, what he
can't take any more of is the trembling, the hot flashes, the shaking of
his own body, and they're constantly getting worse. Everything's gone
topsy-turvy inside him. A whole series of open switches, dead ahead,
and he's clattering along as he goes. Up to now he's never actually taken
a look at Editha, has practically never even noticed she exists. Having
had her wished on him the evening before, as it were, through finding
the whole thing all arranged by Asta for the following morning, and
Asta's having done it with the authority of an elder sister, meaning that
it was done in a legal and licit manner by and large—that approach
had caused events to develop all of a sudden, so quickly that it took his
breath away. But he saw Editha now, really saw her. From below, of
course. She had to be aware that her loden skirt had ridden more than
halfway up her left thigh and past her knee on the right. And now she
was standing with her legs spread far apart, which René had told her
was going to be necessary. She was now standing exactly as René had
worked it out. She couldn't let go with her hands. He began shaking
all over, looking at her white underwear. That was when she said, "René,
I have to go back down."

He helped her cautiously out of the position she was in. When she'd
become free, she supported herself by leaning on him, barely holding
on to the rock anymore, her arm around his neck, resting as if she'd
fled from somewhere and reached safety, as if rescued from troubles

deeper than just this jagged wall of rock with its crest far above her. She turned and looked up. She listened. Very straightforward about it. Then her head moved two millimeters closer and came to rest against his neck. They stood where they were for about thirty seconds or so. Then he started to kiss her, and it was in keeping with the spirit of the occasion when he unbuttoned her white sport shirt and slipped his right hand under her left breast. She let herself be all but carried the rest of the way down. It wasn't so easy, for she stayed pressed up against him, but they managed to make it down the meter and a half to the forest floor. She gave just one yelp of pain, but it was brief and stifled; then she wrapped herself very tight around René, and not only with her arms.

As though by a drumroll across the whole horizon, by quiet thunder somewhere deep in the sunny sky, the space inside Melzer for registering impressions was broken open and every bit of it crammed to the bursting point when he reached the top and looked out from the promontory of the rock, whose nearly vertical cliffs dropped a good hundred meters facing the valley side. Here you could really get a view of the place where you lived, amid surroundings unsurpassed in quietness but unceasingly testifying at the same time to the immensity of their strength—mountain upon mountain, distant rock that the woods down below crept up like moss, all that stone in the milky haze of the sun, ridges diminishing in the distance, outlined against a sky clear as lacquer in the quivering intensity of light. Forests and more forests were scattered among the mountains, as though for all their depth and distance they were nothing, nothing more than the cloth that has fallen around the feet of a statue unveiled.

Like the dot on top of an *i* was how Asta was, and on the verge of looking like a picture postcard as she stood in her colorful local attire before the wide-open landscape, whose undaunted self-possession overall was immeasurably more solid than even its mighty rocks.

Scaling the rock grip by grip and step by step, quickly taking hold and letting go, Asta had scarcely looked in Melzer's direction, totally unconcerned while climbing and not bothering about him in any way. It had made him feel good.

Now they sat down. For Melzer, the moment had finally come that he'd been contemplating for over a year. Still deeper down the spiral of time, as if directly underneath him—far below the express train to Ljubljana, the one that had made hollow roaring sounds as it drove through the Semmering tunnel—and now standing out with a clarity that made it the measure of the present moment, he was recalling the first time he had ever been among these mountain rocks, rutted and washed smooth. At that time, too, Asta, still not much more than half-grown, had been standing before a mighty cliff and an expanse of sky (others had been there as well, but he left them out of the picture for now), in the same outfit, in the same cheerful frame of mind. With that, Melzer slipped entirely away from the here and now. For they weren't laughing now. They were keeping silent and looking into the distance, where the overall color blended into blue-green; only the limestone rocks stood out sharply, flecks of brightness here and there. He wasn't expecting her to talk about Ingrid and Semski, but there she was, already in the midst of the topic. Not only that, she was speaking to him in the most trusting way. The only thing missing was that she should address him with the intimate form, the pronoun *du*. He suddenly began to feel something like a brush with pain, a slowing down and a surface friction, as though he had been soaring in air all the while but were now scraping and shambling along the ground, set ashore by the wave of the hopes and dreams he'd been envisioning, which up to now had had the power to hold him above reality. Now Asta was speaking about herself as well—how she hoped he, Melzer, was taking the view that her concern for Ingrid, and so, of course, for Semski also, was perfectly natural, as she'd been friends with Ingrid since their school days. Melzer sharpened his ear more and more, immersing it in what she was saying. Not without fear. The net of his attentiveness, so carefully spread out this way, might well snare quarry that to his eyes would not look like anything but a monster. He was downright afraid she might now say how willing she would be to stand by him in his hour of need, too, should he ever have one.

Asta stressed how thoroughly convinced she was that Ingrid would be happy with Semski.

And that Ingrid loved him. There wasn't a doubt about it. But it

was just that she had a totally helpless streak, a kind of inertia or block-
age that she had to be carried past, so to say. "She just can't manage
herself. She has to be shooed toward her own happiness, like a goose."

Now they both laughed. At the same time, though, Melzer listened
very deep inside himself again. Looking over the landscape, he suddenly
felt as if he had jumped down into one of those firefighter's nets, but
into one with all these woods and mountains painted on it; now it was
bouncing him back and diverting him completely from his chosen
direction.

Lina, Frau von Stangeler's maid, had always stood as an object of Paula
Schachl's high esteem. Paula called her Aunt Lintschi, though *aunt*
was just what she called her, for their actual kinship, if any existed at
all, encompassed much more. It appears both noteworthy and relevant
here that Paula, from the time she made René's acquaintance in May
(in front of the building called the Blue Unicorn, on Liechtenstein
Strasse) until his departure for his summer vacation, never found out
René's last name. And the same was true in reverse. We know Stangeler too well by now not to suspect one of his—we'd almost like to
describe them as "professional"—safety measures at work; these twists
and turns he could negotiate accurately, no matter how sluggish his
spirit. But in this case we would be wrong. For once, no jury-rigging
was being done. That rapacity of René's, which was bound to seize
every opportunity that presented itself (and in regard to Paula too, just
one more gust of wind had swooped into his always outstretched sails
there in front of the Blue Horsie) and to dismiss any and all objections
by citing the untested axiom that it would never do to miss anything—
that rapacity had already faded from his inner field of vision a half
hour after he met her, while they were still in the bakery having their
first casual little chat; however, that wasn't by any means because the
wind had stopped blowing or because such a seasoned old sailor realized that he was on the wrong course and that the outline of the coast
he was steering for was proving to be very different from how it had
looked when first sighted. It was more because he'd soon found himself
on a course new to him, rather than on the course he'd set, and propelled

by a stiff breeze. We can say it here. But René never said anything, not to himself, anyway. That was just how it was. This new system of tracks took a different set of twists and turns but had never yet stopped off at any of the Pastré's intermezzi.

Incidentally, he paid hardly any more attention to Editha *ab dato*. She also seemed inclined to let slip under the covers that which had happened without any. She had come into René's room late that same Monday night. Whether Asta had somehow decided to contrive, connive, keep the tryst alive, it was something that never came to our boy's knowledge. He never asked, either. Everything went smoothly, very smoothly. For Editha, this must have been a kind of Archimedean point (a δός μοι ποῦ στῶ) lying outside her world but necessary, indeed absolutely essential, for her to gain if she were to continue living her life. In this respect it seems to us that Herr von Geyrenhoff saw the situation quite accurately. That night, by the way, she hung around René's neck a thin chain with a locket. He never looked inside. Nonetheless, he put it away carefully for safekeeping.

The two worlds remained separate, and they turned out just the opposite of how they were supposed to, at least according to formula—the girl of humble origins was not seduced, and it was the young lady who lost her innocence, insofar as any such thing can be spoken of. René drew no conclusions and made no comparisons, though. If we wanted to express what Paula actually represented in the mind of our young friend, we would have to transport ourselves into a world mythically primal, or perhaps just prep-schoolish (which in several regards comes out to the same thing), and say that for Stangeler, Paula Schachl was a kind of local deity of the Strudlhof Steps or dryad of the Alsergrund district.

At one point during the summer she wanted to write to "Aunt Lintschi," and her real aunt, the one she lived with, had the address; here it turned out to be the same one where she sent her letters to René by general delivery, using a box number and an assumed name so absurd that surely no one else would ever have hit upon it—Meningitis Cerebrospinalis. That's the Latin term for a very severe, indeed not seldom fatal, disease involving the brain and spinal cord. Paula copied out the name every time. Needless to say, she inquired of "Aunt" Lintschi, though shyly, as it were, in a sort of by-the-way tone, whether in this Stangeler family whose service she was in—Paula had to write "Caroline Nohel, c/o The Stangeler Family" on the envelope—or among their friends, there wasn't a young man named René. Lintschi didn't volunteer too much in her answer. Yes, there's a René, he's in prep school and has to study a lot, now he's on vacation and is out here at the country house. Period. And no questions in return.

From this source, then, Paula didn't find out much more than René's last name, but the name itself held no particular interest for her. No, her interest had been more on the mischievous side; a bit less rigor and reserve on the part of Aunt Lintschi about anything connected with her domain—with her service, that is—might have made it possible, perhaps, to tease or twit René a little with this or that surprising item of knowledge concerning individual details of his life during the summer. That was what Paula had actually been hoping for, the thought running uppermost through her girlish head, which, however, crowned a soft, slender woman's body, on which, following the fashion of that time, her hemline fell almost to the ankle. We have to toss a pinch of curiosity, of wanting to know things, into a cheerfulness sprinkled atop a jealousy (as a dark forest floor is dappled with flecks of sunlight) that kept itself far off in the background, very sensitive and even vulnerable. That pinch gives us just the right mixture. Sometimes this mixture foamed up a little, making flaky and feathery clouds of anxiety form high up in the blue sky, possibly producing anxiety for no other reason than that they floated so high up. Even so, there was a very solid basis for feeling reassured, although it wasn't really a rational one; because Aunt Lintschi, despite her impenetrable reserve, was somehow part of this whole context (into which she had truly done nothing to thrust herself); it all wore a comforting look and could only come out well in the end. She was a rock of trust for Paula, a child's warm feather bed of confidence; the girl never felt the ax of judgment poised over her neck, and it didn't matter what she went to her with when she was in school, when she was a fledgling just starting out in the office, or now. Furthermore, goodness on the deepest level will cover its own light so as not to blind an eye wandering in error.

So this is what she was like, that patron saint of René and Paula who wanted to stay out of the whole thing. The war, when it came—it landed René Stangeler in a cavalry regiment not long after his Matura—along with the years he spent in a prisoner-of-war camp, caused him to lose touch with Paula Schachl. Nor did he encounter Lintschi any more when he returned from Siberia to his parents' house, where she'd been in service for twenty-seven years; she had moved in with her mother, who, helpless in old age, could not do without the daughter's care, so she turned up only from time to time in the dimly lit house in town to look after Frau von Stangeler's linens and lingerie. It was on one of those occasions, in the small room with the double doors leading out to the balcony (René was living in it again, as he'd done during his school years), next to the room looking onto the courtyard, that he discovered for the first time the connection between Lintschi and Paula, who was now married to a foreman at the government printing office; Lintschi had recently told Paula about René's being lucky enough to make it back home. Paula had sent her best regards, and René sent his in return (it was around five in the afternoon on a day in May of 1921, and the sparrows were chirping loudly in the trees outside, as they always have and always will). Stangeler wanted to see Paula again. But nothing came of it, at least not then. Not till four years later. And in a different context, which belongs in Lieutenant Melzer's story.

Her father had been a quiet, bashful man (she got her reddish hair from him, incidentally), who after church on Sundays would read the New Testament until the noon meal while drinking several cups of black coffee and smoking a cigar. His bashfulness stood in striking contrast to his unusual occupation, which had its dangers but to which he was devoted with extraordinary passion, never so much as thinking of changing to one that would make his life easier; he could have done it in a moment, too, for Schachl was not only fully trained as a carpenter but was also experienced in that trade and was respected for his skill. Anyway, that line of work partly overlapped with the one he liked better, a government job that often kept him away from the house for days at a time. Schachl was what people then sometimes called a river master. The enormous task of regulating the Danube had created and built up this occupation, the real need for which was not felt until a given project was completed and the labor of constant maintenance began. Schachl had grown up in it and with this work—the construction of the locks at Nussdorf and the winter harbor at Prater Point, the blasting near Greifenstein, the flood of 1899, and the breakup of many a sheet of ice formed chapters of his life story at its most intense. The river was its background, its base color. The wide spaces open to the wind, the majestic streaming of masses of water through a countryside divided in two, the gray-green foam of the Au Woods, the work outdoors, winter and summer, in a cutting wind or a pleasantly cooling breeze, the knowledge gained from small signs of what weather was coming, the familiarity with a world of animals that would reveal themselves in astonishing profusion when certain canals were being laid out in the meadowlands around Kritzendorf and Greifenstein—frogs as large as a child's head; pike and huge carp, and once in a while a river crab, a species already dying out from toxic substances discharged by industry; now and again a great crested grebe, most of them chased off to the Lobau, if not transported to Hungary; the oftentimes incredible aggressiveness of biting muskrats—all these made up the indispensable degrees and tones in the chord of his life; as resonant as a harp nearly silent, at most humming softly, its strings brushed lightly, it gave the words of Scripture a tuning hardly perceived, made a sounding board whose vibration was merely felt, but nothing more.

In the section of the ministry with jurisdiction over the department of river maintenance, there were a few section heads who were not only schooled in proper procedures but were perceptive besides. They would quietly ask River Master Ferdinand Schachl to stop by the office and, treating him to a Britannica or a Trabuco, would then hear firsthand about all sorts of matters that could never have sprouted from the tops of their desks.

This River Master Schachl, now, together with his considerably younger and very attractive wife and his little girl growing up all bright and frisky, led a life that never went beyond being unobtrusive and that was, perhaps for that very reason, rising close to the brim of its complete fulfillment. He lost that life very suddenly when little Paula was not much more than twelve—through an accident at his work site (scaffolding was being set up to begin some general repairs on the locks), through an accident, but not really as a victim of his occupational activities, not quite in the line of duty as such, although that was how a gentleman from the ministry expressed it when he gave the eulogy at Schachl's graveside. This accident, however, had nothing to do with the river master's tasks and functions or his supervisory duties. A large, heavy wrench fell from a work platform on the scaffold about seven meters above him—directly above him, unfortunately. The accident didn't happen because it slipped out of anyone's hand, for there was no one above Schachl. The wrench just fell. It had been lying up there (well, there must have been some violation of safety regulations), perhaps near the edge of the planking, and a single vibration or jolt did it. The wrench fell and hit Schachl's head in just such a way as to shatter his skull. The river master collapsed and died. That was on a Monday toward the end of February 1905.

When it was all over—they buried him that Thursday—Paula saw her father's small Bible lying on the table in the living room at which he'd just been sitting the previous Sunday morning; the bookmark she knew so well, a little picture of Saint Mary of Pötsch at Saint Stephen's, was sticking out. She went over and opened the book to the last place her father had been reading. It was the Gospel according to Matthew. A phrase was underlined in blue pencil: "For the workman is worthy of his meat" (*dignus enim est operarius cibo suo*). Paula kissed the verse. She didn't cry, but stayed calm and unmoved, and she didn't consciously think about the obvious relevance of this passage to the deceased. Whatever impression she received didn't linger at the surface of her consciousness, so to say, nor did it become entangled in the network of her nervous system. Through the wedge of that hour it drove straight into the heartwood of her memory and stayed there. After she'd closed the book, she went right out to her mother in the kitchen and asked if she could please keep the little Bible, which Frau Schachl, with a casual nod of her head, unhesitatingly allowed.

The widow remarried before the official year of mourning had fully passed. Paula's stepfather was one of the mechanics who'd been brought in as needed by the department of river maintenance to work under Schachl's supervision—not under him, really, to be exact, but above him—somewhere up in the scaffolding. The new marriage brought three children in quick succession. Paula made it her business to look after them. It gave her stepfather great satisfaction to see the girl taking a burden off his beautiful wife, so happy just to be living, and he was warmhearted toward Paula. However, as tends to happen in this kind of situation, the ground of the home she'd had with her parents began to shift beneath her feet and grow strange to her after her father's death. Inside her, the past came up close and stood too near the present, which now belonged to the new family and almost not at all to her. An elder sister of the deceased river master, Theresa Schachl, retired from the Royal and Imperial State Railway System and residing in Lichtental in a small house of her own not far from the old parish church, requested that Paula's mother let the growing girl come live with her after some weakness or injury in the left hip joint of the aging and rather corpulent (but still remarkably attractive) woman started to hinder her mobility, which had previously always been excellent. Paula's mother gave her consent with no hesitation, whereas the stepfather wanted to keep her at home. But the upshot was that she moved to her aunt's.

They made a happy home. Resi Schachl looked in some ways like her deceased brother, to whom she'd been very attached, only her face was less finely honed. Through several of its features, the river master's physiognomy had stood in apparent contradiction to the physical labor demanded by his occupation (which also frequently required quick powers of decision) and to the build of his body, which was of no more than medium height, admittedly, but which had displayed exceptional strength through the breadth of his shoulders. The man's face had been a refined one on the whole, though, if only because the bridge of the nose was so narrow, almost sharply ridged, in fact, and because there was such a delicate-seeming quality in the area around the temples, which looked sunken deep in; along with her reddish hair, Paula had inherited both these features from her father. Perhaps it was also this resemblance, growing more obvious all the time, that gained her a special place in her Aunt Theresa's heart from the beginning. Paula was easy to get along with, and the aunt was taken care of as she'd never been before. From the solid base of the admiration in which she'd always been held in her neighborhood, an invigorating popularity welled up, fast-flowing and pure, like spring water, all throughout the little world around her after Paula appeared in it and began running all the necessary errands and doing the shopping. They made a happy home; Resi Schachl was one of those who maintained a good mood and had control over a sharp tongue (had control, and so it didn't do her any harm) that could turn and toss and spin the language in all its vigor— in the old neighborhoods all over Vienna, especially back then, it welled up indefatigable and unceasing—imbuing it with concrete vividness in the most exquisitely detailed way. The metaphors she would come out with sometimes really hit their targets, like an arrow shot by an expert archer; when, for example, she once said of a person in a testy mood that the woman "looked like a scorched louse," it must be conceded that there could hardly be a worse mood than the one a tiny little bug would be in if someone were holding a match under it as it went scurrying up the wall.

Two rooms of her little house, along with a kitchen and an entrance area, were rented—in other words, the whole top floor. Here lived Senior Councillor Julius Zihal of the Central Bureau of Revenue and Tariff Computation during the last years of his active service (when he retired, he moved to a less expensive part of the city, ostensibly on the grounds of having to balance his budget). Zihal was a bachelor. They didn't see him too often or hear very much from him. He smoked Virginia cigars, burrowed around in his apartment (at which times his footsteps could be heard pacing back and forth), greeted all the ladies with a dignified air when he met them, and had as his cleaning woman one Frau Zajiček, who now and then did a few chores down at the Schachls' as well. The gentleman she worked for, however, put in an appearance down there only once a quarter, not, as might be assumed, to pay his rent (he never did that in person), but to be treated as a guest for coffee, regaled with the whole array of ruffles and flourishes, nuances of presentation, intermissions, and embellishments that are integral elements of a solemn Viennese *Jause*, or coffee party. The senior councillor's erect carriage, his comportment, his way of kissing a lady's hand and of bowing, his style of conversation—none of these lacked a *grandezza* that had an almost Spanish feel to it, though on a reduced scale, if one will; it was all intermingled, however, with the slight tartness of that irony which can develop—to their benefit—in the minds of individuals who live alone, since people in that situation grow better acquainted with themselves, in response to which fact the quality of their intelligence (if any, and Julius Zihal did have it) is incapable of taking any other attitude. Whenever he came, Resi Schachl would use an exceptionally beautiful gilt coffee service obviously dating from the eighteenth century, a set any collector would have been prepared to make enormous financial sacrifices to acquire, the more so as it was entirely complete, with not the smallest piece missing.

After the First World War, Paula and her husband moved into the apartment formerly occupied by Zihal.

But it was a long time until then. She was in her sixteenth year—at a time in her life, that is, when a girl is still showing a tendency to lose her balance—when she went to live in Lichtental. That moment could well have been exactly the right and proper one for her to sail into the wake of a forthright person like her Aunt Theresa. It was then that Paula started the commercial course which enabled her to fill the position with the lawyer on Marc-Aurel Strasse in which we met her two years later, at the time of her coming to know René Stangeler.

At which time summer is standing in its blue dome over the city, this August of 1911. She practiced waiting, "a woman's chief occupation," as Grete Siebenschein once called it. A woman's? And was she waiting for a man? René was close to a year younger than she, as far as Paula knew. They hadn't had a childhood friendship, hadn't been playmates; they didn't have a love relationship and weren't engaged, she the youthful bride-to-be and he the yet more youthful intended groom. This waiting room of life still admitted of some indecisive hovering among life's categories. But Stangeler of course knew nothing about any of it, said nothing to himself, drew no conclusions, blind in his soul, perhaps if only because that soul was too lethargic to give to things those names they had long held a claim to, or because it filled those far distant names too vaguely and with concepts of an altogether alien kind. Paula, for her part, who came from a class familiar through hereditary transmission with the physical weight of life before it ever settles in, before it even begins pressing, forcefully and purely as a matter of course, down on one's shoulders—Paula was enjoying, and with the most deeply serene conscience, a golden respite of waiting. Had Stangeler at that time awakened to any degree of awareness about the situation, he would have tormented himself, as later on in life he never missed an opportunity to do. Paula knew immeasurably more than he did, and she didn't torment herself. Only now and then would some high-floating feathery clouds of anxiety go drifting across the hemisphere of the sky. Even so, what was happening now was not some temporary game that didn't count for anything, some episode that could be irresponsibly blown away or blotted out; far from that, she was gathering together here, with great painstakingness, and even with reverence, a deep-layered store of delicate, revitalizing substances and essences that she might, in years to come, have to make last her a whole lifetime. That was something else she wasn't entirely unaware of.

The question arises whether René's world, his unknown background or his parentage and social class, had an attraction for her, making him interesting and enhancing his value. Could be. Yet the degree and kind of difference fell too far outside the framework of life in Lichtental to be at all measurable by its dimensions. The neighborhood notables, for instance, were a magistrate and the owner of a small cardboard-box factory located down toward the Danube Canal. With these members of the neighborhood elite and their families, Stangeler—representing his species in the zoological sense, as it were—had not a single trait in common; this fact was solidly rooted for Paula on the level of unquestioned instinct. So he didn't fit in among these leading citizens, but somewhere else instead; to be specific, precisely at the hovering point among life's categories, a point which could not exist in the cosmos called Lichtental—unless in some sort of branch office, as with Paula now—while those categories definitely did exist here, as in other places. That hovering point, though, was Paula's source for the fragrant substances and essences that were being piled up and stored. Therefore, since the vague localizing with which she invested her René indeed and in need served her interests in life right now and, in the deepest way, her future at one and the same time, she was satisfied with it.

But how different he was! We already know that. We would need only to exaggerate and mask things a tiny little bit to reach the point at which we could no longer decide with certainty what attracted him more—Paula herself, or Paula Schachl as just a part of the picture she stood in front of.

This was a time when that picture stood solid in one place, evanescent in another, boxed in the height of summer's parcels of light: morning-white, afternoon-gold, evening-red. For the most part, Paula was needed in the attorney's office on a half-day basis only. That was why it was hard to make her Aunt Theresa understand that it wouldn't be possible to go on vacation just at the moment; the aunt had been wanting for a long time to escape the fierce heat of the city in summer, to beat the heat before it beat her, which was how it felt, as she said over and over. Paula's office would naturally have granted her vacation time without a second thought, and in fact they even asked her if she wouldn't care to take some time off now, as there was so little to do. But there was that matter of waiting for René—not to see him on his imminent visit here in Vienna, to go away before that, was totally unthinkable for Paula. He still hadn't been able to send any definite word about the day of his arrival. So there was some fancy juggling to be done. Paula managed it artfully and gleefully, forever fixing her vacation dates for a time just over the horizon while meanwhile fixing before her Aunt Theresa's eyes some household job that simply had to be tended to right now; at her hands, then, the purely negative factor of the lack of any definite news on René's part was transformed into decidedly positive projects involving numerous particular and exacting tasks, as for example making gooseberry preserves. Again and again, a cloud mass of things to do had to be rolled in between the vacation and the aunt, and each of these was indeed successful in beclouding the aunt's mind with a whirl of busywork activity.

However, the good woman would sooner or later work her way loose from the trammels Paula so cleverly coiled around her, and then something new had to be ready and waiting. There existed in this connection, after all, the possibility and the danger that Aunt Theresa might turn directly to Paula's employer with a request that her niece be permitted to go on vacation sometime in the near future, if not at the earliest possible date. She wanted to go to Vitis (that's a little spot somewhere down in Lower Austria), where she was used to spending a few weeks every summer at a rural inn whose owner she was distantly related to—but in no case without Paula. It was not even up for discussion that the girl might stay at home by herself in Vienna.

And so some underhandedness was called for. Paula practiced it with enjoyment, like one of the fine arts, as it were. She wasn't a melancholy young thing, like René. The gooseberries for the first cloud of entanglement that enveloped the aunt were seasonally provided by their own small garden, incidentally, entered straight through the gateway to the crumbly little house. At the rear was an enclosed glass porch, its wide door panels standing open in the summer. Among the upper panes above the door some individual small panes of colored glass had been inserted, red, blue, and green; some of the rectangles stood on their points, making them look rhomboidal, while others were set in horizontally. Pedestrians passing by on the sidewalk could look straight into the small garden, and if the garden was entered through the low arch of the gateway, it proved more spread out than it appeared at first, and quite irregular in its layout.

It lay between walls that retained the heat, though they weren't high. They weren't blank, either, but had plenty of nooks and crannies and little windows, mostly with yellow frames and green shutters. The sky narrowed only a little as it came down over this patch of garden, which extended leftward along a neighbor's two garden walls, and there stood four fruit trees with a bench and a table in their shadows, as well as a lounge chair Paula had bought herself, blond wood and canvas dyed in several colors. There had never been furniture like this in the house before. Bygone times often give us the impression that, taken with their own self-assured competence, it never occurred to people to make themselves comfortable when they took a seat, as if in those days they had gone through their entire lives assuming stiff postures and stances without ever quite realizing it. The truth is that they lived more comfortably, though, even if they didn't fix their eyes directly on a goal called comfort or coziness, which people can't do anyway until they've grown untrue to life and accordingly arrange it more than live it—of course noting, as if they were outside observers, and eliminating every tiny flaw in their decor, while still, needless to say, never achieving the comfort they seek by doing so, for it dwells inside life and not beside it.

By which we weren't referring to Paula's lounge chair in particular. Lying in it, she would try to think of the next project she could get her aunt all wrapped up in. A high, feathery cloud would sometimes hang in the sky, whose unceasing bounteousness of warm blue was in itself enough to create anxiety. Here in the garden there was very little sound from the city traffic. The streets of Lichtental, narrow and lying beyond the main routes, were hardly traveled at all by automobiles and noisy horse-drawn carts. Once in a while, coming from near Nussdorfer Strasse or Alserbach Strasse, could be heard a horn honking and an engine racing and that grinding, thunder-like noise, with no one single sound leaping out from it, into which the daytime roiling of a large city blends at some distance. Paula's concern was to see to it that her last days in Vienna overlapped with René's impending visit in such a way that she would be able to get together with him a couple of times at least, and this ultimate aim of all her ingenious maneuvering she kept unswervingly before her eyes, kept a tight grip on without letting loose, the way a person will squeeze a pair of pliers. But soon after the middle of August she found a general-delivery letter waiting for her— not addressed to "Meningitis Cerebrospinalis" this time, but more simply to "Strudlhof Steps"—in which René announced his arrival on the twenty-second of the month and asked her if, at three in the afternoon on the twenty-third, she could please be at that bakery we're already familiar with.

With that, a kind of reversal took place. Paula now sat or lay much more at ease in her garden chair than before. Forthwith she reached an agreement with her aunt; it was established that their vacation could begin as of the twenty-fifth, and so their journey to Vitis (to the extent that it can be called a journey) stood fixed on the agenda for that date. It was still a good ten days until then.

Now Paula could lie out in the garden more often, and for longer periods of time, too, because her doing so would no longer be bound quite so inevitably to bring about the concomitant result of causing her aunt, in reaction to the manifestly slight demand for Paula's services on the part of the attorney's office, to break out into lamentations over vacation time that all this while still wasn't being granted. Up to now, that was often the reason why afternoon walks along the Danube docks had been opted for, why at home it had seemed so much more advisable not to provoke, through rest and relaxation, but to enmesh, through cloud masses of busy work. In this regard, Paula was demonstrating in prefiguration the instincts and methods of certain politicians who would not come swooping over Europe until much later. Now she could enjoy the garden. Now she could enjoy waiting; now finally she could enjoy a walk. Somewhere off in a corner of her mind, by the way, she was looking forward to getting out to the country. But that was something that just peeped through, no more than a pleasant backdrop, a kind of consoling thought off in the background and held in reserve, even though it also meant that once again she wouldn't get to see René for a long time. So the anticipation remained faint. With all the intensity of her years, which even inside uncomplicated people like herself are forever betwixt and between in their efforts to make life into something like a poem or some other work of art, Paula deeply breathed in these summer days of white and red and gold. That which is called the art of living, however, is something young people of course do not command; this term has the flavor of living arrangements made by aging bachelors, artists of living where there can be no more art to living, because the person has died in the meantime.

Considering the machinations—difficult enough, after all—that Paula had had to be so involved in and our awareness that any attempt to stay behind by herself in Vienna would not exactly have met with success, it might be tempting to conclude that she was given only a limited measure of freedom by Fräulein Theresa Schachl. But such was not the case. It was more the situation itself than the character of the retired lady that created the impasse. She of course didn't know a thing about any René Stangeler. But she possessed as part of her heritage a deeply rooted understanding of how precious those years are that Paula was just now living through when measured against what would come later, what could not help coming along with the physical weight of life. She was not the least bit spinsterish. Still attractive, if somewhat on the robust side, there lurked in her voice some honey from a past she'd known how to enjoy; a gold-green shimmer like wine gleamed on her lips and coursed along her tongue. Although there was no explicit reference during any talks on the subject—no such talks ever occurred—it was yet obviously being taken into consideration that a girl of Paula's age isn't still hanging around with just her playmates or girlfriends. Ever since she'd made Stangeler's acquaintance, Paula hadn't bumped up against any obstacles worth mentioning when she wanted to go out, even in the evening. Underlying Theresa Schachl's attitude in these matters was what sounded like a triad whose three notes consisted of an almost peasantlike ability to refrain from judgment, the knowledge that one can do nothing to stop what's going to happen sooner or later anyway, and a self-confident trust in one's own kind, which she recognized anew each day in this child who so resembled her deceased brother.

Paula was enjoying waiting, "a woman's chief occupation." Perhaps Grete Siebenschein wasn't so wrong after all with the statement she was to make later on (as of now, she was still in school and growing up in Dornbach, in a villa her father was then renting, next door to the beautiful garden by König, long before he moved his residence and his office to the house diagonally across from the Bohemia Station, the house with all the overdone, showy staircases full of senseless tassels and festoons and mirrors—but returning to the subject: Grete could have said what she later did about the "chief occupation" even back then, which is how far advanced she was by sixteen).

So now Paula was waiting. It was often like a sweet ache, nothing more, not a presence aggravated by resolving into or combining into particular details. One of her dresses was between a violet and a lavender blue. She enjoyed wearing it now. It was her waiting color. At the Danube docks, in the direction of the Kahlenberg or the Bisamberg, there took shape in the evenings a portal filled with blazing colors first layered and then melting into one another. The water would later look as if it had been extinguished, and it appeared to flow more quickly if one looked carefully, streak for streak, eddy for eddy, like very thin sheets of ice. All along the embankments of the Danube Canal, and holding sway until the late hours of every afternoon, life spread out and then literally dismantled into its component parts, into articles of clothing peeled off by people who came to catch the sun and the air and to go swimming. One day Paula walked all the way out to Nussdorf and then rode back on the streetcar. The main river of the Danube, conversely, opened everything out on an incomparably wider scale, would have no part of that heat-shriveled dismantling which people brought to its banks from both sides. It cooled them and flitted swiftly past, however much they wanted to hold it besieged by their troops and swarms. Likewise, the countryside was most definitely divided in two; here there wasn't any tinge of "well, that's the best they can do" about two banks' being joined by bridges quite narrow in their span, as on the Danube Canal.

The garden was glowing. Not until evening began approaching did the fruit trees cast shadows that could offer help. Then at last everything would be set up and lined up just right, green-gold fingers across the grass. There were still roses. The table for the evening meal had been moved outdoors here, and one got the feeling that everywhere else too people were eating outdoors, as voices came drifting from all the other gardens of the nearby houses. These days, Paula enjoyed stepping into this basin of rose-filled quiet early in the morning as well.

Neither then nor later did Stangeler ever make it this far. He wasn't worth it, we'd like to say; it wasn't granted to him; he was never mature enough, as it were. But Lieutenant Melzer, later Major, and later yet Senior Councillor, did sit here once, having a nice talk with Paula and her husband and holding their kicking child on his knees.

Grauermann had been coughing and sneezing in the most pitiable way since Sunday (actually since that beautiful, warm summer Sunday night). His nose was all red and his eyes were constantly watering. His face took on more of a turned-up look, which it was already preformed to have anyway because of a short, straight nose whose tip did not stand out horizontal but instead bobbed back up a little on a slant, so that someone looking into his face from the same height would always see something of the nostrils. And now the nostrils were really visible. They were underlined in red, we might say. "You should lie down," Etelka advised. He could have quoted in reply that line from a ballad by Schiller, "Such thanks, fair one, I do not crave" (*Den Dank, Dame, begehr' ich nicht*), but with the accent on the word "such," meaning "Don't do me any favors." Etelka's nerves were shredded from the coughing and sneezing fits his cold had brought on. "Go lie down in bed," she said. Asta shot her a brief glance from off to the side. They were supposed to travel to Vienna later that very afternoon to attend the garden party at the Schmellers'. That was why Asta packed into that look a whole sentence, one perfectly understandable to her sister: "Don't make it so obvious, or else he'll really want to come." After all, Etelka had already said, among other things, "You can't possibly go and mix with people in your condition. You've got a fever, too, and you belong in bed for a week." Marchetti had gone back to Vienna; otherwise he would have known that he'd been made out to be a liar, that speaker with forked tongue! A sweater and a mackintosh aren't enough to protect against the morning dew high in the mountains. So Grauermann would have been better off if he actually had disciplined and conquered himself.

They set off for an easy, short walk right after breakfast, so Ingrid Schmeller was able to hold her own and even go the distance without getting a stone in her shoe or pains in her knees. Semski had already come up to the house for breakfast. Now he was walking ahead with Asta, followed by Melzer with Ingrid and Editha Pastré, and at the rear, Grauermann, whose explosions could now and then be heard (Etelka's corresponding bursts of indignation remained inaudible); as it happened, though, his condition improved markedly, not to say abruptly, right as they took this little walk (perhaps the exercise and the sunlight did him good, or his cold was now dwindling anyway). At any rate, the most turbulent of his symptoms began to disappear soon thereafter, and with them the bothersome noise that a quiet night of camping out had caused. René was not along. This time there was no duty to perform, no ministrations for him to attend to. Editha was all taken care of.

Semski walked faster. He was on his pet topic and wanted to gain some distance from those behind him. Perhaps he could also feel somehow that Melzer kept looking at his back all the while, right between his shoulder blades. It would have been more in the spirit of things for the lieutenant to look at Asta. The fact was, though, that he knew next to nothing about what direction he was looking in. He drew no conclusions, never. And much later on, still did not. A civilian understanding didn't even begin to make its first rudimentary manifestations in him until he'd been out of military service for seven years.

That's how it carries people along with it. Now he was feeling unpleasantly wedged in between Ingrid and Editha; he wasn't able to start the ball rolling with a conversation, and such few little remarks as he was able to drop sounded like nothing more than a squeaking and a tweaking on the string between the two girls, a string stretched only too tight as it was.

Asta's mood that morning was sprinkled with joviality, the way the dark forest floor here is spotted with flecks of sunlight. That was upsetting Semski. In his efforts to vent his feelings, to come close, at least by talking about it, to a goal that otherwise always remained at the same far distance, he felt thwarted from a sideward direction and impinged on by some irony of a gentle but pungent sort. Accustomed to leaning on Asta in this whole cause of his, what was coming out of her today seemed to him downright unsuitable, something new and contrary to the tacit understanding they'd always had. His egoism, distressed and trapped in a blind alley, did not of course permit him to see except imprecisely and in passing, as if out of the corners of his eyes, and so he didn't take in much more, on the whole, than that something was upsetting him. "You must absolutely try to get a decision now, Stephan," she was saying, "there's nothing else to be done. Do it any way you can. Try new ways. If your mind's really made up, that is. I don't think you should let anything stop you."

"How…?" he answered, understanding her less quickly than she was speaking, like a door being slowly moved on its hinges by a draft until finally it opens. "But you know I can't…" He came to a standstill and looked into Asta's face.

"And why can't you?" she asked briskly and cheerfully, but at the same time with a brusqueness of the kind helplessness often induces. There was pallor underneath her tanned skin, the pallor that comes with overtaxing oneself.

In the meantime Melzer and the two ladies had drawn close.

Of course they more or less knew the place they were living in, though just in passing, seen out of the corners of their eyes—amid surroundings that could not be surpassed for quietness but that nevertheless testified unceasingly to their immense strength. In the ravines and fissures near the mountain walls, in these wounds of the woods, torn open anew each spring by masses of water with their dull grinding, there lay now, when they once more partly healed in summertime, green, fine sand, deposited and dried out in the large basins between boulders washed smooth. Brushwood and branches had long spanned the empty streambed from both sides once again. Nor did time stand still here, either, much though so many hours might be marked off from so many hours by nothing more than, say, the piping cry of a buzzard flying up high. It was just that time appeared to have been brought here to a kind of regularity like the breathing of someone in a deep sleep. In the morning, a first finger of sunlight would point past the trunk of a certain tree and into the hidden rift valley, to a particular stone; in the evening, green-gold and from the opposite direction, another one like it.

Perhaps it would not have been possible to fix all of this quite so firmly before one's eye without first stepping away from life, so to speak, and growing untrue to it—but this latter condition had indeed come to pass, and so one was occasionally capable of the former. "Nature" is just something invented at one time (it was for its sake, really, that people traveled out here on Saturdays), and people remained under obligation to that invention called nature, subsisting in nothing more than that a word which once meant "state of existence" (the ancients understood it in that sense) has now become fraught with some nebulous, aestheticized content—which we are then duty bound as civilized human beings to place a positive value on. It keeps getting harped on and fussed over, and people feel each other out about it in rural surroundings like these by calling each other's attention to various beauties of "nature." If anyone ever said outright that this spinach-green sublimity up hill and down dale was enough to turn his stomach, he would be considered an evil person.

It never crossed the mind of anybody here.

It might have crossed Lovis Konietzki's mind before anyone else's; he was the one Frau von Stangeler always said looked like a dethroned king of Poland. Quite that exalted his lineage wasn't, but his actual lineage was of even greater practical importance for him at the time.

Konietzki was the illegitimate son of a very powerful man, the president of one of the leading banking institutions in the entire monarchy. When the appropriate time came, this man had seen to little Lovis's being placed in a good middle-class family, whose name he then bore from his childhood. He did it in a different way, however—the youthful mistress of the aging bank president had later, with his generous assistance, made an advantageous marriage. As long as the father lived—and he did so most lavishly for the time—he of course held his hand over his son. Sheltered as he was under this kind of canopy, Lovis nonetheless displayed some remarkable talents. Of all the young men who visited the Stangelers' home, no one else was deriving from his own work anything close to Konietzki's income. True, the father had hoisted him into the saddle, but Lovis had gone on to prove how well he could ride. His position in the legal department of the bank was a very good one, and as if that weren't enough, he was able to take yet further advantage of jurisprudence, the subject his father had supported his study of and for which he had just the right aptitude to put to practical use: in partnership with another man he gave preparatory courses for the government law boards and qualifying examinations; and because both men gave their best and charged fees that significantly undercut a competing, long-established operation, the Konietzki Institute caught on very quickly. People said that Lovis earned a minimum of nine hundred crowns a month, and in those days, for a young man of twenty-six, that was more than abundant. Besides that, he was said to be enjoying a large monthly allowance from his father. So if not exactly wealthy, he still had more money at his disposal than did any of the other young people; more, in any case, than the sons of the rich and great houses, who never get their hands on any, because there it has already reached its peak and even gone beyond its highest point, as it were, and now it counts as something harmful, indeed almost indecent, an attitude apparently connected to experiences garnered on the way up the ladder.

Konietzski didn't make any great to-do about "nature," then, and what he loved to do on Sundays, or whenever he had free time, was to sleep late. There was no getting him onto the tennis court before eleven o'clock, and then mostly as a spectator only. If he did play at eleven, then around twelve he would go back to that large inn down in the valley where he preferred staying—because the small, older country inn on the mountain wasn't to his taste, and the nearby hotel was too far beneath his standards—to take a bath and change; by contrast, the young men up at the Stangeler house would all go stampeding into a large bathroom at the same time, twenty minutes before the gong, throw their tennis clothes over all the chairs, and push and shove one another in the shower. As for Konietzki's looking like a dethroned king of Poland, the description fit somehow. When they were carrying Grabmayr around the tennis court and yelling after he beat Semski, Konietzki was the only one who'd remained calmly sitting on a garden bench, gently smiling, with his legs crossed and his chin resting in his hand. He was not fond of getting himself all overheated. Perhaps he needed a cooling layer all around him in order to live. By no means the clotheshorse type, it still wasn't unusual for him to disappear and then fetch back up wearing an entirely different outfit. He would pack an enormous suitcase to go to this mountain village for a week, and he was completely unruffled when people cracked jokes about it. He had what he wanted. When he was dressing casually, he favored violet shirts because of his olive-colored skin and in fact liked this color in every shade for all his clothes. He had knowledge and flair in such matters. Quite a number of men dragged him along to their tailors when they wanted to pick out fabric.

But this detachment, this smiling mien, this gentle melancholy of a dethroned king, these long legs crossed at rest and this chin nestling in the hand—at Grabmayr's victory parade, as on every other occasion—these precisely corresponded to the mode of his simultaneous presence and absence here, to the mode of his feeling comfortable in a social setting totally and profoundly alien to him, to the reason for his returning on a fairly regular basis to be part of this group. He kept his position on the outside here, an Archimedean point, if one will. He retained his cooling protective layer and observed, not without amusement, the doings of people who must have appeared to him harmlessly hilarious and troglodytically oafish at the same time. What's beyond doubt is that his intellect was incommensurably different from that of any of the other young men here, including Buschmann and

Geyrenhoff—the latter gentleman, by the way, since we've just men-tioned him, the one he was much later, during the composition of that chronicle cited earlier, to have a great influence on, even if he was never explicitly acknowledged as a source by Geyrenhoff or by Kajetan von S. Even by the time under discussion now, however, Geyrenhoff had been subjected in concrete form to Konietzski's influence, for it was on the recommendation of the Polish king that he'd been using his particular *eau de lavande* for a long time now. And so that influence wound up extending all the way to René Stangeler. And please don't let anyone say that this connection is merely external and peripheral; doing so would irritate the author of this narrative far beyond his usual measure. After all, it is indeed nothing less than external when one is the cause of another person's coming to stand and walk in a certain scent. Scents are often like bursting bubbles of memory coming out of the depth of the years when they float toward us unexpectedly and we can't quite tell whether they're from the inside or the outside. To modify a person's odor goes right to the heart of that person's life.

Someone who might not have been able to say it like that but who knew it anyway was sitting at the desk in his room and carefully using a small chisel to open a crate that had come for him in the mail that day from a Viennese perfume and fragrance store. Yes, Herr von Gey-renhoff had transmuted his resolution into action bright and early that Monday morning. After untwisting the white cap from the one bottle—two had been packed in excelsior—and removing the cork by means of the little corkscrew enclosed, René took a cautious whiff of the aroma. It was the aroma of a new stage in his life, and what was more, he knew it. He hesitated, as before a decision, to entrust himself to it now; and he felt in the deepest part of himself that there would never be any turning back from this point.

The one person here Konietzki ever actually got involved in conver-sation with was Asta; the way her mind worked, her constantly renewed attempts to be accountable for her actions and to maintain self-discipline, seemed to please him. Each enjoyed a cordial relationship with the other, although it had no further significance than that. She trusted his intellect. She'd spoken to him about Ingrid and Semski, among other things, and had received a real shock when he quite disdainfully and casually declared Fräulein Schmeller to be an individual who in his opinion was entirely incapable of any strong feeling whatever. "She'd never be able to bear up under such a thing," he added.

"With warm regards" was what Geyrenhoff had written on the visiting card enclosed with the lavender water.

Stangeler started a letter.

Dear Herr von Geyrenhoff,

You have guessed a secret wish of mine and done something that makes me truly happy. From now on I will always have to think back on the pond and our talk there as the beginning of something new!

Your
René St.

Geyrenhoff once later referred to these lines as not fully understandable. Stangeler sealed the envelope now; the note seemed to have turned out well, and in the most natural way, with no great fuss; even his penmanship had flowed along neatly and easily.

In front of the house, where the approach road ran level for a stretch, a very strange couple was walking back and forth, and between the two persons composing it, a difference in height of almost half a meter could be noted. They were Frau von Stangeler and Lovis Konietzki.

She enjoyed laughing, this short lady, and she was laughing now, here under the full, unrelenting force of the noontime sun, which she was protecting herself against by wearing a wide-brimmed straw garden hat. It wasn't long before they'd be seated at the table. Konietzki, who'd been invited to lunch like all the rest, had just returned from the village—climbing the serpentine road slowly and pensively, he'd caught sight of his hostess and said hello to her near the top, where it levels off in front of the house. There was too much hustle and bustle on the tennis court. Konietzki preferred staying where he was. He was getting pleasure out of entertaining Frau von Stangeler, doing so through his descriptions of some absurd situations that had not seldom arisen last winter season when they were skiing (a sport whose aficionados back then were still largely incompetent). Frau von Stangeler was bound to consider sports and athletics intrinsically silly and totally unnecessary, for she belonged to the previous generation, which had never gone in for such things as common practice; the next generation then found itself in a sensitive state of tension toward the earlier one, at least as far as this topic was concerned, and found itself holding "convictions" of a sort, just as when people embrace political "convictions," whereupon the first thing that happens is that they forget all about how to laugh and then don't want to talk to one another anymore. Konietzki was lacking any such state of tension, though; his athletic ambitions were too modest and his intelligence too sharp for him to have been caught up in anything like that. So Frau von Stangeler thought of him as being on her side to some degree. But then, everyone thinks of an epicurean like Lovis Konietzki as being on his or her side. Wherever presupposition, impaired vision, or a limited mentality manifests itself, such a person will humbly bring forth whatever vestiges of the same are in himself and present them as his own contributions to the subject. That approach could never offend anyone, of course.

They now heard the gong; one of the maids had come out of the entrance hall and was standing in front of the house. This told the tennis players they now had to start getting ready. It would be struck again in twenty minutes, and lunch would then be served right away. The first players came running down from the court, making white spots in the green grass, and dashed past Frau von Stangeler and Konietzki as quickly as they could with some little greeting, like children hurrying past adults.

Even though not a few of the guests had traveled back to Vienna on Monday (in large part, as seen from the standpoint of a conductor and hence a working man, taking scandalously comfortable trains which would get them to the ministry sometime between nine and ten, albeit not before they'd had a second breakfast in the café and quickly paged through the newspapers)—even though the group at the Stangelers' now, on a perfectly ordinary Tuesday, seemed considerably thinned out, there were still no fewer than twelve persons gathered at the table after the second ringing of the gong; among the young men were, in addition to Konietzki, Grabmayr, Semski, and Melzer, which is to say, those who still had some free time.

Melzer was placed between Asta and René. From where he was sitting he could look out through the window to the mountain facing him; open field below and forest above, it stood in the bright fullness of the noonday sun. But to his right, through the glass doors of a wide veranda, he lowered his glance as he looked the long way across the valley, about six kilometers away, to some distant wooded and rocky barriers that appeared set down just before the flatlands. These elevations lay in another color, in a bluish gray; at that distance the forest looked like moss or fur, and the limestone rocks standing out from the forest here and there as flecks of white made up in their distant and muted sunniness the very quintessence of this full summer day and the ample spaces it enfolded. While the soup was being ladled, Melzer's glance kept on turning back to the right, and in the general hum of voices he was left all the freedom he needed to keep on looking. Until Asta nudged him lightly. Someone had spoken to him from the upper end of the table, and it was none other than the host himself.

Even though he had been almost entirely lost in thought for a minute or two, Melzer now observed—and his observing something like this, or anything else, for that matter, was quite exceptional, perhaps even unprecedented—that the words of a question just then directed toward him, words that had not met with one iota of his attention, were still standing in his ears nonetheless and could now be apprehended after the fact. "Tell me now, Melzer, when are we going to start building railroads down where you Bosnians are?" With no hesitation, Melzer answered, "I'm sure it'll be soon. We're getting just about everything else there. Hotels. Roads. Bridges. It's beautiful country. It isn't right to think of it as just a pile of stones, which so many people do. Of course railroads will be coming, a whole network, and in the next few years, too." "But nobody from the War Ministry or any other knowledgeable source has told you anything definite about it?" "No," said Melzer. "Nothing exact." This answer to the second question was short and to the point, in good military style, roughly like an answer to a superior officer. Of course he heard talk of these matters during or after every meal in the mess down in Trnovo, but indeed nothing definite. Over and over again, however, his host's approach in dealing with the young men who were guests in his home showed itself as

absolutely masterful, accomplished through the simplest of methods.
Fairly often he would sprinkle in the familiar and friendly pronoun of
address when talking to this one or that one, throwing in a *du* here
and there, as he'd just done with Melzer, and without exception the
young man so addressed would always feel very much singled out, if
not actually honored. They could probably sense how much he liked
seeing them all, how friendly his feelings toward them were. Nobody
was left out of the conversation. And because Old Man Stangeler, as
they called him (he wasn't at all old, but he was also nothing if not
old), commanded a virtually encyclopedic knowledge of family trees
and persons in and of themselves; he knew all there was to know about
the father, the mother, the relatives, and the material means of each
one of these young people, and so he also knew the particular way to
take hold of each one and the particular place at which to open a lead;
naturally the person treated this way was going to feel as if this man
really knew him, valued him, and held him in suitably high esteem.
He enjoyed speaking with quite a few of them at greater length and in
more detail, as for example after meals, over black coffee in his den;
among them were Konietzki, Marchetti, and Geyrenhoff, just as in
days to come Consul Fraunholzer would be one of this number. Young
men singled out by their host for these longer talks constituted from
that point on a privileged class in the eyes of his wife.

Etelka, who was alone, as it were (Grauermann ate down below
with his parents), was kept well amused by Semski and Grabmayr,
which latter man, incidentally, likewise rejoiced in the considerable
esteem of his host, who discerned in that young man the representative
of a venerable old family and who further derived great enjoyment
from his energetic way of doing things. When he heard that Benno
had conquered the Rax massif the previous day, on Monday, and before
breakfast at that, all he could do was give a silent little wave of his hand
and then say, first, "That's all I'd have to try!" and then, more seriously,
"Don't bring a heart condition on yourself, son." Semski, who was
talking with Etelka in a lively manner, gave an impression of being
exhilarated. Asta noticed. He seemed to her now to have become
unhitched from anyone and everyone, on furlough somehow, or poised
so that he could get a better running start to confront anyone and

everyone. Ingrid sat there daydreaming. René seemed to be sitting there daydreaming. Melzer was listening to what they—the old man and Konietzki—were talking about at the head of the table, but what did he know about the political aspects of economic policy?

The kind of conviviality that sets in quite on its own as a varied and interesting meal progresses and at the same time rises by imperceptible degrees out of the wine now started expanding around the table and warming everyone. Even Melzer. He was seeing through a veil, and that is what enabled him to see in the first place. It is not in confronting the object itself, which fades in stark daylight, that the eye displays its wondrous abilities; the opulence of light does not unfold until there is refraction. It appeared to him as if the rooms here had unexpectedly grown deeper and that the people in them had accordingly moved off to a distance, in a way somehow akin to what had just happened with the fur-like forest down below on the mountains as they pointed outward and away to a plain which could not be seen. He released himself from his immediate surroundings, as a string being tuned will stretch and raise itself off the fingerboard of the instrument—once it's no longer touching, it can resonate. A kind of dignity was what now crept over Melzer, along with the remote possibility of his composing himself into some other form so as to face what was coming, whatever that might be.

The state he was in, combined with an agreeably mild fatigue, remained fixed in him as they now changed the scene after lunch and left the older people behind. Outdoors, well beyond the stream, there was a round and completely level clearing among some trees, and it was there that the younger people loved to have coffee after meals and lie or doze or sleep on comfortable blankets spread out. Pillows of all colors were brought out here as well. Melzer saw among the trees the white apron of the maid who now came into view with a large tray full of coffee cups and was walking over the little bridge from the house. He was lying next to Asta, but it wasn't something he'd hurried to do or gone to any trouble about. He adjusted his pillow to fit better under his head and looked straight up into the receding blue of the sky; for a moment it was as if he were soaring upward in the wake of this receding motion, rising in an elevator, vertically and quickly. The sweet aroma of Grabmayr's inevitable Capstan now mingled with the taste of his coffee and cigarette. Melzer heard a spotted nutcracker crying in bright cadence and thought how he really ought to shoot one with René's Flobert gun, because of its pretty little feathers—for Asta's green hat. He wanted to turn his head toward her, to ask her about it. His eyes had shut a good while before. Inside their inner purple they enfolded Major Laska, who now stepped closer to him and said, "Be careful that you get along in life and deal with situations, Melzer. I can't be with you all the time. Our political relations with the English are all backward." "But there isn't anything you can do about that, Major." "Yet it's true all the same. And don't you always be leaving a room just because you can't understand what people are talking about, Melzer, just because it might be hard for you, because you suddenly get the idea you're tired. Don't be lazy, Melzer."

Meanwhile, nobody, not even sharp-eyed Asta, took notice of what was going on those days between blond Editha and Melzer; even he hid it from his own cognizance, in fact, put it out of sight somewhere, as it were, just as one will file away an unwelcome letter in the back compartment of a folder. Totally incapable of responding to a few little nods and hints seemingly given by this rich and beautiful girl on this or that occasion, he entrenched himself, one might say, behind his own modesty and behind the overt and even flagrant battle for Semski being waged between Ingrid and Editha. So he wrote off as impossible the very things he was seeing and experiencing. At the same time, a strange feeling of guilt went along with this state. Indeed, it was a kind of doubt about his ability to live his own life; if it was ever possible for a trail and a path to be laid out unobstructed and promising, so they were for him here, and yet he still might not be able to follow them. After all, here was everything a man could ever wish for. And without the hurdles there had been with Mary (which is what he couldn't help thinking, together with all the rest, quickly and in the deepest part of himself). He was denying a possibility that was testing him and that in this case was bound to result in his lying athwart life's current, so that it couldn't lift him up, bear him, take him with it, so that he wasn't swimming but was instead standing with his legs awkwardly apart with the stream breaking against him. Cross-grained, this lad.

The same judgment loomed up from his own depths or inmost chamber, as it were. It's hard to believe how little even actual facts have the power to sway us under certain circumstances. Melzer had come here because of Asta, after all, basically was here only because of Asta, and that was still the case after that combined hike and rock-climbing excursion, which had on the whole ended so sadly up on the flat slab of rock (while René was helping Editha down lower—helping her across the threshold of a new stage in life). A week earlier, Melzer had run into Editha, ditched by Ingrid and Semski, on a bench under some linden trees in the garden; standing there in his porcelain-white trousers, the lieutenant became aware that he could feel how little he was seeing of what he was in fact seeing, which is to say, a delightful picture. She was wearing a red blazer and, amid the sun-dappled green, the distant mountain behind them, and the blue of the sky, she seemed to have leapt forth as the very distillation of all those undeniably fresh, good, and pure forces, with that tinge of peach blossom to her skin, her loose blond hair, and her small, straight nose that fit with her face like one last amiable, masterful little flourish by the Creator.

He got involved with her now—conversationally, that is—out of sheer embarrassment, because he couldn't just turn around and walk away from the spot where he'd unexpectedly bumped into her, truly without having sought her out. Coolly and casually, among some exchange of remarks, Editha slipped in an invitation; perhaps during his next leave—and when would that be? oh, just a short one? this year yet? in November, did you say?—he might like to be a guest of her parents at their home in Vienna. (Melzer never went.) They even took a little walk together, up a hill that stood as vertical as a horn behind the house, and past there on more level ground to the edge of the forest. There they found a bench. Editha sat down in such a way that she was directly face-to-face with Melzer, and her large, gray-blue, wide-open eyes never stopped trying to hold his glance as the two were speaking. For quite some time here, Melzer seemed even to himself to be an out-of-it, dim-witted fool, and he kept looking up and down the tree trunks as though they could somehow help him with his lifeless, unresponsive weakness—not too modest by now to perceive what was pushing up against him, but still much too modest simply to pass over it and set it aside as worthless, as having nothing to do with him, as something that didn't happen to be agreeable to him.

On the same day they went rock climbing, all these matters that it would never have done to speak about came to an unexpected end, and indeed without words. During a break in the game, Melzer was walking along the side of the tennis court to pick up a ball he'd just spotted lying by the net post—not where the slope rose and the benches were, but on the other side, toward the valley. On the strip between the whitewashed line and the green edge, Editha was coming toward him from the opposite end of the court. They were going to have to meet midway, somewhere close to the net. And they did. For Melzer, there was something decisive about their heading straight toward one another in this way, something that would make the real situation clearly visible when they met and then passed one another. That proved true as well. Editha, that day wearing a white piqué dress that made her look less like her old familiar self, but like a stranger, almost like a different person, went striding right past Melzer without in any way coming to a stop, slowing down, smiling, or pointing to the ball lying on the ground. But her gaze had been holding his from some distance and stayed fixed in his when they were up very close, her gaze cold and gray, as it seemed to him, her face devoid of any trace whatever of the least animation. Then she was behind him. Something inside Melzer now fell to pieces and dropped into the dust, as it were; frightened almost to its depths, it was something he recognized as the end of a possibility that had indeed been viable up to this point.

On the day after the garden party in Döbling, Ingrid Schmeller was sitting with Asta in the tiny little room up in the Quartier Latin, which seemed to be underwater; the green light here made it look like an aquarium, light filtered green by the blinds, lowered all the way because of the broiling heat of the sun. The water reached up to Ingrid's chin, and Asta, for her part, was as deeply dismayed and stunned as only an honest soul can be for whom—at least for a long time yet—love is love and the pain of parting the pain of parting. This honest soul believed she was to blame for Ingrid's misfortune. Mademoiselle Schmeller stood up now and then to take a few paces around the little room, between these times talking and crying some more; and once, stopping in front of Asta's white-painted bookcase, she suddenly asked, "What happened to your cacti?"

Several images from the day before kept coming back to Asta, and for minutes at a time she was trapped, whirling inside a veritable orbit of mental pictures. Here came Editha from the back of the house, unexpectedly turning the corner of a paneled corridor on the third floor while Asta, from her hiding place, was keeping an eye out, looking down the stairs leading to the rooms where the party was being held (she didn't know there were more stairs here, a little spiral staircase, just as in her own home, but unfortunately the girl who would later be called Frau Schlinger knew it). At once the bathroom door was flung open, and Asta heard a fairly loud scream from Ingrid. She was so alarmed at that instant that she could summon up no outward movement by way of reaction—she froze at the top of the topmost wall, which she'd been driven up, while Editha walked past her a second later with rapid footsteps, gained the wide front stairs, and went hurrying down them. Asta thought she hadn't even been noticed by Editha (she'd been noticed, all right, but purposely ignored, as it later turned out). What seemed to Asta during those moments to be the unkindest cut of all was the way Editha had slammed the bathroom door shut with such a bang. Then for an absurdly long time nothing happened, until finally Ingrid came tiptoeing out of the bathroom, went around the corner, and ran down the corridor toward the spiral staircase Editha had come up. Semski was still dawdling around inside. Now Asta could hear water running out of the tap and into the sink. He finally came out, slowly and reflectively running his left hand over his forehead and temples, somewhat the way people sweep their hair back to make it smooth. His facial expression was very serious, even somber, one might say, and for the moment it had something strange-looking about it, like the expression of a Slavic farm worker. Or at least that was how Asta thought of it. Even so, he looked all freshly groomed. "You've got to get out of here; go downstairs by the little spiral staircase in the back," he said to her, very quietly and calmly as he walked past and slowly started down the large staircase into the hall below.

Where Herr Schmeller now appeared.

He came walking up the steps toward Semski, coming up faster than the other one was going down, and so they met on a third of the way down, came to a standstill, and turned to face one another at the same height. Of course Asta knew that she was supposed to have disappeared by now. But she stayed. One time, albeit twenty years later, she put a name to what it was that held her riveted to the spot at the time—it was wonderment, even amazement. A tendency to marvel at everything stayed with her all her life, and it was always present, as for example on this occasion, but on countless others as well. She often spoke of it. (Some hostile soul called it the "negroid wonderment of Asta Stangeler" and in a loose, casual way happened thereby to get in a swipe at her outward appearance, at her dark skin and her hair in tight waves, though her face really didn't have anything negroid about it.) It was only in the second place that Asta came to feel a sense of duty, a thought of staying to witness for Ingrid everything that was now about to occur here, so that her friend could adjust her behavior accordingly. Now that was the sensible Asta Stangeler, the head that stays above water. It always stayed above water, not as master of the situation per se, but more as what we might call the lightest part of her body. The posture she assumed as she went through life is somehow reminiscent of one of those bathtub thermometers that stands upright in a cork disc and floats around in the tub. The water temperature can be read above the surface, but the thing itself always stays dry and always bobs back upright (for naturally it's going to be played with in the bathtub, like a toy). Perhaps her honesty and her fearlessness were related to the fact that the waters could never really have closed over her head, not even when she was most dismayed. An invisible inner tube carried this head aloft, like a frilled collar; it could always look around from the surface of the water, and this position, very different from that of the rest of her body, isolated it to an extent as time went on.

Now, however, just as Senior Government Building Inspector Schmeller was preparing to haul off and slug Member of the Executive Committee from Ballhaus Platz Stephan von Semski, there was no question of anything like the smooth hollowing-out and shaping (one would almost prefer to say eroding and washing-out) of Asta's personality later. The temperature at that moment dropped almost below zero out of alarm.

So Herr Schmeller hauled off, whereupon something happened in the same split second that was like a mechanism catching, a bar dropping into place from an iron hinge, a motion so accurate and minimal, restricted to absolute essentials with such precision, that it had almost nothing of a human element left, because it was devoid of any illustrative stance or gesture: Semski was silently holding Ingrid's father tight by his upper arms, and with such strength that there ensued only a very slight straining of the older gentleman's upper body and then a complete freezing into rigidity of the two men's positions. Semski opened his mouth and spoke with a very subdued voice directly into Herr Schmeller's face. Asta kept her eyes trained on his moving lips, which was perhaps the only way she was able to understand the words he was saying. "Please calm yourself now and don't make this unfortunate situation any worse. I'm leaving the house at once." With that he released the older man. "Leave the house at once!" Schmeller managed to bring out; for the moment he obviously couldn't think of anything better than to repeat Semski's words, thereby transforming into an order what the other man had just stated as his intention. Semski's face, pale and Slavic-farmer-like, was completely immobile. He kept staring at Schmeller for another few seconds, and then he gave a brisk little bow and started walking back down the stairs just as slowly as he'd been going before.

Asta knew what was essential now, and that was not to be heard. So she knelt down, took hold of her shoes, and slipped them off (remaining collected and concentrated throughout) while holding them tight. Luck decidedly favored her during this maneuver, for the dance music in the grounds out back, which had been silent all this time, now started again with the prelude to the "Kaiser Waltz," in which there are brass parts as well. Schmeller, alone now, was standing motionless on the half-staircase above the empty, brightly lit hall, into which the waves of sound came flooding from the grounds. Asta vanished down the paneled corridor, making absolutely no sound, and she found the small wrought-iron spiral staircase, but now she came to a stop and looked straight down from there into the cloakroom. Semski went in, took a small ivory disc and a silver coin out of his trouser pocket, and the girl handed him his hat, cane, and gloves. Then he went out through the glass door of the entrance hall, which was standing wide open, into the deserted front part of the garden, and toward the iron gateway leading to the street. Soon afterward came the humming of an automobile driving off.

Asta listened for noises behind her. Not a footstep could be heard.

After standing there quietly for a while longer, she went downstairs, asked the maid for some cologne, and revived herself in the ladies' room.

While Asta was walking through the empty hallway back toward the grounds, she was thinking of Melzer. He was the person she was hoping to find now, not Ingrid or Etelka, say. Here, however, is where we must insert a note to the effect that it would have been pointless by this time to seek out Etelka Stangeler, even though just forty-five minutes before she'd been very visibly standing at the edge of the dance area, talking with Frau Schmeller. But by now she was sitting with three gentlemen and another young lady in the same wine tavern we earlier came to know through Government Councillor Guys; by the way, a drive out to the Cobenzl with him (in an open fiacre, which she loved) had already been arranged for the following afternoon. Etelka made good use of her days in Vienna, and everything was falling neatly into place, the production once more flowing smoothly and brilliantly, so to speak. When Grauermann saw Frau Schmeller and Etelka standing together while he was dancing, he went up and, apologizing to both his hostess and his fiancée at once, asked if he could go home (he was staying at the academy, whose rooms were available to the students under certain conditions even during summer vacation, except for the two-week general cleaning of the whole building in July). He'd been suffering all evening from an unbearable headache, Grauermann confided to his hostess (and what he said was true, at that; one look at him was enough to show that something was wrong). Etelka stated that she'd quite naturally be leaving now too; first they'd ride to the academy, and then she could make her own way home alone in the car. But

Frau Schmeller voiced very kind and cordial opposition to that idea and asked Grauermann to let Etelka stay there with her a while longer, to which he consented on condition that someone be found to see her home. "Of course we will; that should work out very easily!" were the assuring words of Frau Schmeller, who was happy to see Etelka Stangeler, because she was one of "those young girls it's so entertaining to have around," one of those "who bring a little bit of life with them" (which seemed a commodity very much needed in this house, for its wealth was too new yet and its owners didn't know how to be buoyant with it). Besides, Etelka was engaged and hence neutralized as possible competition for her own daughter. Grauermann left, then, and with no big fuss and farewell, since he didn't want to disturb the party; so now the momentary separation of the engaged couple had been given the stamp of authorization by the hostess. Half an hour later, the wine-tavern scheme was more than a dream.

Asta looked for Melzer in the grounds and soon found him; he had been standing somewhat off to the side by himself, and he came walking up to her across the lawn. She immediately told him what had taken place. Heat lightning flashed across the sky; this time it was really vivid. Afterward the starry sky could once again be seen, in its total clarity, all the way out to the edges of the heavy clouds in the northwest. Everyone stood and watched. Nobody was worried about rain, since they were all longing for the humidity to drop. They could easily move into the hall and have the music there, after all. But it wasn't until long past midnight that a brief downpour came.

This was the point around which Asta's distressing memories of the evening before now kept on circling, over and over; she would reach the end every time Melzer appeared, but then it would start all over again from the beginning, with her standing guard upstairs in the paneled corridor by the head of the large front staircase.

"What happened to your cacti?" Ingrid asked again.

Well, what *did* happen to the cacti? Asta could only feel that much more dismayed when she heard Ingrid repeat such an asinine question, which was out of context anyway. Once more she could see the thick, juicy green stain that had been up there on the wallpaper, nearly brand-new, over the white bookcase the previous winter, with little globs adhering to it from the plants (so funny and cute before they all got mashed and smashed) that had once been lined up in a row on the top shelf, each an outlandish and convoluted personality in its own right, each with a totally inscrutable life story full of surprises: one of them, for instance, unexpectedly stretched a little arm sideways, and a long sprout shot out from it; one of its neighbors, as pudgy and stubby as a toadstool, seemed to have arrived at a decision, made in the silent watches, purely and simply to grow twice as fat; at the end of the row, however, there dreamed one less hedonistic in mind and heart—a single blue blossom was all its endeavor, a flower to open like a soulful eye in this arid, prickly company. So, indeed, what happened to the cacti? Smashed up against the wall, one after another, bursting, splattering, the splattering mush mixing with the brown-red shards of the tiny flower pots. Yes—Etelka. We know how she could suddenly have an outburst about one thing or another, as for example when anyone stood out for some attainment that couldn't be played down—in Latin, let's say, or anything else. Still, accomplishment in Latin was strictly peripheral to her sphere of interest. In the case at hand, however, the subject had been a new evening dress that Asta was treated to, and the gift had led to a volcanic eruption of commensurate force from the central crater of Etelka's fury. After it was all over and they'd taken care of the most essential picking up and cleaning, they had to hang a picture over the spot and to try to get hold of the paperhanger on the sly as fast as they could, for Herr Stangeler took notice of any change, especially when he was having one of those days when he would stride through all the rooms with brisk footsteps and an occasional twitch of his squared-back shoulders. As René once put it, his father would not seldom walk through three different doors at the same time, into whatever room one happened to be in. This little *mot* was carried back to the father, and it tickled him immensely; indeed, he gave utterly unconcealed expression to his delight.

Afterward, of course, Etelka swore up and down that she would buy some new cacti for Asta, much prettier than the old ones. But she never quite got around to it. As it was, Asta—who had at first been expecting the promise to be kept—didn't want any more cacti. Perhaps she didn't have the nerve to acquire a new little row on her own; that might have provoked Etelka all over again. And so the top shelf of the white bookcase was empty for a while, but as time went on the space was taken up by other small objects, which incidentally revealed certain traits in common with cacti (but wasn't that more or less how it was with everything that gave Asta pleasure?), for up there came to perch now all sorts of especially repulsive little animals made of glass or porcelain.

Asta didn't bother in the least, incidentally, to answer Ingrid's question concerning the cacti. She had long before made the observation (with wonderment and amazement) that there are people who ask and even repeat a question only to cut right in on the person starting to answer it by talking about something entirely different. Ingrid, as she stood there in front of the bookcase, suddenly looked to Asta like a soggy dinner roll. Hoping to some extent that she could confront a kind of absentminded stubbornness that paradoxically enough is demonstrated at times by soggy rolls, Asta now spoke up in turn with a question unrelated to Ingrid's.

"Did Pastré do or say something? Your father wouldn't have been able to hear you scream, would he?"

"No," said Ingrid, her eyes still red from crying and her expression dull, as if the last of her hopes were sinking fast precisely because of an insignificant detail like that, "she went to get him; he told me so himself. 'I have an eyewitness,' he said, 'your friend Editha Pastré. So don't bother trying to tell me any lies.' That was why he went after Stephan right there on the stairs. He didn't hear me when I screamed. It so happened he was in the smoking room off the hall, by himself, to look for a few packs of cigarettes or something. The door into the hall was open. That bitch Pastré saw him when she came sneaking up behind me. Stephan didn't come up till a bit later. She hid somewhere and watched him go past her. She saw you, too, standing by the top of the steps, which is why she came up the spiral staircase in the back. I found all this out directly from Daddy. He came to my room at eight o'clock this morning and started ranting and raving; I wasn't even up yet. I'm totally done in." She dropped into a small white wicker easy chair. She looked as if she'd lost all her bones.

"Did you and Semski make arrangements in advance for the rendezvous in the bathroom?" asked Asta. She had to have known, really, but she couldn't think of anything else to say.

"Yes," Ingrid answered.

"I never would have believed Semski could do anything so stupid. He knew full well that Pastré was always after him."

They still often fell into a habit they had formed in school of calling one another by their last names, as they'd done not very long before in the lyceum—"Schmeller," "Stangeler," "Pastré."

"Why didn't you just turn Semski down? The two of you could have met alone, somewhere farther off in the grounds. During the fireworks, for instance."

Ingrid was silent at first. "Well, that was what I wanted," she then said softly.

"All right, now tell me—what did Pastré actually see?"

"What do you mean? Nothing. We were kissing. He put the nicest little medal around my neck, an icon of the Blessed Mother, an old piece of jewelry from his family."

"It's quite a juicy scandal," said Asta (and the next words were spoken somewhat severely out of consideration for the sadness of the situation), "but still you two don't have a single thing to show for it! So now what?"

"What time is it?" Ingrid asked, suddenly waking up and coming out of her molten state all braced for action. "Quarter to three? Stephan's at the ministry till four."

She'd run off shortly after lunch, while coffee was being served, despite her father's having forbidden her to leave the house and garden. That same evening she was supposed to take a ride in the car, with her mother and her two younger sisters, out to Fischau on the Schneeberg, where the family owned a large country house, and spend some time there. Herr Schmeller had been called to the telephone, and while her mother and sisters were unwrapping and taking a good look at some of this summer's new photographs, which were developed and had just been delivered from town this minute, Ingrid whisked herself away, just as she was, with no hat or gloves, moving through the grounds to a spot she knew very well, where she could slip behind the shrubbery and get out to the open road; here it led along and past the neighboring vineyards. Sitting now in the little white wicker chair in Asta's tiny little room—where it smelled cool with a pervasive odor of camphor, which at the height of summer wafts through the empty apartments of the city, now turned completely inward, and of Asta's favorite perfume, Bois des Îles—just now, after her agitated question about what time it was, there came floating before Ingrid's inner eye this bush-filled and shrub-filled depth of the grounds, with the narrow, twining short path to the hole in the fence; the powerful heat of the sun; the quietness; the dome-like top of the vine-covered hill before the haze of the sky; and off to the left, below, lightly flung there like dice, the houses encroaching from the city; closer yet, some white villas, the gray-green foam of the treetops among them—all of it held in place through the noonday heat, a tumult under control. This little path was a piece of Ingrid's childhood, then, as later, seldom followed, the border of her world, and sought out now only because she was once again genuinely lost and pushed hard up against that border. She felt pain, a pain with no signpost or directional marker, simply pain and nothing else.

After she left the park, Ingrid made her way via a few detours out to Grinzinger Allee, in just the summer dress she had on, with no purse and no money. An empty taxicab was driving slowly past with its windows open. She hailed it and drove to Asta's house, where she was welcomed by the chambermaid Lina, who'd been sent along to Vienna from the country with the young people and who now paid her taxi fare.

Asta now had the feeling that Ingrid's abrupt falling into abstraction, her sudden subsiding into muteness and silence after the excited way she'd asked about the time, was a symptom pointing to some sort of unchecked and haphazard state of witlessness, some abeyance of the mental faculties. That was what made her take charge now.

"If you can't call Semski at the ministry, as you say, because old Pavlovski is the one who answers the phone and he's in cahoots with your father, meaning he probably knows the whole story by now—which mustn't be very pleasant for Semski!—then we need to find a man, somebody who knows Semski well, who can call and tell him where and when to meet you. Why didn't you quickly plan something right after the calamity with Pastré? You had to realize that a scandal would come of it."

"I don't know...I was so confused. All he kept saying was, 'I absolutely must see you tomorrow, I have to see you, no matter what the cost, do you hear, I have to see you tomorrow, your father's going to drag you away from Vienna, and I have to see you before he does.'"

"Very simple," said Asta. "We'll take a ride over to the Consular Academy right now. Somebody's bound to be there. Pista may be at home now on account of the heat, or maybe Honnegger. He's in Vienna now and staying there. Don't worry; they'll take care of everything with Semski. Let's go. Just take one of my hats and a pair of gloves, and I'll lend you a purse with some money in it. I'm going to the phone now and calling the academy. Why don't you go on into the bathroom in the meantime, sit down at the dressing table, and tidy yourself up? You look like you've been through the mill."

Just as Asta was getting ready to climb the three steps to the breakfast room to go into the front room, where the telephone was, footsteps could be heard next door, in the living room of the Quartier Latin.

"Etelka?" asked Ingrid in an undertone, looking at Asta. "Yes," Asta said softly. "We won't see anything of her. She's busy every minute." They listened. The footsteps went back and forth, and then into the small bathroom of the Quartier Latin, back again through the front room and the living room; after a few minutes Etelka left the apartment, and they could hear one of the house doors outside as it clicked shut.

"She's going out the back way," Asta said; "seems she's in a hurry. Well, we are, too. It's after three. So finish getting ready." With that, she hopped up the steps.

The telephone rang just as Asta was walking up to it in the front room. Melzer. Was she well? He was glad she'd just happened to be coming to the telephone anyway. Where was he? In a café right around the corner. He'd slept a long time and eaten later than usual. Come right up? Why, of course, he'd love to. They were going where? Well, he'd go with the ladies and keep them company. In five minutes.

Grauermann had gone out, but Honnegger was in. "We'll be there in twenty minutes, Ingrid and I. A Lieutenant Melzer will be with us, too. Do you know him? Oh, you do? All right, from the Café Pucher. Good. We'll be there soon."

Ingrid wasn't quite done with the finishing touches when the maid knocked on the door to the breakfast room. Melzer had arrived. Asta had her ask him to wait for just a short while in the next room. At the same time it occurred to her that this whole business with calling the ministry could have been taken care of by René, after all, not to say right here and now by Melzer—except that Melzer and Semski didn't know one another quite that well. She asked Lina about her brother. He wasn't at home, was the answer. All right, then. The two young ladies now quickly bustled back and forth in the small apartment, through the living room—which rested behind green venetian blinds now closed tight and was suffused with the light odor of camphor from armchairs now covered over; only the piano was free, reflecting like a mirror, deeply plunged into the interior of its black-glistening, furniture-like silence. Asta and Ingrid went scurrying hither and yon through the living room and the front room, into the bathroom and back again; a small hat, a pair of gloves, a purse, and a handkerchief were picked out, atomizers with rubber bulbs were squeezed (although Ingrid didn't spray herself with Bois des Îles, which wouldn't have been the right scent for her, even though, now refreshed, the roll did look as if it were somehow regaining crispness), and soon they were ready, fifteen minutes all told, after Asta's miniature phonorama. Meanwhile the maid had gone to call a taxi. They climbed the three stairs, stepped into the room, and greeted Lieutenant Melzer, who now rose from a rocking chair, the very image of stylish grooming and mannerliness, in a very handsome light gray summer suit (he'd worn white at the garden party); in his left hand he was holding a bamboo walking stick with a golden knob, along with a pair of gloves and one of those stiff straw hats, so much in vogue back then, named for the actor Girardi.

Lina came and announced that the taxi was waiting.

"Out front or by eleven?" Asta asked.

"By eleven," the maid said, and smiled. "I only came in the front way because I didn't want to disturb the ladies." Stamped with the greatest of clarity on her face were the signs of total goodness and kindness toward all; they stood out against the more somber background, as we might put it, of a devoutness that could be discerned in her face immediately. It was almost frightening to imagine that a person like that could go through the world so transparent and un-armed—and could yet remain unharmed. But since that was precisely the case, it necessarily had to seem as if this good creature were sur-rounded by some higher protection.

She smiled, this Karoline Nohel (called "the Weasel" because of her quickly tapping footsteps), who at that time, by the way, was number-ing her years in the neighborhood of thirty-five; she smiled because Asta had said "by eleven." In those days a lady would never have put it that way, but would have said it differently somehow—"by house number eleven," maybe, or "in the rear." To say "by eleven," on the other hand, would have been to resort to an expression with something of a technical feel to it, a term used by a concierge, for instance, or a zoning official. Asta had recourse to it with great relish and enjoyment, a relish perhaps akin to the one she harbored for cacti and hideous-looking animals made of porcelain.

"Thanks very much, dear Weasel," said Asta and patted her arm, whereupon Lina turned somewhat red and walked away with quick little steps.

"Maybe I shouldn't have had my taxi pull up to your front door," said Ingrid, suddenly dismayed to a degree out of proportion to the cause. "But, you know, I don't know my way around here so well, what the street number is, or what floor you're on. Come to think of it, I've never entered this house by the rear." "It doesn't make one bit of dif-ference," Asta answered her, with a smile. "But since we're on the subject, nobody except my uncle is ever up on the fourth floor now that it's the height of summer. If he'd happened to be just getting in from Stiebitz's" (a renowned tavern this architect and professor loved frequenting) "he might have seen double or triple of you and, at the worst, told people about a whole crowd of girls driving up in a taxicab, apparently friends of Asta and Etelka."

Melzer laughed. "There's no such thing as what you're saying about seeing double," he said.

"We'd better be going," cried Asta, "or it'll be three thirty before we get out the front door."

So back down the three steps they went. This was a whole new and different route for Melzer to be leaving the Stangeler house; to him it seemed somehow delightful and stimulating. He stood still for a moment in Etelka's and Asta's small, darkened, aquarium-green living room—he'd of course never set foot in the young ladies' quarters before—and voiced his enchantment with such a "romantic" atmosphere. They went through the front room, which always had the cool smell of dust left to settle for a long time, and went out onto the other staircase, the one not inside their family dwelling. Asta checked once again whether she had her key (her head always stayed above the inner tube or frilled collar) and then closed the apartment door behind them.

"There must have been rain somewhere," Melzer said as they stepped up to the open car, more expressing a hope than stating a fact. The heat seemed to have let up a little, but the sidewalks were dry and the sky was blue. A faint breath of air was blowing lightly along the street. This air, along with the breeze that came from the movement of the taxi, had an invigorating effect on the three young people. They rode toward the Ring and through the center of town, whose shadowy old streets seemed to breathe out coolness, past the cathedral, along the length of Schotten Gasse, and beyond, going faster now.

Inside the academy, they went into the small reception room with the Empire furniture. An utterly penetrating silence reigned there, one that seemed to stifle conversation. Now there came resounding into it from the next room—no, not the prelude, but the slow movement of the sonata in F-sharp minor by Schumann, the "Air," as it is called, intimately connected to the prelude by the bell tones in the left hand, falling in sonorous cascades, above which the theme soars high aloft like a lark.

Honnegger really had practiced the piece to perfection. Asta looked at her watch and quietly stopped the servant who'd shown them in and was just now at the door, about to withdraw so as to announce their arrival. "Isn't that Herr von Honnegger in the next room?" she asked. "Yes, madam," answered the clean-shaven footman, whose age would have been impossible to guess, speaking in a voice as subdued as Asta's, and smiling with understanding (could it be that he loved music too?). "Please don't break in on Herr von Honnegger; no need to let him know we're here until the piece is finished; it isn't long," Asta said. "Very well, madam." He vanished.

They took seats in the armchairs, Ingrid facing out to the garden. "Isn't that just great!" Melzer whispered to Asta. She nodded and then noticed that Ingrid's eyes were swimming a little in tears. Oddly enough, that disgusted her. She looked away, likewise out into the greenery, and let the music penetrate deep into her; along with it there penetrated a picture of the way the man playing there in the next room must live. Honnegger had only laughed when they all kept insisting he had to go to the garden party. Now he was sitting at a piano here in Vienna on this summer afternoon, which seemed to be waiting to pour out a cornucopia of seclusion over anyone who wanted it and was capable of accepting such a gift. Summer encompasses it more than any other season, after all.

The movement is over soon, Teddy enters, and it's twenty to four at that point. After an exchange of greetings, Asta is the one who forestalls long explanations and unnecessary back-and-forth by drawing a tight circle around the matter with a single twirl of the compass, as it were. "Herr Schmeller caught Ingrid and Semski in an embarrassing situation at the garden party yesterday. So now there's a scandal. Ingrid was placed under house arrest, but she ran away. She's supposed to go out to Fischau tonight but she promised Stephan she would definitely see him beforehand. She can't call the ministry, because Pavlovski would blab. Semski's at Ballhaus Platz till four. Would you please call him and arrange with him to come somewhere close to here, right after four?"

"It's done," said Honnegger, who asked for the executive committee office in "foreign," and said into the telephone, "This is Teddy von Honnegger. And good afternoon to you, too, sir. Yes, thanks, my father's well. My parents are in Pörtschach, staying with the Lauters. Could I speak with Semski? Thank you very much, I appreciate it." Then, "Hello! It's Teddy. Can you get away at four on the dot? You can? Be at the upper end of the new Strudlhof Steps at exactly ten after four—you know where I mean?—well, good. Ten after four. Order a taxi right now, so you'll be sure to be on time. Bye."

So that was taken care of. It wasn't quite ten minutes to four. The young people stayed sitting together. "How are things down in Bosnia?" Honnegger turned to Melzer. "The heat must be dreadful about now.

When do you have to leave?" "In a week. But at the beginning of August, while I was still here, they even had rain, which is pretty rare, and it was actually cold." "I would love to have seen your bearskin from last summer. Where are you keeping it, anyway? Down there?" "Oh, no, you can't leave something like that down there because of all the moths and bugs. I had it sent to Vienna right away to be treated and preserved and then it went straight to the furrier's. They still have it in storage. My mother doesn't want it because it's too much work for the maids."

Asta felt Ingrid directing a glance her way; she looked over and was startled to see a kind of pleading expression in Ingrid's water-blue eyes. At the same time she signaled Asta. While the two young gentlemen went on with their conversation, Ingrid and Asta went over to the window niche. "Let's set our watches to the exact same time. Please." Asta, somewhat surprised, raised her left hand; their two small gold watches showed the identical time, reading just a few minutes to four. "Asta, I'm asking you to come to the upper end of the Strudlhof Steps by twenty-five after four at the latest. This meeting mustn't go on for longer than fifteen minutes. Stephan gets upset so easily. It would be better if you came even earlier. I promised him I'd see him one more time, and I'm keeping my promise; you're my witness. But you have to come to my rescue, do you understand? I can't stand long goodbyes like this; they're unbearable. Please be on time. Please. Do you promise?"

For a brief moment, it felt as if even the collar or inner tube might not keep Asta's head above water. Four words, only four, went through her head, but they fell like drumbeats with equal rests in between: "She—doesn't—love—him." In the background, hovering over those last few days out in the country, there now flashed a faint light on what could well have been a basic misjudgment all along.

Then she braced herself for a decision she needed to make deep inside, which was to accept this girl's nature as being entirely different from and alien to her own; for the time being, that decision suppressed any criticism (even if it really was for the moment only—to us, this attainment of a new attitude by Asta rates as an achievement quite deserving of respect anyway; it may be that the reader is of a somewhat different opinion, and there would undoubtedly be good reasons why that should be so). She said, "Yes, I promise. You can be totally certain."

Just at this moment, during the second or two it took her to utter these few words, and awkwardly, too, there opened up inside her a simple but incontrovertible insight; it was now blindingly apparent that Ingrid had fully reconciled herself to parting from Stephan forever (at which Asta had to shudder, acting as a surrogate for her friend, so to speak); that none of it was going to hold firm now because Ingrid was refusing to take the ultimate step; and that not the slightest bit of hope was being projected forward into a future that was imaginable, not to say downright feasible, even now.

And as though from a bolt of dim lightning, or only from the distant reflection of one, a light now went on inside her to show the deep-rooted, solid basis of the tacit understanding that will always be found to exist between children of this kind and the parents they take after so exactly below the surface, when all is said and done; she felt as well how threatened, how isolated all people are in their own families. A fiercely empathetic emotion now flew from her to Etelka, to René—wherever they were. What did it matter if right now they were traipsing as free as air through the whole city with its ready and slowly garnered summertime reserves of seclusion? They must surely be caught in some kind of entanglement all the same, just as she was herself.

Now it was time to go.

They said goodbye to Honnegger. Asta noticed—as she walked out into the foyer and started down the first steps of the broad staircase—that he turned back to the music room. When she was leaving the building she heard the first powerful chord struck on the piano.

Ingrid had to turn left not far from the gate. "Don't forget, Asta," she said softly but urgently one more time and slowly went along Strudlhof Gasse toward the steps.

Herr Schmeller was an engineer and a Vienna boy from the neighborhoods.

Those two statements contain pretty much everything there is to say in detail about this not very interesting individual—no small measure of quick-witted, city-streets cunning, plus a certain brutality that was quiet, so to speak, and turned inward, rapidly traveling along its crossings on the inside (οἱ τρόποι, pronounced *hoi trópoi*, as the ancient Greeks called them, turning points or pivotal spots; this term had the same meaning for them as our word *character* has for us) and therefore virtually unstoppable on the outside. At a minimum his elbows would start rising the minute he felt the slightest attempt to hold him back.

So Frau Schmeller had long since given up, or rather had never really tried in the first place. She was one of those runny little blobs of devotedness, the kind men of her husband's kind leave on their plates as the remains of the woman they once chose and courted, a thick gravy now separating, with a few little leftover lumps of a character brought to ruin long before, and now, unfairly enough, that outcome being the very feature in that kind of woman that is quickest to cause offense, simply because these places that are still relatively solid have come to present themselves as something totally pointless and random, with no context.

So it never even dawned on Frau Schmeller to try in this instance— to curb her husband or keep him in check, that is. When he came back into the dining room from his telephone call—here, too, in this spacious room with its furnishings that were so old and valuable and yet unharmonized and untempered, if one will, simply set out on display next to one another, a cool twilight prevailed, closing out the noontime heat of the day—when Herr Schmeller came back in, he at once asked where Ingrid was. They went to find her; she couldn't have gone very far. Her father didn't wait for them to finish looking, though. He drank the rest of his coffee standing up, lit a cigarette, and said not a word as he went out and snatched a hat off the hook in the entry room without stopping. He rousted the chauffeur in short order out of a midday break (the man knew his employer and could tell by the way the wind was now blowing that he'd better get a very quick move on), and three minutes later the heavy car went zooming out toward Grinzinger Allee. In this semirural afternoon calmness, the vehicle alone was enough to make it seem as though some exceptional event were taking its course.

Stop. Scouting left and right. Ahead, a taxi, an old-fashioned closed limousine, drove past in the direction of the city, and at a very leisurely pace, meaning it was probably empty. "Follow that man and catch up to him!" Schmeller called to his chauffeur. The man stepped on the gas, covered the two hundred meters in a few seconds, and pulled up alongside the cab. Stop. Schmeller got in and sent his own car home. "This is for you," he said to the taxi driver, as he handed him thirty crowns, "so listen to what I'm telling you. We're following my daughter; she'll be along pretty soon. That little girl's not doing right. I may have to get out very fast if she makes a move to vanish. But you have your money no matter what. Just pull over by the side of the road now, and let's wait. When I show you the car she's in, be sure you take a good look, and then follow it. All right?"

The unusually generous amount offered as fare, given the ordinary rates in those days; the self-confident way the gentleman spoke with the same Viennese accent as the driver; the frank and plausible explanation; and above all the affinity that sprang up instantly between the two men, as between children who are basically on the same level in spite of differences—all this taken together was more than sufficient to lull into slumber any intuitive feelings of suspicion that might suggest reporting the situation to the police or any impulse to notify officials, such as has animated every petty little functionary who exercises one jot of authority—cabdriver, concierge, or railroad conductor—in Vienna since the days of Herr von Sedlnitzky.

"Thanks very much, sir," said the driver. "We'll wait right here."

As we can readily imagine, they didn't have to wait long.

Traffic wasn't very heavy around this hour, as it would be at, say, six in the evening, and so it wasn't very difficult even in the center of town to follow the cab Ingrid was riding in while keeping a proper distance; checking that they didn't get too close, Old Man Schmeller (he was acting the old man to the hilt, so that's what we'll call him, *mais il ne frisait même pas les cinquantes*) kept turning this way and that, leaning forward from the edge of the back seat in the ungainly old car bumping and lurching so roughly, his hat pushed to the back of his head, and his hands on his knees. I would like to say a little more about the nape of this man's neck ... Herr von Geyrenhoff, later a sectional councillor, whose acquaintance we made out in the country, at the

Stangelers', had a nephew, a certain Kurt Körger, who was still practi-cally a child in those days, very attractive and extremely talented. And in time this child would develop a nape very much like Schmeller's. This area of the body has about it something strongly suggestive of high-impact striking power; its shaved smoothness reminds one of a knee, whose function is not unrelated to the elbow of recent mention. Yes, these Schmellers and Körgers of every generation and social class are a remarkable breed, one whose members take good care at all times and in all places to make sure they are noticed. Sometimes that does not happen, however, until they've turned their back on a person (which they're good at doing), and then one realizes on seeing the nape of the neck who it really is that one is dealing with—oh, yes, so it's like *that,* is it! Then of course one makes up one's mind as of that split second never again to give anyone belonging to this clan even the tiniest bit of leeway and to rap the knuckles (every one of them has fingers that tend to be sausage-shaped) of the offender here and now, whereas normally one would be quick to extend one's hand in a friendly greet-ing. But this is where the clever knack, the trick, the jape of these napesters comes in: you never see their real face until they've turned away—not on a first meeting, anyway—until it's too late, when it's all over. They wear their face on the back of their heads. It's usually stretched tight, because the round head is lowered. Now, it's true that Herr von Stangeler often walked around with his head lowered like a bull's, as if preparing to charge. And yet he didn't have the kind of nape we're talking about here.

Now Ingrid's cab stopped in front of that gloomy-looking house belonging to the Stangelers.

Herr Schmeller asked the driver to keep on going, but slowly, along the wide street (it wasn't exactly a surprise to him that the taxi would come here, because Editha hadn't missed her chance to mention right after the fact that Asta had been standing guard at the top of the stairs). After his taxi turned around and came back, he saw a chambermaid standing by the other taxi and paying the driver. Schmeller now had his old-fashioned vehicle stop diagonally across from the house on the corner ("eleven") in such a way that he could see into the cross street and keep the entrance to the Stangeler house in his sights. It was the first house door on the left, because "eleven" had its entrance leading in from the boulevard.

The driver had gotten out of the car and was smoking a cigarette as he walked back and forth on the sidewalk.

This was the start of a kind of trial by ordeal, the ordeal being heat.

Luckily they were parked in the shade on that side of the street.

Inspector Schmeller got out of the car, too, but he stayed behind it.

The ordeal became more bearable. Had there been some rainfall somewhere? A breeze picked up along the street, weak but steady as it fanned them.

An open fiacre pulled up in the wide street, outside the house diagonally across, but soon drove off again. Schmeller followed it for a moment with his eyes. In it was now sitting a lady in white.

So there he stood, the napester, wondering why Herr von Stangeler, whose financial circumstances he was of course roughly familiar with, would choose to live in such a wretched section of the city. The building might be worth something if it were turned into all rental units, even though it hadn't really been built for that purpose. Or maybe if he just sold it. He calculated the value. The location was good, because the house was close to the city center. (What he didn't know was that the place had a second owner.) Now he remembered that two of those large new villas in the Kaasgraben area had had to be sold the year before, and that the name Stangeler had been mentioned as a possible buyer during the negotiations. Unbelievable. The man would have been able to pay cold cash, right out of his pocket, for a beautiful house in Döbling or Hietzing right after the Alpine rail system in Carinthia was completed. With lots of land. Some people just don't know how to live. The Stangelers didn't own either a carriage or an automobile. And he for one would have arranged better marriages for the two eldest daughters as well. If there are people who don't suit you, why you simply heave them out the door. He brought his reflections to a close with that thought and peevishly turned his glance away. He let it range up and down the street now, over housefronts, sidewalks, women, carts and carriages, children, store and business signs—relaxed yet sharp, casual yet searching and weighing, cold yet interested, the way an expert looks things over, especially at everything pertaining to people, whom he knew the way the butcher knows the calf. An expert on people.

He noticed a young man in a light gray suit and a Girardi, who now turned onto the side street, walked up to the front door, and presently vanished inside.

Well, of course the one family isn't going to occupy the whole house by itself, thought Schmeller—not even close to singling out Melzer in his memory from the swarms of young gentlemen in his house—it's too big. The upstairs is probably rented out.

He took out his cigar case, began smoking, and looked up and down the wide street. But now the front door at the Stangelers' was opening again.

Schmeller wanted to hurry and get back into the car at once, so he looked around for the driver, who had already climbed back in behind the wheel. It was only the chambermaid, though, the same person who'd paid Ingrid's cab fare. She walked across the street quickly, with rapid little footsteps, toward a taxi stand that could be seen farther down by the curve in the line the street made. From there she came right back, sitting in a cab. Now Schmeller really did get back into his own, and quickly too. The cab with the maid in it didn't follow the curve into the smaller street, however, but stopped in front of the house door diagonally opposite.

The building surveyor was very close to becoming enraged at this point. It didn't quite reach that point, which is fortunate, because otherwise we would have to tell the reader what exactly it was that he became enraged about and what was at the bottom of stirring up his quiet, inward-turned brutality. It would hardly be possible to make it clear. He didn't go into a rage, anyway, all the less as the woman made no move to go into that house but instead had the cab wait where it was parked and then walked back along the sidewalk and around the corner to where she'd come out. Schmeller, whose attention was keyed up to strike, found a satisfactory explanation for this sequence of actions; for whatever reason, somebody obviously wanted to be seen walking away from the house on foot and then get into a taxi unobserved—perhaps the Stangeler children were forbidden to use cabs because of some foolish notions about thrift. While deliberating like this, Herr Schmeller was keeping a sharp eye on the front door and the empty cab across the street. "Yes, indeed, with these people anything's possible," he thought.

And indeed it was—including that some of "these people" could come out of a different house from the one they'd entered not long before.

Just for a moment, he was completely at a loss, and then he really did become enraged; it's easy to understand why.

Then they were off and running.

Meanwhile, all the pieces of the puzzle were now jumbled up again in Schmeller's mind, and he couldn't so much as venture a guess as to where this second journey was taking them. Even when the three young people got out in front of the Consular Academy, he wasn't able to fit the school into his calculations right away, plain though it was that this institution had to have some connection with the Foreign Ministry. He told his driver to keep on going at the same speed and to turn around much farther down the street and come back. Then he asked the driver to park on the corner of Strudlhof Gasse, but on the other side of Waisenhaus Gasse, right by the university buildings, so that he could keep the Consular Academy and its entrance in his line of vision. Opposite where he was parked Strudlhof Gasse continued in the direction of the stairs.

Sitting there in his crate-shaped vehicle, Schmeller had to wait through almost the entire second movement of the F-sharp minor sonata by Robert Schumann (we won't begrudge him that), if not hear it, luckily for him; it was about a half hour in toto, at any rate, before the three emerged again, and Ingrid—after Asta Stangeler had gone off to the right with the young man in the Girardi—slowly turned the opposite way, onto Strudlhof Gasse, toward the steps.

Schmeller sat far back in his seat. Several thoughts went through his head. Although he had just been in the grip of an impulse to call out to Ingrid and order her into the cab as she was turning the corner over there, he now decided to wait and not to barge in the second the Polack (as he'd been calling Semski since the day before) showed up for this rendezvous, which it had finally become clear to him was about to ensue. In fact, he'd regained his composure so much by now that he was willing to observe the proceedings himself, if that were possible (who knows what all was being stirred up in him besides curiosity), and to step in only if the Polack tried to take the girl away with him. He was free, after all, just to pop up out of nowhere and put a stop to this whole absurd charade any time he chose. But first he wanted to see what would happen and especially what line Ingrid was going to take.

She was now standing all the way at the end of the street, under the full green trees by the top of the steps.

So all right for now—if she started down them, there would be time enough to get out of the taxi quickly and follow her.

But she didn't. She remained standing at the top of the Strudlhof Steps.

Grauermann's headache during the Schmellers' garden party wasn't, as we indicated earlier, just some made-up excuse to leave; far from that, it was, sad to say, a real and a sudden affliction, very unusual for him. By the following morning he was already free of it again.

What remained behind in him, however—as we see it, that is, for he might not have thought about it the same way—was a kind of yield from the unpleasantness he'd withstood; even though on waking up he wasn't exactly vivacious, he could sense in himself, as a background which was then to dominate this whole day, a new air of something capacious, an elucidating emptiness. Pista's whole mood had about it something of an alarm signal, never becoming audible but silently passing through his body from organ to organ. The abrupt manifestation and subsequent sudden vanishing of an acute disturbance in his physical condition, at all other times healthy to the point of complete unawareness, now left behind two traces like a faint echo—the alarm itself and with it some new realization that the occurrence of such unexpected episodes was possible, be they from inside one's body or from outside, but in either case coming from life, that great unknown so difficult to grasp.

The hour was early. He hadn't slept long. After shaving and taking a bath, and with a hunger he could really feel, he made an effort to escape his own company (every weakness attempts to run from itself, not caring at first what form the escape may take, and we wouldn't feel much credit reflecting on ourselves if we could always see with complete clarity what the company that comes calling as a result has brought along to our doorstep). Perhaps he could have breakfast in the garden with Teddy? But just as he reached the door of Honnegger's room, he heard one of the exercises from Czerny's *School of Velocity* being struck up on the piano downstairs. Teddy didn't like to be disturbed when playing, so Grauermann had breakfast alone and gained some insights while eating into the state and condition of matters as they stood with his own self, thanks to some vistas newly opened inside him (for moments at a time it was as though he needed to step back away from a cave-like space that had been thrown open so that he could make out one by one, and in more detail, all the items inside it). And with that came the first realization of this memorable—for us, that is, but, sad to say, not for Pista Grauermann—day (otherwise he might have drawn a few lasting inferences). "Music," he told himself, "seems to play a negative role in my life; it carries a negative charge for me, so to speak." Now this was a random mental leap, of course, but it was a true and bona fide leap all the same. People who are so quick to complain about such leaps are often the very ones unable or unwilling to take mental steps of any kind (no, they never climb any "gradus ad Parnassum"—I just now thought of saying it that way because Teddy von Honnegger is being so meticulous about executing his sixteenth notes)—no, they don't step with any thought at all into the mishmash of their interior selves, nor do they step with any thought at all into the outside world, either. They just stay sitting where they are.

Grauermann stayed sitting, too, first physically and then pretty soon mentally as well.

It was still relatively cool. The tall treetops behind him in the garden were standing out round and pale before the summer sky, far distant and clear as lacquer. While he ate with a good appetite and started to feel more awake in his physical interior, he also became conscious of the reigning silence, which held its own against the constantly broken off and then resumed passage work from the piano, whose sound made its way to him, clear and solitary, from the music room, and against the slight tapping noises he was making here with his cup and his plate. Only during the longer pauses could any sound be heard coming from the city.

Like a small, compact object hovering in the air right in front of his eyes, and so close that there was no astonishment to make him notice it and remark on it because it was in the very circulation of his blood, a picture of Etelka's little room now suddenly appeared, looking as it would in the afternoon, with the curtains closed, *façon voilée*, Schopenhauer's book and the quatrains of Omar Khayyám; but the image was like any object from the world of the senses only—self-enclosed and self-disposed, so that there was no thread leading from Schopenhauer's treatise *The World as Will and Representation* to anything he was seeing around him.

He should have called for a fiacre, now, while it was still cool, joined forces with Teddy, and taken a ride out to the Prater, where they could have had breakfast in that restaurant called the Lusthaus.

It seemed too far for him to go by himself, when he pictured the trip.

No doubt Etelka was still asleep. She'd sleep late today, because she probably hadn't gone home until very late last night. There was no way he could have gone to see her this morning, say after the trip to the Prater.

"I'll call her at eleven o'clock," he thought.

And suddenly grew very sad.

He was supposed to spend the evening with Etelka; she had some kind of family obligation in the afternoon. And then they had to go back to the country the next day. For several moments he felt the restrictions on him as if they were a saddle on his back. At age twenty-one! There would be nothing short of a big to-do with his parents and grandparents out where they lived if he should decide, for example, just to stay on in Vienna for a while.

On the other hand, it made him happy to think that he was going to eat with his great-aunt in Hietzing at noontime (she was a sister of the publisher, that gross old character whom we've already heard something about—very much by contrast, Fräulein Weygand, an old lady who'd never married, was an outstandingly kind person; she lived in a villa full of curiosities and quaint *objets*, and she liked to pamper Pista, whom she thought the world of, with sophisticated culinary offerings, true festivals of gourmet cuisine and good cheer, whenever he went to see her).

The morning trudged by slowly. It was like an empty serving tray, and any question about what was going to be placed on it had yet to be answered. It's at the edge of such a vacuum that all the things we've neglected like to gather and urge themselves on us to be taken care of and smoothed out. A letter we haven't written. Another good idea would have been to review his Chinese word roots (Pista was studying Chinese at the academy as an elective). An inner capaciousness without any real stimulus to action will sometimes allow room for good common sense. But what's missing from common sense alone is any real stimulus to action, from which we must conclude that it needs to receive a stimulus from somewhere else, and that autonomy is therefore a dubious postulate to make about this faculty in our lives. Pista stared at the toes of his shoes and lit another cigarette. Now he really was floating in an empty space somewhere.

"Good morning," Teddy said, from behind him.

Grauermann spun around. He was taken with a very distinct but absurd feeling that Teddy, in some mean-spirited way, had waited too long to come.

"I'll drink a cup of coffee with you," said Honnegger as he sat down in a wicker armchair.

"Haven't you had breakfast yet?" asked Pista with interest.

"Oh yes, a good while ago." Honnegger took from his case one of those Turkish cigarettes (Régie Ottomane Deuxième) that were the favorite brand here at the Academy. The doorman sold them, and they weren't expensive, because they were smuggled.

"It's pleasant here," said Honnegger, and he stretched. "Not hot yet. And so—" he said, as he pointed vaguely to what he and Grauermann were wearing. Both had on civilian clothes, at this hour just a shirt and a pair of light pants. Teddy was still in his slippers (for which purpose a pair of old *escarpins* served). During the long summer break they weren't so stringent here about the mandatory wearing of the uniform. "Summertime in Vienna has its advantages. It's very peaceful. I'm glad

I managed to get away from Gmunden. My parents aren't there now anyway."

"Are you going to the *Beisel* at noon?" Grauermann meant the tavern and restaurant called the Flight into Egypt, which was only a short way from the academy.

"No. I'm invited to Professor Swoboda's at twelve thirty; he's one of Otto Weininger's few friends, and I'll have an opportunity to discuss a number of topics with him. How about you?"

"I'm eating at my great-aunt's in Hietzing."

"That'll be nice," said Honnegger. "I think I'd pass up a second breakfast if I were you."

"What are you doing for the rest of the morning?" Grauermann asked, after they'd been quiet for a while.

"I'm going to work my way through Weininger's fifth chapter again. It's called 'Aptitude and Memory.' That's what I want to focus on when I talk with Hermann Swoboda after lunch, while we're having our coffee. I should be back here by two thirty at the very latest, because he sometimes takes a nap after his noon meal. I like Swoboda very much. He represents a type of scholar who will someday soon represent the norm again, I hope."

"Is that what his type was at one time?"

"Yes. At least in the humanities."

Grauermann was now feeling separated, as if by a glass wall, from objects and topics with which he considered himself pretty well conversant. So for the moment he couldn't get a grasp on the subject they were talking about; somehow he just wasn't prepared, and he felt awkward, as people can feel on certain days when they're being clumsy with their hands. (On an incidental note, the first person to pursue scientific research into the periodic recurrence of such days was none other than the scholar whose name Teddy had mentioned just a moment before.)

The two young men were quiet for a time, during which the heat of the day began noticeably increasing with that pressure, gentle but irresistible at the same time, which only the passing of time can exert. The glow of the sun reached into parts of the park in which the sharply etched morning shadows had lain while Grauermann was having his breakfast, and the treetops now stood drenched in flaming gold.

"You actually know Asta a great deal better than you do Etelka," said Pista all of a sudden, and he seemed to follow his own words with his eyes as if they were some object falling from the table onto the floor.

"Pure chance," Teddy remarked casually and with the air—based on pure indolence, not implying intent or dissent—of one who really doesn't feel much like discussing the subject and therefore keeps to the most superficial level, where words can be shuffled back and forth and mixed up at will, like domino tiles on a tabletop, as long as there's not a game being played, so that it makes no difference what number of dots is on the tile or what value it has—three, five, or seventeen. "Pure chance," he said again. "I used to go to visit the Küffers a good deal in Döbling, while the old gentleman was still living—I mean the grand-father, the one who had the famous collection of string instruments—and they still played music at home. After the grandfather died, they gave that up entirely, and all they ever played after that was whist, because, oddly enough, the family is totally unmusical except in that one instance. Asta was always there when they played string quartets; she was really still just a little girl at the time. I never saw Etelka at the Küffers', even though by rights she should have been a regular guest there because of her studying music; after all, that home was one of the 'focal points of musical life,' as they call them, even with all the unpleasant conditions and people conjured up by that term—Herr Tlopatsch from the Finance Ministry as the coordinator, and all that. I used to have long conversations with Asta, which I really enjoyed. She's still friends with Lily Küffer to this day, I think, isn't she?"

"Etelka never liked the Küffers," said Grauermann. He felt today as if every door and exit were locked; an invisible wall was holding him in check on all sides; no person or thing wanted to have anything to do with him.

"If people have genuine artistic interests, I mean ones that make a difference, ones they're determined to cultivate above all else, those interests will often push their likes and dislikes off to the side; I think what ends up happening, in fact, is that the likes and dislikes accom-modate themselves to the artistic endeavors and settle in somewhere among them, so to speak."

Finally Teddy had made a real point! And at once he added, "By the way, how was the Schmellers'? How was the garden party? I nearly forgot all about it. I'm surprised you're up so early, come to think of it."

Grauermann told him what there was to tell. Then he tried to pick the earlier thread back up and follow it until complications and consequences ensued, as we might say (he surprised even himself: after all, whatever a man dredges up out of a vacuum, out of a state of absence, will often turn into nothing less than a new stimulation, thanks to the astonishment that now follows from his own actions or that even sets in concurrently with them, for that matter; astonishment because something like a retrospective biography, not officially registered by the consciousness but lived out by the man nevertheless, and with a breadth of scope and a depth of taking root that—or so it would seem in moments like these—emerges into view under such conditions, those being the continuum of our states of absence). "It would be a great pleasure for me," he said, "if you were in contact with Etelka more often."

"I would enjoy that very much, also," Honnegger answered. "It needs to be made clear, though," he added after a very short pause (and so he'd grabbed the bait after all—it's exceptionally difficult for young people to refrain for very long, and, to be honest, it should still be reckoned as a notable achievement in the sphere of mental discipline among persons of more mature years as well!), "it needs to be made clear that Etelka and I aren't, shall we say, at the top of each other's most-likely-to-please list. A trite way to say it is that engaged women are prejudiced against the old friends of their future husbands."

"But Etelka isn't just an 'engaged woman' in the usual sense of the term."

"Whether it's the usual or the unusual sense, she's engaged. All people are subject to, or even subjugated to, whatever laws govern such categories as their outer life has placed them into, and that's entirely disregarding whether their heads are full of true or false ideas about the matter. A man can be a sectional councillor in the Finance Ministry and yet not be a bureaucrat in the usual sense; in fact, he may even have been forced into this career against his will, or he may belong in his very essence to an entirely different human type, the artistic type, for example. Look at Ministry Councillor P., who often played viola at the Küffers'—the world will always see him as a bureaucrat, will do nothing but force him back into his preordained category over and over, keep him captive inside that pigeonhole, make him stand upright in it, and prop him up if need be. And in this case the world really does know what it's doing. You have exactly the same situation when a person has to join the service as a recruit and be made into a soldier or go around as a reserve lieutenant. He may be the most passionate antimilitarist by conviction, but he is subject to the laws of his present state in life all the same. I'm not talking now about just the written laws and the outward force they carry, the civil service procedures of the Royal and Imperial Finance Ministry or the codes of military regulation. To draw on Schopenhauer's terms, one cannot constantly be negating that which one represents on the basis of that which one is or would merely like to be. It is not possible to wear an article of clothing without its being warmed by our bodies, adjusting to its contours, and so on—it enters in, so to say, and becomes a part of us. The unwilling lieutenant, the privy councillor whose function goes against his actual view of the world—they find themselves forming an alloy, indeed a genuine chemical compound, with what they're denying, and it starts the very second they first accept what's due them, whether it's the deferential manner of a waiter's greeting, the brisk salute of an enlisted man, or the nameplate, complete with title, on the office door; or when they first do whatever it is they have the right to do, such as giving an order, leaving the barracks in the evening and not returning until the next morning, which only officers are generally allowed to do, as far as I know, or, as privy councillor in the ministry, making final disposition of some official document through their signature. All of those actions cause the exterior part of them to enter into the interior, and what was originally just an article of clothing or even an overcoat or some similar outer covering has now assumed unique and highly personalized contours; it's become part of the biography. It's inevitable, and that's because people can only live when they've come to fuse or amalgamate with life in some way. They must involve themselves in it. Life consists of involving oneself, of immersing one's very self. No one can relegate outward life to a mask and then uphold his integrity behind it all on his own. The bridge of reality, which connects the inner and the outer, will collapse over a chasm of that kind. But the whole of that outward force, so inexorably certain to be in operation, leads to the inference that all people, no matter how consciously they may think about it, are at any given moment standing on precisely the one point of outward life on which, in accordance with their existence in the realm of fact—not with the existence they live in their minds—they actually belong. And just as it is like this with privy councillors, recruits, and lieutenants, so it is too with engaged women, mothers-in-law, husbands. There is no such thing as a mother-in-law or a married couple who are anything other than exactly that—and in the usual sense of the terms. The most one can hope for is that the categories imposed on a person can be softened, toned down, even cushioned, in some degree, by the person's good qualities. But no one can refuse to accept the role life exacts, whether it be that of lieutenant or engaged woman, master or servant, wife or husband. Only people who know that—whether from primal instinct, meaning from below, or from painstaking discernment, meaning from above (and the first is the more dependable)—should ever get married, by the way. Now of course if the chemical reaction I talked about earlier just will not come about; if an airless gap of space remains between the outer and the inner; that too, then, is just as much a charge in its own way, specifically that of a tragic figure. Tragedy is a concept borrowed from the sphere of the dramatic, though. It's not static and enduring; it has to decide whether it wants to or doesn't want to, has to choose one thing or the other."

While Honnegger was speaking, the difference in the few (but crucial, considering how young they were) years separating them in age intruded between the two men, so to speak, as if they were now at an angle that basically prevented their seeing each other, even though there was nothing wrong with their eyes.

Teddy had just finished when the caretaker came out into the garden and requested that Grauermann come to the telephone; there was a call for him. Honnegger stood up also and quickly told Grauermann he was leaving. "It's getting hot here anyway," he said, "so I think I'll go upstairs and get to my Weininger. Take care, Pista." Grauermann briefly tracked him as Teddy leisurely climbed the broad staircase to the second floor.

The telephone call was from Fräulein Weygand's housekeeper in Hietzing. Madame was not feeling at all well, she said (the old lady suffered from time to time with facial neuralgia, and the attacks could last a full day), and therefore she regretted to say that she would have to deprive herself of the pleasure of welcoming the young gentleman into her home at noon. She wanted to inquire, also, when he would be going back to the country. The following day? His great-aunt sent her warmest greetings. After a number of sympathetic questions from Grauermann the conversation came to an end.

Pista then in turn went up to his room. It was cool there, the blinds closed all the way and lowered, a green twilight; the light was so dim that he would scarcely have been able to read. Grauermann turned on a small lamp with a colorful shade and moved his heavy armchair over to the light. Then he took Weininger's book down from the shelf. Now, after a hearty breakfast, fatigue overtook him. He'd missed his usual full night's sleep by waking up after just six hours or so.

> "A request for their autobiography would throw the overwhelming majority of people into the most embarrassing predicament, incapable as all but the fewest are of accounting, if asked, for what they did yesterday. The fact is that memory is simply erratic for most..."

This was the place at which he'd happened to open the book. He fell asleep.

So it was the Flight into Egypt at noon after all.

Actually, it was later than that, closer to one thirty, when Grauermann made his way there by a slightly roundabout route down the Strudlhof Steps, which at this hour, amid the blaze of noonday and the shadows of leaves, lay as deserted as an untouched place in nature.

He'd reawakened at eleven o'clock, applying that extreme economy of motion, as he drifted over from his easy chair to the sofa beside it, resorted to by everyone who wants to get up and move somewhere else but still stay within the realm of sleep and dreams.

Luckily for Grauermann, they still had something—something good, too—left to eat at the Flight into Egypt, and he soon made friends with a well-chilled Nussberger as well. Those Beiseln, as taverns famous for their good food are known, had something special to offer in those days, and the whole tribe of cabdrivers and fiacre men, teamsters and trolley conductors, would not stand for even the slightest lowering of quality by the management; if any such attempt were made, not one word would be spoken, but at once these customers would all just stop going there. Within a few days a Beisel could be abandoned and its business ruined, for example if the place changed hands and the new owner thought he could do things his way and cut corners. The students from the Consular Academy frequented several of the Beiseln in the neighborhood. That was one of the "in" things at the academy and was considered chic; reserving a table in the restaurant of a hotel located nearby, on the other hand, would be labeled gauche and inelegant, as they were careful to impress upon the "hound dogs" from the very outset. The so-called excellencies, too, and even the demigods, ate at Beiseln. During the semester, the students of course took their meals together at the Academy, but even then some occasion would always arise for a visit to one or another of the Beiseln.

The visit Grauermann was now paying was in solitude, here in this district situated so deep inside the city, so close to the Danube. Right here was where the houses in this area started to climb up past one another like stairsteps, each solitary on this summer afternoon, immersed in its own warmth, in the second half of August. Here, incidentally, in the dining room at the back, it was strikingly cool, probably because of an enormous ice chest against one of the walls which had just been filled with fresh blocks that looked like long prisms of milk glass. At the bar right next to it, the driver of the ice wagon, which could be seen standing outside in front of the tavern, was drinking a mug of beer.

Sleeping before the noon meal when it isn't a habit has a significantly different effect from sleeping in the afternoon, which at this time of year, when the sun is blazing at its hottest, is what would be expected; an afternoon nap, especially if it is too prolonged, can make a person groggy, weak, and downhearted, whereas a little nap before eating lunch irons out in advance the first rumples and wrinkles the day will be bringing. Grauermann had woken up early, seen the morning and the rising sun, enjoyed breakfast outdoors, and then slept very deeply. All that broke through his routine the way calling to a sleepwalker will wake him up. He felt really brisk and cheerful now, despite the food and wine. The only thing missing was coffee. In this regard the academy students were extremely finicky; they were accustomed to the Turkish method of brewing, which was not as prevalent in Vienna in those days as it would become after the First World War, so Grauermann would now have had to go home if he wanted it like that. Here we see how Viennese coffee, otherwise famed throughout the world, was subjected to a negative evaluation on Waisenhaus Gasse in 1911.

What Grauermann did now, though, and without further ado, was to set off for a solid middle-class restaurant nearby, where, after fronting bulwarks of heat as he walked the few steps across the street, he was able to sit, have a cup of black coffee, and read the newspapers in silence, relative coolness, and solitude there in a corner with cushioned seats. He was here even though Honnegger had named two thirty at the latest as the time he would be back from his meal with Professor Swoboda; that may even have been the very reason, come to think of it. There was a possibility, or even a probability, that Teddy would sit right back down at the keyboard. Meanwhile, however, Pista's little boat was off sailing the waters in a new spirit and was no longer attempting, in slightly damaged condition, to make for unreliable—or even well-nigh sketchy—landing places that kept receding, dropping back away from him. His midday meal, for example, was almost as delicious as—and, into the bargain, more relaxed than—at his great-aunt's in Hietzing. Grauermann had reestablished his independence, as it were. He was setting and pursuing his own course, and it was leading him somewhere off the charted pathways; he could sense it now (if only as though behind many walls, deep in the pearl-gray of his innermost depths), even though he was doing ordinary and thoroughly trivial things. With little deviations. Like asking for a cigar with a paper tip and smoking it—instead of a Turkish cigarette, de rigueur for the Consular Academy—very contentedly.

Time stood still. No breeze of purpose produced a flow in any direction. The needle veered slowly in its barometer of possibilities, though not noticeably falling toward the low-pressure zone, as it had earlier that morning. Of all the many points, to which should his attention be directed? This is roughly how the gentle question would have been worded that was dwelling inside him, in among the last, still growing, seed-leaf-moist lamellae of his soul (in moving toward the outside, a person soon gets drier, including behind the ears): that would have been the wording, if the question could have been put into words in the first place and then grown audible inside him. Still, it was present. The dividing walls between the compartments of this young man's soul were still translucent enough that for all practical purposes everything could be placed into relation with everything else, so that all the separate components were still capable of being placed into relation with one whole entity, the person in the making, which process can go on as long as this one condition continues to be met: that the person can inwardly see into all the chambers and the rooms, holding all of them at every moment in recollection, gifted with the possession of memory. As yet, no dark walls, encrusted and grown opaque, divided our young Pista Grauermann into separate compartments of the soul that just go about their business without reference to anything else.

A train whistle sounded from Bohemia Station across the way.

This place was called the Café Brioni.

The broad square outside was filled with unknown dwellings and houses, flights of stairs plain or fancy, decorated with useless gewgaws and mirrors, narrow or wide, with elevator or without. The Danube Canal—two hundred meters from here, maybe, no more.

The clock said quarter after three when Grauermann walked back onto the street. Outside, two intense feelings pounced on him, so to speak, as though they had been lurking; the first one actually hit just as he was leaving the café by the revolving glass door, and it was a keen and distinct craving for something sweet—cake frosting or ice cream or pastries or anything. He really had no choice but to notice it, since it did not have had the remotest connection with his living habits, any more than his headache of the previous day had with his usual state of feeling well. It was also surprising in much the same way. A step off the charted path, a push into the undergrowth off to the side—but what was there to be discovered, anyway? The second of Pista's feelings came to him as soon as he was standing on the sidewalk, and it was that the weather had grown very slightly cooler and a bit breezy.

Pleasantly affected by this change, he now walked uphill along Alserbach Strasse, knowing that ahead on the left, at the end of the street, there was a large—and very good—*Conditorei*, a combination retail bakery and café (even this admittedly minor but independent and unusual little venture also satisfied him). For some time he stayed on the right side of the street after turning the corner by the Café Brioni. It was here that an ancient section of the city gave way almost abruptly to a newer one that climbed high, so that a narrow street Grauermann could look down, for example, had small, two-story houses on the one side (like the Blue Unicorn), towered over by some not very attractive multistory buildings across from them, ones lying on higher ground, in addition. Grauermann crossed the street up ahead, by the market hall, around which the flow of traffic divided left and right. It was a very busy intersection. A light breeze had stirred up here, and the scalloped edges of the awnings that reached far down over the display windows of the bakery were now fluttering in it.

He stepped into the shadows and into the shop, where the aromas were tempting, and he was walking among the little white tables and miniature armchairs toward a seat in the corner (in *Conditoreien*, at least if their decor is old-fashioned, everything always has that fussy, delicate touch of being arranged just so) when someone sitting at a table not far from one of the windows greeted him. "I saw you coming across the street," said René Stangeler with a laugh. A young girl with titian-red hair and a very delicate, transparent complexion was sitting at the table with him. Our friend presently made the introductions: "Herr Grauermann—Fräulein Paula Schachl." He looked radiant and seemed to be having one of those days when all's right with the world—for him, at any rate.

Grauermann sat down with keen enjoyment, across from René, so that he was sitting with his back to the window and didn't have to look into the sunlit street, which he felt as an added pleasure. This chance meeting seemed like a kind of bonus to him, a gratifying bull's-eye he'd scored here in total silence and all by himself. Toward young people, toward "hound dogs," as it were, he harbored a feeling of particular goodwill, about which it would be difficult to say whether it came from his fundamentally good-hearted nature or from his still being almost exactly the same as they were or simply from the unwritten house rules of the Consular Academy, where a certain amount of benevolence—albeit conveyed with a degree of self-complacency commensurate with one's rank—toward all creatures of the hound-dog variety and, as occasion might arise, toward their entangling alliances and love interests as well, was likewise an element of the done thing, the right tone, like frequenting Beiseln, smoking the Deuxième brand of cigarettes, or wearing a pair of trudged-out old *escarpins* as one's slippers.

Besides, the girl René was sitting with struck him as interesting, or at least as very likeable, and that she was truly pretty, but totally modest about it, acted on him under the circumstances as a welcome extra. The hospitable Magyar in Grauermann awoke, and because the other two were sitting over empty glass dessert plates, he went to the rear to pick out some pastries from the bulging display case; soon their little table was overflowing with ice cream and slices of Sacher torte with whipped cream, and the three . . . those three—let's just go ahead and say it—children, blown together by the wind under the hot sky of the city at the peak of summer, gave themselves over to an orgy of sweets, with Grauermann as the instigator, one who, when he did give way and allow himself such rare indulgences, didn't hold back in the least. René was the first to call it quits; he really couldn't eat another thing, whereas Paula, amid many bursts of laughter shared with Pista, let him talk her into trying the doughnuts for which the place was so well known, because he wanted to have some himself.

This was one of those waves in life whose whitecaps, crimped in the baroque style, bend almost all the way back over and touch their curls, or concave undersides, with their curving tips. Each of the three had to feel that way. René was holding forth smoothly, at any rate. "If you've done it wrong," he said, laughing, "then you hear about it, but if you've done it the way you're supposed to, the same thing happens," he added lightly (and it was just this "lightly" that wasn't generally his strong point, as we've no doubt noticed already; he could play any tempo better than a leggiero). "And there are clear outward signs to show me when I've done it wrong."

"Done what wrong, though?" asked Pista, more cheerfully than just facetiously, for he always kept himself attuned to this boy through an undertone of deep and genuine listening.

"Anything, of course," said René. "My basic attitude, above all. Those quick little decisions that are so hard to make—for example, getting out of a chair when it's time or keeping my mouth shut. It's only these little things that count. To keep myself from easing into softness at the crucial moment."

"Myself from easing into softness..." Grauermann repeated, as if he were savoring the taste that clung to these words. He slid his cigarette case full of Deuxième across to René after they'd ordered more coffee from the woman at the counter and been granted permission to smoke—it wasn't done as a rule—in this dainty, even prissy world of the patisserie. No other patrons were seated in the room, and the practice had been introduced by René some time before, in any case.

"For example, whenever I mess up—and my father's wearing his dark blue suit—his shoulders twitch, he's in a bad mood all day, and he comes marching into a room taking three doors at the same time, right when I'm trying—or should I say 'wrong when I'm trying,' because whenever I go to drive a little nail into the wall, say, I always bend it, even though the wallpaper's almost brand-new, just put up last summer."

"And how do you explain that one part—the part about the blue suit, I mean?" Grauermann asked with a laugh.

"There's nothing to explain," answered Stangeler, completely unperturbed, "at least not for me. Because I don't believe in any actual difference between the inner and the outer."

That was taking it pretty far. We needn't conclude that Paula was bored, however. The impression one would be more likely to get was that she was sitting here because, among other reasons, she'd undergone boredom for too long in the course of entirely different conversations.

She looked nice. Summery, in a simple way. Her throat rose, as translucently delicate as the skin of a baby animal, from the triangular neck of her coarse linen dress. Her straw hat was a perfect choice; Grauermann took conscious notice of it, while for René, who didn't yet have an eye for such things in those days, it made up no more than one of the notes blending its music and its color into his whole sense of delight in her. Her hair gleaming red to the left and right of her temples, thick and perhaps a little stiff, stood out from the fine straw, left in its natural color, so that the contrast held the eye.

"Do you come here often?" asked Grauermann.

"Today's the first time since the school year ended; I've been out in the country the whole time. But before that we always enjoyed coming here. Paula lives in the neighborhood. She started her vacation yesterday and is going to the country herself the day after tomorrow."

"I'm really looking forward to it." This was the first time she'd said anything. Her eyes were set at an angle, and now, as she spoke, they were shining brightly; Grauermann could see that they weren't pure blue but had almost a violet sheen. Suddenly the thought occurred to him that this young woman could have sat as the model for some of the newer book illustrators, like Edmund Dulac, who'd done the pictures for the *Tales from the Thousand and One Nights*, or for Alastair, with his strange portraits.

"Are you professionally employed?" Grauermann asked.

"Yes," she said, "by an attorney."

"Here in the neighborhood as well?"

"No, in the center of the city, on Marc-Aurel Strasse."

Grauermann made a mental picture of the Danube Canal and the dock (to which this street leads) for a brief moment and was fleetingly astonished at the unusually intense vividness of the image.

"I love this area here more than anything," said Stangeler. His gaze drifted past Grauermann in an indefinite way and strayed outside to the bustling activity on the street, where the cars and carriages kept ceaselessly rolling by, close to the curb and close behind one another, uphill along Alserbach Strasse (in those days traffic still drove on the left in Vienna) toward the crossing; now and then the movement came to a stop. This was the road to open countryside, to Grinzing and

Sievering (and they would have been out there somewhere, too, Paula and he, that is, if the aunt Paula Schachl lived with hadn't put in yet another request for her help later that same afternoon in some household matter that had to be taken care of before they went on vacation—even so, they planned to meet again in the evening and then go out somewhere green and cool and airy and sit in the garden of a quiet country inn under the leafy dome of a chestnut tree shining in the lamplight). "I love this area more than anything," he said again, as if delivering a soliloquy.

"No wonder," observed Grauermann gallantly, "since Fräulein Paula lives here."

"Why, yes, of course," answered René, perhaps a little clumsy in his effort to snatch at a thought it was only too obvious he hadn't been thinking. "But it was that way earlier, too, before I knew Paula."

"Then it was a premonition" said Grauermann.

"Exactly," answered René, with an unshakable air of saying something self-evident. "I was always finding reasons to come to this part of the city, even though I had absolutely no business of any kind here. And that's how I came to know Paula. This area has always had special meaning for me. I'm at my best here; I feel my potential here; this is where life is; this is where I'd like to live. The gardens! And the way the streets all go uphill and downhill around here. The broad square down there by the train station. To have a room here, to be all by oneself, devoted to some pursuit—thinking, keeping a journal..."

As he was saying all this—his gaze fixed outside the whole time, watching all the comings and goings on the street, looking into a picture framed by the large glass pane of the display window under the fluttering, scalloped, brown-red edge of the awning—a grouping made its way into the rectangle, into the display window (the meaning of which term thereby had the tables turned on it with a vengeance).

Held up for quite some time by the heavy traffic at the corner, an open fiacre had pulled up and was standing near the pavement. In it, leaning back comfortably and for the moment not moving or speaking with one another, were sitting Etelka and Government Councillor Guys; he was holding between his legs a walking stick with a silver handle. Etelka was wearing a white dress and a large hat, semisheer, to match. Guys was in light gray. Soundless when they'd pulled up, motionless as they now sat waiting, there was something like wax dolls about them, since they both kept their heads turned in exactly the same direction. While René now, as he was speaking, watched this apparition drift into the rectangular picture, linger, and then move out of sight, he felt himself in the fleeting but intense grip of a mental picture dredged up quite far from the here and now—he thought of the famous amusement park in Vienna known as the Wurstlprater, and in particular of the *Grottenbahn*, the "Grotto Train," as it was called (its real name was the Whale). There, for the enjoyment of its esteemed patrons, strings of comfortable little cars with padded benches would drive through long, dark, winding passageways as if through underground caverns or grottoes, drawn by a mighty dragon with electromotive power. This little train would stop at intervals, always in front of a brightly lit prospect or diorama arranged like a stage scene, which would present some interesting view or another in the form of a three-dimensional picture, sometimes with figures mechanically animated, like "The Realm of the Dwarves," and sometimes stationary, like "The Gulf of Naples," or else with mannequins that stayed frozen in one attitude, like "The Pasha and His Harem," where the odalisques were made of wax. After a few minutes, when it seemed safe to assume that the riders had by now had sufficient time to view at their leisure the picture spread out before them, the electric dragon would start moving again, the diorama would glide off, and the lights would go out. That's how it was now. For just a split second, right after the fiacre appeared within the picture frame, there arose in René the possibility—though it was soon banished by the couple's posture and physical bearing—that the carriage might stop here and that Etelka and Guys might come inside to have ice cream. Only on reflection did it briefly occur to René to be afraid that Grauermann might happen by chance to turn around just at that moment.

And turn around he did (as though what was coming out of René weren't apprehensiveness but a power, aimed precisely in the direction of wishing the action into being!). But not until the apparition had vanished, a mere second or so afterward. He turned around quickly (with what subtlety and alacrity can a person's perceptual apparatus discern in the eye of someone sitting across from him that his vis-à-vis has now found an object in the same field of vision the person had been looking vaguely into all along!) and then immediately back to René, doing so without lessening the attention with which he was listening to what the boy was saying.

Our friend hadn't skipped a beat in his flow of words, hadn't modified his tone of voice in the slightest. "These are the notions that keep me company wherever I go in this part of town," he said; "I'm just simply better off here than over in the third district. I do a better job; I do everything better. That often holds true even if all I'm doing is thinking about this area. About the Strudlhof Steps, for instance. That's a very mysterious place. The way the steps go reaching down, as from an old city with all its attractions to a new one with attractions of its own! Like a bridge between two realms. It's as though one were stepping through a concealed entrance into the shadowy netherworld of all that's past and gone."

He held forth with particular verve, and while Etelka was visible inside the picture frame he proved even better at perorating than usual, though afterward was when he really came into his own. Not that René was exactly endowed in large measure with any near Indian or Mongolian brand of self-discipline; when it came to a Stangeler, any such idea lay far beyond what could even be imagined. Instead, the tactics inevitable in his family could not but breed and then reinforce at an early stage of the young man's life the kind of alert readiness to hoodwink or bamboozle that will then be automatically activated in every situation, even when there's no actual need for them, like some proficiency that one has mastered cold, some occurrence in the natural course of things; moreover, threads woven of strong imagination and empathetic identification, though held in check here by an accurate sense of boundaries, went quickly and skillfully darting into René's basic sullenness, all of which together make up the complex texture of any hoodwinking.

Right now, though—even during that one split second when he'd been afraid the couple in the carriage might get out and come inside, and then during the moments when they'd lingered in the picture, when, that is, the danger existed that Grauermann might turn around (in time to see them!)—he was feeling as if this smooth-running habit of avoiding the truth had grown into a compulsion only too powerful in the way it went barreling down the tracks; acting like a natural force of its own with no regard for him as it hurtled along, it was trying to make him change course and branch off onto an old, worn-out inside track, to set him in a direction that he just now became aware was on a branch line and that lay diagonal to his real path here. Now, and for the very first time, perhaps, duplicity and untruth did not feel completely appropriate; alongside this technique of living much practiced by all weaklings there opened up another possibility, another track, dim and hazy, to be sure, by comparison with the sharp visibility and the automatic habituation of the customary path, but yet distinctly palpable right at this moment. The smooth old roadway was creating an especially distracting disturbance just now, however, standing as an obstacle to the unfolding of some thought that was stirring up a new and joyous feeling in René.

For inside of him, the picture in the display window behind Grauermann's back, though it had vanished a good while before, was in a way still standing where it had been. The incontestable actuality—he'd experienced.it right at first hand—of being able to look past someone and to see what to that someone are the world's most important matters as if they were a stage set or the background in a painting now made the futility and the totally unnecessary nature of his habitual mendacious exertions only too obvious. What a strain it was, whereas all one really needed to do was take a casual glance beyond the immediate and see what lies behind it, to see what's truly necessary and important, that is, without having to strain oneself in the slightest, without having to lean forward or narrow one's eyes to a squint, without having to shift positions; just stay as comfortable as can be, and they'll set everything into the picture for you! Only now, after the fact, did René grasp that his one split second of fearing that Etelka and Guys might come inside the bakery or that Grauermann might turn around had at the same instant contained a wish, flashing up even more briefly, that something along that line would in fact happen! Now that an exit door had flown open, he was being swept through it as if by an irresistible current that knocked the breath out of him and was carrying him all the way to some point at which it might be possible to have his vision set free; the picture changed out there, and instead of a display window he saw a mirror, one to which his father, sitting at the upper end of the table, had his back turned.

He looked over at Paula. Only at this point did the thread of his conversation snap and drop away from his lips (Etelka and Guys were long gone, meanwhile, rolling along smoothly on rubber tires, with a clop-clop-clop, in the breeze made by the wind and the motion of the fiacre). He looked over at Paula and studied her face, the eyes set somewhat obliquely and her pale temples framed by reddish hair.

The Strudlhof Steps! Yes, that was what she was. Her face had that part of the city as its background, and the background grew visible when he glanced past it; then the face was authenticated on its own. They were one and the same.

There leapt up here (we can say it from the vantage point of some distance) a spark of contact between romanticism and a yearning for truth, two entities which in themselves don't exactly have much truck with each other. Even so, the first of these will make the second more human and keep it from growing fanatical, from standing out like a bone in an emaciated body, while the second will suffuse the first with a pungent and bracing aroma (like certain men's bath soaps) and thereby preserve it from rapid putrefaction, a state this romantic substance is almost as prone to as liverwurst is. These two things can coexist very well, really. But now we should pay some attention to Grauermann and not just keep doing everything behind his back.

In the first place, he had no difficulty admitting to himself that René had been able to lift him totally out of the last few low points of this day, whereupon he added by way of pertinent quotation a passage from Oscar Wilde, who has one of his characters (Lord Henry Wotton) say that a man can truly learn only from the young; and after he shifted the experience he'd just been through, along with the support it had given him, off to a certain distance (a respectful distance from his own self), he found he'd again made room for the Consular Academy's style of benevolence de rigueur toward all creatures of the hound-dog variety. "They're really very nice, these youngsters." Besides, he genuinely like René a lot. But the upshot? That's still the only thing that's really important! So—all of a sudden he had a homey and comfortable feeling in thinking about his lonely room. Yes! Now he wanted to drink some tea there and to resume reading the book that had slipped out of his hands this morning. Then he wouldn't be completely unprepared, so to speak, for his meeting with Etelka in the evening; he'd be in a serene, collected mood. He looked at his watch. It was close to four.

"I've got to get back to the academy," he said. "Wouldn't you like to walk part of the way with me?"

"Yes!" René cried brightly. "We're going up the Strudlhof Steps!"

Walking away from the main door of the academy, Asta Stangeler and Melzer were now—after Ingrid had gone her separate way—slowly heading along the shady side of the street. They stopped turning back to watch Ingrid go, and for the moment they stayed silent.

"It wouldn't do for us to go too far, Melzer," said Asta after about a hundred paces.

And she told him about the promise she'd been forced to make to Ingrid. While she was telling him about it, pushing this object out of herself with her words, almost as we might use the tip of our tongue to work something out of our mouth that's lodged in there but doesn't belong, there very quickly vanished that feeling, born of astonishment, of being hemmed in, and of that acceptance of a totally alien personality type she'd pushed herself to accept. What came now—the words went in that direction by themselves, as if autonomous in their motion—shattered her resolution into the facets of a critical judgment apparently in harmony with good common sense. The frilled collar or inner tube, its function just starting to develop in those days, kicked into operation and began creating a split in Asta; it seems a certainty, on the other hand, that her initial impulse had come flowing out of a person as yet undivided.

Now, though, she got tangled up in her own words, like Wilhelm Busch's magpie, Hans Huckebein, in the ball of yarn. Among other things she said, "Getting everybody running all around, just so she can walk away with her head high! That's all she cares about. She wants to come out of it blameless, to keep her promise, and possibly even have a romantic closing scene—but it mustn't last longer than fifteen minutes, oh no, not one second longer! 'Stephan gets upset so easily'—that's the straw that broke my back. She's the one who engineered that idiotic drama with the rendezvous in the bathroom, and so this whole thing's her fault anyway. No, she doesn't love him. She doesn't love him." She almost said it like this: "She—doesn't—love—him" (*ritmo di quattro battute*, like four drumbeats, the same way they'd pounded inside her the first time, in the window niche).

And suddenly Asta felt that her words weren't grasping onto what she wanted to say. Suddenly she felt as if the emotional upset she'd undergone was now sitting inside her like a pool of black water, its surface risen very high. She put up resistance; she spoke.

"Giving up just like that, without a fight, tells you everything right there. Parting for good, the way she's doing it—just try to picture somebody being able to stand it! That's the most terrible thing there is, parting for good like that. I really don't know if I could bring myself to do it with somebody I really care for. Probably not. And then the time afterward! I can't even imagine it. She's not resisting in any way; she'll cry a little, but then that's it. That's part of how you're supposed to act, just like the perfect closing scene. 'Stephan gets upset so easily.' No, she just plain doesn't love him, and that's the truth."

"And does he love her?" Melzer asked.

Asta didn't answer—Asta, ever verbose, including as recently as a second before. She knew full well she ought to say something, offer some critique, deliver some judgment in harmony with good common sense; doing so would have enabled her to bandage a wound from the outside—not nearly so much her own wound as Melzer's, which she didn't want to see bleeding. But that black water inside her seemed to have risen anew. She didn't offer any more resistance. She didn't speak. The collar or inner tube was just coming into existence back then, so she could still become engulfed from time to time.

Melzer looked into her silence—it had that hardness which can only come from being defenseless—Melzer looked into this newly opened chasm with the facial expression of a dejected young boy who's once again been sent home from school with a bad mark. If at first Asta's critical, coolheaded practicality and uninhibited candor in discussing these matters had been a refined but deeply wounding martyrdom for him, this chasm of silence now grew to be something truly terrifying, because it was driving them apart. Parting was what they'd been talking about, and here was an instance of it coming about right now, untouched by words. Deep down at the bottom of the chasm appeared a red blotch Melzer knew well, a blotch as of raw flesh or spilled blood, that color so full of meaning in his life; the sight of it was what made him now realize what had just taken place, or better yet, had just become obvious, and it was what now banished any last glimmers of hope.

They had come out onto Währinger Strasse and walked along it for several paces, moving a little faster and holding steady to their silence. Still, Asta kept her mind on the time and her eye on her little watch.

"We've got to turn around," she said by Berg Gasse.

They went back and now resumed their talk, bandaging their gashes and wounds by using conversation to smooth and arrange, as with comb and brush, making their way during this pursuit to the corner of Strudlhof Gasse, where a closed taxi was parked in the otherwise deserted street. They reached the upper end of the steps with laudable punctuality.

Throughout the whole walk back it never once dawned on Melzer that his parting from Mary had come about in a substantially different way from this parting now. He was equating the two experiences, just as if he'd been "given the gate" by Mary (which would assuredly not have been the case) and as if she'd sent him packing, more or less as a man lacking, which was how it stood now.

For a few moments he tried comparing Mary and Asta, but that struck him as utterly impossible. True, he didn't know a thing about frilled collars; nor could he know that Mary's very diapers had been made from the same material which was only now coming to be produced, little by little, for Asta here.

Someone was standing at the upper end of the steps.

Someone who now sent his voice booming through the empty street (Asta started when she recognized him—old man Schmeller).

"Ingrid, come up here to me!" With that, he set foot onto the first step but then stopped and stood there, apparently waiting for his order to be obeyed. Asta and Melzer bravely pressed forward nonetheless, she at her fastest pace, he hurrying along behind her, even though he was really not in the mood right now to go involving himself in other people's business.

Now he could see all the way down the steps, and he came to a standstill, since Asta too had stopped walking. In the middle, halfway up the topmost ramp, stood Ingrid Schmeller and Stephan von Semski, who was holding Ingrid by both hands. It looked as though this couple were swaying slightly, like slender trees in a storm. Now, on hearing herself called, she had turned her face up toward her father—she looked completely distraught and helpless—while Semski paid him no attention at all and kept holding on to Ingrid's hands, which she kept trying in vain to pull away with little twisting and twining motions. So he held on to her, his gaze the whole time riveted on her face, until she grew tired and turned back to him; it was as if he wanted to hold Ingrid under a spell and supplant her weaker will by exerting his stronger one to the utmost.

He said "Ingrid" once, and that was all.

Three people appeared down on the lower ramp—Grauermann, Stangeler, and Paula Schachl.

For Herr Schmeller, this state of affairs lasted for just that one second too long that it took for his patience to snap. He started down the steps, vehemently stomping toward the couple. With a few leaps and bounds, Melzer from above and Grauermann from below were by his side. "Herr Schmeller!" said Grauermann in a soothing tone. Meanwhile, Semski had finally turned Ingrid loose, and he took up a defensive stance as he turned to confront Herr Schmeller, who had once more come to a stop, though several steps above Semski. Ingrid walked up to where her father was. He seized hold of her right wrist and dragged her off with him, up the steps, paying no further heed to anyone else present. Ingrid's physical bearing as she followed her father had something like a broken plant stem about it. Everyone kept watching those two until they reached the street above and disappeared.

Melzer was the only person to observe, and with no slight degree of astonishment, that down below, where the ramp turned, René Stangeler was standing next to some girl Melzer didn't know and was holding his arms outstretched, as if enraptured.

Now Melzer quickly ran up the steps so he could continue watching Herr Schmeller and Ingrid. They were already a good distance away. Schmeller still had her clutched by the wrist. Melzer then saw father and daughter get into the taxi parked all by itself at the farther end of Strudlhof Gasse, so he now understood the connection. The cab drove off to the left.

Melzer turned back again and saw that all those present, the involved and the uninvolved alike, had trickled down, so to speak, to the lower ramp, like extras when the scene has been played. Semski was standing gloomily off to the side. He said goodbye abruptly, went down the stairs, and vanished onto Liechtenstein Strasse.

"First he followed her in the car, most likely all the way from Döbling, and then he followed us," Melzer said to Asta.

She nodded. She no longer seemed to be showing any particular interest in this episode as a whole or in any particular element of it. Her glance came to rest briefly on Paula Schachl in a testy sort of way, sizing her up, as though looking for the weakest point her critical faculty could quickly isolate. All of a sudden Melzer discerned Asta's resemblance to her father (and perhaps there might even have been visible, for just a fleeting moment, a more general, a remote affinity with ... with old Herr Schmeller). Melzer thereupon felt some relief from the heaviness and seriousness lodged so deep and so oppressively within him. Asta had now turned to René and was asking in a tone that suggested he was very definitely being required to account for his presence, "And just what are you doing here?"

On top of everything else that was happening, all of them—except for Paula, who tactfully kept herself off to the side—went on talking constantly and all at once; Melzer was vividly aware of how truly pointless all this talking was, but he joined right in anyway. Grauermann would intermittently deem it appropriate to bring the civilized niceties back up to the surface from the receding waters of the situation, so he introduced Paula Schachl to Asta and Melzer (which came off as a more or less disconnected action), while René, cutting right in, replied to the question his sister had just asked him with the incomprehensible words, "Here I have found something long foretold in me, and it is wondrous." His face was manifestly full of joy. Melzer felt only too keenly that all of them were standing perplexed about their own gathering, totally unforeseen as it was, and he was now trying to bring it to an end more quickly through an expatiation on or explanation of the matter which he thought he was obligated to give Grauermann. "It never crossed our minds that there was anything to worry about; at the very last minute it did occur to me to be a little suspicious of that lone taxi up on Waisenhaus Gasse, but by then it was much too late." On the whole, these remnants of the scene were in the same state as a pond into which someone has tossed a stone—a dash and a splash and little crisscrossing waves. The situation as it stood didn't seem very satisfactory to René Stangeler now; his face gathered a bit around the base of his nose, like a knot.

It was Grauermann who brought matters to an end, and Melzer was grateful to him for it (we know, of course, that Pista Grauermann did not easily let go of something he'd made up his mind to do—unless he was overpowered, for example by sleep—and now wanted to get back to his room, to his book and a cup of tea). Turning to Stangeler and Paula, he asked, "Will you walk me back to the academy?" "Of course!" said René, and Paula nodded and smiled (up to this point she'd been very somber the entire time). So this was how the grouping broke up. While those three were going up the steps toward Waisenhaus Gasse, Asta trailed Paula Schachl with her eyes, exactly the same expression on her face as before, as she again took on that resemblance to her father.

And so Melzer now found himself alone with Asta once more, after that whole hullabaloo had broken up, on a landing of the Strudlhof Steps, amidst green patches of leaf shadow and sun rays falling ever more soft and slantwise, as it was getting on for quarter to five. But it wasn't really happiness Melzer was feeling at being alone with Asta once again. What was gratifying to him now was the sense of being set free from a betwixt-and-between situation, as when goodbyes have been going on for too long and people standing in the hall by the front door keep falling back into embarrassed and unnecessary small talk. During this whole scandalous episode, something else, having no apparent connection with it and admitting now of only one result, had come to pass in Melzer without his noticing—something had closed and locked inside him regarding Asta, the way a safe or a strongbox is locked. And it was only for that reason—because it freed him from pain—that he was then placed into the position of being able to absorb and store up in his memory a noteworthy statement Asta made as they now went slowly walking down the stairs (while Melzer's leave, which was supposed to last eight more days, came to an end inside him and he thought about traveling back to Bosnia, perhaps as early as that same evening). "You know, Melzer," she said in that totally easygoing and companionable tone that resonated, as it were, with cordial good wishes from the time they'd spent out in the country, "you know, Melzer, as Herr Schmeller was dragging Ingrid behind him up the steps, something became clear to me in a flash that I never really saw quite as distinctly before. And where I saw it was in Ingrid and how she carried herself; I almost want to say I saw it in her very body..."

"Yes, like a broken stalk." This, or something like it, was his interjection.

"Exactly!" Asta said emphatically. "That's exactly it! I owe you a vote of thanks for that, Melzer! You said it just right. Like a broken stalk. Total, unconditional surrender. And do you know what that shows me? The difference between so many individuals and families I know—and my own family. Not one of us Stangelers would ever be able to submit or resign ourselves like that; not one could copy Ingrid's way of carrying herself; not one could ever look the way she looked there on the steps. I think I'm right in saying that none of us could ever see our way clear to doing something like that. It looks like weakness, but it's actually strength. Any one of us would go down kicking and scratching to the bitter end, fighting against everything—I mean everything exterior, everything of any importance that comes along. It's like a curse; not only won't we submit, but we can't, either. I'm convinced it's out of weakness. Think about it—I really believe that's a weakness."

They had come as far as the Flight into Egypt on Alserbach Strasse, and while Asta was still speaking, he flagged down a taxi to see her home.

Melzer started up out of his memories, knocking over the coffee things in the process. This little accident didn't produce any bad results, though. The fine grounds had dried out long before in the pot, which the Turks call a *cezve*, and in the tiny porcelain cup with its copper holder, and nothing could fall to the floor, because the embossed serving tray was already sitting on it, next to Melzer and the bearskin from the Treskavica, which he was lying on, asleep at first after eating, during his "kèf," but then half awake and drifting amidst intense images just below the threshold of genuine waking and fond forsaking, separated from them as if by a flimsy, translucent wall, that epidermis or membrane on the surface which he wasn't quite ready to puncture. For some time now, he'd been calling this state his "thinking sleep." Right around this time was when Melzer put into limited circulation a number of other self-coined neologisms, a special, arcane vocabulary for intimate use, we might call it.

A few items now entered, point by isolated point, into his waking consciousness, no longer woven into the whole fabric of swirling images in a half dream, in which everything is taken as much for granted as the warmth of one's own body but is in equal measure causing astonishment as well, the astonishment providing the basis for whatever ends up being somewhat fruitful about states of this kind.

He became aware in the first place that it had been fourteen years since he'd last seen Asta, on the very day of that scandal on the Strudlhof Steps. Now her name was Frau Haupt, her husband a government building surveyor (get out of one family rooted in technology and head straight into another family rooted in technology!), and she had two boys. Melzer had been told this by Marchetti, who even today could now and then be found sitting in a corner of the Café Pucher, leaning against the wall like an abandoned Foreign Ministry walking stick— although on second thought, that's not right; that's not what the Ernst von Marchetti of the year 1925 should be compared to, for he'd grown as plump and roly-poly as a little suckling pig from a storybook feast and hence had only superfluity, but not shape, in common with a walking stick.

It had been in 1911. The year after the bear hunt. Perhaps on the same day. Today was August 22, 1925. Quite possible indeed. On the kaiser's birthday everybody was still out in the country. So far so good, but what about afterward? He'd wanted to return to Bosnia the following day, or even on the very same evening, eight days before his leave was over.

At this point the ground of the past, nearly solid by now, opened beneath him and gave way, and Major Melzer was soaring like a bird over a deep ravine, hovering in the air or suspended in it with pinions outspread.

He thought of the hawks on the Treskavica. A man looking up into the sky was often so dizzyingly deep below them that he could almost go plummeting after his own glance.

The days between the scandal on the steps and Melzer's departure were blank. Later in the evening following that episode, there had been an absolutely ferocious rainstorm, around eight o'clock or so; he could remember that much. He'd been lying on the sofa in his room at the Belvedere Hotel. Rain was gushing down the windowpanes in torrents.

Throughout the rest of that week he'd "mulattoed," which is the way such passing excesses were referred to in the language of Austrian officers—frightened at how meaningful, how serious was the color of life, which he'd been making such a strenuous effort to blend into the kaleidoscope of mindless diversions (that much he knew today, and so now he indignantly rejected phrasing that states, "I just needed a little distraction"—no, it wasn't nearly so much about distraction as about collection; he wanted by all means to have his experiences back then, his "tough luck with Asta Stangeler," collected and gathered up in a different language, one in which it would rest on him a bit lighter). "Laska was on leave. If he'd been in Bosnia, I would have taken off and gone back there, and maybe today I'd be able to remember . . ."

He couldn't remember.

But wait! Now there came to the surface, like a cabbage bit in a bowl of soup, the leg of a prostitute in the City Hotel—just her leg, and then not even the whole thing; a silk knee turned sideways and, higher up, the pale skin of the upper thigh past the top of a long stocking.

Nothing else came up out of the chasm.

But wait! Wallpaper, just a patch, with gold embossing, and next to it some edging painted white, in high-gloss enamel. The foyer of a nightclub; it was Maxim's. Nothing but this patch of wallpaper. Next to it, though it didn't really belong here, the sink from his room at the Hotel Belvedere back then. He let the water run for a long time as he cleaned the white porcelain, washing a broad, ocher-colored stream down the drain. He'd vomited.

Behind all these images there stood unwavering Asta's little room— no matter that he'd caught just a momentary glimpse while passing through—and the living room next door, the green underwater light from the blinds, the gleaming black silence of the piano, the subdued quality of sound, the coolness, the odor of camphor or naphtha from summer storage. Melzer turned over, as if he had made a discovery that could serve to elucidate anything and everything; he pressed his face gently into the bearskin—there, that's where the odor was coming from (his landlady would have been happy to get rid of it by packing it away in camphor for the summer, but Melzer was afraid of the empty spot, plus he wanted to lie on it during his kèf, and so this valuable object, which the major had such an attachment to, caused her a good deal of work in her attempts to preserve it from moths).

And now that chasm in Melzer's memories closed up in a surprising way.

A barrel organ started playing loudly on the street. With that, the country celebration honoring the eighty-first birthday of Kaiser Franz Joseph I became present and immediate to him in a blare of trumpets. It was the same march playing now as on August 18, 1911, at night, during a torchlight parade. The bass drum from the firemen's band boomed three times; then the glow of the torches burst into the summer air, which had been getting cooler; they were large torches, flaming, smoldering, and smoking, carried up ahead by the units of the fire brigade not involved with the music. Not only that, but the cradling and soothing tenderness of the night was pushed far off to the side by the piercing treble and the pounding bass, which was being produced, logically enough, by a mountain guide named Pounder (Rumpler), whose wife, even more logically, was a washerwoman. Etelka and Grauermann took condescending pleasure at the many slight rhythmic deviations in Pounder's bass (and yet only a few days later, in his room at the Consular Academy, it was none other than Pista Grauermann who established that music played a negative role in his life, was "negatively charged" for him, as it were. At this point we'd just like to take note of that fact from a totally external standpoint; we're not joined to Melzer at the hip, after all, so we have a better view of the panorama as a whole). Behind the long parade of torchbearers—it looked from the porch of the Stangelers' country house like a gigantic serpent, all afire, slithering up the valley—there followed as a pale afterimage a line of dots, swaying colored lanterns carried by the summer guests. The local people all stayed up toward the front, though, with the band music and the torches, even those who weren't carrying one; and amid the red glow, which kept bobbing up and down and constantly pressing onward, there was quite a sizable throng of people on the left and right edges of the road, walking along beside the marching band. So inordinately loud because it was so close by, the band had something violent about it, or at least so it struck Melzer, who, along with Asta, had been caught in the full blast, while the others, the lantern bearers, remained in the rear, among the summer visitors staying some distance behind. Dust was flying. They could smell the somewhat musty odor coming from the farm people's holiday attire. And it seemed so much more desirable to go all the way back to the rear with Asta, to be the last ones, with single colored lights up ahead of them here and there.

When the barrel organ began playing, Melzer had jumped up from the bearskin and run to the window, where there was nothing to be seen, of course; even the poor organ-grinder was nowhere in sight, probably cranking away under some covered arch or in some courtyard.

Melzer felt these two trivial circumstances—the recurrence of the camphor odor from Asta's little room with its furniture draped (for him the very camphor itself was one and the same) and the striking up, out on the street, of the same march tune from those days—he felt them both to be an outright enormity of some kind, caused by an optical effect functioning inside him right now that was magnifying everything. It never even remotely occurred to him to analyze it or correct for it—in the first place because that was hardly his way of doing things, and in the second because he felt at such moments in the closest possible proximity to the truth. Just as the music from the barrel organ broke into the "trio," as it's called, the middle section of the military march—and in Austrian marches this passage always has a certain softness and fullness in both melody and harmony—a tiny door popped open, right in the middle of the village parade by torchlight, and through it there suddenly leapt, resplendent in all her natural and unnatural regalia, Frau Editha Schlinger, née Pastré, full-grown, like Minerva sprung from Jupiter's head.

He came close to shouting, though softly. He was supposed to be in the country today, in Kritzendorf. But he'd chosen to "withdraw." At the moment, Melzer was using the word with conscious thought— to the extent that we can speak of thought in his case to begin with— though not actually in the military sense (as when soldiers at times withdraw from a tactical position in battle), but quite literally instead.

Because he thought he couldn't take any more of this.

Since the springtime, she'd been showing up again among the crowd that surrounded Eulenfeld, which Melzer had already been increasingly wanting to move away from anyway. For some time, he'd been honest about admitting it on the inside, to himself. But the route he'd been following in withdrawal was now barricaded by Editha, and it was a route at the approximate end of which he would have had to find a dead man, namely Major Laska.

As for Editha, she was a far more mysterious character, a much smoother operator, than even Eulenfeld himself.

So very smooth, in fact, that Melzer kept finding it simply impossible to forge any connection which might suffice even to begin bridging the identity between the young girl named Editha Pastré, who back then, in August of 1911, had set in motion the scandal on the Strudlhof Steps, and the Editha Schlinger of the present day. Never mind that Editha didn't seem to him to look one bit different today from the way she'd looked fourteen years earlier, as a girl. By now, she must have just about reached her midthirties (when he kept that in mind he felt lighter and happier). How very fleetingly, how strictly only in passing had he known her before the war! At the Stangelers' out in the country in that summer of 1911—now he could see Editha in a white piqué dress walking along the edge of the tennis court.

But no. The Editha of those days didn't mean anything to him, and so his mind soon turned away from the girl and toward images of the woman from this summer right now.

In the Danube meadowlands by Greifenstein. She'd gone ahead of him on a narrow, winding path in the Au Woods, which he was wandering along, together with her and Eulenfeld and several people from Eulenfeld's ever-changing crowd (oftentimes Melzer could scarcely even keep their names straight), all of them in bathing suits and carrying a few things in bags or in their hands—boxes of cookies and other packages of food, the Master of Horse with a bottle of cognac, naturally; "After all, he *is* the Master of Horse," as one of the ladies he'd once brought along put it, more or less as though legitimizing the matter. And basically there wasn't much more Melzer could have said about it, either (people manage to adjust, halfway at least, to a personality that's not going to develop any further; it's only the growing process that keeps constantly provoking criticism). Treading softly on the soft ground in her bath slippers as if on cat's paws, Editha glided down hills and waded through inlets without hesitating, without hanging on to tree branches, and without looking back to Melzer, expecting him to help. A blue rubber bathing cap was dangling from her left hand. Her body was covered by nothing but a swimsuit. But that body, which could thus hardly escape close observation, seemed to Melzer to be fully clothed nonetheless; it seemed also, despite its being a known quantity, to be inviting anticipation of things totally unknown. Her hips expanded a bit more amply in proportion to the rest of her measurements, though it was an effect only hinted at, and he couldn't be sure he was seeing it like this all the time; perhaps it was only when she would walk or take up certain postures. To this unsureness was added (by Melzer) the same feeling about Editha's small nose, which was curved so delicately that at times it looked completely straight.

He would have enjoyed telling her at some point how strongly connected he felt to her by the past, by their youth, by days of long ago (on the other hand, it would have struck him as unmannerly, and—in light of how her appearance had stayed the same—even downright silly), by their previous acquaintance (though it actually hadn't been much of one, really, and at the end of it Melzer had wound up in the opposition party, so to speak), by... by (in a word) the Strudlhof Steps, he would have had to say, and by Major Laska, whom she'd never met. So this was how he tried, on one occasion, to come to terms with the past, with the last years of a Vienna still an imperial capital (every stimulus of the senses causes a warming trend in the use of heightened language, and people with no refinement have generally felt a need to declare their love in such terms; for just such people, indeed, expression and reality turn out to be totally congruent). The gathering had taken place in the spring, on a Saturday evening—on one of the Saturday evenings, that is—in Eulenfeld's room. At the time he was subletting in Josefstadt, on Skoda Gasse. An absurd, innocently god-awful bronze figure stood in the corner, a statue of a girl dressed in only a few flowery tendrils made of brass; they wound around her body and held the electric light bulb above her. Editha was sitting under this lamp with its topaz-colored shade. Now Melzer could see her foot in front of him. The open brown *escarpin* squeezed, if only a bit, so that in front her foot protruded roundly over the leather. Other people had been on hand as well (who?—he couldn't remember). Someone was lying on the rug across from Editha and looking up at her. This evening was one of those times when she seemed to have that extra padding in her hips as she sat there, and the delicate curve of her little nose stood out in the lamplight too.

That was one evening: she came back so vividly now, the way he'd seen her ages before, seated in that American physician's automobile as it stood parked outside the café; and, to tell the truth, he'd been more than willing that day not to see her at all. Just the red seat covers in the car. The blinding red leather. But Eulenfeld's way of zooming around curves, carefree, rough-and-tumble, sure of himself, kept pressing him up against her. And then when the car was standing here, outside his building, only that other woman was left, the one he didn't know, sitting up front with Eulenfeld; no question but that he'd ignored her completely when saying goodbye. And then had his kèf. And thought he knew everything.

Melzer, standing at the window all this time, shook himself suddenly, like a dog coming out of the water. In the chambers of his life's energy, bolts would burst and walls would crack whenever he got anywhere near that boundary line where the customary twilight pathway ends in the possible and peters out, because just beyond its last turning an image of actual realization is gaining unnoticed on the man tunneling and burrowing through his own interior and is about to leap on him and knock him down.

During these few seconds, while his memory was replaying their conversation back then under the lamplight—it had been an attempt on his part to slip some familiar old items from days gone by into Editha's hand, as it were, so that he could then take them back as if they were coming from her to begin with—during these few seconds at the window, here and now, Melzer wasn't trying to foist the role of a martyr or a victim of torture on himself. From the first moment, the very first moment, he ran into Editha Schlinger that past spring after all those years, the line of communication had at once been flung from ship to ship and just as quickly tied tight. And there once again Melzer had to some extent been placed in a dependent position, had been swooped up by Eulenfeld, who in a casual way nudged Editha over toward him this time, too. She'd allowed it to happen; indeed, she'd been completely transparent in showing how keenly she welcomed it, thereby throwing Melzer temporarily into a state that made him feel as if someone had doused him with a bottle of soda water. So he was sitting with her on that April morning in the Café Graben, nearly empty now; Eulenfeld, who supposedly had business to attend to, had made himself scarce after just a few moments (in his turn, Melzer actually had taken care of some official business in town). "I commend you now to the tried-and-true guidance of the major"—thus the dragoon captain; he waved his hat in a wide arc and made quite a display of cocking it back down onto his head from above as he strode through the revolving glass door, proclaiming a finish and a farewell, as it were (this "mouse-gray something," as he called his head covering, always of exceptional quality and high cost, but likewise of great age, for he detested each new hat of his for a good long time). So there they sat. And yet no more than a mere five minutes earlier, outside on the Graben, by the beautiful monument called the Pestsäule, the plague column, in the midst of a stream of passersby and in the midst of his own nonchalant and rather absentminded ambling, the little door had popped open, and there was Minerva standing before him, the captain at her side. They'd both been really pleased, landing here simply because the Master of Horse had declared out on the street that he needed to make a telephone call right away, and besides, one of the waiters probably had a message for him. "I commend you now to the tried-and-true guidance of the major"—and off he went. Later on, by the way, as Melzer was keeping Editha company on her way home, that part about the "guidance" proved to be not entirely without foundation; here in the center of town, she really didn't seem to know her way around very well and made a few wrong turns as she went about her errands, so that Melzer wound up looking after her in actual fact.

But what was now hovering right before his eyes, with the most familiar—for that matter, we're tempted to say the most intimate—kind of presence (such as inheres only in the truth) was that even as of their first seeing each other again out on the Graben, Editha had already started building bridges to him, opening hatches, letting down stairways. And had been doing it ever since on this or that occasion, with amazing freedom. Those were just the times when Melzer would feel more distinctly than ever that she was a smooth operator and then begin once more to feel that he in turn was dependent, swooped up and taken away somewhere, so to speak, like a child being led by the hand. She made no bones about how eager she was to get him to separate from the rest of the group with her in places like, say, Kritzendorf or Greifenstein. "They're walking too fast for me up ahead there, Melzer, so why don't we just let them sprint?" or "How about if we go, just the two of us, and have a glass of currant wine, all right? Wouldn't that be nice?" And with that they'd have stolen away unobtrusively from the whole campsite atmosphere and the picnic lunch in the meadow so that they could sit together in an outdoor tavern at a rough-hewn plank table under some immense old trees, wearing their bathing suits, just as they were, caressed by a lightly rising wind and braced by the deeply chilled local vintage, so dangerous because it looks like a carbonated soft drink but has the effect of a potent wine.

No, he hadn't been tortured.

He—a . . . a man who backs out. Instead of being in Kritzendorf today. The deep gray-green foam of the Au Woods, the meandering inlets with such great variety in their different greens, radiant and yellow-toned in the growths covering the calm surfaces, more muted in the lance-forests of reeds, completely subdued under the low-hanging branches that reached far out beyond the bank. The cry of a river bird echoing as if under closed arches. Dizzyingly high treetops, far off in the distance, resolving to vapor in the golden sheen of the summer sky. The rowboat drifts beneath a canopy of leaves; they have to bend down deep, and an oar brushes against the green bank in the clear, still water. Now the keel scrapes and makes a soft crunching sound. She stretches out on the oarsman's bench, leaning back and giving him a long, calm, friendly look; in time she smiles her little, mock-devoted smile. "What can they do? Here I am with you now, Melzer; we've taken off by ourselves again. Isn't it beautiful here? So quiet! Are you enjoying yourself too?" That's what her smile says without a word spoken. No, he hadn't been tortured.

At first they'd only seen each another here and there.

After the evening in Eulenfeld's room, under the bronze person coiled with vine tendrils, about two weeks had passed before they next met. And then again. But lately, Eulenfeld was paying more attention to Melzer.

He seldom had company. Somewhere around the middle of June his landlady (her name was Rak, widow of an accountant), had announced a gentleman and a lady. For Melzer it had been a surprisingly strong jolt, like a dash of champagne in the blood, when just like that, at five o'clock on a perfectly ordinary weekday—Melzer had left his office just a short time before—Editha came strolling into his living room, followed by the captain, Master of Horse Eulenfeld.

Not fifteen minutes had passed before she was sitting on the bearskin from the Treskavica and smoking a chibouk—inhaling deeply, to Melzer's astonishment, nay alarm, as if she were used to it!—and sipping from one of those miniature Turkish coffee cups.

By the same token, Melzer had naturally begun asking himself exactly what the nature of her relationship with Eulenfeld might be. But any such line of questioning was struck down—with a club, so to speak—as early as the beginning of the summer, for it was at this time that there swam into the ken of everyone, and so of course into the ken of Editha as well, a new entanglement of the captain's, this one with a very young woman of exceptionally fine qualities, though perhaps that may just be how any halfway regular or regulated young lady would have been bound to strike this group. Her name was Thea Rokitzer. They'd known her for a good while; she'd been turning up now and then since 1923. She loved Baron von Eulenfeld. It can't be said in any other way than in a simple declarative sentence like this, and indeed, it simply could never be declared often enough, because it was absolutely simple and indivisible, one of life's prime numbers. She loved this charming old jackass. And since he was making use of that, she became Editha's protégée. Then Editha, in her turn, Eulenfeld's. There was something almost servile in the way Editha behaved toward him; it was only a tinge, but it was noticeable. He seemed quite simply to be part of her very lease on life. She had submitted to him. "After all, he *is* the Master of Horse." He possessed not only freedom and superiority of manner, this man the captain. He also possessed a gentle power. Melzer's makeup wasn't such, however, that he would have been able to gain insight into the true nature of this circle of people, a circle on the periphery of which he settled as a stranger but toward the center of which he felt a magnetic tug. Was there any such thing as an actual center here, though? And if so, where was it? With the captain? Or with that young man who'd been lying on the rug at Editha's feet under the lamp with the person made of bronze? He was called Oki. A vicious goon, easily over six feet tall, with moist eyes like long slits and the mouth of a black man. Leucht was his last name. Melzer was aware of an affair he was having with the elder daughter of a professor at the university. Even so, his having a sense of what all might be possible here, all at the same time and in the same place—with Oki Leucht, with his girlfriend Dolly Storch, with the Master of Horse—no, Melzer's grasp didn't extend quite that far. He probably couldn't have arrived at that point even after five more years in this group, for that matter. And so it was that the part Fräulein Rokitzer had to be playing—very publicly had to be playing, right in front of everybody's eyes and with everybody having their little say—was bound to have a decidedly calming effect on Melzer, at least insofar as it had any bearing on Editha's relations with the captain.

He started bungling things, our lieutenant, our civil service official, or better yet, our major. He started bungling, not for any reasons of advancing age—that was a long time off yet—but because whatever substance he'd always been able drawn on to make his way in life, and above all to furnish that life, so to speak (or to burnish that life), had apparently gone out of him.

It happened, moreover, that this Fräulein Rokitzer was once an eyewitness, as it were, to a quandary Melzer was in, and he was later on—more or less involuntarily, because he had to wait for the captain, who was late—to spend about half of one July afternoon with her, during which he even felt a tiny bit of relief from the predicaments he'd been suffering through. The first of these had occurred on the tenth of the month. Editha was expecting him for tea, alone, on Saturday, the eleventh. Not a shadow of a doubt existed as to the real nature of their appointment, but every doubt in the world rose up in Melzer during the three days preceding. Doubts of all kinds. Finally, he was crushed by them, like grain between two millstones. In his case, though, nothing got milled; it was an empty mill-course, the whole works overheating as they ground so exceeding small, whirling in panic, the whole operation re-doubt-able. He ended up writing Editha a note on Friday to say he was sick. And his condition had in fact really grown so bad that it would no longer have been possible for him to be even remotely festive at the party (and surely it deserves that name!) for which he was now in the process of sending his regrets. Note in hand, weary and ground to a pulp, he was standing in front of the black and yellow mailbox on Porzellan Gasse, late in the afternoon; still another doubt arose now, this one as to whether there would be enough time for his excuse to reach her beforehand at all, let alone with the proper amount of advance notice. And yet Melzer completely ruled out using the telephone; it would have contested his present state, which really wasn't open to discussion, by a barrage of cajolery, questions, rebuttal. But then along came Thea Rokitzer, walking from the direction of the city center, and Melzer, whose thought had just been to drop his note (and all the pain and sorrow of the moment behind it) into the slot and onto the bottom of the letterbox, now held on to it and greeted the young girl, who shone out brightly (any unexpected solution will) as she emerged from the gray of the street while coming closer. She was on her way to see Frau Schlinger. Yes, right that very minute. So he was able to give his note to her, which meant that she was carrying away in her little purse the whole heavy burden that had been weighing him down. And even if it was only a short distance away, he gained some space, got some breathing room, at least for the moment. On the fourteenth of July, though—his morning visit, governed by the strictest standards of protocol, to tender his official apology to Frau Schlinger. He informed her of his restoration to health. With a large bunch of heavy gladiolas that had an oily sheen. "I trust you weren't expecting me after all?" "Oh, no," she said; just that. Nothing ended, nothing came to a close; the whole thing simply remained suspended in air.

Now the major is marveling at his ability to keep the exact dates of those days in his head.

He's been standing at the window this whole time, though he can't see out of it anymore, for his right hand has pulled the little chain that opens the slats of the blinds, and so they're now shut again; he's looking at a green wall, wooden and dry, and he feels the heat that has collected between the windows during the course of the day. He steps back and closes the inner casements. Now the sunbaked wooden slats are again mirrored over, as if underwater, and he can sense the relative coolness in the green twilight of the room—aquarium light. He stays standing there by the window. From where he is he can still smell the faint odor of naphtha from the bearskin.

Why not? Why in God's name not?

Mary? It was the same story.

Mary was indelible. Suddenly he was lifted by pain, as if the hardwood floor had surged up under his feet. Gone. Now the floor was again smooth and even.

It had been the same story. Under the pressure he felt now, he started thinking very quickly and with the utmost banality. Don't we all?

"It was because of my career. Because of my uncle David and his conditional stock certificates. But does that really explain it? Old Man Allern would have taken care of everything. I just didn't want to take on any responsibilities; it's as simple as that. Fräulein Rokitzer looks like that chambermaid the Stangelers used to have. She looks like Lintschi, but only in her facial expressions. She's beautiful, really beautiful. But hold on a minute! A man of my age should be past setting his sights on a girl like this. Her full breasts and long legs! Eulenfeld. That pig. I was a coward down in Ischl. Whose lead was I following? There was nobody I had to answer to. My mother doesn't object to Jews. But I always have to have everything laid out just so; back down to Bosnia, all neat and tidy. Laska. If only he could have heard the way Eulenfeld talks! 'Dontcha know, my good friend Melzer, it much behooves a man to ponder whether he ought involve himself with an individual of this ilk, to wit with one whom surely it would be fair to characterize as more inclined even today toward acting the moonstruck calf. For—as I ask myself—how is one to shake her off?' Laska would have smacked him one. He wouldn't have had anything to do with him, in fact. No, not in a million years. Eulenfeld's turns of phrase wouldn't have impressed him. That makes me so furious—that enticing quality! When a woman's being enticing, when she wants me … me of all men! That's like a mist before my eyes; I lose my head. Mary wanted to, I know that much; I'd have had to marry her; it would have been … why not? Why in God's name not?" Once again he shook himself. Once again bolts were bursting and walls cracking, walls and partitions erected to run right through the middle of him, dividing him, today as earlier. No one will suspect our Melzer of thinking; he was really beyond such a thing, and that includes his "thinking sleep," quite a pretentious term for the states he would go into. He was beyond the possibility, we want to say, of discovering the possibility of thinking (we'd be more inclined to concede the point in reference to even Grauermann!). But attendant on what he was doing here and now— during these moments in front of the closed window, the surface of whose green pane now reflected and thereby took on a spatial depth in no way an intrinsic dimension of it as a flat, blank physical object placed only to create a separation from the sunlit street—attendant on what he was doing, with his glance lost in the depth of the green as if it were a silent pond or a well too deep for him to fathom, was, more than anything, a sense of compelling astonishment.

That's just how it is—we're not confronted with astonishment at its deepest in the face of whatever out-of-the-ordinary phenomena the outer world pours out on us. After all, it *is* the outer world. ("After all, he *is* the Master of Horse.") We are met with that feeling instead when faced with our own inner mechanism, which goes on running, with or without our blessing, and which one day we suddenly realize is an entirely independent entity as little prompted by our volition or intent as a steam engine would be by someone standing next to it and playing a guitar.

This kind of hurtling past our own selves, however, a *revue passée* at the speed of an express train, causes whatever issue is at question to light up with a far more intense glow than would any wearisome ruminations of the tunneling and burrowing variety, to light up at the crossover points that this express train has to travel over in switching onto its designated track (these are none other than those turning points, or *trópoi*, as the ancients called them). Little lights are burning at the switches. We see the track running straight ahead as one possibility that existed at the time, and likewise we see the switch; it wasn't set on "open" for us, and so we thundered past and kept going on our way. We see it. Though only now for the first time. Little lights are burning at the switches when this kind of summarizing streak along a stretch of track is in progress; they quickly flash past, one after another, and vanish back into the darkness. There are machines made, games of luck and skill, in which the ball, once it starts rolling, always has to take one pathway or another (for some time these game machines, through the glass of which one could watch the ball as it scurried along, were to be found in many taverns). To make it even more exciting, a tiny electric light bulb, green, red, or yellow, will flash at every point at which the ball chooses its path. It is to these games, with their rolling ball, that such a one-second *revue passée*—or *revue du passé*—might be compared.

Melzer went traveling along his *trópoi* at lightning speed.

And it happened as he was doing so that he caught sight—for an immeasurably brief split second—of Master of Horse Captain Eulenfeld at one of the crossover points; indeed, he nearly switched over directly into his path, nearly collided. Missed him, but only by a hair. Then he was gone.

But now, on the other hand, Melzer saw Stephan von Semski, looking as he had after that scandal with Herr Schmeller, when at first he'd stood gloomily off to the side and then tipped his hat and gone down the stairs. If Semski had made as much of a theatrical display of tilting his hat down on his head, proclaiming a finish and a farewell, as Eulenfeld had done, back in the springtime, while walking through the revolving door of the Café Graben and leaving Editha and Melzer himself to their own devices—matters wouldn't have been any clearer anyway. As he walked down the steps, his back was already saying enough.

And then with Asta, alone.

Paralysis. Nothing more. No *trópos*. Or only a purely constructed outer possibility—to conquer that territory inside Asta still occupied by Semski, in spite of everything, and now vacated once and for all. But Melzer no longer had in him whatever it would have taken to accomplish that.

She'd shown some resemblance to old Herr Schmeller?!

He'd surrendered to the situation at once, like Ingrid on the steps. Even though Semski was out of the way. Maybe it would have been possible after all?

Those terrible days afterward, until he left.

Now the floor didn't surge up under him, though. No pain.

When it came to this parting, this parting from Asta, that is, there was no uncle with conditional stock shares in a brewery to withhold dividends from him, no disarrangement of his neat and tidy routine (though admittedly Herr Stangeler wouldn't have been exactly overjoyed about our lieutenant), no changes, no risks entailing the need to ponder behoovingly whether a man ought here to involve himself.

There he was again, the captain! At this crossing point he went whizzing by in a blur—clever, cold, lethargic, making himself scarce. Because of his uncle, no, because of "the moonstruck calf," and because of his never having known very well from the start how he was supposed to get rid of Thea.

None of that with Asta.

But with Mary.

No, Asta hadn't had this . . . this enticing quality. It was obvious that she hadn't wanted to . . . hadn't wanted him, him exclusively, him only. Instead, she'd made him into her confessor, as it were, on Waisenhaus Gasse—none other than him, him exclusively.

But today the floor no longer surged up under his feet as a result.

Instead, Minerva popped out of the door and supplanted Asta von Stangeler in Melzer's mental images as easily as breathing.

There she was again, sitting under the bronze figure swathed in vine tendrils, the light falling onto her brown *escarpin*, over the leather of which, at the front, her plump foot protruded just a bit. The light from above her appeared to sharpen the delicate curve of her nose. She sat with her legs crossed, her midsection resting in a broader shadow produced by that light fixture, by its remarkable ornamentation. Farther back in the room, where a sofa stood, were some two or three other people (one of them could have been sweet, heavyset Dolly Storch; her dainty head had the beauty of an odalisque, but unfortunately the rest of her body also corresponded to Near Eastern or Arabic ideals of desirability). Now Melzer was talking about old times. And before Eulenfeld—pretty far gone by this point (they always drank cognac here, and out of large glasses)—could start in with his sentimental reminiscing about his military service, especially about his former camaraderie with the Royal and Imperial Austrian Army, and in that way engulf the whole area toward which Melzer was trying to steer the conversation, Melzer had in turn registered a distinct feeling in relation to Editha, one that didn't just go gently drifting past but that pervaded him strongly instead. The feeling was as if he'd found himself, along with all those memories of his (which, come to think of it, were only a small part of the effort—ingrained as a habit by now—he was always directing toward his own past), facing a blank wall, enigmatic and chilling at the same time, because everything Editha was saying was being delivered as though she were reading from working notes, from an aide-mémoire, so that the only thing holding it all together was some facile power of recall and not really memory as such. It stood in relation to memory the way a few loose pages of notes held together with a paper clip would stand to a book whose narrative, lovingly bent over the past, not only encompasses many more details than would any such appointment-book set of jottings but beyond that also stands out luminous against the shining russet-colored background of what has been, a quality entirely lacking at the present moment, as was, by the same token, on Editha's end, any impetus for prolonging this line of conversation or lingering among these topics. She provided information.

She was able to tell him what Marchetti was doing with himself these days and where Honnegger was to be found; in fact, she even let fall, totally unruffled, that Semski was on the staff of the Polish embassy here in Vienna. Her manner upset Melzer in his deepest depths, and far more than he was aware of at that moment; indeed, the affliction and the turmoil he was feeling were much more expansive and convoluted, as it were, than to have been able to find the room they needed in so brief a time. These feelings all came crowding together, imprecise and impenetrable, under one particular image that would not leave him now—it was of himself walking with Editha through the streets and avenues in the center of town this past spring, after the first time (though in fact the second!) they'd met again. She apparently didn't know her way around that area very well; for example, she'd thought she could walk from Goldschmied Gasse to the Kohlmarkt, where she had something to pick up in a stationery store, by way of Tuchlauben. It was a fact, after all, that Editha had more than once been away from Vienna for fairly long periods, in Lausanne and in Paris. Impressions from abroad predominated in her. When she spoke at somewhat more length and with some continuity, which was seldom, then it could be detected immediately. In any case, though, Melzer didn't obtain from her even one iota of what he really wanted, albeit unconsciously—to receive back from her, now wrapped in the warmth of her person, things of his own that he'd opened up to her. (And while we're at it, most people don't want anything other than exactly that when they speak to us; hence the method of taking part in a conversation that will be of most benefit to all is to say back to people, with some slight variation, whatever they've just finished saying to us. This is the way to make the most cordial relations come about with the least expenditure of energy.)

So this is how affairs then stood—though we're actually not discussing so much a state of affairs as we are merely a state of soul in which the scales were teetering in the balance underneath the person made of bronze, with Oki Leucht lying on the carpet at Editha's feet, with all that cognac, with Dolly Storch in the background, with the captain's memories, all sentimental-regimental (he talked about the war the way other people talk about the "good old days"), having just gained ground, which he then began swamping—when in walked René Stangeler.

Melzer knew him again at once.

"Where is thy fair Grete? Off to Italy already?" asked the Master of Horse with a somewhat thick tongue.

René didn't answer. He looked over at Dolly Storch and then turned to Editha.

"We've met," she said, and shook hands with him.

The effect on Melzer was one of complete relief. (His elation or satisfaction would have been less three days earlier, as Editha had seemed for several moments almost to be waiting for someone to introduce her to René Stangeler—that is, until she said hello to him herself.)

He also recognized Melzer right away. "I can remember exactly," he said, "when we last saw one another, Herr Melzer. It was on the Strudlhof Steps in August of 1911."

"The Strudlhof Steps?" asked Editha. "What are they?"

"Leading from Boltzmann Gasse down to Liechtenstein Strasse," Oki Leucht cut in as he nonchalantly reached up, while still lying on the rug, to shake hands with René, who now, even after having spoken right up in saluting Melzer and thus given himself room to maneuver, so to speak, was acting more or less ill at ease, if not downright perplexed. For the moment, he even forgot to say anything to Dolly Storch—she called to him with a "Hello, René!"—and the others over by the sofa.

Our former "prep-school friend," our gymnasiast, by now a PhD, seemed to Melzer as if he'd hardly changed at all (which René had in common with Editha). But there was one feature about his face that perhaps had grown more marked, though, one Melzer thought he had taken note of earlier (at least he thought so now, looking backward, as in the process he quickly recalled the whole area surrounding the tennis court out at the Stangelers' country house and the stream with the artificial pond). This face of René's, its eyes set a little atilt, had the tendency to gather together like a knot being drawn tight; the specific point of focus was somewhere around the root of the nose. René had taken a seat near him and Editha. Melzer felt a sort of revival or lifting of his spirits as far as that blank wall just mentioned is concerned. His feeling was that he and René shared an alliance here, that they held a secret in common. At the same time it was totally present for him that in some strange way the girl Editha Pastré, who fourteen years earlier had brought about that confrontation (an occurrence which she herself might well have remained entirely unaware of) on the Strudlhof Steps—just referred to in passing by René—was ostensibly the same person as this Frau Schlinger, this darling Editha, sitting here now with the middle of her body in a wider shadow and her silk-covered leg (Oki had only too clear and too far a view up it) coming back into the light, along with her foot and its thick little bulge over the leather of her shoe in front! So Melzer began asking Stangeler all kinds of questions about his family. In those days, however, that was the one sure way to arouse René's mistrust; this young man, struggling—and with immense effort, at least in his opinion—to wrest for himself a way of living that would be all his own, was bound to feel anything coming from that direction as profoundly hostile, and that instinct extended to even the most well-meaning of his family's acquaintances. And if this nearly spastic rejection of Melzer didn't immediately leap to the fore, it was only because he appeared fixed in René's memory as part of an image that belonged among the earliest in that incipient life of his own, the life he really could own. Just now, though, as Melzer started in about René's parents and his two elder sisters, who lived abroad, and their husbands, and on top of that proceeded to one or another of his aunts or uncles, Stangeler's defenses went up, and he tossed over to Melzer whatever meager scraps, if one will, he could scrounge up on that subject. Furthermore, he never knew anything definite about his relatives anyway—not what they were doing, how many children they had, or even how old they were—and so any and all questions along these lines only bored him and made him fidgety.

Of course, Melzer could now feel René's mood growing darker and his defenses going up, and he realized that he was once more left alone, now from this quarter as well, with his struggles to capture what was past and gone. René's demeanor, every second becoming more curt and mistrustful until he was now stubbornly resistant, put him on the wrong track, moreover (and here we see how rivers not spanned by bridges can separate two people sitting right next to each other; we see, in addition, that the most hackneyed and purely material explanations we give to phenomena, though correct in almost all cases, are not by any means invariably so). The notion formed very quickly inside Melzer that the war had perhaps wrought so much havoc on the Stangelers' financial circumstances and family relationships that René didn't care to be reminded of how things now stood and for that reason was manifesting such reticence in regard to everything having to do with his relatives. At that moment he resolved to find out, in the near future, what he could about these matters. Accordingly, under the influence of René's attitude, he placed Stangeler squarely into the middle of the family and all its affairs, whereas René himself had been taking such pains to stress the exact opposite.

Yes, that's just how it goes.

People shouldn't stress things. It will be as if the key that a person wants to strike so as to produce a clear, crisply audible tone will be inaudible to others, though the overtones and undertones will sound and resonate in the ears of even strangers long after the person at the keyboard has stopped thinking about them. People just never hear correctly, and that's all there is to it. And yet they do hear the truth—in their own way.

He wanted to ask about Asta now.

He hadn't wanted to lead right off with it.

From somewhere behind the bundled feelings and counterfeelings now stirred up and spilling in a disordered jumble onto the platform of consciousness at the forefront of the mind, impulses and sensations that vanished before he could even name them; from somewhere behind the small, rapid, niggling little deliberations going on inside him (as inside all of us); from somewhere behind Editha and even from somewhere far behind René, something came drifting, like a restless, bright-colored curtain at a distant window.

Up front, everything was covered in flames—swelling and expanding, fiery inferno, bolts bursting, walls crumbling, Editha. And fear, disintegration.

Farther back, the past, himself.

He asked about Asta. And didn't find out one thing more than he already knew.

He asked about their country house. Oh yes, they were there all the time during the summer (he, René, only once in a while though), and sometimes in the winter, too; it was still owned by the family, as was the house in the city.

"So everything seems to be all right," thought Melzer, and then, "So what's bothering him?" As for the rest, he'd take a trip out there in the summer sometime—good idea! A little climbing around the Rax massif, which would give him the opportunity to . . . No, it wouldn't work! Period. So he made up his mind. But knew perfectly well how cut off he was from his own resolve. "I'm getting wrapped up in this now, but in a different way," he said on the inside and felt keenly the trammels and confusions—to use his peculiar terms for them—attendant on living in the present.

All right, so many things could be so simple. But your hand can't reach that far; your arm's too short. Those damned *trópoi*.

Just like here and now, today, in front of the green mirror of the window. Saturday, August twenty-second. A hot day on Porzellan Gasse in Vienna. Not in Kritzendorf; not in the Rax area, either. Never mind. He'll take a trip out that way. Before the autumn weather sets in. For sure.

Then René had said, "The only thing that doesn't exist anymore is the Quartier Latin. They did away with it after Etelka got married; they bricked up the door to those three steps that led down to that tiny little room of Asta's. I watched them."

"Watched them, you say? How do you mean?" Eulenfeld asked with a noticeably thick tongue. It was certain to be thick every Saturday evening around this time.

"The door was walled up that spring, when all of us were out in the country at the same time," Rene said. "I was the only one in Vienna just then, because I had to report for active duty with the military. I watched the bricklayers at work. The room got all new wallpaper after they finished. Then there wasn't a door there anymore. That was my room when I first returned home from Siberia."

Melzer bumped into this walled-up door like a corner he hadn't quite cleared; it penetrated into him like a foreign body. His thoughts entwined the door frame. Now he could see it filled in with rough-shaped bricks.

"You were in Siberia, René?" he asked politely, extending a conventional degree of interest only so that he could remain undisturbed behind it. "I even heard something about that, in fact," he added.

Stangeler had no chance to reply, for the captain now thought he saw his opportunity to switch back to an earlier track. "Yes, he was, and he fought in the war before that; he and I even spent two weeks together."

Editha listened calmly. Whenever anyone was speaking, and it made no difference who, her bearing was always such as to suggest that she considered it very beneficial, a priority higher than any other, no matter what, to learn something—anything—to garner information on something—anything—whatever it might be. The group gathered around Dolly Storch by the sofa happened just now to turn their attention to the rest of the party here.

"I was his squadron commander for two weeks," said Eulenfeld in a gratified way, and, as Melzer's face took on an astonished look, he explained. Forty Austrian dragoons, a lieutenant, and a warrant officer had been cut off from their unit and had attached themselves to his squadron while searching for their own. "All you men were top-notch together, at that time, anyway," he said to Stangeler, "horses and weapons in great shape, and you still had all your rations coming to you standard quartermaster issue." Then he described the reconnaissance push his unit had undertaken after being reinforced by the Austrian troops. (Now his speech was no longer quite so slurred.) Finally he asked Stangeler, "How much time was there exactly between your successful attack on the Cossack *sotnya* and the battle that split up the squadron?"

"You were part of an attack on Cossack troops, René?" Dolly cried from the sofa, agog and athirst for excitement in a totally unconcealed and almost childish way. "Tell us all about it!" Something that could be called an obligatory interest arose in Melzer. It was his bounden duty, so to say, to be interested in the topic. He'd been a career officer, after all. It was a reaction similar to the one a man will have if he hears his name called. He almost let himself get involved; he almost felt something. He could feel resistance on the inside, though, too. But at least now he wasn't trying inside himself to lean on Major Laska.

Instead, on the Strudlhof Steps?!, in a manner of speaking!

"But Gretl doesn't like it when he tells war stories," said Dolly, who had sat up halfway on the sofa and now dropped back, disappointed.

Stangeler still didn't say anything.

In his face was very transparently and vividly reflected some struggle that he appeared to be conducting with great earnestness. And Dolly had in fact just taken hold of him at a sensitive spot, and in an unprepossessing way, at that. But . . . but—he seemed to get over that feeling as well, so it couldn't become all that critical. Lights and shadows flickered virtually in alternation across his face, breaking through from within. Finally, though, the knot came loose that had drawn so menacingly tight around the root of his nose; and this knot released not just his face, but his whole body as well—his limbs, his neck and shoulders, his arms and legs, his hands, and even his hair, for that matter—into a state of relaxation and of blissful resolution. René smiled, but he still had nothing to say, not even at this moment, during which all heads were turned mainly toward him, expecting a story or at least an answer of some kind—at this moment, during which, in brief, the seven or eight people (at a minimum) present in the room were bearing down with all their weight on the long handle of his need for recognition.

Editha was watching René attentively, garnering information.

The captain was looking at him, with growing antipathy, out of little eyes that soon dimmed until they looked like buttons.

And Melzer—to his own astonishment, which was so great that it opened a chasm here, right down the middle of the room—understood what was happening inside Stangeler. Understood that inside him the Strudlhof Steps had gained a victory. That's how it would have been worded in the Melzerian language of thinking sleep, anyway.

Now, after some time had passed and a clean hiatus marked from the earlier conversation, René answered, speaking lightly, as if in an aside, "Around two weeks passed between the skirmish you're talking about and our meeting. By the way, you couldn't literally call what we fought there a real battle; I mean there's a certain amount of deliberateness underlying that word *fought*, but all we did was sort of charge in on each other, and it lasted no longer than thirty seconds at the most."

After a brief pause, he said, "As we went galloping across a meadow sloping very gently downward I passed something like a small well-house with a tiny little roof down close to the ground, and it looked as though a tap or a handle for a water line had been installed; there was a village nearby. A small ditch led away from the roof, too; the water flashed in it for just a second. I tried to picture what that little area under the roof and above the spring would be like—cool, pure, calm, safe and secure, the water murmuring. We were brandishing our sabers and yelling 'Hooray!' Not that we had anything against that little roof—it's the Cossacks we were thinking of—or that it had anything against us. Endlessly distant from one another, with no antagonism. Distance antipodal, such as the greatest antagonism can never hope to bridge."

And now René addressed Melzer directly.

"It took the bricklayers quite a long time. The wall was thick, you see, a firewall between two houses, and the opening had to be filled in completely. To me, this walling up didn't really feel like a hostile action. They were supposed to make two apartments again out of the one, the way it originally was. It would have had to come out sooner or later anyway that two different houses were making common cause in one place. Everything had been removed from the breakfast room; the rug and the curtains were gone; it was all bare. A hod with mortar was standing there. I saw it at noontime, when I went to eat; the workmen had gone away. Lina, the chambermaid, took me in to show me what a mess it was. Naturally the room was full of dirt and plaster—all the clutter and chaos that workmen always have to make. I had to eat my noon meal in another room, but as a rule I'd have it in the breakfast room whenever I needed to be in Vienna by myself. It was a very bright, sunny day. After I ate I went right back across to the wall. It wasn't very high then, maybe three or four bricks on my side. They'd started from both sides. The apartments were empty. I wanted to step down into Asta's little room one more time, but the hod full of mortar was blocking my path; maybe it would have been too much trouble anyway, because the wall on the other side had already reached pretty far up in place of those three steps. It also occurred to me that everything had been cleared out of there already. I was probably still picturing that little room of Asta's the way it had been before; I left it like that and stayed right where I was. The apartments were empty, both of them. Nothing was stirring. I listened through the bricks. Everything remained quiet. But at what point, I remember thinking at the time, will the two apartments truly become separate entities? Now? Has it happened already? Or will it when the last brick slides into place to close up the last opening? What I was really asking—although I didn't realize it until just now—was this: when will the one state of solitude and silence prevailing here at this moment have grown to be two states of solitude and silence? Endlessly far apart from one another, with no antagonism. And when in time the walls on each side are papered and no one recalls anymore that there was once a door here, then the separation will be healed, as it were."

"It so happens I know your neighbors," Leucht said lazily from the rug as he yawned.

"I should think you do," the captain growled, but his little remark wasn't understood or even noticed.

"Can you really call them *neighbors* in this case?" Melzer asked timidly.

"Otto, go make some coffee," Dolly called from the other end of the room. "Stories like this don't agree with me."

"Ah, yes," the captain said, "these are the various epochs of a family's history and, at the same time, the epochs of one's own biography as it may hereunto appertain." He tottered out to the kitchen.

Someone had opened the window. People were saying, "It's nice out again! It's warm. The moon is shining." Dolly and her group from the sofa leaned out. "It's not raining anymore," she said. Into the cigarette smoke filling the room came blowing the smell of the wet asphalt, and also the scent of greenery from some of the gardens nearby. The mode in which they could be smelled was almost as if someone had stepped into the room with a light.

Stangeler spoke to himself, but as if he were answering the captain, the Master of Horse, who wasn't even in the room. "However, the one prerequisite essential for any autobiography would be to get rid of the concept of epochs in the person's own life. They're all fallacious. The first thing that needs to happen is that one's own life has to drop out of the framework of order we're used to giving it as a matter of habit every time we take a look at it. An architecture of nothing but façades. Constructing our own selves. It's only after this all vanishes without a trace that things can spread out in their true immensity and the solid pieces of the frame lean sideways like flimsy sticks of latticework. Then the view is, more than anything else, astounding. I believe that these are the only conditions under which an autobiography is possible."

René stopped talking, and he glanced sideways out of his narrowed eyes. He was sitting in a comfortable position, leaning back, his hands in his pockets. Obviously he had been able to give expression to what was really in his thoughts, and so now he was finished and had nothing more to say. His face disclosed ease of mind, perhaps even happiness. It was in these moments that Melzer discovered how much he liked him, but the discovery was of a feeling he knew had always been there. Now he could once again see before him the stream with the artificial pond beyond the tennis court at the Stangelers' country house. The prep-school boy was sitting on a sand pile by the water. Melzer had just happened along between two games, curious to see what it looked like back there in the little ravine toward the woods. His doing so, however, meant that he'd made his way into an altogether different realm—he could feel it—here under the tall pine trees that came all the way up to the small sheet of water; into a realm of shadows that no longer had anything in common with the scurrying about on the tennis court, the cries and shouts, the taut, tambourine-like sound made by a racket hitting a ball, even though all those sun-filled sounds, as it were, could be heard here, since they were only a few steps away, after all. On the opposite bank, on the small dam, a meter or so wide, that went across the ravine cut by the stream, a certain Herr von Geyrenhoff, executive committee member in the Finance Ministry, was standing and speaking with René. Now, though, they had both turned toward Melzer, who was walking up to them across the wall.

They exchanged a few trivial words; then Geyrenhoff turned and went back to the tennis court. Melzer himself, meanwhile, had stayed with René for a while; he could recall it vividly.

So it was that Melzer was now able to recognize in René Stangeler exactly the same person, so to speak, who'd been sitting there on the sand pile by the water. Not like Editha. She fell away to fragments. René stayed whole.

A small, quick stab of pain went through Melzer.

Now, months later, in the course of this two-minute express-train dash past his own self, in front of the deep, reflecting green of the blinds, behind the window, closed once more, he felt it anew, and for the umpteenth time...

On Porzellan Gasse in Vienna.

On the hot Saturday afternoon of August 22, 1925.

He felt it again, this pain, but it was no longer small and quick; it was large and slow, had grown to be almost a constant thing.

Editha, sitting under the bronze figure, must have sensed something, though. "You'll see our Editha home, O good friend Melzer," the captain had said with his thick tongue. Editha wasn't living on Neubau Gasse anymore, but somewhere out past Bohemia Station instead. He only found that out now.

"Let's be sure to go down the Strudlhof Steps," she said.

"It's out of your way," observed Eulenfeld, fighting off one fit of yawning after another. "You only have to take one streetcar line."

"I don't care," Editha answered. "I'd like to walk a little; it's so nice outside now. Want to go partway with us, René?"

"As far as the Strudlhof Steps, anyhow," Stangeler said.

So Editha went walking along Skoda Gasse between Melzer and Stangeler, slowly, a pace the weather encouraged. The air was fresh and calm; the moonlight lay in patches on the houses and came down into the streets between them in beams and rays. From Spital Gasse—wide, reaching straight out, leading smoothly onward—they could see a few clouds here and there scudding across a sky grown clear. They turned right, toward the Citizens' Support House, which in those days was still standing—instead of the park that the Second World War then destroyed—plunging in headfirst, so to speak, as they entered narrow Strudlhof Gasse, for everything here lay deep in shadow or was twice as sharp in the moonlight that came flowing down from the edges of the roofs and spread itself along Waisenhaus Gasse (the name of which had by then been changed to Boltzmann Gasse). The academy was to the left, behind the light of the moon; none of them gave it a single thought, not even René. They still had a short length of Strudlhof Gasse to cover, and then came the steps—a breaking off; a dropping down; young, bright-green foliage; scattered shadows, all mixed with moonlight, and the glow from the double-candelabra light fixtures above and below. Up to this point no one had said a word. But now Melzer came to a standstill at the balustrade. The feelings crisscrossing so strangely inside him opened his mouth.

"René, do you remember...?" he asked, since he couldn't think of anything better to say.

"Of course I do"—Stangeler's answer was curt—"perfectly."

Their glances met as they looked at Editha, the focal point of their common reference at the moment.

"So these are the Strudlhof Steps, are they? They're really quite beautiful," she said, but nothing else. Then they'd begun descending.

But what Melzer was doing now was ascending, emerging up out of the green, aquarium-like underwater light. He turned back toward his living room, and no sooner had he taken two steps over to the bearskin than there was a knock at the door, and his landlady's maid came in with the tea he'd requested for five o'clock.

Melzer sat by the tea table for a long time. He felt as if a change had taken place inside him, as people will feel they've changed after some great exertion, though not as if anything had grown more clear, as after a movement of the will. This hurtling dash past his own self had befallen him in a way that wasn't a whit different from what happens when an unfortunate serving maid has a tray with dishes go slipping out of her hands and crashing down to the floor. Right at the start, Melzer had overturned the coffee service. Nothing had happened to it, though; the tiny cup had remained intact, and the results had manifested themselves on a different level, so to speak. He realized now that he was going to get out of his apartment, to go out somewhere, to get away from here at any cost—and stayed sitting right where he was. On the wall facing him, by the bearskin, to the right of the fireplace, there was always an empty spot in his mind. Something should have been there, something he'd been wanting for a long time, but he never quite got around to it. He never quite got around to traveling through the Rax area, either. Some kind of lamp or light fixture should have been there. He wanted to be able to read (the newspaper) while lying on the bearskin. He wanted to have a small bracket or wall sconce with an electric candle there, the kind they had in the reception room at the Consular Academy, the room done in Empire style. That sconce would have to be mounted fairly low on the wall, so that he could reach it lying down; all he would want to have to do to turn the light on and off would be to pull a little chain. This electric candle would look somewhat strange if it was that close to the floor, even next to the fireplace, which was where such lighting brackets were often found to the left and right. Frau Rak would be surprised, meaning of course that she wouldn't think it looked very nice.

When Stangeler had said goodbye back then, at the bottom of the Strudlhof Steps, and he'd walked Editha to her front door—nothing, but absolutely nothing. This walk had been so peaceful, motionless even though they were moving, as still as the leaves of the water plants along the calm forks of the Danube near Greifenstein or Tulln. When they had crossed the broad square in front of the train station—the lighted clock placing beyond any doubt how much later it was than Eulenfeld had thought, and not a streetcar to be seen or heard anywhere—and were walking along the arrival side of the old-fashioned building, Editha pointed forward and upward into the shining semi-darkness of the moonlight. "You can always see the Kahlenberg from here," she said. "I love that." And indeed they could now see the mountain, even the lights from the hotel. The slope of the hill rose up, a subtle blue in the moon.

Suddenly Melzer had a picture of how it would probably make him feel if he were to come home at night and find all the lights off in his rooms except for one place where there had never been a lamp before, but where a strong, bright, and even beaming light were now shining.

To him, there was something downright monstrous about this picture. It conveyed a warning; it conveyed gravity and danger, almost even the nearness of death.

He stood up, walked over to the nearer window, opened the inner pane, and pulled the string to raise the blind, which had only been lowered in the first place because of his kèf. These rooms practically never got sun—only in the morning, if at all. They were located on the shady side of Porzellan Gasse, as was Melzer's new office, too, diagonally across from the Miserovsky Twins.

He opened the window all the way.

The heat came billowing in, thick as a down comforter; inside it was very considerably cooler than on the streets, above which the noise was standing virtually compressed. People streaming away from the center of town, hurrying and rushing in all directions, quick last-minute purchases—Saturday evening. The streetcar, always running past here so quickly, showed its dirty white roof, kept company by a throng of squealing noises. Prevailing over all the rest in Melzer's be-wildered ear, though, was the roar of the motorcycles that went zoom-ing past here with no letup, forging ahead by passing everything in sight, leaving even the automobiles behind. Melzer knew where every-body was rushing off to. Out to the Danube. At the beginning of this week it had been hot, but then the weather had turned rainy and cool around Wednesday, and yesterday, Friday, the temperature had reached not much more than 65 degrees. Today, of course, it was a great deal higher, and tomorrow, Sunday, August 23, promised to be cloudless (which in fact it then turned out to be). Melzer stepped back and closed off the room against the invasion. Here was still wafting the tropical, Near Eastern odor of coffee and tobacco. The sun sat in a russet glow, as if in a deep stratum, on the houses across the street; some of the windowpanes were glinting over at the Miserovsky Twins.

These gleams of light affected Melzer like a friendly wave of the hand and showed him the place where he could now, at the onset of emptiness, turn his feet so as to get away from it. Why, of course—tonight he'd eat at the Beisel (though the major was thinking not of the Flight into Egypt, but of his usual little tavern-restaurant on the Miserovsky side of Porzellan Gasse, a few doors closer into the center of the city). E.P. and Frau Roserl would probably show up, too, he was thinking. She never cooks on Saturday evening; after all, she likes to take it easy after she's been sitting at her desk all week in the mortgage department. This couple doesn't have any children to raise, his job isn't exactly bad, and still the wife keeps on working; both of them have an office to run to every morning. On top of that, he's from a well-to-do family. It must be that they both want to be totally independent. With their hobbies, too. Her collection of old puppets is something truly beautiful.

The very existence of this couple brought calm and strength to Melzer just now. Immediately he brushed up against the possibility of living that way himself. "Some nice woman," he thought, but it wasn't Roserl P. or any other woman in particular he had in mind at the moment. (Well, these are just samples of our "don't-we-all?" banalities.) Even so, and even though it didn't linger for more than a fleeting second, there was no way that this fond but indefinite, unbinding image leaning against him now could possibly have persisted in a state of empty mask and complete anonymity, equipped with only such essential components of a human female, so to say, as could be quickly rushed to the spot. It drew a concrete example into itself as a vacuum draws air. It reached the point of Melzer's picturing a woman who manifested at least two recognizable qualities—goodness of heart and long, high legs. About how those two things managed to combine there's practically nothing one can say, since they don't necessarily belong together from the start, exactly. Who doesn't know people with hearts of gold walking around on stubby little legs atop which is a body built like a tree stump?

Melzer had meanwhile gone into his entry room and had tried calling E.P. But behind the glowing windowpanes of the Miserovsky Twins the telephone rang in solitude and nobody answered.

The major got ready and left the house (and by the way, the days of Girardi hats and lieutenant-style mufti were long past—Melzer was wearing a soft brown hat). The street enveloped him like a heavy mantle. The noise filled his ears to the very top, as the sights kept his eyes constantly on the move, and so Melzer grew full to capacity but still had to concern himself while walking with the middle-class person's image of respectability, something which the streets have a mighty power to impose on all. Nevertheless, he was shortly breasting the tide, forging his way against the current. He had turned right coming out the front door. That was his usual, his old—we might even say his primordial—direction when turning from the door, unless he was walking those hundred paces (or however many they were) to the office, to the huge, tall, dreary limestone building that stood for quantity and nothing but quantity, a quantity of endless corridors, countless rooms, assigned duties (albeit totally humane ones) to be discharged, hours to be gotten through. Otherwise, though, everything that had to do with him lay off to the right—his Beisel, the café, the central part of town. It wasn't until the Master of Horse, the captain, had entered his life and he'd begun taking those trips out to the picnic spots along the Danube that the square in front of Franz Josef Station had actually penetrated his consciousness in any genuine way, that he'd ventured on a more habitual basis past the end of Porzellan Gasse, down to where the wine tavern stood on the corner, and farther on. Past there, somewhere beyond the train station, was where Editha was now living.

So Melzer forged his way against the stream, turned right, walked past the heavy baroque portal giving entrance to Liechtenstein Park— to him, the palace inside always resembled something out of China in its ancient days, a building from the Age of Austerity—and turned right again, crossing Liechtenstein Strasse, somewhat less busy, on an angle.

There they soon were—the Strudlhof Steps.

He stopped at the bottom.

Naturally our major, our civil servant, had no concept whatever of a genius loci, a spirit René Stangeler had been keenly alive to even during his prep-school days (but he didn't have any Paula Schachl, either). For him it was just a place holding some memories which, had it not been for a certain Editha Schlinger, née Pastré—conceivably altogether unaware of what she'd caused—might have remained covered over, hidden forever in the rubble, the stone litter of the years. As the situation stood now, however, Melzer was doubtless approaching something closer to René's manner of relating to this place. And while he may not have seen a stage setting for real life in the flights of stairs and in the terraced ramps ascending smoothly, one above another, the depth of his own existence, however modest and insignificant it might be, was somehow able even so to touch our Melzer while he stood there.

For the first time ever, he examined this feat of engineering (at least that's how it appeared to him in the simplicity of his thought) with a measure of attentiveness, thereby separating himself inwardly from an

unending file of passersby who every day tread underfoot what they—
for that very reason—have never seen. It mounted up, or rather it
reached down, placing into orderly arrangement the steep drop-off,
truncated and abrupt by nature, of the terrain here, dividing the tight-
lipped, nearly barren, all-too-pat statement the terrain made into an
abundance of graceful turnings, which the eye could no longer just
dart downward in a fast swoop to follow but instead had to lower its
gaze as gently as a falling autumn leaf swaying softly through the air.
In this place, it wasn't only that the ear could clearly hear but also that
the eye could clearly see how every road and every path (even in our
own garden) is more than a mere line of connection between two points,
one of which we move away from simply to get to the other, but rather
is a line of connection in our very being itself; is more, too, than just
its direction, showing the point of the compass toward which our being is headed; that's a pretext which can bog us down even as we're still
forging ahead. Up above, on the right, where, deeply immured in its
interior, furniture-like silence, there was a small town mansion one
ocher-golden, towering side of which, as it went soaring up into the
blue sky, was canopied and left far below by an enormous tree whose
top dissolved into finest filaments of twig against the summer sky—up
above, the section leading to the first ramp came sweeping in, majestic
as it curved back along the tree-covered hillside with steps that were
level and smooth, not steep, exhausting, rushed. It was about a stately
pace upward here, and it was about having to be drawn downward in
an easy descent, not about a frenetic scurrying up and down the chicken
ladder of purposes having no form. The steps were standing there for
anyone who happened by, for all the self-satisfied run-of-the-mill types
and even for the great unwashed, but their design was such as to provide
a path spread out to the strides of destiny, which don't always have to
shake the ground with a foot shod in armor but will often come walking, nearly noiseless, on the thinnest of soles, and in Atlas shoes, or
with the short, skipping little footsteps of some poor heart exposed,
running at a steady, ticking pace on its own two feet, tiny little heart-
feet all bare and sore and needing so much care—to such a heart as
well will the steps, cascading down in their splendor, offer companionship and escort; and they are always there; and they never grow weary

of telling us that each path has a worth and value of its own and is always, in every case, more than just the goal. The masterful architect who designed these stairs isolated one small segment of all the paths we millions follow in so large a city, and in doing so he showed us how much every meter of it is imbued with dignity and design. And when the ramps go sweeping outward, level and banked, and curve as they run along the hillside, negating all utilitarian efficiency of movement and rejecting all our chicken ladders; when one of the flights of steps becomes in itself a device of style, a means of achieving expression on these stages ranked here one above the other, so that a man with his self-worth all forfeited now seems virtually compelled, regardless of how far he may have come down in the world, to come down the steps with that much more refinement of execution, then the architect's deepest wish for those living in his own time and those coming after him has been fulfilled—to lay out in its component parts and then reunite in some concrete form the treasure beyond price that is in all their pathways all their days, to persevere in this long, tediously detailed palaver, giving cadence to its rhythms, so that it may carry through, a constraining force for skipping little hearts and stomping boots alike, reaching as far down as the platform, where the solitude of summer gathers in so densely around the babbling and the prattling of the fountain, or even all the way down to the urn and to the mask that looks out onto the warm and silent street and is just as inscrutable as a living face, made of stone though it may be.

Someone was waving to him from the lower ramp and calling loudly, "Major Melzer!"

Here they came as if summoned. Frau Roserl was wearing her bright red blouse again today. Melzer went up a few steps to meet them.

"Now here's something to be really happy about," said little E.P. in his peculiarly melting tone of voice, which joined with the liquid glance of his almond-shaped eyes to bear witness to a thoroughgoing amiability, practically an assault of amiability, we might say, the sincere nature of which could not be doubted. Even so, it was too much; it made people nervous. People somewhat on the sensitive side (and we must surely number our Melzer among them) could at times be alarmed in E.P.'s presence, as if they were consorting with some abnormal creature that carries its heart sac—thus making itself extremely vulnerable—outside the body cavity in which it belonged.

They'd been out for their early evening walk. And of course they were hoping to eat with Melzer in the Beisel later on—what a pleasure it would be.

For the time being, all three of them remained standing at the foot of the stairs.

"What were you studying here with so much concentration, Major?" E.P. asked.

"The steps," answered Melzer in a daze. They'd caught him in the act, as it were. "I just think they're really wonderful."

"Do you? Do you like them that much?" cried E.P. "I'm so glad. Hear that, Roserl? I wouldn't have expected anything else from the major."

"I just wish I knew who designed them and when they were built," Melzer went on. "I bet there used to be one of those plain stairways here, the kind you see so often, like the Himmelpfort Steps, for example, that go from Lichtental up to Nussdorfer Strasse."

Little E.P. looked up past the ramps; he seemed a bit perplexed. "I'm afraid I don't know anything about it," he said, "although there's somebody I know who's an expert on all this old stuff." A twinge of sorrow, even of somberness, quickly passed over his face. Melzer could scarcely help noticing. Frau P. wasn't listening; she had gone back up a few of the steps and was now examining the whole structure with great interest.

"Oh, and who is that?" Melzer asked.

"I think you know him, too, as a matter of fact," said E.P. "It's René Stangeler."

"How about that!" cried Melzer. "Of course I know Stangeler. I'll have to ask him. It's just like that man to know all about these things."

"The history of Vienna was his field of study at the university," noted E.P. in a blank tone, and then he grew silent.

Presently they set off slowly down the street, on their way to their evening meal. They left the steps behind, patched in dappling leaf shadows, their edges broken up and softened by overhanging limbs and by crowns of leafage. Up above, the evening began sifting its gold-red light as it came down through a broad gleaming gateway between the branches.

This was the evening Melzer found out more about René Stangeler for the first time. Roserl was tired and had gone home to rest soon after eating, her husband and Melzer walking her to the front door and the two men then going off to the café, which was close. Their dinner had been a lively meal, made all the more festive by a series of special culinary treats and extras of the kind that a small tavern like that, located away from the center of town and enjoying a good reputation, was still able to offer in those days; everything was kept informal and relaxed, and some good wine stimulated both appetite and mood. Our Melzer even went so far as to talk about himself, which was altogether out of character, and indeed unprecedented, at least in the eyes of E.P. and his wife. And even if, to all appearances, nothing of cosmic import came up for discussion; even if no very great depths of soul were plumbed, his every word was nonetheless met with the undivided attention, not to say the almost rapt and engrossed hearing, of the married couple. There wasn't much to it. Certain things he'd missed out on, certain things that had never come his way. The trip to the Rax massif (it wasn't the first time he was talking about it) and—as though it somehow bore special significance for him, as he in fact believed—the reading lamp to the right of the fireplace, down low, just above the bearskin, the electric candle with a little pull chain for him to read his newspaper by; all this even though it had yet to be installed. Roserl laughed. "Well, if that's the worst item on your loss record, Major, you still may be able to hold your head up! There's something I missed out on too, by the way, and through my own fault; nothing can be done to change it now. Two very nice 'convent dolls,' as they call one kind of puppet, were bought out practically right from under my nose, because I just couldn't seem to get myself to the store where they were." With that, E.P. had given Melzer an inconspicuous little nudge. Later, in the café, our friend found out that the two puppets—an angel with a robe of gold brocade and a Judas Iscariot with a nose phenomenally hooked—had been waiting for Frau Roserl that evening when she went to bed. They were sitting on her night table. E.P. himself had been the buyer, and he'd been faced with the challenge, before he and his wife went out for their walk, of quickly putting Judas Iscariot and the rosy-cheeked angel in place without her catching on.

But what did any of that matter? The almond-eyed René made his way back anyhow, though not until late in the evening, and with him the sorrow and somberness came back into E.P.'s face as well; again they came in a flash, but this time they stayed and struggled with nostalgia, which is thought to ripen as the first fruit of distance in time—and perhaps as the last fruit, too, for that matter, lying beyond whatever insights have been ever so duly and dutifully acquired, ever so successfully processed.

"How did you find out that I know René Stangeler?" asked Melzer.

"You spoke about it once before, I think—something about wanting to go back out to the Stangelers' country house—and you briefly mentioned knowing him."

By now, E.P. had hit his full stride with the topic. Melzer was as absorbed in listening to him as if everything he was now learning were in some way of direct concern to him. Which of course was not the case, not strictly speaking; but that was how it felt to the major turned civil service official. It seems to him now that back in those days a link of some kind between René Stangeler and himself was too much to be taken for granted for him even to go on noticing it or taking account of it. Individuals like Melzer often notice a great deal, but they are certain never to take account of anything, inasmuch as they never direct crucial questions to themselves, demanding from behind a drawn revolver, as it were, an answer from the same person who's doing the asking.

This was probably the first time since his break with René that E.P. had had an opportunity, if not to get rid of the burden of past events, at least to prop it against something as he carried it, or even to set it down temporarily. That's all one can ever hope to achieve through such confessions or confidences, which are invariably based on self-deception, on a desire to escape from one's own center, culminating in a systematic effort to make perfectly clear to some other person, rather than to our own selves, how matters stand. Someone may let fall by way of reply that it would make for a healthful exercise anyway to expound on a subject to a person having no built-in prior knowledge or presuppositions that first need to be sorted out and set in order, to take measurements according to what the English call "common sense." But how can we rightly speak of exercise, healthfulness, exertion, when the contents come gushing out of a person only because he's grown top-heavy and keeled over? Of course he's going to feel easier for the moment, like a sick man who changes the way he's lying in bed. But still the emptiness remains when he looks back into the swirling, smoky cloud of his own words and is now forced to realize that it has not borne away one gram of the mass weighing on him, because it wasn't nearly thick enough to support even a dram or a grain. So the whole thing gets mixed in with the scent of gravy and the smells of broiling and searing that are coming from a different psychological oven, the vapors and aromas blend, thoughts and images go drifting like clouds of steam, and then somebody wants to talk about having made perfectly clear to somebody else how matters stand, which is why he went to the trouble of mentioning this and expanding on that. They're two jolly good fellows, Melzer and E.P., but nothing is coming out of this, at least not for them.

But how had the major gotten around to it in the first place? Around, that is, to being used by E.P. to rest his heavy backpack for now, aside from the convergence of a certain softening of mood in that little man this evening and the opportunity presented by a secluded corner of the café? (People in Vienna go to a café for seclusion, and everyone chooses a seat on the principle of insulation—literally, that is, forming an island—so as to be as far as possible from everyone else; this is the contradictory element of an institution the spirit of which is a legacy handed down to us by the ancient Romans and constituting the last vestige of the civic forum, with its time-honored ideal of public assembly, which formed the actual basis on which Herr Georg Franz Kulczycki was first able to set out his coffee bowls after 1683.) The major got around to being chosen as a shelf to rest on because all people are thought to be living a much more orderly inner life than they in fact are. This undeniable generalization holds true for the simple reason that we see other people from the outside. In the deepest of our depths we are not quite corrupt enough to maintain an involuntary separation, whenever we go to apprehend another, between appearance and reality, outer and inner, so that every time we see a façade we will be sure to see only a façade and not assume there's anything behind it. Taking cognizance of another human being is an act of creation and completion. Out of a sectional councillor or civil service official or other fairly high-ranking bureaucrat earning a decent competence this creative cognizance will fashion the rock-solid fortress of a private life in splendid order, a person free of all pressure, as it were, in his own affairs, a firmly established vacuum, an ideal resting place for such backpacks as may from time to time grow too heavy. What's more, every man also appears more purely to exist than he does. To our own selves, we are always occurring, emerging, forever faltering. But others we see in their static mode, so to speak, ascribing to them far more possession of their selves than they have, more, indeed, than we ourselves have. And yet that's exactly what we claim from them—that they should at all times function as a solid base on which to lay aside backpacks, if occasion should arise—presuming upon them in a way that is both unthinking and thoughtless, and of course very selfish, too. For his part, Melzer was likewise viewing and judging E.P. as more static, orderly, and stable than he'd ever actually been in reality. How else could the possibility, perhaps even the hope, of living like E.P. have brushed up against him while he was still in his own home, when a picture of that likeable married couple entered his mind after he'd gone hurtling past all the Melzerian minutiae of his days bygone and present? So here these two jolly good fellows were, sitting across from one another; but from the outset they'd also been sitting past one another, in a sense, not to mention talking past one another.

"The first time I saw him was through an open window," said E.P., after many other things. "I'm just remembering that now. The squadron he was assigned to usually came back in from the drill field a bit longer past noon than ours." (He was talking about a training school for reserve officers, where he'd made the acquaintance of René Stangeler in 1915.) "It was in a dreadful Slovakian-Hungarian village, or really more like a small town. I was living on the outskirts, on the road into town, with a Herr von Q., from the same uhlan regiment as myself.

Our house was only one story high. Stangeler's horse was a dapple-gray. To this day I still don't know what it was that immediately drew me to René. Perhaps it was a certain 'divine brutality'—that's what I called it to myself then—which I came to know more than enough about later on."

It was really up to Melzer to ask at this point, "And which uhlan regiment did you serve in?" But he didn't. In his capacity as an expert on military matters it was hardly possible to get a rise out of him anymore. It all seemed to be sealed behind a sheet of glass.

"I almost believe today that whatever I loved about him was something completely inside myself, and it didn't have much to do with his 'divine brutality,' which wasn't the least bit divine in any case; it was merely blind, no more than the result of a weakness in René's vision, emotionally speaking. In those days I had the vague notion—of course I never gave it a definite name—that I'd be able to deal so much better with everything that cast any light and had any value for me in my own life if only I'd been graced with his talents, his ways of doing things, his abilities. It was through this notion that I felt as if my whole past were somehow bound up with René, as if I were connected to him. He was the one—he alone—who should have experienced it all, and he was the only one who could have taken possession of it the right way! I know how paradoxical that sounds. But that didn't stop it from reaching down into my most crucial depths, down into all that was most my very own. I wanted to present it all to Stangeler—so that he could experience it over again for me, as it were."

("René must have been sort of like a Laska for him"—that thought flashed through Melzer's mind, but too fast and faint for him to have more than a very remote chance of detecting it.)

"In the town of Bruck an der Leitha, where we were sent in the fall of 1915, after all the reserve-officer testing was over and done with—it was very rigorous, and it went on for almost a full week" (this time once more our Melzer showed pretty much no reaction to this place-name from the military roll call; in these matters he already had inside him something like a heightened moment, no longer subject to his control, during which he would experience blankness and withdrawal)— "in Bruck an der Leitha, also called Bruck-Királyhida, René and I shared quarters in town. We lived in a building called the Schöberl House. But as a former active-duty, you must be familiar with Bruck, come to think of it, Major."

All Melzer did was nod. Nothing more was to be gotten out of him. He was acting exactly like an animal engaged in mimicry. Like a river crab in the water. He's right on the verge of being spotted. But still he doesn't move. So it ends up that the boys think he's only a stone or a piece of wood after all. Camouflage. Melzer had the feeling that one single little word was all that would be needed for the massed weight of outward reference points in his life—a welter of objects and images and aptitudes all his proper due and entitlement, to all of which he could legitimately lay claim—to grow top-heavy and start wobbling, whereupon it would come tumbling down and crush him.

"Stangeler didn't bother very much with me, and in his free time he associated with others—not in his own best interest, I thought, and it's true that he didn't seek out the best company. We were rooming together, along with a third, a Herr K., alert, smooth, a man who treated that whole military way of life with complete success and with no trouble at all, by applying to it the thought processes of a civilian, a civilian mentality, whereas we—René and I—hadn't carried a bit of it over into our situation then. We were just about twenty, too. He was older. For four weeks, by the way, all of us in Bruck-Királyhida were without horses. We were supposed to be learning what goes on in the infantry, which is why the twenty-four reserve-officer trainees who'd passed those tests had been sent there. On the whole, it was a very pleasant life, and our duties weren't especially demanding. Our training course was conducted by one of the best and most outstanding officers I've ever met, a rifle captain—"

"Must have been Rifle Captain Sch.," Melzer found himself saying. A reaction. Like a blink of the eye or something similar. Frightened now, the crab drew back into its hole.

"What, you mean you know him?" E.P. cried happily. "That was one outstanding man. Did you know him well?" (But Melzer, Melzer the crab, all camouflaged and engaged in mimicry, didn't make another move.) "Things went well for us in Bruck, and above all we learned a great deal." (Now then, which of these two was the real military man—

the one who'd left everything about his civilian mentality behind when he entered the service or the one who had somehow lost track of his military mentality when he reentered civilian life and hadn't replaced it with anything?) "In Holič—that was the name of the backwater where the school for us reserve officers was—and in Bruck-Királyhida, I used to observe Stangeler very closely, of course, with that greatly heightened sensitivity we all have toward precisely the thing we think we're missing. I was the observant one of the two of us, anyway. René was blind. I know that today. Perhaps he's still like that—for example, whenever he needs his strength. I've seen it in action. We used to ride side by side on patrol in Holič. He had no ambition and loved to go sneaking off with a certain Brauner, who was just as lackadaisical as he was, to the nearest tavern until the training exercise was over. One time seven of us swooped down on an 'enemy' patrol that was breaking out from cover in some woods. There was a kind of rage built up in me. The 'enemy' riders took flight, because they thought there were more of us. We wanted to capture prisoners, though. Galloping full speed ahead, I grabbed hold of a Hungarian hussar volunteer by his upper arm and tried to yank him down from his saddle. There were severe disciplinary measures for brawling and wrestling around like that on training exercises. But I didn't care. We both hit the ground, the Hungarian and I, right near a ditch; the horses, too. We could have broken our own necks and the horses' legs. Nothing happened to us, though. Stangeler had some very angry things to say against me and about me when he came riding up. I was feeling so offended by his behavior, it left me so full of tremendous fury that I could have smashed my sword over his head. After all, I'd done what I did for his sake. Do you understand what I mean?"

"Well now, you see, in matters like that..." Melzer said, because E.P. had paused and was clearly waiting for a response of some kind.

"We also had the experience of spending our evenings out in the field, in the heavy summer heat, and in the forest, where the river had cut a deep gravel bed in the earth. Three streaks of red running horizontally across the sky; otherwise it was almost totally dark. In the evening we'd take a lumbering old behemoth of a landau and ride out to the brooks that flowed through the meadows, just to have a swim, just to cool off a little at last. That school was exceptionally rigorous indeed—mounted exercises, classroom instruction, drills from morning to evening, and then added field maneuvers at night besides the ones during the day. Frogs in the meadows, an overpowering sound, a choral company in our ears. That's the way Stangeler put it. Maybe he'd read it somewhere. Before he was captured as a prisoner of war, I can barely remember his ever making any statement about his inner life—what sustained him, how he held his life together, I mean, what image of himself he had. I didn't know any of that."

He broke off abruptly. His face twisted in pain, as if his own words were hurting him.

And so it was—as careful as this crab was being, he took notice, with his eyestalks, that these words really couldn't be E.P.'s own. Here he was, just about to take account of something—but we've got a long, long way to go before we reach that point, good Melzer. No civilian mentality.

"Later on, everything about him would turn into purposeful course of action, planning of definite goals, exercise of willpower," E.P. went on, now endeavoring to cover the almost compromising manifestation of a foreign language in his mouth with words or phrasings that originated elsewhere. "Just after arriving back home from Siberia he gave me a very precise explanation of what it was he wanted."

But then he let that go, our little E.P.; he didn't develop the topic. He wouldn't have had much luck trying it on Melzer in any case. His almond-shaped eyes—the whites tinged faintly yellow and showing separate small flecks here and there, always a slight bit too moist, as though he'd been crying—were looking to the side, fixed on a spot right next to his empty coffee cup on the red marble top of the little table,. In his physical bearing, and especially in the way he had his head turned, there was, among other effects, a touch of the attractively unbalanced; and he shrank back into himself, as it were, warding off everything from outside, with that relatively broad back of his—too ready to bend down and prostrate itself—and those shoulders, really solid for his small size. If someone had wanted to imagine him as an animal and then draw a caricature, what would have been sitting in E.P.'s cushioned corner seat was a male squirrel twiddling a nut rather than a cigarette in his busy little front paw, gnawing at it from time to time, taking tiny bites of it between brief pauses. It would be possible to reduce E.P. to a bizarre picture—that of a soft heart with sharp little teeth. He wasn't altogether harmless. Compared to him, René looks to us more like a hick or a stupid oaf. He didn't have that yellow tinge in the whites of his eyes, those flecks, those points of savagery that could gather force and then flare up, wolflike. He was merely blind of soul (in this regard E.P. saw correctly, but that couldn't have been exactly difficult, and he'd been made to feel it personally besides), and for that reason he was also raw, like meat on a kitchen table not yet roasted or broiled.

"More than anything, I would have wanted to see through his eyes," E.P. said. "I wasn't jealous of his past experiences, which I had hardly any knowledge of—and didn't ask any questions about, either—no, I was jealous of my own. Whenever we would go roaming through the woods by the meadows in Bruck—on some exercise or other; they really should have been called something like 'tactical strolls'—or when the two of us would sneak away from some nighttime maneuver, at his suggestion, and lie on the side of a hill directly facing the full moon, I'd think, 'He just has to have seen Dornbach—those unforgettable hikes through the leaf-covered hills!—he has to have been there with her and me.' I wanted him to read the books I loved and to hear the music I loved; I wanted him to look out into the distance from a particular point on the Hameau; I wanted those rather angled eyes of his—and only those eyes—to observe exactly this and only this. Perhaps even then I sensed his blindness down deep and wanted him to see. So I guess it was inevitable for me to make the greatest mistake of my life later on by introducing René Stangeler to the woman I loved. We were in Vienna at the same time, on leave from the front. But he didn't even see her. That's why I had to go and repeat the same stupid move after he came back from Russia."

"Maybe it wasn't such a stupid move, though," said Melzer.

"Really, Major? How do you mean?" E.P. sat up a bit more straight; his small, dark-skinned face with the cyanide-blue eyes was keen with apprehension and even fright, but at the same time it had a look of determination, as though it meant to stand and confront whatever might be coming at him now.

"For one thing, you'd never have married the wonderful woman who's your wife today," replied Melzer, deflecting in a sense.

It would have struck a precise observer—Melzer, though he listened very carefully, was no such thing, because, without even realizing it, he was giving his full attention to only those parts bearing on Stangeler—that E.P. had subsided a bit. It was as though the direction his thoughts were flowing had now been walled up, and in such a way that it would be difficult to raise a protest.

"But you realize," said Melzer in a soothing voice, "if you'd remained friends with Stangeler for any length of time, he would have met the lady we're talking about sooner or later anyway. You really don't have any reason to be angry with yourself. For example—it's only been about six months since I met up with René again; I knew him earlier, when he was a very young fellow, still living at home, still in prep school. The point is, I've run into her on several occasions during these past few months, if just in passing. That kind of thing is bound to happen."

"Who is it you've run into—?"

"Well now, I just assumed it's the lady you mentioned, because René's been in a relationship with her for a few years now. I'm talking about Fräulein Siebenschein."

"Oh, you know Grete Siebenschein, then. Of course. You must, if you have any dealings with Stangeler. Certainly."

"And because I do know her is mainly why I said earlier it might not have been such a stupid move by any means for you to get her and Stangeler together, or at least to introduce them. Not a stupid move for you, that is, not as far as your own life is concerned—I'm not sure how to say what I mean here . . ."

What's this? Melzer! Civilian mentality? No, not at all. He's speaking, shall we say, *pro domo*. All he's thinking about this whole time is Mary. And how it might not have been such a stupid move by any means back then. However—and it's a big however—he again has the same idea now that he had fourteen years earlier, when he was walking beside Asta on Waisenhaus Gasse to while away the fifteen minutes of the Semski-Schmeller tryst, and the idea was that in 1910 he'd been "given the gate" in Ischl instead of having left Mary on his own initiative. "Just one of those things that can't be helped"—these are his exact words as he thinks out loud now. What a civil servant! major! lieutenant!

"You may be right," said E.P. softly. ("But that's not so, either"—this is what enters the major's thoughts the very next minute—"she might have been right for him, after all. Just not for Stangeler; she's not right for him. Or is she?")

"How did you happen to meet Fräulein Siebenschein, Major, if you don't mind my asking?"

"Not at all. Just a minute, now—when did we meet? Early this summer. It was even close to here. On Althan Platz, across from the train station. There's this large building there on the corner of Althan Platz and . . . I can't remember the name of the little cross street."

"You mean the building they call the Stein House?"

"Is that its name?"

"Yes. It belongs to a Herr Doro Stein; he also owns racing stables."

"Coming in from the street is a wide entranceway with a porter's lodge, all elaborately decorated, the way they did it in the old days, with all kinds of gingerbread and mirrors."

"Yes, that's where she lives."

"I didn't know that. We were by the front door in somebody or another's car, picking up a Fräulein Dolly Storch . . ."

"You know her, too?"

"Yes. Her father's a professor of anatomy at the university medical school."

"The Siebenscheins and the Storches live right next door to each other; they're on the same floor."

"That's right. Now it's coming back to me. The captain mentioned it."

"Captain?" E.P. asked.

"A Herr von Eulenfeld. A German, not an Austrian."

"I don't know him."

"Anyway, there in Dolly Storch's apartment was Fräulein Siebenschein, just getting ready to leave. I wasn't introduced to her then; I just saw her in the entrance. But then Dolly told me later who she was."

"And that's your sole basis for thinking that Grete and I wouldn't have been right for one another?" asked E.P., and then laughed—for the first time since they'd sat down in the café.

"No, not at all," Melzer replied. "I had some other opportunities later, too; once when she was at Eulenfeld's. Most of the time, René never brought her with him, though. He was always showing up everywhere by himself."

"And again that's just like him," said E.P., sounding as if he were proud of Stangeler for going it alone like that.

"So you see how it is," he continued after a short pause. "She lives right around here, very close by. And I'm aware of it. I never pass her building. Someone once wrote that such buildings are graves that enclose the living. I don't have any business over near the Brigitta Bridge or anywhere else in the general direction from here to Franz Josef Station, either. My daily round or circuit takes me more toward the center of town—the bank, the Beisel. When I go out the front door, I turn left; it's become totally automatic. Taking Porzellan Gasse past my own building to go toward the station has been very rare for me all these years. Whenever my wife and I go out to Nussdorf, we walk along Porzellan Gasse in the opposite direction—toward the city—and take the bus at the nearest stop. By now, Roserl's used to it. It's part of an avoidance that's forever conscious, or I suppose, unconscious, by now. If you have an injury, you soon get into the habit of protecting the place where it is or of refraining from certain movements. But even so, and in spite of all this, I still think it's remarkable that we've never happened across each other here in the neighborhood, on the streetcar, say—I always ride it, and she, too, would only be able to take this one line to the center of town—or walking along a street somewhere, or in a store."

Melzer was quite astonished at the openness being presented to him, astonished that this man E.P., whom—in keeping with that creative cognizance we mentioned earlier—he'd pictured as the image and likeness of a man in an ideal marriage.

"Perhaps Fräulein Siebenschein does the same thing you do," he said; and no sooner had he spoken these words than they struck him as pitiless, so that he would have liked to swallow them.

"I don't think so," answered E.P., apparently unperturbed; "I'm certain she doesn't bother herself the least bit with any of this, because—well, to start with, she didn't love me. But what it really comes down to is that there's something missing in her, and it may be the only thing missing from a person otherwise perfect in every respect. She has no imagination whatsoever. So her reasoning power has nothing to keep it in check, so to speak; it's without any kind of counterbalance. For that matter, it's probably our faculty of imagination, and not our passionate side, that's the real counterbalance to our analyses and chains of reasoning. If the imagination is missing, then reason doesn't seem to know what it's doing; it has to deal with mere names instead of solid, concrete images, and names can be swept aside so much more easily, as it were. I should observe that this view of the matter originates not with me, but with René. This is how he laid out the whole topic to me once. But concerning what we were discussing earlier—about not meeting over the years even though we live not far from each other and obviously travel the same streets—well, there's such a thing as invisible walls. Now whose expression that is, I can't tell you; I've forgotten. But it's very apt. These 'invisible walls' create wider and deeper separations than any lands or oceans, oftentimes when people are physically just a few paces or a couple of meters apart. If the two paths aren't on a course where they'll meet and perhaps converge, then each person is traveling as if inside a closed tube—in the same city, on the same street, even in the same building. Let me add, though, that I wanted to move out of this neighborhood nevertheless, especially after I got married. But our fine apartment with all the furniture was left us by my mother, and we have lots of books and pictures and every other kind of thing you can collect. Then, too, no Grete Siebenschein is going to run me out of my own home. And those invisible walls are sturdy."

What seemed odd to Melzer and kept striking him as peculiar was E.P.'s way of tending to draw on source references when he spoke and of using foreign terms and expressions at exactly those places where he was talking about the most private and personal matters. Yet the major wasn't aware in any explicitly conscious way of what he was feeling. Even so, the connection linking Frau Roserl to all of this disturbed him, and in particular that one little fact—about how E.P. and his wife would always board the streetcar at a stop closer to the center of town, in the opposite direction, if they were going ride out to Nussdorf—somehow seemed to him to be overstepping legitimate bounds.

"Did your wife know Fräulein Siebenschein?" he asked.

"No," said E.P.

"And does she know any of this prior history of yours, or anything about Stangeler?"

"Hardly anything. I think I briefly sketched in the whole story once, before we'd known each other for very long."

"But when ... well, for example, when you won't board the trolley at the corner by Franz Josef Station but insist on going the opposite way, or ... when you refuse to walk past the Stein House—what does she say? Doesn't she ask questions? Does she know that right in the immediate vicinity ... ?"

"No," said E.P. decisively. "She doesn't know anything about it. Also, she's got one virtue that's priceless—she respects any and every idiosyncrasy in another person. And I've got more than a few." He laughed again. His bearing had regained that male-squirrelish aspect of being drawn into itself.

"And she's never asked any questions?"

"No. She accepts it as one of my numerous dislikes."

All this while, Melzer had the clear thought in his mind that nothing could really ever be greater than just not asking questions, not commenting at all. He was completely filled with amazement.

"I met my wife the same day the final break with Stangeler came about. She'd just started working at the bank and showed up in the office that day for the first time."

"The break with Stangeler ..." said Melzer, hesitating. "Look here, though—there wasn't really anything for him to feel guilty about, so to speak, as far as you're concerned. These are things that just can't be helped, after all. He loved Grete, she loved him, and that was that; it's probably still that way today, although ..."

"Although ... ?"

"I hear they don't always get along so well these days," answered Melzer.

"You could say that. I think it could even be said that relations between them are very bad. I never thought it would be any different." There wasn't a trace of regret in his face or in his tone of voice. He was once more chewing busily away at his nut, and peculiarly enough, the yellow tinge in the whites of his eyes seemed to be standing out more strongly now.

"How do you know that?" asked Melzer.

"Through Dolly Storch. I bumped into her this past spring, at an exhibit."

"Stangeler spent part of the spring and almost the entire summer with his sister, Frau Consul Grauermann, in Budapest," said Melzer. "He didn't come back until just a short time ago, and as of now I believe he's still out in the country. All kinds of terrible things have taken place between him and Grete. They say he drove her to complete despair and that she wrote and told him so in her letters from Naples."

"From Naples?"

"Yes. Her sister Titi married this disgustingly rich man by the name of . . . I forget."

"Cornel Lasch. 'Disgustingly rich' is apt, incidentally. He got to be rich in a disgusting way, at least. He's nothing but a racketeer. And by the way, nobody quite knows for sure whether he's really so disgustingly rich, either. People in the world of banking—some of them, anyway—have a different opinion. Merely pretended wealth. *Richesse dans la lune.*"

Melzer took in these last words, the ones in French, as a pure matter of course, even though he knew—since he had a fine command of the language—that E.P. had quite simply made up that saying, which doesn't even exist in French, at least not in that sense. The sprinkling of conversation with a French phrase now and then, however, is something Melzer recognized as a familiar remnant from the days of the Royal and Imperial Uhlan Regiment Number So-and-So (as an aside, it was Regiment Thirteen) left over in the little squirrel. Melzer said what follows now very rapidly; in fact, he practically cut E.P. off as he was saying his last word.

"So Titi and Cornel took Grete to Naples with them in the spring. One evening at dinner, on the terrace of the Teresa, by the sailboat marina across from the Castel dell'Ovo, Grete ran into an old acquaintance from Vienna, a literary man—I don't know him—and because it still must have been somewhat chilly in the evening that early in the season, he asked her, 'Won't you be cold in that short-sleeved dress,

Grete?,' ran to fetch her cape, and wrapped it carefully around her. The man wasn't looking for anything more from her, nor she from him, by the way. But that was what started it. Tears came into her eyes at once, and of course the man she was with—he knows René, too—asked her what was wrong. Then she began crying in earnest and told him nothing like that had ever happened to her with René; he'd never shown enough concern to ask her if she was all right; he'd never put her coat around her shoulders, and so on. There must have been quite a mass of unhappiness built up in her. Anyway, Grete then started sending letters to René in Budapest, first from Naples and then later from Vienna. She berated him with the sharpest of reproaches. Next were the telegrams, and God only knows what all happened; to make a long story short, she told him it was all over, wrote to him in no uncertain terms that she never wanted to see him again. Then suddenly there he was, back from Budapest; supposedly he'd suffered a complete collapse there. Now everything was fine again. But a week later came another big blowup between him and Grete. It was over for good this time, and he headed back to Budapest, but he went into such a terrible depression that the Grauermanns, who'd been wanting to come to Vienna for a week as it was, got in touch with Grete when they arrived; that must have been sometime in June or July. Etelka—that's René's sister—was just crazy about Grete, and they understood each other very well, but the Grauermanns got exactly nowhere with her, and so they had to be the bearers of bad tidings when they went back to René. And while we're on the topic—they say things haven't been at all on the up-and-up with the Grauermanns for a long time now, either; something's seriously wrong, I hear. Supposedly she loves another man. Anyway, over the following few weeks this whole business between Grete and René was patched up after all, with great patience and tact, by the Grauermanns, and now everything's said to be fine again, just the way it was before. Grete has allegedly voiced the comment that Frau Consul Grauermann is the first person in René's family who's ever treated her in a cordial and humane way. That I really don't understand, because she's never spent any time with them ..."

"Do you know all of this through Stangeler?" the squirrel asked, interrupting him at last.

"No," said Melzer. "I've never talked with him about any of this. In fact, I've never actually talked with Stangeler at all, strictly speaking."

He surprised even himself after he'd made this last remark, but it was undoubtedly true.

"I seldom see him," he added.

"But you know all the details."

"Oh, details . . ." Melzer said, but then he didn't follow up with an answer for the time being. He was feeling as though he'd been run over by his own self, as it were, with his rash, hasty chatter of a moment before; it had come out of him like something foreign (altogether like an actual foreign object in his mouth), a pebble or a piece of gravel picked up somewhere or other. For several seconds he felt downcast. Then he continued. "No, I really don't think you could say I've got all the details. The captain—I mentioned him a while ago—fills me in on some odds and ends. He probably gets all his information from Dolly as well. Then there's a man named Leucht, and he always knows exactly what's going on with that Masch or Lasch or whatever his name is."

"I know that Herr Leucht," said E.P. "He's one of our bank's competitors, and I spent a year in the department that handles pending litigation. You won't be surprised that he's so minutely informed about Cornel Lasch's private life when I tell you that he's close friends with Herr Lasch's manservant. His name is Scheichsbeutel."

"It's *what*?!" Melzer cried.

"You heard me," said E.P. "Scheichsbeutel."

"But how can anybody be named Scheichsbeutel?" said Melzer, affronted.

"Well, somebody can. As you can see." Intense amusement was beaming from E.P.'s eyes, and it had to do with this name. This was a rich moment for him! He'd kept a wonderfully straight face and then behaved with total nonchalance and unruffled calm when he finally led with his ace. He resolved on the spot, by the way, to name the wastepaper basket next to his desk at home "Scheichsbeutel" and to label it accordingly. The first syllable had had too many fecal overtones, the second too many suggestions of a pouch or bag not to be weirdly suitable.

Melzer resolved something, too, after his eyes had rested for a while on the cream-colored curtain now drawn across the large window looking out to the street; it was to have an especially pretty bunch of tea roses sent up to Frau Roserl the following day.

"The Scheichsbeutel family—it's a fairly large one—lives right next door to the Stangelers, incidentally," E.P. added, as though it were a startling piece of information to supplement the startling name. "In the house on the corner."

Melzer dropped the tea roses at once and asked with unusual energy, not to say vehemence, "And what floor do these Beutels, or whatever their name is, live on?"

"Just a second—I know, because I was up there once visiting the Beutels. On the third floor. It was six months after Grete and I broke up, meaning of course after I was on the outs with Stangeler, too; naturally I thought of him when I was up there in Scheichsbeutel's home. Of course I did—I thought, 'Right there, just behind that wall, and on the same floor, lives René.'"

"Behind that wall," Melzer said to himself. "By the way, it isn't exactly the same floor; there's a difference in levels."

"In every sense of the word," E.P. replied. "This man Scheichsbeutel was a large-scale black marketeer, and that's why I was there. Whether he was already in Lasch's employment at the time, I don't know. He may have been. At any rate, he made a few trips abroad and smuggled goods in. I was hoping to get some genuine *chypre* perfume by Sauzé for Roserl; it was relatively cheap, too. Leucht was the one who referred me to him. He looks like a retired civil service worker, which I think is what he is. Very neat and tidy, dignified, a bit sharp, and speaks very slow. The family was just sitting down and having coffee when I showed up. The wife's a good person, certainly, from someplace like Silesia, extremely concerned about her Scheichsbeutel, her wedded husband, and very submissive to him. Their two daughters were there. The older was a typical 'young matron' from one of the neighborhoods in Vienna—quite pretty, around thirty, married. The younger was a very peculiar individual, though. Frail as could be, with a tiny little face, like an insect; the eyes very large but somewhat oblique, an expression in them like nothing I'd ever seen before; impossible to tell whether it was just childishness or brazen impudence and indecency. She was still doing her hair completely in little-girl style. The creature was maybe sixteen or seventeen. She didn't have a single word to say. The son was there, too; he doesn't show the least bit of resemblance to anyone else in the family—dark-skinned, good-natured, simple and unaffected. I'm pretty sure he was still in school. It's that skinny, tiny little thing, combining boundless impudence with maidenliness, who's the star of the family, though; she's been 'sponsored by some art lovers'—which is the way her father expressed it—and has somehow even grown to be pretty famous, I'm told. In her work as a dancer she's naturally not called Scheichsbeutel; her professional name is Angely de Ly."

"She's famous, all right," Melzer said. "She's now appearing at the Ronacher Theater."

"Well, what do you know!" cried E.P. "I didn't know that, because I have no interest in the art of dancing and things of that nature."

"I really don't, either," noted Melzer. "But you see her name on billboards."

They fell silent. More coffee came. In spite of his jovial little anecdote about Scheichsbeutel, E.P. still seemed to have something on his mind or to feel the need for a vindication of some sort. Just as a streetcar went clattering by outside—which indeed made Melzer think about E.P.'s room and that resonating mournful sound that would sing out every time the trolley went whizzing past below—he burst out all of a sudden.

"You say, Major, that Stangeler hasn't done wrong by me and that these are things that just can't be helped. All right. But he's an excellent example of the kind of person who doesn't just sit and do nothing, who takes things as they come, who accepts whatever passion has him in its grip like a finger pointing the way and simply follows the path shown by the signpost. No, not at all. His whole relationship with Grete has consisted for the last four years of nothing but attempts to tear himself away from her. That much I know with certainty; that's how much detail I have. Why has he acted so destructively? What's his purpose? And he's destroyed so much more than just this. He's destroyed an entire epoch in our lives, an epoch that should have lasted longer, that hadn't yet run its course, one that began when we first saw each other again after he came back from Russia. A brilliant epoch. We weren't much past twenty-five or twenty-six in those days. At the time of René's homecoming in August 1921, Grete had been living in Norway for a good while, and she stayed there until the following summer. If she'd stayed longer, or if she'd altogether…"

"How's that?" said Melzer, inside whom a switch now flicked on to illuminate something he'd never understood, even though the threads that had just come unknotted presently joined again in a weave still harder to understand. "You mean when René came home you weren't seeing Grete, weren't in a relationship with her?"

"We wrote to each other from time to time."

"That's it?"

"That's it," said E.P.

"And when she came home?"

"Things started right away between her and Stangeler. I was actually in a hurry to get them together. Then it was all over."

"And your hopes destroyed," said Melzer to himself, in a tone somehow lyrical and lilting.

"I didn't really have any," E.P. drily observed.

"To tell you the truth, I don't fully understand this whole thing," said Melzer, "but then again, what is it that I do understand, anyway?" (An illumination? An inspiration? Civilian mentality aborning? Civilian spirit?) "Forgive me, but I think this is just a case of… let's call it double jealousy. Please don't be angry with me, Herr P.; I hope I'm not being harsh—of course you know that—but you said something just a moment ago that's of great interest to me. I mean your statement about the pointing finger or the signpost. Very concrete, if I may put it that way, very concrete indeed. Do you believe that most people simply follow such a thing?"

"And those who don't—what would make them think they have any better or clearer knowledge of what to do?"

Ten minutes earlier, Melzer might perhaps have countered, however modestly, with, "Well, I suppose they must have their reasons." In the meantime, however, he'd been visited with an inspiration, so to speak, and was no longer likely to say things like that.

It had been the new moon since the nineteenth of the month. The eye looking upward from the ravine of the street sees only darkness at first;

not until the second glance does it notice how clear and starry the sky is. Melzer walked away from the front door of the Miserovsky Twins, which closed behind E.P. A light had been turned on in the stairway and was shining above the door now, through the fanlight. The major crossed Porzellan Gasse on a slant, though not going in the direction of his apartment. He turned into Fürsten Gasse, walked past the heavy baroque portal, and before long he was standing at the lower end of the Strudlhof Steps.

And heard the fountain plashing above him, on the landing toward which the stairs pirouetted. The ramps lay in brightness. Whether there was moonlight or a new moon didn't make much difference here; the stars, when they rose, were better able to watch everything that might go on here than to cast light on it, since that was done, above and below, by the tall candelabra on their slender, barred masts, another at each turning of the ramps, each one entwined with vine leaves, through which they shone in green.

Melzer went up slowly, climbing through strata, in a sense, as though he were emerging up from the ground and not as if plunging downward into the depths of time. The past lay high above him, as something bright and sparkling from which the sunlight of bygone days could be recaptured, not as something dismal and dark. This latter depth was what he wanted to surge from, so he could "taste the sweet air of the surface," as Gütersloh once put it.

Melzer didn't come to a stop until he was at the upper ramp; he had quickly darted past a couple kissing down below. Otherwise, the place was deserted. His visit to the steps now, at nighttime, wasn't quite the same as the little walk of a few blocks people often like to take before they go to bed. And it wasn't some nostalgic journey through memory, either. No, it was nothing other than an inquiry, a way of questioning. His steps had been guided there by some last, deeply buried remnant of the same impulse that had once led devout pagan pilgrims to Delphi. It led him to the genius loci here. Who was asleep. For now. Her small head drooping, the dryad of the Strudlhof Steps now slept, deep in the wood of a tree trunk or some other place.

PART THREE

JULIUS Zihal, a senior councillor in the Central Bureau of Revenue and Tariff Computation, had, rich in attainments and honors, entered retirement status in the year of our Lord 1913 and had soon thereafter, occasioned by that circumstance, changed his place of residence, a circumstance that does not appear comprehensible without some additional elucidation, as we herewith readily concede. He shifted his domicile to a less expensive district, ostensibly as a way of responding with accountability to the margin of difference that would henceforth stand open between his retirement income and his previous compensation, which latter had, to be sure, been higher. It seems plausible as an explanation, but it does not remain so when one gains familiarity with Zihal's financial situation in its entirety. His deceased first wife, a widow named Deidosik, eighteen years his senior, had bequeathed him valuable assets in the form of part ownership in an apartment building and a store, the secured yield from which furnished an income substantially greater than Zihal's pension. For the most part, however, the civil service councillor's living habits had nonetheless confined themselves in the expenditure they entailed to a level below the total consumption of his professional earnings, almost as though he wished to remain independent of his spouse even after her demise. But now, with the end of his active working career, matters could not of course remain quite as they had hitherto stood with this old bachelor friend of ours (more bachelor than widower), accustomed as he was to a measure of creature comfort. And yet Zihal offered spirited resistance to this readily apprehensible fact, thereupon initiating a series of computations, using the amount of his retirement income as a basis, in regard to such expenditures for his personal maintenance as he could legitimately authorize himself; but his need to assess nearly caused him to obsess, to the point that he was quite seriously ready to open an official file on himself. So as to be able, amidst all these transactions and debates with himself, to continue holding the reins in his own hands, at least to a limited extent, he resolved to make a move and found in the same area—albeit in a section still comparatively new and consisting primarily of multistoried rental buildings—an apartment whose considerably lower rent once more consolidated his position, so to speak, in reference to the Deidosik inheritance. Even from the few trivialities adduced thus far ("basically they're nothing but spiteful remarks," as the civil service councillor once expressed it), we can see that Zihal was one of those individuals whose overmastering concern is to persevere in their internal stances, which for them have come to be more decisive than ease and comfort, more decisive, for that matter, than anything idyllic or Arcadian in their lives—after all, who else would so readily exchange an old house with garden in Lichtental for a fifth-floor walkup, much though we must at this point make allowance for the realization that we today, as a consequence of having endured certain improvements to this world of ours, are more susceptible to sansculotte-style rearrangements along such lines than were people in those days, who were still living on a human scale in circumstances as yet unimproved, not to say on a human scale resistant to improvement (incorrigibly human, we might say)—in a word, none of that entered into Zihal's decision; and what may be yet more telling is that even the concrete facts of his financial situation were incapable of bringing about in him the decision, however much they might warrant it, to spend his life as a retired civil servant in the house of Fräulein Theresa Schachl, enjoying his breakfast in the garden during the summer months whenever possible and taking his ease in general, walking around in his shirt and suspenders and smoking a Virginia cigar, which was his habit back then.

Even the simple circumstance of Zihal's having lived in this area at all, as it was a considerable distance from the Tariff Bureau, points in the same general direction we've already indicated. For him, any argument based on a short commute to his place of employment carried no weight. He regarded such deliberations as appropriate for a mechanic, perhaps, but not for a Royal and Imperial civil servant. And to live right by one's place of employment itself was quite suitable for, say, a tavern keeper or a grocer. So it was that throughout all those years of living on the upper floor of Fräulein Schachl's house in Lichtental, he would make his way each morning to the bridge across the river; be swallowed up at that point in the station of the city rail system, present his long-term government-employee pass with a gesture restrained in its dignity as he went through the turnstile (which was unnecessary, though, for most of the conductors manning the turnstiles knew this character, a man by whom they could confidently have set their official clocks); and descend the wide, ample stairs to the platform below.

The cars belonging to the city rail system, the Stadtbahn, which is what the network of elevated trains and subway trains in Vienna is still called today, were driven by steam locomotives back then, which made for a significant roar when, storming and bellowing out of their tall, broad black chests, they would come hurtling into the narrow station building and along the platform, a line of brown cars behind. These, however, were pleasantly warm in wintertime; if anything, they were most often a little too warm. Zihal always took up a position at exactly the same spot on the platform, directly underneath a sign reading, "Second-Class Cars Stop Here." And there, in accordance with his social standing, is where he would get on. The government as it was in those days (unimproved and unimprovable) never thought twice about offering its subjects something in return for the fares they paid—the passengers could see it with their own eyes and grasp it with their own hands, no matter where those might range. Demand for vehicles of public transportation was met by a supply more than adequate; indeed, Zihal was almost always by himself in one of those slightly overheated compartments, sitting alone under the gaslight, which burned at all hours because of the tunnels. In the winter months, this trip to his office made for a self-contained pleasure of its own, for he could read his morning newspaper and smoke the one cigarette our civil service councillor would allow himself all day; everything was beautifully laid out as if custom-tailored to the purpose, filling in quite nicely the brief trip of four stops.

That was all history, though. Café Simberl, near the Tariff Bureau, was the only place he still frequented.

The dogged preparations for moving that Zihal made after his retirement remained undiminished in the matter of expense and value, at least as far as upholding inner attitudes is concerned, and that even in light of a fact that effectively pulled the ground from underneath all previous considerations or, if one will, shifted them all to a new ground of calculation—to wit, that not even six months after going on pension, the counselor entered into matrimony.

So along with the wheels of Zihal's moving van, a good number of other wheels got rolling too, and along tracks that had not been spotted in advance. Due and proper foresight was shown only by Fräulein Theresa Schachl, who immediately began, after the departure of the civil service councillor, to regard (and then very quietly, by way of this or that little renovation or improvement, to remodel somewhat) that upstairs apartment in her house as the future conjugal home of her niece, Paula. Meanwhile, however, she rented the apartment to others, even if only on a temporary basis during the war. But in 1920 the rooms were once more standing empty, though they now had nice furniture in them; that was the same year the whole apartment was totally refurbished with the finest of everything. And in 1921 the young woman—whose name was now Paula Pichler—moved in.

Just as Supervising Postmistress Rosa Oplatek had been going by the name Frau Rosa Zihal since 1913.

Much of this, now, does in fact have some connection with Lieutenant Melzer's history. As does Frau Zihal, remotely. Not so, however, the events leading up to her marriage—a brief prior history of barely six months' duration. The way the relationship came into existence is of no significance for our purposes here and would make a whole book of its own, as the saying goes. As of 1925, at any rate, the events prior to meeting his new wife in person had long since been forgotten (and, indeed, cried out to be forgotten), even by the civil service councillor himself (who, however, in regard to the point under discussion here, harbored a remembrance and an awareness that occasionally still flashed a bright bolt of lightning behind the thickly drawn curtains of the past). All these origins and "here begins the story of" lay deep under the waters of the many years that had flowed over them, peaceful waters in spite of the First World War, inflicted in the meantime on these good people, who had nothing whatever to do with it, by a few self-inflated pooh-bahs from Ballhaus Platz—still waters, for that's altogether what Zihal was. His marriage was a good one; it turned out to be happy, as they say. Now by this time our civil service councillor was really quite an old gentleman. But here is where the realm of the exceptional begins once more—he was only so on paper, as it were, old only in theory. Anyone would naturally believe that the attainment of such age as must result in the entry of a civil servant upon the honorable estate of retirement must mean that the "golden years," as people like to call them ("although basically they're nothing but spiteful remarks"), of said civil servant's life, the recapitulation and coda, the epilogue of his existence, are now beginning. Not so with Zihal. His physical dexterity had increased remarkably since his wedding. It would never have occurred to him earlier in life to go walking through the Vienna Woods for hours at a time. Yet the married couple was now to be found on the highest elevations of this delightful retreat, on the Tulbinger Kogel or on the Troppberg. Frau Rosa—whom we do not, however, view as the motivation behind this newfound mobility of Zihal's—liked going along; she rejoiced both in having a husband with all the freshness of youth and in the opportunity to maintain her figure (structured in several capacious but agreeable stories; the mezzanine in particular drew the admiring eye of many a connoisseur) in proper form and to a degree that would be noticed. Surely no one will think ill of Frau Rosa for having aspirations this mundane. In the first place, she was twelve years younger than her youthful spouse and felt obligated to maintain her own youthful and slender—insofar as there could be any question of such a thing in her case—appearance for his sake. Second, she was an attractive woman to begin with, and mankind has not been commanded to hide its light under a bushel; quite the reverse, in fact. Third, this couple remained childless; and should the natural prolongation of a marital union into historical time—that is, its continuation until such time as the family line is defunct, so to speak—be lacking, then the partners, after so many fruitless conjugal moments, will stop going down the path of growing distant from their individuality and will now come to be that much more self-directed; in this effort, everything depends on the charm the partners possess (or don't possess). Many have it. The life line, in the process of hastening down to a new generation, starts to bend, making a slight curve at first—still open to that other future—but now closes entirely by turning back on itself, functioning as a kind of decoration, and with filigrees and curlicues, as far as that goes, among people with charm. So then come the long walks and the good, honest ways of treating oneself; then come the books, the lovely antique furniture, angels with little robes of gold brocade, a Judas Iscariot with a phenomenally hooked nose, and more puppets besides those.

However, this physical activity on the part of Julius Zihal, civil service councillor (ret.) and gentleman of matrimonial estate, was not a self-illuminating phenomenon, so to speak. The Council of Vienne, which convened in 1311, promulgated an extraordinary decree—*anima forma corporis*—one which delivers a slap straight in the face of all such shallow physiognomic constructs as wish to maintain that the body is an outward form of the soul (like a schoolteacher's "outward form of written assignments"!) and which might be translated in layman's terms, if one may put it that way, as, "The soul organizes the body." Such was what manifested itself in Zihal, after his retirement and his second marriage, events we accordingly cannot allow to take on the appearance of an exclusively private matter turning back only onto itself. He didn't just marry. He managed somehow once more to send his own self flying, as it were, out of the catapult of a newly created situation, and that impetus seemed to carry him all the way through a long stage late in his life, one which most people just slide down like it was a slope. It wasn't simply that he was an older gentleman who'd come into his own. It was more that he'd once again come into an ownership (of self, that is), had gotten back his very being and the posture that goes along with it.

There is a portrait of Zihal dating to that time. He commissioned it at one point but then, when it was finished, he rejected it, and so it stayed in the possession of the artist responsible for its creation. The writer Kajetan von S., who incidentally, for reasons unknown to me, published from time to time under the name Dr. Döblinger, saw it, described it, and judged it to be altogether excellent. He was on good terms, perhaps even outright friends, with Julius Zihal, who was entirely wrong in looking upon the portrait as a caricature. Our friend the civil service councillor really should never have become involved with the arts and literature and pursuits of that kind in the first place, but he enjoyed them, especially in conversation with that Dr. Döblinger, who took too much pleasure—or at least so it seems to us—in these pronouncements of Zihal's and went so far as to goad him into making them. It was with great pleasure in her turn that the painter Maria Rosanka—who later lived in Stuttgart and then afterward made a name for herself in Paris—kept the picture, which could be seen framed and hanging in her studio. It portrayed Zihal at full-length, posed in an attitude of stepping toward the observer while speaking. The right arm was lowered but at the same time being raised in an upward motion visibly still in progress; this impression was very forcefully conveyed in the way the thumb stood up by itself, making it look to the viewer as if Zihal were hoisting the imaginary subject of his conversation up through the painting, from below to above, as though he had pushed it down, with his upper body bent slightly forward, and were now in the process of letting it rise again to a certain height so that it could end up being placed on display. What Rosanka had done, however—she could have been no stranger to the movement known as expressionism, by the way; Zihal's picture was painted in 1923—was keep herself well hidden, so to say, behind the actual purpose of the laws of perspective, with the result that her choice, totally absurd in and of itself, to compose a portrait such that the right arm is reaching straight out to us provided her with an opportunity to seize on any feasible exaggeration or pointed overdrawing of objects in their relative proportions, and in particular with regard to the thumb. And it was a fact that this portrait, with its genuinely "speaking likeness," had been composed around the thumb, to some degree laid out as a whole arrangement behind that rising hand with its uplifted thumb, and that is probably what Zihal found caricature-like about it. Yes, our friend the civil service councillor should never have become involved with the arts, for it was fixed in the deepest part of his being, as a foregone conclusion, that he was bound again and again to import into this area of interest a category that assuredly does not belong there a priori—specifically, he demanded dignity and decorum; that was his one criterion. And that was the basis on which he passed judgment on the objects depicted in a painting or on the events narrated in a book. With that, however, we come to a significant change in his living habits. Ever since his marriage he had taken to reading novels. On closer inspection, this development proves to be only the next logical step in a consistent process. His justification for having avoided—indeed, having fundamentally disapproved of—such reading material in the past was in part because most books of that sort contained scenes that could in a certain sense be called stimulating; which utterance at the same time entailed a fleeting, if also a slightly embittered, sidelong glance at his own state as a bachelor and a celibate. But that had changed now. He read the complete set of Paul de Kock's novels in German translation. A somewhat outdated pastime, one might say. In any case, though, the books belonged to his wife, who gave them to him to read; and only the stars above know how it was that the collected works of Paul de Kock had ever wound up in the cozy, comfortable apartment of Supervising Postmistress Rosa Oplatek! This is where our couple lived; Zihal had moved into his wife's place and had thus of course given up the fifth-floor apartment which he'd been renting for such a short—though very crucial—time. But now once more, as far as that painting of the civil service councillor is concerned, it almost goes without saying that Dr. Döblinger was the one who talked Frau Rosa into thinking that her husband really should have his portrait painted; how else, after all, would any connection between our civil service councillor and the painter Maria Rosanka ever have come into being? For the artist, by the way, the hours during which Zihal sat for her still remain unforgettable, thanks to many of their conversations.

Patience! Sooner than you think we'll have worked out way back around to Lieutenant or Major Melzer. Frau Zihal had two elder sisters. One ran a tobacco shop in Josefstadt, while the other had been married for more than twenty years to the proprietor of a large stationery store on Alserbach Strasse, across from the Liechtenstein summer palace with its famous collection of paintings. The store may have had a different name, still going by the one it had had earlier, but Herr Rokitzer, Rosa's brother-in-law, who had bought it and was the current owner, ran it jointly with his wife. And here we have the parents of Thea

Rokitzer, mentioned earlier; we will recall that in the summer of 1925 she gravitated, in a questionable enough manner, toward the indeterminable midpoint of the circle around Eulenfeld.

Even after his departure from the Schachl household, Zihal retained his custom of paying visits to Fräulein Theresa at set intervals; these always proceeded with decorum—in the bearing of the civil service councillor there was something of a delicately veiled, almost Spanish brand of etiquette, beyond what of it he displayed, more could be inferred—and they always featured the gold coffee cups trotted out for use and the good old days of yore for discussion. Only in a general sort of way, though. Our civil service councillor, who as a married man now of course turned up in the company of his wife, dropped hints, with easygoing openness at this point, to the effect that his bachelorhood struck now him, in retrospect, as a pathetic state of existence. To be sure, he did not intimate such sentiments to Fräulein Theresa Schachl while his wife was in the room; instead, he would wait until she was in the garden with the Pichlers and her niece Thea, whom she'd brought with her.

That had happened for the first time early in the summer of 1923, and Paula had first caught sight of the young girl from her lounge chair (it was still in good condition and was still in use), in which she was lying out past the four fruit trees in their little garden when Civil Service Councillor Zihal came through the archway with his wife but also, unexpectedly, a third person behind them. She was tall, slender, and energetic, and she exuded that air of having turned out splendidly, or at least that simple sense of being unblemished, that can affect a discerning individual—and such indeed, within her own limitations, was Frau Paula Pichler—like a kind of projecting rock cover, a challenge looming overhead. The roses were in bloom, and the garden was saturated with them; but it was only now that the spots of color and the perfumes were given their true reference point, which was this twenty-one-year old, whose vibrant womanliness completely overshadowed the more subdued nature of Paula Pichler, who was downright flustered and—as she candidly admitted to herself later—happy her husband had gone out. It's known, however, that women who make such a strong impression on other women are always less dangerous to the male of the species. That rule of thumb applied perfectly in this case, and master mechanic Alois Pichler could never see anything more in Thea than that she was unusually stupid.

In this respect, though, he was spoiled by his wife, in a sense.

Even so, Thea Rokitzer was much more than "stupid," as our good friend Alois called it (he was the total embodiment of what is known as a "really great guy," the type formerly just about the most frequently encountered among all the common people in Vienna). The argument could also be made about Thea, however, that she was far from stupid. She was missing two traits needed to attain stupidity as our age recognizes it; they were brazenness and hostility, neither the faintest trace of which was evident in her face or her person. One might, accordingly, call her callow. Very well. Call callow shallow, but though soft as a mallow, it's not fallow. No, it's a bud that arose when the spring sun's warmth grows and falls low on the callow in the hollow while the cow lows, a bud not just in the physical sense, the kind, for example, that René Stangeler, his hand skillfully guided, had in earlier days learned to find under Editha Pastré's unbuttoned tennis shirt. A bud was what Thea was in the highest degree, and the roses in the garden had instantly made her their focal point. It was slow to blow in that one furrow (unfallow) her callow being would show, but for her it really was a slow go (but then she'd so glow) rather than a no-go, and there was more to her than you know; so what ensued for the time being, though only in the summer of 1925, was the low blow of the captain's entry (and, to elevate the incident to a level commensurate with higher social rank, in an inebriated state) through the natural gateway. Yet for all that, if we were forced to make a choice, we would prefer to opt for the assertion that Thea was far from stupid.

In our estimation, after all, a more general significance attaches to this kind of unassailable blankness. If we take a good look at the group of people who now and then congregated in the garden of Fräulein Schachl's house, all sitting around an old table fetched from inside and now set with a liter bottle of new wine and a few glasses—if we observe this gathering of women in light summer dresses, of men in shirtsleeves and suspenders, whose moderate and subdued chatter and laughter fill this green basin of quietness and self-enclosure in which glowing patches

of color from the rosebushes are suspended in repose while the blue
sky far off in the heights casts its reflection all the way down to the
wine in the little glass, then we will notice a good many distinctions
among them, indeed almost a sharply differentiated stratification. It's
beyond any doubt, for instance, that Fräulein Theresa Schachl and the
civil service councillor fit into one and the same category, along with
Paula and her husband; Frau Rosa Zihal, née Oplatek, seems to us to
constitute a transitional phase leading not so much to the Rokitzers—
inasmuch as the lines of stratification now being traced are following
neither family relationship nor chronological age but are instead demarcating a phenomenon which in a more general sense is of simultaneous occurrence and should therefore be arranged by epoch, as it
were—leading, then, not so much to the Rokitzers as to Paula's stepfather, Loiskandl, an assembler, and to Paula's mother, his wife; of
course this couple also turned up here from time to time. The man
Loiskandl, however, even though his age in years was far greater than
that of Alois Pichler, nevertheless fit into a later stratum, and we can
say the same about his wife in spite of her being a grandmother—Paula
was the mother of a little girl—as well as a daughter of eighteen, the
eldest child from the second marriage, who was now engaged, young
as she was, to a good man, a dedicated police administrator named
Zacher. Young Hedwig Loiskandl didn't show up too often; had she
been really attractive, she might have functioned as the basis of a smooth
lateral transition, remaining in the same stratum, to all three of the
Rokitzers, especially to the parents, for it was already self-evident
enough that—if only she had revealed equivalent external advantages—
she would have been on exactly the same level, which is to say in exactly
the same condition of blankness, as Thea, whose domain was the
apartment behind the stationery store across from the Liechtenstein
summer palace. She lounged on and against all the furniture (there
was too much of it), with special preference for an art nouveau sideboard
along the rear wall of the dining room. Everything was in perfect order
here. Even the stationer's cash reserves in savings accounts were more
than adequate, and life-insurance as well as fire-insurance premiums
were paid up well in advance of the due date. Nobody ever got sick here
or had any doubts about anything or was at all dissatisfied with his or

her own self. Thea was the only child. In soil this rich, given a healthy tree, what other kind of fruit could possibly have ripened but some variety not unlike those picture-perfect specimens from California that can never quite measure up to the intense, piquant flavor of a mountain berry? But the flawless blush of this downy cheek in its re- splendent colors lures and entices the worm as though the fruit had been grown expressly for it to bite. Thea never came up with any thoughts. But there was one thought that did come to her—she wanted to be a movie actress. It came to her from the street, through the win- dow, or maybe the store, among all the magazines and postcards, or straight from some movie house. The thought was able to make its way to her because her blankness was in a state of balance absolute, but at the same time unsteady. To make this point as it correlates to lines of stratification: of the specimens of all the strata represented in Fräulein Schachl's garden, the Rokitzers—father, mother, daughter—made up the most recent, so to speak, strictly alluvial matter long removes away from being newly formed rock. And if, as it would be altogether right to do, we were inclined to place River Master Ferdinand Schachl—the finest of the lot, to be sure—on the same level as his sister, Theresa or Civil Service Councillor Zihal, then it seems to us a certainty that he would have communicated very well with his posthumous stepson, Alois Pichler; tolerably well with Frau Rosa Zihal; only through a struggle with Loiskandl; and not at all with the Rokitzers.

Nobody goes to the dogs all at once or by a direct route. First you go to Eulenfeld, and that's where the matter will be decided. After all, he *is* the Master of Horse. "Oh, mankind, do penance! For here is the cow's hoof"—these are the words of an inscription dating from the Middle Ages in Vienna; it is equally incomprehensible, at the very least. But that was just how it was, and Frau Mary K. was definitely right when (we've made mention of it already, I seem to think) at a later date, and by that time in possession of only her left leg, she stated that Eu- lenfeld was far less a person than he was an illness which certain organ- isms simply have to undergo. But who is a person anyway? Most human beings today are illnesses or odors, and always mere functions of some- thing or another. Eulenfeld was like some kind of sieve or colander (*passoire*). Whatever went through, went through, but whatever had a form and could maintain it did not go through. Furthermore, illnesses are institutions. Oh, mankind, do penance; for here is the Disaster of Course.

For the same reason, the various interlocking causalities that conveyed Thea to this stop on the line are completely meaningless; I never inquired about them and so I don't have any information. But at any rate, Thea (one of many) had to get off here under any circumstances. As early as June or July of 1925 her suffering ("soffering" was how it sounded when Paula Pichler said it) had blossomed to the point of being full-blown; though slow to blow, it was now on full show. We can only assume that through this whole process she was still convinced she was on the right road, which is to say on the one that would carry her the farthest possible distance away from that sideboard in the dining room and the farthest possible distance away from . . . Thea Rokitzer—who never came up with any thoughts (it's high time to get ruthless about resuming our story here). So she wouldn't have understood. She thought this was the right road, because on it there occasionally appeared among the Eulenfeldean fauna (sometimes almost a "*societas daemonum aliorumque damnatorum*," which the great catechism cites as one of the punishments of hell) this or that person from the theater or the newspapers and because the way they lived there rarely came close to matching what the flickering images on the screen showed her to be an escape route, a doorway leading out into the world, even if it was no more than two-dimensional and thus a walled-up escape door, if we can say it that way.

Between those two friends—which is what Paula and Thea had soon become—there was a difference of eight years; Paula was going on thirty-two. Early in the summer she began reliving, more or less, the experiences Thea Rokitzer would bring to her from some unknown quarter and pour out to her, following that untested belief of the young according to which it really is possible, even normal, to give some other person a part of one's own burden to help carry, so now the two people sharing it have it in common, and the other one will handle it and hold it just as one is doing oneself; this is how far sideways the egoism of callow ephebes will fling the reins when they go into a panic instead of grabbing the reins themselves and pulling the cart out of the ditch. Even among adults, too, however, we know of attempts, from time to time, at least, and equally between the two parties, to set down their backpacks when those have grown too heavy; so it does happen once in a while, when the situation seems to invite it, as for instance in a secluded café, one hidden in the depths of the large city, where two people are sitting together but in fact past one another because the person going to confession is bound to believe that his confessor (except that both are both at the same time) has a much more orderly inner life than he himself has. But at that time, Paula Pichler actually was in good order, a *point d'appui*, an Archimedean point. Such things really do exist, relative, interim, situational though they are. Good order is nothing more than the water of life rising up through the arteries, the veins, and the capillaries; when it fills them to the brim they form the most beautiful network of branchings. And when it recedes, then you can bundle them together or smooth them out any way you like but they'll still be all tangled and snarled, in great disorder. That person is best engaging with life whose apparent command of good order is handled with discretion and can barely be discerned for what it is. It wasn't so much that Paula Pichler had ever created order in her life as that she had grown into it. She didn't lose her balance when Thea came swooping down on her, either. Her acquired knowledge enabled her automatically to translate that familiar cry of distress, "Help me to get out of this!" (a cry uttered in the language of infatuation) into its opposite. But she was imperturbable in promoting neither the one nor the other; and on the whole she didn't say very much, which was the greatest possible favor she could do Thea, who more than anything else needed to talk, to talk and get away from herself, to talk and get it away from herself, to get some breathing room for a while. Quietly and to herself only, Paula very soon (and very bluntly) started calling the object of Thea's infatuation an old reprobate, though her doing so didn't jettison any ballast for Thea, so to speak, or take any weight off the seriousness of her plight; as far as that goes, it would never have entered Paula's mind to expect that appraisals of this kind might bring about even the mildest relief in a case as glaring as Thea's. All she did was ask at one point whether Thea had ever paid an unexpected visit to Eulenfeld or had gone to see that Frau Schlinger in her apartment out past Franz Josef Station. "I think I'd do that sometime if I were in your place." Just from the way Thea looked at that suggestion as an utterly colossal feat of daring, Paula Pichler was able to deduce the whole emotional basis, as it were, of the situation, which was that Thea was in deep waters there, that she was being terrorized.

Melzer was constantly mentioned among Thea's chaotic outpourings. Paula would have liked to see a few more strokes added to the picture of this man, a stranger who'd caught her interest. But she didn't ask many questions about him, and none at all about Stangeler, whom Thea mentioned only seldom (speaking briefly once about his troubles with Grete Siebenschein); even so, that little was soon enough for Paula's alert ear to match the identity of this man with René beyond the shadow of a doubt. Now any questions were omitted entirely, and she gave no sign whatever that she knew him. It was a kind of spice amid the heavy burden, though, an impish little pleasure for her to hear this or that item about René from two sources, not just from Aunt Lina on rare occasions, and then very sparsely. Of course it goes without saying that once Thea had begun telling her these stories it didn't take Paula long to figure out quite clearly the nature of the established and continuing relations between Frau Editha Schlinger and the captain (while Thea fervently went on construing every sign as its opposite), quite by contrast with Melzer—as we know, unfortunately—who, in this instance, was thinking (if we can say that of him) in too orderly a way, too much in accordance with the laws of physics, inasmuch as he was applying the axiom which states that two objects cannot occupy the same space at the same time. That law may well hold true in physics, but it all gets written down very differently on the schedules of local railroads (running on the erotic track) with a separate set of fares for short distances. And in this regard Melzer was like a man who tries to reach the conclusion, based on eating but a single noodle at any given meal, that there could be no such a thing as gluttony. Well now, Paula was a woman of thirty-two, while Melzer was a lieutenant, first lieutenant, captain, major, then Melzer the civil servant, with the first tiny shoots of a civilian mentality beginning to sprout. Besides: "Men, well known for being obtuse and awkward …"—something that a lady wonderfully dear to me used to like telling me, and today I know (too late, unfortunately) she was right.

It was as early as July that the texture of all these affairs began to grow more coarse-grained—literally as well as figuratively—for it was then that the first slaps and blows were landed. One day the captain had said, "Thea, sweetheart, you've got to do me this big favor." Only too happy to! Thereupon he handed her something that looked like a passport, a very elaborate and beautifully executed identity document, asking if she would please go to the main post office and inquire, after presenting this document, whether there was a general-delivery letter waiting there. Then he hustled her straight out of his apartment and sent her on her way. Thea stood at the streetcar stop with a passport in her purse that she hardly even wanted to look at and with the inescapable feeling that when she got to the post office she would have to represent herself as a different woman, the one to whom the letter was addressed that Eulenfeld was trying to get hold of. She hoped there would be no letter. Without uttering a word, she placed the open document on the smooth counter at the window, and a minute later it was given back to her, along with a letter, which she likewise didn't want to look at. What's more, however, she got the impression—in the brief moment she waited at the window, but she could never erase it thereafter—that the photograph on the passport was a likeness of none other than Frau Editha Schlinger. Preparing to go back, she opened her purse to take out the money for her fare, and her glance naturally had to fall once more, and almost against her own will, on the envelope, on which she could read nothing but a very foreign-sounding name that later escaped her memory and the marking "General Delivery—Main Post Office." What happened next was something she herself never came to comprehend. (And for our part, we'd rather not risk any definite psychological diagnosis for now, if only because pretty much anything can come breaking in on a condition of total blankness when its balance is so unsteady; it may be a safe assumption, however, that what follows was an action directed in essence against the captain, the Master of Horse.) She got off at the train station, walked past the front door of Eulenfeld's building, and kept on going in the direction of Editha Schlinger's apartment. "I just couldn't seem to help"—she said to Paula—"thinking of Herr Melzer the whole time I was covering that short distance. That wasn't because of his letter to Frau Schlinger, which I was still carrying in my purse! What do you say about that? If I'd bumped into him, I would have been sure to ask him what I should do with the letter from the main post office." She rang Editha's bell (and so she really did show up there unexpectedly, knowing all the while that Eulenfeld was at home, waiting for her to come back).

Editha came and answered the door herself, looking as if Thea had roused her out of another world or another set of problems, or as if she'd been expecting someone entirely different; at any rate, her face was unprepared, so to speak, and for a moment it presented the aspect of a person who is all alone (alone on a July afternoon in a small apartment with several boxy little rooms, all painted high-gloss white or cream color). Nor did this aspect seem very friendly. However, a smile now quickly flitted across Editha's face and reassembled its features, which had been standing with open gaps between them. "Well, now, Thea dear," she said, "what brings you to my door? Do come in!" She held on to Thea's hand and led her inside through the hallway. Thea, now in a state of almost complete vacancy (but vacancy from what? from a vacuum? and does that mean vacancy to the second power?) and close to shedding tears as well, went toppling down into the situation and stayed lying helpless where she was, amongst all the small, smaller, and smallest of its inner and outer circumstances in a manner comparable to a serving maid who is lying speechless all alone on the floor next to the pile of shards (speaking loud and clear on its own) from all the china that smashed into a thousand pieces when the tray went crashing down. Oh, the poor Viennese chocolate girl Thea, who's taken a bad spill—as if painted by Liotard! She could see the whole Kahlenberg standing at Editha's windows. She reached into her purse without saying a word; by now her eyes had filled up—in spite of her action (an attempt at making up for underhanded dealings, at making good for them, at making off with them and herself along with them, if the truth be told), she looked like the very personification of bad conscience—she reached into her purse and handed Editha first the passport and then the letter.

Within a few seconds, Editha's face came plummeting down from the penthouse of the decorous composure to which it had mounted into the subbasement of darkest fury. Neither woman had taken a seat yet; both were standing in the middle of a kind of living room, which, in addition to the entrance from the hallway, had identical white double doors left and right—a good many doors even for a more spacious room. "Just how did you get your hands on this passport?" Editha shrieked. She went straight into a screaming fit before asking any other questions or demanding any explanations; perhaps the way Thea's face was displaying a paradoxically bad conscience made Editha just itch to let loose even more.

"Answer me, you idiot!" Editha snarled; she was now speaking conventional standard German rather than Austrian colloquial, which probably intensified in Thea a feeling of special danger about this particular situation and about the whole situation in general. At least what she emitted now, instead of an answer, was the whimpering sound peculiar to a first gush of tears, a sound with some resemblance to a foal neighing. Then Editha stamped her foot so hard that the white doors rattled. "I won't have my mail delivered here because of the riffraff in the building, and then what happens anyway is..." All of a sudden she began speaking very rapidly in a foreign language Thea didn't understand, her voice rising in pitch as she stepped closer, and then came the sound of blows and a burning on Thea's cheeks, on the left, then repeated, and then one on the right. Now the poor head-over-heels Viennese chocolate girl literally did go tumbling down, dropping into a white upholstered armchair behind her and burying her face in her arms as she started to howl. Editha said (to the degree that one can refer to such hammer blows as saying something): "You bitch! Available for use in an affair like this! Our own Little Miss Goody-Goody! But don't worry; I'll be sure to tell them in all the right places about what kind she really is! No more than a week ago Herr Melzer was sitting in that very chair and kept referring so warmly to this good, estimable, unspoiled person; he couldn't say enough! Now I can't wait to tell him a thing or two about what a no-good, sneaky animal..." At this point she broke off, and, what was odd, she sat down calmly on a chair and had nothing more to say.

Thea, even though she was sobbing out loud, had very clearly registered the two elements in Editha's outburst that were most unusual, had cocked her ears, as it were, right in the midst of the turbulence she herself had caused. One of them, to be sure, was not quite so distinct; that was Editha's odd, almost outmoded way of expressing herself, one that sounded, even when she was in a rage, as if she were speaking a language she'd learned and practiced more from books than from actual use. Now, this item was one she didn't mention when she was recounting this whole episode to Paula Pichler. She probably wouldn't have been able to put a name to it anyway; for her it fit into the whole incident more as a background element, like the Kahlenberg through the window and those two white double doors, tall and stiff. But the unexpected reference to Melzer in the midst of the whirlwind struck her very forcefully and very consciously, on the other hand, leaving behind in her an echo, a feeling that lingered, as if something had thrust deep into her internal—or even, as they say, vital—organs, more or less like a palpable hit from a foil, which can slide right in and penetrate once it has pierced the surface layer of the body, toughened and tautened by the muscles.

With that, everything grew still, except for Thea's sobbing.

Editha sat with her eyes blazing, probably no more able to understand her own words and actions than Thea was able to understand why she had come here. If it was seeing the passport—and she had to realize how and by whom it had been purloined the previous night—that had sent Editha into a fury, that fury nonetheless did not keep its direction focused on the captain; rather, like an emetic acting indiscriminately on all the contents of the stomach at once, everything gathered there, whether it was part of the immediate problem or not, came spewing forth, scoring a direct hit on Thea Rokitzer, who to now had done so good a job of making herself her own protégée through self-effacement and eagerness to please. In this process, Editha, bent on revenge, burst out of the dark, deep subbasement of the mad rage she'd plunged into and came back into the light of day. So then came the tongue-lashing, the flying hand, the reference to Melzer.

Awakening now, however, losing the thread of the real connections here and robbed of a deeper and better logic, all she could do at that point—and it frightened her—was read the mere names of things; so it occurred to her only now, after the fact, that she should have been giving Thea a vote of thanks. Thud! There she was up on dry ground now, sitting on the beach, as can happen at some of the ocean spas off in the west, at Arcachon or Biarritz, say, when the heavy Atlantic swell roughly heaves the swimmer out of the water. That was how Editha was sitting in her easy chair now, unable to understand her own self because she'd been cast off by the swelling wave and pinned between the two irrefutable facts that Eulenfeld had stolen her passport and that Thea had returned it, though not at once; first, that letter had been wrongfully obtained. Her fury was on the point of breaking out once more, especially when she thought about the captain's incredible nerve in taking advantage of her being fast asleep—apparently he even must have had the lamp on the nightstand turned on!—to search through her purse and her official papers, both of which she always placed on a small white étagère she had standing at the head of the bed. Yes, her fury was at the point of breaking out once more, provoked by concrete images like these. But Editha escaped this outburst of passion by taking flight into a different one; now it was her turn to be awash in tears as she flung herself at Thea, almost falling down at her feet, and with a flood of affectionate hugs and an even greater flood of words—words that spoke in an altogether indistinct but urgent way of her "emotional despondency," of her frequently not being in control of herself and her need, overall, for somebody she could trust—asking Thea for the love of God please to forgive her. Which she now did. We can understand why when we bear in mind that she had reason to feel both elated and blessed at this chance to withdraw her foot from the trap she had blundered into here, and without having to walk away from an enemy at that. They ended up having tea together, and Editha treated Thea to marrons glacés from Demel's.

Still hanging as a loose—by which we also mean licentious—thread: the captain.

That didn't bother Editha Schlinger too much, though. While now enjoying the unbounded pleasure that came of having staged this dramatic scene as a way to help get past the frustration of waiting in vain for Melzer to show up—he'd simply stayed away, that is, and hadn't sent one single word of excuse, which didn't fit his style at all, and he certainly wouldn't be coming now!—she opened the letter, working adroitly and quickly with a little steam and a miniature opener she took from her white secretary desk by the window, and then read it through, carefully and slowly, taking a seat at the tea table. It was a letter of some length. After reading it, she sealed it back in the envelope exactly the way it was, so neatly and skillfully that no one would ever have noticed anything wrong. During her reading she had jotted down several passages into a small notebook bound in green leather; then she locked it in her desk. "I keep the letters I receive for a long time anyway," she said, now again holding a teacup in her hand and pointing to the desk piled up with mail. "At least I took notes on the most important parts of that letter. So now you can just go back to the captain and give it and the passport to him as if none of this had happened. And it goes without saying that I'll keep it strictly to myself. That's the least I owe you by way of thanks. And I mean thanks that you've forgiven me, too." She kissed Thea after she finished these words.

"But your passport!" cried Thea. "How are you ever going to get your passport back?"

Editha smiled indulgently and merely observed that her passport would soon find itself back in the very place from which it was now missing. With that, Thea left in a hurry, in the street still sucking on one of the glazed chestnuts that Editha had slipped into her mouth at the apartment door.

"Well, in what foreign language was she cursing you out?" Paula asked.

"I don't know. Maybe French. They all speak French once in a while, kind of back and forth; Otto too" (she meant Eulenfeld), "and Stangeler, but not Melzer. He knows it, though."

"And you—didn't you ever learn French?"

"No. Can you speak it?"

"Oh, I can get by. My English is better. My aunt had me sign up for it in my commercial course. I learned some more later as well. What did you go to school for, anyway? Or didn't you ever want to?" Thea didn't answer, and Paula quickly deflected her own question. "If you'd thought to give Frau Schlinger the letter from Melzer first, and then the passport with the letter from the main post office, she might not have gone off at you. Or maybe she would really have let fly! How long ago was that, anyway?"

"Saturday afternoon."

"So it was on the eleventh. And today's Saturday, the eighteenth. That's a full week ago. Have you seen anything of Herr Melzer in the meantime?"

"Twice, in fact, and both times by chance; on Wednesday on the street, for just a minute, and then on Thursday at the captain's."

"And he never asked you any questions about his letter?"

"No."

"He might have if you and he had been alone."

"We were alone, and I was dreading he might ask. He came to see Otto on Thursday. I was in the apartment already, and Otto was supposed to be back soon. I asked Herr Melzer to wait for the captain a little while, because I know how fond of him Otto is."

"Oh really?" said Paula, and nothing else.

"Yes. I suppose I should have been happy for the chance to get him out of there quickly; all I would have had to do was tell him the captain wasn't at home (I was just straightening up the place) and wouldn't be back until evening. Otto didn't show up until two hours later than he'd promised as it was, and he was really glad to find Herr Melzer there. Then the three of us ate together."

"So you were with Melzer that whole time?"

"Yes. I did some sewing, and we made ourselves tea. It was so quiet and pleasant. I forgot all about that stupid letter, put it completely out of my mind, and he didn't ask me a thing about it. He was so sweet."

"And you never did take a good look at the passport?" asked Paula. "Not even after you got slapped around?"

"No," Thea answered. "All I wanted to do was get rid of it, along with the letter, by leaving it at Otto's."

The older woman did nothing but shake her head.

The spot along the riverbank where Thea Rokitzer and Paula Pichler were lying on a blanket was half shaded by shrubbery and half in the sunlight, so they could roll into it if they turned slightly. Paula avoided it, however; because she got freckles, she was no devotee of the cult of broiling. Sunbathing didn't really yield successful results for Thea, either; her rosy-pink skin would rebel every time, and only too fiercely, against the unnaturalness of this radiation treatment, which had the effect—but only when gradually and carefully increased and, in the last phases, undertaken for long hours at a stretch while not moving a muscle—of transforming the delicate coloring of a blond into the oily brown demanded at every turn, even in those days, by the uniform regulations for females. Also, the captain was the kind of man who needed the support of the majority in order to feel comfortable, a fascination dictated by the masses but applied to a genuinely personal matter. And yet he wouldn't have been capable of upholding the personal at all had it not been for the general. So it was that Thea began dabbling in all sorts of nostrums and concoctions, smearing them onto the velvety, peach-like epidermis nature had given her body. For now, though, as the intensity of the talk she was having with her friend grew more concentrated, she felt distracted by the glare and the heat of this July afternoon, and she drew closer to Paula in the half shadows of the bushes.

A soft breath of wind blew in from the river. And the water was flowing swiftly. Coming around the side of the Leopoldsberg, it left the other mountain, the Bisamberg, off to the left, receding into the sky behind it, the edge of its face blurring the checkerboard of fields and forest along the extended foothills, which opened up the distances of summer into a depth even greater than an unrestricted view out to Jedlersee would have done, with striding electrical transmission towers, with house and heath far-flung. Everything here was grouped around the river. It was the foreground, the background, the prime color. Everything was blue and gray, everything went off into the distance, borne along the expanses opened out to the wind, borne along the stately surging of the watercourse that divided the prospect and split it in two, in fealty to the river god, as was the foam of the Au Woods that trailed behind him. And the god spoke unto the dryad, unto the dryad Paula Schachl from Alsergrund, and what he had to tell her, as he gently spluttered and sprayed, came from her father, a man who had been his faithful son.

Now it wasn't that Paula was giving any thought to the departed river master. And yet she was encompassed by him, we might say—here and now, often, two days before, in a dream. She was perfectly secure, for example, in the unquestioned certainty that he would have really liked Alois, her husband. Every time she had a dream about her father, she would make it her firm purpose to ask him a question the next time he appeared. But what question? This was the strange way she came to the realization one day that her life didn't hold any questions. She had been in the garden, three weeks earlier, just getting ready to lie down in her lounge chair. No, there weren't any decisions to be made. "I'm happy," she thought, more a statement of fact than a feeling. The last time she'd dreamed about her father, he'd said, "Make me one more cup of coffee when I read in the morning. It's not as easy as it used to be. I won't always be able to be with you."

At the same time, in a way strangely charged with intimacy, these days of summer she was living now—each one came to an affectionate close with her husband's warmhearted return from work, his whistling in the garden, the brief, strong pressure of his arm around her shoulders when he kissed her, a kind of pressure lingering from other days, as though he were calling something back into her memory each time without saying a word—at the same time, these very days would blend and melt into the ones from fourteen years earlier, when she would be restlessly but happily waiting for René, who was supposed to be coming to Vienna from the country, while at the same time doing what she could to hold back Aunt Theresa, who wanted to escape the heat of the city by beating a quick retreat. In those days she also spent much time down at the river, just like now, in her conversations with Thea, only by herself back then. Whenever images from those days came into her mind—at times a few of them would come fluttering out, like a curtain in a gust of wind—they would appear to her standing against a delicate lilac background. One time the scent of René's lavender water emerged out of this color with sharp distinctness. Her walks with Thea had also not covered very much ground in the beginning; first along the Danube Canal, and then later as far as the lock. But now they stretched half the distance from the lock to Kahlenbergerdorf. On occasion she could go out and stay away without worrying; Aunt Theresa looked after her child in the garden, not just as "the apple of her eye," but even more as her new and already well-established and indispensable reason for living. The little girl was almost four years old.

Paula pictured René in her mind as though he were still in prep school, were still a gymnasiast, as close to her, as much a part of things, as comforting to her, in a sense, as everything from a good childhood is; and today that is what she felt hers had been, including those years around the time she was eighteen. She was unaware of the contradiction in her mental image, a contradiction because of the past fourteen years (although we know better than does the thirty-two-year-old and altogether mature Paula Pichler that her image of Stangeler was still very largely congruent with the actual nature and state of his person-hood as they were then). Somewhere to the back Aunt Lina was there too. Perhaps this was the deepest and most solid reason why all this recurrence, all these questioning and resounding overtones and un-dertones of the person she'd once loved, never created the slightest uneasiness in her. It could only be good. She was listening to Thea's conversation not only patiently, but eagerly.

"When did Melzer give you his letter to Frau Schlinger?" she asked now, turning onto her side and facing Thea Rokitzer as she squinted into the sun a little, which made her eyes look very slanted and catlike, though gentle, above her slightly high cheekbones. She was turned more toward the slope of the riverbank now, toward the regulating jetty made of massive granite blocks, from which they were about forty paces away, lying on a kind of little peninsula formed from the bot-tomland, covered with bushes and with the water now at low level, standing free and dry. Behind and above the jetty stretched a length of railroad track and a road right past which, on the other side, the terrain climbed steeply, part of it tree and shrub, part of it abruptly broken, sliding hillsides from which lines of stone stuck out like ribs. The downward slant of the afternoon drew near, and in the folds of the mountain wall, shadows were now painted. A truck drove noisily past on the road beyond the track bed.

"On the afternoon before the episode with the passport," Thea answered, "so I'm talking about Friday, the tenth, since you always like everything figured out exactly. My unlucky day came early, though, on Saturday. It should have been on Monday; that was the thirteenth. I was going along Porzellan Gasse on Friday, because there was some-thing I had to ask about in a store. Then I was supposed to go to Frau Schlinger's and meet Otto there. A little farther along, toward the train station, Herr Melzer was standing in front of a mailbox, holding a letter in his hand but not putting it into the box, not moving at all, just frozen where he was. He looked strange—very sad or even desolate somehow, I want to say. He didn't notice I was there until I stepped right up to him, but then, when he did see me, he went through a complete change. Paula, he was openly and honestly happy at our meeting. He said, 'Oh, hello, Fräulein Thea! How are you, and where are you headed?' 'I have to go up to Frau Schlinger's for a quick stop,' I said. 'Really? In that case you could do me a very big favor,' he said; 'this letter is to Frau Schlinger, and it probably won't reach her until tomorrow morning if I send it through the mail. Would you mind simply handing it to her?' 'Of course not,' I said; 'but it's a shame you already put a stamp on it.' He gave a little wave with his hand, so tired and downcast, you know, but then he laughed and said, 'What's important is that she get the letter on time,' and then, 'I thank you very kindly, Fräulein Thea.' He gave me a warm goodbye; he's very courteous in his way, a complete gentleman, and not just on the outside; I always get the sense he's the real thing. I put the letter into my purse—but then what happened was that I never made it to Frau Schlinger's that afternoon anyway. I hadn't yet reached her front door when here came Otto and Stangeler slowly ambling along toward me; they were having an animated conversation. Stangeler had just gotten back from Budapest and looked terrible. Right then he was having some serious problems with his girlfriend or fiancée, Fräulein Siebenschein. I think I've already told you something about that. They weren't seeing each other, and he was madly unhappy. Otto and he talked about practically nothing else the whole time, right into the evening. I had the feeling, also, that they'd both been drinking cognac up at Frau Schlinger's place; you know how unhappy it makes me when the captain starts boozing it up like that. Then we went for a little walk along the Danube Canal and went back to Otto's after that. He brought Stangeler with him. I made myself some tea, but here came the bottle, of course trotted out by Otto. He made me drink, too. I always feel so woozy and stupid the next day. Well, anyhow, when I went up to Frau Editha's all of a sudden on Saturday, the only thing I could think of was that letter from the main post office, not the one from Herr Melzer."

"You forgot it, then?" Paula asked.

"Yes … no," Thea Rokitzer replied, hesitating noticeably as she answered. Between her thoughts or feelings and their outward manifestation on the surface, whether in gestures or in words, there almost no vigilance at all was interposed, because the person who could have exercised it and stepped in between was to a large extent missing. She was good at lying to herself but totally clumsy or even downright incompetent at lying to others, because inside her the requisite machinery was in a rudimentary stage of development. And so her speech represented an exact and perfect replica of her actual being, which is something one seldom encounters, as a general rule. Paula was familiar with this trait, of course, and her instincts also recognized it as being significantly different in origin from, say, the honesty and truthfulness of her husband, on which she placed a very high value—compared with it, Thea's brand was no body of clear water through which one can see the stones all the way at the bottom; no, it was so shallow that the stones rose well above the surface.

"Didn't it ever enter your mind just to say to Herr Melzer, 'I forgot all about your letter; here it is back'?"

"No."

"Maybe you … wanted to forget it?"

"I don't know. But what does she need a note from Melzer for anyway? They get along so well as it is! And she already has … she has … the captain," and now suddenly—her eyes had already begun to fill up during the last few words—she burst into tears and began sobbing heavily, slowly, as if someone were dipping from a barrel and spattering the water; she'd hidden her face in her arms. Paula stroked her hair. It was soon over. Thea's good-natured face, when she turned it back toward her friend, looked like a little country garden with its flowers all fresh after the rain. So that was how the child's milk curdled when she had her first heartbreak.

"Do you still have the letter?"

Thea just nodded. But in answer to Paula's question about what was in Melzer's note, her friend replied, somewhat bewildered, that she hadn't opened it. "Why don't you bring it with you next time?" cried Paula eagerly. "There's no way you could give it back to Herr Melzer now, and he certainly isn't going to ask you about it if he hasn't by this time." Well, she had the note right here in her purse, said Thea.

Out it came, of course; nothing else would do. Paula was somehow ready with a small pair of scissors (Thea plucked up her nerve just watching her) but for a moment she didn't do anything but inspect the outside of the violet envelope. There was no return address. She slit the note open.

Dear Editha,

I've been so much looking forward to Saturday afternoon, but I'm in horrible shape right now and would only spoil the occasion if we got together. I'm sneezing all the time, even while writing this note; probably I picked up a cold last Sunday evening in Kritzendorf, but I know I just have to rest in bed over the weekend. I hope my coming to visit when I'm feeling better will be in order—I'll wait to hear. But given the nature of the information (concerning the procurement of tobacco products in wholesale quantities), preferably by word of mouth, not in writing.

Very respectfully yours,
Melzer

The date was the ninth, not the tenth, of July.

"He wrote this note on Thursday of that week," observed Paula, "and then he let it sit till the following day. Or else he was trying to fudge the dates in case his letter arrived late. But besides all that, I don't understand why he wrote to her in the first place."

"What do you mean?" asked Thea; it really did sound like the bleating of a tiny little lamb.

"Well, because she has a phone. I know that from you; I don't miss anything. And he probably has one too. No, there's nothing going on between them. In that whole note there's not a single intimate *Du* or a single businesslike *Sie*; he doesn't know quite what approach to take with her. But there was something happening earlier between those two, and maybe Saturday was supposed to have been the clincher. Anyway, he didn't try reaching her by phone, that way she couldn't argue and tell him he should come even if he did have a cold—which we know he didn't. As you must have seen . . . ?"

"I didn't notice anything like a cold," Thea said hastily, now completely cheered up again.

"Well, there, you see? But now what's this about tobacco products?"

"I have no idea what that's about," Thea replied.

"Are you going to keep the note?" Paula asked Thea by way of closing as she slipped the sheet of paper back into the envelope and handed it to her. Thea grabbed it quickly and put it safely away in a side compartment of her leather purse.

So now she could stop and catch her breath—that is, as long as Editha Schlinger held to her solemn vow of silence regarding the captain (though Paula Pichler tended to be pessimistic about this in her thinking). Meanwhile, there soon took place another event that was fundamentally every bit as incomprehensible as the one we've just outlined, or as that old exhortation to do penance because of the cow's hoof.

It seemed as if there was nothing Thea could do to avoid the captain's wrath in the long run. But at least there were no blows landed in that quarter. The Eulenfeldean surface was polished much too smooth with courtliness for anything of the kind, and on the serving tray of his inner self—on his interior surface, we might say—were displayed gleaming objects and unauthenticated heirlooms of the very same types as the beautiful bowls and plates found on a shelf. People own such things. Even the greatest skeptics have such *objets* of the soul, their patinas carefully burnished, in their possession. That makes everything just wonderful—though only if nothing falls. Furthermore, Eulenfeld's disposition was cheerful, like that of many drunkards. Even aside from that, the sort of sharp edge we might call Pastré-like never manifests itself in men; if it did, they would be hermaphroditic monstrosities, something our old Master of Horse (as he enjoyed styling himself) most assuredly was not. The latest trial by ordeal decreed for Thea Rokitzer, even before July was over (she failed it), had some connection with her Aunt Oplatek, her mother's one sister—the other one was Frau Zihal, wife of our civil service councillor, as we will recall—the one who ran the tobacco store in Josefstadt. Tobacco products? Oh yes, that's which way we're headed. We might begin by asking if the members of this group were such exceptionally heavy smokers. Answer: not at all. Frau Pastré-Schlinger smoked only on occasion (but when she did, she liked something strong) and Melzer with utmost moderation, Stangeler and Eulenfeld being the only two real consumers.

But still and all—tobacco products! One day the captain had said, "Thea, sweetheart, you've got to do me this big favor." Only too happy to! Thereupon he directed her to ask her aunt, Josefine Oplatek, whether it would be possible for her, at her next "fixing" of merchandise—this was the term long used in Austria (the imperial military services included) for the process of receiving consignments of government-regulated goods, and the persons charged with overseeing this process were called "fixing members," which conjures up a vividly concrete image of prehensile tentacles of some kind—whether it might be possible, anyway, for the aunt, at her next "fixing," to order and take delivery of a larger shipment—quite considerably larger, for that matter: some fifty thousand cigarettes and five thousand Virginia cigars, to be specific. That higher quantity could be disposed of at once. The aunt didn't seem to fix on anything being said when her niece laid out this proposal; all she did was scratch her head reflectively with a knitting needle through the bun in her hair and calmly listen to Thea's rather far-fetched rationale for the increase in demand. It went like this: the gentleman on whose behalf Thea was making this inquiry was contemplating a change in his employment situation and would perhaps not be in receipt of any income over a considerable period of time; accordingly, being a heavy smoker, he was hoping to make provision for himself in this matter (all right, but could there ever be such a thing as a genuinely logical reason for a private citizen's all of a sudden requiring mountains of cigarettes? The captain might have done better to hide behind the proprietor of a large café or a hotel, but apparently he was just too lazy to go to that trouble and tried working his scheme through Thea first). Several days after Thea had gone to visit her aunt, Eulenfeld received a postcard with the following message:

To the Addressee:
    Regret not being in a position to provide the consignment per your request, as it exceeds the quantity authorized me in my

fixing. Please make application in this matter to the main tobacco distribution point.

Very truly yours,
Josefine Oplatek
Tobacconist
Vienna, District VIII

… and so on. But Eulenfeld never so much as dreamed of turning to Melzer, an official in the tobacco administration, convenient as that route might seem. Instead, he suffered a (medium-strength) attack of rage—not because of the tobacconist's refusal but because of Thea's having communicated his name and home address to her. So he kicked Thea out for a week, placing her under banishment in sackcloth and ashes. For the most part, she spent these days of penitential observance discussing the situation with Paula. On this subject, however, Paula felt as though she were standing on a side track, uncoupled and with no plans for further use; her powers of judgment simply couldn't connect to anything at all in that isolation. The one point that came to her once when she was alone and had time to think things over in her lounge chair—the four fruit trees, the colorful bursts of flowers in the curtain of quiet, the warm yellow walls, and a feathery cirrus cloud were at rest inside her like a trusted weight, like a tuning fork whose note can be relied on to remain the same—the one thought that came to her was that if occasion ever arose she could ask Civil Service Councillor Zihal why the tobacconist would have refused that shipment and whether it would have been violating some regulation for her to accept it. But then she forgot all about it. What the captain did, when Thea was allowed to see him again, was triumphantly brandish a newspaper, proceeding to use it to furnish her additional proof of what a pathetic little simpleton she was; there was a story (really an altogether parenthetical, insignificant notation that stuck to generalities) reporting that several times recently, sizable quantities of Austrian cigarettes had been stolen from the factories or warehouses of the state tobacco administration and apparently smuggled across the Italian or German border, which had prompted increased vigilance on the part of customs authorities abroad. Eulenfeld was now seizing on the newspaper article to place Thea's lack of forethought and her carelessness into the proper light; because, after all, now her aunt—at least as he saw it—knowing the name and address of the party who'd been interested in placing that order for a large consignment of cigarettes with her, might start feeling downright uneasy in her conscience and could make some passing mention of the matter, something just short of an official report, on the occasion of her next fixing, and then he could wind up under suspicion of being in some way connected with this business about the smuggling, and wouldn't that be all he'd need? Chances were that her aunt had a background of experience with such matters anyway—when illegal activities were being planned, however; that was the difference—and had turned down the idea for that reason. With Thea, though, all you had to do was get the tiniest bit involved and trust her with the smallest and simplest errand; right away one disaster after another would follow and the worst kinds of difficulties would ensue (what exactly did they consist of in this case?—but Thea never got a chance to say a word). Anyway, he had a very hard time imagining himself living with a woman who had two left feet; what a terrifying thought it was to go through his whole life yoked together with Calamity Jane . . . and more of the same (the sharp thorn ended up piercing deep). When she was at last able to work her way through the ground-swell of his words and the cataract of her own tears so as to say something herself, it was of course all mixed-up, too. "But I would have had to jot down your address for her so that she could check back with you." (This last expression proves that the captain had penetrated deeply—linguistically speaking, also—into Thea Rokitzer, because even overlooking the conditional "would have had," the term "check back" was still extremely unusual in those days in Vienna). "She didn't want to have to make up her mind right then and there." (Whenever Thea spoke with Eulenfeld, his way of using language dominated hers, whereas Paula never desisted from warbling her native woodnotes wild—in either case, the vacuum would be filled with whatever material was at hand; after all, something had to come rushing in!) "What a ridiculous explanation!" cried the captain, holding his hands to his temples, as though stupidity on so large a scale had gone beyond the capacity of his head to grasp it and he were now forced to hold it together so it wouldn't explode, "what a ridiculous explanation! Anybody can sense right away whether a person wants to do something or not! So why did you have to start right off by telling her who needed the shipment? All you would have had to do was first sound your aunt out, as it were." "But she's such a totally good and innocent woman!" cried Thea. "Oh, is she really?" said the captain; "the only innocent one around here seems to be you" (at this point we might say that her quiet little existence was indeed innocent, but truly it wasn't without its share of sorrow). "Innocent or not, those are words it might behoove one to use not only for people's characters but for situations as well." (He was anything but stupid.) "Beyond that, your aunt's probably afraid for the simple reason that the shop she runs is under government supervision. And you Austrians all have a screw loose when it comes to the police or other authority figures. It's in your blood, a holdover from the long-ago days of Metternich." Here we have one of the very rare cases of Eulenfeld's making any disparaging remark about the country in which he was living. But then he'd become angry enough to "see red." Anger turns up what's at the bottom and brings it to the surface, as when we lift up a flat rock and watch the thousand-leggers and other fuzzy little bugs go scurrying. As sure as it is that the adage *in vino veritas* is untrue—in wine is just hot air and bibulous babbling—that's how certain it is that *veritas*, the truth unvarnished, will be dredged up and dragged out into the daylight by anger.

"But listen to me, Otto. If I had told her nothing about you and not given her your name and address"—Thea moved closer and was trying to answer him now in a cello-like voice broken by sorrow—"she would have asked me to come see her anyway, that is if she'd decided to do what you wanted, and then she would have given me the third degree about who was putting me up to this, what they thought they were doing, and all that. Can't you see? I had to tell her something."

"Yes, I can see. But then why not just something, as you say—any-thing? You could have thought it all out ahead of time. And whatever you told her would have provided the clearest proof that she's letting her imagination run away with her; why, we'd even know at what point her crazy ideas began taking on definite shape, so to speak. Anyway, it's all just preposterous."

"Of course it's all just preposterous," replied Thea, infiltrated by Otto's linguistic substance.

"But you, dear child," he said, "are well and truly cut out for simpering birdbrained ideas of every sort and kind. It's totally within the realm of possibility that had you in fact not imparted to your aunt on a first visit the personal data of your humble servant—'to the addressee,' if you please!—you would have very much have compensated for the omission the second time, under questioning, and without saying a word to me in advance. Totally within the realm of possibility, I repeat; indeed, I'd even go so far as to say that one will always be safe in assuming the rottenest of all possible outcomes to be the one that will actually occur. Your little story told to justify my need for that drastic increase in the supply of cigarettes—owing to a change of jobs and my making advance provision in case I'm not earning a salary for some time, and so on and so forth—all that can only be labeled a tale told by a blithering idiot." He emitted a deep grunting sound that underscored and reinforced his words; it was a noise peculiar to Eulenfeld, somewhere in the middle between the belling of a stag and the squealing of a piglet.

But then Thea suddenly scraped and bumped against the very bottom of her patience. "If only I knew," she said, "what you want those dumb, stupid, god-blasted cigarettes for anyway!" (Her few acts of rebellion were always accompanied by a linguistic emancipation of self). The captain, however, reached into his left vest pocket for his monocle and fixed it in his eye with an inimitably suave gesture, whereupon he turned his (literally and figuratively) glassy stare to her and replied serenely, "That's got licorice-flavored shit to do with you, in my humble estimation." With that, he walked into his study and closed the door behind him (and Thea went slinking through it ten minutes later, all repentant of mood, to beg his forgiveness for her impertinent and inappropriate question; said forgiveness he granted at once and with good cheer, and he even sealed his word, if not right there in the study).

These exchanges and episodes between the captain and Thea Rokitzer were of course not recounted by the latter to Paula in quite as exhaustive detail as they have just been by us. It didn't matter, though,

for what Paula did hear was enough to make her "prick up her ears"—
an expression applied to humans from the behavior of horses (primal
reaction of a wild horse on hearing even the farthest, most distant howl
of a wolf in the steppe)—even though human beings cannot possibly
perform any such exterior action, in that they have lost the capacity to
consciously control the fan-shaped musculature around the ear; instead,
they now do the same thing, to a certain extent, on the inner wall of
the cranium, and the exterior organ still twitches, if very slightly, in
memory of the long-vanished motility of the ear muscles. So it was in
this sense that Paula pricked up her ears—small and beautifully shaped—
under her reddish brown hair. Somewhere in the blurred and jumbled
accounts Thea gave of her mishaps, Paula had caught the sound of that
distant howl, or at least she thought she had now and again caught it
for a fleeting moment. Presently, however, her previous basic understanding of the matter, extremely well-grounded and very well hidden
from Thea as it was, began to have superimposed on it a more distinct
feeling, and she started to form the opinion that the captain wasn't so
much interested in using Thea for nefarious purposes of some kind as
he was in getting rid of her, of aborting her, so to speak, by means of
increasingly strong dosages of meanness and bullying; and perhaps the
nefarious purposes were concocted and set in motion for that sole
reason alone! Alois, Paula's husband, by revealing masculine secrets
(for men—make no mistake about it—when they are operating in this
realm, namely in the weed-choked field of love, men, considered simply
as men, constitute a criminal organization precisely like the one made
up of all women), had made a substantial contribution to this way of
interpreting the matter. What he'd said was that Thea was of the variety of fruit which—provided its type attracts a man to begin with—
seems to be just made to bite into as long as all one is does is look at it,
but if it is bitten, one can only despair of having done it, because it
tastes like food in a dream—like air, that is. So it might well be that
the dragoon captain had bitten into thin air. That can be as unpleasant
a surprise as biting into a stone. Then again, Alois Pichler had another
theoretical addendum or contingency clause to the effect that for each
and every man and woman there was just one right man or woman.
They weren't necessarily fated to meet and get together in every case

(though naturally his opinion concerning his own marriage was that he'd had the good fortune to have exactly that happen). But it followed that for a girl like Thea there had to be a man out there to whom she wouldn't taste the least bit like air. As far as the words of Alois.

In Saint Valentin, near Upper Austria, there lived in those days a relative of Civil Service Councillor Zihal; she was related to him not just in the formal, familial, genealogical sense, but also in a way that fulfilled on a much deeper level the shades of definition and the strictures of stipulation governing the term "related." A chemist would have called a saline compound of this kind a Zihaloid, and a zoologist might perhaps have given the name *Zihalidae* to such a kindred grouping of animals. Still, she'd never been a civil servant. This is the right context, then, in which to point out that here in our country, the circle of salient affinities along these lines has a greater radius than that within the immediate area illuminated by the light of employment in the government bureaucracy. And even if we were entirely to overlook a little fact that lies on a different plane anyway—it is that no one born of mortal can achieve transcendence solely by being entrenched in a bureaucratic structure but instead must, with no exception ever granted, be subject to the judgments of performance assessment (and most particularly if any question should ever arise of incompleteness or insufficient accuracy in the preparation of one's reports and other paperwork)—overlooking that fact, we say, the actual bureaucratic bailiwick as such, when under illumination, is surrounded by a kind of aureole, a solar corona, a halo, in which, albeit under somewhat dimmer light, the separate individuals who make up the balance of the population, the nonbureaucratic segment, appear as dancing motes of dust. In its turn, this halo has an inner band (usually situated around the center), a middle band, and an outer band. It is in the innermost band that the Zihaloids are most frequently encountered. Next there are, of course, building superintendents and concierges as quasi police officers more or less thrust into private life, and after them—along with letter carriers, railway conductors, cashiers for the gasworks—many specimens which, by contrast with the functionaries just mentioned, are identifiable upon the very closest of scrutiny as private persons entirely outside of any civil service capacity; nonetheless, like a resonance, an epiphenomenon of the life at the center—which is the one true life—they give the distinct appearance physiognomically of being formed from and shaped by it even so, and hence of living with their internal organs of sight facing completely toward that central sun. This is the one hypothesis capable of accounting for the strikingly frequent extrabureaucratic occurrence of Zihaloidic phenomena. A prime example was the civil service councillor's cousin in Saint Valentin. She was a widow over fifty who owned a house with some ground and a garden. Her deceased husband had for many years been a gasworks cashier in the seventeenth district in Vienna.

Now Frau Rosa Zihal was thinking that Thea's appearance had for some time been worse than bad—it was downright awful. What's more, the gooseberries had long since ripened in Saint Valentin, and there were also quite a number of important jobs to be done in the house and the garden, especially the kinds of chores that required a good deal of bending (weeding, scrubbing floors), which wouldn't have been easy for the Zihaloid resident there or for the Zihaloform Frau Rosa, either, owing to the architecture of their exterior persons; Frau Rosa was nevertheless giving some thought to spending a few weeks in Saint Valentin with her husband again this year, though not without a strong protective shield against the plethora of domestic activity she feared might be expected of her. The cousin of the civil service councillor had been writing letters all winter pretty much directly soliciting the help of Frau Rosa's niece and coaxing them to let her come out there and stay for a minimum of two weeks sometime during the summer, the more so as the girl was living in Vienna but "didn't have a job to go to," (although yours truly would be happy under any circumstances to welcome Thea, whom she hadn't seen for such a long time and who had grown so attractive, she heard).

Paula Pichler strongly urged her friend to go.

That alone was the one thing needed for Thea to make up her mind. However, in her imagination she saw shining before her, as of the end of August—as of the morning of Saturday, the twenty-ninth, to be exact—a bright star. It was finally going to be her turn to be introduced to some people from a movie agency, an event Thea had built up to be in essence nothing short of an actual screen test. She very emphatically

requested permission of her parents, of her aunt, and, through correspondence, even of the Zihaloid resident in Saint Valentin to return
to Vienna on the express train the evening before, and she was constantly
seeking reassurance. Perhaps they would offer her a part; at least that
was the backdrop of serious purpose that seemed necessary to her—and
she was probably quite right—for proper performance and due security
throughout the time up until then. The change in her whole way of
living couldn't possibly have escaped her parents or her other relatives—coming home late at night so often and with such wildly irregular explanations; dropping out of so many activities she used to
enjoy taking part in; looking so much less alert; showing such sadness
when people would happen to bump into her. Yet the really significant
effect, even though it never reached consciousness or expression in
words within the family environment, was manifested by the changes
in Thea's facial expression and in her language. So it was that her
forthcoming trip to Saint Valentin met with universal and understandable approval, as likewise did, when all was said and done, those fixed
plans she had made for returning. It was Paula who added in advance
a nice enhancement to those plans by promising to meet her young
friend right at the train platform on the evening of August twenty-
eighth at the West Station; and what's more, she would bring along
Aunt Lina, who for a long time now had been yet another object of
high admiration for Thea Rokitzer. And so off she went to Saint Valentin, our Thea—to the extent that one can call it going off somewhere,
in this case—on the very first day of the month and by this means
vanished for a time from the arena of events (provided one is willing
to grant that such is what these tempests in a teapot in fact deserve to
be called) and of course, accordingly, from the *societas daemonum
aliorumque damnatorum* as well.

So we're rid of her for the time being. Grete Siebenschein too, while
we're at it. She was off somewhere abroad again. Of course with Cornel
Lasch and his lady wife, Titi, née Siebenschein. It's not hard to detect
an unhealthy state of affairs in the way—which even by then had become a habit—the man would stick close to home while the woman

kept flying the coop. And in some way or other, after all, Grete and René had to make a deal to get along with one another like man and wife; they did it like wife and man, not like man and wife. She dealt with his frustrated lack of independence by going away. She, and not he, was the one who would pound through the thick wall of her familiar surroundings to fashion a window, but then the very act of her doing so would turn it into a narrow slit, not a decent-sized opening, through which came pouring and peering whatever she would have wanted to see in the first place (and often it was the diametrical opposite of whatever he would have wanted to see). Then he had to deal with her way of dealing. As he did with all the books and magazines she brought back from Paris at his request, thus establishing a cross section which was scratched into the surging wall of time with a nail scissor, as it were, the result being that a Marcel Achard or an Henry de Montherlant ended up emerging as a writer of significance, if only because Grete might have felt particularly at ease during one of Achard's farcical parodies on the Rue des Mathurins, behind the Madeleine, or somewhere else, and because the beautiful name Montherlant seemed as if it stood for something like the utter absence of anything and everything that had her trammeled and tangled here in Vienna. No, René was very far from being able to do any of this, never mind how overpowering his effect otherwise on whatever he had to work with! "*Voulez-vous jouer avec moi?*"

This time the whim of the millionaire *dans la lune* had been to rush from the August heat of Vienna directly to that of Paris—though admittedly there also beckoned in the background some of the cooler seaside resorts, Dinard or Deauville. What's more, hindsight makes it very easy to understand Grete's eagerness to accept the invitation for this trip. Ever since that energetic attack she'd mounted in the spring as a measure taken to separate herself or, more accurately, to free herself from René (the first glimmer of which probably flashed into her mind in Naples, on the terrace of the Teresa, while she sat taking in the sight of saddled Mount Vesuvius, the sailboats, the Castel dell'Ovo, when a man she knew from Vienna wrapped her cape around her shoulders, as reported by Melzer); ever since that energetic attack in the spring and its far-reaching consequences, including some truly unbelievable

letters full of ranting and—as far as that goes—partly incoherent vi-
tuperation directed at René and all his kith and kin; ever since that
time, when she'd made an attempt to drag herself across a threshold
of life, one she considered to be of the utmost importance, through
methods that had no correspondence whatever to her actual disposition; ever since then, having retreated back beyond that threshold when
assailed by René, she had been glutted, made apathetic, demoralized
in the very deepest part of her being. Glutted from her own victory,
too—how pitifully abject in subsequent capitulation his assault had
been, after all, with supplications, beseechings, efforts at reconciliation
via the Grauermanns, telegrams, telephone calls, letters, gifts! René had
to put up with the most extreme behavior from her; and, as far as she
was concerned, he fully deserved to have the heels of her shoes grinding into his neck. Nonetheless, she'd "come tumbling down" (which
was how she expressed it to Etelka); she'd ended up by giving in.

Don't ask, "But did she ever love him in the first place? Did she still
love him then?" Don't say, "But she couldn't have loved him!" However
a person is—tall, straight, short, clean-cut, hunched over, a pain—is
how that person's love is. It's that person's love and no one else's. Nothing about a person could ever be more distinctive. And there can be
no such thing as reaching common agreement in this area. Everybody
suddenly dashes off into his or her own corner, and in the middle there
comes tumbling down—crash!—whatever effort of the normalizing
sort they'd just been trying—all together now!—to erect like a formal
reviewing stand; there it lies, all ruins and rubble and lumber, the
catafalque of the course from which all we've ever done is go astray.
Love is the swerving declination from the other pole. As it was, though,
Grete Siebenschein's magnetic pole, which drew the needle in the
heart's compass to point in the wrong direction, had the peculiar attribute of being similar—and similar enough to induce despair—to
various mechanical devices calibrated to exactly the same degrees of
declination inside the emotional makeup of Herr René von Stangeler.
It isn't the convenience of undue oversimplification that's tempting us
now to say what we have to say as briefly as possible; no, it's the much
greater danger of venturing too deep into the thick undergrowth of
particulars and then of not being able to see the forest for the trees. To

sum up, then: had René simply accepted his passion for Grete (like the "finger pointing the way" or the "path shown by the signpost," as Herr E.P. had expressed it in such an illuminating way for Melzer), rather than constantly tear himself loose from it and push her away for the sake of some delusional image called freedom; had he, on the contrary, gone about his work unconcerned, exploring the limits of his intellectual capacity rather than interrupt his studies by accepting this or that position or taking state certifying examinations and speeding up his PhD, which is what he had done earlier, in the spring of that year (and lucky for him that it had been before the "disaster" with Grete), these being the lines along which he kept on seeking, over and over, some acceptable and honorable involvement with "practical life"; had he let all this go, she would have stayed by his side much longer, and without rebellion—in fact, she would have been there with banners flying, in spite of and along with the families on both sides, and without their having to be married, either, since her feminine intuition would have told her in any case that this boy was going to meet with success and would then be ready for her to bring him around to what she wanted. But the half-heartedness of his mental and civic endeavors kept her trapped in her own, so that the two of them wound up blocking each other's way, standing athwart one another like crisscrossed, looming barriers. And even if this Fräulein Siebenschein isn't entirely to our taste—any more than is Herr Nose-in-the-Air René—does that entitle us to overlook her lovable and winning traits? What about her almost childlike demands, including on herself—demands for truthfulness, sober judgment, diligence and industry—and all flooded once again with feelings hurt (how many countless times) until they're bleeding? After they got back together during the summer, Stangeler was of course biting into nothing more than transparent crystals like these (a terrible diet for a man in love); not long after that time he was caught in an eddying whirlpool of that second kind which burst in on him again, and he got his head back above water after a fight, only to muddy it quite soon after and in a way deserving of reproof. It's our firm belief that what passed between René and Grete—as reported by sensible people (and here we're by no means confined to just Major Melzer or the Grauermanns)—is what dissolves a love relationship;

what then starts to resolve, after the sentimental overture has been played through, is what makes the real relationship emerge into view. In economically better ordered times or situations, two people will go through this second chapter once they've settled down nicely inside the marriage. But that's what was lacking here, with the result that everything was much more likely to be questioned or second-guessed whenever the least occasion arose. They were lacking any and all outside support. The whole mess ended up putting a roadblock in his way and her way alike and set them whirling and swirling around one another like little slivers of wood in the inlet of a stream; this was a state of affairs Grete's feminine intuition recognized sooner and more clearly than did René's head, to the extent that in his case we can speak of such a thing in the first place as of a body part normally located on top. By now, at last, at the imperative behest of the organ twice referred to, the severing of the thread between René and herself had begun, though of course in an entirely different place.

After all this unraveling and refastening, Grete was now strolling along the beach promenade at Deauville with a (less attractive) friend from her school days, one who had moved away to Paris long before and had made arrangements to meet Grete there. Our Grete was sauntering along with a swaying motion, the weapons and insignia of her femininity all worn so as to be clearly visible under her thin summer dress, and her high heels were clicking on the springy boards laid along this walkway, which was slightly elevated above the sand. Even so, that desirable state known as clarity was far from reigning inside her. Everything had clouded and clotted edges with no strength; nevertheless, they lay under a vigilant and even severe oversight—except that at the most crucial time of all, in the face of the heartrending and nerve-shattering assault launched by René, who'd acted as if his life were literally hanging in the balance, that oversight had itself become clouded. She had had the sense to run away, though, and now here she was. She longed for René, but at the same time she swept aside this longing, hardly able to believe she was feeling it. Her friend Eva, who had met him, naturally asked questions, but Grete's comments on the subject—the two had come to a stop, facing the sea; the wind swooped down and was whipping the skirts of their dresses between their knees, while off to the left, not far from a lone gentleman reading the news-paper, one of those canopied and basket-shaped wicker beach chairs that lose their balance so easily fell over—the comments she found it proper to make to Eva struck even herself like foreign words in her own mouth, as if she were speaking about some subject alien to herself; in her words there was nothing about this very summer. Defense and prosecution alike were halting and hampered. She looked out across the water, which now showed some stronger whitecaps here and there, and felt she wasn't completely present here, either, and for that reason far from ready to plunge into all this resort activity as into a relaxing, flowing bath. Her ability to focus on her stay in Paris had been limited this time, her critical faculty anything but flooded with new impres-sions. When, every morning at eleven, a gymnastics instructor held classes for ladies, gentlemen, and children, classes that consisted far more of teaching the participants to strike poses than of running through exercise routines designed to limber up their muscles, Grete found the cry *"Lancez la balle!"*—after which drawn-out command everybody, all of them with their weight on one leg and trailing the other behind them, would be standing posed as if a balloon were just then drifting out of reach—every bit as absurd as Cornel Lasch's pre-dilection for speaking English, especially if the sentence structure didn't involve all that much risk; should he accidentally bump against another couple out on the floor at the five-o'clock *thé dansant*, he would never fail to utter a murmured "Oh, so sorry!" while at the same time giving a decorous nod of his massive head.

Naturally she didn't believe in any such thing as a new era in her love relationship, the very belief on which Stangeler was basing his whole life—his right, as it were, to get back together with her—though after a round at the conference table things read quite differently. After all, Grete was above such childish notions. She simply went back to bearing up under it all. The era that had in fact commenced, how-ever—not the reform Stangeler had thought through and even gone so far as to commit to writing ("the official file" was what Grete rather Zihalistically dubbed his half-pound letter, which she never read, in-cidentally)—was quite closely connected with Grete Siebenschein's having entered upon the thirty-first year of her life just that past July.

They walked into the lobby of the hotel, where Titi and her husband were just now making an appearance, not having left their room until ten thirty in the morning, Titi, as usual, apparently in the best of moods, her lips slightly parted at the corners of her wide mouth as if all set for an ironic exchange, more of a sensory organ than a speech organ, as if she were using it now to taste a sample of everything humorous that might just be floating in the air. Lasch, by contrast, conducted himself with gravity and decorum when traveling abroad, even down to the kind of suit he wore—solid, if a little behind the fashion, a crotchety, wealthy foreigner with his young, lovely, elegant wife. It's conceivable that he adopted this style after reading about it somewhere, and we really must admit, if such is indeed the case, that he put the fruits of his reading into practice with intelligence and a genuine feeling for detail.

Of the first of these attributes, above all, he was anything but deprived. This remarkable man—to dismiss him as merely a "racketeer" or a "wheeler-dealer" was the sloppiest but most convenient approach for many people who, had they been in possession of his talents, would most surely not have refrained, on grounds of moral scruple or intellectual conviction, from putting them to use—this big, healthy-looking regular guy and shipmate signed on for a cruise to anywhere (he looked like that, in spite of his irrational and irregular way of living) must have been in his midthirties at the time. Peace to his ashes. Even his last horrible night in a hotel room in Pera lies back in the distant past by now; healthy in body, he succumbed to deprivation while withdrawing from morphine, which a Polish actress had gotten him addicted to . . . for now, though, we still have him before us in the flower of his days. It's quite possible that his exceptional vitality was the result of his having come to realize early in life where he should concentrate his main emphasis for optimal effect, of his having determined in what direction he could exercise his greatest strengths while encountering the least resistance; and from then on—with a kind of shameless but clear-sighted indiscretion in regard to his own self—having kept his qualities in his grasp for dear life, like a carpenter holding on to his tools and making sure that not a one of them gets filched, but keeping a constant watch over them all, especially when he's working outside and has to carry his toolbox with him. His doing so is a matter of simple practicality, not of his being distrustful, insecure, or self-inflated, which latter thing Cornel was, but on an entirely tangential plane that lay outside his fundamental nature. This nature, in turn, can only be called a very distinctive one, and, for that matter, somehow a brightly illuminated one, in comparison with all the conventional and contemptuous dismissals he had personally been subjected to by the type of human being alluded to a moment ago. As for us—unlike those others —we'd prefer to see him without having the light of our own critical remarks focus back on ourselves in a soft reflected glow. Oh, so sorry.

Scheichsbeutel appeared. In accordance with the concept we have just finished formulating and applying, we have to describe him as a Zihaloid, at the least, if not outright a Zihaloform phenomenon. And the fact is that he was indeed said to have once been some kind of petty bureaucrat somewhere (it couldn't be ascertained with any certainty, and a long drawn-out investigation just didn't seem worth the effort in this case). But a Zihaloid without a core, a seedless fruit of baroque culture with no inner principle of decoration, one that—even in a completely casual gesture, in an incidental exchange of conversation now and then, in the manner of lighting a Trabuco cigar—would imply the unifying atomic core of one of those sprawling, episodic dramas of Jacobean violence and intrigue, erotic and political, that ultimately reveal a remarkable inner consistency. That was what was missing here. The center was empty. What resonated now, but without any strings vibrating—resonated because he was standing, through no merit whatever of his own, on the immense resonance chamber and violin belly of a culture two thousand years deep—was the accumulation of all the individual Zihaloform qualities (*virtutes et facultates*): a minute observance of punctuality; an ability to appear at exactly the right moment, even when unsummoned and unbidden, but when in fact bidden, to step forward at the precise minute, like those moving figures in the clocks of old town halls; a capacity for disappearing in the twinkling of an eye and leaving not a trace behind when one's presence is undesired (a distant echo of olfactory powers that can sniff out from a crack under the door what is wanted in a room in which one's superiors are sitting, so as to allow the possessor of that power to turn on his heels in front of a tall, closed double door and vanish, noiselessly and smoothly, into his own quarters); a virtually absolute order and reliability, extending to the uttermost boundaries of what is humanly possible, no matter what the agenda; an eye of glass and an ear of iron—any power behind which is impossible to detect—turned toward all petitioners and supplicants; an affable demeanor toward everyone else; an inscrutably Oriental smile and a perpetually lubricant-smooth secretion—all these qualities existed, and they were all, in their complete range, consciously held in possession, nurtured, and cultivated, except that all of them, taken together, had picked up a negative sign in front of them somewhere along the way. For Scheichsbeutel, so different from his employer, Lasch, who held a variety of interests—at one time, for example, having acquired a valuable scholarly collection of books on alchemy, and at another having procured for a small fortune a microscope incorporating the very latest features and used it to pursue (and with great single-mindedness) a serious research project lasting several months—Scheichsbeutel was a mere common crook operating just within the law; he faced anything and everything between the earth and the sky, unless it fell within his area of specialization, with callous indifference and dead coldness, strictly a recording instrument of the most objective kind, one who never saw a connection between anything and himself and for whom it would have been totally outside the realm of possibility to ever ask himself what it was that his boss thought he was doing when he spent hours and hours at a time in the Louvre or to consider whether he himself could possibly enter the place if he ever felt like it. No, Scheichsbeutel wasn't the inquisitive sort. At one time, and no doubt quite early in life, he must have reached the point of denying, on a fundamental level, that there could ever be anything, anywhere at all, that was new.

His recording capability, however, was utterly exemplary, and—overlooking for our purposes here certain doubts on the part of some philosophers about the existence of an objective external world in the first place—we must say that external realities entered into this man completely unimpeded, as into a mirror. He simply took to cognizance whatever it was and never made a judgment; he refrained from doing so to a degree that bordered on the inhuman, in fact, and the reptilian coldness of his gaze, looking out of the parched and empty window of a soul that was exactly the same way, seemed as if it had never been animated by sympathies or antipathies of any kind. One can picture Scheichsbeutel as a corpse whose limbs and organs and faculties— rhythmic heartbeat, logical ability, retina, tympanic membrane—would all continue functioning (unimpeachably; oh how perfectly unimpeachably!) after the soul has flitted away. One might conclude, on making such a picture, that the whole splendid range of optical, acoustical, intellectual powers we are endowed with is never actually disturbed except by life itself, which, when considered from that standpoint—the Zihalistic viewpoint in its highest and strictest sense, perhaps—must of course appear to be an anomaly, if not a manifestation of sheer nonsense. (For basically these are nothing but spiteful remarks!) Scheichsbeutel took part in such nonsense to only the minimum extent. Nonetheless—and this is something we won't have any trouble understanding when we give it a passing glance, after all that's been said—he was tolerant of nonsense of all kinds; not just people who haunted the Louvre, but also people who kept busy pursuing totally unlucrative activities and went through pointless contortions, which would have been out of the question for him. He was even accommodating in these matters and went so far as to support indulgence in nonsense—if it didn't cost him anything—not for the sake of the nonsense, but out of callous indifference and because he was immeasurably far from jeopardizing good relations through good advice. He had never, at any time, ever said anything whatsoever to anyone soever. Everything stayed inside him (*apud notas*), with no centrifugal tendency, and in that respect he was like certain defunct celestial bodies which no longer rotate on their axes but would be able to retain their form in their present state anyway, even without gravity—which does not have to counteract centrifugal force—because the body is hanging in a vacuum, like a motionless outer-space cream puff. If any one of the people he knew and had lined up on the board and never placed so far to the side that he wouldn't have been able to retrieve them comfortably had all of a sudden taken the stubborn notion to make a large purchase of some kind, one that would apparently be pointless and surely unlucrative— let's say one hundred thousand Austrian cigarettes, the government's own brand—and fifty thousand Virginia cigars—Scheichsbeutel would have extended a helping hand; indeed he might well, under certain circumstances, have seen to all the arrangements (for a guaranteed sum) himself, have drawn on those helpful connections of his, have set in motion his various agents and underlings—of whom he always had enough in his pocket—and have had the consignment together and ready within a brief time (never mind the shortages that back in those days, seven years after the war, could now and then still arise and persist for an interval), with no risk, attracting no attention, legally, for the specified amount, and all the while considering the whole affair to be unmitigated lunacy, unless one had somehow been able to ascertain with certainty that an announcement of new price increases for tobacco products was forthcoming. Then again, though, Scheichsbeutel wouldn't have regarded such a dealing as a genuine business transaction, if only because it would mean trespassing on the government's domain, which proved to be simply unnecessary in so many other—and better—arrangements. Yet, as we said, he would have seen to everything and not—this is the essential point, it seems to us—ever even shrugged his shoulders, the way Paula Pichler pricked up her ears, a purely internal reaction.

Grete Siebenschein detested this Beutel, and far more than she was willing to admit to herself, all eager for clarity, sober judgment, rectitude, and reasonable motives and explanations as she was. After all, she knew nothing at all about Scheichsbeutel and had never had anything to do with him. What she found repellent about him, what tasted like vinegar in her mouth when she had to look at him—right now, for example, as he stood in the background speaking softly, in fluent French, with the doorman, since Lasch didn't have anything for him to do—lay on an entirely different plane from all the Scheichsbeutelian maneuvers, always sure to be tacking under the proper wind, which she had no knowledge of anyway. It was the man's clerical appearance. He could have passed for a sexton or a verger. It's not at all rare to encounter this variety among Zihaloid phenomena, by the way, this variety likewise traceable to that violin belly of two thousand years' depth we mentioned earlier; there are people standing on it who, with their iron ears and their callous indifference, never did learn how to play the violin and who, out of everything there is in music, have held on only to the question-mark-shaped and questionable physiognomy of the violin clef; but whereas it may be a clef, for them it can't be a key, and so they're locked out of major, minor, and modal alike. It's exactly this kind of thing that can sustain itself quite comfortably and contentedly on the very verge of the metaphysical (which is what a verger also does with the modest service he renders). Everything else just falls into place. The man makes the clothes. Scheichsbeutel liked to wear dark, wide ties with collars that recalled the 1880s; the look might have been a little out of place in Deauville, perhaps, but not anywhere else in France.

They stood together, there in the hallway, for a minute or two, and discussed what they would most enjoy doing next—they could go swimming right away, although it was windy, or, as Lasch suggested, thinking of creature comforts, it might be nicer to go and have a second breakfast; he liked doing as the Americans did here, which meant a half bottle, *goût américain*, naturally (how much better the invigorating, bracing power of champagne when its effect is called upon in the rested, relaxed mood of an intimate breakfast than it is for effects of detonation, of cork-popping explosion among the roistering din of banquets and routs! We're unreservedly on the side of Lasch in this case. We don't always have to be seeing absolutely eye to eye with Grete). He, however—we mean Cornel—may not have been in possession of quite so extensive a legacy as Scheichsbeutel and thus was unable to subject the violin belly to quite the same extent of misuse; on the other hand, that was the very token that made him enormously better suited to learning things. Not just strictly a recording instrument. No, this lively individual effervesced, foamed up, and washed out the uncertain boundary (as uncertain as the boundary between sand and water here) marking where the external world begins, and in this foam a covalent reaction took place, a chemical marriage. A man without imagination doesn't make millions *dans la lune*. That was also something of which Scheichsbeutel was perfectly aware, and he looked out, himself unmoved, into all this movement from the vantage point of a combination jetty and breakwater—they kept out the surging waves altogether—made up of his bank (or perhaps it was a postal savings) account, held ever and anon in clear view. When he ventured out on the water, and then only when the weather was calm, visibility clear, and all due and proper Zihalisitic safety precautions taken (and when it came to the winds, they were something else our Cornel had a very thorough knowledge of). To be brief, Scheichsbeutel was a coasting vessel and not an explorer—in neither large undertakings nor even the smallest ones. Not one to unlock new delights. Lasch, however, had been empathically observing an older American gentleman who, after his solitary breakfast at a table with a full view of the sea, would end with "half a bottle." So why couldn't Cornel do the same? It always impressed him to see anyone, anywhere, enter any kind of Louvre.

As if it had emerged out of the brown paneling in the hallway, a picture, complete to its last detail, now appeared and hovered before Grete Siebenschein just as she was turning her eyes away from the doorman's post and from Scheichsbeutel, so as not to have to look at him anymore; it was a picture of René on the platform of the West Station at the very moment when the express train for Paris had imperceptibly started moving and, very slowly at first, even more slowly than the people walking along, began the journey along its route, measured against whose expanse not only this train station, tracks branching in every which direction, but also the whole section of the city here, or, for that matter, of any large city anywhere, with all its neighborhoods and districts combined, can only dwindle to a dot, a point with no measurable dimensions (so greatly—think about it for just a bit—does the countryside spatially outbalance the city, the quantitative mass outweigh the head, which is what it is in the age we live in now and which is what it will continue to be as long as this age endures). Lasch had been standing beside her at the lowered window in the corridor, and Scheichsbeutel, at the next window, was looking out with an unchanging facial expression. Cornel could have joined Titi in the compartment; he must have known that Grete was standing here at the window because of René. But he stayed where he was.

René was waving his hat, a light gray summer hat with a narrow black band. For several seconds his eyes fairly pierced into hers as they leapt in her direction, once more vanquishing and annihilating the distance between them, which had expanded over quite a few meters by this time. And in those moments, glimpsing out of the corner of her eyes, she noticed that Cornel was smiling a tiny little bit; he was looking down at René from his elevated position, gliding away, slipping off, leaving the world behind. His smile wasn't scornful, but it wasn't gentle, either, nor was it a superior smirk; instead, he was merely smiling the way a graven idol smiles. Grete had the strength, however, to force her gaze into a vigorous countermove—now her eyes darted back, once again reinforcing and rebuilding with all her strength the bridge just then being constructed by René but already collapsing because of the distance growing between them; and since René was now running more quickly along the platform to keep up with the moving train, the span became firm and complete again; one more kiss flew, one more word fluttered; and right before a gentle switching over of the train hid Stangeler from her sight, she took note with the most extreme clarity, and as if once more recognizing them anew, of his ways of moving and the unique aspects of his physical bearing, and then . . . she felt respect, from the bottom of her heart, for every one of these individual peculiarities. This was how Grete herself later described her feelings at that time, at least, and she was right, it seems to us.

So it was that even today this graven-idol smile of Cornel's stood between her and him at times.

As if he were smiling into her exposed entrails, into her pulsating flesh.

And why was he, René, down there anyway? Why hadn't they taken him along? Or, much more to the point, why wasn't he in a position simply to decide to travel with them? No matter what she saw in Paris, she thought of him. Why was he so weak? Why was she so weak herself? So weak that she'd been—taken along? But one of the two of them had to be strong; otherwise they'd be sure to go under, both of them, and then nothing else would ever be able to happen! A fierce pain moved and stirred somewhere in her depths; she allayed it, full of fear, not letting it rise up and emerge. She wanted to turn back. Back to René. But it was as if the train were giving the orders, plain and simple.

Even now, as late as nine thirty, the summer morning seemed hesitant. The mountains were standing as though newly created in delicate wisps of haze, which was also drifting under the dome of a sky otherwise cloudless and dimming the blaze of brilliant sunlight, whose full power could be expected to burst out any time now that the day was so far along. At the zenith, a great arch of the firmament was already at its brightest blue of day, clear as lacquer and shining free. Everywhere else, though, a mellowing held sway, the kind one feels in the afternoon when the aroma of coffee with milk is wafting through house and garden, a milk-drenched mellowing made by the white veils of mist floating still on the air and keeping the high mountains from unfurling their sweeping range with a flourish, as if with a roll of thunder from within. The square in front of the high-lying little church was bounded by a railing, a barrier against a steep drop-off that had steps set into it and led down to the valley and to the road. The church square was nearly empty now; only at its edge, where people could lean against the railing, were a few men lolling around in clusters, people whom custom and habit had brought this far from their mountain farmsteads on Sunday morning but who then wavered at the church door and simply could not haul themselves across the threshold. So they would wait outside here until Mass was over and then join their cronies from the village in a companionable walk to the tavern. They whiled away the time in between by puffing on their long pipes.

Soon after the end of Mass, followed today by Benediction of the Blessed Sacrament, the soft, sunlit emptiness of the graveled square was breached, and the church door, which up to now had kept the sacred ritual closed off, was set moving by a few homemakers, black cloths over their heads, eager to hurry back up the mountain to their cooking pots. Others began straggling out as well. So it was that those waiting out on the square were able to share some part in an event now unfolding inside. Except for the four persons involved and the local music teacher, who was sitting at the organ, no one had had the faintest inkling in advance, and those involved had kept the pastor just as totally without a clue as they had kept the congregation.

Cornelia Wett and three of her fellow artists from the Vienna State Opera—ones who, like herself, had amassed laurels from all over the world and across the sea—now launched into the "Tantum ergo" after an organ prelude, while the members of the congregation couldn't help letting their own voices die in their mouths as their ears were filled with such richness and force of sonority. The people on the church square—the pipe smokers, the farm women just then scurrying away, others arriving really late—all went rushing toward the door, through which the venerable hymn surged out in a burst of sound into the muted sunlight from the humble little church, while inside the metallic timbre of the tenor and the immense power of the bass made the walls and columns quake as the soprano voice of Cornelia went soaring high aloft, almost flinging the separate compartments of the vaulted ceiling open to the freedom of the sky.

The impact was overwhelming. People in those Alpine regions set great store by the art of singing. What was more, they knew the soprano; she owned a country house there. So now, during the slow dispersal of the congregation out on the church square, our Brünnhilde—which is what she was not simply on stage, but also very manifestly in her private life—formed the center of gravity for the group drifting out of the place of worship.

This dispersing company, with people lagging behind, breaking up at a leisurely rate, shifting around in little clumps, slowly began to spill down the wide steps of the steep mountain drop-off, across from the church door, down to the tavern, though some also took a path on their left which cut crossways—more gently, too—along the slope to the road, while over at the right of the church door others were making room hastily and even to some degree with clumsy eagerness, for that was the quarter in which Cornelia Wett had heaved to, and her flotilla had veered around accordingly. The path narrowed here as it dropped, under tall fir trees, into a side valley, which the singer's small house lay on the opposite slope, hidden in the forest.

Etelka stayed standing where she was. She had to return to the country house because of her son. Everyone was loud and lively in lament because of the tennis game scheduled after breakfast on the court at the W.s' down below. Karl von W. was the one assigned to see Etelka, the wife of the consul, home; he was the elder son of the man who owned the handsome silver *tabatière* that Baron von Buschmann—killed in the war—had once so admired; thus he was the grandson of Minister von W. Etelka and Karl climbed uphill and disappeared now among the tree trunks; Cornelia dropped ever lower as the path did; likewise her party, in the midst of which was Grauermann, who would have been denied permission point-blank, as it were, by everyone present, to join his wife, because then the whole idea of playing tennis before lunch, with Etelka missing already, would have fallen through. It was easier to get along without Karl von W.; not a poor player, really, but a lazy one.

They almost all took leave of Cornelia down at the level bottom of the valley; she was feeling tired and wanted to get home. Grauermann was the one she let walk with her to her house. The other distinguished singers from the opera left the valley, heading for the W.s' place, where they were to have breakfast with everyone else. Altogether, there was a considerable number gathered, including some young people, among them Karl's younger brother. The singers, led by their host and hostess, walked at the head of the party. Herr von W. was glowing a bit; that was easy for him, since his keen intellect was of the kind that stayed polished and honed at all times and that therefore only needed to be drawn out of its scabbard and exposed to the common light of day a little for it to achieve every object it was aiming for—and right now, the remarkably attractive and celebrated mezzo-soprano from the Vienna State Opera seemed well worth the effort to him. He was one of those men—regrettably, they're an extremely rare type—whose exceptional ugliness can only be kept in evidence by the senses as an abstract concept; one has seen it with one's own eyes, after all, and hence knows all about it, but in reality it works like a magic spell and ends up seeming nothing more than a bizarre habit or whim of the person whose trait it is.

Grauermann was silent as he climbed the slope side by side with Cornelia.

Down deep, he felt as though he were walking next to a lioness, and a medium-heavy swipe of her paw, part annoyed, part well-meaning (of about the same strength Cornelia was used to landing on her housekeeper once in a while), wouldn't have been any great surprise to him. Whatever it was that she, for her part, saw in Consul Grauermann, we'll let remain an open question for now; it may just have been that time was passing for her if she was still going to find anything at all after her first marriage—to a Hungarian nobleman who, three years earlier, had died in her arms, really and truly in her arms, like a child; one of the sweetest and gentlest men who'd ever lived. It wouldn't be silly to ascribe a fairly high degree of attractive power to Grauermann's impeccable orderliness and correctness. He was looking out of those bluish-gray eyes he had inherited from his mother. They didn't so much lead inward, into his head, as they extended over his face like saucers or betting chips. They were large. They worked in tandem with his little straight snub nose to produce an effect that one could well imagine might be exciting for people with a special fondness for such things. The man was clean-cut, proficient in every way, and physically very intrepid. From a critic's view, Grauermann seems almost entirely unimpeachable when it comes to particulars. People of his kind have to be faulted in toto, along with the foundation they're standing on—only, who would ever take it upon himself to do such a thing? Besides, the critic would be running no slight risk of absurdity, for what if it turned out that this big, solid foundation is nothing more than a flimsy plank, the kind toy soldiers stand on?

They walked past the picket fence enclosing Cornelia's small plot of ground and went into the woods. Her house wasn't even visible until anyone approaching it drew very close; it was situated almost as if by a concealment ingeniously planned, hidden away in a narrow clearing planted with a trim country garden full of brilliant colors. Grauermann stepped onto the veranda with Cornelia.

"Sit down over there for a minute," she said. He asked if he could smoke and took out his cigarette case when she said yes. She looked at him in a well-meaning way, blinking lionlike from her powerful face, crowned and built over by a thick, billowing abundance of extremely blond hair and marked by eyes that sat on a light incline, their outer corners higher than their inner; just the opposite was the case with Grauermann, although by no more than a hint.

"And how long do you think this is all supposed to go on?" he asked in an even tone, leaning forward in his lounge chair and blowing smoke down toward the ground. She looked left and right, listened for any sound behind her in the house and then stroked him briefly on the head. "Think the whole thing over once more, Pista," she said. "There's nothing to think over," he replied. "Etelka has spared me the trouble, I'm sorry to say. That became very clear—and not just to me; to others as well—in Budapest, after our trips to Vienna during June and July. What a frenzied way to live. Etelka spent the winter—and the spring, too—under wraps, as it were, withdrawn; she suffered terribly from insomnia then, and she never wanted to leave the house, didn't want to go anywhere. It got to be too much even for me. If it hadn't been for Teddy von Honnegger and those musical soirees he sometimes used to hold in our home, we would have lived like hermits." Cornelia watched him pensively while he spoke. She always had a look as if she were thinking about something anyway; her finely sculpted face had no doubt been able to bridge many an intervening vacuum. "Honneg-ger—how is it he's in Pest?" she inserted. "He married a woman from there, plus he's a consular attaché at our legation—or actually that should be vice versa," said Grauermann; then he stopped and had nothing more to say. He kept his eyes fixed on the ground.

Sitting across from this powerful woman, who was also much ahead of him in age, he could well have given the impression that he was sit-ting between her mighty paws, a tourist at the Sphinx. He may have felt, too, as though she were turning him over and over, in a way. People will often speak because they're trying to stifle a thought; their speech doesn't grow more thoughtful as a result, of course, but it can grow more animated.

"I purposely went along and took an active part, instead of just letting Etelka have her way when the big change set in for her; I con-sidered it a welcome thing that her vitality had reawakened at last. We were somewhere different every night. And every night ended with champagne. It suited me that way, except that Etelka went totally out of control, with incredible speed, especially for several days in July that I had to spend in Vienna for professional reasons. That was when all kinds of people in Budapest dropped hints my way about rumors of tremendous turmoil. I can tell you it was really embarrassing, and I'm putting it mildly. Etelka had no consideration at all as far as I was concerned, none whatever. Our boy was already here in the country, so she was alone."

"Listen, Pista," she said, softly and very calmly, "a whole lot can happen, a mountain of things, and it's like nothing; then some little thing can happen, and it's a major event—if they can prove it. That's how it always is. The one thing that counts is what people can prove, not what really happened."

Cornelia was recalling his own nature, which she held in some esteem, to his memory, and she knew it, too. It was clear to Cornelia without a moment's thought that he would never reach the point of arguing for a genuine rebellion against the circumstances of his marriage unless he could see a clear way out of it through a new object of desire; she knew the arguments and counterarguments of all men to be nothing more than smoke that's disavowing its fire. But now something had to be done to provide for the proper venting of those clouds and puffs of smoke, and that didn't seem difficult to her when working with a sharply categorizing mind like Grauermann's, all alert for taxonomy and rubric. "You've got to get back down there now," she said, stroking his head once again. "But while we're talking—do you know anything about Fraunholzer?"

"Not just at the moment," he said, now completely cool, detached, expedient. He kissed her hand for a long moment and then started down. Cornelia stood and watched him from the veranda. Because he wouldn't have a chance to change into his white tennis trousers until he was at the W.s' and hence now still had knickers on, the one flaw that had ever been discerned in this man was visible. His calves were too short and his thighs correspondingly too long, as his legs as a whole were the right length in proportion to the torso they supported. Of course one will say, "That's only a minor flaw." Cornelia didn't see it as quite so minor, though. It wasn't that her classical and ancient-sounding name placed her under an obligation to apprehend more keenly what conditions prevailed in the realm of the somatic; it was more that being on the stage had trained her eye to notice fine points like that. How rarely men wear long pants in opera! And in Wagner, never! Just think of Thor, Wotan, Siegfried—that whole raft of heroes and gods. But to us, a slight disproportion between upper and lower leg will seem too small a defect to worry about in a man. What's he supposed to do about it? What could come of it? What could go wrong because of it? No, a man can walk a straight line on straight legs like those; it's just that when he goes to buy a pair of athletic socks, they may be a little bit too long. But that can always be fixed. An inconsequential defect.

Cornelia looked up. The rocky face of the mountain at the end of the valley gleamed through the tree trunks; single white patches of mist were still clinging around rocks and in crevices there. Grauermann had just clicked shut the lock in the gate of the picket fence. Those last vestiges of mist looked like the shrouds of ghosts who had not fled back into the realm of shadows in time to escape the dawning day and were now stuck hanging in suspended animation in the bright morning light. Was that autumn wanting to arrive, or was it Indian summer come early, as August was just beginning? After the gate closed, it was totally quiet for a good while, until far away, from down on the district road, the next automobile horn beeped.

It was in Pastor's Woods, high above the church, near some rocks thick with moss that lay all fallen and crumbled among the fir trees, that Etelka's and Karl's walk together ended—on the smooth, needle-covered ground far away from the path. She now heard the darting, perpetual hum of insects as she cradled his head on her left shoulder. Karl lay still. The vulnerable feel of this hour and the remoteness of this lonely, untrodden place in the forest were keenly, and even piercingly, sensed by Etelka, while a whole series of linked images kept on trudging along the edge of her inner horizon, as though she were hearing a ceaseless drumroll from off somewhere in the distance. But here was the pause, the middle now, and it held no meaning; here was a good place to rest, and the unbounded wonderment and loving rapture of a twenty-five-year-old led—with calming results in regard to everything else, all of it unimportant—into this welcoming space and the sun that had dominion in it.

While she stroked his hair and looked into the sun-flecked underbrush, however, she was thinking about the mail from Pest. Had any come today? They had to go pick it up on Sundays. The groundskeeper or one of his children would see to that errand and would then at once hand straight over to Asta any letters for Etelka. Moreover, Grauermann was highly discreet; he made it a point. He would purposely not see letters addressed to his wife and had never turned one over to read the back. Customs of high courtesy, in the style of those bygone days of Omar Khayyám and of the earlier *façon voilée*, which latter mood had once more held Etelka in its grip through the winter just past, only to yield later on to a frenetic mania for living and to a series of escapades compared with which any of the previous ones, whether with Guys or with the evening dress hidden in the bowl-shaped copper vessel, were bound to seem nothing more than innocent tripping and skipping in place.

Yet there's no room at all for doubt that Etelka loved Imre von G. Otherwise, what was she doing waiting for a letter like that? (Like what? Out in the woods with another man? No, just forget that. Don't say, "She couldn't possibly have loved him." But let's not start that old song and dance all over.) She said, "Karl, it's time. You have to get back down below." He grumbled and tore himself free with difficulty. Safeguarding this secret intimacy, so precious to him, was close to his heart, however, so he obeyed.

She watched him go and then climbed uphill through the woods alone. When we think about the last days of people whom we knew well and who are now departed, each of the thoughts they may have secretly harbored at the end becomes precious to us, and then it's almost as if death had made them all sacrosanct and set them on the highest peak of authority. Doesn't death lend an aspect of immortality to all those who, however lacking in merit, have passed on before us—even when it's of their own volition—and in that way, our pictures of them still blossoming and growing, have been saved from the wasting and leveling powers of life? She walked with no effort, with speed and power. What was this root-filled and rocky woodland path to her, to a woman who had known how to climb sheer walls and to creep along narrow rock ledges above the abyss and who, when the time had come, had proven ready and able to perform these feats, even though they may have been required only to get through one of her escapades? She would have known how to find her way to Imre even along the Inthaler Band, that ledge reputed to be so treacherous, or up one of the sheer faces of the Predigtstuhl, the Pulpit, as that famous mountain is called.

So who can say she didn't love him? Everything has to happen at the right time—Omar Khayyám, *façon voilée*, Robby Fraunholzer, Karl von W. There was only one thing that would never work, and that was to live, simply to live, without the excitement, without the fulfillment, even if living meant being ground down. The afternoon passes apace, a milk-drenched mellowing comes pouring out from the more slanted rays of the sun. The aroma of coffee wafts through the house; some person whose work is finished now goes to drink and enjoy, some ordinary person—the hardest thing a person could ever be. They had no great gift for that in the Stangeler household.

This path, running right along the dividing line between two valleys—one sprinkled with village dwelling places, heights and hills all settled with houses and homesteads, the other, to Etelka's left, where the slope fell steeply, uninhabited through its whole extent, dominated all the way to the bottom by timber woods with separate crags and peaks of jutting rock—this path, on the exact boundary between the rugged, self-contained solitude of nature turned so deeply in on itself and the submissive spreading out under the sky of mountainsides plowed and planted every year, led along and beyond the silent tension of this contrast, bent to the right as it parted ways with the line of division, and, after a climb of considerable steepness, the last of which went over a massive escarpment, ran into the road through the pass, so freely winding along at that height and now so easily widening out the viewer's gaze to a broader vista. Now everything unfolded here, and truly as with inner thunder from beyond the sweeps of sky, grown clear and blue—a mountain wall in brilliant sharpness and the swelling curves of an Alpine range going out to forests that cling like fur far out at the edge of the sky, seeming in shadow again by the sheer splendor of sunlight and dotted all over with rocks.

She walked downhill. What was she thinking? Did she look around? Yes, she stopped and looked around. She leaned against the railing at the banked shoulder of the road before the steep drop-off. Was it the conventional thought that held her there, nature's beauty, as it's known, before which people have to stop a moment, if only for the sake of appearances, and present their quick act of devotion, reminiscent of a sexton or a verger making a little bob of genuflection when he has to

pass in front of the altar? Why had she stopped and why was she standing there? What was she thinking about? Only about the mail from
Pest? Or was she looking at the very starting point of her life, at the
place where her roots were, where her family's house stood, but without
seeing it? Was the gap separating her from it, was the distance not great
enough even now? Through the other end of a telescope more than
two decades long, we can see her there on the road winding through
the pass; we're according her too much freedom, and we see how the
happiness and the peace of this beautiful August morning are lying all
around her in whole sweeping vistas encroaching on her, indeed even
engulfing her, though she still had governance of her every footstep.
Then again, no—she was only thinking about the mail from Pest after
all, she had not the slightest hint of governance, and the horizon didn't
extend in a circular sweep but was narrow and cramped instead, like
a trench.

Right as she walked into the yard, Asta told her she had a letter
from Belgrade.

The lighting for the day switched to the "low" setting.

She went into her room. The letter lay on top of the desk.

She felt tired, exactly the way Melzer (another one who of course
had no idea what was in his own actual best interest) had felt in that
room at the country inn fourteen years before, when Buschmann,
Geyrenhoff, and Marchetti had talked about life and death and England. Even so, she lost no time in opening the letter. For the space of
just a breath she was lifted above and flung out of the situation she was
trapped and bound up in, and the heavy shackles that keep a person
fettered in situations like that strained for so very minute a fraction of
a second as to make it, in its brevity, seem scarcely a particle of time at
all, but of a different medium entirely, outside of time; what lifted her
was the sight of Fraunholzer's handwriting, which made the past come
palpably surging toward her like a curtain suddenly whisked to life
and sent swirling outward by the wind, and in that surging, which she
could feel was calling her very self back to life, were heartbeats that
had—how often, too!—quickened by rushing toward that handwriting
as if they were scampering toward her from somewhere outside, like
footsteps of the heart able to make their way alone and with no feet.

But the bonds didn't burst. They just stretched a little. That was enough, though, to make Etelka now feel she was moving closer to the possibility of at last answering Robby's letters, which had been growing ever more urgent. It was like an awakening, a renewed calling back into life of limbs that have fallen so totally asleep we no longer realize they still belong to us.

Well, we're not as discreet as Grauermann. We're going to go right ahead and read (over her shoulder, her powerful shoulder covered by the bright-colored silk shawl of her Alpine clothing—and while she was reading, the geese by the bank of the stream, as innocent as their white feathers and for that reason all the louder, set up a cackle).

...whatever may have taken place after you went back to Budapest from Vienna is something I don't know anything about, because I've only received a few lines from you that whole time. For now, too, all I can do is assume or speculate that you're staying at your parents' place. Etelka, what is going on with you? When I was in Pest the time before last—a good many months ago now, back in the spring, before your brother René came (and, incidentally, the tales of woe from his love life are of no interest whatever to me, so you don't have to write so much about them, the way you did the last time you were in Vienna; write about yourself instead!)—I had a downright ominous feeling of doom all the while. You were apathetic, and Pista was as cold as an icicle, including to me. It felt very much to me as if he were on the verge of doing something completely out of character. But Etelka, why do we have to continue cramming our lives full of problems we don't need to have, like a window full of cacti that haven't had a chance for a long time now to be what they're meant to be? And all that simply because we made a wrong judgment? And because we can't shake off the past and start over? I could have filed divorce proceedings at any time during the last few years, and I could still do so today. How often have I nagged you about this? But I've been growing less and less sure of you. Is it passivity with you, is it nervousness about making any kind of change, or are you afraid you're going to be faced with a need to live in less comfortable circumstances, which would never even enter the question, I'm sure you know, or—and it's this last "or" that's tormenting me beyond all words here in this broiling city where I'm counting the days until my leave begins and I can get away from the Ulice Kralja Milana and travel to Vienna to see you. Unfortunately, it's still a long time till then. And that's why I don't want to wait until I see you to say to you yet again once more, and yet again once more after that: put the whole thing behind you, lay it all out to Pista (something tells me you're not going to encounter one bit of resistance), and don't be afraid of your father, for I know how to make it all square with him. Let me know when you have those things taken care of; then I can take a trip straight out to see my wife in Gmunden even before I come to you. She and I have been in agreement about these matters for a good while; it's a lot easier for us because we've already been separated by distance on a day-to-day basis for so long. Go into action now; today would be better than tomorrow. And send me news tomorrow, by telegram if you have to. Better tomorrow than the day after. So get moving…

Her upper body bent slowly forward until she lay with her face on the desk. Her cheek was touching the sheet of paper the letter was written on, and out of its cool, dry feel on her skin came a kind of purely physical comfort, as if it were a sheet of paper and nothing else, as if it were blank, as if nothing on the sheet of paper were speaking words into her own life, like water trying to collect but pouring into a sieve instead. Now, because she found it impossible to stay alone here in the room with this letter and its demand for an immediate answer, it popped into her head that she had to go and see how her little boy was, to check whether he'd drunk his milk, and to find out where the children—Asta's two boys were out in the yard as well—were now. She put the letter back into its envelope, not even having read it all the way to the end, and slid it under her lingerie in the dresser drawer, which she then locked.

The boys were out on what had once been the tennis court, and Asta and the nursemaid were with them; glasses of milk and slices of bread with butter had been brought out to them a good deal earlier, and their empty glasses, with a bluish tinge now, were standing on one of those benches up above on the embankment, the place from which, fourteen years earlier, the deciding match between Grabmayr and Semski had been followed with such intense excitement.

The little man came dashing over when he caught sight of his mother.

Asta had also received a letter from Robby Fraunholzer.

He was asking her for news about Etelka.

Who was sitting here, right next to her, while their little boys were playing at the edge of the tennis court, already more than half overgrown with grass, and talking about Imre von G. in a spirit that declared her love like a branch in full bloom—rather than the way Thea spoke about Eulenfeld, say—an approach that brought all sorts of little details along with it (examples: it was his job to oversee a heavily mortgaged estate and a sugar refinery in equally precarious condition; as if that weren't enough, he was a poet, too; that in turn made him even more sensitive to the conflict he was having with his wife, who loved him still), details that were more than sufficient to have Asta prick up her ears à la Paula Pichler, even if what she thought she was hearing here was far less about a dangerous wolf than it was about a mere schoolboy, a gymnasiast.

It was basically her frilled collar or inner tube which led Robby Fraunholzer to place such great trust in Asta, even though he was unaware that this device existed, so gradually had it come into being and use. On the whole, he essentially respected her as the daughter of her father, whose stretch of track she seemed to extend and lengthen directly, whereas Etelka, charged with the same energy, just took off and went bolting up hill and down dale. The outcome was what he got to see in Asta—he hadn't been introduced to her until about 1920, after all—and he saw in it something with the same amount of polish and skill he'd soon come to recognize, in earlier days, as characterizing Grauermann's proficient air, all his own, of going about his business both inside and outside the office in Constantinople. He was quite friendly with Asta; they liked one another very much. "I'm asking you to please give me full reports" (he was blunt in writing), "because things simply can't keep on going as they are. Keep an eye on Pista as well, if he should happen to be out there, too; I've got good reasons for asking. Please give me whatever news you have right away. And of course not a word to Etelka about this letter." It's remarkable how firmly confident he seemed about being able to cut across the bonds of the criminal organization subsisting among all women, including between these two sisters, at that (or could the bonds have been weakened by their common blood?). On the other hand, he may well have realized that Asta's reasoning power always singled him out as the one contact with reality in her sister's life, as it were, and had come to deem him indispensable as a result. It was the father in Asta that kept clinging to him. And that was how Fraunholzer's oversimplified viewpoint resulted in his hitting the target so accurately nonetheless.

"What does Robby have to say?" asked Asta.

There was no helplessness displayed in Etelka's features. In fact, they didn't open up at all. She would certainly have told Asta everything, for that was how she always operated; not just because of the closeness between sisters, and also not for the sake of the advice she could expect to be given or because she knew how highly she should value her younger sister's judgment. No, it was because, without giving it a moment's thought, she considered Asta under an obligation, a purely self-evident matter of course, to lavish attention on her. Now, though, on this particular occasion, she herself didn't want to hear anything, not about Fraunholzer, at any rate. Her face, basically rough-hewn and structured with strong curves when looked at more closely, disappeared behind the hasty gloss of arrogance. "It's always the same thing with him," she said; "he's insisting I get a divorce. But why all the fuss? I'm not as naive about things like that as I used to be. A marriage is a marriage. Building superintendents. Fuel bills. Better to leave everything the way it is. He'll soon calm down." The truth, presented on a cushion made of complete misunderstanding of the situation, confused Asta at first, but only for a moment; indeed, it had been a long time since she'd fallen headlong into the trap set by what we'll call Etelka's theoretical or philosophical posturings. Her answer diverted the arrow in its flight and sent it in an entirely different direction; and even without knowing any of the specifics, she shot it straight at the weakest point.

"Pista seems strange to me these days," she said.

"You don't know him. He has his moods." Etelka's voice now seemed to be covered over by a layer of the same substance that was on her face.

Actually, Asta knew him—Grauermann—better. She knew him better because she could see more clearly and could fill in details of what she saw, thanks to a talent for drawing she'd inherited from her father. The proportion of the lower leg to the upper won't escape an eye like hers; nor will the stubby straightness of a nose in which there dwells a quality almost akin to denial; what's being denied is the vast assortment of odors that exists in our world, and following from denial comes the belief that it's possible to sort the ones that really are there under taxonomy and rubric. Putting it differently, such a person's astonishment at any given odor won't be very deep and is likely to bring about an immediate retreat—on short calves—from the sphere it is occupying. Asta saw all that. And even more. For the time being it was surrounded by a swirling current; it wasn't fully immersed and had no trouble looking out from where it was, but it was standing in the current, like a flower pot when its saucer is filled with water. It would have been completely inundated otherwise.

Naturally it was hard for Asta to say anything at all just now about a situation she felt to be so contradictory, and Etelka would have been totally unable to register even the gist of her words anyway, at least not now. But she knew her own kind and was well aware of the state they would go into when in quest of thrills and excitement, during which time their true and abiding needs and interests would drift into the blind spot of the optical equipment they were making use of. Excitement is nothing more than the beating of a blocked artery, and perhaps it had been stanched in the first place because there was no longer enough blood for the whole circulatory system. But with compression, the patient will at least be amply supplied with blood in one place instead of being anemic in them all. On the other hand, an occluded area like that will of course cease operating as an integral component of the system as a whole, which is still going to have to keep on functioning somehow, no matter what. Asta had also grown cautious when it came to René and all his efforts to tear himself away from Grete Siebenschein, for whom she had never quite been able to swallow her dislike entirely; in fact, she had at first welcomed the various initiatives he took to break from her. Later, though, she recognized what René needed better than he did himself, even when that need was lulled into a stupor by some other craze or passion, whether for his university work, for scholarly knowledge, or for literature.

She was also aware how much Etelka needed to be known as the Frau Consul; she estimated the weight of that "Frau Consul" correctly and would even have been willing to go along with the title "Frau Consul General" for the sake of Etelka and her weakness, and in this attitude she wasn't failing to take into consideration that revamping whole structural elements of a life already quite definite in form always entails risk, even when the renovations are excellent and offer genuine improvement. At this point, though, the entire structure was shifting its crushing weight off two pillars that had lately seemed to be diverging ever farther, as if exploring an alternative, shifting onto a third support that would prove to be only a broken wisp of straw. Meanwhile, Asta saw mitigating and extenuating circumstances in Etelka's involvement with Karl von W., much as we find it understandable when someone resorts to chain-smoking at times of great nervous tension. This liaison was tolerated by Asta as just a concomitant lesser evil—well, that's how she saw it, anyway—with no consequences. The sweetness of her nature and a desire to make life easier even led her to start flirting with Karl's younger brother in a meaningless kind of way, and so the two sisters would walk along their secret paths together, the one in full flight, as it were, and the other protecting her as she went.

Grauermann could now be spotted walking along the winding path up to the house. At the same time the nanny, who had left the two ladies with their boys out on the overgrown tennis court to go into the house and follow up on some work she'd been doing, came back out to fetch the children inside and get them ready for lunch. The gong sounded not long afterward. Amid all their settled arrangements, their standing and running arrangements, mealtimes constituted an abruptly decreed stoppage of everything and anything, just like the timpanist in an orchestra suddenly cutting off the sound by laying his hand flat on the drumhead. Herr von Stangeler had become the victim of a severe illness; once a daunting original character, now an estimable one. A bad case of arthritis, no longer treatable at his time of life, placed a heavy burden on that powerful body of his, weighed down enough by old age as it was. But the pain his burden inflicted every day was not able to grind this man little by little to a pulp and to make him go trickling down the last slope of his life without shape or form, which is how it happens only too frequently to old people, even ones in good health. On the contrary—the fire of his spirit crackled and blazed furiously under pressure, so that this old gentleman remained a very focused conversational partner and by no means an insipid one, either; especially not with his own children. Whenever he sat bent forward in an armchair—an eagle with drooping pinions that he still keeps trying to flap even though they've grown useless; then he remembers and regains his composure and once more smooths down his feathers—he gave the impression that he was able to see before anything else every weak point, every soft spot, in the person he was conversing with, and that, free of all repugnance, he was pondering whatever he saw with a kind of outward-looking, clear-sighted, and almost shameless degree of indiscretion. About his own self he knew a great deal less. That's important, too—not the whole of it, but at any rate an essential part of the difference between him and our friend Cornel Lasch, who was versed in exercising precisely the same skill, although in the opposite direction.

The old man had to be lifted out of his chair and set back down in it, which required a considerable amount of strength and a great deal of delicate treatment, in spite of which he suffered pain each time. It was all very complicated. A faithful servant girl from the area, one who'd been working in the house for many years, was adept in helping out with this task. Still, it wasn't only the physical weight of his body and its pain that bore down, as if it were a restraining mass, on the scurrying, scattershot movements and words of their daily life here— no, it wasn't that somebody was suffering, but who was doing the suffering and how; nor was it even that it was the father, much though that fact did manage, in the long run, to break the tips off any pointed objects heading for their mark (more than a few had been deflected in this family and sent ricocheting toward its head, the strongest member). Today, though, it wasn't the invalid, it wasn't the gentleman far along in years, it wasn't the father—it was just the person, pure and simple, who was triumphing, that aged eagle whose impotent wing twitches they seemed compelled to keep thinking of, contrary to their better knowledge and to all appearances, as the onset of a soaring flight.

Yet the more essential achievement of this man's old age, his invisible late work after so many visible deeds in a life directed entirely outward—even today, after all, the trains hurtle past the latticed girderwork of his viaducts, whose fine tracery, delicate enough to make one's head whirl, spans chasms—these, his last projects, deep in his own interior, which may well have remained as foreign to him as some ancient specimen of a man from the days of long ago, revealed themselves in quieter signs on the visible surface. His hand, once always balled up into a fist, now rested with outstretched fingers no longer capable of flexing. But that hand seemed more thoughtful, more aware of itself, more familiar with itself; hence it had the capacity even to execute with grace tasks that would on first glance have lain beyond possibility, given the condition it was in—with unbending fingers he was still able to write neatly and to roll a cigarette from his old tobacco pouch. And his entry—made possible by an illness of years' duration—into a completely new state of being, with all its new discoveries, bisected this man, as it were, accorded him a gradual access to his own self, and transferred (inasmuch as there had come to be two of him, split into a sick man and a well man) many an earlier standard of his, too simple and pat by far, into the realm of the questionable. So here at the end there blossomed an astonishing fruit—not quite ripe, admittedly, but coming into its full development. It was tolerance.

Nevertheless, people still had to tread softly, especially those who had remained in any way dependent on the old gentleman. That was the case with his children, and it caused him more pain than it did anyone else, because it hardly allowed him to appraise these adults as adults. Only Etelka found herself more or less outside his orbit; Asta, in spite of being married, was inside it, and our boy René deep inside. Their father's condition as it now stood, however, would not have prevented him from turning over and over for his inspection letters clearly addressed to Etelka, or even possibly from opening them under some circumstances. The strict precautions introduced in the course of their postal paranoia had been devised with the head of the household in mind.

On the following day, a Monday, a letter arrived from Budapest with the afternoon mail.

Asta brought it home. While she was at it, she'd dropped a letter of her own for Fraunholzer into the slot; Etelka hadn't given her one for him in spite of Asta's inquiry before she went to the post office in the village. Her own solution to the problem of how to answer Fraunholzer is more or less reminiscent of the proverbial Gordian knot.

Dear Robby,

I understand very well both what you've written and what you're hinting at. Take your leave time as soon as you possibly can, but be sure to do it earlier than you were planning. That would be best. What's the sense of my writing you pages and pages now? You wouldn't be any wiser than you were before. These are the kinds of things you can only talk about face-to-face. But don't send any mail for me here anymore. It's only by lucky chance that Etelka didn't see your letter, just because she didn't go to the post office yesterday, Sunday. Of course she'd want to know what's in a letter you'd be writing to me. Apparently you didn't stop to consider that. Then if I couldn't show her the letter, a difficult situation might arise. Write care of my husband at our apartment in Vienna, and tell us whether you're coming earlier than planned. But make it soon, though. Just let me know when.

Now she'd put the letter from Hungary into her jacket pocket and pushed the one to Belgrade through the slot. There hadn't been any mail for her. She kept standing there in the sunlight and looking down at the white dust of the road as she reached deep inside herself for several moments. Her scrutiny was close and clear. She was doing the right thing in asking Fraunholzer to come. Neither party should get too carried away in this affair with Karl von W., either. Grauermann was here for only a few days; he would probably leave soon. But suppose he didn't? Suppose he stayed? Didn't it seem as if a contretemps or even a confrontation with Fraunholzer would be almost for the best? It could set everything running smoothly again, item by item. Including with their father. Fraunholzer would do a good job of handling that situation. He couldn't just turn up unexpectedly, though. But there was the closing of her letter. Wasn't it too alarmist? And would Fraunholzer indeed notify her in Vienna? Or would he start harboring suspicions of some kind—and then really take it into his head to show up here with no advance notice? Once more she reached into herself and savored how the end of her note—she knew it by heart—tasted. She became downright engrossed, as if her inner self could supply her with information about all that was happening or might happen, as if she could bring it all out of herself, because it had to be as good on the inside as on the outside. She didn't come to any definite answer on this point, though. Of course Asta knew she could rely on her husband, Government Building Surveyor Haupt, as could Fraunholzer, who knew him well. Haupt was to be counted among those persons who rotate on their own axes to only a slight degree, which is to say very slowly, as a result of which almost no centrifugal force is released. That's the secret of their prudence. Unlike others, those whirling madly about, they aren't compelled to hold objects as if clenched, lest everything go flying off, humming tops that need to keep spinning at a high rate of revolution in order to remain upright at all. In more slowly rotating bodies, however, ones that are cooler and have ceased long before to be give off their own light, gravity is by far the more predominant force. Every object stays in place on them, prudent and silent as the grave. A place where all that pertained to Etelka and Fraunholzer had lain for years now, prematurely buried along with all the details.

When Asta reached the point at which she became unable to dredge anything more out of the interrogated inside of herself, she felt conscious of being bothered by the sunlight on the white dust of the road and also, every bit as much, by the chance that someone might bump into her now and involve her in a conversation. She got off the road by turning left onto a side path and entered the woods. Here the path went steeply uphill to the ridge separating the two valleys, where Etelka had gone walking the previous day. This climbing path was taking Asta on a considerable detour, to be sure, but time wasn't at a premium just now.

She sat down in Pastor's Woods, on a mossy bench, a number of which were set here and there along narrow trails and little steps that had been placed many years before, apparently out of a feeling that this wasn't just an ordinary patch of farmers' woodland but a place of relaxation and perhaps even of meditation for the good keeper of souls. By now these thoughtful amenities had long since crumbled and fallen back into the earth, the benches existing only in pieces, the steps made of trimmed logs broken. Here Asta took the letter from Hungary out of her jacket pocket, turned it over, and looked at it from every angle. The writing on the envelope told her nothing; it seemed to have been formed more by convention than by anything distinctive about the writer's hand. The envelope was long and grayish-blue. It felt pretty full. On the back were written the initials I.G., with a small five-pointed crown above them. She slid the letter back into her jacket pocket. "What's this supposed to mean?" she thought, and then, right afterward, "Do we have choices? Can people go to search out their own options?" Here in Pastor's Woods, with the declining rays of the late afternoon sun coming down through the trees, Asta felt opening up within her, quite early in her life, a vista that her father had been able to attain only as the last one he would see, and then only after he had stepped across that bisecting line, the boundary separating sickness from health. This was the very moment at which, if only as a byproduct, the borderline marking two distinct eras had been handed off to Asta—a line drawn by the end of the war and the change in every single circumstance bearing on happiness and prosperity—something the old gentleman was struggling for under the pressure of his physical suffering and the attendant pressure on his whole consciousness. That's all well and good, the reader might want to chime in at this point, but why is everything always happening in Pastor's Woods, matters touching on the lives of a Protestant family, at that? Well, it's simply because everything that occurs at all occurs more or less in Pastor's Woods, a place it's very hard to find one's way out of, even when riding in the vehicle of excitement

at its most intense, for riding only means that one is bound to leave a
great many things behind and will then wind up having to go back
and retrieve them—from Pastor's Woods. In the meantime, though,
we're just about to leave the woods ourselves anyway. Asta had no duties to perform here, no ministrations to see to. Her errand to the post
office was all taken care of.

She followed the ridge, from which one could see down into the solitary,
scarcely inhabited side valley. The slanted rays of the sun shone onto
her face from among the trees. The path continued on as it took a slight
bend by a stand of young birch trees. Past the birches, to the left, the
hillside broke off, steep and bare, with no trees, a sheep pasture all the
way down to the valley below. Asta stepped away from the path a little,
though not as far as the edge of the woods. There was a narrow paved
road down below, and because the first stretch of it was a favorite place
for summer guests in the village to take their walks, some comfortable
benches had been set up here and there, including a few facing the
slope, right before the place where the woods began and under the first
of the trees.

Asta wasn't thinking a single thought just now, not a single solitary
thought for the time being. With the optical sharpness of an eye that
could not only detect short calves with precision but could instantly,
even at a great distance, distinguish a ram standing at the edge of the
forest from a doe, she was observing a conversation being held on one
of the benches over on the other side of the valley and proceeding as
though she were going to have to infer the inaudible words from the
few gestures and motions visible to her, just as earlier, on the village
street, she had tried to draw the entire exterior from the entire interior.

Cornelia Wett and Grauermann weren't moving very much, at any
rate. He was leaning forward while he sat and blowing smoke from his
cigarette down toward the ground.

Now it looked as if she were speaking, because he stood up and
looked at her. At one point she lifted her right arm to make a circular,
all-embracing, hauling-off movement. She talked for a long time. It
was a discussion, not a casual chat, that Asta was witnessing here, her

sharp eye like a spyglass. That realization came directly to her conscious mind and moved whatever she was seeing away from the realm of the incidental and the insignificant, although not into any discernible course. Now it looked as if Grauermann were giving her some answer, since he was moving his hands. Just a second later the spatial distance that separated Asta from this mute pantomime came caving in on her, so to speak, and was smashed to pieces—in the sun-filled silence of evening, Cornelia's bright laughter came audibly resounding across the valley. Asta shrank back deeper among the trees, as though they were going to be able to see her now, which was hardly possible.

She turned away and continued walking.

Asta's errand to the post office wasn't quite so completely taken care of after all, as it turned out. Her long absence pushed the nervous tension Etelka was feeling about the mail well beyond the limit of the tolerable. Indeed, she snapped with fierce joy at the letter Asta held out to her in her room, but the excess pressure had to escape somehow. For years, Etelka had been used to being the midpoint and the centering sun around which Grauermann, Fraunholzer, and other, lesser planets and asteroids of the household, such as Ziska and similar bodies, orbited, such orbiting an entrenched and cherished tradition of Hungarian life. Here, though, on her parents' turf and in their home, Frau Consul Grauermann was something along the lines of a celestial body struck from the lists in astronomy, far lower in status than a dethroned king of Poland, and in any event less capable of being formed into decent shape. Cause and opportunity met and overlapped; and as if that weren't enough, she saw some mushrooms Asta had gathered in her apron. Her dissatisfaction caused her to vent the actual claim she felt inside herself entitled to make, but to vent it with the purpose of giving offense. That claim was purely and simply that she should be waited on. "What took you so long?" and "Were you just with Egon?" (she knew full well that Asta was trifling with the younger grandson of Minister von W. only for her sake) and "Stupid mushrooms, no less!" Asta turned and left, the most prudent action she could have taken. That spark of pride in Etelka's eye, which was never able to accomplish anything but set the roofs of other peoples' peace on fire while they were sitting in their houses, was intolerable to her, arousing outright hatred in her and drawing the frilled collar, the inner tube, the water wings—they could still fulfill their function in time of need—all the way up around her neck.

Etelka devoured the letter well before dinner.

Meanwhile, Grauermann came into view; he'd arrived from the village and was climbing the stairs to a large attic room which was really René's but which also held a second bed. It wasn't always possible to give married couples the same room, but nobody considered it a high priority, either. By the time the gong sounded and Grauermann's footsteps could be heard coming back down the stairs, Etelka's rage to impart the latest had long since come to outweigh her detonated wrath. She ducked into Asta's little room with its balcony, asked her forgiveness in a manner that involved quickly pouncing on her sister and getting it all over with at once, and then said in haste that Asta absolutely had to read Imre's letter, since it was even more wonderful than any of his earlier ones. She'd bring it to Asta's room when everyone had gone to bed.

In the summertime, high up in the mountains, one can come to understand what an "ambrosial night" really is. The streaming in through a balcony door's dark rectangle of exhalations from countless plants intense in fragrance, a release and an outpouring grounded in silence of all the vegetative breath decocted by the sun throughout the day and now streaming into the night as day's epilogue and variation; this expansiveness of a thing silently good, and the plashing of the fountain as well, were eminently suited to prompt full assent in Asta's mind to what she was reading. If, on the other hand, when we're trying to form an impression of a thing, when we're focused on the work of sampling and assaying, we should happen to encounter an odor not deemed pleasant by our individual sense of taste—it can be an odor far from inherently repulsive, too—then we most assuredly grow more critical. From this example we see the kinds of subjective forces objects can be dependent on. And so Asta was all disposed and composed to be receptive, lying in bed by the lamp on the night table, a brown moiré robe over her white nightgown. What's more, in this case it was all about love, which she really did know something about; it wasn't about, say, language, which struck her as less important. And here is what Imre wrote:

> ...I am still not yet able to grasp this miracle, the miracle of union between two persons who only found one another at so late a time in their lives. And perhaps I don't want to grasp it quite completely, for then there steps before my inner eye the tragedy inhering in our never having come to know each other earlier, in our not having been granted the bliss of encountering each other sooner. Ofttimes, when it is quite silent all around me, I can feel your childhood. It is very close to me. To me it is like a precious jewel I hold somewhere in my possession without being able to recollect at the moment in what secret drawer it is locked away and protected. Or else I feel we must have known each other as children. Ofttimes, when I have had to do without the sight of you for weeks and can live only in the thought that we will see each other again, I fancy we must have shared childhood secrets—hiding places, passwords. Of an evening I sometimes feel as if I could bring them to utterance and find them once again. Ofttimes, when I'm about to fall asleep, my lips try to form one of those words from our childhood...

"Why 'ofttimes'?" thought Asta.

We would call it a rise in temperature, starting from the bottom up, whenever his use of language was involved. Asta continued reading.

> All of this brings to my spirit a new life, one of which I knew nothing throughout my whole previous existence. It is you I must thank for this new life; it bears your features and is stamped by them, is illumined by the rays that stream out from your unique personality. Only now do I begin to fathom what Dante really meant by the expression "new life" in his *Vita Nuova*. Ofttimes now, when I read poetry, poetry by one of the great, revered masters, it seems to be yielding up its meaning to me for the first

time, as if it had been translated—by you—into a new language
I can comprehend on a very profound level. Ofttimes is such the
case . . .

Ofttimes.

Asta nodded out of respect. But after that her face froze over with
the first layer of objection, became coated with the frost of disenchantment. Now a name could be put to the revulsion breaking loose within
her, throwing open and exposing the situation Etelka was in, like a
breached cave revealing waters that deeply disturbed Asta as they welled
up from its floor. She set the letter aside and looked at the ceiling. The
silence broke up into the sounds audible in the room. A moth kept
tapping against the taut lampshade as it fluttered toward the electric
light. From far off in the woods came the piping but penetrating call
of the nightjar. Then, closer, a tawny owl, again and again.

The ceiling—Asta was now looking straight up at it; she had forced
her head back almost to her spine, as if to tense up like an archery bow
so she could offer some resistance to a heavy burden lowering itself on
her now; to tense up so much, indeed, that her back muscles were
slightly involved in making the arch. The ceiling was a faint ocher in
color and blank in its lack of movement, not, as could often be seen
here at night, befluttered, beflitted, and beflown by one of those winged
creatures with long legs whose artificiality, fragile and clear as crystal,
virtually erases—when looked at more closely—whatever it is numb-
skulls think they're taking refuge in as an adequate observation when
they say the word "nature," which comes out of their mouths like a lazy
yawn reduced to only the two sounded vowels, the rest masticated
beyond recognition. The blank ceiling now made a serving tray for
Asta's disturbance, principally on realizing—it was so totally obvious,
too, at least now—how far away she'd been, right up to this very moment, from perceiving Etelka's true state. There was no telling what it
must be like, thought Asta, if a letter like this didn't wake her up from
it! She had seen pictures of Imre; the passages she'd just been reading
seemed like notes written in the margins, as it were. Hence he didn't
look merely handsome and languishing; he looked noble and deep as

well. Her feminine intuition now mounted relentlessly, though, rising up past the frilled collar, the water wings, the inner tube. So what had been the point of Etelka's reading books, even back in the early days, with Pista? What had been the point of her Schopenhauer and Ibsen, a large edition of whose complete works had always been on display in the piano studio up in the Quartier Latin? Why any of the rest of it, for that matter, if all she did now was go into raptures at the kind of poppycock that was being dished out now?

Yet there was one point she became conscious of when she concentrated all her energy—it was that as matters now stood she could say exactly nothing to Etelka. In fact, the seam ripped further, and her lonesomeness thickened around her, as if it were pouring into the room from outside, where up till now the call of the nightjar had encircled her, dark as a bowl inverted over her: she realized she could never say anything to anyone. Not even to her own father. And not to René—to him least of all, in fact. Never at any time say anything whatsoever to anyone whomsoever, was what she thought all of a sudden, and everything around her grew more distinct, as if the light had been turned up, while she lay calm in the midst of it all and yet somehow as if shunted off to the side. One and the same skill—if innate, it's nothing but pure callous spitefulness; if acquired, it's a goal worth keeping in sight. In their two different ways, Asta and Scheichsbeutel coincided and met at the same point. It appears, then, that there are certain virtues it is granted to a person to obtain only as convictions, but not as actual qualities, and not with any certainty, either.

Asta relaxed. Well, she was over thirty-three, and you just can't help becoming a grown-up little by little, a grown-up into whose head there now entered forthwith, after the generalities, a specific that was easy to grasp—small at first, and as clearly rounded as the head of a knitting needle, but enlarging and at last exploding with a burst of insight. "Cornelia values Robby very highly, and she's so fond of his letters." That was 1920 or 1921. Back then, and later on as well, Etelka used to deposit her valuables at Cornelia's; Fraunholzer would write to Etelka at her address, and the replies were ordinarily written in Cornelia's apartment. Asta remained cool and calm. Here was something—though it may have been the only thing—she could question Etelka about if the right opportunity arose. There was a soft noise at the door to the next room, which now opened darkly, like a toothless mouth. Then Etelka's nightgown gleamed out in white as she stepped into the circle of lamplight. "Did you read it?" she asked as she sat on the edge of Asta's bed. "I'd like to have it back to read again before I go to sleep." Asta said nothing. She sat up, put her arms around Etelka, and kissed her. What was there to say? So what they did was exchange loving words. Then Etelka vanished with her letter. Asta now noticed that she was glad not to have it on her bed anymore. She turned out the light and lay on her back. The rectangle of the open balcony door, dark before but now relatively light, began to extend and enlarge itself.

On the following afternoon, Tuesday, August 4, when the sun was already beginning to lower in the sky, René was walking at a slow pace up the winding road. He was carrying a light backpack and, in his left hand, a briefcase filled with papers. In front of the post office, where the bus made its regular stop, he'd run into Asta (who again today had undertaken the errand to the post office, since Etelka was being so totally blatant in parading her lack of interest, at least for now). Brother and sister had exchanged affectionate and happy greetings. It looked as if Asta were hoping to take care of some other business while she was in the village, though, and so René started off by himself. As he turned away from the main road and walked past the hedges in the lanes, as he began climbing the twists and turns in the serpentine road, the vapors in the pure air exuded by all the vegetation filled his nose and lungs to such a degree that the city atmosphere he'd left behind now departed from him completely, like something deceased and defunct, like something truly dead and gone.

A clear chord with widely spaced intervals came surging out from the piano, filling the air above the tops of the old apple trees. Like all people affected—or infected—by music (we have good reason to be very explicit here about leaving the choice of word up to the reader!), the one chord René had caught was enough to give him the feeling that he had heard some irrefutable statement and that he need never make the faintest additional effort to express it in any other terms. His bearing at that point does not appear to be entirely unrelated to what Melzer would exhibit at a slightly later date, namely on August 22, that sweltering Saturday afternoon, in his room on Porzellan Gasse in Vienna, by the bearskin from the Treskavica. True, it had been a barrel organ and a military march then, as opposed to the twenty-seventh measure (counting backward from the end) of the second movement of Brahms's Symphony No. 3 in F Major now. The difference, however, is far less important than it might seem to a music-loving reader (and almost to the author as well) on first glance, whereas the fact that Melzer had been thinking about something definite as the organ-grinder was playing his tune (the odor of camphor from the bearskin also helped that process along) put the whole experience onto a smooth and solid track for the major. During this moment, meanwhile, Stangeler was feeling as close to truth as he would ever get, but without thinking anything at all; that is exactly wherein lies the unspoken accord, as paradoxical as it is natural, that subsists among all musical people. Thus he came to a standstill and followed the twenty-seven measures of that altogether remarkable phrase—which launches a totally new idea only toward the end of the movement—through to their conclusion, the orchestral palette underlying the piano sound, in particular the lightly compressed stringendo in the soft notes of the trombones. René was nodding his head the whole time. It's in just that way that a person will put a period right in the middle of the blank white space on a sheet of paper, a period after a sentence that hasn't been written yet but that still signifies "period" anyway, something nobody would hesitate to call idiotic. Stangeler's nodding was no less so.

Only now did it strike him that Etelka—she who knew of his humiliation this summer—must be the person at the piano.

And it was only at this point that he indeed arrived, got to his destination, reached his goal, truly achieved separation and severance from the starting point of this brief trip lasting no more than two hours; off like a shot, as though he were a rubber band stretched for a long time and then suddenly cut (he didn't notice that he was picturing the West Station in Vienna as his starting point now, even though he hadn't left from there at all but had been left behind instead). It wasn't just the city atmosphere that now took flight, deceased and defunct, that dipped below the edge of the horizon, far out in the open country, truly dead and gone; it was everything else as well, without exception, that he'd lately been listening to, talking about, learning there, as if there were no other option than to burrow deeply into the silliest pastimes he could find, simply so that he himself wouldn't have to be driven silly anymore: spending time (hours at a clip) with the Siebenschein family and its natural point of gravitation, Cornel; swallowing back his own opinion as obediently as a child swallows medicine (after the big capitulation—it was his, not hers!—Grete felt this point to be no joking matter, and our friend René regrettably lacked the intelligence to grasp how healthful it was for him to follow these exercises); to top it all off, though, being treated to a few brief intermezzi, such as, for example, the purely well-meaning utterance confidentially delivered not long ago by the mother of the Siebenschein family vis-à-vis her (as of this day forward) quasi-officially designated future son-in-law, so to say. The view of this astonishingly agile little lady was that if only they could have had the knowledge a few years earlier that they had today as to how everything would eventually straighten itself out so completely between him and Grete, then he would still have had time to switch over from a PhD program to the study of law and hence would have gained the prospect of perhaps taking over his father-in-law's legal practice at some future date! Kindhearted Dr. Ferry Siebenschein was quick to add, though, "I think all we need to do is congratulate him in hindsight; people can be whatever it suits them to be—not just lawyers."

There are those, however, who hold the opposite opinion. In any case, we are left with absolutely no choice but to agree with Frau Siebenschein in view of the situation that had been created here. That absoluteness was missing in our friend René, and perhaps as a general point—in every respect, that is.

The piano fell silent. René walked on.

Some days later, the Charybdis of the postal system began to swallow and then disgorge him, too, ingesting him and spewing him back out twice a day in an alternation as regular as the sea tides; it started when the time came to expect and then actually receive Grete Siebenschein's first letters. Even so—as if he had undergone a decrease in specific gravity—he swam with relative ease on the surface of the postal waters, like a mere cork, we might say, bobbing and dancing; those waters no longer hurled him down into deep-hollowed troughs between waves, troughs made of agonized waiting followed by depression, which people dismayed by a vacuum in their mail delivery can work their way out of on their own strength only with great difficulty. This weight reduction set in shortly after the morning on which Grete's first letter arrived from Paris. Asta had laid it on top of the desk in René's room; he was the only person staying in it now, because Grauermann had gone back to Budapest before René arrived, the day before, in fact.

He bent over the letter without picking it up from the desk right away or touching it at all, for that matter, and felt shock, soon yielding to fear; at first all those feelings did was quickly flitter down his back, but it wasn't long until they penetrated and lodged deep inside his chest. Now, however, like a countermove effected while he was examining Grete's handwriting—light and pointy but at the same time flyaway in forming the name "Stangeler"—he felt disgust at the sight of her penmanship.

And only then did his feeling offer its own elucidation or commentary—it was because this handwriting of hers purported to be merely that of a woman; yet there was an unwritten something, or actually more an unwritable something, set down firmly in her hand and mailed from Naples or Vienna when the letter was slipped into an envelope, addressed (as now), stamped, taken to the post office, and registered. So now this handwriting kept on writing, in a sense, unswerving in its demand to be considered merely the handwriting of a woman.

Helpless, René looked around. He left the letter sitting.

It couldn't be anything too terrible. This was a regular letter, not registered. Although he wasn't thinking in any very definite way, he still felt the full horror of systems like these and, beyond that, something worse yet—that he had grown totally conditioned to them, as it were, drilled to the point of reacting like a horse to pressure from the knee.

A dreadful somberness, indiscriminate from the moment of its onset and thus all-engulfing, began to consume his face, which in a short time tightened around a knot at the root of his nose. It felt to him as if some disaster were occurring right now but that it was unable to withstand him; he looked for a way out—no, not for quite that much, but just for a way of deflecting it instead, a way of retreating, just as a man who can't get his breath tries to do nothing more than gasp for air first, before asking himself what might be blocking his windpipe. An archery bow and a quiver were hanging there on the wall. He took them down from the hook and went out of the room. As he went sweeping through the hall downstairs, Asta stepped through the open door from the driveway; at once alarmed, she walked straight up to René, and the question she asked him—"What did she say in her letter?"—was completely obvious and inevitable, because what he had just been through was pouring out of his face like gravel, like those wagons for hauling pebbles or gravel that have a board in the back to allow the hissing stream of stone to come rushing out and grow into a pile. "I haven't read it yet," René answered. She sensed that this incredible answer was nonetheless true. As quickly as that, he was out of the hall, and she watched him rapidly climbing uphill among the fruit trees. After he'd passed out of her sight, she turned toward the stairs and went up to his room. She picked up Grete's letter from where it lay on top of the desk, just as she had laid it there. It was unopened. As she set the letter back down in exactly the same spot, she couldn't grasp anything other than that a severe disturbance of some kind was in progress here. As, indeed, all around her everywhere, upstairs and downstairs, throughout the whole house.

Above which house there rose a hill, a kind of slope with a crescent shape, one flank falling off abruptly toward the valley side, easing gently down on the mountain side into the fields and meadows, over the boundary of which—a girding of rock barely two hundred paces wide that resumed a steep ascent after a small hollow—the woods against the sky made a dark wall to close off the view. This elevation, covered by only a few sparse mountain ashes and an old pear tree gone wild, got the brightest sun, and for the longest time each day. In addition, it lay out in the open, offering the widest panorama, and from so high up that one could look down onto the roof of the house. Such chances to get a look all the way out and a look all the way down made the spot quite suitable for putting some distance between oneself and whatever conditions and circumstances were prevailing under that roof at any given time—for distancing oneself and then discussing them. In particular, Asta and René enjoyed withdrawing for that very purpose to this lofty watchtower of objectivity. They would lie in the sun for hours here.

Even so, René's frame of mind wasn't exactly objective when he reached the place today.

The broad expanse unfurled in a cloudless sky amid brilliant bursts of late-morning sunlight, pale flecks of single rocks in the moss-distant forest at the lower end of the valley, before the lowland plain—this whole vista crowding in on him lay now behind some uniform, smoky gray, as if he had sunglasses on.

René seemed quite determined to break through his benightedness, however, and under no circumstances to shrink back into what we might call an inner state preserved in mothballs. He was now as eagerly rushing to get out of his clothes as if they were the evil causing his trouble—shirt, pants, socks, all flew onto a bush that stood there patiently catching them, and Stangeler wound up with nothing on but swimming trunks and a pair of light shoes. There might well be an element of the totemic or fetishistic discernible in this transference of one's condition into one's clothing, so to speak. In one of those remarkable stories of his, Franz Nabl tells of a man who, for the moment, knows of no other way to move past the revulsion—appalling in its intensity—that he's now trapped in after a bad experience than to strip naked and sit in front of the fire burning every relevant letter or document. Whatever condition we're in has ever and anon become caught up in whatever clothes we're wearing, however—to say the least. In any case, René's were now draped over a bush here. He slung the quiver on by the straps with the arrows protruding over his left shoulder. Then he rested the lower limb of the bow on his shoe, tilted it forward, and set the bowstring into the nock. This bow was a wonderful piece of workmanship, made of two different kinds of wood. Eulenfeld had sent it from England at one time.

Directly across from him, at the same height on the opposite slope, and not exactly gracing it, a target made of tough wicker densely woven and painted in harsh colors stood at a distance of about a hundred meters. The center was black, the next ring red. René couldn't see very clearly, and the difference in vision between his two eyes—he'd inherited it from his father—prevented him from becoming a good marksman. In archery, where willpower has to substitute for the sniper's scope, as it were, it's better to keep both eyes open.

Here and now, though, he was hardly worried about his archery skills, or if so, not about this one single shot. His body suffused by the sun, as if a warm hand were holding him, René lined up the arrow on the string. Carefully, too. The fletching perpendicular to the nock pointed upward, the correct way. As he drew his arm back to tauten the string; as he took a deep breath, his chest expanding and his weight shifting onto his heels; right before his hand reached back to meet and press his chin; just as the tightened string was about to touch his left breast—that was the split second at which, filled with dark rage and with hatred rising from a deep well of powerlessness, that was the split second at which he knew this shot had as good as hit the bull's-eye already. The target changed its shape, becoming elongated as if it had somehow hollowed out in the middle through the pressure of his taking aim and were now almost crimped or buckled. The red ring jumped into pitch-black, but the bull's-eye glowed forth in rosy brightness; and now, as if jolted by an ax blow, the target standing over there shook with the dull thud of the impact. And yet the marksman, as if he himself had been the mark, collapsed and fell to the ground; still on his knees at first, and then lying on his side with his body doubled up, he twitched as he kept on emitting a quiet sound—for a good long time, too—that very much resembled a dog's whimpering. Then he lay still.

When Stangeler got back up on his feet, the smoky gray had vanished. The light fell in shrillness up above, over the rock walls at the end of the valley, and then softened, becoming more misty toward the lowland. He unhitched his bow and took a few short steps toward the target, placing his feet like a person at the seashore walking along a narrow strip of sand from which the water has just then receded. The arrow was stuck dead center, in the middle of the bull's-eye, buried almost up to the fletching. Considering that René's archery skills were generally quite weak—most of his shots would whiz right past the target—his result now, so strikingly unwonted, scared him, as if it were proclaiming some irreversible deed he had done, in some very remote way like a murder he'd committed without even knowing it. He stopped and didn't go any closer to the target but left the arrow buried in it while he moved back away to the hill—and away from the sorrow gripping him. It, too, he avoided, backed away from, looking for some place to escape the hardness all his surroundings now seemed to be taking on; what offered itself was the letter on the desk in his room.

Of course a big rush now. He hung quiver and bow back up on the wall upstairs.

The letter contained nothing threatening—more than that, it was good, indeed full of love. No objective depiction, rendered superior through distancing, of surroundings in which one could now deem one's own self objective and superior; moreover, Grete hadn't written the letter on stationery from her hotel in Paris but on her own note-paper instead. He kissed it in several spots. There was weariness in her words as well as a tendency to recall earlier times, in fact the earliest of the times she'd spent with René. She spoke about how indefinite Cornel's plans were, about how unpredictable he could be, and about how she really wouldn't mind getting away from those two in the near future; at any rate, she was giving some thought to coming back sooner than Titi and her husband. She almost wanted, she wrote, to ask René to be in Vienna as of the twentieth and to wait there for a telegram from her—well, after all, a telegram would naturally be a source of comment in the country house and his immediately ensuing departure seen as connected in some way; what was more, she was genuinely sorry to curtail his vacation time and his relaxation out there. But she was really longing to see him, too. That came right at the end. René had scarcely finished reading the letter when the gong sounded for lunch.

Mealtimes were all the more blithe and chipper the more everybody had something to hide, as all of them felt perpetually constrained to flail about and keep the surface always in a flurry through constantly renewed little waves of laughter, lest a calm sheet of water treacherously expose a view of the bottom, which contained rifts and fissures and cracks with things moving around in them that—everything without exception being measured according to the father's standard in this part of the world!—couldn't be talked about. Except for the mother and Grauermann, who was of course gone by this time, they all seemed anxious to close ranks against the intrusive thrust of some impropriety that had burst through to the outside and was now trying to pierce to the very marrow with its gaze; anyone called on to symbolize this mirthful gathering in a manner favored by certain trends currently pursued in the art world would have placed a shiny round metal disc into each figure's hand and shown them all sitting lined up at the table, each holding his or hers upright, every one of them absorbed in the effort to flash reflected light into the father's eyes so that his vision would be impeded by all those discs kept gently but unceasingly in motion. They were all doing everything in their power to give the appearance of being more orderly and untroubled than they really were. Etelka was the one who went to the least bother to do so, René to the most, and Asta, in a mood that had often grown genuinely cheerful a long time ago, held to the operative degree of dependence on the father of the house. With all three of them, the means, eternally being brought forth anew, would go streaming out onto an end that always remained the same and into a bed already dug for it, thus making it impossible to see to the bottom.

Beginning on the first evening they were together, the sisters and brother, and especially Asta and René, soon had talked over everything in his room. There she emphatically, but greatly counter to her actual inclination, took on the role of advocate for Grete, since René's uprisings against her, and the state of a binding engagement—which he was apparently incapable of so much as conceptualizing, let alone actualizing, at least for himself—pushed their way out from inside him to the point of open speech, and all the more so after her second letter, a cooler one, from Deauville, which was also cooler. In this case, moreover, as indeed in any case involving family, his relationship—devoid of any basis in reality—was placed beyond even the faintest possibility of ever being discussed (although that was precisely what was expected, and with some justification, in the Siebenschein household). "You're going to have to make many changes—lots of them—when it comes to her. Considering your living circumstances right now, anything official would be completely ridiculous for the time being, of course. But she isn't the one worried about that; it's her parents. How old is Grete? Thirty? She is? Well, there you are. Things can't be so easy for her." The reasoning power of a family as a whole is not unlike that of a certain organ referred to rather frequently by now; what they have in common is that they start to function at the exact place where the thinking capacity of the individual undergoes disruptions as the result of a momentary predicament. As early as the day after his arrival, René, too, was shown Imre von G.'s letters and pictures, and the strange communism of feelings that prevailed here quickly lifted him out of a certain aura of oppressiveness in regard to Etelka. Now she seemed to be the one whirling in the midst of the floodwaters that had engulfed him. And as for the letters, they were at so far a remove from anything Stangeler considered it in any way possible to discuss that he was able to tolerate them with relative ease as a phenomenon entirely foreign to him, thereby producing, simply as he walked past, a well-nigh perplexing effect on Asta, who might have been anticipating sharper disapproval here.

It was still bright and sunny in Pastor's Woods; each individual pine needle on the ground could be seen. Etelka was moving slowly and keeping herself bent far down the whole time. And indeed she did see every pine needle on the ground, but, although she was decidedly on pins and needles, the needles were all she could see, not the gold pin set with a medium-size brilliant-cut diamond she'd evidently lost the day before. But to tell the truth, we can't really say "lost." After Karl had stuck himself on it, Etelka had unfastened the brooch, put it aside, and then forgotten it.

Now she needed to find where she'd mislaid the pin, which was why she was stooped all the way over while retracing her footsteps—and she'd been at it for a long while. This particular posture; her strenuous absorption in a gaze that drew the ground up to her, so that she felt for moments at a time as if she had grown very small and were barely three handspans higher than the brown needles she was walking among all around her in the forest here; her strict concentration on the purpose that bound her now—all these elements caused Etelka to immerse herself deep into this place, the solitude of which might have been calculated to make a frame of mind like the one she was in even more acute, especially because of the silence, which filled her ears like thick padding.

Meanwhile, the sun reached noiselessly higher into the trees and marked off this or that trunk with a reddish glow.

She stood there before the long shadow and the imprint of her earlier visit. They seemed restless now, like a sheet of water when the calm surface is broken, the smoothness of the forest floor agitated, as if slain. To her right, at the very bottom of one tree trunk, she had sighted a small, upright stranger—the brooch; it was tilted in such a way that it could easily be overlooked. Etelka didn't reach for it right away. She knelt down first and fixed her eyes on the spot where she and Karl had been. It looked like a rumpled bed. Suddenly a spark flashed up in her eyes from behind, from somewhere deep inside, and then the scalding ring burst into a flood of tears; now she was crying without any restraint, sobbing heavily, curled in a ball, hands flung to her face. All the while yearning so passionately and fearfully for Asta. At one point she even wept out her sister's name, half swallowing it between two sobs.

There was a time when the overnight train between Belgrade and Budapest used to be scheduled in such a way that passengers wouldn't arrive in either city until a reasonable hour in the morning; the actual journey did not take that long, but it was protracted and prolonged somewhat by a series of layovers. No one would have dreamed of demanding that travelers get off at the South Station in Budapest at five thirty in the morning, their business associates still asleep in their beds, hotels still closed for the night, and no chance of finding any breakfast. Demands like that would be made today without a second thought, however—if such a train even ran at all, that is, in which case its very existence would be touted as a sign of enormous progress. The austerity measures taken at any given time don't remain fixed in place as purely negative factors. It isn't just that somewhere or everywhere there's a shortage of something or everything, and that's the end of it. No—it's more that those whose task it is to take necessary measures will often far overshoot the original goal because of having developed an attitude that makes them turn around and invoke their regulatory measures against exactly those persons for whose benefit the measures were supposedly enacted in the first place. That's how they wind up making other people's lives not merely as inconvenient as is unfortunately necessary, but also as inconvenient as is at all possible, no matter how deeply the logical-sounding rationale of necessity may be covering over that latter truth.

Fraunholzer had never been one of those people who can't sleep at night. He was unconcerned about having Turkish coffee after dinner before leaving Kralja Milana for the train station. Always in a first-class sleeper and hence alone, he had rarely crossed the wide bridge over the Sava and never the one over the Danube near Novi Sad in a state of complete wakefulness but had instead often gone to bed the minute he boarded the train and fallen into a sound sleep before the journey even started. There he would then lie, our Pompeius, our *civis romanus*, still looking not just full of vim and vigor but even a bit peevish as he slept. Today, too. But he wasn't sleeping soundly. Just at the edge of a submersion he had brought about in the midst of his extremely noisy surroundings (outside the train was a bedlam of stomping, running, shouting, and screeching), amid which one would have thought he were retiring to his rest all alone on a desert island, just at the edge of a submersion shallow that night at best, every number on the deafening program—repeated in order each evening—of this railway departure was played through to the end.

And this time he could clearly make out the bridge. Those hollow dragging sounds of tearing along and then past something, as though the train were being escorted through the darkness by gigantic arms reaching out ahead of it.

Fraunholzer had received Asta's letter, of course. Nothing at all from Etelka, on the other hand, neither at the same time nor later. He lay on his back and could not escape the feeling, however much effort he expended to apply systematic thinking to it, that he was a kind of target for flying arrows he somehow drew toward himself. He jumped up when the train was standing in Petrovaradin, turned on the light, and looked into the corridor. The sleeping-car conductor, who knew him well from so many previous trips and who might have been surprised to see a sound sleeper like this—he never moved a muscle—now awake and about, asked whether the Herr Consul General might perhaps like a cup of coffee, since there was some ready. Yes, he would. He didn't feel like lying back down and sleeping yet. It seemed better to him to wake up fully than to lie there amid all those dreams and schemes. He sat on the bed and lit a cigarette. Like all people who are bright—bright along the same lines as Karl von W.'s father or as Herr von Stangeler or even (why not?) as Cornel Lasch—he thought in a language of intellection common to them all; this language gives voice to itself and never really to what the speaker means. It wasn't very well equipped to dispel his foreboding, for it could not reach down anywhere nearly as far as his roots.

Despite all his brightness, though, Pompeius continued traveling along his *trópoi* all the same, and they were independent of that brightness, which was likewise the case with Herr Schmeller, or with Major Melzer—functioning in the case of this latter gentleman as nearly autonomous phenomena, since it's unlikely we'd have cause to talk about mental brightness on his part (for lack of a civilian mentality)— or with all the rest of that whole crew lumped together. At one of the train's crossover points or switchovers (*trópoi*), Pompeius all of a sudden collided with his wife; remarkably enough, there was nothing the least bit unpleasant about it. He didn't run up against any sharp edges (and in fact Mädi Küffer—that's what they'd called her as a girl—had never exhibited any). Not only that—he felt a gentle cushioning on impact. For the first time, perhaps, since his young years in Constantinople— or, to be more accurate, since Etelka Grauermann had set her right foot onto the platform as she was stepping down from the train there— he wasn't looking at his marriage and his overall domestic relations with only a dutiful glimpse out of the corner of his eye (while otherwise preoccupied with those features of his life which he deemed indispensable and toward which he'd steered his course); instead, he was now soaring or drifting above the topography of his life like a cloud through a sky grown clear, and he could look down on it from a high elevation. A strain he had until now always carried upright as if it were altogether a matter of course, never asking himself what justification or necessity there might be for him to do so, now slackened and lost all its essential meaning simply by declining from its peak level.

The marriage between Fraunholzer and Fräulein Küffer from Döbling had come about in the simplest manner imaginable—a textbook example of concupiscence and convenience in tandem. His position as new vice consul in Constantinople; his family's affluent circumstances (although Robby came from a line of officers); the young lady's wealth; her parents' desire for this alliance with Fraunholzer: it was on a nearby serving shelf cleared in this way that her love—and that's what it was (right up to this very day)—stood on offer to his infatuation as well as to a real obsession he had with her pallid but profuse Oriental style of beauty, heightened all over somehow by dark but delicate shadows that began around her eyes. The lack of any obstacles, the absence of any barriers in an open and welcoming space is often enough of a temptation by itself to make someone step inside; and in this case desire hurled him through the entrance with full force. Search high and low in the wide world—no one could ever have found a reason for failing to take this step into marriage with Mädi Küffer; and Fraunholzer hadn't been doing any searching. Children followed quickly, three right in a row in the first four years.

But then came that moment on the train station platform, as of which everything else got brushed off, even before it all began deteriorating on its own. Just as the dove in Kokoschka's famous painting *Monte Carlo* sweeps through the air before a background of sea and land, just as sweeping in his own flight was Fraunholzer as he soared up to a level of existence he'd never known before and submitted himself to its laws, starting with the three years of undeclared love in Constantinople, as if those years had been a period of preparation or a kind of novitiate. We don't know when his wife began to feel the intense pain of it, but it must have been back there, back then, and not just starting in 1920, when she was in Gmunden. If what Consul Fraunholzer experienced was a complete entity he could skim over all at once, however, the negative manifestation of it, like a sharp-edged stamp pressing down hard into someone's heart, found that heart to be no less full of determination and amplitude; in fact, if it were our job to make judgments instead of just turning in reports and then to organize a ceremony at which we could confer laurels accordingly, we might perhaps be most inclined to award the wreath to the heart of that beautiful long-suffering woman, whom the name Mädi, as she was still called in her family, was by now far from suiting. No, she was no girlish "Maidie" anymore. In Constantinople she found out about all the places where crabs hibernate, and she felt the lacerating crab of jealousy in the deepest and farthest hidden recesses of her heart, to which it was heroically exiled for the time being.

And later on as well, even when he was no longer dwelling exclusively in his interior, delicately but steadily plucking his life's sustenance—always uncertain still—from the sinews of his heart, but was constantly receiving fresh supplies in profusion from the outside. She suffered like an Indian chief at a stake expressly erected for torture. Any such idea as her communicating each and every news item to her relatives, the way Grete Siebenschein used to do at home, where the tidings of Stangeler's most recent criminal outrage—whatever it was this time—would quickly make their way through the family, or any communism of feelings like the one prevailing among René and his sisters was totally foreign to this woman with her fair, pale skin and her thick ebony braids. She stood by her husband's side, however much the ground shook under her feet. Here's what we want to come right out and say: nothing got skimmed over in her case, not in any way, shape, or form; so by that token she never forgot the nights that had been hers. Throughout this ordeal she was actually bereft of hope (at least it seemed so, for example to Frau Mary K.) and maintained a stony reserve toward Robby that could also be called unapproachability (that's exactly what appeared so wrongheaded and so utterly mistaken to Mary K., and she tried to oppose that stance on one occasion when she happened to see Mädi at her parents' house in Döbling). So it was that the whole attitude with which the Frau Consul General conducted herself—and admittedly it had its failings, but they only make it the more estimable—was bound to guarantee that the state of her marriage would emerge only very gradually, and never quite distinctly, to the view of the Küffer family at large, and Frau Mary K., as the older friend, was the only person who knew somewhat more—maybe—though far from anything very precise. But of course it all comes out in the end. It would really be advisable sometime, by the way, to bring that fact to the attention of all swindlers and frauds—a breed that's forever, and always with the same boring earnestness, making use of materials like flimsy cardboard, wet tissue paper, and frazzled old scraps of yarn as if they were wooden planks, leather, and strong ropes—finally to bring that fact, and pointedly, to the attention of all swindlers and frauds, which unfortunately can only be done, however, by the inimitable situations of life itself, at least when they're opening windows and offering views inside, views into the cabinet of wax figures or, say, past the venerable pulpit of some orator and into the true mirror of the situation located behind it. Enough of this—when it comes to Fraunholzer's wife, nothing was being hushed up through fraudulence or false pretenses, and she wasn't pretending to be in a better state or less distressed than she really was. On the other hand, outward circumstances also did their part to block the way toward any view emerging rapidly of how matters stood. It's true that their life in Gmunden after the war didn't take the couple as far away from the home she'd grown up in as the years in Constantinople had. Still, they weren't in Vienna. And then when Fraunholzer, after his official severance from government service on the strength of connections he'd made earlier in Belgrade, began casting about, until he ended up taking charge of a large Austrian firm's business affairs across a wide area, with his headquarters in Belgrade, well over a year passed while they were still considering whether the rest of the family ought to follow him and relocate there. Everything stayed up in the air. The older boy was enrolled in boarding school, and not long afterward so was the daughter, to whom her father seemed to have imparted the same solid understanding of how to get along in life that he possessed. And of course didn't Fraunholzer just have to go ahead and choose—after he'd undergone that serious illness of his, and that was only in 1919—one of the dustiest cities anywhere as the site of his professional work, which aroused understandable misgivings and in turn delayed his family's move, for they believed or hoped that in the course of his duties with the large firm that employed him an opportunity might present itself to relocate at any moment. It's conceivable, too, that Fraunholzer himself fostered this kind of speculation on the part of the Küffers, even though he had to have known that his knowledge of languages and his personal connections would be sure to point the way toward an ever-widening field of activity right where he already was, in the south. His yearlong stay in Belgrade didn't damage his health; the air is still more wholesome there than in Vienna. His illness after the First World War didn't actually fit any category of the type our Pompeius belonged to; it was like a stranger in his life, transient and then vanishing without a trace. Come to think of it, though, it wound up genuinely perfecting him in his type by causing him to grow stockier.

Only at a very late stage did Mary K. learn that the woman involved in Mädi's unhappiness was the sister of René Stangeler. By no means do we simply come to find out everything that's close, closer, closest to us. Somebody has to make mention of it first. Even in our conversations there are invisible walls, placed as though at random, and if they should now and again crumble when we're speaking, they'll just be thrown up once more as we're listening. That summer, in any event, for the duration of René's pathetic, hangdog campaign, about which Grete would naturally furnish Mary with periodically updated news bulletins, Grete began speaking a great deal about Etelka, after the time her new friend had spent in Vienna; it was on this visit that Grete had become acquainted with not just the Grauermanns, but also with Fraunholzer, even though fleetingly (but that's all a bright woman needs; it's only men, "well known for being obtuse and awkward," who require in detail all the minutiae that emerge from repeated contacts only to come away from them having extracted nothing but inessentials). The consul general had traveled to Vienna for a few days, and strictly for business reasons. But it was during that visit when Grete said to Mary that she got the impression Etelka didn't love this man—meaning Fraunholzer—anymore. A woman like Grete Siebenschein would have had as little need of René's past improprieties as of Etelka's present confidences to show her what kind of position Robby occupied—but was already in the process of losing—in the life of her latest friend.

That alarmed Mary, who after all was in Mädi's camp, as it were; at that point she was already thinking about having a talk with Mädi and finally trying to prevail on her to give up the obstinate attitude which was both detrimental and incomprehensible, in Mary's eyes, and which Mädi would have to drop now—but right now—if she wanted to keep the path of retreat open for her husband or even to make such a retreat possible in the first place.

Those who are plugging and patching away at a marriage—whatever it may be like, or even if it's over and done with and no longer like anything—will always develop that certain cheery tone of righteous goodwill toward themselves and the associated flatulence they so enjoy releasing. That gas wasn't heating Mary's legal efforts at restoration and rehabilitation all by itself, though. More of her energy was coming from the sad fact that she herself had been living as a widow for eighteen months—Oscar having died of some kind of cancer-like illness in February 1924—as well as from her (rightly) considering Mädi to be a very beautiful woman, and (even more rightly) herself, too. And as a result of parallels that she suspected might exist—and which for that matter actually might have existed—between the Fraunholzers' marriage and her own (more specifically, as far as the basics were concerned), Mary remained convinced that nothing whatsoever had really come to an end with the couple but that they still had a strong basis to build on. Following indirect routes like these, then, pursuing her tendencies toward restoration, was her way of staying true in her deepest self to those nights with Oscar.

Not mentioning a given matter can grow to be an unconscious habit; and as if that wall, invisible to her own self, weren't enough, Mary was hauling a second one behind it, that of deliberate silence (by itself it's much less stable and can sometimes reveal weak spots), when she came to realize how everything was connected, namely that the maiden name of Frau Fraunholzer's rival was Stangeler, which made her a sister of that René. She'd first begun maintaining real discretion in her behavior, though, as of June of that year, 1925, and as of Etelka Grauermann's stay in Vienna and the beginning of her friendship with Grete. We can see one of the most significant differences between men and women in the way men, granting that any of them know as much about life as women do, are loath to put their knowledge to use but will on occasion nonetheless get all caught up—by way of natural history or physics or whatever their interests may be (basically they're made up of nothing but spiteful remarks anyway)—in arguments full of irate disputation, in the course of which they keep on taking the data they've cobbled out of nothing more than some hobbled notion about congruity with settled laws and slamming them up against some concept or other about how things are supposed to be (meaning how things happen to suit them), just like a little child's fist that gets hurt by its foolish pounding—whereas no daughter of physics will engage in debate with her sweet old mother but will instead be constantly profiting, through her receptive attitude, by what Mama has to offer. (Scheichsbeutel's nature feminine? Where is this leading us? What an odious name in this context!) Yes, when physics' mannerly daughters share even their bedchamber with a hopelessly unmitigated metaphysical ninny, that is with a truly valid specimen of that other vexatious breed, the male of the species, then provision will be made to ensure that they can have whispered consultations on a daily basis off to the side somewhere, at the kitchen door or by the entryway, with their dear, gray-haired mother, whose arrival has been so quiet, and thereby dispose of the most in-comprehensible cases. Nothing like this was actually part of the way Grete Siebenschein was built, though. All she knew how to do was grab the bull by the horns, but that accomplishes nothing in the long run; to begin with, it's cruelty to animals, and it will only make the beast turn more stubborn.

And so Mary had a solid enough grounding in natural history to know (and to act in accordance with the knowledge) that between two people in love there's no such thing as discretion or indeed discreetness of any kind—unless in matters pertaining to that criminal organization referred to several times now, that is if there's cheating going on, though it will all come out in the end anyway!—but that the rise in tempera-ture where the use of language is involved, a heightening brought about by dual proximity, will in its turn cause the crystals of every such good resolve to lose their clear edges and finally to dissolve altogether.

Anyone familiar with (taking care to note) the physics of a person or a situation will never burden that person or situation beyond the weight-bearing capacity. It isn't humane to leave the cashbox open long enough for someone to rob it. "Nobody has a right to subject others to hard tests," as Dr. Ferry Siebenschein used to like to say. Whatever you tell to one member of a couple, you've already informed the other one about as well. And it was for that reason that Mary K. never mentioned anything to Grete Siebenschein about her association with Frau Consul General Fraunholzer and about those inclinations to attempt to restore her friend's marriage.

Throughout the whole summer, incidentally, Mädi never came to Vienna, nor did she go to the estate her widowed mother had in Wolkersdorf, where the older woman ordinarily stayed until around the middle of September.

Mädi had also changed in her outward appearance since the war; Gnaeus Pompeius wasn't the only one. And just as with him, to her advantage, if such a thing were possible. We want to say that her attractiveness was underscored; it grew more noticeable and more sharply silhouetted, as if outlined and contrasted more intensely by a retouching brush. The shadows grew deeper. Her figure had become somewhat more filled out, though only by a very little, but her face, oddly enough, was more spare; it may have just looked that way, because her features had been exquisitely sharpened by pain until they became exactly the opposite of what people call puffy. There vanished from her entire being, spiritual as well as physical, the last remnants, if one will, of shapeless, contented-cow baby fat, of which she had once been endowed with her fair share. Her filled-out look had always had about it at the same time a slenderness in her limbs, especially in those beautiful legs of hers (just like Frau Mary), and that feature, now that she was a bit more full, was even more distinctly marked. Along with the modeling of her face, and thus of her whole head, her hands had also developed a more delicate shape; they'd always been long and narrow, but now they appeared almost gaunt and yet very refined and spirited. (One might well recall poor old Herr von Stangeler here.) Dr. Döblinger, who had seen and become slightly acquainted with Mädi in Gmunden, was enthralled almost to the point of paroxysm but still said all sorts of scurvy and vilifying things about her, which was just the way he was (he couldn't keep from doing it in regard to Mary K., either); one of the observations he made at that time was nonetheless very pertinent after all—what he did was compare the Frau Consul General to a woman older by quite a number of years, namely Frau Pastré-Meriot, Editha's mother.

And indeed Frau Fraunholzer was also one who had something of the fanatic far down in her depths; she was possessed of a penchant and a passion for the art of pain, and she practiced it not to reap any of the benefits of narcissism but simply because she was pursuing her talent. She, too, had about herself the air of one of those beautiful martyrs in rare old hagiographic paintings, though not "standing with one foot in the realm of death," as Geyrenhoff had expressed himself fourteen years earlier in referring to Frau Pastré, née Meriot. Her store of meekness seems to be concentrated in the deep vales of shadow that begin around her eyes and then again to be suffused all about her with utmost gossamer fineness like an aura suffusing her wax-pale skin.

Our sleeping-car train is still en route; just now it's in the stretch between Novi Sad and Subotica. Pompeius, our Gnaeus Pompeius, out of character, is still sitting on the bed in his pajamas and, much more out of character yet, chain-smoking Serbian cigarettes. Yes, he was thinking just now about his wife, whom he'd never called Mädi, but always Lea, which was her real name. He began a descent from that sky grown clear, coming down lower over the topography of his life and not looking at it any longer from so high aloft; now, details skimmed over from a great height and submerged for many a long year rose up to meet him out of the ground mist, which itself was enfolding him like a cloud, a cloud formation on a totally different layer from the one he'd been on before his descent, himself a cloud for so long a time, a high cloud sailing rapidly and far above such contact with the ground as he was having now. Now it was all blending. Now the mist of palpable remembrance came surging left and right around his temples, swirling around his forehead and eyes, gathering in more thickly, making shadows like old chestnut trees in a promenade one can see running along the depth of space, deepening the vales of shadow even more and bringing them alive with the burnished and fragrant russet of memory. And as Lea now emerged so distinct and manifest, surrounding him as though from all sides at once, she also brought along an intimate familiarity with herself as a whole person that he alone could have had (and that Frau Mary K. lacked entirely). At one blow she would again be his completely, and he knew it, if only he himself could bring the same thing to her, resolutely leaving a long and high-spanning arch behind him as a form resolved and closed off at the place where it once more made contact with the ground, the solid earth. Lea wasn't just long-suffering; she was long-enduring as well.

And faster than the split second between breathing in and out, or even before his next heartbeat, for that matter, Fraunholzer, traveling along his *trópoi*, had already followed his thinking (insofar as we can call it thinking, in a case like this) to its conclusion, down to the last detail, in the same hurried, hackneyed way we all do. He was already in Gmunden. These really are basically nothing but spiteful remarks.

And only the Higher Zihalism can deflect them, parrying through adroit counterthrusts that turn back the tomfoolery and reduce it to an absolute minimum—in every given instance, by virtue of its charge, and as a matter of principle, to go fully bureaucratic here. This Higher Zihalism—even where scrutiny of the most punctilious would appear to present no possibility of containing, even by implication, the atomic nucleus of a formal, stately baroque political drama (whereby it could attain to outward coherence of design, to form, that is)—will proudly forego everything else and systematically interdict the tomfoolery through resort to appropriate measures. That, after all, is exactly what people are lacking today: dignity. The *austriaco-hispanicus* variety of the Higher Zihalism is the ultimate force of opposition able to counter what is known as "the present day"; hence it belongs in the Museum of Counterexamples, curated by Herr Kriegar-Ohs (the character in Christian Morgenstern's *Gallows Songs* to whom von Korff presents that august institution with a copy of the score of *The Marriage of Figaro*). Dear senior councillor, you strange bird! If an ancient and honorable air of lofty Spanish ceremonial is not what animates you, then your ways are just Greek to me. Please remain on your guard so you don't end up allowing them to come at you jabbering their uncouth demotic tongue. That would be the end for certain.

Having come back down to earth in the speeding train somewhere between Novi Sad and Subotica, but without really admitting it to himself, Fraunholzer found himself sleepy, crept into his berth, and turned out the light.

At eight thirty the next morning he rode from the South Station to the Vadászkurt, the Hunting Horn. He was partial to this eminently solid and slightly old-fashioned hotel—even though he didn't completely fit in—because there is where the conservative Hungarian estate owners stayed. During and after breakfast he called to confirm three or four appointments his business affairs had required him to make even before his vacation trip to Budapest, and the same would be the case during his equally short upcoming stay in Vienna as well. Everything fell into place conveniently, all the preliminaries lining up in proper order, dovetailing exactly as he'd hoped (because for a few of his meetings he needed to draw on information he'd gathered while arranging the one before it). Nothing else arose to cause concern, either, and he had all he needed in this capably managed, carpet-quiet hotel imbued with a seigneurial style of living. This was Fraunholzer's own style, too, though it wasn't inborn; he had acquired it painstakingly and by his own exertion instead. It was not even remotely the style of an Austrian officer's family, not even that of a general, which is what his father had been. This original character, who could at times be downright boorish, belonged to an exceptional type, one the old Royal and Imperial Austrian Army seemed to throw up once in a while at almost regular intervals here and there. That fact would make it seem as if the very existence of these Galgótzys and Fraunholzers, singular as they might be, were nonetheless grounded in the deeper structure of the whole system on which they were based rather than in mere chance. That note was rarely struck, to be sure, but it was always within reach, just as certain instruments of the orchestra are called on only sparingly—the xylophone or the celesta, or the contrabassoon (the instrument with which the elder Fraunholzer could most aptly be compared). There were once people in this world who could somehow contrive to give a rough tongue-lashing to a member of the imperial family after large-scale troop maneuvers but who would find an opportunity the next time around, whether they were still occupying the same rank or now holding an even higher one, to switch course and issue a commendation to the very same archduke. What was most out of character for Artillery General Fraunholzer, however, was the weakness of the force with which he thrust his family to the side; men of his kind generally tend to establish a reign of terror and set great store by upholding it, after all. But it didn't bother our military commander in the slightest that he spoiled his son, for example. And plump little Pompeius would graciously consent to his father's personally bringing him breakfast in bed and gently waking him, whereupon the boy would improve the shining hour of encroaching reality with a pained and jaded comment suitable for one tested so early in the fires of experience: "*Oh, que la vie est dure!*" Yes, he could chatter away in French quite rapidly; for that matter, he learned as quickly as a sponge absorbs water. It might be tempting to say, then, that Pompeius's seigneurial manner was founded on solid bedrock from early on. Not quite, though—what was missing was the fragrant, lustrous undergirding, the foundation conferred by a long tradition of which the recipient is entirely unaware. What Fraunholzer actually owed his father more than anything was the unbroken continuity of a self-regard never called into doubt; his talents and abilities, able to twine themselves around the sturdy trellis this acceptance provided, took care of all the rest. It might well be that the father had intuited the boy's proficiency early on, cautiously safeguarding and nurturing it on the strength of his possibly housing in his own innermost self a delicate and easily wounded nature. The general's pedagogical strategy would prove later on to be the proper one, at any rate. If today Pompeius made seigneurial demands on others, he was himself more than capable of living up to the effort needed to fulfill them, and quite offhandedly at that. Later on, for instance, his coworkers in the company that employed him and the one large department which he supervised would yet once again be astounded— as if for the first time, never mind that the same result transpired year after year—when they verified that his salary, which had over time been boosted by generous increases, along with profit sharing and travel expenses, made up only a paltry fraction, in fact merely a drop in the bucket, of the business he brought in through the skill with which he could close deals.

So things had been running smoothly ever since he'd set foot in the Hunting Horn; everything he needed was right at his fingertips. All the more clearly did he become aware, then, that the same feeling he had had yesterday evening, which had made him feel like a target directly in the firing line of arrows whizzing toward him, was now coming back.

He could feel tremendous pain ready to burst in on him, very close, as if behind a thin wall already bulging from the pressure. He was afraid. Yes, it was as simple as that. He wanted to go running to Lea. He was standing wide open, like a city facing the enemy when its walls have fallen.

His situation manifested itself negatively at first: he refrained from placing a call to Városligeti Fasor or to Grauermann's office, although he took it as a certainty that Pista was in Budapest. Usually he made it a point to get in touch right away and let them know on Vilma királynö út that he was in town.

The heat of the day was moderate for Budapest in August; it had been known to happen, after all, that the asphalt paving, half melted and gooey in the blazing sun, could cause a woman's shoe to get stuck by its heel and pull it right off her foot, so that the poor lady would nearly go sprawling in front of one of those gigantic double-decker buses just before it came rumbling by and be saved only through the extreme dexterity of the driver, in whose nimbleness, by the way, could perhaps be discerned a holdover, albeit in quite altered form, from the tradition of those master coachmen in the Hungarian countryside, able to lead a four-horse hunting wagon at top speed straight along and through a deep ravine—uphill and downhill, across and athwart—talking to the horses the whole time and never a single one ever stumbling or falling . . . Fraunholzer got out of the vehicle and strolled along for a while. He'd already finished his first business meeting. More than that, in fact. In the course of it he had found and with apparent nonchalance seized on an excellent opportunity to earn the gratitude of someone with whom he considered it important to keep on friendly terms; it came about simply through his agreeing to take care of a few little matters in Vienna (which, thanks to his connections, he would be able to arrange to complete satisfaction and with no further ado lying comfortably in bed in his hotel room: of course he didn't mention that part of it but instead just amiably stated his willingness to do whatever he could). In this way he was able to spare one of his business partners the need to procure a visa that would involve losing time by having to make a trip to Vienna with an uncertain outcome (Fraunhol-zer even went so far, after everything had been taken care of within three minutes from his room at the Hotel Ambassador in Vienna, as to convey the favorable outcome on the same day in a friendly little note to Pest). All right, then. He liked Budapest every time he went there, even though he wasn't very fond of the Hungarians; that said, however, their full-blooded capacity for living life on every front and in every nook and cranny could have a really captivating effect. Seven years after the country had lost a war and had had its borders drastically truncated, this city was living as if at a peak moment in its history.

Meanwhile, cold, dark floodwaters began encircling the bustling, sun-filled islands of his activity. And they were rising. Why did he go down the steps of the Oktogon subway station and take the next train that came along? Did he really want to spend his free time taking a walk in Városliget, the city park? Robby rode only as far as Bajza utca, though. From there it's just a short way across to the boulevard. But he didn't head that way, either. Why should he? Totally senseless. How often he'd walked along here, but in a different frame of mind. He got back on the train and traveled as far as he could, which meant to the last stop, Vörösmarty tér. Once he'd gone up the steps and was back at street level, he noticed Honnegger standing by the monument with an attaché case under his arm (so that was it: this is where he'd had to wind up). They hailed each other at exactly the same moment.

Here is the place to say a word about how Honnegger's musicality and general temperament had developed. It became apparent even in his earlier years that he was not, and did not want to become, one of those types who proceed along the increasingly sterile, uncreative path from music itself to musical monomania and go sliding further and further down it as if into the ever-narrowing mouth of a funnel, de-positing inside the world of mathematical and musical forms whatever in their lives is unclear and not in their control, as if none of it demanded incessant effort but had just magically crystallized on its own into something definitive. The gates of music stand open only too wide. Honnegger had by and large taken the opposite route. Deeming it impossible that such a degree of precision could correspond with everything else about his nature, he drifted ever further away from music in favor of substantiating life's situations and circumstances directly while managing to overlook totally the immense expanses of precision lying in wait just behind him. Which didn't make his life any easier, it goes without saying.

Openness on that scale, after all, can soon turn a person into a glue trap that flocks of birds keep fluttering around. All sorts of creatures get stuck to it and flap their wings frantically, because more and more of them become that person's concern, while on the one-to-one level, paradoxically enough, individuals like that appear less and less interested. We might say that a person with such a disposition becomes a target for arrows that are in no way intended to pierce the flesh and that indeed do not wound, but simply cling instead like pins to a magnet. Through this power of attraction, however, that man or woman, even though a weak shot, gains the ability to fire off a bull's-eye, as it were, and ends up in fact being able to exercise power over bird and beast or whatever else is whirling and swirling in the air. Without fear, too, because not a one of them poses any danger any longer as it goes whizzing past and buzzing about wounds and pains before the arrow strikes.

So it was that Honnegger often knew a great deal he didn't want to but always what he needed to, a capacity which, we might note in passing, benefited his diplomatic career, just as he—born to music, lofty of pedigree, that is, but striking out on a path into his real life—gradually forged closer and closer bonds with his professional side.

Which was the kind of encounter that started as soon as Fraunholzer and Honnegger began approaching one another by the monument, a meeting of two people who need to sort through issues long kept in mind—for they weren't blind—and whose time had now come, through the coincidence of their bumping into one another. Without exchanging many preliminaries they sought out a quiet space and got down to essentials at the Café Gerbeaud, all the way at the rear. While they were being waited on, Honnegger was thinking calmly and fluidly, like a person writing in a clear hand: it was plain that Fraunholzer would at some point have to confront the aftermath of the raging fire Etelka had ignited here this summer; he was going to have to examine the scene and inspect the damage closely, especially where it might not be so visible to the eye. A great deal would depend on who would now guide this hapless man toward that path, and by what approach he would come upon it, through the clarity of speech or the torture of silence. It was important here to forestall the wrath of women who would now feel themselves entitled to cast the first stones of facts (there they lay, so close to hand) at one who had dared to take actions they compressed ever so tightly with their knees. The odium of being the first to break the news, of stepping directly into the field of kinetic tension between a couple, of treading onto the fruitful soil where pungent herbs of insecurity thrive but also artful blossoms of distrust are cultivated in trim rows—Honnegger was indeed aware of this odium as a circumstance he would just have to put up with, a grudge directed even toward an aristocrat at times, though a mere mosquito bite, provided his bearing maintained the stability proper to his station. It was out of the question that Fraunholzer could remain ignorant of facts being so widely circulated here in Pest. He would surely be calling on the Russows on Döbrentei utca, where Frau von G., a close friend of their daughter, was a regular visitor; the full weight of this family's prominence and distinction would help shield matters behind protective armor. So now, what Honnegger had to do was talk.

And he did.

The first arrow hit the target, shaking the stand it was on as if struck by an ax blow.

He also told him everything about Imre von G. and answered every ensuing question as well as he could.

It was not very bright in these somewhat prissy rooms but rather cool and hushed instead.

Honnegger saw something he would never have thought it possible even to imagine (and he was well aware of his reaction even at the time): Pompeius was crying. A moist gleam welled up quickly in his eyes, then a mighty wave was forced back, and it was over.

"Just think," said Honnegger, "that perhaps you don't know even what you're being spared."

"I think I do know, though. I was never one to carry a spare."

Honnegger advocated for Etelka the whole time, playing a role in which he would once have had a hard time picturing himself. "Our friend Pista isn't named Grauermann for nothing; he's a real gray man, chestnut-brown hair or not; that's what he always was, but now what he really was these past few years is coming out—or rather what he *wasn't* and has never been. This woman has been driven into a state of extreme conflict, which is her way of trying to keep hold of something she could never become as long as she breathes the same air he does. That explains her excesses. That's what you have to look at; that's the key, not that there are men involved. Everybody plies the instrument he or she is given to play, and for a woman that of course means love affairs. But I believe in this case that's a secondary symptom for Etelka, as it were, however paradoxical that might sound. Who is this Imre anyway?! Nothing. It's really not about him at all, or about any of the others who thought they were next in line. What we have here is a remarkable woman fiercely rebelling against the dictatorship of mediocrity while admittedly plunging at the same time into the deepest damage she can inflict on her own. I'll show you what I mean in its purest form, like a textbook specimen, by telling you about an incident that marks the peak of this extreme heightening and of course led to unforeseen consequences—for Pista too, sorry to say, because he really didn't deserve anything like this . . . They had guests at their place on the Fasor for some reason or another, probably related to his business; people from out of town were there, too; I didn't know them. They were invited along with other guests from here. It was a supper with ten or twelve people. Etelka did these things very well. You could say on the whole that in this regard she and Pista worked outstandingly well together through a kind of—let's say cold calculation. That's what I've always called it in my own mind. The fact is I admired it. They operated the gadgetry of life with skillful management, the way you handle a bath heater. Oh yes, she was very versed in things like this and had the knack of being a gray wife to her gray husband. Completely. But not exclusively—there's the rub. Because it seems you need to be able to function that way exclusively, that one way only and no other. A few days before the gathering she begged me to come. She was afraid she might not be able to get through it. I had to sit next to her at the table. Parties like these are a horror to me, and the very few I can't get out of are still many too many. But I said yes. Maybe I had the feeling I could prevent a disaster, but I was duping myself badly. Well, to keep it short: the meal hadn't proceeded very far when all of a sudden she jumped up from the table—I can see her strong round face in front of me now, all pale and virtually overpowered by sheer despair—and showed all her guests the door. She would have stopped at nothing to throw out each and every last person, literally, should a single one have hesitated to leave. I could outright see the potential for physical on-slaught in the way the muscles of her bare arms were working. But nobody hesitated. A uniform crowd of silent guests poured into the reception room; it reminded me on the whole of those diplomatic conferences with a disappointing outcome, or none at all. Pista gravely shook hands with each and every person outside the door: 'You see,' he said calmly, even placidly, 'how very ill my poor wife is at the mo-ment.' He conducted himself exquisitely. He put me in mind of a man in a burning house who stays unruffled while pondering what items lying around here and there it might be possible to take away in the face of destruction already in progress and no longer avoidable, clearly conscious that little things can make a significant difference in easing the hardship of having to make camp somewhere near the scene of the blaze by providing comfort that's twice as soothing because it's makeshift ... I was among the last to leave. The door from the front salon into the vestibule was abruptly flung open. For a brief moment Etelka appeared in the doorway. 'Teddy, you stay with Pista,' she said in a strong voice that ruled out any disagreement, and then she vanished. I didn't see her again that evening. What struck me at intervals was the absolute invisibility of the servants. Nobody hurried into the an-teroom to help the departing guests into their coats. In the kitchen they seemed to have been fully aware that something appalling had happened. In Hungary yet, land of hospitality. The serving maids had just been at their duties in the dining room. Once we were alone, I began right away to look for the lead-up, for anything that might have precipitated the whole episode, for the *déclic*. After all, even though I was sitting right next to Etelka, I had noticed absolutely nothing along those lines, no warning sign, no goading, no snide remarks, not even the most mildly controversial topic of conversation. Pista couldn't think of anything either. After a few minutes he turned on an electric hot plate and prepared Turkish coffee for us. He asked me, too, if I didn't want to eat something, but all I could do was simply laugh. He paced back and forth, looking solemn but sharp as well. 'Etelka is sick,' he said at one point, and then, 'I'll go and see how she is.' He was talking himself back into something he had tried talking himself out of not long before. That worked out well for her, though. He did the right thing. I went back the next day. Not one single word was spoken about the incident, neither then nor later. So that's how Etelka Stangeler threw her guests out."

"She was right; she was totally in the right," said Fraunholzer. He was now crying with almost no resistance. His eyes were wet. Where they were sitting, the two men were screened off by themselves. Pompeius was crying. On the battlefield.

He kept shaking Honnegger's hand for a long time as they said goodbye. And from that moment on he drifted through Budapest like a ghost for two days. He visited no one. Kept to his hotel, avoiding even his usual café along the Danube, by Petöfi tér, where he ordinarily enjoyed sitting looking out at the river, which cools the city along its banks, there exposed to the wind, observing the whole array of bustling activity on the water and the large ships advancing with pitiable slowness toward the mountain into the mouth of whose tunnel everything that passes the Chain Bridge and makes it lively will unfailingly disappear . . . in Fraunholzer's mind this image had always made up the distilled essence of Budapest, and perhaps what he felt here was what we could more plainly call the romantic spirit of this city. Once he had gone swimming at Margaret Island in the Danube and was sitting in one of the wide inner stone rings that encircle the hot springs and separate cooler from warmer basins, beginning with the farthest one, refreshing and cold, and moving to the innermost one, which is hot; switching back and forth while stretched out under a blue sky brings about a sense of well-being all its own, as if the sulfurous water were transmitting it through the open pores. There he sat, *Pompeius in thermis*, and that's exactly what he looked like. Even so, he found the earsplitting noise all around him unbearable, a ceaseless racket throughout the entire sunlit swimming area, a constant din produced by children and adults alike . . . After he'd dressed again he walked along the island under the old trees. It was here, and then once again during his journey to Vienna, in Hegyeshalom, known as Strass-Sommerein in German—the name never fails to prompt in a speaker of that language the reply *Sommeraus*, for symmetry ("summer in" and "summer out"); to live summer in and summer out at the gateway of the East as it commences here and as if under its colossal overhang would be bound to draw the most mournful sounds from the lulling pan flutes of melancholy—it was under the mighty old trees of Margaret Island, then, and again in Hegyeshalom while waiting in the railway carriage during the customs procedures at the Austrian border that he very nearly succeeded in making the leap to Gmunden. It came over him, the cloud, and enfolded him. One moment he pushed it away; the next moment he pulled it back.

Things went better in Vienna, where the ground wasn't burning under his feet, as it were. Nonetheless, he kept to himself here, too, as if isolated, proving totally powerless, for example, to make a telephone call to Asta's husband, Building Inspector Haupt, as he'd meant to, if only because he'd never answered her letter and then because of the need to bring them up to date so they'd be better informed of developments. For the rest, his business dealings went so very smoothly, almost strikingly so, that he had them all taken care of by Saturday afternoon (it was August 29) and was sitting in his hotel room at an empty desk, a notepad in front of him that showed only crossed-out writing on a sheet he didn't bother tearing off so that a blank new one, pure white, could present itself. He'd read almost everything in the newspapers and bought the usual idiotic magazines, too, and he'd already put into his hand luggage a large package from Kugler's for Etelka and some marrons glacés from Demel's. Now there began a concentrated attack of emptiness from all sides, its spectral battle formations on the move, pressing in on him ever closer. A car horn sounded. Fraunholzer reached the night express in plenty of time. It would be too late for him to make a connection with one of the postal buses out there, but that made no difference; Fraunholzer was almost never able to summon much patience for hustle and bustle anyway and preferred taking a horse-drawn carriage from a country station.

On Friday, August 21, at seven thirty in the morning, René Stangeler woke up in his room in Vienna and was met with an intense scent of lavender. The marble washstand holding a small, tightly closed bottle filled with lavender water was about four and a half meters away from the bed. Also, the sensation lasted much more briefly than we can indicate here. The scent seemed to have entered his nose on its own power, directly from his head, as it were, even to the extent that he found the process and himself to be identical in some indisputable way: he and it were the same.

"That would come in handy," he thought with pleasure, "then I wouldn't have to buy it on the Graben."

He lay on his back without moving, as though he were waiting for something.

And it came.

He suddenly thought of the little gold locket Editha Pastré had once given him.

Where on earth was it now? He felt his way backward, tracing a path through the bottoms of boxes and a little storage chest where he'd seen it not so long before. Yes!

Now he jumped up, brown as a faun.

René liked sleeping without nightclothes.

The locket was where he remembered it. He opened it by cautiously inserting the blade of his penknife. The cover popped open. There was her picture. "Unchanged," he realized. "She's just as she was then."

Then. When was that? The year of the *tropidonotus* serpent (that's what his chronology looked like). The year of Paula.

The year of the Strudlhof Steps.

Like a curtain fluttering high up in the wind and opening a view to the rooms behind it, the sound of the words now drifted toward him and a picture of the place hovered above him. He stood in the middle of the room with his eyes closed, the small bauble on its chain in his hand. There was space around him here, and inside him, too, for that matter, opening far out so that he could turn around in it like a weather vane, all depending on which way the wind was blowing. Now more than ever before. He stood waiting. No worries. Not about finances, either; seven payments for various jobs of tutoring and coaching had come his way all at once—the largest fees arriving, oddly enough, when he was going through a bad time, having no idea how he was going to drum up money and hardly ever leaving his room. (Only on the evening after he returned from Budapest—he'd spent it with the captain, unburdening his heart, with Thea Rokitzer on hand and listening, by the way.) He now felt free again for the first time since those awful days when Grete's dreadful rantings and ravings from Naples had kept bursting in on him like miniature bombs, so to speak, in his garden room at the Grauermanns' on the Fasor. It even seemed to him now as if he were tasting freedom for the first time in his life.

Fourteen years ago, then.

In August. Around the twentieth.

Maybe even fourteen years to this very day or the next. He felt coolness on his skin like foam from a bath; the air held a morning freshness, since this room faced north. He looked up and out, past the mighty spread of the foliage at its fullest, over toward the buildings opposite. A sharp white gleam flashed out from a window sash somebody was closing. The sound could be heard in the stillness.

Faced with such freedom inside him and such emptiness all around him as they unceasingly called to him in silence and seemed to enclose spectral regiments of forces waiting in readiness, on alert for valid orders, there suddenly struck him like an arrow shot from the ceiling an idea so utterly astonishing that he—right there, and as he was—slowly sat down under its weight, growing heavier as it ripened, on the nearest stool and remained sitting there like a new rendering of Rodin's *Thinker*, albeit somewhat weaker in every respect.

Well, he could turn this freedom to account by... making his mind up about Grete and honorably letting himself in for whatever that decision entailed. After all, she'd been... been... *shown* to him (he couldn't think of a different or better word at the moment); it wouldn't be right just to disavow that fact, and bypassing it through a simple "No, no" without some solid reason was downright unthinkable.

At no time had he ever made his mind up about Grete, and he realized that now.

The telephone rang sharply through the empty apartment.

Just by the sound of the ring René had a feeling that the call was for him, not for his brother-in-law, the building surveyor, now occupied at the ministry, or for Asta, in case somebody or other thought she was back in Vienna ...

He went out through the corridor to the front room, undressed as he was and still holding the locket in his hand. But what he was really doing during these few seconds was in fact walking into and through himself, the way a man might walk through a long, straight set of rooms, leaving all the doors open as he passes through, so that at the far end his glance can turn back unimpeded to the beginning: the time before he had met Grete, the time when it would have been entirely possible for him to live without her. To be able to return to that point and find a hold there, to click into place as into the notch of a tautened crossbow seemed to him now to be the only way of truly returning to her, and of his own free will, so to speak.

"Well, as I live and breathe!" boomed a jovial voice on the other end, after René had said hello. "Redivivus. Allow me as the first order of business to extend the most heartfelt of salutations, Cadet." (Eulenfeld often called him this; in his language it meant something like "a creature on the whole still endowed with the disposition of a moonstruck calf." His attitude was not entirely unrelated to the de rigueur manifestations of goodwill—known to us from earlier days—accorded to creatures of the hound-dog variety at the Consular Academy, while it contained at the same time a kind of general pardon for understandable youthful excesses—they had good cause to be understandable, after all!—to which the older well-wisher was himself not disinclined to succumb even today and which thereby included the elder's own little peccadilloes within the general pardon.) "Are you doing tolerably well? I've been trying over and over, though in vain, to reach you. The last times were yesterday and the day before. Are you all right? Went through a good deal in July, didn't you? Our little Grete is in Paris, as rumor has it. Well, good. I imagine you've been out in the country up to now? Working? Very well, then."

He told René that they—meaning his whole crowd—were thinking of driving out to Greifenstein on the Danube on Saturday at noon. Did he have anything planned for Saturday morning? Was he free? Yes, René said, but he'd rather not go away this coming Saturday or Sunday because he was expecting a telegram from Grete from Paris; she was going to be returning to Vienna. "I imagine she's had her fill of Cornel and company!?" Eulenfeld commented. ("But she probably won't come back for a few more days..." was what now ran through René's mind.) "But that's just what I wanted to ask you—not to come with us, but to stay in Vienna. Here's the explanation—I want to make the trip; I've had a hard week and urgently need some relaxation. And I've already made some arrangements in Greifenstein for Saturday anyway—you know what I mean; we all need a little recreation to soothe our nerves. Editha most likely won't be coming out until Sunday, if she comes at all; she's got various irons in the fire, and she gets those headaches of hers now and then, so—long story short—she's staying at home on Saturday afternoon. She'll be left all alone, all by herself. So I was wondering if you would stop by and keep her company for tea. She thinks very highly of you; I'm not sure you know how much. You'd be doing me a big favor. You did say you're free. There's no relying on Melzer; he might even want to come with us. All well and good, then. She'll give you a call soon and invite you."

Stangeler went back into his room.

He'd been holding the locket by its chain the whole time.

On the following day, however, Saturday August 22, in the afternoon (Melzer is just now beginning to gather momentum and speed through his *trópoi*), he was wearing it around his neck, next to his skin under his shirt, low on his breastbone, for the chain was long. He was damp all over, his hair, his handkerchief, his underwear all fresh and cool from lavender water. He'd been lavish with it after his bath. Moving in a cloud of fragrance, he turned off Währinger Strasse and walked along Waisenhaus Gasse—long since renamed Boltzmann Gasse by now—on the right side, by the park wall of the Clam-Gallas Palace, headed for a detour down the Strudlhof Steps: not to take them was utterly out of the question; the afternoon absolutely mandated it.

Much as his actions right now had basically been of his own arranging, at least to some extent—the little golden disc resting on his chest, scheduling ample time to take a completely different and longer route— he had in essence been led here nonetheless by a kind of unconscious process that obviated any other choice. And now, because he felt as if he were being more or less pushed and shoved along, he hesitated before the corner around which, dropping straight and short and downward into greenery, the inconceivable stage was standing and waiting where events unfathomable to him had once taken place; now, though, the encounters he'd once witnessed as they played out before him, as well as the whole lead-up and background to them, which he would later learn about from Asta, no longer struck him as unfathomable—rather, they were past and gone; rather, Old Man Schmeller wasn't going to turn up again with Melzer behind him, above, and he himself with Paula Schachl and Grauermann, down below.

The street was empty, the sun shining down on it and irradiating the domes of greenery to the rear.

René went along slowly. He sank downward. Like a swaying autumn leaf. He remained alone. He encountered no one on the ramps; chance had it so. His ear, keenly attuned, had already caught the fountain's murmured soliloquy while he was still above it. He tarried even more. The warmth came closer in on him, and with it the silence. Down below, on Pasteur Gasse, he turned back and examined the site, marveling at how it lay as if embedded miles deep in the late-summer silence of a city now emitting no sound, uttering no word, and now—now of all times—keeping perfectly silent for moments at a stretch.

Then he went on, walking in the direction of the Bohemia Station. The doors of the buildings along the street behind it were standing in the heat like the open lids of crypts. But the stairwell was cool, holding the civilized-subdued odors of decorous living, the mask the genius loci wears in the city, a last remnant, now just a reduced symbol, of the smoky scent of the penates. The stairs and landings were still damp from the concierge's Saturday ministrations with bucket and brush.

The bell sounded shrill, as if it were ringing in an empty house.

"Oh how nice, René," said Editha. She let him in, not opening the door all the way, and ducked behind it smoothly like a fragrant cloud; a full-bodied, sweet-smelling aroma came up against the odor of lavender, tangy and almost bitter by comparison, with no mingling at first, like adjoining solid bodies. The outfit she was wearing struck him at once as somehow foreign in its bright, iridescent colors and its cut, which augmented her figure and enfolded her in swathes of material. "Plenty of tea to drink, as much as you want, you old Siberian, no limit; I've also made maté if you'd like to try it." They'd stepped all the way inside. Just now, this room, with its two tall door panels left and right identically painted in white enamel and the Kahlenberg visible in the background through the window seemed to Stangeler in some peculiar way like a vehicle for transportation rather than a fixed and immobile spot; it was more like the gondola of a hot-air balloon or something of that kind. "Maté," he said, "that's South American, isn't it?" "Yes," she answered, "would you like to try it? I drink it all the time." She poured him some. He leaned without self-consciousness over the flat, broad cup, now colored by the peculiar green tinge of the beverage, and breathed in its aroma while raising his eyes to her, still bending over in the same position. She smiled. From the other side of the tea table her face came very slightly closer to his as she leaned down a bit more. Seized with a distinct feeling that this whole room, along with its occupant, was now somehow making its way inside him through every pore and from every direction and coming back out of his mouth like a streamer, he improvised, but as if reading from a text:

> "Oh smoky, far-off ports, expansive spaces;
> The anchor chain runs rumbling, then lies still.
> Distance means crudeness, yet it is my will
> To go; a gentle pull within impels me to new places.
>
> An empty sky. A palm as if of glass
> Stares out from some remote, haze-blurred horizon.
> My own land rasps my heart, can but harass
> Me, yearning for the secret home my vision lies in.

Hoist all the anchors fully. No longer cleave the salt waves!
Airborne, the gondola ascending shows
Both strand and land receding. From high up
Objects are small. Space cramped. What hurts us here just goes

Its way, dispersed in light now breaking in upon us
Here in a room or gondola; broken years unravel,
Talks long past and forgotten. But it's once more assembled—
The easy burden and the freight with which I travel."

He was perplexed when he came to the end. She looked at him in
sheer amazement, and they both kept complete silence, not moving a
muscle for a time.

"What is that? Who's it by?" she finally asked.

"By the maté," he answered, feeling guilty and explaining, though
guardedly; for a time he had in his mind's eye the picture of Etelka,
Government Councillor Guys, and a Latin poem his father had made
him translate.

"They've all driven out there," she said, and pointed in the direction
of the mountains. "Nothing but noise and crowds. Don't we have it
nicer?" She held René's lower arm while she was speaking. Then she
stood up and took a few rapid, almost vehement steps toward the
window. "My desire is to be somewhere far away," she said, only half
aloud and as if singing, "being somewhere far away again. Oh, René,
we all need to avoid returning to what's past and gone. When we do,
it turns its back on us and shows us an empty hillside covered with
debris and dead brushwood, the back of a flat slope where we'd been
expecting a significant elevation, the back of an empty space, nothing
more. And it's because we didn't turn our own backs with enough
resolution. So now there's almost nothing to see except a 'haze-blurred
horizon,' as you just put it . . ." René was nowhere close to sharing her
viewpoint (and on this subject he was in agreement with the major),
but his astonishment at her peculiarly bookish or archaic way of expressing herself was much stronger and more to the fore. It never dawned
on him that she might have been quoting from something she'd read.
What was much more present in his mind was the enormous appeal

of the whole situation—that someone right here, not even very far from the Strudlhof Steps, come to think of it, could be soaring high up in a white-enameled gondola and speaking in such a distinctive manner. He was paying no heed to the content of her words, to the effect that she wanted to be far away again or that she'd spoken about returning to old haunts. Now she again started moving briskly, the rich, delicate fabric swirling in every color of the rainbow around her limbs. Not only could he see them clearly; he also realized she wasn't wearing anything underneath. The heat made that seem reasonable enough. She took a few steps closer to him once more, her face confronting him before the distant backdrop of the vista outside like that of a hovering dragonfly or some other strange insect with tunnels and towers of the unknown stored behind its unfathomable eyes. She was very far from still being the same woman as that Editha Pastré from the rock-climbing episode in the country, but he would naturally speak to her the same way, even if she was making use of the formal address *Sie*; she probably didn't want to treat him as though he were still a schoolboy by keeping to the familiar *Du*. And that was exactly what caused René to toss his inhibitions aside and in a split second prevent the situation from going stale or lumbering to a halt.

"Drop it!" he called out, and loudly, too, pointing to his own clothes to show what he meant. Sliding out of the chair and dropping to his knees with his arms raised as he now did might have affected her like the primitive worship of an aborigine.

She was standing three paces away and did what he asked, then kept standing there and looking at him with her arms opened wide. That went on for several moments. René rushed over to her now, put his arms around her back and the hollows of her knees, lifted her off the floor, virtually hoisting her, and called out: "Where?!" With a movement of her head she pointed to one of the door panels, not, as he was expecting (but why, after all?) to the hidden door on the side wall behind him. The vista to be seen through the window filled and dominated this smaller room even more. "The curtain," she said. It rustled red-brown, the color of Mediterranean fishermen's sails; all the rest white-enameled here as well, the dressing table, the small chairs, the wide French bed, and the little étagère at its upper end—now, however, a deep tempering and assuaging.

The gondola lifted, soared, caught the wind, ascended slantwise.

She picked up the locket (the couple had set it swinging quite a bit on its long chain) and turned it this way and that. "Do you recall it?" René asked. She looked at him from the side. "On the little desk over there," she said when he asked for a penknife. Now they looked at her picture for a long time. "Rock-climbing . . ." said René, "remember?" "Yes," she replied, not falling into common ownership of past events as people like to do, especially in situations like the present one, but speaking hesitantly, almost guardedly, "though I'm not very fond of dwelling on memories. I thought I'd said that a different way earlier. I want to see the ballast fall away, get tossed overboard. It's not that sadness is over-whelming me right now, but everything over and done with is sad." She gave him another sideways glance and looked up at the ceiling, her hands crossed behind her head. Her language sounded sweet and strange to René. Now for the first time he grasped the nature of the white-enameled gondola (had he just this minute detected a faint, cool odor of naphtha or camphor here . . . ?). It wasn't being guided. It had been turned loose, unmoored; it was floating free. It was drifting in the wind, climbing, making for the Danube, unfolding the patchwork of meadows and woods on the Bisamberg, all of it now seen from above. Seen from the Strudlhof Steps, however, reposing deep within their domes of leafage left and right now, its fountain murmuring faintly, immured in its miles-deep summer stillness of the city, this gondola looked like no more than a tiny, high-flying cloud. René saw—with astonishment, but as if only from the side (the way Editha looked at him)—that yesterday and today he had once more come really alive for the first time in a long while, without inspecting a squad of intents and purposes rigidly standing at attention but also without collapsing, which is how it had been as he was finishing his studies, the screws tightening ever more until he'd made up with Grete, until he'd wreaked havoc on his nerves by forcing himself to complete a major seminar paper out in the country in the shortest possible time. Now, though, now he'd been set free, was living as his own master, moving out to very different places, for the Strudlhof Steps themselves could be a stairway, a gangway leading to the balloon gondola, in which there would be no more thought of the stairs now submerged in their depths of summer. Here's something he did not say: "Just think, Editha, a little while ago I came down the Strudlhof Steps on my way to you; that's where the relationship between Ingrid Schmeller and Semski came to an end—more or less your doing; I bet you still think about it . . ." At this point he didn't want to remind her of anything (hadn't she said something like, "Do not summon up remembrance of things past"?). He didn't ask her anything. He had hearkened, heeded, not hesitated, not stuffed himself on the inside with intentions, resolutions. And now he'd landed up in a new light that showed him there was nothing to land. The gondola swayed. He started covering Editha with kisses, moving downward from her shoulders and collarbone. When he reached her thighs, he saw how extremely delicate her skin was— gently fanned, like water over which the wind is skimming, bright, satin sheened, a scar from some operation almost totally vanished, probably an incision from an appendectomy. He kissed that spot as well, along with many others. Soaring high aloft in this white-enameled enclosure, inwardly mingling with all that was most foreign to him as it seeped into his pores, he allowed it to release him from himself in a way he had never felt before: that meant even more than being able to go back to a place where he had not yet even met Grete Siebenschein and to snap into the right groove there somewhere. In their sheltered conveyance they drifted into sleep, head on shoulder.

On the following morning, Sunday, August 23, Melzer rode the local train out to Greifenstein on the Danube. On the way to the station he remembered the talk he'd had the evening before with E.P., the squirrel sitting hunched over, busily moving his rapid little paws, and the abandoned, buried, forgotten café.

No sooner had he boarded than Editha called out to him. She was dressed very lightly and looked to be flourishing. She delivered nothing but fully formed and elegantly trim sentences into the air, still relatively cool. The carriage wasn't very crowded this early in the day. They found seats next to one another. "Melzer, old dear," she said, "this is charming"—she lay her hand on his lower arm for a second—"we'll be thrown together out there again, right?!" She looked at him from below. And in this glance there was a kind of rounding off. Since the evening before he'd been feeling something like a right to have ... the release button pressed, as we might put it (was that a term the squirrel had used? did it sound like something he would say? could Melzer picture it coming out of his mouth? hadn't he been feeling since their talk that there was on deposit somewhere inside him something like a credit balance, a coupon he could redeem?!). Editha suddenly turned her head and looked out the window. Someone on the platform had called "Mimi!" in a loud voice. "Are you waiting for someone?" Melzer asked. "No," she replied somewhat hesitantly, and then, with her bookish pronunciation: "The voice sounded familiar to me; it was an error, however."

The train began gliding away.

As it does so often.

As we all do.

Past Nussdorf and beyond the locks, the Danube curved in closer. The coves and inlets of the marshes also went sliding past lightly and rapidly; this was where Thea Rokitzer and Paula Pichler, née Schachl, had lain a few weeks before, holding one of their many conversations and reading Melzer's note from Friday, July 10, to Editha Schlinger. The little stations followed in quick succession, wild grapes growing along the bustling platforms, and by the small town of Höflein, rails and river were briefly separated from the flat land lying before hills whose blithe-looking crests stuck out in the silver-gray foam of meadow reeds and woods: the flagpoles on the airy wooden houses of the rowing and regatta clubs; the untold number of colorful, cheery log cabins belonging to Danube habitués, some of the houses looking like small villas, a few even rivaling that status fully ... This was what they saw, but as more than fleeting images flitting by, for they were keeping silent. She was observing him, but he hardly noticed, because her way of looking was dispersed, as was her way of listening when someone was speaking; even so, she heard and saw things accurately. What opened up now inside Melzer on this Sunday morning was something genuinely simple people accomplish much earlier and with less effort: he yielded. Not overestimating his own hopeless judgments and estimates but instead keeping his ears open for the word our surroundings are so much more irrefutably addressing to us directly. He—the major, the civil service official—now gave in completely, profoundly; the booming and the zooming, the whooshing and the swooshing past all his *trópoi* stayed in the background, were shunted aside.

"Weren't you back in Salzburg around the middle of the month?" he asked.

"Yes," she said. "In that general vicinity."

Now they arrived in Greifenstein and made their way out of the station, not as part of a large group but among only a scattered few. The larger crowd had gotten off the train piecemeal at earlier stations. It seemed they were being asked to shed their clothes right away so they could start wading and swimming even while headed toward the site they'd arranged; that one particular location was their usual spot, but it lay quite far away, out in the wetlands. At the swimming area they found a changing booth for Editha and then, after searching around, one for the major as well, at the other end of the shelter, which stood on cement pillars like a bungalow or a stilt house because of the high water. When Melzer emerged with some kind of improvised carryall under his arm, Editha was already standing ready, holding her colorful straw basket by the handle. They started off at once, not barefoot, but wearing thongs with sturdy soles because of the stones along the regulating dams.

He was feeling her physical presence more strongly than usual. And although her presenting herself at these swimming parties almost completely undressed made him nearly apprehensive every time, it didn't register with him now as the least bit daunting, as it always had before. It surprised him that he was walking beside her so calmly. Now the wetland woods closed around these two, the groves of the river god enfolded them, the pale silver tops of ancient trees hovering over them high as clouds, as if about to resolve into vapor in the upper distance of the summer day, along the lowest ground of which they were making their way amid tall reeds and rushes. Now there meandered through the wooded depths the first bend of a river arm gently curved, its first channel shaded with dense overhang. They took special pleasure in being able to step into it properly, to enter the water, to wade through it—the soft ground, the water splashing only up to their calves at first, then above the knee, then mounting halfway up their thighs; they carried their bags and robes on their heads. "Like native columns of bearers in the African jungle," Editha remarked. Melzer's eyes were fixed on her swaying hips. As if it were past and gone. As if it were all over and done. As if he'd finally reached that point the day before, August 22, in the afternoon, in his room on Porzellan Gasse, when it had been so hot. (Deep within the depth of the green-reflecting window.) But things looked different when they stopped for a rest. Her ear stuck out from her hair a little like rose-colored edging, and her nose once more seemed slightly curved as her foot swayed back and forth over her thong. They'd made themselves quite comfortable lying on the bathrobes. "There are two things I keep wishing for," she said, looking up at the treetops, while her head rested in her hands crossed behind it. "One of them I can have, the other I can't." She reached into her basket off to the side and rummaged until she took out a silver case, thin as a disc; it held two or three cigarettes of the strongest brand. "What would be the other one?" Melzer asked. "Don't remind me, Melzer." "Oh go ahead; tell me." "Right here and now, in the woods, where it's so nice, not a single mosquito, total calm, dear old Melzer sitting beside me—what more could anyone wish for? Here's my glorious dream—a cup of Turkish coffee, right here and now, a postlude to breakfast, so to say, to enjoy with this Nile cigarette. I'd even smoke another one. And inhale as deep as I can. All right, so now you know. Hopeless, like all our deepest wishes; I mean the more substantial kind, ones worth wishing for in the first place." She looked at him with a totally open gaze that became more and more filled with everything unspoken, which at once went flowing into the silence. As this was happening, she could only construe the extreme astonishment in his features and the silence he was maintaining to be a symptom of possibility immeasurable in its extent though just now grasping for the first time what was being laid out in front of it or even being outright pushed toward it; on the other hand, that stupidity might be winning out, after all, and in overpowering measure at that, thanks to the un-imaginable degree of modesty behind it . . . Pertinent as any of that might be, however, Melzer's unbounded amazement was based on something entirely different this time, something visible, completely tangible and solid, something that in the twinkling of an eye popped out of his bag of supplies without his uttering a word: he let things themselves do the talking. And not just to Etelka. To himself as well. A Turkish coffee mill of the smallest size, two tiny porcelain cups in copper holders, the little polished pot, the fuel capsule, the coffee itself, the sugar: they were talking loud and clear. There was even a small, lightweight bronze tray. They spoke roughly the same language to Melzer as the odor of camphor from yesterday or the organ-grinder with his military march on August 18, 1911, and August 22, 1925, re-spectively, a language just as indisputably communicative, at least to Melzer, as music is to a musician. And how else could he possibly have interpreted the present moment?—here and now, where for the first time he'd brought along his complete little coffee set, more or less as a kind of trial run so that he wouldn't have to do without his beloved black coffee out there, perhaps anticipating that he would need it es-pecially on this particular Sunday, after all he'd been through (mean-ing the *trópoi*), after all the overstimulation . . . Just now, however, a new chemical bond had been forged as quick as lightning, an instan-taneous chemical marrying of naphtha, bearskin, Treskavica, and coffee grinding. He stopped turning the crank. He thought of Major Laska, now dead and gone. He felt pain. He was staring into space but looking deep into the unfeeling spinach green of nature in its forest exaltation. It was as if the dead man were now dying once more inside Melzer, but slowly, in stages and by degrees, as if Melzer still needed to absorb a measure of pain not yet admitted, of grief as yet ungrieved. On the Lavarone Plateau. This is it, Melzer, God bless you, go see my wife.

"Well you old Bosnian, you!" Editha had cried out, sitting upright and clapping her hands: "Just like a traveling Turkish merchant!" Then she noticed the change that had come over him when he'd stopped grinding the coffee. "What is it, Melzer dear!?" she asked, leaning forward on the palms of her hands. She crawled over to him and looked into his face from below. "What are you feeling, what are you thinking about, friend? You look grief-stricken!"

He was in a state he himself was at a complete loss to understand, a loss that made him diligently start turning the handle again (the more so that the sugar water would soon begin to boil). Besides, there was nothing else he could do; any chance of giving her an answer simply from his own resources was proving to be an utter impossibility. He wanted to answer her. He wanted to tell Editha Schlinger who Major Laska was, if only a few details, so as to give her at least some kind of an answer: a treasured friend and comrade, killed in the war, died in his arms on the battlefield. It was impossible. Iron silence filled his mouth. It was outside the realm of possibility for him to speak to her about Laska or even to say his friend's name.

He served the coffee. She'd observed his simple, skilled movements with interest and not without pleasure or even deeper emotion. "So our boy Melzer is still a soldier at the campfire," she said. "And he's got everything all neat and squared away. Apparatus for preparing Turkish coffee at the ready, as per regulations. I am so grateful to you!"

He took her hand and planted a quick kiss on it as if to ask pardon for his puzzling behavior a moment before and then with a smile held out to her the tray with the full cups. "Happy again?" she asked, and then added nonchalantly, "what's past and gone is never anything but a burden." She sipped her coffee and inhaled the smoke from her strong cigarette with the rapacity of a drug addict. Melzer kept his head bent over the tray.

Her last comment made him feel revitalized and demoralized at the same time. Pressed to the ground by the heavy blanket of the summer day, he could clearly see that he was at the same point he'd been at yesterday or that time in July, standing at the letter box on Porzellan Gasse just as Thea Rokitzer had appeared. She came flying toward him now like something suddenly and very alarmingly near. This is how a person must feel who watches the moon fall into the garden and lie there on the lawn like a large yellow quince. It made absolutely no difference to him what Thea had done with the note he'd given her. And Melzer quickly applauded himself inwardly for never having asked. Or perhaps it might have made a tiny bit of difference after all, to someone else? No, nonsense—what possible interest could that young girl (his emphasis as he drew on this expression in his thoughts was along the lines of "like any other") have in that note? She must have delivered it. How else would Editha have known he wouldn't be coming? But he didn't ask, even though the answer was literally lying before him. Now she drifted away once more, Thea Rokitzer, whom he hadn't seen for such a long time; now everything having to do with her, whatever happened or might happen in and around her, withdrew once more to a remote skyscape whose tempests were incredibly far distant, whose dew did not wet his hair.

By now they were on the third cup of the concentrated beverage, Editha still silent with mute euphoria, that deepest conviction of an addict. The coffee started to have its effect on Melzer as well: stronger disposal to inner mobility, more dexterous disjoining of antitheses, plus a more physically immediate grasp of his external situation, this strange and singular *Déjeuner sur l'herbe.*

"Do you know a Frau von Budau?" Editha asked, setting down her tiny porcelain cup.

Now, as we know, our major was one of those who live close to the Strudlhof Steps, so of course he knew at once whom she meant. Her question—or more exactly that she had asked it in the first place—now rose like a sharp spike out of the murmuring creek bed of this conversation in the woods. Images flashed up quick as lightning—the tennis court out at the Stangelers' country house, the garden party at the Schmellers', and in the same instant their meeting near Saint Peter's on the Graben, her smart gray suit, the corner by the bookstore—while her words had already propelled the major across the line where something mysterious as far as mere feeling is concerned has been stamped and minted into an incongruity the understanding is able to grasp. In a flash he now thought he knew why he had met Editha in the train this morning—for one single reason. Only for that reason had he ended up here, only for that reason had he brought along his coffee service, only for that reason were they sipping coffee out in nature: to open a way out—through however utterly baffling and astonishing a turn of events—of the humdrum evenness produced by being constantly rolled around between two glacier crevasses, as it were, squeezed just as tightly between them yesterday, August 22, in his room on Porzellan Gasse, as when he'd stood by the mailbox in July, and then during the whole time in between as well. Now the heavy blanket of the summer day had been lifted in a totally unexpected place. Something new entered Melzer. Along with it, however, a most extraordinary degree of caution, comparable to that of a child in the process of creating something audacious with his building blocks and taking special care not to bump against the table. (The first structures of a civilian mentality?) He stood up slowly, casually, under the pretext of gathering up the coffee things on the bronze tray so he could wash them, which he then made it a show of preparing to do, walking back over to the same small, clear brook made by a branching off of the river, from which he'd fetched the water for boiling. Melzer stood up, then, no longer lying flat on his back on the deep forest floor under the farthest reaches, high as the clouds, of treetops heat-hazed. He stood firm on the two tan, slender, muscular legs of an infantryman, legs that could at once be pictured as limbs on a Greek sculpture. He stood on them firmly, as on the pedestal of his silence, which emitted a single concise word only.

"Yes," he said.

Nothing else could be gotten out of him. Nothing like, "Oh, of course; her maiden name was Schmeller!" He clearly felt (at least as clearly as any feeling allows) that even one single additional word would be enough for him to cause the entire mass of all the associations in his life—knowledge and experience he was entitled to, as it were, he could lay claim to, his by right (and not just military this time, either)—would cause the entire mass to start lurching and then toppling over, by which action the unstable opening that had at last appeared and shown some green among all the scree and that could lead him out to what was really essential (as it seemed to him) would be buried, filled in, his exit sealed off, the brightly shining gap once more entombed in darkness.

"A peculiar person," said Editha, still lying on her back. "A soggy sandwich." (By this stage, however, we have to say, a somewhat more generously proportioned soggy sandwich, one made with a whole round peasant loaf.) "The captain and I were out not long ago; he'd dragged me off to go dancing at that stupid casino in the City Park, and there were the Budaus with some people he knows. Making introductions at gatherings like this is always so haphazard, all jumbled together and topsy-turvy, everything happening at the same time. People who already know each other are introduced, and people who don't are left hanging. I was just about to shake hands with this Budau woman when I noticed her pulling hers back as she looked me up and down in the most brazen, arrogant way and then simply turned her back on me. At first I didn't understand…"

She broke off suddenly. In her face now appeared a look she seldom displayed, a strenuous effort to stay composed, shown in tiny wrinkles above her nose. It looked winsome and cute, but it was caused by vexation: she wrinkled her nose in much the same way when she'd dropped and broken something through carelessness. This dialogue in the woods has quickly put us into the position of having to communicate not what the two parties were saying, but what each of them was choking back instead. So Melzer didn't say, "Are you surprised—?" but, "Oh well, things like that happen." (Just like yesterday with the squirrel, when he also had to come up with replies now and then.) He was standing holding the coffee set and looking down at Editha. Her face, still strained, was now expressing outright anger.

"Ancient history! Ancient history!" she cried, "always this ancient history I have to wrestle with, first one thing and then another!" She sat upright and her way of speaking turned forceful; at that moment he could sense that she had somehow now found a way to break through, a chance to vent properly. "What am I supposed to do with all this?! Am I meant to keep in memory everything that ever happened?! No matter when or where?"

Melzer now heard the rustling sound of a curtain closing and cutting off his view of the unbelievable development he believed he had seen just now without the need to analyze it for the time being. The day leveled itself out once more, as it were. A pathway that seconds before seemed to have led directly to this point, and this point only, now widened and smoothed out into an open road. He turned to the water with the coffee set and said, "It's been a good long time if you think about it—fourteen years!"

"That's what I mean!" she answered, lying back and falling silent again. When Melzer was finished, they left and make their way to the site where they'd arranged to meet the others.

To be sure, though, some sores that heal quickly can leave blisters behind, and even though the major lacked any point of reference that would help him get past where he was through organized thinking or anything resembling it, there had been rising up inside him ever since the *Déjeuner sur l'herbe* a growing disgust at the shoddiness—only brazen people would have thrust the whole mass of it on him anyway—that had been spread out before him here, exposed to the light of day so openly that its full reality truly appalled him, never mind that he'd caught whiffs of it at every turn and throughout the years among the captain's acquaintances, if never more than faintly. To bear hatred for a person (and then only because you'd once played a dirty trick on her), to continue defaming her years later, as on the Graben in September 1923, and then, just for a change, to forget all about it two years after that and to be surprised when the injured woman refused to shake hands: to Melzer, Editha's being so heavily weighed down by the past without at all feeling the weight of any corresponding obligation on her part went totally and deeply against the grain, whereas he was always exerting himself to comb and brush with it; for that matter, it went against anything and everything he fought for in his humble, unassuming, Melzerian way.

Having reached this point, he thought of Asta Stangeler. Anything along these lines would be completely out of the question with her.

Meanwhile, something about all this was still unexplained and was pressing on him from below; even though Melzer had the day before, on Sunday, seen everything mysterious about Editha at least gathered together into one spot, altogether incomprehensible as it was—no healthy mind could ever perform that task, but could grasp the result when completed—today the components looked scattered again and occupied his limbs more than his head. That meant the situation he'd been fearing had arisen anew; the two glacier crevasses were turning him around again, grinding away the hours just as they'd ground away the days and weeks in July and August.

That was what made Melzer leave his apartment that Monday, after finishing at the office and having coffee at home, somewhat earlier than on the Saturday before, but in much the same frame of mind. And he chose the same route for his evening walk.

On the lowest landing of the Strudlhof Steps, by the fish-mouth fountain, he saw someone leaning against the stone balustrade and writing in a notebook. It took him a moment to recognize Stangeler, any thought of whom had admittedly been extremely remote but who, now that he was standing right there, struck Melzer as the one person he would most have wanted to bump into today. And at this very place, too. He fixed René in his eyes the way a person reaches for a hold. Only when Stangeler put his notebook away and looked up did that feeling recede.

René looked pleased and came toward Melzer. "This is great," said the major, "and I also have a request, Herr von Stangeler. But how are you, anyway? I didn't know you were in Vienna! Any news from Paris? I heard Fräulein Siebenschein's in France with her sister and brother-in-law."

"Grete's coming back on Friday," Stangeler answered curtly, but it didn't sound abrupt or cut off, more or less resonating instead like a chord on the piano when the pedal is sustained, for there was so much tangibly unsaid lying behind the words, everything he was dreaming and fancying as he uttered them. "I got a telegram at noon today," he added, tapping the left side pocket of his jacket. That's where he was keeping it. The text couldn't have been any more to his liking; the message was earnest. "Arriving alone Friday August 28 six p.m." She'd even given the number of the train, not generally the rule for her. And then, "All love Grete."

"May I ask what your request is?" he said to Melzer.

"Yes," the major answered cheerily, "it's about the steps we're standing on right now."

"And where we were likewise standing at the same time fourteen years ago," Stangeler replied.

"Here at the bottom, too, all of us on that landing," Melzer added.

"After it was over and done with," said René.

"I love these stairs so much and the whole surrounding area as well,"

Melzer continued. "And I can't even begin to understand how people just rush up and down the steps so thoughtlessly and with no respect for their artistic quality. They are a work of art, after all. Am I right?"

"Exactly, like a poem," Stangeler said. "They embody the mystery of this place in having manifested it and given it form. The genius loci unveiled. This is the main feature underlying any significant structure, deeper than even its foundation: the Palazzo Bevilacqua in Bologna or the Church of Maria am Gestade in Vienna. In both cases the locale sat back, was recessed. That's true of the Strudlhof Steps as well, even if they don't mark any special point in the history of art, at least not today and not for us. But that could take a very different turn in the future."

Melzer had already lost the thread.

"What I wanted to request, though, Herr von Stangeler," he demurred modestly, "was for you to tell me when the steps were built and by whom; true, I don't know if you've ever made a special study of the subject, but I thought you might possibly know a lot about them through your study of Viennese history. You are a historian, after all."

"Why 'after all'?" thought Stangeler, and he answered: "Yes, I can tell you something about them. The Strudlhof Steps were constructed in 1910—that is, just one year before we had our very own little dedication ceremony through the scandal with Old Man Schmeller—according to designs drawn up by Johann Theodor Jaeger, who's now on the staff of the city's building department. Jaeger is exactly the kind of man it would be very right to call truly cultivated; a fine painter, by the way, and a musician as well. That's all plain to see on the Strudlhof Steps."

"Do you know this architect Jaeger?" Melzer asked, and because Stangeler was shaking his head, he added: "And then how do you know all this?"

"From my father," René answered. "I asked him. He has all these facts at his command, plus he knows Jaeger personally. Jaeger also visited my uncle quite often, too, a professor at the Technical University; he lives in the same building as my parents."

"I know," Melzer commented. Stopping now and again, they very slowly made their way up the lower ramp. "What was here before? Before the steps were built?"

"Just empty ground, a *Gstetten*, to use our special Viennese word," Stangeler answered. "There wasn't a different or an older stairway. The area was just simply part of the hillside running down from the Schotten Point, as it's called, to the old neighborhood called Am Thury, which used to lie outside the city. A shortcut of sorts. Young boys probably played cowboys and Indians here. As far as the project manager of the steps is concerned, the architect Jaeger, as you call him, I know a few very instructive details about him through my father. In the first place, he's not an architect at all; instead, he's an engineer and was originally an assistant professor in the division of bridge construction at the Technical University. Then he went to the road maintenance section of the Municipal Bureau of Urban Construction. Jaeger originally attended a humanities gymnasium, not a technical or vocational school, and only after that a professional school. That's something it might not be hard to gather from the contrast between this work of art and a purely engineering approach. The design of these steps was being nourished from the deepest levels of its creator's mind, ones that might have been considered useless and were later discounted. But what would any foreordained engineer know about a genius loci? The most he'd ever be able to do, no matter where, is knock one out by applying standard procedure. Certainly not discover it, as Jaeger was able to do here, and to compose in the form of a stairway a four-stanza ode in tribute to it. Only a humanist would be able to do that. These stairs speak about life at its deepest and most intimate, not about some kind of official biography, intentionally official and officious. The heart's desire of a distinguished and high-minded man has been given voice in stone here. Something else, by the way, something my father even made it a special point to underscore: Jaeger must have known exactly and in the minutest detail how to go about the project, really and truly understood how it's done, because his design conformed perfectly to the strictures of the stonemason's craft and the exact methods for cutting stone. He apparently had a profound familiarity with the subject, or else it was somehow second nature to him—just as the classical poets commanded the most complex meters and the deployment of quantitative syllabic distribution they required with such perfection that there is hardly a single error detectable anywhere in the whole corpus of ancient Roman literature, for example—so that Jaeger was able to move with complete freedom inside his material when composing his masterpiece. The result says everything. Here the steps are, in the grove of the genius loci, more or less incidental for passersby."

"And why are they called the Strudlhof Steps?" interjected Melzer somewhat abruptly. They had come to a stop and were leaning against the balustrade.

"After a painter," said René. "Peter Strudel, or Strudl. People didn't used to be as exact in the spelling of their last names as they are in our age of bureaucratic documentation. I know of an Austrian baron from the fifteenth century called Gamuret Fronauer who spelled his own name a different way almost every time. It's only recently that we began being so persnickety about spelling as the mark of a supposedly educated person. This ABC-fixation of teachers will apparently soon be all that's left of our language. In 1705 Strudl founded the Academy of Fine Arts in Vienna, modeling it on the one in France, by decree of Emperor Joseph I, or rather of Emperor Leopold I, who didn't live to see its opening. Above here, where the building of the former Consular Academy stands on the old Schotten Point, Peter Strudl (he later became a baron) built a large house, a villa and studio, plus a farm: a whole estate called the Strudl Hof. That's where the name of the street and the stairs comes from. Do you know the Church of Saint Rochus, on Land Strasse?"

"Yes, of course," Melzer said. He may well have been somewhat bewildered by this cloudburst of detail pouring down on him. At the same time he felt put off by the tone in which all this was being delivered: a bit dreary, the words just rattled off, as if the speaker himself weren't committed to them or considered all these particulars to be mainly just a waste of time.

"The large painting over the high altar is by Peter Strudl—Saint Sebastian and Saint Rochus looking down on Vienna. Strudl is also represented in much more official quarters, by the way, some of them what you might call trouble spots. When an Austrian finance minister of the present day is bent over his cares in his study just past the yellow salon of the Palais Eugen on Himmelpfort Gasse, he has looking down at him from the ceiling a rather wanton scene painted by Baron Strudl—the abduction of Orithyia, daughter of King Erechtheus of Attica, by Boreas, god of the north wind.

"I might add that after all this about the past, we're now standing right at the most recent and most dismal spot in Austria's history," Stangeler commented after they'd been silent for a while, taking in the view across the park at the palace of the Princes Liechtenstein and all the distant features of the city beyond it. He informed an astonished Melzer that not a few of the residential buildings here on Strudlhof Gasse were the property of the Austrian foreign minister responsible for the outbreak of the war of 1914. "On the left when you come up is the Palais Berchtold," Stangeler said, "and the smaller one, the ocher-yellow one on the opposite side—the house of my dreams, by the way—belongs to him as well."

"You mean you'd like to live there?" Melzer asked in a lively voice.

"Absolutely," cried Stangeler. "Here you have everything at once—deep in the depths of the city but with distance from it, thanks to the green drop-off of the terrain and the wide-open view. It's not the country or 'nature,' or whatever they like to call it, that entices me, but on the other hand, these relentlessly built-up city streets keep me constantly crazy with fear throughout spring, summer, and autumn. But what's Count Berchtold getting from any of it? He understands nothing. If he did, he'd be living here and not in Bohemia as he does. He understood nothing about any of the things he'd been entrusted with."

"Do you really believe that?" Melzer asked.

"Yes," answered Stangeler with complete calm. "In Berchtold's time and indeed from time immemorial the old Austrian state took a totally wrongheaded political approach to England. The situation with the assassination of the heir apparent, Franz Ferdinand, that critical moment where everything was teetering in the balance, was the last possible chance Austria would have had to turn onto an entirely different track without letting down the Germans; it would have been to their benefit, in fact, because they wouldn't have been drawn into a war because of us."

René made a few more statements expressing flatly the opposite views of every discussion that had been held in the officers' mess at Trnovo on the Jelesnitza in Bosnia just after the assassination of the successor to the Austrian throne; Melzer had taken part, too, and always in the same confrontational but optimistic spirit of hankering for revenge, while they were all preparing to set forth as if on a chivalric exploit or to avenge the abduction of Helen by the Trojans . . . "But war would have come no matter what," said Melzer, though not feeling very well as he spoke the words, if only because a few insights were scrambling around inside his head that had weaseled their way in, since the collapse of the monarchy, anyway. "Don't say that," René answered. "It's impossible to argue that persistence over time could ever be the hallmark of a critical state; that would be a contradiction in the term itself. Suppose we could have gotten past the critical point, keen as it was, just this once, without a war—who knows what solutions were standing waiting in the next room of the future? What changes coming from other levels might it have been possible to work into a situation that stayed receptive and malleable right up to the point of its hardening into a disaster? No, there's a certain sense in which it all depends—depends on surviving, on holding your weapon to the throat of death, which at that moment is trying with all its might to force itself on us, and then, as we enter that next room already opening up to us, to leave death behind in the place where it's been waiting in vain, to slam the iron door of the past on its caved-in nose. There was never a European situation that was bound to result in war sooner or later. Those are solemn fabrications by interested parties, by professional politicians, generals, busybodies, historians; they're the hot air produced by people who have the language of the newspapers sloshing through their brains like water when you flush the toilet. That's how they always drag down everything, of course. There are seats that people have occupied for too long, including ministerial seats, or rooms people leave too soon, maybe only ten minutes too soon, or telegrams people have been holding in their hands too long . . ." He made a short, angry motion with his chin up the steps in the direction of the Palais Berchtold.

Melzer had lost the thread again this time, though not because he would not have been capable of following René, but because from one particular point during this conversation something significantly different, though still related to the topic, had been seeping into him and collecting, so that now everything was starting to float and swim, in a sense, and by now was drifting over an area not at all anticipated. That particular, pinpointed moment was marked by Stangeler's observation about Austria's completely wrongheaded political approach to England. No sooner had he made it than Melzer was of course seized by the memory of that conversation in which Buschmann, Geyrenhoff, Marchetti, and Lindner had taken part in exactly fourteen years ago in one of the rooms at the old inn by the rushing mill, everybody in colorful pajamas, with wineglasses and coffee cups, Benno Grabmayr looking at that time (by now, he had long since been laid to rest in Serbian soil) altogether like a Tyrolean devil, in his red pajamas and his pipe between his strong white teeth . . . But this memory, vivid and easy to grasp, was frustrating Melzer. It wasn't what he was really thinking about; the wrong political approach to England was intruding like a cover or a screen in front of a completely different image. For a split second Melzer pictured the intensely sky-blue feathers on a spotted nutcracker's wing, but it proved to be only like a nearby mosquito taken for a high-flying bird by mistake. While Stangeler had turned in the direction of the Palais Berchtold so he could continue his polemic against it, Melzer had become a little more deeply immersed in the Strudlhof Steps, as it were.

"Do you believe, Herr von Stangeler," he said after they had been silent for a time while taking a few more steps up the ramp and reaching the turn to the next one, "do you believe Editha Pastré later found out everything that had happened here on the steps that time fourteen years ago, we might say as a direct result of her actions?"

"Certainly she found out all about it," answered René.

"But how do you know? Did you ever talk to her about it?"

"Not on your life," Stangeler said. "She doesn't like that; she doesn't want to hear any of those old tales. 'Herr Melzer, do not summon up remembrance of things past!'" He had turned toward the major and imitated Editha so perfectly and convincingly that Melzer was totally overcome by a fit of laughter but—even while bitterly resenting himself for laughing like that—couldn't help feeling a relief that could almost be called a deliverance.

"And so, Herr von Stangeler, how does it come about that you have knowledge of Editha's knowledge?" he said, suppressing his laughter with some effort.

"It was quite obvious," René answered. "Old Man Schmeller had an affair with Editha—later, I mean, because it hadn't quite ripened into that at the time of the scandal here on the Strudlhof Steps. I just happened to find out about it." After saying this he laughed in a way Melzer couldn't understand. "Pretty soon after, though. I can tell you I saw them walking together one evening that same autumn in the Prater; they were shaded by the chestnut trees, but there was no mistaking the situation. It would be absurd to assume he never told her anything."

"As you say," replied the major. "Tell me, Herr von Stangeler, do you remember a certain evening earlier this year, in the spring, when the captain was still living on Skoda Gasse? You and I saw Frau Schlinger home that evening."

"Of course," said René. "I came along as far as here."

"Exactly. We were standing up there" (he pointed up to the platform) "with Frau Editha between us. I imagine we were both thinking the same thing, that is, we were remembering the same thing. I even asked you a question at the time, but all Editha said was, 'Oh, so these are the Strudlhof Steps.' Up at the captain's place, after all, Oki Leucht had to explain to her what that meant—'the Strudlhof Steps.'"

"Yes, you're right," René commented, stopping and looking to the side through narrowed eyes. "Look here, though, look here," he said with great introspection, as if determined to dredge ruthlessly inside himself, "that's an example of a case in which we're . . . too exact. I feel that; in fact I know it. It does injustice to the charming disarray of feminine sensibility and consciousness. Of course she knew about the Strudlhof Steps and what they mean and all the ins and outs of them. But just at that moment she *didn't* know. Can you still call it knowledge, though, if it's there one minute but not the next, especially when it seems totally natural to the woman and isn't upsetting her in the least? Sometimes it seems to me that two different dictionaries would have to be created, one feminine and one masculine, as a result of which two different languages would evolve over time, and anyone who falls in love would have to learn the other one instead of garbling his or her own. Or speech between couples would die out entirely, and only a kind of touch-language would remain, like insects have; they speak through their antennae—yes, an insect language ..." They'd continued in the meantime and had now reached the middle of the upper ramp. Stangeler was hardly looking at Melzer anymore. He was speaking as if reading a prepared text from some source. "Yes, that's what's behind the face filled with tender meaning, though it's only itself, nothing more. They write letters and don't know what they've written. Do not summon up remembrance of things past, because I don't have any. Those are the faces of women from large cities—much more distinctive, personal, and exceptional than is allowable, I almost want to say. The face is only too individual, standing out and presented to view like a bubble with only hollow space behind and beneath. Overindividualization, generated by the natural force that remains consistent in forging ahead as it constantly gestates new classes, varieties, variations, and special cases of physiognomic manifestation in its constantly renewed processes of refinement. Yes, they all want to take on more and more detail. They want to become 'limb-real,' as Paracelsus says." (René was by now verging on crass incivility by no longer paying any attention to Melzer.) "That's how Oscar Wilde's 'Sphinx Without a Secret' comes into being. That is how women in Buenos Aires, Vienna, Paris come to have faces whose effortful individuality they can no longer justify, for which they have no personal warrant, and whose enigmatic promise they could never even begin to fulfill. Indeed, it is that very face that so engrossed us" (Melzer saw with amazement that René now had his arms outspread and was speaking upward, into the steps above, as it were), "framed by the dark and yet light-sprinkled windows of the underground, its glance outward into the tumultuous breadth of a city seething with numberless creatures of light when the train would glide out onto a high viaduct: yes, the aspect an enigma, the path and the journey's end unknown. But there was neither an aspect nor a path nor a journey's end. It was and is only the fearsomely tormenting uniqueness, thrusting deep and bringing happiness, that sits in the memory like a stake and penetrates to the deepest heartwood of remembrance. That is Editha. But there is nothing like memory there, nothing like remembrance. There is the gondola hovering and then, when torn loose, reeling over the city submerged miles deep in the height of summer. There is Editha."

Melzer, who had really and truly lost the thread this time—by miles, and ten times over—stared completely mesmerized at René; he had understood not one single word. Not as a word, really, but more as a color when you take a good look or a sound when it enters the ear. But only with the last words did he realize that René was talking to someone actually present, so he moved his head back and looked up. There on the platform, leaning lightly with her gloved hands on the stone parapet, Editha Schlinger was standing and smiling down on him and René. At this moment Melzer was taken by a forcefully insistent feeling that Stangeler had been reading to him from Editha, so to speak, as if from an open book.

"Bravo, Stangelboy!" she cried (had she been there a while, and had she really understood the last words?!). "Hello, Melzer, old dear! There's a novel by the Danish fairy-tale author Andersen called *The Improvisator*; our friend Stangelboy-Stangelkid really ought to read it. So what kind of strange conference or confab are you having here? Aren't you a little embarrassed? You're acting as if you were all alone here!"

Then Editha started down the steps. She could only have been referring to herself when she mentioned the presence of others, for the Strudlhof Steps sometimes managed at this time of day to lie completely deserted among dapples of sunlight and shadows of leaves, now gathering more deeply even as the evening glow from the entrance gate at the end of the street above them broke through with resonance of light.

They walked back down the steps with Editha. Melzer wasn't able to grow calm, not even slightly; everything was pitching and heaving, pushing at his mouth from the inside, and he wasn't at all far from turning to Editha right this second and forcing on her "remembrance of things past." Stangeler gave the impression of being totally unburdened, sauntering along on Editha's left, hands in his pockets, hat back on his neck. René's whole bearing had an disquieting effect on Melzer; the lad was practically an object of envy. Just as they came to the fishmouth fountain on the lower platform, Editha said, "This morning on the Graben I saw someone who made a strong impression on me. A

tall man, slender, his skin almost olive-colored, very easy in his movements, with an intelligent and slightly melancholy air, a man of genuine breeding—he could have passed for an Eastern potentate or
something similar. Fabulously dressed, by the way..."

"In what color?" asked Melzer, abruptly cutting in.

"Pale lilac or mauve or whatever it's called. Suit, shirt, and hat."
(Here we can see how exact her supposedly scattered powers of obser-
vation were.) Now Stangeler interrupted the interruption. "What else?
What was the King of Poland doing on the Graben?"

"I might have looked at him too blatantly—long story short, he
tipped his hat as he was passing me, bowed slightly, and said, 'I kiss
your hand, dear lady.' Then he was gone. I turned back, but he didn't.
I really don't think he knew who I was. I may be imagining it, but I
don't thing I've ever seen him before in my life. The strange part, though,
is that the second he had gone past me I thought very vividly of you,
René. And now I've hit on why—this King of Poland apparently was
using the same lavender water you do."

René was obviously determined not to let Melzer get a word in
edgewise (or at least that's how it seemed). "Scent and memory! There
are deep connections between them. But you're exactly right when you
say you only imagine you've never seen the gentleman before. Of course
you know him, or you once did, anyway, at some time and some place.
But are we offices of vital statistics, deeds and registrations, certificates
of birth and death? It would be a terrible thing if we were all constantly
pulling along wagons full of old materials. Of course you knew him,
the King of Poland, but at the moment when you saw him this morning on the Graben, you were free from that knowledge, untroubled by
it—and that was exactly the reason he was able to impress you so
strongly. You saw him completely anew. A requirement for living is to
break constantly with everything past. This breach runs through time
and splinters it; only then is there the present. Every genuine resolution,
every decision annihilates the past; if it weren't so, nothing great would
ever have happened..."

Only in these moments did Melzer recognize how much Stangeler
meant to him; otherwise he couldn't have been so deeply affected by
what René was doing here. The man's devious, deceitful play of words

and ideas, not a single one of which lacked falsity, seemed filled with horrible coldness toward Editha, whom he was apparently dismissing as a case so hopeless that it apparently wasn't even a consideration on René's part to present her with anything other than this downright unseemly reinforcement of her nature. The major kept silent. Anything he might have wanted to say had long since vanished. Escorting Editha, they were now walking along Liechtenstein Strasse. "Come to my place," she said, "or do you have plans? Otto's coming too. He'll be so happy! I have plenty to eat for all of us. René, you'll get between eighteen and twenty liters of black tea." "Since you put it that way, I'll take a chance," Stangeler said. Melzer accepted the invitation too. They hadn't yet reached her front entrance when the captain joined forces with them. "These two lads are coming up as well, are they, Editha dear!?" he cried; "when folk like these foregather, then all is well. There's ammunition aplenty."

This evening proceeded for Melzer in unchanging close proximity to those ten minutes back in the spring when he went with Editha from the Strudlhof Steps, where Stangeler had parted company with them, to the entrance of her building here behind the Franz Josef Station: nothing, nothing at all. The illuminated clock, the moonlight, the distant lights of the Kahlenberg Hotel, the silver elevation of the rising hills out there. Here they were, sitting in the white-enameled room with the tall double doors that seemed even higher because of the panels over them, likewise painted white, with clusters of grapes and angels. And while they were busy with the improvised but varied meal—Melzer had already started feeling a little hungry out on the street—everything smoothed out again, so to speak; the closed-in road or narrow path soon seemed to get lost among their sense of lively give-and-take as they got back onto the hilly terrain of their accustomed topics and gestures, conversation, and laughter. The view alone, with the evening sun, the castle, and the mountain facing them, kept on serving as a background before which nothing else would now obtrude as it slowly subsided into the dusk.

The captain, in such a good mood at the start, drank heavily as the evening went on. That sent his mood on a steeply downward curve. He grew taciturn, slightly stiff, placed his monocle in his eye. In parting he quickly separated from Melzer and René, and even though he shook their hands heartily, the other two were now left with no opportunity to see him to his door, which would have been the obvious thing for any number of reasons.

During this same week Melzer saw Editha Schlinger again, a few days later, on Friday. He had left his office building at one o'clock to go to eat, when she quickly approached him, coming along the sidewalk from the opposite direction, clearly happy at their meeting. "Oh, Melzer dear," she said, "first off, it's delightful to bump into you, and second, I think I'm in luck. Just tell me, are you by any chance possibly going into the center of town this afternoon? Maybe even somewhere in the vicinity of the Graben?" "Is there some errand I can take care of for you?" he asked, "Yes," she said, "there is, Melzer dear; you could absolutely be my salvation. For days now I've had no success in getting my fountain pen in to be repaired; something always comes up, and this morning I wasn't able to get to it either, and on Monday I was on the Graben but without the pen; I forgot and left it at home. Could I give it to you? I need it pretty urgently even now, but it often takes two weeks to repair." "I'll be happy to help," Melzer answered, "I have to go into town after the office anyway to shop for a few things." She took the longish brick-red leather pen case out of her small handbag. Melzer then saw her home before going to the restaurant. "I have some urgent things to take care of this afternoon and tomorrow as well," she said, "so then it's Monday again and the pen still not in the shop. It's a good thing there are such trusty soldiers in the world who can be counted on to take care of things like this, and a good thing meeting them at the right time like this too. People are always bumping into you at the right time, Melzer dear, or it's more that you're always bumping into them at the right time. Then there's the other kind of person; it's the exact opposite whenever they cross your path, no matter when or where they turn up. If you're anxiously waiting for somebody else, of if you've started cleaning your kid gloves with ammonia or kerosene, or if you've just cut your finger or tipped over an inkwell—that's exactly when your bell rings and there's somebody standing at the door all clueless, friendly, and innocent. But I believe, in all seriousness, that behind it all is a deeply hidden, inherent spitefulness. Because there's no doubt that this way of turning up is peculiar to certain kinds of characters. Once I've noticed this happen two or three times, the offending party is finished in my book. Then there are the others, ones who turn up and ring the bell at just at the right moment, as if it were timed. How do they manage that? Then again, unfortunately, there are those who never ring and are never standing outside the door."

Just now, however, during these moments in which once again a certain invitation, coming on him suddenly as if from around a corner, leapt out at the close of her comments—even in his modesty there was no denying what she meant—an enormous tension swelled up inside Melzer, making the walls really bulge and the barriers crack. They went along the last stretch of the sidewalk to her building entrance, and the light wind blowing on this relatively cool day felt almost cold to Melzer, as if he himself were some hot object it was rippling around. He didn't fully recover from the onslaught. As they parted, he held her hand longer and the kiss he planted on it had a tiny bit more pressure than is either usual or automatic on such occasions.

Around four o'clock that afternoon Sectional Councillor Geyrenhoff was descending the magnificent flights of stairs in the palace of Prince Eugen of Savoy (which still houses the Finance Ministry today), took the few steps to Kärntner Strasse, and crossed it, but he didn't go to the Graben. Contrary to his habit at any other time, he stayed today on the side of the Stock-im-Eisen Platz for once. The sole cause perhaps was the forcible impression he had to the effect that a panopticon of the past was bursting in on him at this very spot, an uncommon phenomenon he would have no doubt been spared on the other side of the street. First Marchetti appeared. Then Konietzki. Not long after that, Langl. So they went walking along as a foursome, chattering away and moving with correspondingly annoying slowness. Then when Herr von Lindner turned up, Geyrenhoff could only say to himself in all sincerity, "This had to happen as well."

He had his rather crotchety notions, quirks, and Higher Zihalisms (more *austriaco-hispanico*), this sectional councillor of ours. In the first place, he'd become absorbed not long before in exuding page by page his lengthy and bulky chronicle. Second, there had recently appeared on the horizon for the first time the chance that his sequestered English fortune might be released. But third, and connected with the first two points—his position and his duties were no longer gratifying to him at this stage, or perhaps not at all anymore. Now, for the first time, and in retrospect, he was painfully beset by an awareness he had not acknowledged in its full dimensions and with such distinctness as a young assistant in the court president's legal division: the great mission of the Austrian administrative official from former days, the qualities and mandates (*virtutes et facultates*) bequeathed him by virtue of his function had to be exercised these days as if someone were trying out a new tennis racket in his office. As it happens, however, the Higher Zihalism has a notable tendency and ability to transcend itself, to become crotchety toward its own self, even to take an ironic view of itself. So Geyrenhoff was exasperated because he knew so precisely what was causing him worry or sadness and what was weighing on him—he even had it all itemized. If it was all subject to being outlined and perused, however, then there couldn't really be all that much to it. Unfortunately, that applied to the chronicle he'd begun some time before. Turning critical, through deliberating in this vein, the sectional councillor noticed on taking a sidelong look that Marchetti's bushy beard and pointy nose had grown conspicuously incompatible with the rest of him and were sticking out like little promontories from a continent all the rest of which was submerged in fat.

Langl's voice fit right in with the unashamed—we won't say shameless—nature of the appearance being presented here. "Yes, I was in Salzburg. Guess who I saw walking around the Collegien Church on Monday morning? Editha Pastré. Her name is Schlinger now, I think." Konietzki turned his head quickly and looked at Langl. Just then somebody called out, "Melzer! Melzer!" He came around the corner of the Kohlmarkt in a hurry without noticing the group and was about to pass by. "This had to happen as well," thought the sectional councillor. The whole lot of them ended up in the Café Pucher.

Melzer asked to be excused for fifteen minutes because of errands he still had to take care of, and after that time he came back. It was cool inside here and almost deserted. The group entered into a lively discussion about the stabilizing of Austria's currency, for which ample reason was at hand in those days; they cross-questioned Konietzki. He gave his information slowly. He claimed there was a good deal he didn't know. Melzer looked over to an unoccupied table; it looked empty, tidy, and caught in the maws of the upholstered velvet banquettes. It took him a while before he realized with perfect recall that it was none other than that table at which he'd sat in the high summer of 1910, before the bear hunt, with roughly the same people as now, even though Geyrenhoff and Konietzki hadn't been present and Benno von Grabmayr—no longer living—had been, though only for a short time. Melzer had taken the train that same evening and met Major Laska in the compartment. It now became strikingly and unassailably clear to Melzer that he would simply be unable to spend the last part of the week on Porzellan Gasse, but not in Tulln or Greifenstein, either, something for which the weather wasn't exactly promising right now anyway. A ceaseless rain continuing into today had now swamped the earlier part of the week. The Danube was at a menacing high-water point. Even so, the weather seemed to be wanting to clear up. Tomorrow, then, Saturday, out to the country to visit the Stangelers or climb the Rax, or both! He had the headwaiter bring him a train schedule, and a comfortable afternoon express train jumped out at the very first glance. At home he would reserve a room on the telephone—a nice large one, not in the country inn near the mill (which had utterly no appeal for him just now), but in the hotel farther below! Having reached this point, he said his goodbyes and left.

Before five thirty that afternoon René Stangeler set out for the West Station to meet Grete Siebenschein. Sunlight broke through now and then, ranging and threading through the streets, spreading pensiveness everywhere, setting small incidental objects aglow in an intense gold, accentuating them in a way somehow inexplicable—a signboard here, half a row of windows there—and rising up to meet the viewer on every side, opening out a vista with its radiance and closing it again as it faded. In the small, old-fashioned concourse the late arrival of the train from Paris had already been chalked up on the noticeboard;

another train, late as well, though only a few minutes behind schedule, was just due to enter the station at any moment, and people were already making their way through the open double doors to the platform. It was the express from Salzburg. "René!" someone called out in a low voice just as Stangeler was buying a platform ticket. He registered this soft and very warm voice with something like pleasure and looked around without spotting anyone, but then here was Paula Pichler coming up to him from the right. She had already been on her way out to meet the train. Behind her, Lintschi now came into view and was immediately swept into René's arms after he'd greeted Paula properly. Lina was very embarrassed by Stangeler's behavior but was obviously very happy, too. They went back outside to wait for Thea Rokitzer together.

René now found out all about her friendship with Paula Pichler during the fifteen minutes they still had to wait for the Salzburg express. For Stangeler, who had never bothered himself about Paula in the least—to him she was just an appendage of the captain and nothing more—Thea suddenly began to acquire a meaning from what he was hearing, as if she were being annexed to or fused with his life, in a manner of speaking, while at the same time a dividing wall now crumbled that had kept them separate up to now for lack of any connection. He was struck with an inkling, if only a dim one, of the general way such networks manifested themselves as life went on and reached out in every direction, in any of which outcomes emerged that could look as if remote worlds were meeting, as when his sister Asta and Paula Schachl had met on the lower ramp of the Strudlhof Steps fourteen years before, while Grauermann, a real pontifex of the conventional, had made a ridiculous effort at building bridges by introducing people back and forth.

Of course there was a great deal Paula wanted to know on this occasion—including about the captain—and they spoke quickly and intensely, like a brother and sister who hadn't seen one another for a long time, and with a level of trust that was entirely beyond question. Lintschi, for whom their conversation soon slipped into unknown territory, stepped off to the side, as it were, and, tactful as she was, turned her initial listening *to* them into a listening *away* as she set those grave, gray-blue eyes of hers—which signally combined solitude and engagement with human nature to a rare degree—wandering over the platform, the waiting people, and the tracks.

Paula had been pressing forward, meanwhile, and reached the topic of Melzer; that is, she asked flat out what kind of person he was.

"Melzer, well let's see!" René said, and looked up to the high ceiling of the concourse, to the smoky-gray iron supports and bracings of the thick glass roof through which the sun was hardly able to penetrate. It looked as if he were now trying to fetch down the right word from up there. At the same time, the way he was choosing his words showed how important he considered it that Paula should understand him. "Melzer," he said, "now, he has a deep-down integrity that can make anything possible. Even the greatest step. Even becoming a genius. It's forever standing in its own way, though, because first and foremost it shies away from anything that's not simple. But then what's simple anyway?" He looked down in frustration, in frustration with himself, because just when he was so eager to have Paula understand him, his word choice struck him as a failure! As if hoping to earn her forgiveness for his demonstrated ineptitude—inept just where he should be ad-ept—he took Paula's right hand, kissed it, and looked at her sadly for a minute. That latent genius Lina, standing next to them but completely *not* listening, had picked up nothing of their conversation. "Well, ev-erything's simple when it's over and done," Paula now asserted, "but anybody who believes that when starting out will always be a fool." René felt extraordinarily relieved at her words, now thinking he might not have totally missed the target after all. Paula then went on to ask about Editha. "In reality she doesn't even really exist," Stangeler an-swered, partly serious, "she's just a ghost, a kind of dream, a fancy. I think Melzer's afraid of her. It's possible she's in love with him."

"Attention! Step back!" the railroad men were calling.

The empty, dead tracks and the rail beds came alive from the thun-der of the train pulling in. At first it seemed to be made up of only the locomotive, in its immense height, but now it pulled into the concourse at what technically unschooled laymen always think of as a frightening rate of speed. Only a few meters from the buffer stops at the front wall did the long-practiced dominance over the monstrous beast and its total submission become apparent. The dragon stood still. Now it was all domestic, part of the home, so to speak.

The contents of the train immediately came pouring out by the many open carriage doors, and Stangeler joined the searching attentiveness of his own glance—it quickly impinged on dozens of strange faces, one after another, only to glide lovelessly past them for not yielding what he was anticipating—to those of the two women, engaged in doing the same. They had not positioned themselves in a very advantageous place and had scarcely paid the requisite amount of attention to that fact, caught up in their conversation as they were (whereas with a latent genius it's well known that questions of tact not infrequently take precedence over anything else, and so the one we're talking about here refrained from interrupting their discussion by pointing out that they were too far away from the exit and were by that token close to incurring the risk of allowing Thea to pass through it unnoticed). The flood of travelers pouring out grew stronger, so it was now easy to lose track of individuals in any case. But at the very moment when he heard Paula Pichler's resonant voice (autumnally gold-burnished, as it were) calling "Thea, Thea!" and could spot the girl herself responding to Paula loudly while coming down the steps of her carriage—at that very moment René recognized an entirely different person among the passengers leaving the train, someone he wasn't at all expecting to be among the arriving travelers: Editha Schlinger. Another woman hurried up to her immediately and hugged her. After a brief stop to talk to the porter, the two then stepped forward, plunged into the stream of all the other travelers, and were swept along toward the exit. Being in the crowd made them less clearly visible to René than when they had been standing by the carriage and then made their way along the platform, where the exiting passengers were backed up. But then the right amount of distance gave him a clear view, unobstructed for the moment, of the two women, and what he now saw with his own eyes hit him in the head like a stone, in the shape of irrefutable optical evidence to the effect that there were clearly two of Editha Schlinger-Pastré walking side by side, that the woman who'd hugged and the woman doing the hugging were one and the same person; they were dressed almost alike, so telling them apart would require painstaking scrutiny of the small differences, something there was no time for now. He blinked hard, opened his eyes again, and even shook his head as if to put them back into focus. The redoubled lady (or two ladies?) now passed out of his sight, even though that meant they had to come closer to him on their way to the platform exit, but then he located them again in the crowd for a moment, the two faces of two heads he had known only as one up to now.

Thea had come up to them in the meanwhile, hugging Paula and greeting Lintschi; René, whom Thea may have been somewhat surprised to find among the others, turned to greet her as well. She struck him as very beautiful, which he registered on a strictly objective level, not feeling any attraction. Her face was aglow and her eyes like fresh water sparkling in the sun. In her happiness, Paula couldn't rave enough about how well her friend looked. It wasn't until René, searching with one eye among the stream of passersby for the redoubled ladies the whole time, vigorously tugged at Paula's sleeve and whispered to her with such rapidity and insistence that she immediately had to realize something very much out of the ordinary had just occurred and then told her what and whom she should be on the lookout for—not until then did Paula turn away from Thea and look among the crowd along with René, suddenly letting out a short exclamation of surprise but then, facing away abruptly, said in a low voice to René, "Turn around quick, René; make it fast. It might be better if they don't notice you and recognize you; you never know." René immediately did as she said, deeply astonished from the bottom of his heart at Paula's presence of mind and her ability to think her way in a flash into and ahead of an obscure matter that had left him standing there dumbfounded with his mouth agape.

It was Paula too who now dragged out their departure from the platform as if intentionally. Staying put where they were standing, near Thea's few pieces of luggage, she first asked her friend for details of the enjoyable time Thea had spent in the country, and then (this was not really like her at all!) she absolutely couldn't find the platform ticket she would have to turn in at the exit, rummaging around in her bag and producing it from her jacket pocket only after she'd hunted high and low several times. So the stream of travelers had ebbed and dispersed almost completely when the three women finally left the platform along with Stangeler; he left with them because by now the Paris train was going to be well over an hour late. Paula Pichler now told Thea how they'd coincidentally happened to meet up with Stangeler, who had come to wait for somebody (René had of course mentioned it) arriving on the delayed Paris train.

René was left behind by himself after Paula and Lintschi had set out to see their companion home. They went to the city rail station. As they were saying goodbye, Paula Pichler and Stangeler made arrangements to meet within the next few days, on Wednesday afternoon, in fact; after all, they were certainly feeling the need on both sides to talk over this strange event. Thea had noticed nothing about the incident on the platform; her distraction was brought about in part by Lintschi Nohel, who understood that she needed to engage Thea in particularly absorbing conversation while Paula and Stangeler were standing off to the side and whispering.

René looked once more at the noticeboard announcing delays, set his watch precisely to the official time on the station clock, and went to a nearby café.

Here was where it was borne in on him, to his intense surprise, if not with a sudden jolt, how drastically the frame of mind he was now in had changed compared with his outlook while on his way to the station, a realization that again struck him like an arrow shot from the ceiling, at once forging an intimate connection with every single object in his immediate environment, no matter how small or insignificant; this cushion covered in green was more deeply hollowed, his glance across the street toward the trellised gateway of a small park took on a more densely spatial character. He also recognized at once that he had been brought to a point past and beyond Grete, so to speak, outside her range, beyond her validation and authority. Even more, it dawned on him that he downright owed her this new understanding, which had not come about for him alone but for her as well, or actually for them both, as a couple, so that they could really become one in the first place. For only now (so it seemed to him) was he capable of really and truly setting out to meet her, of going to her—and that was exactly what Grete needed. Drawn back this far (like a bowstring) and functioning under its power—even snapping and locking into place—he would now, thanks to this power, set out joyfully to join her, to conjoin with her for the first time.

His tension left him when he had come this far; he dropped away from it like a ripe piece of fruit falling from the tree, a bright shining spot to mark the short drop.

It contained a core so inconspicuous he scarcely knew it was there, though it yielded as a totally unpremeditated ramification his maintaining the most absolute secrecy toward Grete in regard to the incident at the West Station earlier in the day.

It seemed to René somehow as if Paula had left with him the charge, as it were, to keep silent on this matter. He started off for the station again half an hour later. He was taking into account the possibility that the Paris train might have been able to make up at least half its lost time, and assuming that would be the maximum. The sun had by now withdrawn from the streets. A moderately warm summer evening was growing grayer. The delay turned out not to have been reduced. After twenty minutes of René walking back and forth in the small waiting area the doors to the platform were opened once more.

Everything worked out in the couple's favor. From the first moment on, all the imponderables fell into place, starting when he folded her in his arms on the platform—like a cloud flashing lightning, he thought, a baroque cloud with liberally rounded curves, as her slender body nestling against him kept heightening and even overheightening his keyed-up emotions, causing an aureole, a radiant halo, to gleam forth at every point of contact. "Just to have you back again," she said, her arms around his neck. Somehow they found a taxi, and after a ride they were hardly aware of—each an uninterrupted explosion side by side in the back seat, detonating over and over without producing coherence—after a ride during which they were incessantly flinging words and syllables back and forth, the elevator went up through the middle of the stairwell with all its senseless festoons and tassels (surprisingly, none of the luggage had been lost; it was all there) to the Siebenscheins' apartment, empty now in summertime, as even Grete's parents had treated themselves to a few weeks out in the country and were staying at Goisern in Styria, though they were expected back the following day, on Saturday afternoon.

Grete's flat suitcases were stacked in a corner of her room unopened, clothes were lying on the rug, and Grete's delicate lingerie slipped off the chair onto René's shoes.

But this was no gondola unmoored and reeling through the air but instead a ship on a steady course, with the many calculations that went into determining it complicating matters. René knew that beyond any doubt. The dark spaces in the room had long since been gathering snugly around the colorful, dimmed lamp next to the wide bed, and they confirmed René's knowledge almost as clearly as did the shadowy coves of his lover's body, scattered parts of the core, the central shadow, which was a gate and a gateway signifying that everything about this moment was leading to somewhere. It wasn't only the past that took on concentrated form and went into hiding under this smallest of particulars; the future came surging up and placing a strain from inside as well; thus doubly fraught, the shadow kept moment by moment taking in and taking on greater weight, as well as haunting or even daunting proportions that cried out for meaning, though almost silently, barely whispering.

On the following day, Saturday, which brought better weather in the form of a windless late-summer day—a faint hint of imminent autumn, still entirely without any of its visible signs (perhaps it was the air alone, the echoes from the distant street noise, the sky between the roof edges) would drift into the soul of anyone looking down the street toward and over the Danube Canal—on this Saturday morning, Grete Siebenschein was busy getting the apartment ready for her parents' return, which meant in part airing out the bedroom, so it was here that daylight and noise from the street first broke in as the window catches snapped into their hooks and dust motes swirled in the sunlight while the beds were being made, the fine cool dust stirred up that had collected here and there, the vacuum cleaner set in motion and run back and forth across the rug just now unrolled. Stangler helped her with all these chores and looked through the linen closet for a long time and started waving large bedsheets around, which sent Grete into one fit of laughter after another. She was wearing a silk head cloth and an apron. Her body, always *fausse maigre*, now seemed after her stay in France to be underscoring even more emphatically whatever statement it had been making from the start, or at least this was how its decrees were being promulgated from underneath her thin housedress; and it might well be that after all turmoil of the of the previous months it actually had filled out a little. They decided to tidy up the dining room too and so to start in one more room, at least as a preliminary, the more methodical and laborious work the household staff would get down to when they returned next week. It was from here that they had a view along the street to the Danube Canal. Grete and René stood arm in arm at the window for a while. She was holding a feather duster with a bamboo handle in her left hand. Just now—they were looking right down on that taxi stand cut in two by the street (the same one that drew our attention earlier, of course, in connection with Frau Mary K.)—they watched as a cab slowly and noiselessly crossed from one side to the other. The tops of the trees lining the Danube Canal were still deep green and covered the lower rows of windows of the houses over the water on the other side.

Stangeler went home in the afternoon. Grete had gone shopping to make sure there would be food in the house on Sunday and then got ready to go meet her parents at the station. René was not invited to come along, even though he would have been a great help with organizing luggage and finding transportation, but experience had shown that whenever Frau Siebenschein traveled, and especially when the journey was over—indeed on all such occasions—she would be even more susceptible to becoming unglued, whereupon one or another of her many and varied ailments would without fail be called into requisition, though only in most cases to be forgotten again (happy to report) once the situation had settled down. It seemed to a degree as if this woman's physical weight—she was slender or even emaciated, very bright and vigilant as well—were too slight and would not let her press down hard enough to leave her impress on her milieu, especially on her husband, always much too pleasure-loving for her taste. Her way of augmenting that inadequate weight was through sensitivity to the faintest sign that the attention directed to her from anywhere in her surroundings appeared to be dwindling.

Stangeler was scheduled to stop by the following afternoon, on Sunday.

Dr. Siebenschein had planned on being back at his desk in his legal practice on the day after that, Monday (his professional offices were directly connected with the residence, which isn't the standard arrangement among lawyers in Vienna), because he had arranged an important consultation for that coming Wednesday afternoon at which Grete was supposed to aid her father as his secretary, on hand to take detailed minutes. She'd already been involved in several capacities in his business affairs but always to a minor extent and free of any soul-killing daily grind; her father thought her talents lay more in "dreaming and doing" (to borrow his own expression) than in being steadily occupied with a barrage of tasks. Dr. Ferry respected everyone's idiosyncrasies, including his children's. Given the lack of a son, or at least a son-in-law, with legal training (something Frau Siebenschein missed as well!), it was something of a disappointment that Grete had not studied law. But she had encountered significant learning difficulties even in high school, and hers was a father who rejected force or coercion in any form. Meanwhile, his elder daughter had grown familiar with every case of any significance in his practice, and the father even went so far as to ask her advice, and rather often, at that; yes, her complete lack of specialized legal knowledge often caused her to miss the essential point entirely, much to her father's merriment, but from time to time her corresponding freedom from preconceptions would lead her to an answer so exactly right that it opened up new perspectives. Here is the right place for us to remark that Dr. Siebenschein's legal firm was one of those practices, proliferating more and more in those days, whose main activity increasingly shifted to out-of-court settlements via enmeshment with industrial disputes and a myriad of other such business matters, so that it was hardly possible anymore to refer to such an attorney as a man of the forum.

So René was unexpectedly sent home with a date to come back the next day, Sunday; being caught off guard like that thrust him into an empty afternoon and evening.

Only now did the duplicated ladies, the twins (our captain, the Master of Horse, was in the habit of referring to this phenomenon, long familiar to him, in decidedly different terms, but we'll be hearing more about that later from his own lips), enter his mind again. It had therefore been easy for René to keep quiet about this matter to Grete. As he now turned the subject back and forth and rolled it this way and that, as if playing with a ball, it would first flash forth like a point of the gravest concern, but then it would appear absurd and petty, some kind of trick, much ado about nothing. He meant in any case to keep maintaining silence about it but had a hunch that the centrifugal force of his communicative nature was in and of itself going to make his preservation of that silence a powerful dynamic through the extra energy any item of information, no matter what, will accrue when we don't share it with anyone else. He sensed, too, that accruing the energy from a good many such items could eventually come to play a significant or even decisive part in producing from those numerous tiny bursts a burdensome aura of superiority.

With newborn thoughts of this kind lodged in his midriff—all in all they represented a not very exalted and in fact an outright Scheichs-beutelean category of those virtues gathered under the heading of discretion—he bumped into his brother-in-law, Building Surveyor Haupt, who had made himself comfortable in his pajamas, an English pipe between his teeth, and was just in the act of leaving the hallway, from which he'd fetched his briefcase, as Stangeler opened the apartment door. They said hello, and Stangeler stopped to chat with Haupt for a moment, wondering somewhere inside why the man had spent the entire summer so far in Vienna without taking any kind of longer vacation. He asked him about that later but received an evasive answer with an offhand remark to the effect that the Vienna telephone system, in the process of being fully automated (a development carried through at that time in several large cities), was now nearing completion and had kept him stuck in town. (The building surveyor was an engineer specializing in this branch now, but he had originally come from a different field, metallurgy; this had been his area of expertise in 1914, and so he had been assigned several times by the War Ministry to travel to Germany, including once to Hamburg, not long after the well-known Battle of Jutland.) René chattered away and rambled on about who had been on hand at the country house and what all was going on there, and soon enough he was talking mainly about Etelka. He didn't feel quite right while doing so, however. He became clearly aware of a wide gap that seemed to have opened up immediately and more or less automatically and had separated the way he was conducting himself now from the principles he had been contemplating a short time before. What emerged with less clarity, however, was his uncertainty about how to read the other man, whose impact he was feeling intensely and unremittingly, even though Haupt had done nothing except sit at his desk—stacked with a pile of thick professional books lying open and an adding machine next to sheets of paper covered with tiny columns of figures—smoking his pipe and looking quite affable as he took off his horn-rimmed glasses and lay them on one of the open books. To be sure, this man, left alone in the empty city apartment and now studying at his desk, looked on the whole like an English ship's captain, tall, lanky, athletic, easygoing (as a young engineer, by the way, Haupt had in fact spent a number of years in English-speaking countries); nonetheless, he unremittingly projected some perceptible attribute that seemed to be the settled essence of the man and not just a momentary outlook triggering a temporary reaction: projecting it right now, perhaps, because René's chatter might have been getting on his nerves, which could easily have been the case, or because he wanted to get back to what he was working on, or because he really didn't want to be regaled with details concerning Etelka—at any rate, he was emanating deep-seated rejection, whether of the latest developments from the country, of René's way of presenting those developments, of such developments in general, of the fact that developments of that kind existed at all, of anything and everything whatever. Deep inside him must have dwelt different standards and ideas about human affairs, but he never discoursed on them, partly from good-heartedness, though possibly also from passivity, to avoid getting tangled up in a dispute, but even more essentially because he would not have been able to achieve release had he voiced the contradictory views he might have expressed under other circumstances, for they would have been held fast by a gravitational pull which there was no centrifugal force to counteract, rendering him incapable of sustained equilibrium in his environment if he made his standpoint clear. So there wasn't even a hint of confrontation, which is often provoked only to set off fireworks as an antidote to loneliness that otherwise never sparks: that was the situation with Haupt. That refusal to engage lodged in the back of his mind as a standard of measure, which was exactly what Stangeler in all his effusiveness was feeling as the reason why the paper fire of his words died down so quickly. Along with all his good-heartedness, Haupt also projected a sternness well suited to antagonize and provoke deep opposition in a young person like René, who had never been confronted with such a thing, never been exposed to a risk, never had a knife blade brandished at him, or if he had, had seen it withdrawn again at once. In short, it would have been up to Stangeler to say, with all due respect for Haupt, that simply holding any standpoint, however slight its value, by that very token obligated the holder to engage in dialectic down to the most minute detail. But where was René, that pipsqueak, where was his espousal of logical principle? He merely drooped in Haupt's presence. He withered. He suddenly felt very tired, downright sleepy. And we could indeed look on this effect brought about by Haupt as a kind of biological manifestation of self-defense mechanisms, just as a cuttlefish makes the water murky. At any rate, René's resources were nowhere nearly equal to this mechanism, so it overpowered him, even though not a single step had been taken, their differences had not given rise to tension, and not even a fleeting thought had been wasted on the matter.

Still, René was asked about Fraunholzer—whether he'd already shown up there at the country house or whether anyone knew when he'd be coming. Stangeler could answer only with a simple "No," which calmed him to an extent. He told Haupt that Asta had already written to Fraunholzer, but Haupt had known that for some time anyway (it seemed impossible to read from his expression, incidentally, whether that was sitting well with him or not). Maybe he rejected that too.

Only at this point, more and more overcome by the power of his urgent need to sleep—which seemed, paradoxically enough, to be an anesthetizing poison administered by Haupt—did René feel a force beginning to relent that until now had been constantly building pressure from inside as his mouth kept talking; holding up under that force had represented to him a last stand, a last chance to hold out against

Haupt, so he held on to its tail end with great effort until fatigue made him let go of it as well; still, he had parted from his brother-in-law without telling him anything about his experience earlier in the day at the West Station (however advisable, not to say crucial, he thought it would be to mention it under the guise of wanting to ask this level-headed and to all appearances well-balanced man for advice as to what to do about this incident, what action to take, if any). He held it unspoken inside himself, though, and it felt as if in doing so he were holding his own self intact in his hand, guarding his strange reaction to these duplicated ladies, which were no concern of his anyway, but the undeniable physical, manifest fact of whose existence still kept appearing in different lights, sometimes trifling, sometimes consequential. Then suddenly something hurtled across his memory, like a meteor of the mind—he saw the pond at his family's country house and himself sitting next to the sand pile, with Geyrenhoff standing in front of him in his cream-colored tennis trousers. An aroma of lavender. He had told Geyrenhoff nothing about the large snake, either, and however weak his own position was at the time (these are the exact words he was thinking), he had held his ground and not yielded, had even then held reserves in his hand (note how deeply and enduringly, by the way, military or battle-related images and metaphors had penetrated into people's general outlook as a whole, pounded deep into the heartwood of memory by many an ax blow and now persisting with a life of their own, even among the notoriously civilian-minded—doesn't that fact oblige us to find it remarkable that none other than Major Melzer was growing more free and easy in this regard?!). At the same time, Stangeler could now see with astonishing clarity that his conduct back then had been exactly right. In this one point, at least, he had not failed, for Geyrenhoff would undoubtedly have been the antithesis of a person to whom he might have reported his experience in the ravine earlier that day. Melzer, on the other hand, who had come along later, was just the right type. Stopping at this point, at this spot now so sharply illuminated—René had in the meantime made his way across to his rear bedroom, densely filled with the odor or vapor of the wild grapes and other plants on the long balcony in front of the windows, the aromas really lush, almost arousing—on this spot, then, before he turned on the light, standing in the darkness of the cool room, he could feel, as if they were the colossal stresses and releases of a stanza written by titans (didn't the parquet floor in fact virtually swell underneath him?!), the giant step life had since taken, catching up to and long since having passed by the man who was then Lieutenant Melzer, who thereupon at once became for René, in clarifying contrast to those former days, the next example of a person toward whom silence needed to be maintained, no matter what pretext should start talking him up and trying to talk him into believing that it would be desirable and even necessary for him to tell the major or civil service councillor about the bizarre sight at the West Station, which after all could possibly or even probably concern Melzer. But the flood of silence and concealment had caught up with the major and submerged him, a clear flood below the surface of which René now saw Melzer floating. He looked unpity-ingly at Melzer down there. With his trousers pure white, like china. And much more clearly than usual, gleaming as if in crystal, while the flood continued on toward a horizon beyond which "no one would ever again at any point say anything at all to anyone whosoever." With that, the single right answer was formed, ready to be conveyed at any given time to any and every imaginable version of Government Build-ing surveyor Haupt, without exception! And René Stangeler resolved, with a kind of passion blazing here in the dark, his eyes firing like small guns that kept ceaselessly flashing, to fulfill this deferred obligation at the next right place and time with more conscious intent and thus better (as he supposed) than he had back then, where he had merely scraped through. All he had to do was get used to it. *Not* mentioning something, *not* imparting it, could with no great effort soon enough come to be an unconscious habit, ingrained, seasoned, no longer a strain, no more need to hold onto some tail end for dear life …

He slept late into the day and turned up at the Siebenscheins' around four thirty, in a good mood. Besides Grete and her parents, one of Frau Siebenschein's sisters was present, a Frau Clarisse Markbreiter, who bore not the faintest resemblance to the hostess. She had a great deal of feminine grace, plump little white hands, unusually abundant and beautiful ebony-black hair with occasional single silver threads that looked as if they were actually made of that metal. What was most remarkable about Aunt Clarisse was her figure, in particular when she stood next to her slender and almost wasp-waisted sister, which at once made her contours almost border on walking caricature. Frau Clarisse, whose shapely legs could well have held their own alongside those of Mary K. or Lea Fraunholzer, retained her trim look on the whole up to the middle stories of the building (how much her corset maker may have contributed to this spruce architecture is not a subject we can research at this time). In the upper mezzanine, however, a monumental style surged forth with such unexpected abruptness that the general effect could best be described as the shape of an upside-down drop. She was cheerful, even funny, and by no means dull, but she had one of those spirits (insofar as we can speak of such a thing) that instantly lose all their good qualities and their affable inoffensiveness the second they're confronted with something they don't understand, which apparently causes such people to become highly insulted. There probably inheres in them a demand that the world must under any and all conditions run smoothly, in a manner they can understand, and that it is to be reprimanded the moment it should in any way deviate from that course. Now, Frau Clarisse seldom saw René Stangeler. But it will be easy to understand that when they met, he didn't come off too well in her eyes, no matter what he had to say for himself (and it wasn't much). She had brought her daughter, who was universally trumpeted forth, so to speak, as especially pretty, elegant, and bright, along with the young woman's husband, who had resigned himself to the accolades bestowed on his wife as well as to his assigned role of model husband, which his mother-in-law had been passed on to him once and for all en bloc and which he was now making every effort to live up to—a modest man not yet thirty, very well dressed and groomed, with a culture of restraint met with over and over in Vienna among middle-class persons with old and well-established businesses.

Grete talked about Paris and France as a whole. They were sitting in the dining room; the actual parlor was still in mothballs, locked and dark. René, for whom people like Frau Clarisse Markbreiter had the somewhat calming effect of an outsider, a clear standard of measure at the outermost limit of his horizon, meaning a purely familial range—never mind that as a possible provider who could make genuine provision for Grete he dwindled by that very measure to a size whose measure could no longer be taken and to a place beyond the pale—René was rendered far more uneasy by these stories and the thoughts (if we can call them that) exchanged among the younger people, after he had listened to them, than by the unwavering, silent protest against his whole being by Aunt Clarisse. With those around his age, however, he felt only too close a proximity, forged by the conventions of their educated and more sophisticated colloquial speech, and he thought it was much to be feared that Grete, turning nimbly back and forth on the same level between her cousin and her husband on the one hand and himself on the other (insofar as he could take part in the conversation), might in that way inwardly be tossing him into the same pot with the others, as it were, and to use this pot to concoct a stew forcibly struck him as a hopeless fraud: a fraud on his part, a swindling of innocent people who adopted viewpoints and expressed opinions the same way they did anything else—cleaning their fingernails or taking snapshots, say—but certainly not as the result of any systematic evaluation resulting in the eventual articulation of their individual stances. The young couple had been in Paris several times, to be sure, not just on their honeymoon, but on business trips later, most recently to the South of France. On the other hand, René Stangeler lacked any experience that would have enabled him to keep up with a conversation that at every moment, as is customary, passed far beyond its actual subject to yield sage generalities. He fell into the very dubious state of having to judge utterances on subjects he knew nothing about as nonsense. Had he been capable, as any genuinely mature person in fact is capable, of leaning for support against the comfortable and insurmountable balustrade of irony and urbane detachment, of leaning into a conversation of this kind, so that he could now and then—more for the fun of it than because he was in over his head—let his own light shine by tossing in, just for a brief second, some witty, aptly formulated comment, he would have experienced his ignorance of the topics being spoken about with much less embarrassment, would have been less affected by the tight squeeze his youthfulness again and again made him feel compelled to work himself into, and, strangely enough, with a deep consciousness of his own guilt at his life's circumstances.

As it turned out, though, the talk and his reaction to it didn't last long. Moreover, Stangeler was imbued with so palpable a sense of physical well-being today that every discord quickly subsided after it arose, smothered by the positive, as it were. He felt cleansed and cleared inside, at home in his own skin as in a new suit that fit well, and it was exactly this kind of feeling that bound him gratefully and intimately to Grete. As he looked out the window at which he was sitting, he saw two or three of the taxis at the end of the street, where the divided cabstand was located, cross one by one to the other side. This movement, occurring at roughly similar intervals, had a disconcerting, admonishing effect, like a clock ticking, like drops of water falling, like a fixed measure against which to assess everything here in the foreground, a measure even more severe and foreboding than the one dwelling within the monumental bosom of Frau Clarisse Markbreiter. Now he started feeling once again, even more keenly and painfully, that sense of constriction in his life from just before, especially when facing out from the Siebenscheins' apartment into this day, autumnal to its depths and nursing in its vaulted breadth at the end of every street. The telephone started ringing insistently in the hallway. Grete went past René quickly and gracefully with her typical gait that thrust her hips to the side with every step. Now they heard her talking into the phone for a good while and laughing out loud several times, after which she called through the door, "René!" She handed him the receiver as she whispered, "It's Eulenfeld. Make arrangements with him for Wednesday; I'm not free all afternoon or evening. He wants to get together with you. So Wednesday, all right?" she repeated, disappeared back inside, and shut the door behind her.

After saying a few words to Stangeler, Eulenfeld passed the receiver to Editha.

As if at a single blow there burst in on him here in the Siebenscheins' hallway the faraway places he had missed out on, all the trips he hadn't taken were made up for, the time-measuring taxis were overridden and rendered meaningless as the gondola went reeling high up across the sky, over the city and the mighty river. For a brief moment he felt separated from Grete in a very unwelcome way; something thrust itself between them that apparently wasn't content to remain a single point but was running along as a line instead. All of a sudden, however, he felt this line fading away, no longer a marker for him. Anybody who's double couldn't be real in the first place, it seemed to him now. And Grete had run off to Paris, too. They both had to return, to come back from being away, if they were going to be able to meet on equal terms. Not just Grete.

He promised to come to tea on Wednesday afternoon.

The room was large, cool, spacious, aglow in the shimmer of the thick greenery by the windows; it stood almost as if in a kind of underwater light, and the reflections of the treetops from the old-fashioned mirror in the background expanded the room further. There were scents of wood and fresh bed linens as well as the air from outside, suffused with the fragrant breath of all the plant life. The murmuring of the stream, clearly audible, was now interrupted by a brief noise that started and stopped with surprisingly precise timing—it was a chorus of geese.

When the chambermaid left, Melzer stayed standing there motionless, in as astonished a state as if he had not arrived here of his own volition but had been somehow unexpectedly catapulted into this place like an asteroid into the orbit of a strange planet. He kept looking out at the greenery, which filled everything here. He looked into it as if gazing into the surface of a deep pond. The incomprehensibility of his present position, commonplace enough in itself, now struck him with a feeling almost like happiness at the thought that he'd been transported here only by an impulse from inside himself, alone and with no external rationale or practical purpose whatever. He felt like the monarch of all he surveyed and accordingly had a very clear sense that even on the physical level he was the midpoint, so to say, of a world he himself had created.

Melzer drifted for a few moments, though of course he couldn't stay afloat for long. He opened his shaving kit, washed his hands, ran a brush through his hair, and went down to a table in the garden to have coffee. As he was leaving the room, he saw a newspaper, purchased at the South Station in Vienna, crisply folded and still unread, lying next to a small leather case on the sofa. He left it there. The sight of it was enough to satisfy him. For a moment he had a picture of the station café, where he'd sat before the train left, and the wide, half-empty room now seemed to him to be stretching far to the back and vibrating like a resonance chamber or the sounding board of a violin, alive and familiar. The garden was tidy and shadowed by leaves, the old waiter's footsteps crunched briskly on the gravel, and from around a sharp bend in the village street, made invisible by a tall living fence of hedges, there came past at ever closer intervals, each time like a fitful breath or a gushing noise, the rumble of automobiles and motorcycles that had driven out from the city and were now hurrying toward the high point of the pass. Melzer was taken by the thought of writing a picture postcard to Thea Rokitzer, but because he didn't know whether she was in Vienna and didn't even know the house number of her building on Alserbach Strasse, it remained undone.

He walked slowly up the village street.

Asta was standing in the sun by the post office.

They greeted each other warmly, with undisguised happiness, and as if they had been together just the day before. In these first seconds each recognized in the other a kinship, in the respect that even physically they had both successfully withstood the destroying and leveling work of fourteen years and had kept themselves intact instead of falling apart, as happened to so many, after all (we need think only of Marchetti!), who go rolling down the hillside of time, turning as they tumble into one of those formless blobs that remain lying there at the bottom. It took no effort for Melzer to see the girlhood face of Asta in her somewhat more distinct and distinguishable features; it even jumped out at him with good humor. And as for the major, he had set his civil service councillor onto the legs of an infantryman who was still present and accounted for. Inescapably there flashed across Melzer's mind a fleeting thought of Editha, whose unchanged appearance could never have caused him such happiness but on the contrary induced a dizzying feeling of emptiness every time he tried connecting her with the girl who had once come walking toward him in a white piqué dress by the tennis court above the Stangelers' country house.

The mail Asta was expecting had arrived by the same bus that had brought Melzer from the station; now it was being handed out at the counter as acquaintances greeted each other and mingled; Melzer was recognized here as well; he was even addressed by name; it was Herr von W., the son of that minister, the man whose almost novel ugliness appeared to be a quirk, a prank played by his own intelligence, perhaps because he considered it also would be boring to be good-looking. When Asta and Melzer had broken free of this homey rural hubbub, Asta holding a few letters and the evening edition of the newspaper, they began walking up the road. They didn't follow it for very long but soon turned left instead, climbing the same steep trails and sloping meadows Asta had crossed twenty-six days before, leaving the beaten path of the general foot traffic in the village, where there was always the danger of bothersome encounters; their turning off the road came about as a result of the turn their conversation had taken. Quite contrary to Melzer's expectation, by the way. In the very first moments of their reunion, Asta, through her attitude alone, and secure in her instincts, picked right back up at the exact point where he, not she, had broken things off fourteen years before, and the generosity of her manner in overlooking his fault lent her a kind of dignity and graciousness that led Melzer to suspect she was displaying those qualities to so exemplary a degree not for his sake, but only for her own, meaning she was not acting like a woman. She didn't touch on the past in words at all; it was totally obvious that she looked on any reversion—even one merely courteous in nature, let alone sentimental—to memories they shared as entirely unnecessary to the renewal of the connection between Melzer and her; instead, she simply took that connection for granted from the start, in no way needful of restoration, and filled in her friend, again as if they'd met only the day before, on everything happening here that he needed to know, and indeed he had a genuine right to know. In this way, their talk of the here and now contained within it a full validation of what had been.

This here and now wasn't called Semski or Ingrid this time, but Etelka.

They sat down in Pastor's Woods on a mossy, rickety bench that called for some caution (Melzer did not catch himself as a nonsensical idea dashed through his mind as quickly as a little bird flutters its wings: it was that nothing could happen here, no matter how much the bench wobbled, because he was so light these days). Just as she had once done in the reception room at the Consular Academy, when she had brought Teddy von Honnegger up to date about the current situation and thereby forestalled long explanations and unneeded palaver, Asta now again marked off with a single twirl of the compass everything that pertained to Etelka, cutting out anything unknown and uncertain (was it her father inside her, who often listened so impatiently when she was speaking?). About Fraunholzer, whom Melzer didn't know: "A good heart, loyal, hot-tempered, and smart, looks like an ancient Roman, like Gnaeus Pompeius—my father, even if he was completely different in so many ways, might have been somehow like him when he was young." She went on: "Pista Grauermann you know. He hasn't changed one bit. Capable, correct, cold as an icicle."

"What a contrast!" he said with spirit, even though he was doing so just to have something to say, in an effort to hide his actual, genuine emotional reaction to the woeful, upsetting, and ominous reports he was hearing—for his mood was that of a happy man. As if he could see the footprints, as if he could run his finger along a fresh, sharp edge: that was how vividly there lay in front of him now the step life had taken in these fourteen years—toward the better, toward liberation, it seemed to him. A warm sense of the deepest gratitude and empathy toward Asta came over him, for keeping a place open and free for him through all those years, for him, a man who hadn't had the ability to occupy it at the time but who felt happy and real to be back in it today (and—the civilian mentality was flourishing in its fresh forward development!—perhaps he even had an inkling that such a place, when a woman like Asta directed him to it, would measure up with well-nigh equal value to the one she hadn't been able to accord him). Something had moved forward here; there had been no turning round and round in place, but real strides taken instead, and it seemed as if he had reached the opposite end of a very elongated ellipse, where the curve closes harmoniously. He could have taken Asta by the shoulders and given her a hearty shake.

"The contrast is exactly the point," she now replied, in answer to his comment. "The fact of the matter is that the whole contraption only keeps on running by this point-counterpoint. I find it pretty boring sometimes, downright tiresome. And of course it's exactly the same thing with this Imre, but in a different form."

So here our Melzer was sitting, Melzer the crab, creeping out a bit from his cave under the stone, his beady little all-seeing eyes at rest, here on this bench at a high elevation with Asta, in freedom, having escaped from the terrarium back in the city, where all sorts of objectionable creatures slithered around one another, where glacier crevasses rolled and ground away—Editha and Eulenfeld, Scheichsbeutel and Oki Leucht (regarding Scheichsbeutel, Melzer was completely off the mark, however; the man was still in Paris and was standing at this very hour—with pachyderm-like indifference perfected to the point of an absolute, immeasurably filled with ennui but altogether imperceptibly—behind Lasch in the salon of a well-known dealer in semiprecious stones, newer ones as well as antique gems and cameos, from among which his employer had been choosing for an hour and a half). Here he was, sitting, our Melzer, looking out at the beauty of nature and calmed by knowing it was as it needed to be. Calmed even more by having again encountered that recognition here and not placed in confrontation, say, itself all floppy and sloppy, with a purity bordering on absolute emptiness and a hopelessly spinach-green sublimity. Nature wasn't mustering him with dismissive self-sufficiency and amid noiseless inner thunder in the sunny sky; no, it bent lower, it stood up, it breathed, it took the great stride with him; it spread its wings and made proffering signs, such as through an open forest aisle the eye could see along if he turned his head a little; it showed not just the rock walls of the mountain graying upward to the sky but also the valley flowing into itself from many green heights and the sun on the roof of a farmstead on the opposite slope.

Asta didn't tell him too many details. She stuck to a line drawing or croquis, a sketch made with almost military economy. Melzer would soon be seeing Etelka in the flesh, incidentally; down in the same hotel where he was staying, a dance or some such entertainment was scheduled for that evening; Etelka and Asta intended to put in an appearance too, as well as young Herr von W. and other acquaintances of theirs. For the rest, they could expect a mixture of summer visitors and local people, which was usual at these not very frequent events and provided an innocent charm of its own. Asta then invited Melzer to come to lunch at the Stangeler house the following day, Sunday.

They stood up and followed the crest in the more slanted rays of the evening sun, making their way silently and slowly along the level stretches of the path. For moments at a time Melzer almost imagined he was walking past his own earlier life through a gallery or along its roof ridge, as it were. What was playing itself out on his first day here now struck him as a gain that had accrued more value through his procrastinating all summer long—so in the long run hadn't he come out here at just the right time after all? Walking along the divide between two depths, two valleys, as they were caused memories of the Treskavica, of the bear hunt, and naturally of Major Laska to well up inside Melzer as if rising up from this ridge itself, so to speak, out of its exact center that cut directly through. He began telling Asta about his dead friend; using few words he talked about Bosnia and, in the end, about their last farewell on the Lavarone Plateau.

She listened wholeheartedly. "How sad," she remarked, "how very, very sad. He must have been a good man." "Yes, he was indeed," answered Melzer. Meanwhile, they had reached the peak and the bend in the road along the pass, stepped up to the guardrail, and were looking down into the valley at the densely threaded weft of sunlight. Then Asta started for home. Melzer wanted to linger up here for a while, and he watched her for a time as she started walking downhill along the road. So now she knows about Laska, he thought, in quiet wonder. He felt he had stored something precious in the right place. He still needed to see from down below the multicolored regional garb mottled like the lower edge of a gigantic mural, which the entire landscape was now applying layer by layer, as he saw it, almost without perspective at times, soaring vertically upward from the dark base tones of the forest to the topmost rock edges, whose gray-blue arched off into the distance at a dizzying height.

Dr. Negria was an unknown quantity for Melzer, and in lederhosen he looked no different from any other handsome man who'd been sweating lightly. Conversely, the major—just like everybody else here—

couldn't help noticing Angelika Scheichsbeutel (Angely de Ly). Her way of presenting herself had the same effect as the faint, high-pitched whine of a mosquito or a gnat—downright unbearably intrusive, even with her lowered eyes and childish ways. These features just referred to immediately call back to mind an epidemic that was underway at the time among the female pupils of the famous dancer W., among whom, for all their exalted cultural attainments and limberness of both soul and body, there was manifest in the emerging women no dearth of that indestructible childlike aura, an effect underscored by their hairstyle, a backswept pixie cut. Fräulein Scheichsbeutel of course picked the pixie, too; she wasn't one to be cut.

Basically these are nothing but spiteful remarks. At this point we would like to align ourselves unreservedly with Zihal for once and to assess his inveterately recurring, semibureaucratic parenthetical remarks as not a disruptive factor but a constructive one. The old summer waiter, meanwhile, exhausted like a worn-out nag nearly ready for the glue factory, though nonetheless having been forced some time before, in 1918, that is, when he was already in his declining years, to leap across the barrier between two eras, both totally Austrian, meaning across a mess—this waiter still preserved in the meager space between skin and bones those instincts that allowed him unerringly to recognize even at a passing glance a true gentleman as measured by the standards of the past, a prime specimen being Major Melzer, on whom he accordingly conferred his eagerness to serve and his goodwill at once. He thus considered it only fitting, while leaning over to Melzer's table, to draw this guest's attention in a discreet murmur to the celebrity seated nearby, none other than the dancer Angely de Ly, and he added: "The gentleman having dinner with her is more or less her protector and her physician at the same time, a Dr. Negria from Vienna; I think he's an uncle as well, in fact, the head of the family." Now there's no doubt a head-of-the-family uncle is something quite over and above a run-of-the-mill uncle; any oaf could claim to be that. Even to people who aren't real notables but have a knack for getting close to those who are—just as is the case with a famous woman artist—there can under certain conditions be granted the right of patronage by a head-of-the-family uncle; besides, it adds to the luster of the establishment and its dining room. "More or less her protector; that's who's with her," was what was being whispered about the pediatrician and old steersman, who had as a change of pace now advanced to an identity as munificent patron of the arts.

Melzer had been accorded the insight only eight days before, incidentally, that someone could be named Scheichsbeutel.

From the room where Melzer was eating there was a view of the adjoining garden salon, whose glass-paned double doors had just been opened and in which the lights were soon turned up brighter. At Asta's prompting, the major had reserved a table there. Various groups started getting up from dinner and moving to the other room. Just as Angely de Ly was crossing the threshold with Dr. Negria, there arose from the salon—for a country inn, it was disproportionately large and high-ceilinged—a rousing fanfare from the band waiting there. Whether this was just coincidence, a touch the owner had planned, or an arrangement made by the boatman (navigator) remained uncertain. As Melzer started through as well, the old waiter went bustling ahead of him and pointed out the table he'd reserved. There was space for about eight to ten people, and even more, if need be . . . It was a good spot, somewhat closed off by wall dividers, almost like a theater box set up in one corner of the room, around the edges of which tables had been set up so as to leave the middle free for dancing, the floor freshly polished and gleaming. In the corner diagonally opposite from Melzer was the tall, spacious bandstand, but instead of rural musicians with brass instruments, a twelve-piece dance band was set up this time, all complete and ready. Obviously they'd been hired especially for this evening. Almost right away, guests took to the dance floor and began tripping the light fantastic.

Melzer took all this in stride, but not without astonishment. It all went against his expectations, didn't even remotely correspond to anything he'd imagined this short trip would be like (climbing the Rax, for example, followed by a short visit to the Stangeler house). But the complete mutual understanding he felt with Asta—undiminished by her not being present at the moment—dwelt within him like a gift he had newly been given.

Melzer had asked for some wine to be chilled, but he was drinking

black coffee now, two or three cups, one after another, which was quite
a significant departure from his usual moderate indulgence in that
poison. But inside him was an urge to be more wide-awake. It seemed
to him that present circumstances required it somehow—but what
kind of "present circumstances" did he mean anyway? And could he
even refer to this rather prosaic situation by so portentous a name? As
in a container that someone has been carrying and then puts down, so
that the liquid inside has not yet come to rest but is still sloshing back
and forth, there was now still rippling in him the green from their walk
in the open on the lofty ridge and the truly sublime images presented
to each glance down; and while the electric light, too harsh as it was,
shone on these absurd doings, some of the villagers, by no means
clumsily, either, began swaying in English rhythms (which by that time
had already come to monopolize dance throughout the world in the
same way the three-quarter-time infection from Vienna had spread in
the preceding era): while these gyrations were taking place, inoffensive
in themselves though not lacking a smattering of pretension, there still
glowed inside Melzer the slantwise evening sun from up on the heights,
the gold in which the green was dissolving as if vaporized, and the
cooling blue of the bowl that was the deep-curving, wide-arching sky.
From time to time he observed, with no interest at all but only because
it was happening directly opposite him, several good-looking men
being turned down, one after another, when they asked Angely de Ly
for a dance. The dancer wasn't dancing here. (On the other hand,
several highly acclaimed vocal artists had sung in the village church
not long before; but then the less you have, the higher you have to hold
it up, it would seem.) It amused Melzer to note how each man would
first turn to Dr. Negria and bow slightly (to the "gentleman protector,"
that is, borrowing a phrase from the skin-and-bones waiter), in that
way seeking permission to approach his protégée. Negria replied every
time with a careless, lazy little wave of his hand in the lady's direction,
whereupon she would gently shake her head no with a childlike yet
womanly bearing and lower her eyes. While the major was still caught
up in watching all this and thinking that the young lady would surely
dance with all the greater vivacity later on, after delaying for so long,
his empty table was virtually deluged by a great wave; Etelka and Asta

had arrived, plus a whole group with them. It included not just the grandsons of the minister but four or five others, among them a middle-aged married couple; most of them had just happened across one another here, in the entryway or even in this room. Etelka said hello to Melzer without quite knowing right away who he was. What followed next was that crisscross, back-and-forth introducing of people who didn't know each other, a ceremony worn down to a mere symbol or shorthand, made up of names no one ever caught and little bows everyone kept making; it reminded the major vividly for a moment of the breakfast postlude out in the marshes the previous Sunday and of Editha's objection to this custom. The table was now almost completely full. Melzer next to Asta. The thought would not let go of him that "present circumstances" were in progress and that he had to be alert and watchful. Etelka danced with Karl von W. Then Dr. Negria was at the table suddenly to step out with the lady who had come with her husband. Of course it didn't take long for Asta to size up Angela de Ly's galling way of conducting herself and to complain to Melzer about it. Everything in the room started to get more and more jumbled and tumbled together, which is what happens at these kinds of gatherings. For the local people, dancing was serious business, and they pursued it with hardihood; Asta too was soon whisked away. Then she danced with Melzer. Etelka, unusually vivacious this evening, was making a considerable amount of noise with Karl von W. and two other young people when she wasn't dancing with Karl, which now began happening almost without interruption. All of a sudden they saw Karl's younger brother, who apparently felt neglected by Asta, go sailing along with Angely de Ly. Because this young man proved to be an outstanding dancer (had she somehow detected this about him?), Angely now came fully into her own, with corresponding displacement of everyone else as people here and there stopped their own galumphing to watch. They noticed, incidentally, by her brief whispered comments, that the lady was leading her partner and successively alerting him to the next steps and figures of an amplified and glorified South American tango. Their finale was outright sensational. People applauded. Meanwhile, a rather harsh comment made by Etelka might have been audible beyond their own table: "I could throw up!" she said, leaning over to Karl. Asta realized that her sister was not sober. Finally the dance number was over. The waiter seemed unable to make his way to the table through the crowd, and Asta wanted something to drink, but because she completely refrained from wine for the sake of her physical training, she asked Melzer to do her a favor and bring her a mineral water.

So he wove his way through the salon and the dining room to the taproom, its door standing open to the hallway.

The square bar was almost empty except for a corner in the rear, in which three drinkers were silently hunched over their glasses. While the young bartender moved a few wooden crates so he could open a side compartment of the icebox, where drinks not exactly in constant demand were stored, Melzer stepped into the doorway; there the cooler breeze of the summer night met the thicker air of the barroom, saturated with the cellar-like whiff of beer kegs. He could also smell the dust from the road and the odors of plant life drifting in from outside.

Lights and a rumbling suddenly came around the curve in the road, but they didn't go sweeping past; instead, they stopped with a squeal of tires and a crunching of gravel, while the car's motor kept running and thereby seemed to be announcing that someone had pulled up and a late-arriving guest was now at the hotel entrance. And indeed the waiter soon put in an appearance to take care of registering the guest and doing everything related, as the owner and manager seemed more occupied with his farmers in the taproom. A chambermaid also turned up at the bottom of the staircase. The new guest walked past Melzer as his flat suitcase was being carried in, but he dragged the major along with him, as it were; Melzer could positively feel himself being tugged behind the man. He had the astounding, indeed the overwhelming sort of sensation that very seldom leaps out at us—as if out of a little door flung open suddenly—but if so, then out of everyday routine, when an image dwelling in some remote corner of our mind is verified by abruptly manifesting itself in the outside world and approaching us as an actual, real perception. The Roman citizen Gnaeus Pompeius, clothed in a casual suit from our own day, was meanwhile disappearing up the steps with the maid leading the way. Melzer was so keenly aware of how pointless it was to ask the waiter about this gentleman that he at once almost regretted having done so, but the old man then gave him the expected but altogether unnecessary answer, "Herr Consul General Fraunholzer from Belgrade."

Melzer had fetched Asta's mineral water, in the interval, and slowly went back inside.

So here they were, then—the "present circumstances."

And he had some responsibility here, as it were. Just for a moment, without his becoming conscious of it, a feeling deep inside him left over from the war came back, one he'd had whenever he was confronted with the decision to issue an order. It moved in close and grazed him, dark and dull; he was remembering with his organs, not his head, so to speak. Now it struck him as a good thing after all that he had asked the waiter the newcomer's name. Healthy common sense had at once leaped across a gap of astonishment even as it was opening ever wider; there had been no faltering. It would have been impossible, Melzer thought, to transfer to Asta alone the certainty with which he had instantly grasped who the new arrival was, even if it was brought about by her concise and apt characterization of his looks (the major of course didn't know René had coined the nickname). But now he was bringing her the proof. For a few minutes he stood holding the bottle in the empty dining room, now only dimly lit. He seemed as if he were running all around his own center from every direction at once; now he was consciously recollecting the war. This was the same feeling he used to have back then, at least under certain—"circumstances," but now only stronger, clearer. It was as if he were falling through time, rapidly, propelled by a sharp blast of wind. He went into the salon. The noise had grown greater, and the table he'd reserved was doing its part. The minister's younger grandson was now sitting over with Negria and Fräulein Scheichsbeutel.

Fraunholzer was to be expected at any moment, thought the major, because he surely couldn't have had dinner earlier, and then the noise and music would draw him here from the dining room, if only to find out if anyone from the house had come. Melzer struggled to weave his way through the dancing, which had just started again; fortunately, Asta had kept her place at the table. When he was sitting next to her again and had poured her a glass of mineral water, he quietly told her the news, briefly but urgently. But then, even while they were whispering and Asta was questioning him again just to be sure she was getting it right, Karl and Etelka stood up and left the salon together. Asta looked after them in amazement. Their departure got lost in the whirl of the dancers; still, it took a lot of nerve, and it didn't escape the notice of some. Dr. Negria, for example, seemed to fall into deep reflection as he watched them go. Asta and Melzer, on the other hand, were overtaken by momentary bewilderment. They were simply at a loss. Asta might have been able to hurry off in pursuit of her sister. But even now it was too late.

Because Fraunholzer had meanwhile taken a seat in a corner of the dining room closed off by wall dividers like the ones in the salon—they too created something like a theater box—and was waiting for his dinner. The condition to which Etelka and Karl had succumbed a moment before would have been described by the captain, Baron von Eulenfeld, as a "considerably moonstruck impulse." They were both drunk, too (as Karl von W., in a state of innocence and ignorance, confidentially divulged later on, in grave distress). After they closed the salon door behind them, they came to a stop right behind it in the apparently empty dining room and started smothering one another with kisses. Then they walked through the room only to disappear swiftly into the garden, lying abandoned under the waxing moon and in the nighttime chill, which can now and then be quite noticeable in the high mountains toward the end of August. The couple hadn't spent more than thirty seconds total in the dining room. Just after they left, the skin-and-bones waiter appeared with the consul's dinner.

Fraunholzer picked up his fork but then laid it back down. With all the force of a gigantic press, the weight of his age—he was getting close to fifty—came bearing down on him, casually and easily crushing his mounting rage from the humiliation he was enduring, even though he was looking down at Karl from the height of his years as nothing more than a scamp, a whelp wet behind the ears, and someone he could line up to be the target of that rage, at least initially; but then that feeling soon dropped away and disappeared from view as well. The wreckage-strewn battlefield of a whole lifetime, on which the last legions were perishing, lay gleaming in the moonlight; it shed its light on the broken shafts of weapons hurled in vain and now jutting up high above the ground; in its bluish light glowed armor that had been flashing in the sunlight not long before; it cast a pale glint on a fallen warrior's knee—now grown stiff, but once limber in youth—raised motionless against the pale starlight. Here it was, then, the total defeat unfolding right before him now, though he had felt its approach even as he was leaving Belgrade. He had already decided to retreat behind the demarcation line into the last bastion, the border fortress (Gmunden) that safeguarded against nothingness, and his decision sat on him easily, because he was no longer making choices about what had to be put in order but merely catching up with what the facts had already ordered. And if there was anything that could help him now, it was this: seeing. Until his eyes dried up completely and could no longer overflow. And until he vomited, which for a moment he came close to doing, when he looked at the food set out before him, at which point he pushed his plate away. He tossed the fork he was still holding onto the table and stood up. He needed to drink a healing elixir, and he could get a dose of it here. For the first time in his busy life there arose in him the wish to do nothing, but instead to have only eyes all over his body, as it were, and to be healed by what they absorbed, by whatever came flooding in from the torrent. He left the dining room, crossed the hallway, came to the same open door Melzer had been standing in before, and wound up with the farmers in the taproom, though no conscious thought had been involved. This was good, reliable guidance on the part of his subconscious, now revealed for the time being through the collapse of the gridwork and the superstructure. Determined to stay and to see and to swallow, which would help him hack his way free to a retreat, as it were, but a complete and final one, he found in this resolve a benign and indeed merciful way to bridge the gap still open in him between an attack of deep-seated weakness and the determination to spare himself nothing for the sake of freedom. Here were the first drops of the elixir: Styrian slivovitz. It kept his stomach settled. The consul drank four shots standing up, and the bartender poured them in a cheerful mood, gratified that even distinguished gentlemen didn't spurn this local brandy, in which dwelt the tutelary god of plum trees, who also protected against the larger and smaller sufferings of body and soul. Meanwhile, Fraunholzer asked if there was any champagne available. This painful festival of freedom needed to be celebrated to the fullest. And because nothing less than a French vintage was hospitably waiting in storage, he had some of it chilled—not just a split, though (this wasn't a brunch, after all), but five magnums at one go.

Good!

Pompeius, OMNIBUS BENE COGNITIS REBUS, DEDECUS PUTASSET, SI QUIDEM CLADE IMPERFECTA REM RELIQUISSET: SED EO MAGIS NUNC ANIMUM ADVERSIT. In other words: Our Pompeius—unlike that other Gnaeus at the Battle of Pharsalus—did not run away in view of impending defeat on the battlefield. Let there be no doubt: in view of all the babble and the gabble, the nattering and the chattering, plus the rank psychological odors emanating from this brew, the best way of holding things in check and keeping this particular situation under proper restraint would be to have recourse to Latin prose. But then where would that take us? From naturalism to classicism. In other words: to misplaced oversimplification. We can't continue writing in Roman *quadrata*, those square capitals. We look good enough as it is.

Adding everything together, the following situation had resulted—six people came to the table at more or less the same time: Dr. Negria and Angelika Scheichsbeutel, who together brought over the minister's younger grandson from their table to keep them company; in addition, Fraunholzer; and immediately after him, Etelka and Karl. Not long after that came the champagne. The return of Etelka and Karl appeared to be totally outside the bounds of possibility, because the very brevity of their absence—in fact not actually very long, to be sure, but judged foolhardy—rankled all the more (they had used their time solely to gawk like calves at the waxing moon). Even so, Etelka allowed herself to wallow in resentment at Fraunholzer's sudden arrival; she felt put-upon, and even as they said hello, her features froze over exactly as they had done on a related occasion three weeks before, when we had occasion to witness the sisters' debriefing at the overgrown tennis court; nevertheless, Asta was now flabbergasted in spite of how well she knew all that Etelka was capable of. Asta and Fraunholzer greeted one another wholeheartedly. To all appearances, he was completely unflappable. After he'd made sure the whole table had full champagne glasses, he treated the musicians to the wine as well. Asta studied the masklike face of Angelika, who happened to be sitting right across from her, and asked herself on and off if she hadn't blundered into a madhouse or a dream; all this while, Fraunholzer could be seen dancing; he'd asked that married woman at their table, about whom there's nothing to report except that he found her suited to his purpose. Then Karl soon started dancing with Etelka again, or actually vice versa. The noise kept rising, and not just here at this table; the popping of champagne corks appeared to act as a catalyst for the whole salon. Asta and Melzer stayed seated. They were sitting out their own perplexity, so to say, as this ever more frenetic hubbub unfolded before them, deeply convinced that nothing good could come out of it. They saw that handsome Negria and Etelka swinging and swaying, and a bit later but they couldn't help but admire how Fraunholzer and Scheichsbeutel were dancing a foxtrot; she'd instantly accepted his invitation, apparently because she'd heard he was a consul general. In the course of an intense conversation with the not-sober Etelka—they kept it up the whole time they were dancing—Negria might have been plied with further vital statistics. The five magnums were soaked up as if by the desert sands, but new ones were brought. Now strangers began showing up at their table, and Melzer couldn't tell if they were acquainted with somebody or other in the original party. That could be assumed about some of the local residents, who had by now barged in past the wall dividers, but in no way about the young married couple—the woman in a red summer dress, her hair yellow as a trumpet blast. The consul general had vanished in the meantime. For a time there was no let-up; the uproar was continuous; Asta was extremely tired. When they finally prepared to leave—the salon had already started to empty out—Melzer walked the two ladies up the village road, the moonlight thin and the water murmuring on their right—to the turnoff for the Stangelers' property.

Etelka hadn't asked about Fraunholzer when they left, and they said almost nothing as they went on their way.

The major was supposed to meet Asta at the post office at ten; it was still the hub of village life around here.

Melzer awoke that morning relatively early and ordered a bath.

Lying in the hot water he felt as if the events of the day before were a small hill of golden-brown schnitzels, breaded and deep-fried to a turn, now piled up on his body and stubbornly adhering, so to say, to his own golden-brown flesh (tanned from a good many swimming trips to Kritzendorf—and more recently to Greifenstein!), clinging to the exact spot between his upper abdomen and his thigh muscles that offered a flat shield-like surface to bear this light but astonishing burden (a Greek would have said he was pondering deep within his diaphragm). This trip out to the country, intended as a getaway, was now turning out to be more of a gateway to a whole other set of complications. Admittedly at the same time he was feeling a curiosity. Not long after they'd exchanged greetings, Asta had invited Fraunholzer to come to the house for lunch the next day; her father would be so pleased. This meant the consul general and Etelka were about to spend a longer and calmer span of time in one another's company. Only at this moment did it occur to Melzer that Fraunholzer was staying here, in the same lodging. He'd probably still be asleep. It was barely eight o'clock.

Melzer had breakfast in the garden. The air was crisp, the sunlight thin, and every sound—the clatter of silverware and the footsteps on the gravel—came to him clear and isolated, as if surrounded by great stores of silence gathered abundantly in the forest above the valley. Once in a while a roar from a car coming around the narrow curve beyond the living fence would punch a hole in the stillness. Once quietness was restored, it was broken again briefly by the chorus of geese from the stream; this time, too, it was precise and simultaneous.

The major finished his coffee and left the tavern garden with a cigarette in his mouth. He was almost completely unfamiliar with the area down here. His visit back in 1911 had been confined completely to the Stangeler property, from which they'd tended to go on walks and hikes that would take them even higher up, into the more solitary woods and mountain elevations. At that time there had been little occasion to go down to the village below the inn by the mill. They'd seldom come to the bottom of the valley, broadening out here, unless it was to visit the W. family, whose estate lay directly across from the inn, but lower down. When Melzer left the garden, he was facing a wide path, so he followed it, as there was plenty of time for a little walk. A small bridge led over the stream, rushing powerfully here, and past it, the way was crossed by a level promenade with benches, almost all of it shaded by overhanging branches and shrubbery, since the mountainside again rose steeply beyond the path. This was a kind of discovery for Melzer, because to a certain extent it didn't fit into the rest of the surroundings, the forest primeval and the steep ascents—instead, it was more like a feature that had somehow wound up here from a summer vacation setting much closer to the city, including its charm tinged with melancholy, especially when the first days of autumn or even late summer drift in; and indeed, there now came the fragrance of the many flowers cultivated along the path, left and right, crossed with the pungent scent of kitchen herbs, while farther along he now saw colored glass balls on top of stakes in a late rose bed among narrow gravel paths, the house behind them hidden by a garden deep in the grass, covered by the crowns of fruit trees, though the old-fashioned, dried-out brown wooden verandas could still be seen as the sun lay on its windowpanes.

Melzer sat down on a bench, looked into the rushing stream and the speckles of sunlight, and for a few seconds went deep into himself, as it were. But soon it was time to go. He followed the rising path and came back onto the village street, pleasantly surprised at being right near the post office. Asta came out immediately, letters and newspapers in her jacket pocket. He felt at once very clearly that they had a good understanding and that everything would go smoothly.

"So what do we do now, Melzer?" she asked. "I want to catch Robby Fraunholzer alone and have a talk with him before the three of us go up to the house. After everything that went on yesterday, that seems advisable, or necessary. It could be that even more went on than we know. His quick disappearance at the end seemed very suspicious to me, anyway."

Melzer pointed to the promenade and the path he'd just arrived by. "Here's what will work best," he said, "I'll go take a seat on a bench near the little bridge over there, and then you can come for me with the consul general. There's a direct route between the gardens; you surely know it. I took it this morning." "Yes, of course," she answered. That was the plan, then, and they shook hands. "This may take a good while, Melzer," Asta added. "It doesn't matter; it really doesn't matter," he replied, looking into her eyes after he raised his head from kissing her hand.

They nodded cordially to one another.

Melzer turned back to his bench on the small promenade.

As soon as he stepped out of the sun and away from the street, back onto the narrower path in the green shade of the trees, suffused with that disconcerting underwater light near the rushing stream, he realized that when he'd been sitting here earlier his recollections had ranged across much wider spaces than he'd been aware of, but it entered his conscious mind now, and the melancholy charm of gardens in late summer lay collected in the warm sun on the dew-damp grass and gravel, still exuding a faint morning vapor, in front of his mother's house in Neulengbach, near Vienna; so the dragging anchor of his memory suddenly and unexpectedly struck ground, much farther from the shore for which Melzer was making, much farther from where he had wished to be. He stood before the bench, looked down, was alone here and knew it, mindfully owned his solitude and the distances it now instantly sent radiating outward in every direction through his world, like a ribbed structure becoming visible, like *the* ribbed structure of life as a whole, in fact. For the first time, however, it was now about to be held together by a sturdy truss positioned somewhere outside the occupied and occupying space itself, for he still knew almost nothing more about his memory of Neulengbach than that he had been a schoolboy on summer vacation. After all, this was the first time he was purposefully reaching so far and so clearly back in time; that autumn day at the end of school vacation returned in total vividness. A colored glass ball was shimmering in the rose bed. But under the veranda, in deep shade and with the mugginess of rotting leaves, where he keeps his bicycle next to the garden tools and a few old chairs, the light is the

same green as here or in Asta's little room, say. Or on the Strudlhof
Steps. Sometimes. If the evening sun didn't happen to be breaking in.
He suddenly felt a painful yearning to fix the anchor of his memory
in even more solid ground, not just in that of his lost childhood years,
so fully at the mercy of random circumstances that it always looks like
their reflection, and a deep reflection at that, the way the stream here
was reflecting bushes and trees, or his window on Porzellan Gasse—but
everything, for that matter, his whole life. Somewhere inside it there
had to be a place—to find it he needed to reach farther back from the
here and now and from Asta and that deeply muted green light in her
room—a place where the truss could seize or engage, bringing together
and holding together everything, right up to the present day, that had
ever been part of him. He had stayed standing there, perhaps taken a
few steps back and forth, and steps were what he now heard coming
toward him across the bridge, so he looked that way. Asta was coming
alone, returning surprisingly soon. In the few seconds it took her to
reach Melzer, he felt a totally uncontrollable amazement at her ability
to come closer, unimpeded by the ribbed structure of distance radiating outward from him in all directions that should have created an
immovable barrier, as it were, keeping her at more than arm's length.

She looked serious. There was just the hint of a hollow over the root
of her nose. They both sat down on the bench. "Robby's gone away,"
she said. "I have to read his letter. Do you have a knife, Melzer?" He
opened his and handed it to her. It was flat, enclosed in a matte silver
sheath, and honed to sharpness. "This knife looks just like you," she
said, looking at it briefly, then she took out the letter and opened it;
she hadn't put it with the rest of the mail but had kept it in a different
pocket. The hollow about her nose deepened while she was reading.
Now she silently handed letter and knife to Melzer, leaned forward,
and looked down at the ground, her elbow propped on her knee. Melzer read:

Dear, good Asta!
No sooner had I arrived yesterday than I came to the realization
once and for all that my presence here is totally pointless, so I
left early this morning for Gmunden, back to my wife. Thus ends

what has been the substance of my life for nine years. Remember me to Etelka. I'll write her later, but it will be a long time. And say hello to your parents; tell them I got an urgent message from Belgrade and had to travel back at once, and to accept my apology for lunch at noon.

Hugs from R.

"What are you going to do?" Melzer asked after a while.

"Not a thing," Asta answered. "But of course . . ." she hesitated.

"Of course what?"

". . . I'll just simply give it to Etelka to read."

"You probably don't have much choice," the major said. They got up from the bench to make their way back to the house.

This day at the Stangeler house: at every turn there prevailed an outward resemblance to all the minutiae of those bygone days, and here in the sunlight of today they were standing all crowded together and as if recreated in miniature, so to speak, yet without being connected to each other or moving toward their common vanishing point back in the distance of time. Rather, it all remained a world without a midpoint, with numerous objects side by side, a museum. Only in looking up at the neglected tennis court did it still seem to be as it had been. He was waiting here. (Asta was upstairs in Etelka's room; she wanted to give her sister Fraunholzer's letter.) Under this level expanse, overgrown now, he felt so much moving and swimming, as if he were below the surface of a body of water. Not least Asta's little room. Suddenly he was seized by the thought that people should relinquish back to nature every location they'd ever ventured onto so that it could take the place back to itself with grass and weeds and eventually with undergrowth and trees, take the place back to itself through the never-ceasing inroads of the forest against all the time-bound felling and clearing, against sites sanctified by us, where we left the last marks of our presence, returning to the forest what had been uprooted before other passersby could cross over it and cover it over and tread it down. Were the forest to take back unto itself in this redemptive and merciful way all that we left behind, we would never again chance in the bright light of day upon scattered, rigidified artifacts along erstwhile paths; instead, they would remain buried, sunken in greenery as if deep underwater, and our paths would not be hedged with exterior memory in the form of dense thornbushes indeed separating us irretrievably from what has been, jabbing us and making us bleed when we try to penetrate them, which we are always under a compulsion to do. And for a few seconds Melzer saw the Strudlhof Steps deeply immersed not only in the underwater light of their green leaf shade but overgrown with grass, weeds, and bushes, the small yellow mansion above it on the right crumbled into stone walls no more than two feet high, as in Italian vineyards. And above it on the left, where the larger white mansion belonging to a foreign minister of most unblessed memory once stood, were woods. Deep woods. Trunks tall by now.

Asta came back. She reported coolly and matter-of-factly that Etelka had simply shrugged her shoulders and said, "He'll come back. I'm off for Pest, by the way. No more than a week from now, to be exact."

It was at this moment that Melzer thought, in precisely these words, "Things are going to go downhill from here in so many ways."

Seeing the older family members was an absolute delight for Melzer.

The old eagle had looked up, flexed his right claw, and fluttered his wings a little, as if he wanted to get up, although he couldn't anymore.

"Well, look here! This is a pleasure, my friend, a great pleasure, Major—or have you been promoted? How are things these days? What are you doing with yourself?"

"I'm a civil service councillor now," said Melzer, smiling diffidently.

"Well, let's stick with 'Major' anyway, my boy! Come and sit with me for a while. How are things in civilian life?"

"I think the military is a good preparation for civilian life."

"Hmm, maybe you're right. You could be right, son. But does that mean all young people should serve another term?"

"God forbid!" cried Melzer, almost alarmed at this inference. "All I mean is that if you had to be in the military anyway, it at least had that one benefit."

"Understood; now I get it. Right." He looked at Melzer in a friendly way. The major's modest but solid way of presenting himself seemed to please the old man. Frau von Stangeler came in, bringing slivovitz distilled from the fruit of the plum trees on the property, and the same god who had sustained a faltering Pompeius in battle the day before now warmed Melzer to his deepest depths.

But the news Asta had just brought onto the green surface of the overgrown tennis court seemed to the major to reveal the petrified state, the irreparable nature of this whole situation. But he said nothing; he looked down at the carpet of low grass coming through the gravel, along with scattered white and yellow weeds here and there. He could see that the plant shoots, working silently but strongly, had moved aside some of the flat stones and split the surface, once rolled so smooth. It once more seemed to Melzer as if this were all floating on water. Right now, he wouldn't have been surprised by water lilies; ranging freely in the deepest level of his imagination, the former tennis court was lying at least a few meters deep. They had meanwhile walked around the slope and sat down on one of the benches; there were a few left, though they were moss-covered and rickety by now.

Suddenly he saw Editha walking past in her white piqué dress on the opposite long side of the court, exactly now as it had been earlier, with the glaring white of the lines in the sun cut by the outstretched net and surrounded by high retaining nets stretched between poles, because any ball struck the wrong way would go flying far down the mountain. He could even smell in the sun the faint and clean odor of creosote used to preserve the nets.

"Do you think about the Strudlhof Steps now and then?" Melzer asked quickly, only so as not to remain alone with his vision, so to speak; it almost seemed as if he'd caught sight of a ghost in broad daylight.

"I was thinking about them just now, in fact," said Asta without turning her head. She was looking at the mountainside opposite.

"Editha Pastré," Melzer said. Nothing more.

"We had strange girlfriends," Asta replied after a few moments, her eyes still on the mountain now shining in full sunlight, fields below, forest above.

"It was more for Ingrid's sake," she added.

"Ended up being a mistake," Melzer said.

"You can't really say that," Asta retorted calmly, even a bit distantly, as if she were casually observing something very far off and to the side. "After all, Editha would have been just as capable of engineering that whole episode with Old Man Schmeller if we hadn't been friends or she hadn't had any dealings with me at all."

"You're right," Melzer said in a lively voice, "she certainly would have been able to, but she might not even have hit on the idea if her fury against Semski hadn't been gathering force for the previous two weeks here at the house. The two of them were right before her eyes morning, noon, and night."

"You might have a point," said Asta in an even tone meant to close the discussion. She was finding Melzer disconcerting or even strange at this point. Her sense was that by his present close attention to such completely trivial items from the past he was far exceeding any degree of appropriateness the topic warranted. She'd noticed not infrequently in the course of the past years that quite a few of the young people who'd once populated the house and garden here were still anchored by lively memories of this place, which would often be quick to surface when she happened to meet up with someone or other from the old days, whereas it struck her that Melzer, who had just been making every effort to patch together scraps of detail that were all ancient history, was treating these issues like a specialist, which brought about in her a feeling almost of futility and tedium. Despite that, she was again marveling even today at her past association with Editha; it had arisen mostly out of her closer bond with Ingrid, who was Editha's best friend, but also in part out of a dynamic Asta was now understanding clearly; it had been one of those deposits of sediment and infiltrations of foreign matter that a personality belatedly achieving self-awareness and some critical distance from its surroundings does not fight back against in early youth, the result being that alien and alienating layers can pile up on top of one another to a significant height until the peak they form rises above a spirit by now much better enlightened about itself, that light now revealing the astonishing nature of the whole edifice. She realized, of course, that she had always found Editha un-pleasant, even at school, the Luithlen Girls' Lyceum. Asta had enrolled only in the upper class, for her senior year, where she had encountered Editha basking in a kind of fame often found in schools, whether acquired by whole classes—ones that include a full share of talented but rambunctious pupils, say—or isolated characters good at spearheading successful pranks. Editha was far ahead of the rest back then in having teamed up with her twin sister—now deceased—to outfox the faculty repeatedly and to a degree never seen before or since; the Baronesses Buschmann were especially familiar with stories about them. Asta gave the matter a passing thought. Then she went on to change the subject. For his part, though, the major had almost nothing to say after she began talking about Editha. By no means did his sudden tight-lipped approach to this topic of conversation arise from any lack of interest, however; it came instead from his being permeated through and through with the absolutely irrefutable realization that this whole matter was finished and closed off, as though a barrier had dropped into place or a glass window lowered, as at a counter. It was sitting in him like a stone that could not be carved down to something less or built up to something more.

It was only at noontime that Melzer had a chance to realize how much the father of the family had really and truly aged: the cumbersome way the old man was brought in, supported by the maid, and then had to be cautiously lowered into his armchair, made it obvious, and he now saw the few streaks of gray in Herr Stangeler's hair and beard. Yet the first flash of lightning in his eye, the first word he spoke, scattered that impression at once. Etelka still had not turned up as they were taking their places. When she appeared, Melzer followed her movements with curiosity, or really more with tension. But her facial features, having had so much practice in presenting a deadpan exterior at family meals, did not allow his searching glance to detect any trace of events from yesterday and today. Melzer was thinking that perhaps the disastrous totality of the situation had taken root so deep inside her that she was feeling nothing whatever for the time being.

They did not have their coffee on the other side of the stream, with its flat round clearing among the trees, but in front of the house instead, in the sunlight, on the side where the driveway was located. The old gentleman got to talking with Melzer about Bosnia, the association prompted by uncompleted projects organized but then interrupted by the war. The civilizing development of that country, accomplished in its entirety by the old monarchy, had now been bequeathed to those least entitled to it by any effort of their own: "Every good bed or clean towel in a hotel, a train departing on time, a room without bugs, or a well-maintained public toilet—all Austrian provenience," the old man said. At this moment, though, there drifted over to Melzer no scent from that prehistory of his life, which was how he was now beginning to think of his Bosnian time; it loomed, to be sure, a peak strangely illuminated by today's light, last remnant of a sunken mountain range (almost the same light in which her friendship with Editha now appeared to Asta Stangeler!), high above it a solitary vulture from the Treskavica.

So the rest of the day fanned out and drooped as if it had made its own self tired, no longer able to take anything in, overfilled with yesterday and today. Melzer left at five o'clock. When he looked at Etelka's face after kissing her hand, he saw that it was presented to him unmasked, with no layer applied over it: a generous face, intelligence and giftedness speaking out of the wide distance between her eyes, as it were. Was she only now feeling that Melzer, with whom she had found as few points of contact today as at any time previously (she'd always seen him as somebody just tagging along with Asta), wished her well and was silently trying to signal rapport? She suggested to Asta that they walk with him to the bus stop by the post office, so off he went with the women. He was with both of them at once for the first time, the three of them together for the first time; a new bond was being forged in these few minutes, during which—there was of course no way Melzer could have known this—he was seeing Etelka for the last time in this life. "Goodbye!" they both cried, standing side by side in the costume of the region. The heavy bus went whisking around a curve in the road and then barreled so quickly downhill through the visibly widening valley that it seemed to be falling, while the friendly moments he'd just experienced echoed and lingered, but as if on solid ground made of rock, and he knew that he was somehow going to have to hunch down toward it and let it graze and scrape him. He closed his eyes for just a brief second, while the valley seemed to be dropping away under him due to the speed the vehicle had reached. And just now a deep red seemed to swell up to his inner eyelids, a terrifying color like wounds or fresh blood.

This had nothing to do with the war, however, as he was surprised to recognize clearly; nothing to do, either, with the blood of Colonel Laska that had gushed out all over him as the man was dying in his arms on the Lavarone Plateau.

As the train came closer to Vienna and passed through the small stations, passengers could see wild grapevines twined along the platforms and people standing crowded together, heading home from their Sunday outings.

Melzer, as though ahead of the moving train, could feel himself subsiding back into the city, felt things already not counting as much here as they had out in the country. Entangling alliances he'd been part of now released him, but not for long, didn't turn him loose from his own in any lasting way. Even so, he felt as if he were returning from a long break, not just from a weekend stay. From the conventional side of him, the correct and proper exterior, there again emerged—it had cropped up a few times before, but now for the first time more distinctly— a kind of puzzlement at his having made no move at all this year to take his usual vacation; with no conscious intention, he'd adapted himself to Eulenfeld and others who had recently started visiting the fashionable settings for winter sports, even though none of them seemed to try them out in any noticeable way, let alone become proficient. So it was that as of today, August 31, Melzer had his whole vacation time unused without any real intent to take it. What was firm in his mind, however, was that he would not be choosing as his destination the place from which he was just coming back.

It had long since grown dark when the train pulled into the South Station, the air filled with smoke, but milder, warmer than it had been out there. He went down the broad stairs and onto the street. The city seemed deeply hollowed out, reverberating, expansive, lying as if deep below sea level in what is known as a depression, crept upon by numerous lights; now his brightly lit streetcar pulled up, jingling its bell. As he rode along the Ring Strasse, past the Hofburg, the imperial palace, everything from out in the country had entirely subsided; only the form as a whole remained, turned to stone, undeflectable. It was housed inside him like a model. The familiar spruce atmosphere of the stairwell, that stable smell for humans, the home. The keys jingled. He didn't touch the switch in his entryway; the light coming through Frau Rak's glass door was bright enough. When he opened the door to his front room, where the fireplace with the bearskin was, the opening didn't lead into darkness. There was light here. New light never seen in this room before. Sharp, clear, and solitary, down close to the floor, as if an eye had secretly grown in this unnoticed place and it were wide open and now looking up from there, beaming, turning back shadows, throwing upward what was lowest, what was hardly ever seen—chair legs, as if folded together over the seat, the base of the fireplace thrown so highly into relief that it struck one at once.

Melzer leaned back against the inside of the door as if he needed support, and he stayed that way, holding his flat suitcase in his left hand.

Now came a knock behind him. Frau Rak had come along in silent slippers. She'd been waiting for him so she could eagerly explain what he now already understood.

Her face, its separate features not unattractive, looked oversharpened when seen as a whole; it had something of a Kasperl about it, and especially when she was speaking, her narrow black eyes gleamed all too intensely, almost as if in oil. She was always pale into the bargain. An interested Pierrot. That expression came from Eulenfeld.

After the new light fixture had been installed exactly according to Melzer's wishes, Herr and Frau E.P. had arranged with Frau Rak to turn on the electric candle on Sunday evening, before the major returned from the country, so that the surprise would be perfect.

And it was. When Frau Rak left, Melzer saw once and for all that the illumination he'd received only seconds after he'd entered the room, even before the landlady knocked, was of no use at all. The eye in the wall had immediately forged a connection with that model inside himself, that model turned to stone, as it were.

Somewhat later Melzer found on his desk, exactly in the middle, a calling card:

Herr and Frau E.P.
have taken the liberty, Major,
of spreading light in your home.

PART FOUR

GOLDEN domes of late summer vaulted over the city and its wide-reaching districts; not yet Indian summer, autumn had as yet given no sign of itself.

The air was so utterly calm that if someone had pictured the gently hovering gondola of a hot-air balloon more or less directly above the Strudlhof Steps, it would have remained aloft at the same spot for hours without drifting away across the river and the long slopes of the Bisamberg, its checkerboard of meadows, fields, and forest not yet showing any change of color.

Dwelling places were very quiet; those deserted and locked at the moment now were looking open. Every shimmering object left alone dreams of distances, and especially where the windows present a more intriguing view of the substantial cityscape, the sheen reflected off a solitary music stand or an abandoned piano seems intimately molten and fused with the gleam lying far-flung and fleeting on unknown roofs.

It was very quiet in Frau Mary's apartment as well.

Nothing had changed here since the death of her husband, Oscar K. (in February 1924, we will perhaps recall).

The long suite of rooms was still laid out as it had been earlier.

The furniture was still standing where it had been standing earlier.

When Marie, the faithful and always cheerful maid, wasn't officiating in the kitchen and quiet reigned there—gleaming quiet, for the kitchen lay on the sunny side of the apartment (not so the other rooms, just as at the Siebenscheins') and all the pots and pans sparkled in silent but powerful testimony to domestic virtue—when, in other words, the quiet compacted itself around all the objects standing and lying in the kitchen, there was never heard the clocklike regularity of dripping from a faucet not altogether tightly sealed. It was tight. This noise-making mouth was firmly closed.

Passing time also detectably broke in on the forever sunless rooms to the front, more noiseless than clocks, almost as soundless as a sunbeam wandering between the closed piano deeply reflecting its furniture-like stillness and the polished music stand, making them gleam, linger in full resplendence, and then once more pale and fade. Almost as noiseless was the threading of the taxis, like beads being strung, as they occasionally crossed the roadway at the end of the street just below that led straight to the Danube Canal. It stayed unwaveringly empty and still. The wide canal opened up the prospect. The trees on the opposite bank were still green. And not far away stretched the Augarten (with its tennis courts), the pale façade of the palace seeming to recede, mother-of-pearl inside a shell.

Frau Mary K. had gone back to playing tennis.

Herr von Semski was still showing up at the club from time to time as well, along with Frau Sandroch, that Russian lady of German background. To Mary they both still seemed somehow to occupy a higher sphere, although she would never have admitted such a feeling to herself. She would sometimes watch them as they strolled along the wide promenades between pruned-back trees. Frau von Sandroch usually draped a lilac-colored silk shawl around her shoulders after a match.

Son and daughter were growing up very satisfactorily.

The boy, though not yet fourteen, had already become a young man advancing toward the upper grades of his prep school, studying three languages, and resembling his mother. But between her and him nature had slipped in, all unawares, a masterpiece of a variation and thereby made two different modes of beauty out of a single type, so to speak. What was a Rachel in her showed up in him as a young King David—except for the underdeveloped upper body. We prefer to imagine the princely shepherd, the wielder of the slingshot, the vanquisher of the giant Goliath, as having a youthfully bulging chest. That is the picture the artists of the Italian Renaissance have spread out before our souls, and we can't jump into and over its frame the way clowns jump through tires. Young K. was a shepherd. Tanned and handsome. From any picture of him would have been heard the sound of a reed flute. An English horn.

His sister, older by a year, had inherited favorable traits from her father—the reddish hair and the common sense that lived underneath it. Nothing else, though. Which was all to the good. A girl with the features of the late Herr Oscar K. would truly have been something like an outburst of rage on nature's part. As it was, she didn't resemble her mother or her brother or anyone else among their relatives. Her ginger-colored hair went very well with a skin tone like milk glass. Her figure was slender and agile. Her little snub nose with its bridge drawn completely straight. A well-defined face, but with no sharpness. Dark eyes amid the white and reddish-blond features. A twinge of the exceptional, lacking any special physiognomic significance. Not yet fifteen, she looked at least eighteen: a perfect young lady.

It's easy to understand a mother's pride in such children. It had recently been laid on a little thick, though. The whole family, three members strong, oozed quality from every pore.

In sum, then, nothing had changed, because everything had remained impeccable. In cases like these, the center of gravity is located above the ruff binding their necks together, so that all are in a state of equilibrium creditably upheld, to be sure, but nonetheless precarious when seen from the mechanical functioning of life.

There had been a change in one small matter even so.

Mary's daughter no longer slept in her own room. At night she was now occupying the empty bed next to her mother's. She herself had initiated that change almost immediately after Oscar's funeral out of love and a desire to comfort her mother, shielding her in this way from the gaping maw of a marital bedchamber now dead. So the two ladies would be lying side by side when Marie came in, usually early (Mary loved having breakfast with her children now and then). They lay side by side, ginger and brunette (with a shimmer of titian red), and if it had been granted to some old reprobate like Eulenfeld or Kajetan von S. to have a look inside the room and contemplate a sight Marie saw every day—any such appalling specimen, now cast in the incongruous role of Paris faced with making a judgment, would not have known into which bed he should toss the golden apple.

The substitution of conjugal fundamentals now taking place through their product was possible, of course, only on the basis of a relationship between mother and daughter that had mutated into pure friendship and sisterhood. Mary did not find herself at all disturbed by the new sleeping arrangements in the activities of her life, and if any such danger had arisen, her daughter would very likely not have been the one to bring it about. Whenever she went out in the evening and then came home, no matter how late or early—whatever the situation yielded—she would be considerate of her mother by being quiet and careful; most times, however, Mary would wake up in a good humor and review with her daughter in the dark, before falling back to sleep, all the psychological details of an evening spent with young people. Here is where lessons in what could be called interior physics took on the most affable form possible; no gray, dampened, muttered wisdom at the back door of youth. These were two women. Men and boys who idolized the younger might perhaps have been much less at their ease had they been able to listen in unobserved on these debriefings by the general staff.

One floor below, at the Siebenscheins', similar conferences also took place about whatever topic was at hand, and the language used was basically the same, although here the participants always stood or sat opposite each other, never lying parallel, in spite of the same kind of mutual understanding, which Herr Nose-in-the-Air René was ever so slowly starting to pick up with those long ears of his, making him set them back distrustfully.

After a year of genuine and deep mourning had passed, the widow did nothing to change her dealings with the world—but let's just say it right out, with the "world of men," as this often irksome, not infrequently absurd, and unappealing crew is often referred to. Mary had admittedly always felt a gravitational pull in that direction, even during the time of her marriage, and as much toward Dr. Negria, for that matter, as toward Lieutenant Melzer. But when the water level in the reservoir of virtue has reached a considerable height—as for example here, through almost fourteen years of marital fidelity, all told—then any decision to drain it back down to the zero mark is very hard, even though that might ultimately seem down deep to be the most right and proper course of action. A person's barometer of self-esteem has to be reading high for that to happen, though. Parting from our virtues, after all, can demand just as much self-denial as taking leave of our ingrained vices. Anyone who's gotten into the habit of gazing down from the height of his or her ruff onto the qualities and merits gradually piling up underneath will be very reluctant to climb back down, even if he or she registers what amounts to a warning, when the whole building is shaken to the foundations, about how precarious the equilibrium is on which that treasure chest is perched. In addition, by nature normal people think (insofar as thinking can be spoken of here) in commercial terms and set their highest value (this way of expressing it still confines us within the realm of marketable commodities!) on features which, once liquidated, cannot be reacquired or reassembled: chastity, fidelity, honor, virginity, all entities by which the irreversibility of time is made manifest. So Frau Mary K. stayed put up there in her peaceful bay window, where even as a married woman she had enjoyed sitting and observing the various turbulences (breakthroughs) enacted within her narrow horizon; nineteen months after her husband's death it was even starting to seem, in fact, as if this bay window were turning into her permanent widow's perch. Not that her interest in such turbulences and affairs as were played out in her immediate surroundings had waned; it had increased, if anything, and she had even procured—if only inwardly—a "busybody," as those mirrors are called with whose aid it is possible to see more from a window than the unaided sight lines allow.

Around this time—the beginning of September 1925, that is—Dr. Negria turned up once more, and in two different places at once, no less; within the orbit of Captain Eulenfeld as well as, after a long absence, at the Augarten Tennis Club again, but in neither place did he achieve a breakthrough or even take measures to instigate turbulence along these lines, since he'd after all had the good fortune of scoring a breakthrough just shortly before in his capacity as bountiful patron of the arts. In Vienna it's possible to traverse all sorts of circles in succession and in the end to wind up back at the one we started from; we proceed as through the circle of fifths in music; it is an en- rather than an un-harmonic modulation in a city whose main boulevard, the Ring Strasse, circles back on itself, after all, much like three-quarter time, which induces a similar perceptual orientation. So here he was again, our Dr. Negria, having circled back around to Editha Schlinger and Frau Mary K., though he was now more subdued, as we've suggested. Sometimes, incidentally, he would bring the object of his latest artistic interest to the club with him. What specific impulse had prompted him to renew his membership here remained mystifying at first. The art object understood as much about tennis as an artillery colonel about microtomy; she conducted herself accordingly, too, merely looking on at the matches—with her mosquito-like face and an audacity so deep-rooted it might be thought of as completely internalized—and managed much later on, by following a recipe we're familiar with by now, to achieve a breakthrough right there in the clubhouse, where there was dancing some evenings. It wasn't with Dr. Negria, however, inasmuch as just at this time a fresh turbulence had burst in on him, instantly sweeping him past both Angely de Ly and Mary K. and propelling him straight toward mellow Frau Sandroch, knocking Semski for a loop in the process. To be sure, these are all expansions of our foreshortening vanishing points that signpost the further course of these various minor matters, although they have as little to do with Major Melzer's life as do, say, the special circumstances of Julius Zihal's becoming engaged in 1913.

When Mary and Negria caught sight of each other in the Augarten, they were both seized by bad conscience, which they then strove to bypass or cover over, but that only made their contact proceed more smoothly. People never converse more vivaciously than when they tacitly set out to offset whatever had set them off at the outset. She'd stood him up in 1923 (the Nussdorf "date"), and he'd never followed up. In general, though, Negria wasn't surprised by anything at all these days, not even, for example, after once more coming across Editha Schlinger, somehow changed and now in Eulenfeld's clutches. Besides, what was holding him in thrall at present was the languid way Frau Sandroch's hips swayed when she walked, and so it came about that he ended up having a sensible conversation with Mary K. for the first time. And she wasn't so terribly displeased after their talk, either.

She did take umbrage at the mosquito, though, as did almost everyone else here, by the way.

Until Dr. Negria took steps to put himself in the running for Frau Sandroch and stopped bringing the mosquito to the club.

During the breaks that came about between the end of the first and the start of the second match Mary even strolled now and again with Dr. Negria along the paths in the park; that was around the middle of September. Visitors walked in the mild sun here as if dissolved in milk though they felt the draw of the autumn undertow tugging them toward faraway places, the tug at its strongest in the city, since they knew it was enclosing them all around. On the same path where she and Oscar had kissed that day two years before while Dr. Negria waited in vain (love's labor's lost—and found) in the café in Nussdorf (whereas in Oscar's arms she had been recalling the first days of their youthful marriage and their kiss on the Strudlhof Steps)—here at this very spot, secluded, between rows of trees tapering off toward the pale palace in the background, Negria told her about his trip to the mountains during the last days of August and about a curious dance he'd attended at the hotel out there; Fraunholzer's and Etelka Grauermann's names hadn't slipped his memory.

Inside Mary an alarm bell started shrilling.

It immediately wrenched her out of the inner state she'd been enjoying with the more than presentable Negria, a state she could never really have sanctioned anyway. Right here and now, though, a way out presented itself, but it would mean getting busy at once. Though she pricked up her ears, she took care to affect at first a demeanor simulating merely slight attention during his report, indeed almost absentmindedness, and only after listening for a while did she toss in a question here or there so as to gain more clarity about the complete set of circumstances. She had no doubt about her need to step in; a decision was standing right at Mädi Küffer's door which would give her a onetime opportunity to turn everything around for the best. Or on the contrary, a disaster which could never be made good again if Frau Lea were now, at the very worst time—yea, verily!—to take the wrong approach to her husband by persisting in what had to be called the frozen, rigid bearing she'd adopted.

Mary would have liked more than anything to rush back to the clubhouse that second and get on the telephone at once. As if it were a physical reordering inside herself or a change of surroundings and atmosphere, just in the same way the sets are shifted in a theater, this was how she was now experiencing her more solidly fixed position toward Negria, raised on the spot to a higher stage level, here and now on the wide promenade, on the gravel, before the pale pearl-gray of the palace to the rear. She now had a task to accomplish, and Negria's role had been merely ancillary. When he expressed a wish to see her home, she found an excuse to wriggle out of it—instantly, without a moment's thought, quick and smooth. Behind this reaction there opened up deep within her a kind of empty space for a split second, and that astonished her.

But that's what will sometimes happen when we go speeding at a mad dash along our *trópoi* and have to catch up with our own selves, as it were.

Now came the second alarm in regard to Lea Fraunholzer. Mary started feeling something close to a bad conscience when she thought about the weeks before summer was at its height and about Grete Siebenschein's occasional assertions that Etelka Grauermann's love for Fraunholzer basically seemed to be over and done. Then would have been the time, she was now thinking in her eagerness, to enlighten Mädi-Lea, to temper her severity, to put some spirit into her. It seemed to Mary that this exact moment, right here and now, was holding out the very last but also the most promising chance, and from now on it was in this light and no other that she would be ready, willing, and able to view her surprising and almost remarkable renewal of contact with Negria. He was no more than an errand boy of life, as it turned out, a bearer of important news at the right time! And accurate news, not just a casual opinion tossed off by Grete. The doctor had also noticed that Fraunholzer had departed promptly the very morning after his arrival, and now he told Mary that as well. But where had Fraunholzer gone? Vienna? Belgrade? Or even Gmunden?

The moment she reached home—the slender newel posts of the stairwell enclosing the elevator as well as all the silly tassels and festoons and brass rings on the walls presented the chalklike emptiness of a pale, abandoned snail shell—she lost not a second in rushing to the telephone, which was located in the bedroom. Lightning flashed across her path. Marie had opened the door to the kitchen, now flooded with the evening sun, to let her know that neither of the young people were at home. Mary's white fleece jacket dropped onto her bed. The sun was shining in here too. This room was the only one not in the row along which the others were lined up; it had a wide window at the rear that faced some unassuming treetops in front of the partly windowless walls of the courtyard. Frau Mary placed a call to the Küffers' family home in Döbling. It became apparent in short order that only a factotum was on hand, though; the mother and the next generation of Küffers— meaning Lea's younger sister, the woman with whose children Mary's boy and girl were friendly—were still in Wolkersdorf, which, considering that classes were about to start again any day now in all the schools, struck Mary as quite surprising, even on the verge of being frivolously relaxed. The housekeeper seemed to know exactly what was going on—that Frau Mädi was in Gmunden and Herr Consul General had been there as well, but she didn't know whether he had returned to Belgrade in the meantime. But Frau consul general was expected in Vienna, for a short stay at least, sometime after the middle of September. For now, however, "nobody had the faintest idea" that Herr Consul General had paid a visit to Gmunden. Very well. Frau Mary asked the woman to write down a message to the effect that she was urgently requesting an immediate telephone call the moment Frau Consul General arrived in Vienna. After that, she decided to write a letter and went straight to the parlor, where her secretary desk stood, each of whose compartments, like its writing surface, could be closed with a smaller or larger roll top and was for that reason always tidy and polished. When Marie came in with the tea tray, it entered Frau Mary's mind that she could have had tea with Negria here, after which she might have been able to find out this or that additional detail from him. The letter wasn't turning out. It couldn't, for that matter, and she should have known that from the start. The full urgency of the situation could only be expressed in a face-to-face talk, and the whole story was too complicated anyway. She ended up writing a few lines repeating the essence of the request to Lea that she'd already placed with the housekeeper. Plus a few extras—about the weeks spent in Velden am Wörther See, about the children. A window was open. From the empty streets, like an uninterrupted, steady tone came the calling of boys playing ball.

It had not taken long for Paula Pichler, née Schachl, to create a tentative mental picture of Captain Eulenfeld; we could call it a simple black-and-white sketch, with more black than white. No opportunity for verifying the image ever came about, nor did any need to do so emerge. It was enough for her to be an interested party—on behalf of Thea Rokitzer, of course—and that she was unstintingly. Her never having seen the captain or made his direct acquaintance was all for the better; otherwise the possibility would doubtless have arisen that his exotic appearance and language—as seen by a girl from Lichtental—his charm and ingratiating, slapdash elegance might have had the effect of diluting the concentration of her single-mindedness; by that same token, she would no doubt also have been capable of discerning not only Eulenfeld's intelligence but the man's additional qualities besides, not the least of which was his capacity for friendship, as manifested for example in his dealings with Melzer, concerning whom in Paula's mind a bias in the opposite direction prevailed, specifically a very favorable one. At any rate, she felt downright drawn to this man she'd never met, although in effect the captain was nothing more than a devious old bounder as far as Paula Pichler was concerned, a man who had never deserved the love of a girl like Thea, persecuting and tormenting her into the bargain and apparently exploiting her for shady dealings.

Her suspicions had been roused just after they'd picked Thea up at the West Station on Friday, August 28. The following Monday afternoon Thea had shown up in the little garden in a more than despondent mood. It was then that Paula was made privy to everything Thea had undergone in the meantime, and it was quite a bit, at least in Paula's eyes. It was not without a certain amount of pleasure, though, her genuine compassion notwithstanding, that she saw herself placed among all these interconnections, sitting (she thought) like a spider in the middle of the web. She was looking forward with special gusto and curiosity to her get-together with René, which they'd planned for Wednesday afternoon. They had arranged to meet at the Café Brioni, the place where fourteen years earlier Pista Grauermann, then a student at the Consular Academy, had started coming to terms with his loneliness and thereby acquiring a degree of independence, as well as some thoughts or ideas that today would probably have struck him as extravagant. Paula Pichler had at once agreed to the choice of meeting place, since it was so close to her apartment. And that would make things work out conveniently for René, too, because at five o'clock that same Wednesday he was supposed to board the gondola, which is to say have tea with Editha Schlinger. It was Grete's busy afternoon, when she was always booked solid. That's how it would end up being for René as well. Regarding Paula we must not fail to mention that her husband, the foreman, knew all about everything and everyone, right down to the duplicate ladies and the upcoming get-together between his wife and René, her friend from the old days. He followed all these developments with enjoyment and curiosity.

Two rocks, one crashing down right after the other in a double blow, shattered the smoothed-out surface Thea had regained in spite of everything during her halfway involuntary stay in the country and a spell of intense and at times draining physical work imposed on her out there just as a matter of course, without giving it a thought, by her aunts, by the Zihaloid lady in Saint Valentin but not less by Frau Civil Service Councillor Zihal, who dogged Thea's heels even more unrelentingly than did the hostess herself. This kind of exertion on the physical plane is often more draining in a literal than in a metaphorical sense, the best example of this truism being found in the use to which the gasworks cashier's widow turned Thea's presence by finally seeing to it that all the floors in the house were scrubbed spotless, setting her to this task on the advice of Thea's Aunt Rosa, in this way reimbursing the woman of the house at her niece's expense for her own visit. Weeding in the garden was even more laborious, as was picking, cleaning, and making preserves of the gooseberries, and superimposed on all that toil, starting from the first days of scrubbing and scouring floors, was the loud and clear protest made by her bent back feeling even the slightest aches and pains—they sat deeper in every sense—imported from Vienna. The one countermeasure Thea Rokitzer was able to undertake this whole time was the meticulous care of her hands she made it a point to carry out faithfully in secret every night behind the closed door of her room before going to sleep. Her unfailing attention to this countermeasure, which she took every single evening without exception, revealed the compass point the depths of Thea's heart were facing day after day—toward the morning of August 29 and her scheduled appointment to show up at the film agency, which her imagination was showing her to be something like a fully staged show she would be asked to put on; her passion and talent would make a showing so triumphant as to show up all the rest and raise the curtain on a great career in show business. That was all she was living for, sliding as if down the inside of a funnel as it restricts more and more the view of anything outside itself and contracts into an ever narrower point a patch of light already isolated as it was, like keeping an eye on the distant exit of a tunnel or shaft we daren't lose sight of, since it is showing us the only way through and out. But it was precisely in front of this opening that the first rock crashed down, sealing it and creating total darkness, because what happened at her appointment on the morning of Saturday, August 29—to which Thea, by having prepared so conscientiously, brought the fullness of her whole being—lasted a scant three minutes, in the course of which she had virtually no chance to strike her own attitudes and none at all to declaim the passages from classical drama she'd so zealously rehearsed; furthermore, she had to give her tiny scraps of line readings—they flashed by like lightning—in company with dozens of other girls, and nothing more came of the "show" than that they were all thanked in a businesslike way, dismissed, and left to stand together in little groups on the sidewalk for two or three minutes, strangers with strangers, each awkward and uncomfortable with all the others, sticking together for a moment only because the watercourse along which each had been steering her life's fragile bark to her intended destination had now been swamped, which left every last one standing mortified at a temporary backwater pending the new course each one's trickle of water would find, since this was how things had turned out and that was all there was to it.

The second rock came hurtling down on the very same day, at five o'clock that afternoon. Who should turn up at the apartment behind the Rokitzer Stationers store, Alserbach Strasse . . . (we don't know the house number any more than Melzer did), but Hedwig (Hedi) Lois-kandl, Paula Pichler's eighteen-year-old stepsister and onetime foster child, asking to speak with Thea, now hopelessly forlorn and hiding away in the room where the well-known art nouveau sideboard stood. The parents were busy and simply shooed her in. Thea began to fear that nothing good was in the offing the second she saw it was Hedi, who wasn't very prepossessing to begin with and who seldom put in an appearance but had now popped up so unexpectedly. Since there was no disguising how unusual this visit was, on none other than the day after Thea had come home at that, Hedi thought it best to blurt everything out at once. She greeted Thea warmly and declared (she was lying) in the very same breath that her Aunt Oplatek didn't even know she'd come to visit, let alone that she was acting on the aunt's behalf—which our Thea, roaming in the far-distant mists of her own inmost terrain, had not as much as intimated or even grasped, since for hours past she had been seeing herself in her fantasies (and never mind that she'd just flopped) as a brilliantly radiant comet streaking toward a great career, leaving the captain far behind as he observed her passage with eyes dulled to buttons (which is how they were when he was plastered). A much different light started shining on her now, however. The aunt was troubled because of the cigarettes. Once again the news-papers had recently been full of stories about large-scale thefts and smuggling operations with the police in hot pursuit; Fräulein Oplatek felt duty bound to report to the appropriate authorities the remarkably large quantity someone had sought to obtain from her before her "fix-ing" in July, including information about who had made the request and so on. It so happened that Thea "was in a relationship with that gentleman," though, and the aunt was afraid that grave awkwardness could come about in the family, because no one really knew how deeply Thea was involved in that particular matter or with Eulenfeld in gen-eral. The smartest course of action (so Hedi said) would be for Thea to tell her calmly where the whole situation stood (she didn't go so far as to say, "Now make sure you really come clean") so she could put her aunt's mind at rest just in case. It even seemed to Hedi, as far as that went, that Fräulein Oplatek, tortured at the moment by unwarranted scrupulosity, might be more inclined to reconsider recording a report and might perhaps even change her mind completely if she could only know once and for all that Thea had had nothing to do with the whole episode.

This last part wasn't so stupid. Hedi made clear through her manner of speaking the full certainty with which she was simply assuming Thea's enmeshment in criminal activities and was now emphasizing her desire to help spare her. That was why nothing had needed to be said about "coming clean." Hedi's face, not a whit more intelligent than Thea's—and we'll venture to say that both visages were positioned in front of an almost unimaginable vacuum—Hedi Loiskandl's face, to which life had displayed even at the start a different face from the one glimpsed by Thea Rokitzer, whose path was always illuminated, after all, by the reflected light of what effect she was producing: Hedi's face, we say, young, but far from being especially attractive and not the least bit regular, had given itself permission to accrue some swampy or greasy shadows among its recesses in a way that men who are drawn to such looks (and these evidently included Hedi's ambitious fiancé) even find in them a distinct attraction, one diametrically opposite to the appeal Pista Grauermann's orderliness and his trim, straight little nose had for Cornelia Wett, the diva. As for the rest, people don't always have sensible and easily understood reasons for becoming "cops" (as police officers are known in Vienna); they sometimes have more valid ones as well. On the other hand, it can't be said that Hedi was conducting herself in a very police-like manner here in the sterile back room with the sideboard, because what she was hoping to obtain seemed to be anything but a confession; she was striving for the opposite, in fact, a kind of blank check, meaning an explicit statement that Thea had nothing to do with any of it and knew nothing more about it.

So what else could Thea do but tell the truth, run over roughshod by Hedi Loiskandl as she had just been, and by that very token running roughshod over her in turn by the only means possible, not least for the sake of Aunt Oplatek's peace of mind? (Hedi's psychological ploy, as reported above, had struck a chord with Thea.)

This entire unexpected scene had been set in motion though a directorial error by Paula Pichler. When it comes to this odious (but not odorous) matter involving tobacco, we feel entitled to put it like that, with a slight change of meaning. About ten days before Thea came home, Hedi had shown up at the Schachls' little house, or actually in the garden, to talk to Paula about the same concern, emphasizing that Thea's best interest was what had motivated her to seek information and advice. She met with good fortune in that Paula refrained from asking a given question in return; it had run through her head, but she didn't voice it, perhaps because it struck her as too direct (which was what was now holding Hedi back from saying anything about coming clean)—the question was how and why Hedi had all of a sudden trotted off to the Josefstadt district to visit Fräulein Oplatek, a relative, to be sure, but one she could scarcely claim more than passing acquaintance with. This point had struck Paula Pichler, but not Thea in her cinema-diminished condition. Hedi would have told a lie, but in all likelihood not readily and smoothly enough, because, to tell the truth, what was behind the whole thing would have been embarrassing if the Schachls were to find out. But what about? Frau Rosa Zihal's clandestine baskets of fruit from Saint Valentin, two of which had been packed off to Vienna around the middle of August (a transaction with which Frau Zihal, who as a rule bore down heavily on her niece, did not tax the girl in the least, so that Thea never even noticed what was going on, and no one else was called upon, either; all on the quiet, Frau Rosa had found the two baskets, the only two suited for the purpose, in the attic). One of the clandestine fruit baskets was dispatched to the Loiskandl family along with a request to make sure that a certain amount of it went to her sister, the tobacconist (and so Hedi was charged with making delivery). The second basket, also not small, had been sent to Alserbach Strasse, to the much less numerous Rokitzer family (in fact consisting of only the parents at the time!), but without the addition of a request to turn some of the fruit over to the Schachls, close as they lived. Frau Zihal apparently considered the four fruit trees and the short row of gooseberries in the Schachls' garden ample justification. She really meant it down deep, too, and not just on the surface. Seen officially and from the outside, she should have had closer ties to the family in the Schachl household, where her husband had once lived and where she and he were guests at regular intervals, than to Paula's mother, stepfather, and stepsister. But in a very general sense—it could literally be called epoch-making—she was much more strongly allied with the Loiskandls. There was no way her sisters could be overlooked, of course, and that included Frau Rokitzer, though Frau Zihal had gradually become quite estranged from her. Beyond these family circumstances, however, ones that admitted of no appeal, the time to which Frau Rosa Zihal-Oplatek belonged—it was equally adamant in barring any appeal—made her decisions for her, and that time was different from the one that flowed through the young people in Lichtental, the foreman and his wife. Not at the level on which clocks strike the hour, needless to say. That ran the same for the Pichlers and the Zihals.

Paula's directorial error consisted of her having failed to tell Thea Rokitzer anything about Hedi Loiskandl's exploratory feelers some days before, so that the girl's appearance had come as a surprise. Only to Thea, though, not to her parents. Hedi had already been to see them, and they approved her plan to start off by touching in a friendly and confidential spirit—young girls just having a little chat, we might say—on a subject that had borne for Herr and Frau Rokitzer, ever since Hedi had broached it, not nearly so much the official stamp of the Austrian Tobacco Administration as it did the name of Baron von Eulenfeld. He now became the key that opened up an explanation of all the baffling changes that had come over Thea during the last few weeks before she departed for Saint Valentin. For the time being, Thea's parents remained closemouthed after their daughter returned home, as they'd previously arranged with Hedi, who indeed didn't keep them waiting very long. She could have found out the day of Thea's return just easily from the girl's parents as from Paula Pichler. There was another point on which Herr and Frau Rokitzer exercised discretion toward their own child—anything connected with the basket of fruit from Saint Valentin. Frau Zihal, naturally aware of the friendship existing between Paula Pichler and Thea, had tossed out a little hint about keeping mum. The fruit from the Zihaloid in Saint Valentin had long since found its way into glass preserving jars, incidentally.

Surely Paula should be excused for her slight omission. All the chatter on arrival, the presence of Lintschi and René, and not least, the spectacle of duplicate ladies in plain sight on the platform besides—

all this caused more important matters to be left unsaid in the jumble of conversations crossing back and forth. So they'd gone their own ways after arranging to meet on Monday afternoon, for Saturday afternoon and all day Sunday would no doubt be reserved for the captain, however much Paula was aching to hear details about Thea's experience at the movie agency; Eulenfeld was in no particular hurry to see Thea Rokitzer on Saturday, however, and had given some excuse over the telephone to postpone until evening. She reported to him in two phone conversations, one on Friday evening and another brief one on Saturday, that she had had a good trip, had arrived safe and sound, and had been met by her aunt and her cousin, according to plan, at the station, where they'd happened to bump into Herr von Stangeler, who was there to pick someone up (his Grete?) and had had to wait around a long time because the Paris train had been so seriously delayed, by over an hour. They then scheduled their first reunion for today, Saturday, in the evening; poor Thea took it with good cheer and wound up not going to see Paula, staying stuck by the well-known sideboard in her hopeless condition instead, only to be trapped by the expeditious Hedi Loiskandl.

It seems worth mentioning that immediately after Hedi took her departure from the garden, Paula Pichler hit on a plan, one she couldn't act on at the moment, but that Thea was able to effect at practically the same time: it consisted of having a talk with Civil Service Councillor Zihal at some suitable time about the whole business involving Josefine Oplatek, the tobacconist. For Thea, the opportunity came about on its own in Saint Valentin. And here once again a directorial error was made in the management of this production, this time by Thea Rokitzer, who has never given us just cause anyway to assume she was able to maintain order on the small stage of her life. Still, she really might have mentioned to Paula Pichler that she had already asked Zihal some questions; then Paula would not have done the same thing over again later, which could only have struck Zihal as odd, of course. The topic and everything pertaining to it came up for discussion often enough among the two women, after all. Perhaps the reason for Thea's forgetfulness lay in her complete lack of success in receiving from the retired uncle any answer that really delved into the matter. It had been toward evening, in the garden, where Zihal enjoyed keeping busy by watering the flowers at this time of day and was just returning from the faucet in his shirtsleeves. These water processions had very soon solidified into a ritual Zihal executed with rhythmic precision and a certain degree of inflexibility, so that his back-and-forth shuttling along the garden paths began displaying features of an undeviating circuit while his facial expression turned inward, so to speak. These movements amounted to a language. The way he carried water constituted a discourse, its topic dealing with the nature of the method for proper performance of mandatory assigned responsibilities in general, and the calculation of the movements which are to be regarded as absolutely necessary in the furtherance thereof. Thea met up with him along his route, on one of the gravel paths (she always had to come right out with whatever she was thinking and act at once on whatever entered her mind); this was not a clever move, its result being that Zihal, in full-blown formal bureaucratic mode, gave her short shrift after an equally short hearing, as if she were being a troublesome party, even though he was really very fond of his wife's niece and enjoyed seeing her (in the literal sense), which appears understandable: he would even watch her unobserved sometimes and would smooth his moustache and seem for several moments to be wrapped up in memories of some kind . . . (He would also not infrequently stand up for her against the two women when they were about to saddle her with too much work.) Now, however, inasmuch as a ceremonial proceeding had been disrupted, something else immediately came to the fore, and the councillor—in shirtsleeves or not—was now every inch the Spanish grandee. He set the watering can down on the path. "A purchase of this kind," he said, "is to be regarded neither as contrary to law nor even as dubious, assuming that the legally fixed price, and neither more nor less, is levied. Nevertheless a licit purchase could in certain cases be capable in and of itself of giving rise to a suspicion of illicit manipulation or speculation with the acquired goods." He picked the watering can back up and resumed his interrupted regular circuit. All Thea could do was stand there with her teeth in her mouth. Meanwhile, Zihal had already advanced more closely toward that fine dividing line along which the Lower Zihalism ceases and the Higher begins, even though he had never in his life set foot on the magnificent flight of stairs in the town palace of Prince Eugene of Savoy, and a directorate overseeing the finances of a province had always represented for him the most rarified azure of what bureaucrats consider heaven, a sky where nothing goes awry, eternal blue with nothing askew.

Hedi Loiskandl, cheerful bearer of bad tidings (the kind of messenger to be recommended highly!), was no sooner holding the blank check Thea had handed over than all suspense and interest drained away from her, a change Thea really would have had to notice, but didn't, as a consequence of her cinematically impaired state. The police inquiries—conducted with utmost cursoriness and haste, seemingly more just for form's sake, so to say—were dropped after a short time. So off Hedi went, but she left behind in Thea, or on Thea, a streak of dirt, caused not least by the question she'd languidly put forward at the end—who was this Eulenfeld anyway? Questions directed toward someone in love about the object of his or her love can only strike the lover as egregious, for the simple reason that it will awaken in the person being questioned a suspicion that he or she is exactly the one least in a position to furnish an adequate answer. Thea didn't give any. So off Hedi went through the clean kitchen after making this last soiling blotch. Frau Rokitzer was there. Hedi filled her in, quickly and quietly, on the outcome of their conversation, telling the older woman she was certain her daughter had had nothing to do with this business. But Baron von Eulenfeld? He might well have. It could be, though, that he merely wanted to secure a stock for himself personally. Regarding Thea, she would set the aunt's mind at rest. And about everything else, too, as much as possible.

It was impossible, but only because Aunt Oplatek had never upset herself about any of these matters in the first place. She had merely asked about Thea in a casual way, calmly scratching the back of her head the whole time with a long wooden knitting needle, and then told Hedi about how the girl had come to see her in July and about the large quantity of tobacco products Baron von Eulenfeld had been hoping to obtain. She had refused the order, she added, because her store was a retail shop. None of it made any impression on her, not even when Hedi pointed out all the newspaper reports about large-scale thefts and smuggling activities. "Well then, that's just as well," she said; "who knows who the cigarettes were intended for. Or the Virginia cigars. They're a favorite of smugglers. So it's just as well I didn't act on the order. It would have stood out." She knew nothing about it from the papers. There are people who have a newspaper in their hands all day long and yet are mightily astonished when someone talks to them about what's in it—they have read and seen exactly nothing. From which we conclude that for them, reading a newspaper has nothing whatever to do with learning or finding out anything; it's a sort of physiological process instead, one that stands in closer connection to voiding, digesting, and perspiring—with sleepiness, when all is said and done. A woman who runs a tobacco store but doesn't know what's in the papers appears paradoxical, since these stores stock every imaginable newspaper and magazine. But that's only at first glance; looked at a second time, such a person seems totally natural. For example, Thea Rokitzer didn't know "who this Eulenfeld was anyway," even though she lived in and with this material as much as the tobacco-store proprietor lived with the printed material stacked up on her counter. Hedi wasn't one to let loose too soon, meanwhile, and certainly not in this room behind the tobacco store, where it was nice and cozy, and even pleasantly cool in the hot weather, since the windows looked onto a shady courtyard. In this courtyard or garden, enclosed by several old trees and an attractive lawn crossed by gravel paths, a photographer had set up his workshop, or atelier, to use a term whereby that occupation acquires a tinge of artistry, like painting. And indeed it could be said that at heart only a photographer has the ability to create full and complete correlations to every feature envisioned under the heading of art or artists, basically because his life and profession are openly and by outright declaration aimed at the functional creation of works the daring and the compositional organization of which would immediately make any artist nervous. As for our craftsman here, a tall, ironic, and enigmatic man with a goatee—strangely enough, he bore the same family name as one of the most renowned English naval heroes—he quite frequently used the garden for open-air pictures, especially since it housed a pretty little pavilion (the Viennese would call it a *Salettl*) that could function as a background if one was wanted. So there were interesting moments from time to time; for Fräulein Oplatek they could even be exciting, because some bridal couples, for example, wanted to ensure they would be commemorated on the great day and in their nuptial state not only in the pale overhead light of the atelier but also out in nature. Since access to the photographer led visitors along the corridor right next to the store, Fräulein Oplatek often knew in advance about such events by seeing the festively decorated wedding fiacre pull up in front. Here, inside her sphere of interest—which is what she had at once recognized this whole set of developments to be, of course— Hedi got into a state of her own and was behaving in a distracting, irritating, disruptive way. Fräulein Oplatek set her knitting down on the table and perched her glasses on her nose. "Don't you think a report should be filed or information provided anyway? I mean such a large order—it really does stand out, now all the more ..." "She's really not very attractive," Fräulein Oplatek was thinking. The double door of the atelier had just opened and the couple glided down three smooth steps and into the garden, hesitating somewhat, while Nelson (not the Eagle of Trafalgar, only the tobacconist's neighbor) hurried ahead of them with an assistant to set up the camera. The bride and groom about to be immortalized in black-and-white were meanwhile trying to do the same with their own selves in front of the pavilion, the photographer stepping in to suggest slight improvements. A chair was fetched as well. Everything went quick as lightning, and the picture for the annals of a lifetime was produced as quickly as a form filled out at the post office. Luckily for Hedi. Otherwise the following conversation would have gone on longer. "I'm only saying somebody could make an accusation later on, because what we know today might have given them a clue precisely when they're searching for the criminals but not getting anywhere." "She gets too worked up about things; that's why she'll never be pretty." "Isn't there some kind of regulation or law about cases like this?" "But she's a very nice girl. Very good figure. When will it be your turn?" "Maybe in the spring," Hedi said fervently, "he has to become an inspector first." The group in the garden had meanwhile been absorbed back into the atelier. All her solid common sense notwithstanding, Fräulein Oplatek was a species of Zihaloid after all, conscious that her proprietorship was licensed and governed by the tobacco administration. And so that marked propensity toward subservience in the face of officialdom and that suspicious mentality receptive to filing police reports—traits endemic hereabouts ever since the days of Herr von Sedlnitzky, feared police chief and head of the censorship bureau under Metternich, and capable even today of softening up and loosening the tongues of all those smaller fry to whom any little post or function is entrusted—were also alive and well in Josefine Oplatek. That was why she was now listening with one ear while her tongue was elaborating what her apprehensive eye was seeing. She took off her glasses. "I don't see what any of this has to do with me?" she said, but more in the tone of a question. "We have to find out exactly how Thea fits into the whole story," Hedi said. "That would be a job for you," her aunt answered. "I'll try my best," Hedi answered. "But make it soon," Fräulein Oplatek replied, "because if you look at it right, you could start worrying about the girl. So will you come back and tell me what you find out?"

"I will," Hedi assured her, and she left soon after, continuing along the track of her cautious exaggerations, if we may put it like that, ever the cheerful bearer of bad tidings as she exercised her distinctive method of stepping up to someone a little too closely for comfort, which then undetectably hampered the other person's freedom of movement and exerted a constraining force that in turn produced unease; this had happened to Thea's parents as well as to Thea herself. That of course didn't mean Frau Rokitzer wanted to go running right off and advocate for Thea to a sister she had relatively little contact with as is was, but that was roughly the idea about how matters stood in Josefstadt that Hedi Loiskandl imperceptibly insinuated into Frau Rokitzer's mind; and yet if the two Oplatek sisters had in fact met without delay, Hedi wouldn't have been made out to be a liar. Paula Schachl-Pichler was the only person Hedi could get nowhere with. (It's quite significant that something of the same kind happened to a person not unlike Hedi Loiskandl—specifically Wänzrich, graduate of the Commercial Academy—in his dealings with Civil Service Councillor Zihal, though this is more relevant to the story of Zihal's engagement, and so a different department, nay a whole different book, has been given accountability for that tale.) Hedi's being party to the hint Frau Zihal had sent from

Saint Valentin about not mentioning the fruit to the Schachl-Pichlers was in itself enough to make her feel superior to her stepsister—she knew something the other didn't—and she behaved accordingly in the garden. As it turned out, however, Hedi, while sitting on a rickety chair amidst the four fruit trees and in the vicinity of the lounge chair (from which Paula had not seen the least reason to get up), was in effect brought down, like a hunter's quarry. She wasn't able to tell Paula anything new, after all—because of the captain, Paula had long since pricked up her ears and had been well acquainted with Thea's oblivious-ness ever since—and so the only actual revelation for her was Hedi's interest in this whole matter. That seemed totally understandable to her. In addition—and circumstances like these really are important—the lounge chair, and her being stretched out in it, lent distance; Hedi couldn't get too close to her and was therefore obliged to sit there on her little chair while still positioned out on a limb, placed on display. All this time, in the calm of a relatively cool and overcast late-summer evening, Paula's imagination was captured by a rather peculiar image. Hedi was sitting to her right at the foot of the lounge chair (here we have to give due credit to Paula's silent authority that the girl hadn't moved any closer). While her stepsister was talking and the shadows from the indentations long since lodged in her face now deepened even more, Paula felt as though the entity on the garden chair by her feet were almost a peripheral part of her own self, a body part extended outward, in the same way she could see her feet in their brown loafers on the footrest of the lounge chair; and just as they were simply there, something to be taken for granted, that was how Hedi Loiskandl's presence was to her now as she eyed up the girl the way you look at a shoe, turning your ankle this way and that, after stepping into dirt or a puddle. Paula's instincts were suggesting that she would really need to treat Hedi nearly the same, but right now, because nothing was definite, she bumped up against the unresolved nature of the situation, as it were, and kept looking very pensively at her own right shoe. But as far as clear understanding was concerned, it included both in equal measure, her shoe as well as Hedi, perched there on her little chair like an appendage to Paula's bodyscape, extended outward, kept at some distance and for that very reason easier to see. It was clear to Paula that a blank check for freedom of action was being requested (also, though, that there were still inhibitions) but equally clear that it was not her part to bestow any such permission; nor was it her charge—one she could have fulfilled in an instant—to pierce through the exposed midpoint of Hedi's objectives, as it were. She kept looking at her shoe, turning it this way and that, and was in fact somewhere else entirely in her train of thought; she casually said she was sorry, but this was the first time she was hearing any of these stories, how foolish Thea had been, how much she hoped nothing unpleasant would come about. "When are you supposed to get married, by the way?" "In the spring," Hedi answered. Nothing about her fiancé's promotion. But for all intents and purposes she'd just been given the brush-off; she hadn't been able to step in close enough, to cause distress, to wangle an assurance that Thea hadn't had anything whatever to do with all of this. It took no time for Alois Pichler to appear in the garden after Hedi left; he'd been watching her from the window. "Is that girl gone?" he asked. "She looks like she always leaves a dog turd everywhere she goes." Husband and wife talked things over, needless to say, and it was Alois who suggested to Paula not only that she should ask Councillor Zihal about this matter when he was back from Saint Valentin and came to visit the next time, but also that she should also talk to that lawyer on Marc-Aurel Strasse she'd once worked for. She said she would do both.

It can confidently be attributed to Hedi Loiskandl's drawing a blank (but not a blank check) in Lichtental that the Rokitzers—both sisters and, even more, the Loiskandl family—began regarding Paula Pichler as the champion of the love affair between Thea and "that Eulenfeld," as they called him (they referred to Paula in more caustic terms). Paving the way to that attitude had required only a single comment from Hedi to the Rokitzer parents timed just right, at a moment whose natural impulse (preening) was suited to reinforce this somewhat less natural one (demeaning): it was in Frau Rokitzer's pantry, as the woman of the house was proudly showing off the clandestine fruit from Saint Valentin, by now packed in its own juice in the gleaming jars with their slightly magnifying effect. "There's no getting anything out of Paula," Hedi said, "she's put herself in charge of the affair between Thea and the captain and is probably thinking she can make a Frau Baron of her.

I'll have to have a talk with Thea myself. Some baron—" Then she broke off all of a sudden. Frau Rokitzer was looking too preoccupied, she thought, more than was really warranted by the jar of pears she was holding and contemplating; she seemed to have fallen unexpectedly into some sort of well or trench. Hedi leaned over the edge in fright and yelled down, "—a swindler!" whereupon Frau Rokitzer resurfaced, though slowly.

So the dividing line ran along the fruit, we could say, and indeed it does seem legitimate in this case to differentiate between who had sent and received fruit and those who'd remained empty-handed. Councillor Zihal was the only one who remained aloof, soaring above it all in his sky-blue, never-awry-blue bureaucrats' heaven. That was because Frau Rosa had managed to dispatch her shipments without his knowing anything about it (and how often, alas, do people just tiptoe past the "noble simplicity and quiet grandeur"—in Winckelmann's words—of government departments and divisions). Basically these are nothing but spiteful remarks. Even so, the Schachl-Pichler family was standing on the outside in this instance.

This day, Saturday, August 29, 1925, wasn't over yet for Thea Rokitzer. Best never even to think, "What a day this has been," because events can always come thicker and faster. What came next was a testy exchange with her parents as she was preparing to go out, which she had to do, because Eulenfeld was expecting her.

After all, he *is* the Master of Horse.

Rokitzer trailed grousing and grumbling after his wife, about whom there's been so far a complete information gap about what she looked like, for the simple reason that she had that look of someone who never looks past herself; she was wrapped up in her own cleanliness, a cake of good domestic soap with moderate lather and muted fragrance. All the ingredients for being attractive were on hand, but still she wasn't attractive, even though entirely undepleted (and where inside her would there be any place to produce friction?). Her husband was nowhere within range of a breakthrough—Rokitzer breaking through; that would be the day!—but only exuded a thin, uniformly spun filament of worries and fears instead. His wife was exhibiting uncertainty. It might well be that she still hadn't managed to crawl back all the way out of the ditch she'd toppled into right before Hedi Loiskandl's eyes. As for the rest, though, our innocent lamb now recognized Hedi's intrigues for what they were.

Thea got away around nine o'clock—by this time, no more than a cup that runneth over with woe—and was at Eulenfeld's door ten minutes later. It was painted olive green and had polished brass fixtures. After she'd rung the doorbell, Thea stared into the depth, as neutral as it was fathomless, of the enduring material solidity the door seemed to symbolize, and into this vacuum of a vacuum there intruded sounds from inside, soon resolving into voices all talking at the same time.

Eulenfeld wasn't alone.

Very much the contrary. There weren't just a few people there, but a whole crowd.

Thea was distressed at realizing she hadn't lied to her parents when she kept repeatedly assuring them that she was going to a rather large party scheduled this evening at "the baron's."

It was only five after nine, but he already had button eyes, and there was a special reason why.

For aside from the duplicate ladies—present here and now in their one-woman configuration, however, and going by the name of Editha Schlinger, as usual—aside from this bothersome phenomenon, something had happened to Eulenfeld that absolutely, positively must under no imaginable circumstances whatsoever, regardless of what they may be, ever come to pass in Vienna, owing to the unforeseen and unforeseeable consequences which could ensue; something that must be categorically avoided but concerning which the captain, foreigner that he essentially had always remained, had to all appearances not found himself in a state of sufficient clarity, of which in turn, to be sure, he would have had to possess an extraordinary measure so that it might substitute for the ingrained instincts he was lacking, instincts which apply the brakes—in fully autonomous mode and at any price, as it were—when approaching particular danger zones. Even at the price of being in the right and able to prove it.

Eulenfeld had had a falling-out with the concierge in his building.

"You're a creature from another planet." That was the considered judgment of good-looking Dolly Storch (she was present this evening as well), an example of how the rest were weighing the situation.

After the captain had reported on his vexatious mishap with much harrumphing and all the embellishments at his command, Leucht looked at him but could only laugh and shake his head at this incurably droll specimen.

"Laugh all you want," Dolly said, "but this is going to be taken out on poor Editha."

Nobody understood at first, but then they realized quite soon that it was an irrefutable insight. "After all, I see them together every Sunday!" Dolly exclaimed (she meant the two concierges and their families, the one from the building where Editha Schlinger lived and the other one from here). "How it is, I don't really know, but these are the kind of people I keep constantly running into, either on a Saturday afternoon or a Sunday. Either Frau Wöss—that's the name of yours, Otto—with the other one, yours, Editha; what's her name—?"

"I don't know," Editha said sheepishly.

"What, you don't know the name of your concierge?!"

Editha didn't answer and kept looking at Dolly as morosely as a schoolgirl looks at her teacher when she's at a loss for the answer. From the sofa, which Editha and the captain were sitting perched on the edge of, while a young man from Dolly's circle of friends was half stretched out behind them (it was the same writer who had wrapped Grete's cape around her shoulders at the Teresa in Naples that past spring)—from the sofa, then, there came two words: "*Nil admirari.*"

"A person could learn that from you," Dolly answered. "To make a long story short, the two concierges are always in contact. I recently saw Herr Wöss with Editha's—"

"Hawélka," interjected Eulenfeld, accenting the name on the second syllable, which instantly triggered a burst of uproarious laughter. "Do you also say 'Swobóda' or 'Jerzábek'?!" cried Leucht. These accentuations were German, completely alien to the Viennese.

"At least the first of these is correct," replied the captain with imperturbable aplomb. "In Slavic phonology, dontcha know, this word, which means, more or less, 'free,' is pronounced paroxytonically."

Nobody here except the literary man on the sofa knew what that term meant. The bar set by the Master of Horse was too high for anyone else to reach.

Dolly continued. "Not long ago I saw Wöss and Hawekla together at a card table in the coffeehouse on the same side of the street as the train station—I live on that side—not in the Café Brioni. I was walking past, and they were sitting right by the window."

"Now a few things are starting to come clear," Editha cried suddenly. "The woman who looks after the building has really had it in for me these last few days. Yesterday she even removed the light bulb in the stairway, because there's an office opposite where nobody comes or goes in the evening. 'The bulb is needed elsewhere, and the concierge won't give out any more.' I handed her a new bulb today and asked her in a very friendly way if she would mind screwing it in. She said absolutely nothing in reply—neither yes nor no."

"There we are," said Leucht. "But that's just the beginning. If anybody leaves the street door unlocked some evening, then right away, you're the one who did it. And so on. Nip things in the bud right now, Editha; find the right opportunity to give the woman a generous tip, and find it soon, but don't make things too obvious. As for this business about the lighting in the stairwell, it seems to me you handled yourself perfectly according to the code of conduct governing relations with a concierge."

The captain growled faintly and gave out a loud snort that sounded as if he were out of countenance; then he placed his monocle in his eye. That fall from grace illustrated by the unlocked main door was exactly what had befallen him. And it was connected with another fall, this one physical, that had happened on the stairs and had been preceded by a merely moral one, so to speak. The captain—fortunately it fell out, by the way, that Eulenfeld had only fallen or stumbled forward on the previous Monday, after spending the evening at Editha's with Melzer and Stangeler—the captain had not neglected to turn around on the staircase, cursing as he went, and carefully lock the building entrance, which he hadn't done before. He'd been shaken awake, as it were. The concierge, too, thanks to the noise and Eulenfeld's loud, bad-tempered monologues. When Frau Wöss then found the entrance door open at six o'clock the following morning, logic suggested an evident chain of causality, so she felt only mildly put out by how much noise the captain had made in heading back down to the front door. She appeared that same day in his entryway, a very Zihaloid expression on her face, and requested that "Herr von Eulenfeld" lock the building door when he came home late. So far, all was running smoothly. But the captain was not about to take the fall, and in direct reply to his objection she allowed herself to allude to "circumstances" under which he might not be able to say for certain whether he'd locked up behind him or not. He took the Herr von Eulenfeld part in stride; he'd never been one to set much store by titles, not even after noting long before that Frau Hawelka, Frau Wöss, and all the rest, *tutti quanti*, did so to the very fullest extent. Herr Hawelka, for example, in addition to his other occupations, was an official of the Watch and Secure Association (a kind of privately organized police group alert to prevent break-ins) and was accordingly referred to even by his own wife as the Herr Inspector whenever she mentioned him to the tenants; in addition, Frau Podiwinsky, her mother, never spoke about her son-in-law as Leopold or Poldi but always called him Herr Wöss instead. Titles were omitted in one direction only—up, when climbing stairs. This was the trend here. Eulenfeld had tolerated it easily. But never his interlocutor, who was taking aim at his "circumstances." At this point he began speaking in standard, formal German—this was his true first language, after all, insofar as we can speak of language here to begin with—and the rest proceeded like a sharply falling curve, which it might soon have literally turned into: he threw Frau Wöss out and came close to knocking her down the stairs. Heavy drinkers are sensitive; above all, not one of them ever thinks he is one.

"And you're only telling us the whole story with the concierge today?!" cried Editha, seeming to catch up with the astonishment into which she was just now falling.

"Never mind, though, because at least this gave us a way to clear up the household code of conduct," said Leucht with total seriousness.

That made for no more than cold comfort as far as the captain was concerned. The whole story had by and large slipped out unintentionally or accidentally. He'd in fact aired a smaller concern instead of a larger one, the significant pressure of which had pushed the smaller to the periphery and through his mouth, even though Eulenfeld was not ordinarily the most talkative of souls. But the ensuing broad discussion of the topic, swirling like a spillover, was having an essentially adverse effect on him; in the first place he construed the episode to a notable extent as a sign he'd suffered a comedown, a decline after his fall. He considered it seriously unbecoming to be wasting words on a Wöss or a Hawekla; it offended him. In the second place he thought he could sense that the admittedly toned-down version of his fall on the stairs as portrayed by himself was being supplemented on the spot with a more realistic narrative, perhaps even nearer to the way Frau Wöss had seen things . . .

So he growled again, though even more faintly than before (this was roughly his answer to Editha's astonished exclamation) and then fell back into a persistent silence.

During all of this Thea Rokitzer was carefully maintaining her balance on her little chair, more or less the way someone holds a glass that's filled to the brim. Throughout this pother about concierges and their ways, she felt as if she were on furlough, as it were, not really present, and freed from any obligation—such as telling the captain about Hedi Loiskandl's visit. He had welcomed Thea very cordially in the entryway, incidentally, and had asked her to come back the next day, on Sunday afternoon, when they'd have peace and quiet; he couldn't have done anything about having guests today. "I have to be home by evening," Thea had responded, completely without advance intent. "And you certainly will be," Eulenfeld said in a very friendly and yielding tone, "you'll be back home by seven o'clock, and that's a promise." This quick whispered conversation by his door, right after she'd come in, was now resonating inside her with a sad sound. She could see herself sitting here tomorrow, darning and mending the captain's laundry. There was Melzer. That afternoon in July. Here; she'd been sitting on the sofa. Now she felt as if this spot with the sofa, even though a half dozen people were lounging and lolling in it now, were vacant. She didn't ask about the major. She looked at Eulenfeld, who, even considering his present and clearly visible state of button-eyed obliteration, gave the impression of being troubled. When it occurred to her that it would be better not to tell him anything tomorrow either, but to wait until Monday instead and have a talk with Paula first, her mood lightened and grew more lively. That was exactly the thought that lent her great comfort, and it stood for the time being in no connection with Melzer that a name could be put to.

The Pastré twins, having seen each other over the summer only in Salzburg and other points west, including Munich, had scarcely been reunited in Vienna before a squabble broke out between them, in spite of the tender greetings and embraces at the West Station, or precisely because of them, among other reasons. Editha—she was the arriving twin—considered it a very bad idea indeed that her sister, whom she'd recruited to be what we might call her surrogate in Vienna since the spring, had shown up at the train station, for she was thinking she might prolong the current situation, specifically the singleness of her person, for some time to come. That was why an appearance in duplicate could not by any means be endorsed, no matter where, and least of all at a train station, with people bunched in tight clusters. Her sister, Mimi, was hoping to put an end to this burdensome farce, however.

The person to let loose on was the captain, who was supposed to take care of picking Editha up but who in all probability, she assumed and stated, had gotten drunk before the actual weekend started and as a result had become too lazy or too immobilized to go to the station. It's easy to picture the forceful grunts that must have resounded after such outrageous indictments by Editha.

It did not perturb Editha in the least, on the other hand, that Frau Inspector Hawelka—draping herself, as is the custom, in the mantle of her husband's title—crept out of her underground lodging and started up the stairs at the most opportune possible moment, just as the taxi they'd taken from the station was pulling up to the door; toward her, it would hardly have been possible to maintain the fiction of singleness anyway, and if so, only with the very greatest strain and under conditions that would seriously inhibit day-to-day living; that was why, after Editha's departure in the spring—she wanted to meet her sister's ship, which was landing in Bordeaux—Mimi Scarlez, née Pastré, who arrived alone in Vienna two weeks later, fulfilled the legal requirement without delay by having herself registered through the concierge at the district administrative office under her real name and using her Argentinian passport as proof of identity. Of course she could have altogether spared herself the trouble of registering and simply gone about as her sister, coming and going as she pleased; Frau Hawelka would have been the last person able to tell the twins apart. But Editha was already looking ahead toward the end of summer, when she was thinking of returning to Vienna herself, and thinking about legal considerations, too, namely the ones that pertained to Mimi. That called for having solid ground under her feet and putting all the formalities in order so that she could present herself with no constraints and not have to live for months in Vienna unregistered. There had also remained the option of registering at the district office in person, without involving Frau Hawelka, allowing her to believe Frau Schlinger had returned after a short absence, but this would only have meant waving it in front of her face at the end of the summer, in the form of a distressingly abrupt duplicate appearance, a sight far outside the framework of a concierge's everyday life; as it was now, though, she had a few months' time to get used to the idea that Frau Schlinger's twin sister, who lived abroad, was currently occupying her apartment, instead of later having unexpected clarity harshly thrust upon her. In addition—perhaps most important—this way of handling matters avoided circumventing Frau Inspector Hawelka when officially registering, an evasion which, considering the Zihaloid mentality nature had conferred and nurture confirmed, would have had little to recommend it and might even have aroused suspicion.

The fact was, however, that the captain had indeed turned up at the station upon Mimi's arrival with masses of flowers, deeply touched, eminently charming, and all the rest of it, as though there were only one side to him, the very best one. A full year of his life—even more, and it hadn't been one of the worst, either—stepped out from the long carriage of the express train, surrounding Mimi Scarlez like a nimbus. But Mimi, filled with anxious, even dismaying emotions on arriving once again in Vienna after seventeen years, quickly found a piece of

Buenos Aires waiting for her on the platform at the West Station, just as if she'd seen the captain on the Calle Florida only a few days before and not as if a separation of four years were standing between them.

A scant half hour after embracing Mimi on the pier at Bordeaux, Editha Schlinger was embarked on a thorough contemplation of the code of conduct, protocol, or rule book mentioned above as governs relations with concierges; the two had hardly arrived at their hotel, for that matter (this was Editha's curious, desiccated way of carrying the soil of her homeland on her heels even when abroad). Yet it was the one arriving from farther away who immediately began prodding her nearest and dearest. It is at this exact point, in fact, this new point of departure and beginning, that there promptly—but without any prompting—emerged what it was that constituted the actual difference between sisters whose physical appearance made them indistinguishable (and which had never so much as entered the mind of Herr Georg von Geyrenhoff fourteen years before, however much he thought he was in sole possession of the facts or at least knew more about the subject—and many another as well—than anyone else). So they hadn't even set Mimi's handsome luggage down in her hotel room next to the great opera house before she stated one condition—a single one—for her stay in Vienna: if she was prepared to impersonate Editha for a time in her relations with that civil service councillor or major from the tobacco administration (she literally called him "that major from the tobacco administration"), she demanded unconditionally in return that she be allowed to exercise propriety and adhere to all the formalities with him and everyone else. Her passport was in order, and she was considering making use of it, even calling at the Argentinian consulate general in Vienna, because she had some business to take care of for her husband, and so on (it's quite possible, too, that Enrique Scarlez had cautioned his wife about suitable conduct in regard to the externals already mentioned). Mimi's words had induced Editha at the time to evaluate with all due haste the whole situation touching on occupancy rules and police regulations, whose complexity we (as tried-and-true Austrians) foresaw immediately. During her contemplations, however, Editha Schlinger's feelings were mixed, and they were painful as well. Here, in this "mania for order" (as she now swiftly and secretly dubbed it) on her sister's part, lay the true root of the separation seventeen years before; she clearly sensed it now and had sensed it even then, perhaps, known it on an intuitive level, even though still half a child.

So she agreed to her sister's condition.

Back in Vienna, Frau Hawelka was given Mimi's completed registration form and even her passport: up to that point—the documents were handed to her the day after Mimi's arrival—the concierge had not believed a single word Frau Schlinger said about a twin sister living abroad; she'd entertained the more plausible surmise that Editha was returning from Paris with all new outfits (for how could she have missed noticing the change) and that whatever this whole stunt might mean, she'd get to the bottom of it soon enough. Now, however—nothing makes a more forceful impression on a Zihaloid than documentation, government forms, and official stamps!—now, however, she started directing her vigilance to a different realm, scrutinizing Mimi's wardrobe as carefully as she could, recording each new item as it appeared or identifying an article she'd seen on Mimi before.

Mimi's way of behaving just after she'd landed in Bordeaux gives rise to a suspicion that she'd been infected in early youth with a strain of *Zihalismus endemicus* viable still today and now undergoing reactivation, emerging from the latent phase and manifesting itself in full force the closer she drew to her birthplace. Other aspects offering rebuttal need to be taken into consideration, however: that neither her father nor her mother had been born and raised in Vienna, so different viruses had populated her family dwelling years back; that she had left her home and her country while still in the full malleability of her girlhood; that here in Bordeaux, in April of 1925, she was still far distant from her native heath. No, this resistance of hers, this effort to construct a barrier of order against Editha—she launched it immediately—was grounded in much more personal reasons.

As was the pain it caused Editha. It can be stated with certainty that there was only one single person on whom she had ever fully bestowed her love: Mimi. So now she was resuming a struggle—it started as soon as they left the dock, and extended far beyond anything related to codes of conduct or other, more opaque stratagems—to achieve total congruence, indeed nothing less than a complete fusion and unity of personhood, a possibility she believed in from the bottom of her heart even today just as strongly as she had when they were girls, and every deviation from which—inevitable, of course—was magnified tenfold in her eyes.

Conflict comes about most readily when one of the parties secretly considers the other one obligated to be closer than is the case.

Being picked up from the train station was the least of it. There were essentially two altogether distinct factors in play here, the Pastré parents and Major Melzer. And on this latter point Editha was to be confronted by a resolute adversary, specifically Eulenfeld.

The prospect of subsequent reunion and reconciliation between the newly duplicated lady Mimi Pastré-Scarlez and her aged parents was not without its terrors. But it wasn't connected to anything about the major, and action on the parental front came about only after matters concerning Melzer had been resolved and all the horses—meaning all the ladies—had been let out of the barn and, to an extent, off the hook. As for the culminating point and end result of these double monkey-shines—at least we'd be tempted to call them that if the delightful twin bundles of joy with which their parents had been blessed weren't so abundantly charming—it would have been much more to Editha's liking if this thunderbolt had struck much earlier and in a way completely different from how it actually did (full reports will follow in due time; we can't just skip over the episode, after all). Nothing impromptu, she hoped, but well prepared in advance. There would have been a whole summer to arrange it; that was true of the business with Melzer as well. Even so, what Editha had once more learned from Mimi around the middle of August in Salzburg was that nothing had happened concerning their parents, absolutely nothing whatever, and there was no tangible outcome of any kind with Melzer, either. (Mimi ended up meeting Editha at the station to make up for that!) At Bad Wildungen—strangely enough it was at this very same spa in the Waldeck region where the Pastré parents had in bygone times annually pampered their Calvinist gallbladders or spleens but had in the meantime long since given up (this is according to Geyrenhoff's chronicle)—at Bad Wildungen, Editha, who for good reasons of her own had enjoyed extended stays there since 1923, was in constant receipt of letters from her parents even after Mimi's arrival in Vienna, and she had to answer them and give full accounts of what therapies she was undergoing, what physician was treating her, if this or that group of people was still frequenting the place or whether certain stores or bakeries from the old days were still in business, and in which pastry shop she had eaten those delicious German fruit tarts, and so on and so on. Nothing would do but for her to answer every last question, which meant wearing out her pen by dashing off page after page of lies, which Editha had always had a special knack for concocting, but which often grew to be too much here. She neither had the remotest need of treatment at a spa, nor did she bother her head about anyone except for a very well-to-do cigar dealer from Wiesbaden, who had another store here in Wildungen he considered important, vitally important, in fact, for the very reason that it gave him ample excuse from a business standpoint to spend the summer with Editha in Wildungen and environs, far from his home in Wiesbaden, where he was only too well known. Of course he had to go back from time to time, because it would be apparent even to someone with no special knowledge of tobacco, or even to a non-smoker, that a shop in Wiesbaden would be of much greater import than one out there in Waldeck, even though it's a very popular resort area . . . Enough! Her parents' letters kept on coming and coming throughout the summer, and the invariable and unmistakable testament they bore was that Mimi still hadn't gone to see them, hadn't embarked on her temporary impersonation of Editha just for this visit, a time frame offering Mimi the best opportunity to grow somewhat used to her parents again and to sound out the territory, if only in regard to putting the inheritance in order; the subject would have to come up for discussion within the foreseeable future in any case, and it was essential, not least for Mimi's benefit, to settle it soon. The issue entailed nothing less than having to change a will! But no amount of insisting and expostulating helped in the least whenever the twins met in Salzburg or Munich. Sooner or later Editha was going to have to step forth with her Pastrésque severity. To say nothing of Melzer.

For it was none other than the admirer from Wiesbaden, Herr Wedderkopp, who could have used the cigarettes from Fräulein Oplatek

to supply a private, select inner circle of customers he had special connections with; it happened that there were two or three people in that
group whom Herr Wedderkopp set great store by (in every respect)
and whose wishes and individual tastes he strove hard to gratify. For
these purposes, though, the small quantities of Austrian cigarettes and
Virginia cigars, never more than a couple of hundred at a time, which
the recently duplicated Editha would bring across the border, by ap-
propriately farcical methods (the captain will soon be heard covertly
grunting about them)—those small quantities were totally insufficient.
This whole state of affairs made the trips to Salzburg and Munich a
torture for Mimi Scarlez. But she went along. Direct opposition to her
sister had never been her way. She exercised resistance more by omission, by passivity, and these came to the fore every time she was supposed
to go see Editha.

The idea was not simply to obtain large quantities of cigarettes at
one time but also to find a secure way of transporting them. And Wedderkopp was pushing.

He meant a great deal to Editha—everything just now, in fact—and
it would be a mistake to believe this was the case in only one respect,
the commercial one (to express it gently). Wedderkopp captivated her,
he swept her up and away, he gave her zest for living. This even though
the man looked the way his name sounded, and that's enough said. But
this bull-necked stability, an attribute that meant he understood how
to make a life stand on its own two feet, how to give it a good swift
kick in the rear, so to speak, if it's taking too long to get into its stride
or start its wheels turning, this happiness that builds up a head of steam
for a life was something Editha Schlinger-Pastré was soon no more able
to do without than a warm stove in winter. She may have sensed that
to feel at ease—in any way at all, provided it's the person's own, authentic way—is what really opens up life as life, and it was in exactly
this respect that she had so often stood before closed doors.

This blithe bull-neck (altogether the opposite of a bearer of bad
tidings!) caused every wellspring inside her—at least insofar as she had
any (basically these are nothing but spiteful remarks)—to surge up,
and it was important to Editha in the early months of 1925—just as
Mimi Scarlez was deciding finally to take that trip to Europe she'd

been postponing time and again—it was important to her, especially now, to spend time close to Wedderkopp. His divorce, just about an accomplished fact even before he'd met Editha, was now being set formally in motion, entirely on his initiative and completely without pressure from Editha, the upshot being that he was clearing up his affairs so he could propose to her. She'd gone about things the right way, letting the proposal come to her unbidden without ever at any time having given the slightest hint—and now there it was. So far so good. What she did wrong, on the other hand, was not to call at once for a long period apart—although she did travel in the meantime to Geneva and Lausanne for eight weeks to visit relatives, incidentally—for absence does indeed make the heart grow fonder, a truism about which there isn't the least doubt; after a few weeks a warming trend becomes manifest in the language the lovers use in their letters. Besides, only those who are together can move apart, which is logical if you think about it. But none of this wisdom quite pertains in Wedderkopp's case; you could take a few swipes at this mass of man when he was sizzling hot—it wasn't just cigarette smoke that was producing the steam—and score a bull's-eye smack-dab in a life on fire even when you missed. He was aflame. These days, with his verve immense and his nerve intense, he not only would have administered a good swift kick *in podicem* to the world but would also have smacked it in the chops (he loved this expression) a few times if only that could help move his concerns forward. Long story short: the Pastré sisters were together for a brief two weeks in Paris, and then Mimi traveled to Vienna by herself, which fit in with Editha Schlinger's plans, by the way, as she, for her part, took a trip to Switzerland.

She had been to visit Mimi in Buenos Aires in 1923.

Not very long at all after Negria's breakthrough in Nussdorf, the ride along the river, the tipsiness from the Greek wine, the ensuing full consummation of the breakthrough soon thereafter by the old boatsman in medias res, the first argument, the second quarrel, the third and final farewell until further notice. To pinpoint: Editha's trip took place in November of 1923, and she stayed until March, through the hot season, that is. But Enrique Scarlez lived in the Recoleta district, not very far from the water. When she would lie in bed in the dark, she felt, almost more than she heard, how loud and dynamic this city was at night.

Strangely enough, she had often (according to her own statement) thought of Schlinger during her stay, because she was having dreams about him: she would be approaching their apartment on Rudolf-von-Alt Platz in Vienna the way a person steps up to a still pond, but the square, closed in on three sides by buildings, *was* the apartment; she wasn't in a house; the square was filled with water and had greenery around the edges, very fresh greenery and young trees; she was standing between two of them; opposite her on the other side was her former husband. They said nothing to one another; they didn't call to one another; they didn't move; he was wearing a dark suit, not evening dress, but just something like what a man would wear to a *thé dansant*, with striped trousers. The silence was very strong in the dream. That was the strongest thing about it. It kept coming back to Editha Schlinger during the first nights in Buenos Aires and was connected in some way with the window blinds, the *persianas*. Whenever a powerful *pampero* would blow, which was not seldom the case here, it produced a rattling sound that reminded her of that apartment in Vienna. It had been years, incidentally, since she'd heard anything about Schlinger. Soon after the dreams we've mentioned, Editha moved to a different room because of the heat; a fan ran in it, and the dream images never came back.

Nothing even approaching a fusion of personhood with Mimi ever came about in Buenos Aires, even though Editha's head had been full of such notions as she set off on her journey to her sister and brother-in-law, a man she'd met fifteen years before in Munich and knew even less than slightly.

Mimi had undergone an appendectomy not long before Editha's arrival, we might add.

Scarlez worked in the same line of business—only on a somewhat larger scale—as Wedderkopp, with whom she wasn't yet on such a familiar footing at the time (she had nevertheless fixed Melzer in her sights in September 1923 in this connection and had also told her sister about him): she had an immense liking for Scarlez. All in all, a rich family with no children. That was completely to Editha Schlinger's taste. The cigar wholesaler was a soft-spoken, smooth-skinned man with a graceful figure and an unusually symmetrical face; his eyes were quickly cast in shadow by his long, dark lashes. This part of his face could have belonged to a beautiful woman. But his mouth was disproportionately wide and always shut tight.

In summary, then: the Pastré children were up to their necks in tobacco. And they had a strong tolerance.

Needless to say, Editha had taken her trip to South America without her aging parents' knowledge. The captain would receive their letters (forwarded to Vienna from Munich, where some relative of his had furnished an accommodation address), answer them (insofar as he didn't forget) using a small typewriter and stationery signed in advance by Editha—he wasn't skillful at forging her signature—and send back his letters by the reverse route, routed through the other wayward family member in Munich. Arrangements had been made to use cablegram or radiogram in case of emergency, but otherwise Editha wanted to be left in peace. Nothing drastic happened, however, no urgent developments. That was how it was, then, that an old hussar, a Master of Horse, ended up for a large part of the winter from 1923 to 1924 writing genuinely kind letters to a pair of lonely parents, trying to make plausible why their child always stayed away for so long. This turned into a habit, and he spent many a cozy winter evening corresponding with "his" parents; he even stopped procrastinating with answers. As time went on, there even crept into them a warm-feeling tone. Shrewd, as an old Master of Horse always is (boatsmen are the same way), he would often look back in these missives with deep emotion, or even with honest grief, at the unhappy course of his marriage with Sectional Councillor Schlinger—against whom he never directed a word of accusation or belittlement (after all, he was in equal measure unacquainted with and indifferent to Schlinger)—and he understood how to convey a very serious attitude on the subject, according the parents a fleeting glimpse into a deeply wounded heart that needed to keep away from Vienna primarily because the city was still today a place of painful memories. And if around this time compassion for their child and her unhappiness, her shattered love and broken marriage, gradually began outweighing in the hearts of Herr and Frau

Pastré their puritan outrage at the scandal of a divorce by their very own daughter, it was in large part thanks to the captain's letters, not to mention that the parents were also taking a more lenient stance because there was now only this one child remaining to them.

By the time Editha's visit to South America was drawing to a close, Eulenfeld had become carried away by his epistolary zeal; it far exceeded anything Editha had had in mind when she'd asked him for this favor. Her intent had been that the correspondence be restricted to a bare minimum, though she had an inkling that the captain would prefer to take care of his letter writing on Saturday afternoons, at a time when his routine during the winter months was to take a seat at the chair by his desk after a refreshing siesta and a bracing stirrup cup. The episto-lary steed he would then ride had the advantageous trait of holding still enough—whether at a walk, a canter, or even a gallop—to enable the ongoing intake of additional medicinal spirits and cordials. The resulting state contributed to a release of feelings toward the Pastré parents—complete unacquaintance and total indifference here, too, as with Schlinger—and the bracing warmth in his stomach would transfer over to the language he chose and produce a comparable effect. Every action to which we at first had to force ourselves with consider-able expenditure of energy reliably acquires the foggy quality of habit as we stick with it, whether letter writing or shaving, and Eulenfeld had always been one whose acts were governed by such small habit patterns. Only he took things too far. He sat at his table swathed in fog and clouds, and not just from cigarette smoke, either. That was exactly what Editha had been afraid of, and in fact he'd once made a bad slip-up after accelerating from a brisk trot to an invigorating gallop, quickening the pace too abruptly for him even to realize what he'd done. "No, no," he wrote, "I've recognized for a long time that you can't flog a nag into climbing the Irish bank when it likes to jump; that's something my first squadron leader (!?) always said." Fortunately, Editha had at one time had the benefit of riding lessons, and her first teacher had been an uhlan captain, another master of horse. The "nag" was understood to be Dr. Schlinger in this case, and exactly what the "likes to jump" phrase referred to seems rather open to question. The whole metaphor (with which Editha meant to say more or less that she herself had ridden her husband straight into his own mistakes, as it were) was a horse lame in all four of its legs. But the letter had already been posted by the time its content emerged from Captain Eulenfeld's patch of fog on Sunday morning. Of course he immediately thought of chasing down the letter by a telegram to his cousin Joachim in Munich, which would prevent it from being forwarded. But then he just let it go. At heart he didn't care one way or the other. Later on he confessed this lapse to Kajetan von S., grunting lightly all the while. It remains admittedly (and unfortunately) unknown to this day what impression that turn of phrase made on the Pastré parents.

This whole time, Editha was living in Buenos Aires, where a clear demarcation of dual personhood was upheld and an orderly routine maintained, which engendered a certain hospital-like barrenness inside her, sterile as a sanatorium and scrubbed of all potential for sensation. That was the point at which she had begun bringing up for discussion a possible trip to Europe by Mimi, advocating for it to her and Enrique, even though Mimi at first only listened with one ear, if that, and acted skittish in a way that seemed to go beyond simple resistance to reviving a sunken past. Editha, always alert, felt almost as if something were being directed against herself here. Very soon after her arrival in Argentina, the old impetus to achieve total congruence or even fusion with Mimi was once again powerfully reactivated in her. On her side, though, Mimi instantly rejected habits instilled through basically innocent childhood pranks, the last of which, however, fifteen years earlier, in Munich, had ceased to be innocent and had taken a fateful turn—auspiciously so—instead (it was in Mimi's bathroom, during one of their chats about the old days, that Editha was shown the clearly visible scar left over from her sister's recent appendectomy, from which she'd recovered well). Mimi exhibited open dislike of her parents and keen distress at the thought of seeing them again. Enrique would lower his long eyelashes when she spoke like this. Just the notion that Mimi had never once managed in fifteen years to write them a letter was hard enough to understand. She might have wanted to do it earlier; afterward she may have kept putting it off. And then for that very reason, starting at some indefinite point, she never again wanted to hear a single word about it. For his part, her husband had given serious consideration to establishing contact with a father-in-law he didn't know, even if she wouldn't, just to inform the old people at least that their other child was alive and doing well. But it was as if Mimi could guess Enrique's thoughts, and one day she abruptly burst out with a declaration that she would leave him if he were to dare reforging family bonds behind her back. "Chaining me to this disaster again?!" Her exact words. Husband and wife spoke only Spanish between themselves. This flare-up took place at the window of Mimi's large drawing room (used only during the cooler months), a salon whose lightly curved furniture and almost rainbowlike iridescent fabrics evoked a feeling that everything here was airy and movable. There was a direct view of the water (because it is more than forty kilometers wide here, the mud-brown Río de la Plata gives the impression of being open sea; its mouth is a gulf of the Atlantic Ocean, for that matter). Far off to the left, the outermost points extending from the Barrio Parque section of Palermo were visible. No large oceangoing steamships like those in the harbor and the Riachuelo Canal were found here, but perhaps the sight of any water at all was enough to satisfy Mimi. "If you write to them," she said more softly, but very vehemently, "you can call me your ex-wife. If you write, they'll insist I come; and they might even send Editha for me. Everything would start all over again. I will not have that!" She shouted those last words in a strong voice. "Nothing will happen, dearest love (*mi adorada querida*), that you don't want to happen," said Enrique with eyes wide open, lashes not lowered. They held this conversation in the early summer of 1923. And seven months later Editha did indeed arrive, though of course without her parents' knowledge. We must say that Scarlez would have been bound to develop a strange conception of the Pastré family over time had his manner of thinking—a deep, unruffled placement across from and in front of his own life's background and experience, which would thereupon recede, of all the pertinent incompatible and inexplicable elements for as long as it took until the first thread of his understanding wove into the weft of the foreign mesh—had his way of thinking not kept matters in a state of constant fluid reassessment. But it was by this window and in the morning sun—falling from the right, the side the Naval Academy is on, through the streets with so many mansions in such disparate styles, through their front gardens and among their treetops—that Scarlez was presented with undeniable proof (Mimi had spoken in great turmoil) that a kind of aversion toward her devoted twin sister dwelt inside his wife, but he had never come so clearly to notice until now.

This was a onetime occurrence. When Editha actually arrived in person, the most genuine fondness came flooding out of Mimi Scarlez.

Any observer would have had the same impression Editha had about the Scarlez couple—that their marriage was happy; and it was. The crisis Eulenfeld had ushered in during 1921, which he spent in Buenos Aires, never brought about an open rupture. After all, Enrique was following a few paths of his own at the time, and we can say that the time was exactly right; the fact was that for months and months both partners, each in a kind of slight numbness, lived not with but past one another in the most harmonious mutual agreement. What became more important was that they rediscovered one another at almost the same time (scarcely a week after the captain's ship had sailed, by the way). That rediscovery verified the stability of their union and the good favor conferred by the stars under which it stood.

Soon after her arrival, Editha had of course dropped all hope of being able to awaken in her sister a longing for her old home, at least by a direct route, so to speak. So she spoke into someone else's ear—Enrique Scarlez's, naturally—along lines that guaranteed he'd have to listen. The Pastré fortune, grounded almost entirely in Swiss currency and securities—everything Herr Pastré had acquired in Vienna, above all, the proceeds from the factory in Simmering, which he'd wound up selling because he lacked a successor of his own, he had transmitted to his old home, namely Geneva—this fortune had undergone hardly any devaluation after the World War and the extinction of the Austrian imperial state. All in all, taken together with what we have already found out from Sectional Councillor (at the time, Executive Committee Member) Geyrenhoff, this is not a matter any normal person could ignore or would be willing to forego. But the pedestal Editha pointed to when trying to appoint Scarlez to anoint his wife's trip to Europe—perched atop it was not just filial devotion but also the necessity of assuring Mimi's part of the inheritance—this pedestal seemed all the more solid and lofty, at any rate, in that it was made of nothing other than selfless love for her sister.

Now then: all of this was being talked about in the bright room with the white-enameled door panels and the insets above them with grapes and angels, likewise painted white, the window framing the distant, sun-flooded Kahlenberg, while the captain—grunting softly at times, louder at other times; utterly exasperated at times; virtually distraught at times—was dashing back and forth between the duplicate ladies like the hare between the hedgehog and its wife in the Grimms' tale, for Mimi was sitting at one end of the room by the small white secretary and Editha by the door panels at the other end in a chair that belonged at the tea table (the same chair into which Thea Rokitzer had crumpled under Mimi's rain of blows on July 11). Now that we have this information, it becomes understandable that the captain had felt obligated to place a phone call to Thea, who had just returned, and postpone their reunion until that evening, even though he would be having company.

"If that's what I want and Mimi agreed to help me in this business…"

"Bidness, bidness!" Eulenfeld shouted (his making a little game of using dialect pronunciation shows his disposition and mood as tolerable for the time being—Frau Wöss had been regaled with the most excruciatingly correct formal pronunciation). "I know you and your monkey bidness; you stampeded her; that's how you always do. Boring in like a power drill; boom, she's done. What else could she say but 'All right, I'll do it!' Everything is set up here just to satisfy your wishes, though they're as idiotic as they are outlandish. But things don't always work out in such a jiffy." He grunted. That might have been a sign that he was preparing to leave the homey territory of dialect speech. "Scheichsbeutel will take care of everything for you," he added.

"That's all I need, this Sch…creature," Editha cried (her exact words). "What's in it for me if I get involved in situations I don't know how to handle?!"

"Well," said the captain more calmly, and with a superior smirk, "our little caper à deux in Salzburg wouldn't exactly be large-scale enough for the quantities we have in mind. Coming up to the toll barrier with an innocent little travel case and opening it with no prompting to show three brushes and two perfume vials—no customs inspector could be bothered. But lo and behold! who should turn up out of the blue but your sister, dressed identically! Unquestionably a most affecting unexpected meeting! And just fancy, the identical little valise. Of course everybody will marvel at the twin sisters while the first one is busy switching luggage in a flash, the second then batting her eyelashes and ever so sweetly presenting for inspection the overnight case that's already been inspected, along with the affable remark, "I have exactly the same as my sister." "Cleared!" says the inspector. What else would he say? Meanwhile, the cigarettes are well on their way with her sister; by now they're in the railway carriage with the little valise reserving a seat. All well and good, and it could work perhaps twice in Salzburg, once in Passau, and one more time somewhere else; in the long run, though, sixty thousand Memphis cigarettes or ten thousand Virginia cigars would hardly be transportable by trivial maneuvers like these, haha!

"Of course I don't exactly need you to point that out to me, birdbrain! But wouldn't you think somebody who has a friend sitting only a stone's throw from here in the headquarters of the tobacco administration and in a rather senior executive capacity at that, would be able to get him to point the way or even to clear one? But no, an entire summer passes and nothing happens. I'll tell you something, though: if you wind up having no success all summer in bringing that stupid Melzer around to your side, I'll take over and have the job done in no time."

For the moment, the old hare checked his running back and forth between the two hedgehogs (whose bristles, as we might expect, were visibly growing more erect) and pricked up his ears instead of covering them à la Paula Schachl. Eulenfeld's face, its features essentially altogether out of place in this day and age—they resembled more those of a somewhat dubious chargé d'affaires with a taste for high living from the early years of the eighteenth century—clouded or even glazed over, taking on a disquieting and disagreeable rigidity, as if to monitor with even greater concentration its own degree of alertness. What he was searching for in his vest pocket was not only his monocle but also a wrench that would open a treasure chest of the purest formal language he would need to tap quite soon.

He looked sharply at Mimi, at this moment in fact more clearly transparent to him than the twin so vainly striving for the fusion of two persons. Mimi was comparable to someone who's sitting in a glass house but never threw stones; the first shards and slivers from outside are nonetheless tinkling at her feet. Her face emerged from behind the shattered glass, the rainbow colors of its polished but now smashed bevels glittering still, the daybreak gleam of mounting secret joys leaning against it even yet, the sunset light of a sweet look back at everything that remained unfulfilled . . .

Eulenfeld knew all that, of course, knew it deep in his lethargy, though he trod it into the mud (like all the rest of us). Mimi's endorsement of his relationship with Thea—and just now, in an image that was manifestly speaking to, nay shouting at him, the relationship looked in his eyes like the short slime trail of a slug—had made him long since realize *how* things stood *where* he stood. But whatever knowledge came through his *trópoi* was vastly heightened and for the first time coming truly alive through the brief, glittering and shattered surprise (though it was more like a demise) in Mimi's features.

He wasn't stupid. No old hussar or Master of Horse ever is. No more than boatsmen are. Even Negria was a great deal less stupid than Frau Mary had once considered him (that wasn't her opinion anymore, and she wasn't even so down on Lieutenant Melzer these days). On the contrary: both of them, the hussar and the boatsman, suffered from incurable shrewdness.

Even so, Editha squeezed right in—into the open breach, into the gap, into the shards and slivers.

Neither the monocle nor the wrench just referred to had been retrieved yet, but the captain's facial expression resembled that of a dog at the mouth of a fox's lair; some of his ancestors had gathered in this face, and we must say they must have included a number of oafs who'd gone belly-up. He waited. He'd learned from his first squadron leader, after all, that you don't flog a horse into negotiating the Irish bank when it likes to jump.

Editha jumped—on all fours, that is, and straight onto Mimi, without balking for a second. Ever since that evening in Buenos Aires in December 1923, when her sister had told her about the appendectomy and her full recovery from it while pointing to the scar from the work-manlike incision (still reddish at the time)—this was in the noise of the hot-and-cold shower, in the brisk coolness of water streaming down abundantly—ever since then, when something in Editha had surged up against Mimi on the spot, that delicate salmon pink seemed like the color of a dividing line, a cut Mimi had purposely made between them. A sign of separation, even of betrayal. It was the hot season by now, so on the evening in question they had had dinner on the roof garden once it grew dark; and all throughout the hours at the table and afterward the image of an ever-present rising and sinking fleck of color drifted across the inside of Editha's eyelids: the white, still almost childlike curve of the abdomen above her pelvis, the fine red scar. Enrique passed her a bowl of strawberries; it came at her as if from some place barred to her. The red line linked the couple; Editha was the third party. Now it rose up again, rose up from the bowl with the fruit, up from a potted plant whose fronds, set in motion by an air vent, were casting trembling shadows above the white table linen; it pierced through her dress like a needle, striving in vain to stitch a stitch in her heart, ever present.

Even now.

"I'd finally like to know once and for all what's been happening in regard to the Melzer business, what you have and haven't accomplished, and above all, what you've botched. Would you be so kind as to tell me?!"

It was probably only now that Mimi was gaining full insight (by reviewing facts and figures) into the actual state of affairs, meaning that precisely nothing had been undertaken to advance matters. She couldn't do anything but turn her attention to an infinitesimally tiny mosquito buzzing about, pretend it was a large bird on the wing some-where off in the distance, and talk about it accordingly.

"I asked the major about this business of yours in July, but he wasn't able to give me exact information right away. He promised to look into how the purchase of larger quantities is currently managed. I was hop-ing to talk to him about it, just the two of us, so I invited him to tea here. But he never came."

"In July—that long ago!" exclaimed Editha. "And he didn't come! You poor thing! Didn't he come later?!"

"No," Mimi answered simply, since Editha was already standing on her soul with all four feet. She was hardly still able to move.

"And what reason did he give for not showing up for tea?"

"He was sick—a very bad cold."

"That's right," Eulenfeld noted offhandedly, but in a tone of complete certainty. "I went to see him around the middle of July, and he was in bed."

"But you never told me that," said Mimi; at the same time she looked at him as if at an old friend who's just proven how much you can rely on him. Her ill-timed little protest sounded so genuine and so marked by a reproachful but gentle tone of concern, however, that Editha could place only one construction on Eulenfeld's comment, and it had nothing to do with doubting its truth.

Mimi had also lied, incidentally. The fact was that Melzer had indeed come to see her; it was on the Tuesday following the Saturday on which she'd waited for him in vain and had later slapped Thea Rokitzer around, partly as a result. The major hadn't quite made a tea party of it, to be sure, but showed up only at the official eleventh hour instead— on the dot of eleven in the morning, specifically—and not empty-handed, since he'd brought flowers. But then he'd stayed for perhaps all of ten minutes, if that . . . Mimi could see it all before her eyes:

"Dear lady, I've come to apologize once more . . ." (She didn't quite understand the "once more" part.) "Oh good," she had answered. And he: "You weren't still expecting me on Saturday?" "Oh no." "I went back to the office today. I was in pretty bad shape. I just stepped out now for a minute; I wanted to stop by in person."

It had been hot, the morning like an empty, clean bowl heated in the oven.

When she was alone again she kept holding the flowers—heavy, succulent gladioli—in her arms and pressing them to her body. That was all of it, then.

"But what about later on?" cried Editha. "You must have seen Major Melzer again! Fine, he had the flu or whatever in July, but he didn't die of it, did he?"

At this point, however, the meager store of events Mimi could recount had run out completely. She couldn't even spot a tiny mosquito to make a bird out of (let's not even mention an elephant). Now she'd been backed into a corner, sitting here opposite her opposite number, her mirror image, wide chasms of air woven with sunlight, the Kahlenberg, its distant treetops somewhat gauzelike, an evanescent line across the horizon, almost dissolved in air and afloat in the late-summer sky.

"Of course I saw the major again," she said, "but . . ."

"But?!" Editha cried.

Mimi must have become aware once and for all as she paused that there was nothing else for her to do but to hold out her empty palms.

"We never said anything more about it. I was expecting him to bring it up again, since I'd asked him for information. But he never mentioned it. And I didn't want to start in on it again."

"Very nice of you, I'm sure. And is that all?"

"Yes," said Mimi.

Suddenly the captain was wearing his monocle.

He'd literally flipped it up to his eye, executing the move like a Prussian weapons drill. At the same time he seemed to have plied the wrench and unlocked the not very comforting treasure chest of a mother tongue that no longer was one, since mothers are not by nature persnickety about dotting *i*'s and crossing *t*'s; if they were, they would have become old maids, or at least remained without issue.

"So would you be so good as to tell me now, Editha dear, just what it is you want from Melzer?"

"What a silly question!" she cried. "Exactly the opposite of what Mimi wanted from him. Any and all objective dealings get boiled down to love stories with her, and it was basically no different four years ago, with that ridiculous coffee business you wanted to start in Buenos Aires."

"Better than the other way around," the captain calmly retorted. "First Wedderklops or Wedderkopp, then Virginia cigars. But you haven't answered my question."

"Because it's so damn stupid. What do you even mean by it? You surely don't think I'm a big enough idiot to believe in all seriousness that the Austrian authorities, all the way up to the general directors of the tobacco administration, would have any fundamental objection if cigarettes from here were to find their way abroad? It stands to reason that the country to which they're shipped will protect itself, just as we don't admit German cigarettes! But not the reverse, not export. That would go against plain common sense. The Austrian Tobacco Administration has its own production facility in Munich, but the goods naturally have to be sold at a much higher price there, because otherwise people would think they're not getting the real thing, the original; no Austrian subsidy in Germany. But what do I know? Still, the government here sends huge amounts to trade fairs in Germany—Frankfurt, Leipzig—and I believe the samples come from here, because not all brands are produced in Munich. The diplomatic staff in Berlin gets plenty of cigarettes, too; at least that's what I've been told, whether it's true or not, I don't know. These supplies have to get to where they're going somehow, I should think, either by postal shipment or rail, with some kind of relevant customs declaration or accompanying paperwork; or else I picture some employee or other traveling with the shipment and showing inventory forms to the German customs officials. He could take them by the crateful; he's allowed to convey across the border as many as are on the declaration forms. I don't know if it happens quite this way or not. But surely it would hardly make any difference to write down or hand over or just supply a few thousand more or less—however it's done, especially when it's all been paid for in due and proper order. These are the kinds of particulars I'd like to find out from your boy Melzer. He could be a great help that way. Everything could have been taken care of a long time ago.

"A great help..." the captain repeated. "With the aid of your plain common sense, Editha dear, you're making yourself out to be more stupid than you are and concocting an outrageous palaver aimed at making matters appear harmless. Meanwhile, however, you have, I should think—since you're enamored of this expression—crossed international borders a number of times in your life, and it will surely not have escaped you, particularly in light of such focused attention on your part, that the authorities germane to our present topic work to a large extent in reciprocity, hand in hand, that is, like good colleagues, which appears understandable considering the mutuality of the entire enterprise and the pertinent governing formal agreements and stipulations. In addition, the Austrian Tobacco Administration is its own exporting agent; at present its products lie not inconsiderably under the world market price; you wouldn't want to see how quickly supplies of Mimi's Nile cigarettes would grow scarce if it were to become possible to transport "smoking articles"—as you Austrians call tobacco products—out of the country unchecked and on the sly. In addition, your production center in Munich would very soon have to close its doors. And my final estimation is that difficulties not inconsiderable in scope would ensue if the sovereign Bavarian state of the Prussian nation were, just like that, to start tolerating or even abetting the illegal export of tobacco products: they'd quickly put the kibosh on it. All due respect to your plain common sense, but it's not quite as simple as that. Yet the real catch is located elsewhere. As an avid newspaper reader it perhaps did not escape your notice during your various perusals at the Café Tomaselli in Salzburg that an outcry went up here in July about widespread disappearances of tobacco products from the government's warehouses—defalcations or abscondments, or whatever you want to call them—and the supplies then supposedly shipped abroad black-market style, which is what the higher echelons of the police claim. Italy or Germany, they're saying. The first guess is probably nonsense, which is readily deduced from the current state of the lira. Germany is more likely, and an attempt may be made, perhaps especially right now, when the brouhaha has abated somewhat. If the police can bring the shipper to grief, they might have hopes of finding the thief. Your Austrian customs officials at the border—don't you call them "spinach guards," because of their green uniforms?—will have to give their full cooperation. Summing up: the increased vigilance not just by the police but in particular by the Austrian customs authorities will now be focusing on exactly the same spot as that of the customs police from the great sovereign state of Bavaria. *Compris?!*"

His manner of expression had been growing a little more relaxed, and he'd let the monocle drop. In the meantime, however, while Editha and Mimi just sat there in silence, it came back up in the ensuing pause.

"The upshot: I'm asking you one more time what exactly you want from Melzer."

"You already know. Turning this little matter into a clear and present danger to the state is absurd."

"Not to the state, but to Melzer—a clear and present danger to Melzer, that is. Have you come to some kind of an arrangement with Wedderkopp or even made him definite promises?"

"Seems as if you've been eating hallucinogenic mushrooms," Editha said. "Wedderkopp doesn't know a thing about this; in fact, he died a thousand deaths in retrospect over a few boxes of Virginia cigars I brought to Bad Wildungen from Salzburg, even though nothing bad could have happened." (She was never at a loss for details when lying.) "But I know for certain this undertaking would mean a lot to him, not because of the business aspect, which is minor considering his circumstances, but for reasons of some cordial personal relationships he wants to keep up. I know he'd be very pleasantly surprised, because that's how it was at the time his profitable connection with Enrique came about through me."

"You can't even begin to place the two side by side," Eulenfeld commented. He kept the same distance away from both women as if rooted in the ground and didn't move from the spot.

"So you're not under any kind of coercion or pressure," he added as conclusion.

"Nonsense," Editha said.

"Well then, why?"

"Do you have to hear the same thing twenty times?"

"No. Once will do nicely." (What the captain was saying was now coming from a sour face, a real sour puss, and not as a statement or comment, but more as if he were taking something like a medicine, a nostrum that didn't taste very good. But he was the one in charge of administering his own words to his own self, during which process his ancestors began receding and withdrawing from the face that looked so sour, which made it then seem to be growing much younger; in fact, something disproportionately youthful began appearing in it, an adolescent gymnasiast, who now emerged to view along with a very wrinkled but basically sweet-tempered Saint Bernard.) "I know what you're doing; how well I know what you're up to! Yes, indeed! Why take a straight path when a crooked one's available? Editha, dear, I can read you like a book. She wants to play detective story. A hopelessly stupid, amateurish one at that. Scheichsbeutel never says anything. But this time he boiled over. Boy oh boy did he boil—shucks! Shy to boil? Not him. But only this once. That's how you always are, though! Mimi should have gone first to see your parents by herself, pretending to be Editha. But of course taking the simple course of making a pilgrimage to the family apartment on Gusshaus Strasse in the Wieden district, one going ahead and preparing the poor parents and, then, 'Here's your prodigal son, or I mean, daughter'—no, out of the question. Better dead than living without a scam. Tobacco administration. Another romantic fancy! Unspeakable nonsense." His tirades began to grow more unbridled; neither of the women ventured a word. Perhaps the captain's monologue was turning on a light of some kind. It affected them very differently, at any rate: Editha iced over, but Mimi thawed and was looking at Eulenfeld with wide-open eyes, which allows the conclusion that she hadn't closed her ears. At this point, however, the captain made the decisive move, the spirited one—he reached backward into his hip pocket, out of which emerged a thin flask, sterling silver, like a cigarette case. He took a careful sip and stowed the pretty little container back in its resting place. Then and only then was the actual cigarette case produced. Whereupon, after some deep grunting:

"It's pathetic that we even have to be talking about things like this. Did you travel to places like Paris or Buenos Aires just so you could think up such paltry, lame, lackluster, vulgar escapades? Smuggling cigarettes into Germany indeed! Might as well smuggle in sauerkraut! You've missed the boat; things aren't how they used to be. Go buy yourselves Gibson Girl cigarettes from the Manoli Tobacco Company in Germany; that's just one of those ridiculous, awful brands aimed at women. As for women—how about two of you affecting to be a single person. Heartwarming scenes at the customs barrier in Salzburg. And essentially the same thing here in Vienna, but in a different form. And for absolutely, positively nothing; nobody can tell why you're doing all this. Oh, but this is her way of taking revenge on the world for all the successes that have passed her by (!?). Thinks up a monumentally imbecilic cloak-and-dagger romance novel, but only halfway! 'The Exploits of Editha,' Wedderkopp saying, 'My heroine!' Then Melzer's supposed to star in the other half. He won't, though. You don't know what old hussars are like!"

Editha's patience appeared to be worn so thin that she couldn't snap back with a real rejoinder; instead she asked him, quickly and abruptly:

"What do you mean by that?"

Her question come out like hissing from a valve.

"What I mean is clear. You're not going to be able to string Melzer along. Neither of you will succeed in exploiting his good heart and his unsuspecting nature. The man is a government official. Perhaps he still hasn't tumbled to the game you're both playing, so he's trying to be accommodating but is getting tangled up in your stupid schemes in some way he doesn't even realize. All well and good, but he'll be through as soon he catches on. And he *will* catch on. If only, Editha, because your complete ignorance of what you're talking about and your total lack of any plan are oozing from every syllable of your obnoxious jabbering."

"Why are you saying 'neither of you' and 'both of you?'" Mimi was finally piping up. "I don't want anything to do with this."

He looked directly at her. As if the shards and slivers from the glass house she'd been sitting in were made only of ice, and as if their razor-sharp edges were now dripping and melting away, that was how dowsed and drenched her face looked. No doubt at all: she was crying. As if to block what he was seeing, Eulenfeld turned to Editha.

"I wish there to be no remaining doubt that I propose to acquaint Melzer fully with the game you've been playing all summer and the contemptibly stupid tricks you have in mind. He'll laugh! So will I, Editha dear, if I notice you trying to make serious attempts to badger him relentlessly about it; and as you well know, my vigilance in this matter won't let anything get past me. Stop all this nonsense and step forward as the pair whom, after all, your august progenitor—unfortunately, I'm almost inclined to say—brought into the world..."

"Don't you dare say a thing to Melzer!" Mimi suddenly cried out.

He couldn't avoid her glance any longer; he had to look her way.

Through that move, our dabbler in wrongdoing, Editha, gained a little time to start turning and examining, as if it were a ring on her finger, one of the particular deeds of malice she had thought up; it was her revenge on a life in which her youthful years hadn't been youthful, and it would both restore the balance just lost and overtake the gap of past years so she could take over. She had become familiar with Eulenfeld's arrest record from Munich. Such a thing as formal expunging of criminal records does take place, to be sure. But anyone who makes a concerted effort to find out all the particulars can get beyond that paper shield, provided a few connections exist and are drawn on. Editha had had an exact transcript in her possession for lo these many years. Now, aware that she had the power and the potential to oust the captain from workplace, food pantry, and comfort zone all in one fell swoop, like flinging aloft an unearthed rodent from a shovel (after all, his home office in England wouldn't exactly be amused), she backed down inwardly and felt already as good as revenged on Eulenfeld for his threat, which he had unsuspectingly (or perhaps not so unsuspectingly?) ventured.

Mimi was crying. Like a child who can no longer hide what she's done. Her protest and her outcry had brought everything back out into the light of day. Eulenfeld at once went over to her, sat down on the rug in front of her, and in that position, half lying at her feet, rubbed his right cheek on her hands, just like a Saint Bernard.

And kept on saying the same thing over and over: "No, no."

Editha looked on as if glutted from the banquet of revenge she'd been enjoying in her imagination.

The captain stood up and plied both little containers, which involved ritually consulting first the one with the screw top, then he took a seat, closer to Editha this time, which seemed to require a bit more alertness or even scrutiny. Her staunch facial expression couldn't be overlooked.

"Well, all right," he said in a placating tone, "at least you know about Melzer now—I mean what my thoughts are about the matter. Let the thoughtlessness and scatterbrained schemes—punishable by law as they are in their current state—come to a stop right now. And all involving such childish nonsense anyway!"

"I would be ever so eager to know, Otto dear, how I have reached a point of allowing you to say such abusive things to me without letup," Editha objected. She was now completely calm as she spoke. "You're acting as if I were trying to get Melzer into my clutches or to 'badger him relentlessly,' or however you put it, and only because I'm hoping to obtain some information from him as a favor to someone. What's more, you can always call someone else's business 'childish nonsense' for the simple reason that their concerns are of no importance to you. And as for 'thoughtlessness punishable by law' on my part, you have yet to furnish me with any proof. You're the one who delivered him into our hands by placing Mimi directly into his path."

"True enough," he cried, "but who would have believed you'd really want to continue acting out the same absurd charade in Vienna?"

"It's just getting started!" Editha said. "And why? Because you haven't done anything. Neither with our parents nor with Melzer. Everything could have been taken care of a long time ago. I've said that before."

"Yes, but damn it all," Eulenfeld started blustering. "Why this whole game of hide-and-seek around the major? Forgive me if I'm woolgathering here, but your motives are inscrutable to me, and wherever I strive to ascertain a single solitary one in this connection, I can find nothing that answers the strictures of reason. Why didn't you just stay here if these things were so important to you? 'Everything could have been taken care of a long time ago!' You could have simply taken matters into your own hands. What's more, I find it strange, even paradoxical, that you should decide to go off on a trip at the exact time you could have been with your sister once more after a two-year separation!"

She looked at him the way one looks at a dolt who has just proven to an alarming extent how much of one he is. Her glance was shifting from astonishment to horror to forbearance, like discs of different colors being drawn inward by the eye, until it finally settled on a look that can't be spoken of in any other terms than: after all, he *is* the Master of Horse.

"What's it like for you, Otto," she asked in a calmer tone, "when you fall in love? Doesn't she seem unique to you? Even that ninny Thea?"

"What's with the theoretical discourse?" grunted Eulenfeld. "Very well, then, if you say so."

"Very well, then," she imitated, "and if there were suddenly two of this unique being, would the attraction be doubled? There you are. *Compris?* I had to go off on my travels exactly because Mimi came. Which is also the reason why we will now be continuing for some time to appear as one person only, not redoubled."

"This gets a man's brain boiling," said Eulenfeld as he grasped his skull. "This nonsense is rising to the height of Mount Chimborazo in Ecuador. Thirty thousand Virginia cigars, five thousand Egyptian cigarettes, third variety. And Weddeklops."

"Yes, and Wedderkopp, Gustav Wedderkopp," Editha quietly corrected him.

"Accursed wretches of duplicity!" the captain burst out again (and so there it was, the term of art, the *terminus technicus* he had only ever used in his own mind, at least up to now, to refer to the twin sisters when he was traveling through his *trópoi*, rapidly and with utmost triviality, like the rest of us). "What a weight on my shoulders! Like a heavy pack! Not a thought in their brains! This can all be proven, goddamn it! Stupid correspondence! What the hell do I care, though? Go ahead and scratch my eyes out, explode in front of me if you feel like it, *éclatez toutes les deux*, but I never felt quite right about all your letter-writing to Mimi from Wildungen. Around the middle of July or so there seemed to be this strong pressure about how time was galloping away, about Melzer and all that gibberish about the tobacco scheme. Pangs of conscience. I know all about it: one time I intercepted one of your letters, Editha. Right from the main post office, with Mimi's passport. You thought general delivery would be safer. I'll confess right here and now that this represents a serious violation. But I perpetrated it only in Melzer's interest. And what a fine how-d'ye-do met my eyes . . ."

"Dimwit," Editha quite casually remarked. "You couldn't have presented yourself at the post office as a Frau Mimi Scarlez. I bet you sent Thea."

"Indeed I did," said Eulenfeld. "But let's keep to the main point. You go traipsing off to Wildungen, Lower Wildungen, Bad Wildungen, and stay with your heart's desire at the Fürstenhof Hotel, then you draw up yet another set of general instructions for Mimi—they constitute a warning letter, too—in which not only is my real name heedlessly bandied about in humiliating terms—supplemented by the *epitheton ornans* 'Otto, that old fool' ('he should help you instead of standing right in your way'; that's how it's worded in your missive)—in which, as I say, not only is my real name heedlessly bandied about in humiliating terms, but Major Melzer's is as well, and even if not quite so heedlessly in the full sense, nonetheless set down in a context that is nothing less than perniciously compromising, meaning that it's woven right into this crackbrained, ridiculous scheme with the cigarettes. I really wouldn't have needed to keep asking what exactly you want from Melzer, because the whole thing is all summed up crystal clear in your letter, tricked out in addition with a wealth of none-too-affectionate admonitions and remonstrations for Mimi. More than a little uncouth, speaking *entre nous*. Just wanting to hear from your own lips if you haven't by chance come to feel any differently on this heading. *Quod non, ut videtur.* That would be even more asinine, thoughtless, and scatterbrained than the entire saga of the Wedderklopsiad. All that has to happen is for a letter like that to be left lying somewhere, to get stuck somewhere, to get lost, to be opened and read, and you've wreaked more havoc and worse damage than you are even remotely capable of imagining in the hereunto appertaining dizzy little head of yours."

"Don't be silly. There's no more censorship. This isn't 1825. We have secrecy of the post."

"There's something to that. But we're in the land of the whilom archcensor Herr von Sedlnitzky, who departed this earth not all that unimaginably long ago. Given the exigencies of official business there could surely be exceptions made in this regard."

"Oh stop; that's just muddy thinking."

"If you want to call it that, but let's not even worry about officialdom. Bureaucrats don't have to be involved. Take a look over there at Mimi's secretary, where that unholy agglomeration is lined up, even neatly arranged in compartments, wide open and easily accessible. And after my little sample it takes no effort to surmise what there would be to see in that collection of screeds as a whole. A star of ill omen would appear to have been shining down upon such brains as might have been at your disposal, if any. Your serving woman comes through here every day and, as I have had ample opportunity to observe, you allow her to putter about completely solo. But why talk about just that? A letter covers a long distance, and there's always a good enough chance that it will make its way into the wrong hands through some diabolical coincidence or other. The Evil One rides a fast horse and never sleeps."

"As far as I'm concerned you may in essence be totally right," Editha now commented quietly and matter-of-factly, "in saying that this letter you stole represents a great imprudence. Even so, it remains an isolated instance, I can assure you of that. The business we're talking about now is not mentioned anywhere in any of the other letters Mimi received here, nor is Melzer's name stated. Definitely not. Don't play dumb; you know that perfectly well. After all, if you're going to steal a passport so you can extract via one of your chippies a letter not addressed to you, then you will surely not have balked at reading your way through Mimi's correspondence there in the secretary from one end to the other. You had more than enough opportunity when taking your siestas, Mimi in there and you here on the sofa, just the way she told me once in a letter this summer. If you look at it carefully, that second situation made the first one unnecessary, so why you went through all the fuss with the passport and the girl when you had the letters here to hand in the first place, I'll never know. Unless you wanted to keep my letter completely away from Mimi. But you didn't succeed."

Now she had bowled him right over, mowed him down. His monocle dropped. For a few moments, prodigious astonishment flooded over the Eulenfeld face, making it seem to have flipped inward. At first it was unrelated to the comment with which Editha had just made her closing point. His astonishment was a reflection of his own self instead, having to do with his own person and his conduct in this matter. It was a fact that it had never even entered the captain's mind to take the letters from the desk while Mimi was asleep in the next room. This would have seemed to him—on the inner surface, so to speak—dishonorable, conduct unbecoming a gentleman. But while she'd been sleeping right next to him rather than in the next room he'd dived below the inner surface, as it were, and had taken her passport as a way, if a rather laborious one, to get hold of a letter through Thea. We could put it this way: a mischief it would never have dawned on him to perpetrate on the woman asleep in the next room, not even if left alone in her apartment—he was a friend, after all—he had no trouble outdoing when they were now covered by one and the same blanket. In the former case, the comradely code of ethics was still in force, at least more or less, whereas in the latter it was a whole different story. While he was thinking about all this, climbing up and down between two floors of his personality—just now they didn't seem to be connected in any very clear way—Mimi took a small green notebook out of a drawer from the right compartment of the secretary, which she'd opened with a little key. Eulenfeld raised his head, and it was only now that Editha's last comment, arresting as it was, come back into his mind.

"Whatcha mean 'didn't succeed'?" he said quite offhandedly, still turning over the earlier thoughts in his mind.

They both seemed to have emerged out of a deep well or trench—not just Eulenfeld, but Mimi too. Editha pointed to her sister: "Let Mimi tell you," she said briefly.

Picking up the green leather notebook, Mimi was just now climbing back out from the shaft of her thoughts; it had opened beneath her like a pitfall during those admonitory disquisitions by Editha to which the captain had in his exasperation given the name "theoretical discourse" because of her penchant for expanding into the realm of the paradigmatic (just the trait likely to make her look like a Little Miss Know-It-All in the eyes of an old hussar!). She was resurfacing, but slowly, like Frau Rokitzer with the jars of preserves; Hedi Loiskandl had been frightened at watching her subside, so she had leaned over the edge and called after her. But Mimi had descended even deeper. Back to 1908. Her memory wasn't as bad as Major Melzer must have thought it was (and to him, neither hussar nor boatsman—what would an old Bosnian trooper of the Royal and Imperial monarchy have had to do with the cavalry or the navy anyway?—to him, these things were very important). Mimi's memory operated very much in fits and starts, however, so it wasn't really a memory as such, at least not according to Herr Nose-in-the-Air René. Most often its contents would explode in bursts of rainbow-hued streaks or stripes, as happens at times in the evening sky when all the clouds look as if combed back from a single point, thus causing the horizon to lie configured as a bold exclamation point at the end of a silent (and accordingly incomprehensible) sentence. Not this time, though; it all held together: Munich 1908. She'd just barely turned sixteen. And their companion, a young lady from Neuchâtel in Switzerland, was herself no more than twenty-five at the oldest (she was too pretty for the girls' father and therefore suspect in his eyes, but his wife had a high opinion of the young woman). She mainly enjoyed sitting in the writing room of the Hotel Regina on Maximilians Platz, where she spent endless hours composing letters of endless pages. As one can imagine, she was often diverted and deflected from this activity by the twins' need to be forever going somewhere, as for example to museums, especially the Neue Pinakothek. Come to think of it, though, the companion could write her letters there as well, sitting on a velvet settee in one of the galleries with a little portfolio and a pen. Scarlez was standing in front of Henry Scott Tuke's painting *Sailors Playing Cards* and took a step back when the twins paused at it in the empty, silent gallery. (It is a very large picture, almost two meters long and more than a meter high. The Bavarian State acquired it in 1894. It shows the deck of a sailing ship on the high sea. In the foreground the card game is taking place right on deck. Behind the players sits an old man sewing. His physiognomy is perhaps the most masterful element of the painting. To the left rear a young fellow lost in reverie is sitting on the rail, holding onto the shrouded sails and looking at a little monkey perched in the lashings with his paw outstretched. This all behind the old man's head—his face, diffused, as it were, amid its many remembrances of things past, his lore of times and lure of tides: the far-off horizon line, the little monkey brought on board from some tropical island, and the young dreamer, a youngster the old-timer sewing with such absorption might once have been.) Scarlez lowered his eyelids. And with this one flicker of his lashes everything was decided; that is, a landslide was immediately set in motion, a veritable avalanche of rapidly succeeding events and occurrences played out at so rapid a pace and taken to cognizance by Mimi in so intense a state of bedazzlement that she found herself incapable ever afterward of registering very clearly how all of it had progressed or even been made possible in the first place. The clearest image in her mind remained that of the picture by Henry Scott Tuke; it was her last distinct impression, and from then on everything began whirling and swirling. The outer contours can be reconstructed roughly according to the following pattern: during the next two or three days they left their companion increasingly to her own devices in the writing room of the Regina (this was the real setting of her travels as she went describing in installments what she'd never seen, drawing the images entirely out of her imagination, thereby in complete contrast to those many travelers who merely dash from one place of interest to the next without the slightest capacity for describing what they, no less blind, have failed to see). The young Swiss lady began yielding to temptation, and it must have seemed to make no difference at all to her whether she sat and wrote in the Schack Gallery or here, where it was more comfortable. So the twins went off to the collections by themselves. Now and then, however, either Editha or Mimi (in reality it was always Editha) stayed with her under the pretext of being tired. Then sometimes Mimi had gone to her room for the evening and would then ask the companion to please stop by for a minute. There she really would be lying in bed when the young lady and the twin sister came in. Not on the last night, however. Editha had taken complete charge, intimately involving herself in every detail of this full-scale hoax (all their old tricks at the Girls' Lyceum paled by comparison) with such gusto that it never even occurred to her how effective all these contrivances and subterfuges were going to prove in robbing her of her beloved sister! Scarlez had at first wanted to travel straight to Wildungen to see the twins' father. But he was forced to realize almost at once that this would have been tantamount to forfeiting all hopes of winning Mimi: both sisters balked, knowing how futile his approach would be. Enrique originally hadn't been able to grasp their viewpoint. According to the ways of his homeland, Mimi was long since of marriageable age and he himself—a wealthy heir and the independent owner of a thriving business in his own right—more than man enough to step before the girl's father and sue for her hand. But because he had been consumed from the first moment on by fire and flame (for Mimi, mind you: it is worth mentioning that he was the only person who had never, absolutely never, confused the sisters, even if he often acted in jest fifteen years later as if he had); because his intense passion was rendering him almost helpless, he abided by their advice and now set out with high resolve on the romantic path, so to speak, because the conventional middle-class way was barred to him. (As far as that goes, just imagine even trying to picture Herr Pastré—a figure straight out of a painting by Jean-Baptiste Greuze—as he's being confronted with the unthinkable proposition that he should consent to his sixteen-year-old daughter's being whisked away across the high seas, at once and *prestissimo*, by a Catholic Argentinian.) Enrique had traveled by way of France and had brought back to Europe from Buenos Aires a young blond French woman who had been in his mother's service; the girl wanted to go back home to be married. Scarlez had to spend some time in Bordeaux for business reasons, but the girl lost her patience and ran away to the South of France, around the vicinity of Mont-de-Marsan, where she came from. She left her passport behind in his hotel room, since she wouldn't be needing it anymore, and he had held onto it. Now Mimi was traveling on this passport; the picture did portray someone not too unlike her, and wretched as it might have been, the image of an attractive young blond who looked somehow like a French type could be made out after all. On the crucial evening, Mimi (Editha) said she wanted to go to bed early. And Editha (Editha) came back downstairs to chat with the companion. The next day Mimi and Scarlez were long gone, ensconced in Paris. Only at around this point did it become unmistakably clear to the epistolary-minded young Swiss lady that one of the twin sisters was missing. Off the couple went to Lisbon, where Enrique had the Argentine consul general—whom he knew—stamp a reentry visa into the passport of Mademoiselle Yvonne Dufour.

But all these outer contours—if Mimi, aided by her memory, had ever grasped them in any even halfway orderly sequence or arrangement in the first place—had long since been shredded among its flying streaks or shreds, we might say. What remained, however, was nothing less than a glance backward at a course of action that amazed her still today, because by it she had for the first time in her life, and before her own eyes, come into existence as an individual entity in herself, more or less through an external impulse, through Enrique Scarlez, that is, the single-minded purposefulness, the lightning-fast determination of whose actions were directed entirely toward her, and her alone, not toward her sister, with whom he stood in so little danger of confusing her that Editha simply began silently dropping all the little jokes—they'd been quite frequent in the beginning—she once used to make about it. Only at this late stage had Mimi been birthed away from her and was now able to see herself as distinct and separate, as a focal point toward which came storming all the strength and resolve of this handsome man, who all the while merely lowered his lashes as if he were hoping to hide the glowing fire in his eyes and who had suddenly entered Mimi's life from an unfamiliar but nearby room, stepping as if down from a wall, calling her with total confidence by her name, one he would never disclaim: Mimi. And she herself realized for the first time that she was Mimi. In her depths she felt that Enrique had emerged from the picture by Henry Scott Tuke, across the horizon of the sea, then climbing over the bulwark, stepping onto the planking of the deck, whereupon he left the group of card players on the left and the pensive young fellow with the little monkey on the right and was now standing beside her in front of the picture, looking out at the sea, as she too was doing; the sides had switched, so that the young sailor was sitting on the left and the players on the right. The ship went sailing on. Here is the place to bring back to mind one Herr Georg von Geyrenhoff, whose surmises about certain chains of romantic imagery in connection with Mimi's flight—he had been thinking of the model of a large steamship, an ocean liner he'd seen in the window of a travel agency, we may perhaps recall—might at this point not seem so very wide of the mark after all. So it was, at any rate, that two had become one, as it were—through a separation from outside, overpowering in its force, through the decree of a man who recognized her as his. "When you fall in love with a woman," Editha had said not long before, "doesn't she seem unique to you? And if all of a sudden there were then two of this unique being, would the attraction be even stronger?" For Enrique, there had never been two of Mimi: out of two he had instantly made one, but not by confusing them. One—she quickly became a separate entity by means of one final hoax to redeem every other hoax. And here is the place to bring back to mind one Herr Edouard von Langl and his assertion that the nature of a doppelgänger has nothing to do with biological twins; even so, Mimi's makeup embodied some of Editha's more questionable potentialities, to which the long-lost sister had patently once more succumbed in Vienna: her scruffy life with the captain, escapades like the one with René, and the cooperation she'd promised her sister back in Bordeaux in working the deceit on Melzer. So Herr von Langl doesn't seem to have gotten it entirely right; it's possible to have a twin who does indeed possess isolated traits of the doppelgänger.

It was exactly this insight that lay closer to the surface of Mimi's conscious mind and in a relatively brighter spot than the deeper-seated and more primal memories from the Munich days; those were memories of a physical personhood emerging, a second birthing, one that had over time gained a moral component, which was now right in front of her. She held onto it tight; around it the situation (insofar as we can speak of such a thing in light of its bestreaked and beshredded nature) arranged itself; here was the point of departure for her constantly renewed but utterly hopeless attempts to bring order into circumstances that were themselves propelling her along and to stabilize forces that kept slipping and sliding under her feet like pebbles.

Through these efforts, however, Mimi had finally arrived back at the outer surface of events and turned to the captain, who had been looking at her expectantly the whole time with no tension despite initial signs, weak and gray, of button-eyed oblivion in his glance, which had in the meantime been ameliorated by renewed requisition of the elegant silver object with the screw top.

"The letter," she said, looking in her notebook, "was from July ninth. In addition to everything you've already referred to" (she took out a little pencil and drew lines through her notes), "Editha wrote as follows about our parents. It's especially awkward for her that she never knows if she can or should answer a letter from Gusshaus Strasse or not, because I might suddenly have bestirred myself in the meanwhile and gone to see our parents as her representative, so to speak. This state of affairs is getting on her nerves badly, all the more because news from me arrives sporadically and after long periods of silence. She simply can't endure this. I should settle on a definite day for visiting our parents; they're not planning on leaving Vienna until the end of August this year and will travel to Merano for three weeks. This matter has to be taken care of by then. 'Send me a telegram immediately after you've been to see them, so I know you were really there'—Mimi was reading from a text she'd copied word for word—'you've got to realize that the way you're doing things doesn't work; I'm about to jump out of my skin here. I'm asking you to pull yourself together and stop torturing me with your free-and-easy way. Also, answer the questions I ask in my letters! When you write back you need to go to enough trouble to set my last letter in front of you and look through the main points…'"

"Ridiculous," grunted Eulenfeld. "Not since the dawn of time has a woman ever done that. Impossible expectation."

"Yes, and then," Mimi continued, after tossing just a quick glance at Eulenfeld, "there's more in the letter about what I should have been wearing for my visit to Gusshaus Strasse. None of the Paris creations" (with great deliberation and thoughtfulness she now started scratching out everything she'd referred to so far), "but Editha's dark-blue suit out of the wardrobe here…"

"Good; just leave it at that!" the captain cut in, "we've heard all we need to! Yes indeed, it's that letter all right. Damnation take us! Females running the show! Poor old hussar! Thea. Minx. Flibbertigibbet. Rokitzer, if you please! Hold on a minute. Heavy pack! You could almost blow your stack. Accursed wretches of duplicity. Shucks! Scheichsbeutel a sheikh. *Schaykh al-Islām.* Beutel and the boodle, can only shake my jam-packed old noodle. Moss-covered head. *Sunt certi denique fines.* Packed, I say, kit and caboodle. Heavy pack, this Thea! Posted off straight to the main post office. Of course she was here first. Irish bank. Now just a minute, I'll get them jumping. Gently, though, gently! Later on, *peut-être.* For tonight we just need to stomach it! 'This is the very curse of all foul deeds, that they must go on giving birth to evil!' Old Freddy Iambic, alias Schiller! ὦ πρὸς θεῶν (Oh, by the gods!) Riding circles and figure eights! Such a nag! Stepping out on the wrong leg! You know me."

"Thank you," said Editha.

Her sister turned to her.

"I completely understood the part of the letter having to do with our parents and answered you at once to say I simply didn't feel able to go visit them but that quite soon and with ample advance notice I would let you know exactly when I intended to follow through."

"Too bad that an intention was all it ever was."

"Yes," Mimi said calmly. "But as for that letter of yours Otto withheld, I have to say I'm of exactly the same opinion as he is. What did you ever do with the letter, by the way, Otto?"

"Well might you ask!" the captain said. "Burned immediately, it goes without saying."

"Good. Then I'll do the same with these three pages from the notebook. They're not from the notebook itself anyway, but from a tear-off pad next to it. So there's no damage if I take them out."

Mimi tore off the three sheets of paper, clicked a silver lighter, and held the pages over the large stone ashtray on the desk as they flared up and burned completely. She crushed the still-glowing remains with a letter opener.

"You surely are worried about your dear major!" Editha said casually.

She was taken by persistent astonishment at something about her sister that on first glance appeared to be totally insignificant but that now struck her suddenly and forcefully, a trait that had not been in evidence either in Buenos Aires two years before nor in Paris this past spring, even though she had then occupied the same room with Mimi in the small Hotel Opal on Rue Tronchet. There was now a certain prissiness about her. The little notebook, the little pencil, the fussy crossing out, the prompt and punctilious recourse to burning pages. Prissiness and timorousness in her sense of order, by this time no longer carrying enough energy to draw a separating stroke or dividing line and by that very token to point to its decisive boldness, but instead merely deploying feeble little stingers now, as it were, leaving an only too carefully documented record of their inability to effect anything (and in turn giving rise to yet more dithering and disorder). Editha felt as if the stingers were pointed toward her, however. And at the same time there seemed to be a certain poignancy about Mimi, the way she defended and defended herself with her scant resources, blond and scatterbrained in a rainbow-colored sort of way as she sat before the broad backdrop of mountain and castle, which Editha only now apprehended all of a sudden, an abyss of air and space no longer in full sunlight, since the afternoon was waning slowly. During these brief moments she truly loved her sister no less urgently and compellingly than a man who's head over heels about a woman. An exotic flower against a homespun background. Strive as she might to step into this mirror image of herself, it would not make its way toward her as it should have (in her opinion, or in her creed, we almost have to say) so as finally to obliterate the very last, minute gap in the crystal surface; instead, it backed away from her every single time she approached it, receding to that inaccessible deepest space in the mirror that Editha wanted to know nothing about, that space that Editha denied.

The captain considered it anything but a comedown that in reprimanding Editha for her carelessness he had been obliged to admit withholding a letter; far from that, what he viewed as his acumen in recognizing the inner surface of the particular idiocy that brought him to his act of suppression in the first place had forestalled a quick grab at all the letters already opened and lying around; at this juncture, then, he thought he had due and proper justification to let flow from his fount of wisdom a few instructions relevant to the practical implementation of that unity of personhood, as we referred to it some time back, or that "singularity of appearance," to use Editha's expression, a state apparently substituting for an ideal condition that could never be attained in reality and representing a pragmatic activity only on the inner surface of the matter, practicality of execution in any endeavor always and unfailingly identical with a hoax or intrigue of some kind, as far as Editha Schlinger was concerned.

"Listen," he said (after once more fortifying himself), "I should like to recommend that you, if you're at all minded to, continue to play the part of a single woman without underwear—I mean under the weather, no, damn it, not underhand—let there be just one of you, I'm saying, though nobody knows why—all right, it's so you can put one over on Melzer, and if that is indeed your hereunto appertaining intention and plan (a manifestation of utmost idiocy, I might add), then I advise you to turn some of your attention to the—how shall I say it?—language-guided modalities as well. Because that absolutely will not do. *Si ex duabus una facienda et loquendi mos congruere debet.* Got it?"

"No," said Editha, adding, "Fool. But I do know what you mean even so, because after nearly five years I'm used to your way of expressing yourself with 'utmost idiocy.' Otherwise your babbling is totally incomprehensible to me."

He assumed a sweet look, offended in a truly charming way, good old Saint Bernard. This made Editha so happy that she stood up quickly, planted a kiss on him, and then sat back down in the white chair that had figured in the hail of Thea-directed face-slappings.

"Thanks very much," said the captain after kissing her hand in return. "So, circles and figure eights. 'The Grand Tour' was what they called it in your cavalry of truly glorious memory. Oh me oh my, where has it all gone to now! Heavy pack! Suffice it to say for the moment that your own mode or manner of expression diverges to a degree that cannot be missed, that is to say very considerably, from Mimi's. 'Damn stupid, dimwit, fool,' and all the rest of your favorite red-blooded, no-nonsense lingo. To be sure, however, there is more to it than the rather coarse invectives immediately heretofore instanced. Rather, she, I mean our dear Mimi, is on a rather more familiar footing with German grammar in general. She speaks more correctly. Otherwise, I'd say you two aren't so very different in tone. Weathering Wedder—listen to that!—weathering Wedderkopp has had no discernible linguistic effect on you, nor has Spanish spoiled Mimi's native woodnote wild. In any given instance of relevancy or pertinence—damn it, I mean to say in any relevant or pertinent instance of what I'm talking about, to wit, when you speak German, your rootedness in this native heath, meaning of course Vienna, is likely on the basis of all the pertinent and relevant layers and strata hereunto appertaining to be detectable in a trice. It's basically the word choice, the vocabulary, that constitutes the *differentiam*, in addition to a more correct or less correct, as the case may be, observance of grammar" (Eulenfeld always accented the word "grammar" on the second syllable), "Mimi's greater accuracy doubtless deriving from her having for many long years had recourse to the German language only *legendo* rather than *dicendo*, meaning to say she surely must have read it but practically never spoken it. Am I right, Mimi?!"

Mimi nodded. After Editha had, almost as an aside, commented: "When this old moron starts a sentence you can go off to the post office, fill out the paperwork to send a registered letter, come back home, and he's still not finished"—after this comment she turned to the captain, taxing personality that he was, and said:

"Easy, Otto, easy! I don't doubt that you've observed or, better yet, heard correctly. But this is such a small thing! I command another language as well, one that doesn't call the past back to mind. I have the ability to detach myself—I might even say to dissolve myself—as if I were strolling along the Avenida de Mayo and knew it better than I know Kärntner Strasse and a white facade with twelve columns were more a matter of course than the Giant's Gate of Saint Stephen's Cathedral (oh, if you could only make a less stupid face right now, but that's unlikely to be possible). I'm no stranger to dressing in rainbow colors either, and I know how distracted a person can be when wearing them, even with the Leopoldsberg in the background (or some other such thing—whatever). I don't have to put on an act to talk like Mimi; all I have to do is take back my conscious decision to refrain from totally being Mimi, even though in the end I've never in fact refrained. I need only forget that a thin red needle inside me is trying to sew a stitch in her heart, even if always in vain, and then I'm happy, and then—how easy it is for me—I speak Mimi's language!"

This (if we pass over all the interpolated side comments) was the most authentic truth she could tell. ("You take my breath away," said the captain, then grew silent.) Editha had stood up, and now she was across the room and on the floor, kneeling in front of Mimi and putting her arms around her. Everything was quiet now. It had seemed while Editha was speaking as if she were singing herself into the beloved, to put it that way, for at the start her intonation had not yet quite accommodated itself to Mimi's manner of speaking. Her last sentences, on the other hand, had the effect of appearing to have been devised by her sister, uttered in her mode, suffused by the warmth of her voice and its rather plaintive timbre, one that could suggest or create in recollection the sweetly nasal sound of a clarinet.

It was Eulenfeld who spoke the concluding words when the sisters had finally released each other from their mutual embrace and Editha had gone back to her seat in the post-face-slapping chair. Her resuming that seat produced in the captain—even as he began talking again, even while he resumed (not without satisfaction) his typical parlance and speech pattern—the effect of imagining that Editha had returned to a previous point, not just in space but also in time, before she had lowered herself at Mimi's small feet and before their ensuing embrace. As she sat in the chair, she seemed to have taken back upon herself, like a task or a burden from which she'd enjoyed only a short respite, the decision to refrain from attempting that total unity with her sister to which she herself had alluded, as a result of which the membrane between the two women again grew taut, its tension palpable once more. The captain, nattering the whole time, saw or felt this all taking place far below him, as it were, just as a person on a wooden bridge, higher up and exposed to a wider vista while passing over the deep, slow current of the river, sees the meadow between the struts while walking high above it, crossing the planks and not stepping over the grassy ground itself. This was how he was now registering his exposure in general, mainly to the absolutely indissoluble bond created by the highly sensitive affinity between the twins, stretched to its utmost at this point in that the one was virtually wooing while the other was shrinking back, the one constantly trying to bring into existence challenging situations and exchanges of roles which the other one could not tolerate and kept running away from. It may well be that the gin (it was this potable that filled the flat but quite capacious glass container—not betokening an abstainer—inside the silver sheath) he partook of in such generous measure was what produced in Eulenfeld a kind of second sight, double vision, that is, even though (hmm! hmm!) he never saw four Pastrés, always just two); it is well known that mysterious gremlins dwell within the juniper berry and the bush itself, sturdy, dull green, thriving in forest solitude, fraught with the ill repute of witchcraft. At any rate, the captain was an old and phlegmatic tippler (not in the least sanguine, which temperament he called "*sans*-gin" and accordingly rejected with vehemence as pertaining only to people not enjoying that bewitchment!); any intoxicating substance, however, will disclose its secrets to strict moderation only, never to chronic indulgence. In this connection, Johannes Viktor Jensen calls habitual smokers "zeros made flesh." Sparsity is what lends nuance to anything. Whoever (like Wedderkopp) goes around puffing unrelentingly has a whole ring of stale cigarette odor enveloping him, in his clothing and his hair, on his hands, in his linen and laundry. And he is not wafted on his blue clouds to Manila or Cuba, for the clouds are no longer delicate wisps of tropical fragrance, no smoky, far-off ports, no *fumée des îles*. Enrique, the husband of our Mimi, did exactly the opposite, on the other hand (he had professional reasons, of course, for not wanting to deaden his sense of smell, a concern that loomed much less large to a jolly roisterer like Gustav). Whenever Scarlez drifted toward and then immersed himself in his peculiar manner of thinking—which on first encountering one would scarcely be able to believe how well it had served him time after time in his business dealings (but do kindly step closer and consider it more carefully, whereupon you will concede how indebted a merchant would be to a mindset that could be called case-by-case deliberation rather than some general poetic, pastel concept like "imagination")—whenever Scarlez exercised his individual manner of thinking—that deep, unruffled juxtaposition across from each other and in front of his own life's background and experience, which would thereupon recede, of all the pertinent incompatible and inexplicable elements for as long as it took until the first thread of his understanding wove into the weft of the foreign mesh—then during these exertions nothing would be too strong for him: Puerto Rico and Havana, the most intense tobacco from Paraguay, though his favorite was a short black Dannemann (that's a brand of Brazilian cigar that sells very well over there). But his indulgence in smoking was a discrete enjoyment, intermittent only, an accent, an occasional spur. Hence too Mimi's comparatively sparing habits, although on the bearskin from the Treskavica she had at once plunged in with great gusto by inhaling so greedily from the chibouk, as if drawing the smoke all the way down to her navel and only then exhaling, that the major had been almost horrified.

"Enough!" said the captain. "Linguistic subject closed. Regarding the matter at hand I am now convinced and thus completely easy in my mind. Duplicity apparently rendered null and void. Nothing but a heavy pack. Sheikh. Strange, Editha—that a man would come to apprehend the truth if he were so drunk as to see double, for instance. *In gino veritas*. Accursed wretches of duplicity. Other vexations abounding as well. Concierge romanticism, tobacco administration. Lose track entirely of the hereunto appertaining nonsense." He let out a grunt so forceful, indeed so prodigious, that Editha flinched. "Stop that!" she cried out, "we're not in a pigsty." "Oh yes we are," the captain replied in a more moderate tone, "indeed we are. I'm just a poor old pig." "Well, maybe you are," she said, "that could well be the case with you. And there are plenty more vexations besides, and they're mainly your fault. It's still a question whether that René Stangeler saw us at the West Station or not."

"Probably not," said Eulenfeld, "if we, to wit, admit into consideration the pertinent characteristics of said Stangeler, that worthy."

"That worthy...the language you spout, Otto, is sometimes enough to make me jump out of my skin. This baroque, magniloquent nonsense. A person would think one of your ancestors had been something like a court master of ceremonies."

"Master of correspondence. Overseer of dispatches and couriers. At first for the mother and, until 1688, legal guardian of Landgraf Ernst Ludwig von Hesse-Darmstadt, Elisabeth Dorothea von Sachsen-Gotha."

"Good," said Editha, "you may put yourself down for a bright golden gulden. But don't let it prevent you from prying out of Thea whether she or Stangeler saw us on the platform yesterday. And who those two other women were who were with him, the one young, tall, with reddish hair, the other shorter, elderly..."

The exchange that followed deteriorated into something almost like a grilling. The captain, even as he went on prattling incessantly, dubbed it a "minutiae-fixated flea circus" and answered at various points with, "Yes, Mr. Sherlock Holmes," and later, when he was being confronted with very strict orders, "*Jawohl*, Colonel." If there existed among the punctuation marks of our writing system a capital grunt mark and we were reproducing verbatim this part of their conversation (heaven forbid!), we would have to place such a mark after almost every phrase or sentence the captain uttered: he stood up under it, though, that is, he held up under Editha's third degree, during which she addressed him once again by the honorific "idiot" ("powerfully philoprogenitive locution!"). Her exclamation ensued upon his airing the view that "it wouldn't have mattered one bit" if Editha had happened to bump into Thea on the train. It's not hard to imagine how furious this made Editha, who had gone to all the trouble of putting in an "official" appearance in Vienna (in the form of Mimi) at just the crucial time and on the day before—on Friday afternoon, that is, on the evening before her paradoxical arrival—had dropped off her fountain pen at Major Melzer's on Porzellan Gasse (Mimi would seem to have done a good job of reporting fully and clearly!). And then of course, thanks to his "giniality"—insinuations along these lines were always especially hurtful to him, whether their source was Frau Wöss or Editha Pastré—Eulenfeld had totally forgotten about everything, although he knew perfectly well, as he freely admitted, on which train Thea would be arriving... long story short—a telegram should have been fired off to Salzburg! And then Stangeler into the bargain! That's all they'd needed! And how had the captain come to be aware in the first place that René would also be turning up at the station to meet his Grete? From Thea? Had she called on the phone? And what about those two women, those aunts or whatever they were? All in all, what was needed now was to find out by hook or crook if anyone had seen her and Editha together. First by quizzing Thea. Editha decided that she herself would deal with René—at tea (Mimi flatly refused). Thea was assigned to the captain for the "hereunto appertaining" full treatment, to be administered the following day, on Sunday, because he was expecting guests tonight at nine o'clock ("I'm happy Mimi has promised to come by," the captain noted). So Sunday, the next day, then. When Thea would be doing his mending. "If I know you, you'll wait no matter what till the very last pair of socks is darned before setting in motion any measures meant to retaliate for the letter delivered to Mimi. How do I get hold of Stangeler, though? At home would be senseless. He probably first has to arrange with his Grete about when she doesn't need him to be on hand. Mightn't it be better, then, at the Siebenscheins' tomorrow around five? Didn't you find out from Dolly he'll be going there tomorrow? Good. You place the call, not me. And then give me the receiver."

"But I'll be with Thea at around this time," the captain protested.

"What difference does that make? You can come by for fifteen minutes while you have her busy darning socks. Then you can report right away whether you have the impression she saw something at the station. And as far as René's stupidity goes—you keep on claiming he never takes notice of anything—you can't count on it all that reliably..."

Eulenfeld repeated with a touch of malice, "Sunday, August thirtieth, three o'clock in the afternoon, reconnaissance effort to be launched simultaneously with cleaning and mending, reporting for telephone service at five in the afternoon."

"You can't really count with any certainty on that stupidity of René's," Editha said stubbornly, "any more than you can on his chattering constantly; you're never sure 'if the whole kit and caboodle he's got stored up will come bursting forth all at once,' as you put it. Has he had any direct dealings with Melzer?"

"Not until recently," Eulenfeld answered. "But lately they seem to have established some kind of connection. People bump into them together. This past Monday, for instance, Mimi happened across them on the Strudlhof Steps. And holding the most animated conversation."

"The conversation being about me," said Mimi.

"On the Strudlhof Steps!" cried Editha with evident astonishment. "And having a conversation about—you?! What were they saying?"

"I could only hear René talking…"

"Stands to reason," said the captain.

"So what exactly was he saying?" Editha asked tensely.

"He was discoursing to the major about how women don't possess memory or even faces, for that matter, if I understood him correctly. He mentioned my name and Editha's, too. Then when he spotted me he kept right on talking, turning toward me and addressing me directly. He was standing down lower; I was higher. It was really quite strange."

"And what did he say to you?"

"Something all gushy and overdone. I couldn't catch it."

"Gushy—hmm, well that's all right," Editha commented to herself. "What he said about memory, though—I bet there's bound to be some kind of preceding reason or prior occasion that prompted it."

She broke off but then jumped right back to the topic.

"We have to start out by cutting the ground away from Stangeler's feet so the major won't believe anything as outlandish as what René might tell him, or maybe has told him already…"

"Melzer's not in Vienna," the captain said.

"Oh that's right. But he'll be back tomorrow evening. So how do we take away Stangeler's credibility in the major's eyes, if I can put it that way?"

"René will very likely take care of that all on his own," the captain remarked. "I don't think there will even be much to it. While René Stangeler is drinking between twenty-two and twenty-five cups of tea at your place—which he does—all you have to do is fill his head with something he'll be happy to hear and will want to pass on to others. Tell him you met a gentleman last year in Lausanne who read an essay by him in a newspaper in Zurich about some ancient-history hogwash or other—I'll ponder what it's supposed to have been and then give you details; some pieces he wrote actually were published in Zurich, after all—and the gentleman in question gave a very laudatory assessment, etc. etc. He'll be sure to tell Melzer. And in all probability he'll also specify when and where you recounted the episode to him, that is, here at tea with you, on whatever day. Mimi and I will make it a point to get together with Melzer, perhaps at his place, perhaps at mine, or perhaps out for a walk when he's free after work, around four or five. I'll keep myself in readiness expressly to make this happen. René will believe the whole time that his story about Zurich has put him on an even more solid footing with Melzer. And if I know Melzer, that cautious old trooper, he won't say anything at all. But he'll be doing his share of thinking, though he certainly won't contradict or dispute, won't object, 'That can't be true, though, because that same afternoon I was out for a walk with the captain and Frau Schlinger.' The most he'll do is ask you or Mimi about it if occasion arises—in either case you know nothing from nothing, not about Zurich, not about Lausanne, not about any gentleman or any newspaper or anything about Stangeler having tea with you."

"Is Melzer that cautious? That reserved?"

"Yes he is. Wasn't always like that, maybe. Got that way. Seems to have cottoned on at some point that the light in his upper story doesn't burn so blazingly bright. When a person comes to know that—and I consider that a far-reaching act of self-discovery—it's really just about equal to a manifestation of intelligence, and so the person conducts himself for all practical purposes like someone of great intelligence, which is what I deem he should be considered. A great enigma. That is just how matters stand with Melzer, that worthy. He's cautious. But not distrustful, which makes a great difference. More likely to distrust himself than another, to an extent. Perhaps apprehensive of falling back into his own hereunto appertaining state of stupidity through an incautious remark."

Editha looked at Eulenfeld in astonishment.

No, he certainly wasn't stupid.

An old hussar, a Master of Horse.

Easily leaning against a bar too high for anyone else to reach.

ὦ πρὸς θεῶν. (Oh, by the gods!) A humanistic hussar. Heavy pack.

"This whole approach seems a bit risky to me, though," Editha said.

"Not a bit," replied the captain. "These matters are just going to be touched on, not laid out or paid out side by side and analyzed and compared and specified with precision. Nothing remotely like that. Melzer will pull back at once, like a crab. But he'll never again believe a word René says. People in general are happy to spare themselves painstaking analysis of situations by anticipating the outcomes of said situations in the form of judgments as rapid as they are inflexible. Once they've assembled even a few little relevant items, they turn inward, *in domum*, and make their conclusions, *pro domo*, obviously."

They now stayed quiet for a long time. To an uninvolved witness, if this conversation had had one, it would have appeared as if the captain finally, after a great deal of banter (and a great deal of impudence from Editha), now had again come into his just due, regaining, if one will, the rights of a gentleman over these two women.

"Somehow or another you have to take matters like these to their utmost extreme if you want them to be effective," he added in a tone suggesting a scientific, methodological finding. "Every fraudulent act makes the head spin anyway, so it's got to be extrapolated with optimal proximity to the very limit of the possible, always with uttermost approximation to the edge. It's what's called a limit value, like Ludolph's number, pi, and similar transcendental-number hogwash. Vertigo over the abyss of the impossible, the manifestly incongruous. The word 'fraud' always makes its planner's head spin, and that should tell us something about how to perpetrate one."

And the two Pastrés listened with genuine attention. Particularly Editha, whose obstreperous quicksilver would seem for these moments to have solidified. To be sure, it could become liquid again at any moment; all that was required was that the temperature of her temperament rise just slightly.

In the meantime, Mimi, who had been present for this conversation as no more than a silent third party, like a basin into which excess content or an unintended spatter will splash or overflow—Mimi was being subjected to a process that the two partners actually taking part in the discussion were not even remotely aware of: she became caught up once more in a whirl, a vortex, a miniature cyclone of imaginings, and went noiselessly spiraling deeper and deeper, this time almost entirely, into a funnel of despair. But then was heard with sudden sweetness the clarinet's lament. No grunting cut across it. An old hussar seemed to be moved from the bottom of his heart in hearkening to her lonely descent. And then it rasped at Editha's heart as well, and she made no effort to resist that voice which "kept in memory everything that ever happened."

Mimi said, "Otto just spoke the truth. That's it. A life on the edge. We have to practice fraud here and now because we practiced it there and then, and at some third point it's also a matter of getting by *à tout prix* without the truth, because it was abandoned at the first stage. None of our steps are taken freely. Everything is connected with everything else. The ground we stand on is totally eroded and hollowed out everywhere with cavities and tunnels, like porous limestone. In front of it, too, are fine spiderwebs we're not allowed to brush against, because everything relies on them. With their flimsy but taut filaments they're holding together the rabbit hutch that would otherwise fall to rubble right before us. It isn't just that we're walking on raw eggs but that we spend our nights asleep on bedding made of raw eggs, a catafalque teetering in the balance, a lying in state over the abyss. Life simply ceases, because you can no longer make a move—you will not and must not budge at any price—can no longer shoo away the fly that's walking around on your nose, because the movement would be too much effort. Too much, at any rate, for a corpse lying in state over an abyss. All this falseness and lying, all this fraudulence ends up like catalepsy. Even as a child I had a horrible fear of that." (Her voice gradually became a little stronger and the anguish that now came as she contemplated her own life provided it with something almost like a vantage point.) "And I knew that with Editha nothing else would ever be in store for me throughout my entire life—that and that alone, over and over, never anything else. I knew that even back in school. At the lyceum. Always to walk along the edge. Chained by spiderwebs. Balancing. But never lifting a hand. A bad dream. Always vertigo. Finally we were placed in two different classes of the same grade because the teachers had too hard a time handling us. When we had tests in English or mathematics and I would be sitting there instead of Editha, I would so yearn to be back in my real seat in my own classroom and afterward be able to follow the lesson and do my assigned work at home and be well prepared the next day. But there was nothing I could do. I could never find out later from Editha what had been covered during my own lessons. What could I have done? I couldn't ask anyone; after all, I'd been present. Oh, the hundred disturbing little things at Luithlen and at home, and I trudged on through all those years as if wearing shoes full of pebbles and sand. It defeated me. Somebody had to write Editha's English essays, or else she would have earned bad marks and caused a hue and cry at home. And somebody had to tell Papa in detail how the new production of *William Tell* at the Burgtheater had turned out, even though I hadn't seen it because Editha wanted somebody else to sit in the seat next to her, and I had to come back at the right time during the last act before the governess or one of the maids would be waiting down below in the foyer to see us home. I always went for a walk during the play, always quickly around the Ring Strasse, afraid somebody might see me, so I never dared go into a café. I never liked my father, but it offended me that he was constantly being hoodwinked. At the same time I held grievances against him and still hold them today" (grievances from the "memory of everything that ever happened . . . !"), "because he never ever noticed anything amiss and left me stranded in a life where I had not a moment's peace with what seemed like nary a qualm about expecting me to continue bearing up under it for the duration. And that's why I ran off with Scarlez: away from fraudulence, from that need to slog forlornly from one lie to another. One time I came into the Burgtheater during the last act, but the boy Editha wanted to have sitting next to her and who always waited for me outside so he could give me his ticket wasn't there. Some attendant or usher gives me the ticket, I go inside and take a seat next to some totally strange young man I've never seen before; in the semidarkness he immediately takes hold of my hand and squeezes my arm.

Editha showed up at the very last minute, after the performance was over and I was coming down the stairs alone and just about distraught, with the governess already waiting in the lobby: lo and behold, Editha slips in through some narrow door, coming in from the street, and waves at me. I don't know even to this very day where you were, Editha, but you must have said something or other to that young fellow, because he acted as though your temporary absence were completely a matter of course—or did he know he was dealing with the sister now and decide to try behaving the way he did on the off chance? It was impossible to keep track of these things all the time."

She stopped talking. The others didn't say anything either. Apparently both Editha and Eulenfeld considered it more advisable at this juncture, when a whole life's situation had been thrown out of balance, not to set or toss anything onto the scales until the beam had stopped teetering and the pendulum swung back into calm regularity from the extremes.

Mimi continued.

"It was my salvation to be far away with Enrique, even if I didn't like it very much in the beginning and a few small things seemed foreign or incomprehensible to me—stupid, stubborn little things, practical or impractical: as, for instance, how children had to put on a kind of artist's smock or dust coat when they were in school (they're called *guardapolvos*), or how traffic policemen were forced to wear heavy dark-blue uniforms in spite of the prevailing heat, or how anniversaries and other special occasions were observed by giving festively decorated pieces of parchment as presents ... even today I'm not one who thinks everything is wonderful where I now live, and everything over here is shabby or petty. That's not true of me at all. Of course we're more prosperous over there, especially since the war. There's no comparison, as you know, Editha. But otherwise there's so much that's simply unique to Vienna; it could scarcely be duplicated over there ..."

She seemed to have lost the thread and to be looking for it now, whereupon that woeful tone peculiar to her crept back in. It was growing noticeably darker in the room. Mimi was singing like a caged nightingale, a bird famed for its especially spellbinding melody.

"But the ground was solid beneath me. In the evening I no longer had to expect a shock to my nerves to come bearing down the next day, even ahead of time, there was no more array of disreputable schemes involving exchanges of identity, where I could expect basically nothing but a repetition of the way we would once more unreel the same old paltry tricks we used to watch everyone trip over. Was there any value in our playing those tricks or any success resulting from them? No, it was simply dreary. Now I was always able to tell Enrique exactly where I was going. And I was always eager to meet him somewhere when I was out of the house, somewhere in the city by myself, which didn't happen very often. One morning, as I lay in bed—I'd been out there for two years—I suddenly became fully aware that I had nothing to keep secret. Nothing whatever. From anyone. You can hardly even imagine what that meant to me. I was like a newborn. I felt polished and transparent, like rock crystal."

Both her listeners understood her; there was no doubting that. He who remains silent is expressing consent, as the Romans used to say (and it's a safe bet the captain knew this little maxim in Latin). But that's not true. (These days, definitely not.) Perhaps it would be better to say: He who remains silent appears to have understood. He who is quick to dissent is offering a defense against what has been asserted. Editha didn't defend herself. But she couldn't agree with the rock crystal part. It was too adamant. It would have made an impenetrably mirroring wall with Mimi sealed off behind it as if in glass. In a glass house. But that was the very edifice that had just been shattered. She, the beloved, had brought that wall with her, had hauled it across the ocean. It was here. There was no denying it, and there was no changing it. Let her sing like a caged nightingale all she wanted! The Pastré inheritance had to be put in order! Naturally that was what Enrique was confidently expecting, no two ways about it; it was on this stout hook— holding steadfast—that Editha had from the outset, with poised and irreproachable skill, hung her plan to bring her sister back. Cogent, and irreproachable from the moral standpoint as well. And everything was still hanging on this hook yet today; Mimi was hanging securely. This security elevated Editha's stimulus threshold quite significantly or it diminished her sharpness. So she could bear up under a great deal; she had a higher tolerance, red needles stitching away at her heart or not. Sweetly rasping song! Let her sing! They let her sing.

"Those letters you wrote me, Editha," the clarinet resumed, "so many of them, loving and dutiful and good—they all ran beside me like a conveyer belt, like flooring laid next to me that I would never have to stand on anymore. How happy that made me! That was because I saw things had remained the same, even without me, even without the exchange of identities, even without the romance of creating intrigue. I saw what preoccupied you. It was a way of being that no longer existed in my life. I saw it next to me, from letter to letter, but I didn't have to enter into it anymore, no longer had to stand on that ground. You were a great help to me in taking the measure of my happiness. Otto's turning up somehow thirteen years later as your emissary—of course I knew all about him from your letters—was powerless to thwart anything, on one hand, but at the same time it was the seed from which grew the end between him and me. That and nothing else. And I knew that right from the start, strangely enough. I'll always remain grateful to Otto for keeping me completely free, as it were, from actually experiencing Enrique's infidelity. It was like an operation under anesthesia, and after it everything really was healed." ("Anesthesia—hmm," growled the captain. The container with the screw-top cap emerged once more to sight.)

"And now here I sit. Right in the thick of it. After this summer. And what a summer it's been. What a setback! I feel enclosed like a pupa, a cocoon. All summer—nothing but bad conscience and loneliness and pain. As if I'd again lost everything, everything. Oh yes, it's beautiful here in Vienna. More beautiful than in Buenos Aires. I know that today. I admit it to myself. But the fact is I'm sick. I need to go back to my sanatorium. Where I'd been able to recover. It's beautiful here. I really enjoyed being in Greifenstein. Where the current comes flowing so fresh and youthful around a bend and resolutely courses on its way with no faltering, flowing and flowing as it gains mass. The lowlands begin here. This is where the last mountains are." (She gestured behind her, but there was not much more to see outside; everything was subsiding into an evening turned ash gray; points near and far were by now converging as a rising and limiting wall of deeper dusk.) "I've enjoyed being here. It's been really lovely. But the ground is all eroded and hollowed out again, the holes filled with spiderwebs. You've been very sweet, Otto. But you steal a passport by night, and then along comes a girl crying, and I attack her out of sheer frustration, slap her face, even though she's done absolutely nothing wrong. So much has to be kept secret. Did Stangeler meet Thea's relatives on the platform or in the waiting area—that is the question! And the answer has to be drawn out of her while she's darning socks. And all summer long I've been under pressure to go see our parents so I can once again dupe and hoax Papa—and Mama too, for that matter. I keep putting it off because I can't do it. May turns into July and then it's hot. I'm not getting anywhere with Major Melzer, either. I can hardly even talk to him. He's always bringing up old episodes I don't know anything about. Stangeler seems to stalk me somehow, too. At the casino in the City Park, at a dance, or even at tea, a certain Frau von Budau acts totally brazen-faced to me; the captain was there; I ask Melzer who she is. Even that little was too much. The whole mountain of raw eggs started slipping and sliding. I am thoroughly frightened and horrified by every bit of this. Not only do I have a lot to keep secret, but I have to keep the whole of myself as a person secret, I'm nothing but one big secret . . . Ah!" (Her voice dropped, and her whole body crumpled; she wasn't sitting back in her chair, was no longer upright as she'd been up to now; she was drooping forward as if wilting.) "Down deep what I'm yearning for is only to be far away, to be far away once more. Oh Editha, people should avoid returning to what has been. It's as though a person were sinking down into the grave while still alive. I want to get away. Travel. Back. I'm chained, broken on the rack, shot through with holes, tortured to death. I have to wake up from this dream. I have to find my way back to my other dream. In my hospital. In my sanatorium. The haven I really and truly did reach. But it could meanwhile be a thing past and gone, my hopes all forlorn there beyond the horizon, which means I'll never get back to the street of my dreams, the Avenida Leandro Alem, and I'll have to wake up, and the sweet, evil dream here is the only reality."

"Let's turn on a light," said Editha. Her voice had a smudged, uncontrolled sound, like a lamp globe someone has bumped into and cracked, so that it doesn't ring anymore but merely clanks.

She then let herself in for only a few questions about the Budau situation. And when she found out that this had taken place on none other than the day preceding that peculiar encounter with Stangeler and Melzer on the Strudlhof Steps, she nodded slightly and said:

"That must be what it was." She spoke the words to herself in passing and then fell silent. Her quicksilver had once more frozen, as if in astonishment. It's quite possible that the uncontrollable mechanism of life, gazing for perhaps only a few seconds into her consciousness, had cowed her for just this brief moment in time.

"Of course you couldn't have thought of everything," Mimi continued, speaking her palliative words in a tone somewhat colder nonetheless; and now that the electric light was sharply demarcating the room's interior from the outside, her descant seemed completely finished. "I've restored total order to the whole mess." (She now described approximately how.) "But I ask myself if it was worth going to all that trouble. And the answer is no. It even strikes me as totally pointless. Tell me honestly, Editha—what's behind all this for you? Nothing but material interests. And not even large-scale ones at that. You've said your friend in Germany considers this whole affair with the cigarettes a mere trifle from a business angle; for him it's much more about favors he'd like to do for this person or that. I don't believe it. I believe it's really a business matter after all. And why are you pursuing it so eagerly? Does this Herr Wedderkopp really not know how far you're extending yourself? You talk as if he wouldn't want to know anything about it, as if he mustn't or daren't know. I don't understand why you're going to such great lengths with this matter; you're a rich woman. Our parents—you've said it yourself—have placed you in a position of total financial independence. I have to add, incidentally, that the way you achieved your goal was masterly; I mean how plausibly you pointed out to them that they would avoid the inheritance tax. I remember even now how happy it made me when you wrote to me about it in 1911. Otto talked about it as well. In Paris you showed me your bankbooks and explained them. So what do you need money for? Why all this complicated wheeling and dealing on poor Melzer's back, if I may put it that way? The only thing behind them is money, nothing but money pure and simple. Suppose he somehow or other sends you a couple of cases with all the proper customs declarations or however you imagine it taking place: that's not just a trifle, is it? And doesn't that make a difference in the long run?"

Here in the glow of the electric light, however—it wasn't harsh but shone softly from the tea table—Editha's stimulus threshold was now rather quickly exceeded, the Edithian sharpness awakened from latency and brought to the fore after all that patience and restraint; it pierced through a surface that had been only as thin and pleasant as a pastry glaze anyway. And so the thread of Mimi's descant—she'd very nearly lost it, just as the room here had been split into isolated segments and virtually fallen to pieces after the artificial light was switched on—was now completely severed by Editha.

"And are you saying you're *not* rich?!" she asked. "I should think you're a good bit wealthier than I am! And yet you're here in Vienna for no reason other than material interests as well. Yours are more extensive than mine, for that matter, and if these financial affairs weren't so essential for me, if they weren't the only crucial factor, you wouldn't be sitting here, Mimi, believe you me, and I'd never have taken the trouble to get you to come here. Quite the opposite, in fact!"

This oddly vehement turn, this outburst building up throughout Mimi's discourse—with its air of being conclusive, somehow derailed, seemingly parenthetical, and not entirely logical—was now enough to trigger off a complete panic attack.

"Get me away from here!" she cried out, sitting up straight with her hands at her temples. "Let me clear out. Let me go away. Tomorrow." Her posture stayed rigid, as if a terrifying fear had seized her. Editha said nothing and did not move. In her gray eyes was the concentration of a marksman taking aim.

"Yes," she finally said. "You'll be going away. You have to go away, in fact. Beyond and below the horizon once more. To your sanatorium. It's not a thing past and gone. It's been there the whole time, waiting for you." (Now the pain in Editha's voice was audible; it made the smooth, cold tiles of her calmly flowing words bulge a little.) "It's waiting for you; depend on it. Enrique is waiting for you. But not with empty hands. That should be clear."

"I'm your prisoner," Mimi said half aloud, her hands still at her temples. "Yes, that's the truth of it." She didn't have a sword to unbuckle and hand over. That would have made a greater impression.

"Sweet prisoner!" cried Editha, jumping up and hastening to her. "Most dearly beloved of all prisoners! Yes, I've got you now. I've accomplished it, and you just have to surrender." She knelt on the rug in front of Mimi. The rest was the silence of a long embrace, a silence that silently swallowed up the room. There was a short interval, and then the captain could be heard unscrewing caps, opening containers, snapping a lighter—performing his ritual in proper sequence, *secundum ordinem*.

We recounted earlier how Paula Pichler, sitting in the garden with Thea on the afternoon of Monday, August 31, heard about everything the girl had gone through since Friday. As of Sunday at six thirty p.m.—five thirty marked the return of Eulenfeld, who had just stopped over to see Frau Schlinger for a minute; the last pair of socks had been darned by six—Thea found herself placed under obligation to do penance for an unspecified period. Reproach, interrogation, confession, and sentencing had required barely half an hour, so that this time Thea really had appeared at the family dinner table right on time (even though she hadn't promised that for Sunday). Not drenched in tears; no sign of any such thing, in fact. Instead, she was wearing a kind of leaden overcoat—invisible, it goes without saying.

Thea's composure, amounting almost to imperviousness, was being nourished the whole time by a reservoir that had opened up inside her, to her profound amazement, and provided abundant sustenance during the captain's half-hour absence; so this corner of the sofa, now genuinely vacated, as it were, could be filled and occupied with all that was entering into Thea in the silence of an interval during which she was fully, completely thrown back on her own devices. It wasn't that she "lowered her mending and stared pensively into space" (as we could for better—or really for worse—write at this point). Not by any means. She went on quickly and skillfully plying her needle, busily darning stockings and socks without even a faint inkling that she was thereby hastening along the primrose path to her own execution. She was going about her business exactly as she had back in July, when Major Melzer had been seated here; no idling then, either. And that was exactly what had made those hours so cozy, so intimate. Melzer hadn't sat here as a guest whose presence brings everyday pursuits to a halt, but for the most part more as a companionable someone by your side, fitting in so perfectly that you never really notice him until he's gone once more. The truth was that she had indeed *lived* with Melzer throughout those hours, entering—and specifically just then—onto more or less higher and more wholesome terrain than that on which her existence was otherwise passed. But that terrain hadn't been exotic in any way; according freedom of movement from the outset, it was eminently habitable and not just a rostrum erected for some brief holiday, which was why Thea hadn't been in a holiday mood at the time, but had simply continued stitching rapidly and expertly, just as she was doing now, when being granted the major's presence only in spirit (insofar as we can speak of such a thing).

That was something else Thea talked to Paula about, since saying whatever came into her mind was the very shortest pathway from her most recent and most intense emotion to her already moving lips, just as a ball thrown against a wall bounces back to the thrower. This pathway was too short, in a sense, to accommodate lies, and the resulting openness accordingly shielded the love of truth from all temptation; it couldn't even be established, for that matter, whether or not any such temptation even arose. Paula was lying in her lounge chair with Thea sitting near her, though not kept at foot's length, if one will, like Hedi Loiskandl not long before, but right by her older confidante's ear, into which she as good as tunneled, whispering, murmuring, from time to time heaving slight little sighs and sobs. It's practically a foregone conclusion that after Thea's account Paula must have had the impression that on the very afternoon before, on Sunday, this Frau Schlinger had broken her promise and given Thea away when the captain had briefly stopped by her apartment; Paula had been expecting it to happen sooner or later and had taken always a pessimistic view of Frau Schlinger's discretion, as we will recall. Ditto in regard to Thea's aspirations for a film career. Though she was poles apart from that field, it seemed to her nonetheless that her younger friend was lacking precisely those traits of temperament that should and indeed must somehow make themselves manifest, an inner verve or zest, even if it's just a tiny smidgen, the small, hidden nucleus of the personality. On this point she had an easy time cheering up Thea, who, Paula's instincts told her, had been virtually saved from embarking on a crooked path. Naturally she didn't voice that feeling. There were other points to consider anyway. Her parents. Hedi Loiskandl. Now, however, she was free from having to ponder whether the captain should be filled in or not. Thea was banished from his presence, and a period of penance was a period of penance, which is just as it should be: Paula strove gradually to bring her friend around to this view. In the older woman's mind, the major more than anyone else remained the key figure. She listened with the keenest interest to Thea's idyllic solo about her moments in the sofa corner on Sunday, the preceding day.

She was absorbed this whole time by an idea that had recently come to occupy her mind and spirit (and in the case of Paula Pichler we most certainly can speak of such a thing, as we've already noticed). This summer, especially these last months, had opened up to her a deeper insight into the heart and soul of a person like Thea than she'd ever had before; as these months went on, they were more and more deeply suffused by an admonition perhaps just now materializing into full visibility, no longer merely darting out at random times and places from an open fissure in her conscious mind, but at this point emerging into the realm of words like an object shoved into a room at night, later coming into view, in tandem with the morning light—and along with the room as a whole—in its full dimensions, now standing as a visible, tangible object among other objects. It seemed to Paula today as if all the people with whom Thea Rokitzer had contact were in some special and increased measure accountable for this aspect of the girl, to so large an extent, in fact, that there was really no room left for answerability on the part of the Thea she was envisioning. It was not owing to any lack of intelligence on Thea's part, nor to her good-hearted and defenseless nature, but to one particular factor and to it alone—her emptiness. Everything depended on who deposited this or that item inside her and what the item was. She seemed to Paula to be like a display case made entirely and exclusively out of totally transparent, perfectly clear, untinted glass, almost as invisible as air itself. What did become visible was whatever was placed inside it, even ultra-visible, as it were, and from every angle, conspicuously highlighted on a serving tray made of glass and hermetically sealed in a glass compartment from which it could no longer be removed. Possibly entailing a serious indictment, too. A corpus delicti placing on display, on pitilessly unsparing display, the person consigning the object, not the person on whom it was consigned. It was in this spirit that Paula Pichler began not just exercising prudent caution but on a much deeper level also feeling a kind of diffidence, as if confronting something inscrutable, possibly even facing the immensity of the role this girl might be playing—without a trace of guile but doing so all the while—toward everyone, including toward herself, her closest friend. Paula was weighing her words at this very moment. And if, as Captain Eulenfeld had opined, the recognition of one's own limited mental capacity amounted in effect to the same thing as keen intelligence, then the paradoxical effect produced by our meek little lamb Thea was evidenced by Paula Pichler's behaving toward her as cautiously, indeed as cagily (though not trapped in caginess, we'd like to note) as if she were dealing with a person who exacts heightened alertness from others, thanks to the exceptional agility of her intelligence. "Just don't let on that anything's wrong"—this had become Paula's constant caveat to herself in her exchanges with Thea, and not only because she considered the girl indiscreet. Paula held a low estimation of the discretion of others as it was—and of the discretion of her fellow females, very low indeed (as we observed in the case of Frau Schlinger). When it came to Thea, however, she soon got the feeling she was placing on record an irrevocable memorandum of anything she said to her. That was how strongly Thea's utter naïveté affected her! She really did seem to Paula like a showroom, a display case into which several people had placed objects, had exhibited highly compromising portraits of themselves: the captain, Hedi Loiskandl. All of Thea seemed to consist of such display items—those and better ones as well. To Paula, naturally on the lookout for points of comparison as she pondered these matters with increased awareness in light of recent developments, Aunt Lintschi Nohel seemed by contrast to be a woman armed with a strong shield and armor and safeguarded at every turn.

It was as a direct result of these vague impressions, mounting admonishments, and clear-cut points of rationale, above all that our Paula didn't tell Thea anything—just as one example— about that manifestation of duplication (in this instance, duplicitous) she'd witnessed at the West Station.

She met René on Wednesday at three o'clock.

This was her corner of the world, so to speak. Her domain, her bailiwick. Not neutral ground (nothing neuter here, if you please!) occupied neither by him nor by her. He entered her realm. This was her sphere of influence, her native heath, the sacred grove of the dryad Paula Schachl. René felt it again today from the moment he made his way into the neighborhood. In this regard nothing about him had changed in all these many years. That tipped the scales in her favor right from the beginning. Whatever it was that now slightly mortified him was the force that fortified in her the biases she considered self-evident truths (the mightiest of the monsters that slumber by our side, that sense of the self-evident!)—but not quite "considered," come to think of it, because she lacked any realization of it in the first place. She stood inside her world, in no way different from an Amazon Indian in his rain forest or a Kyrgyz from the steppes against the copper-brown horizon, round as a disc. She stood inside her world—astute. He alternated between worlds—*tropidonotus* trenches and Siebenschein salons—stupid. Only little by little, and by laboriously crisscrossing borders between territories with no apparent common features, did he acquire whatever was lacking in him; she was able to dispense with such a course because she'd possessed unity of spirit ab ovo (to use a pet expression, one to which Sectional Councillor Geyrenhoff constantly resorted as a verbal tic, since it recurs with such frequency as to start jumping out on prolonged reading of that weighty, scrupulously well-organized volume comprising his chronicle—we've mentioned it before). To our way of thinking, one of the saddest facts about this aspect of Herr René von Stangeler's biography is that he had never set foot in, had never reached, never even glimpsed that little garden well known to us; seemingly minor chance misses would appear to have kept him away from it, as will emerge, whereas the truth lay in a more basic circumstance: he was unworthy of the little garden.

All these points taken together gave Paula Pichler the ascendency during the first moments of their exchange in the Café Brioni (while a sudden torrential rainstorm poured down the windowpanes for several minutes). Two factors came into play, however, to shake her superiority.

The first immediately. She could feel here and now—it had not struck here with anything near such impact and conviction at the station—that he still loved her, exactly the same as before. And, as if a weapon had just recoiled, that she still loved him too, exactly the same as before.

To a certain extent, that surpassed her understanding (not his, though, insofar as we can speak of any such thing; it was a matter of course to him). There was no comprehending what kind of a love it could be that came surging over from him, that she herself was feeling as well, and that now reappeared in this life of hers, though without any spatial dimension, inasmuch as it pushed aside nothing, diminished nothing, entered into conflict with nothing, suffered from nothing, and thus desired to alter nothing.

As they were exchanging greetings, he kept her whole hand in his, holding it firmly and looking at her from his somewhat tilted eyes with great delight, as if he were contemplating some lustrous object of special beauty, a work of art that sets one's gaze alight.

She would have had exactly the same reaction, or a closely kindred one at any rate, if her greater sense of decorum had not curbed her and kept her joyfulness from flashing out at once, like those reflections young scamps make in school when they wave hidden little pocket mirrors to catch the blackboard.

The second factor initiating Paula's descent from higher ground was of a completely different kind. Because René had asked a question about it, she assured him with certainty that Thea Rokitzer had been completely oblivious to the strange double apparition at the station that past Friday; likewise Aunt Nohel, for when she spotted that he, René, and she, Paula, were whispering with their heads together, she had begun engaging Thea in an intense conversation. This was how Aunt Nohel was. And on Monday, the day before yesterday, when Thea had come to see her, Paula, and had talked on and on about everything under the sun, the older friend would have been bound to notice something. No, Thea was unaware. And she, Paula, had of course not said a word on the subject.

"Why 'of course,' though?" Stangeler asked, because the phrase struck him as odd in this connection.

Paula, to whom it was completely foreign that anyone should seize on this or that item in a person's whole speech inventory—like practically everyone with her level of education, she said what she meant not by enlisting separate words one at a time but by blending masses of them together, adding this or that touch as they go, in a process comparable to watercolorists working wet-on-wet—Paula, then, for whom such chopping and parsing of words could only appear incomprehensible, was rather perplexed for a moment but finally answered:

"Because it's better not to say anything to her. It would do her harm, I think; it would be too much for her."

"And so because of—her nature," Stangeler said with deliberation (there were indeed occasions on which he could turn genuinely deliberative). "So is that why you said 'of course'?"

"Of course!" cried Paula with spirit. "Because of her nature. You're right. That's nothing for her. But Major Melzer has to be told. And you're the one who has to do it, René."

"No," he said decisively, in a voice clear and calm.

"Why not?!" Paula asked animatedly. "He's not a scaredy-cat like Thea, after all!"

"Not because of—his nature," Stangeler answered. Then he fell silent, steadfast in his refusal to make any disclosure whatever to Melzer about the double phenomenon (about the attendant duplicity).

"Why do you want me to tell Melzer about it?" he asked.

"The reason is clear. I grant you Thea doesn't know what she's saying, but this much I've been able to get out of her—the major is somehow unhappy because of Frau Schlinger. He'll be less unhappy when he finds out there are two of them. Besides, Thea has got to get away from this captain. He's nothing for her. The fact is she loves the major. I know it for certain. Since Monday. It's probably mutual, too."

He seemed to himself to be like a man who's dropped something and who, now looking on the floor for the collar button or the pencil that fell, gains a whole new perspective on the room he lives in: the top of his desk from underneath, like a ceiling, the feet of his bed from sideways, large and close-up, all the more if he has a flashlight; it reverses shadows, throws the lowest-lying objects, almost never seen, to the top, makes the legs of chairs look as if they were folding themselves over the seat, casts light so strongly on the base of the tile stove resting on the floor that it leaps to the eye. This was the way in which Paula, whose projects and objects were now causing her to approach from a whole different direction the little circle of people among whom he lived and who reinforced his underlying biases—this *tropidonotus* Indian and Siebenschein Kirghiz, who had accordingly taken to cognizance very little indeed of what was standing nearest to him.

"And why do you want Melzer not to find out anything about this?" Paula followed up.

"No, no"; René put this misunderstanding right. "I have no objection at all to his being told that Frau Schlinger exists in duplicate. But that knowledge won't come from me. Not from me."

That was the point at which Paula finally came all the way down from her higher vantage, for here she could sense something she couldn't understand but that she knew was present and fixed, not merely whim or caprice; there was something solid here. It surpassed her understanding in the same way as did the indestructibility and the imperturbability of his love for her, of hers for him.

"Nothing would come of it if I were the one to tell him," he continued. "Something needs to come of it, though, and I want to see it. But if I butt in and make a to-do, I won't see anything."

She seemed to respect what he was saying without balking (notable enough in itself). After they had spent a short while leafing through the newspapers lying on their table, Paula expressed a wish to make Melzer's acquaintance. "I want to invite you," she said (and briefly described the little garden in Lichtental). "You, Thea, and the major. How should we best go about it? Suppose you ask him? And then Thea should ask him too. My husband will be there as well. You don't know him, but he's known you for a long time, because I've told him so much about you."

"Yes," said Stangeler (and Paula seemed to him now to be enviably bright and independent, altogether mature). "That's really good. An excellent idea. So—unexpected. Yes. That's how things will go. That's how they have to go..." He spoke these last words more quietly, as if he were talking only to himself. He looked out onto the square, where streetcars and automobiles were turning and curving in a jumble. "Everything's close by," he said, "including the house with the blue unicorn, in front of which we first met, Paula." "Yes," she said, "and here we are once more, sitting side by side, thank God." With slight pressure, she laid her hand on his, which was resting next to her on the red velvet of the banquette.

Stangeler had taken the Strudlhof Steps to come to the Café Brioni for his date with Paula and had made himself ready pretty much the same way as he had on the occasion of his first visit to Frau Editha Schlinger: bracingly chilled, if we may put it like that—the late-summer heat had in fact let up in the meantime—and enveloped in the strong fragrance of lavender. Deep silence on the stairs. The tree branches motionless high up and far away against the sky. It had also been silent on Liechtenstein Strasse; the plashing of the fountain behind him could be heard. Paula had at once become pleasantly aware of the lavender fragrance, flaring her nostrils in a way that formed alluring little wrinkles along her nose.

After he and Paula Pichler had gone their separate ways, he struck out from this landing spot as if embarking on a distant journey to faraway ports of call. His whole mood, in fact, felt like that of someone off to his travels with a long, swaying car of an express train waiting for him. It really did feel as if he were leaving the city and everything he was connected to behind, about to soar aloft at a great height, reeling and set adrift from it all. Before he left home he picked up the locket Editha had given him in days of yore. That memento would have been perhaps out of place in the gondola (as a token of what's past and gone); and yet, because he'd worn it last time, he wouldn't want her to miss it now. So even with his shirt buttoned up and his necktie pulled tight, he drew the chain over his head and stuck the pendant down his collar, letting the long, thin chain slide down as well as it could.

Paula had turned left. She waved one more time and went around the corner.

He gazed out over the heavily trafficked square in front of the station like a swimmer looking across the wide water before shoving off.

Into these empty moments there now dropped an overdue thought.

Which of these duplicate ladies would be waiting for him now?

Which one (at the other train station, that is) had been Frau Editha Schlinger?

The one arriving or the one fetching?

Probably the one fetching.

Why? There wasn't any difference, after all. Which was which?

He gave a sudden brief smile and plunged cautiously into the pool of heavy (admittedly, only by the standard of this city) traffic. And now, resurfacing on the other side, as it were, he had only about three more streets to cross. Here, too, the steps and flights of stairs lay quiet and empty, breathing the building's most secret reticence.

Now came her footsteps. "Oh, you're here!" she cried; "I'm so happy." He considered it only natural that she should proceed from the start to the intimate *Du* form of address (to tell the truth, we almost went ahead and wrote "ab ovo" à la Geyrenhoff. Basically these are nothing but spiteful remarks).

So it's the same one, he thought. Not so sure I'd want to bet on it, though.

He lacked the time as well as the small expanse of interior space necessary for him to ponder and expatiate. René was in the position of a man who needs to jot something down but doesn't have a slip of paper. She steered him to the tea table. She poured him a cup. She wanted to know what he was up to, what he was working on, telling him all the while how she'd wanted to ask him recently when he'd written that essay about medieval memoirs—he knew what she meant, didn't he? She'd never known there was any such thing as memoirs from the Middle Ages; the word had such a flavor of the eighteenth century, after all, but she'd found out about it in Geneva, because one of her friends, a gentleman from Zurich, had read the article in the local newspaper and mentioned it to her as highly praiseworthy, along the lines of "a very mature and weighty piece of work." But now she broke off suddenly and said more slowly and in an almost plaintive tone, "It's hardly possible to fathom how much study and expertise are often required to bring even the smallest effort of this kind to a successful completion."

He'd heard all he needed to. Even despite his usual inability to connect things rapidly, her language alone was enough to give him complete understanding. But Mimi's way of expressing herself, which Editha had recalled and reverted to, was now, in retrospect, presupposing the presence of the original throughout the spring and summer, the steady manifestation of an earlier phenomenon known as Editha Schlinger and before that, as Editha Pastré. He, René—well, he'd been with the other one. With this one here as well, however, down at the foot of the cliff Asta and Melzer had climbed fourteen years before.

She leaned in close to him all of a sudden and took hold of his neck.

"What's that little gold chain sticking out from your collar? Are you wearing a lorgnette or something?"

"No," answered René.

He loosened his tie at once, unbuttoned his shirt, and held the pendant out to her. "Open it," he said.

But she recognized it just as it was.

"No!" she cried, "how sweet! It's so nice that you still have this, René!" She was now sitting on the armrest of René's chair; she hugged him and kissed his neck three times. "Now let me see if my picture's still in there!" She leapt over to the secretary to fetch a tiny penknife. "What do you know!" she cried, touched and excited, as she looked inside the open locket. Then suddenly: "Can you make love to me again today?!" She took his head between her hands.

Strength comes bounding at once out of people this young, like dogs from a kennel when the gate is opened. He didn't carry her this time; they went arm in arm.

Editha drew him off to the right and opened the built-in door.

They were in a smaller bedroom, a charming little box, a discreet abode where favors could be quietly bestowed. Next to the bed was an appealing rack, white with metal trim and a number of glass shelves cluttered with an array of letters and books.

René knelt on the floor and began taking off Editha's shoes and stockings.

"Why were you trying to turn left earlier?" she asked as she bent down to him.

"I thought—the sofa," René said quietly (a second later he caught up with himself and the quick thinking that had made a smart answer pop out of him so abruptly and easily despite his addled state).

"No, I don't think so—it's so much nicer here, after all," she cried, in a voice that sounded cheery.

Everything fell away. He pressed his face against her body. There wasn't even the faintest mark of a scar on her loin.

It was almost dark when René came back out to the street.

He stood there as if buttressed. Solidly supported. Thickly padded with insulation.

The irrefutability of the facts enfolded him up to his hips, as it were. It offered security, released what was often a merely interior state from the danger of becoming trapped in a demonic or ghostlike existence, proffering a fixed point for any doubts that might still surface from the maelstrom of astonishment, confronting turmoil with a firm hold. The point lying in the distant past, at a time before he knew Grete Siebenschein, the point to which he had been trying to make his way back a short time before, so he could take proper aim at her and strike: this point was now secured; the bow was at full draw, and the arrow clicked in, as when a crossbow comes to rest.

He kept standing there, rooted to the spot (near the corner of the café behind whose tall windows, bowed at the top, Dolly Storch had once seen those building superintendent folk assembled at the card table) by the weight, crashing to the ground, of this visualization. René weighed in his hand what kind of arrow he should place in the socket. Twice the string seemed to him to be fully taut, extended to the utmost, the first time drawn back into the distance of space and faraway lands (though it would have been a random shot, fired from the gondola!), but now even farther and deeper back, into the distant reach of his own years, before which the present lay like a future that could be freely chosen. That's where he had to strike. Into the black center. The center was glowing red, but then the red ring leapt back and gave way to a black cloud mass. He now felt he had been transformed into the arrow meant for Grete. It was meant to strike her.

Without saying anything to anyone, however.

Firing the costly projectile senselessly.

He saw Melzer once more drifting as if underwater or swimming under glass, in the wide white trousers he wore in those days.

Now that the field of fire lay open and the target in clear view, now that no quarry had to be flushed out and run to ground, an incalculable variety of memories, all in sharp detail, came rumbling forth out of the last few hours. Behind many of them was a bright background, like far-off tufts of golden heather. He was now seeing the departure and the way back from the foot of the cliff after Asta and Melzer had climbed back down, watching them walk through a forest still partly strewn with rocks and into a secluded clearing (in the middle of which another boulder stood, but a smaller one) with Editha moving in front of him, Editha as the main feature over the following two days, even though he had paid no attention to her. Yet she had now returned, and so he must have seen her after all. And that night in his room came back to him not by his own doing, and there was no chasing it away. He believed what he was feeling was that life had to a certain degree kept its word here. The Strudlhof Steps had never lied, either. Yes, he came back to them as well and grazed them briefly. Editha was contentedly splashing around in those long-gone times like someone soaking in a bathtub, and just as we enjoy handing a child its whole aquatic menagerie, its plastic seals and fish and crabs and crocodiles, to play with while its smooth white body is immersed in warm water, in that way Editha had sat on the bed with her toys on the blue silk spread, as it were, giving Geyrenhoff a nudge, making Konietzki sit next to Marchetti, dodging Grabmayr, shoving Semski aside, and simply tossing Ingrid Schmeller onto her back. She hadn't been able to get enough. And it didn't bother Stangeler very much that she kept on pausing and asking this or that question in the midst of it all: when Grete had come back; what it had been like picking her up at the station; whether they'd really been happy to see one another or whether there might have been a certain amount of strain; how long Thea had been back and whether he'd seen her yet—this all bothered René very little. It soon became plain what she wanted from him, what she was trying to find out, what was worrying her. It was so obvious that he was able to feign gullibility as easily as turning his hand.

Now he turned and released himself from the spot. The picture of the darkening street with its constant movement all around entered him again after some seconds of almost complete absence. There was just one way for him to go, the arrow flying before him—diagonally across the square. Even if only for five minutes.

He raced up the steps so quickly that the separate floors were like carousels slowly circling below him, still in rotation as he ran past. As in the saddle, on skis, or in bed: the body of a person this young is an apprentice nearly full-fledged (except as it pertains to denseness) that never gives advance notice but still jumps in to do everything. The heart pumps, the chest heaves, the thighs extend or contract, strength comes bounding out of the gate. With no shortness of breath René was standing at the brown door of the apartment. The bell rang. The steps coming toward him, though, didn't seem to fit his scenario; they weren't conforming, weren't placing themselves correctly. Damn it, just like the objective outer world (hereunto appertaining), which only allows itself to be fully subsumed to rear the inner one (hereunto appertaining) for the briefest of times. Frau Siebenschein, who ordinarily didn't answer the door (the maid had probably been sent off somewhere), looked into the corridor, like a rat peering over the top of a wall; at least that was the not very amiable image under which she appeared to René, ready to barge in as he was. The agile little lady was obviously surprised to see him. "Grete is very busy," she said, at first without moving aside. Stangeler produced a few shards of a surface smile on his face; we could say he was smiling through shards instead of through tears. "I only wanted to see her for a moment," he said, now given room to step into the entryway just as Dr. Ferry and two gentlemen did the same, talking loudly and laughing. Grete was behind them with a dossier under her arm. She was wearing a white smock; it was an excellent garment for her, incidentally. The two gentlemen were already leaving. Dr. Siebenschein waved to René, vanished back into another room, and called out as he was going, "Gretl, don't be long; we have to finish up." Only now were Grete and René finally able to exchange greetings, while the mother's reproachful gaze rested on them, as well as on the rear door leading to the law office. Nor was the small woman about to budge from the spot. "What is it, René?" asked Grete, "I'm really very busy at the moment…" "I just wanted to see you for a minute," he answered, in a subdued voice, strangled, if one will, by the presence of Grete's mother behind him. "Is anything wrong!?" she asked, warmly and with genuine interest, her eyes protruding a little. "No, nothing," said Stangeler. He took her hand, squeezing as he kissed it, and then turning to Grete's mother so he could bow and leave. When he opened the door, Grete quickly came after him. She'd come to realize by now that no external situation had brought him here; she cast off her inhibited state and was about to confront his. She kissed him. The door slammed shut. Walking back down the stairs, René was struck with amazement that having the brakes applied as abruptly as they'd just been upstairs hadn't caused even a small spark of anger to fly out of him, something otherwise inevitable, considering his nature. But whatever it was he'd experienced on the street earlier seemed to have placed him somewhere outside of himself. He was still holding the arrow in his hand; he hadn't been able to fire it. He stepped through the street door just as Major Melzer was coming along the sidewalk from the right, thereby so completely quashing the lively movement of our René's interior observations that a flat decision ended up crushing equally flat all his cross-grained turbulence, the way a steamroller presses the asphalt smooth.

"Were you just up visiting Fräulein Grete, Herr von Stangeler?" asked the major in a friendly tone. "Yes," answered Stangeler, as they continued walking together. For the first few seconds, Melzer's face appeared somehow craggier to René, having a look he'd never seen before. Now he caught on. Now it struck him that it had probably simply been an effect of the light coming from a gigantic wrought-iron lantern suspended from the vaulted ceiling and hanging high up in the entrance of the Stein House, a fixture that would have been better suited to a sumptuous mortuary parlor. "I took a walk this afternoon," said the major after they'd gone a few steps side by side, "along the river path as far as the lock at Nussdorf with Frau Editha Schlinger and Herr von Eulenfeld." At this moment Stangeler felt something like gratitude toward Melzer. The bluntness with which outward facts were being presented here, like a bludgeon being wielded, precluded from the very outset any possibility of discharging the arrow in reverse motion or the opposite direction ...

As it stood now, after all, any impulse to tell Grete about the duplicate ladies, if any had been present in the first place, somehow, during those moments on the street (in front of the concierges' card-party café), had been rendered null and void inside René, had died away completely, had become an exterior manifestation serving as the vehicle of his most intimate and interior concerns, and so he now firmly believed he was feeling that the reason to act swallowed up the occasion for taking it. While they were headed toward the corner of Porzellan Gasse, Stangeler reached the point of asking himself, as if struck by lightning, what exactly he'd intended to say to Grete, what words he would have spoken to her had the opportunity been more favorable. Then, of course, he was forced to realize what had really happened: he *had* told her, and furthermore, she had understood him.

Let it be noted as a marginal comment that one of the unusual features—suspicious, too, if you will—of this couple's relationship was how readily each of them kept secrets from the other. They didn't seem to find it the least bit difficult.

"Are you getting onto the streetcar?" Melzer asked.

"I don't know," replied René after some confused hesitation. "I may just continue walking. This way ..." He gestured casually in the direction of the Strudlhof Steps.

"If you don't have anything planned for this evening, Herr von Stangeler," the major said, "I'd like to invite you to a simple evening meal. I have everything we need at home."

"Of course, I'd like that," René said. "Nobody's expecting me." He quickly dashed through the highlights of the afternoon, which now seemed jam-packed to him. Paula. Then Editha. The stop off at Grete's. He was suddenly seized, as if it were a new feeling, by intense thoughts of fidelity (something it would really not be possible to claim on his behalf). And now Melzer. That was like the finishing flourish in the calligraphy of time, which had been writing him since noon.

René gladly agreed to drink Turkish coffee instead of tea after their meal.

Then they lay down on the bearskin.

Stangeler had to take notice of the electric candle that had been installed hardly a foot above the floor. "For reading," Melzer said. René was naturally (in keeping with his nature) very taken with such things.

In this connection, it might have been observed (though not by René) that Melzer took an ambivalent attitude toward this new roommate of his (meaning the candle). On the surface, the inner surface, he could assess the object easily and favorably: a fixture he'd long wished for as an aid to his special comfort, a handsome and practical gift he'd received from dear friends, a considerate token of their thoughtfulness, worthy of those who'd bestowed it and not to be underappreciated. Indeed, Melzer had stopped by the apartment of Herr and Frau E.P. on the very day after his return home and had thanked them on the spot with all his heart and with all due gratitude.

Below this inner surface, however, a mood held sway to which entirely different courses of action would have corresponded, such as standing a chair next to the fireplace against the wall in such a way that the candle would be less visible—a paradoxical image, almost reminiscent of the well-known light hidden under a bushel. Or, to trim down a long list, to drape something over this wall fixture, such as a silk scarf. But Melzer didn't own anything like that. And it wouldn't have looked right anyway. When he was in the center of town the preceding Tuesday, his attention had been caught by the display window of a toy shop in which a charmingly decorated room in a dollhouse had been set up; in it was a three-panel screen or paravent. Its height would have been perfect, but placed down on the floor next to the fireplace, it would have looked even more peculiar than the wall fixture itself.

Melzer had pulled the little chain only once before, on Sunday evening before he went to sleep, which finally switched the light off.

Now Stangeler switched it on with delight.

Melzer looked at him sadly.

René could feel it, turned around, and now realized how indisputable it was that he hadn't been mistaken in front of the Stein House, when the major's face had seemed disconcertingly changed.

He made an effort to collect himself, to hold together everything he knew, as it were, to keep everything facing in the right order and compare it piece by piece (in the process, Paula Pichler came into his mind, along with what she'd said about Melzer and Thea). He inhaled deeply from the chibouk and took a sip of the coffee, but no sooner did he have an intimation of the truth ready to swirl up from the fumes of his rapid, pungent giddiness than René's barely formed thoughts were quashed once again, this time by Melzer speaking to him (perhaps to distract René from the candle, to keep him from turning back to it, perhaps, in addition, to recompose his face once more, as it were, a face whose ungoverned features his guest had seen for a few minutes), deflecting him as follows:

"I've been wanting to ask you something for a long time, Herr von Stangeler," he said, "and I hope you won't consider it indiscreet. Is Fräulein Grete your very first love, as they say, your first experience along that line?"

René clearly recognized for what it was the diversionary tactic the major was consciously or unconsciously deploying; he himself was supposed to serve as the lightning rod for a storm that had gathered over Melzer. More than that: Stangeler could now feel that the brief spell he'd experienced on the street an hour before was now furnishing distance in retrospect, dissipating mist and fog, cleansing the atmosphere. Given how clear his vision had grown, the possibility did not escape him that the major, for the sake of taking cover or retreating back into himself, might be applying a method he thought would result in opening the floodgates of his guest's loquacity. It's well known, by the way, that anyone who has spoken somewhat more volubly than usual at a party or said something animated or even witty, interesting, or stimulating will from then on be confronted with demands by all and sundry to pipe up once more for their entertainment, and if he doesn't, he will be queried outright: "Well, Herr X., aren't you the quiet one today!?" René had a hunch he'd unknowingly installed such a mechanism in the major that past Monday on the upper landing of the Strudlhof Steps, when he'd held forth with such vivacity and had fostered in Melzer a belief that such disquisitions were a matter of habit with him. (For this reason alone, if no other, it is always an act of stupidity to present oneself as anything other than an utter bore in company.) His vague suspicion, his faint sense of being warned, was very slight at first, still off on the mist-shrouded horizon of his inner perception, as it were, but it rapidly shifted front and center, directly into the beam of light illuminating a power of observation that now functioned effortlessly and lucidly, assigning everything its right place, displaying matters hardly pleasant or flattering in a rather amusing light, if only through the beam of truthfulness now shining down on it all. That was the feeling that came over him, and he was relishing it. And that was exactly why "the whole kit and caboodle he's got stored up" did not come "bursting forth all at once" (we always enjoy quoting the captain); instead, René stayed comfortably leaned back, totally at ease, and saw each aspect in its proper light, including, we might add, an article from a newspaper that had just arrived from Zurich that very afternoon and was standing out a little, since it was so new and crisp. But strangely enough it was completely obvious to him throughout that a certain someone—of whom there were two—would never be able to convey a genuine statement or pass on any genuine piece of news in the absence of any genuineness herself. The newly arrived item from Zurich, fresh and crisp, had turned in the twinkling of an eye into nothing more than a useless old dust-catcher, scrap paper (so these memoirs from the Middle Ages were exactly what the captain had called them, "ancient-history hogwash!"), something you could only keep shoving farther and farther off to the side until it's pushed beyond the horizon.

He finally answered in a slow, relaxed, laconic way, as if scrutinizing the backs of his words (because of possible contraband?) as they came out of him:

"On the physical level, not by any means, of course. Though what I didn't know previously was that the apparatus isn't automatic; it requires power from an outside source. And even today I don't know that as well as I should. Not every cell is aware of it. Not in anyone."

He fell silent. Melzer felt roughly dismissed. Instead of being able to draw the protective layer of René's volubility over his own ears, the lad had thrust some cold object between his neck and his collar, so to speak, and it was now sliding down his chest, uncomfortable and strange. The thought occurred to him rather clearly that he shouldn't have started out with Grete Siebenschein as a way of setting René in motion and that it would have been better instead to introduce some literary topic or other. But he wasn't versed in such things.

Then, however, Stangeler's words seemed to melt against his skin; the cold liquefied into warmth and began fitting itself to his bodily contours; moreover—though admittedly in his own way—he now understood. The connection to his own self was restored, and he answered with a question, totally involved again:

"Have you been seeing Fräulein Grete for a long time?"

"Four years," René said.

"And—please forgive me for asking these questions, but I'm doing it to a certain extent on my own behalf" (now I've got him! Who else but Melzer would ever even think of immediately announcing a change of venue, so to say, and all in good order?)—"and has the relationship met with your full consent or agreement the entire time? I mean: have you always considered it to be right for you? As far as I know that wasn't always the case, or was it?"

"Only as of this afternoon," said René in a tone seeming to communicate something absolutely commonplace.

"Did you spend the whole afternoon with Fräulein Grete?" asked Melzer, quite as if an affirmative answer from René would make clear this incomprehensible answer he'd just given.

"Five minutes only," said Stangeler.

At this point the conversation broke off, which will surely be understandable. Fresh chibouks. Fresh coffee. They lay back down.

Melzer wasn't lying just in a comfortable hollow there on the bearskin, however, but much more so in a pit he'd dug himself. And now, by contradicting Stangeler, he dug himself in even deeper:

"Excuse me," he said, "but I really can't believe that in a love relationship—if I may express it that way—there can be upheavals of any kind or fundamental changes . . . not ones deliberately brought about, anyway. Everything is bound to remain the same. Because the conditions don't change. Outside circumstance can only be changed if new possibilities arise. But that's usually impossible. I believe there might be only one exception."

"What would that be?" René asked, without moving.

"Getting married," Melzer answered. "Because then the love relationship stops being merely that. It seems to me a fixed point is placed."

"And do you consider that so crucial?"

"Yes," said the major.

He was surprised (at the exact same thing we are: at catching him for the first time—and of this there is no doubt—in the act of actually saying something, finding a way to express a general viewpoint, speaking on a theoretical level; had his burgeoning civilian mentality broken through the barricade of language?). He was surprised at the resoluteness with which he'd just spoken, and he felt underneath it an even deeper basis than experience and common sense provided. And at the same time he realized—perhaps for the first time in his life—about his own words that they were indeed his very own and not quotations, so to speak, like the statements little E.P. made, not simply copycat slogans and sayings like those opinions voiced at the outbreak of war in 1914 in the officers' mess at Trnovo on the Jelesnitza, what we might call shots of linguistic schnapps.

"I can't quite picture what you mean," said Stangeler, unsure of himself, feeling as he must that he'd been struck with a powerful blow. That came about unintentionally, for the major had intended to go in a different direction entirely, but René had blocked his path with the barrier of his curt answers. René had suddenly succeeded, meanwhile, in incorporating Melzer's fixed point into his Indian territory (it was the habitat of the *tropidonotus* Indian). He commented succinctly:

"We both mean the same thing, Major."

Here Melzer had no choice but to ask for a clarification, even though that seemed to him to mean veering even farther from the direction he'd originally meant the conversation to go in. But Stangeler kept it relatively brief—for him:

"Marrying a woman," he said, "entails taking upon yourself her personhood in its entirety, along with all the outward and inward circumstances of the relationship, the detrimental just as much as the beneficial. All of it, just as it is. Your own desires and wishes aren't going to revamp anything. From then on, you have this relationship in the same way a man has brown hair and blue eyes. You're given the power to observe the detrimental aspects calmly, even the hopeless ones, as far as I'm concerned. Your compass has led you to this place, and that entitles you to believe—or rather it obliges you to believe—that it will carry you right through it. When you clearly see the shortcomings in the light of truth and choose to live with them instead of rebelling against them, then they're no longer shortcomings, because you've gone to the heart of the matter. Besides, there's no way you can know of what use they might be to you. The captain once said to me that a stupid person who realizes his stupidity is demonstrating great intelligence by that token alone. Such a person would even be capable of asking the question—and probably would ask it—what actual significance his own stupidity is supposed to have, why it should have fallen to his lot. The very question places him outside his limitation. He can't get rid of it; he can't chop it off, can't amputate it. But every clear recognition has a strengthening effect, so I think he shouldn't dodge it, because that's exactly what always lends him the power to bear up under what he's come to recognize, whatever it might be. Except for certain borderline cases, perhaps. But these won't pertain to someone who has made a valid effort at the right moment. Life will not knock him flat just after his recognition dawns, and certainly not by means of it; what it will do instead is grant him enough range to savor the pleasure he takes in his recognition. The pleasure is enormous. And pleasure is needed for everything; it's as necessary to life as air. In everything, whether it be a well-aimed shot with an arrow or a moving funeral oration or the advance of a squadron for the attack. Only someone who feels pleasure is in command of the situation, and vice versa. As long as he feels pleasure, he's in command; life continues to grant him the range he needs. That pleasure is the sheer voluptuous ecstasy that comes about through the marriage of life with recognition. If it's lacking, then anything we know hangs in an empty room like charred rafters. But achieving recognition presupposes that we let a thing be whatever it wants to be, in keeping with its nature, without pushing and pulling it, tweaking and tugging, pecking at it, smoothing or straightening it, not to say trying to get rid of it altogether. If a teacher writes a formula on the board during the mathematics lesson, then the pupil must solve it as given and can't demand that $16b$ should be changed into $4b^2$ or $12xy$ should become $3yz$. He's got to calculate what's there, even if it turns out at the end that it wasn't an equation but an inequation causing a nonsensical postulation to result—which in turn is precisely what the teacher was trying to determine, I mean whether the pupil was confident enough in his ability to calculate that he would hazard that conclusion. The formula itself remains as intact as any maiden lady, however, and it's necessary to proceed step by step from it, and only it, as the starting point. No intellectual action can be fully executed except on an absolutely conservative basis. I know that today. In your way of speaking that would mean I married Fräulein Grete Siebenschein this afternoon."

"Not yet," said Melzer and fell silent. He was lying on his back. Stangeler's words, which were no longer at all unfathomable to him, were moving somewhere high above him in the room, like bright, foaming eddies and circles on the surface, while he lay here at the black-tinged bottom and looked up. Stangeler was lying next to him. He too was lying on the dark bottom and high up above him was what he was saying.

"You've struggled a great deal here," Melzer resumed, cautiously steering a path out of the *tropidonotos* reservation and back to his own concerns. "And so you ended up giving in. Accommodated yourself. You gave in to her inclinations. Which might have been the most natural course right from the start. Should people always give in to their own inclinations? Follow that signpost? Might there perhaps ensue a good deal less unhappiness in the end than if you resist?"

While it was now dawning on Melzer as he spoke that he was simply attempting to continue with another partner (but the real one!) his conversation with Herr E.P. from the Saturday before, it became clear from Stangeler's ensuing words that he felt misunderstood:

"I did not give in to my own inclinations; they weren't exerting pressure on me at the key point. Instead, I finally caught up with them. And now I trust this signpost, if that's what you care to call it. At any rate, I've been of the opinion since this afternoon that a person should and must follow it while interpreting the direction in which he's going. Anything else is revolution, a change in the assigned formula by the pupil's clumsy hand—a hopeless point of departure, that is. But as far as your 'signpost' is concerned, there's an important caveat to keep in mind, as I've recently found out."

Now at last the conversation was switching onto the track Melzer hoped it would; he felt very clearly how his discussion with E.P. on the evening of August 22 was being continued here and now and being taken by René a step beyond where that previous conversation had reached, a step his earlier interlocutor would likely have been incapable of taking. And here once again a wariness coming from his innermost chamber kept Melzer collected and self-contained, Melzer the old crab hiding under a stone. He ventured: "And what caveat might that be?" Not another word about it. Not a syllable more to be gotten out of him. Not another word about it. In all seriousness. As if it were a matter of staying alive, like a crab some boys might spot in a stream. But now Stangeler leapt before he looked, took the bait, jumped right in. How hard it is to do the opposite! Perhaps the very highest attainment the mind can reach, the one most worthy of respect. René did not achieve it. He lacked a suitably broad view. René, the lad who could refrain from at least the most egregious jabbering when he really had to—hadn't he said to Paula Pichler earlier that afternoon, "If I butt in and make a to-do, I won't see anything"!?—now intervened (just like Negria!), tinkered, exerted influence—almost force, for that matter—didn't hold his tongue, anyway, but now let it weigh in almost like the pointer on a scale.

"The caveat is," he said, "that the signpost, the compass, the magnetic needle, the whole contraption itself not become subject to distortion or malfunction, roaming instead of homing, fluttering instead of uttering."

"And what would throw it off or make it malfunction?" asked Melzer, already more confident; he could see that things were moving forward.

"Placing too much reliance on it," René answered.

Melzer was now feeling with uncanny precision how they were

lying underneath this discussion they were having, as it were, how it was drifting along in the bright light above them. He, Melzer, now found he was somewhere beyond either his military or his civilian mentality, or else that he was lying underneath his own mentality on the bearskin from the Treskavica, if one will. Because he had never before in his life been presented with any such state of being, he felt diffidence, almost awe, in its presence, and he thought of it as being evanescent, fragile as glass. He wouldn't have dared change his physical position by even the slightest movement, proving to us through the person of this ordinary man that to every genuine awakening of the spirit is given straightaway a condign physical manifestation of the mechanism that is the essential core determinant of said spirit. Melzer didn't move a muscle; he maintained a literally conservative position, to draw on Stangeler's term, so he was able—without lifting a finger— to put to use at once a piece of knowledge he'd just now acquired: people don't think by means of their heads and above their collar buttons alone (the way scholarly specialists do), but with their whole body.

He said nothing for the time being. He saw the smoke from the chibouks hanging over the bearskin in a straight diagonal line. He felt as if his sense of smell had suddenly grown keener, the wraithlike aroma still mounting from the Turkish coffee like light radiating from the dark corners of the room. He heard the streetcar approaching from far away, down below on Porzellan Gasse. The aeolian tone of lament was resounding in E.P.'s study too, where Stangeler had in earlier days come and gone at will, only to have the contact suddenly cut off one fine day, so much so that he was now as good as dead and gone. A picture of René could have hung on the wall as if of someone departed. Perhaps with a little slip of paper on the lower edge of the frame, with "picture" written on it. So that it wouldn't get mistaken for a serving tray or the desktop. It seemed to Melzer now as though René Stangeler had only really entered into E.P. since the day they made their break and went their separate ways, as if E.P. no longer had any external need for René, an expendable appendage that had been retracted, so to speak. Which was why he sometimes spoke from out of him—René from out of E.P., that is. The smoke above the bearskin gathered to a cloud. Then it dissipated. The streetcar had passed over the mountain peak of its own noise and was long gone by now. Far. Just faint traces still audible.

"Yes," Melzer said at last.

"Yes," Stangeler repeated and then went on talking. "That is the borderline, thin as a hair, one daren't cross, because that's where things begin to get really hopeless." He too, though rearranging his shoulders on the bearskin to be more comfortable, give the impression of speaking out of a twilight sleep in suspended animation, a genuine kèf, and it wasn't so much that he spoke the words as that they spoke him—and in the most flawless manner. "That's just it: merely bending over this apparatus disturbs the needle; the wind rising from our inclinations can't be consulted like a pocket watch. Every one of them proves only that any of them can come to the fore and make all the others invisible or that any one of them is just as capable of disappearing all of a sudden so as to yield place to a different one. The reality is that we've stepped too close to the machine, we've bumped it and pushed it without meaning to, yet it still shows no meaningful deviation, because it now lacks the current that would allow the needle to register an accurate determination. So we end up playing our inclinations against one another and measuring their comparative strengths. But they're constantly shifting, and they're all equally weak. And here we are, sitting right in the midst of them while fancying we're going to make decisions by continuing to follow this path of indecision and then looking only from the side, into the bargain, letting one measuring device take over from another. We've gone astray among machines; we've become thinking matter. Voltaire says somewhere in his *Lettres sur les Anglais*: 'I am a physical entity and I think—that is all I know. Shall I then ascribe to an unknown cause that which I can so readily ascribe to the sole effective cause I do know? Indeed, what man would be in a position to warrant without foolish godlessness that it is impossible for the Creator to endow matter with thought and feeling?' Oh yes, matter can think. But what it thinks will necessarily be insanity. The light of consciousness placed thinking matter somewhere or another among the rods and levers, the wheels and gears, but then moved away from the spot where it was providing moderate illumination of the complete workings in their interrelated functions only to have separate parts of the machinery shine out with harsh shadows, their perspective gro-tesquely distorted, while all the rest sinks into darkness. Like a room lit only by a candle placed in a corner and underneath a chair."

Melzer was following him (as we surely must know).

Stangeler now fell quiet. He lay totally motionless; even so, some-thing seemed to be agitating him, blowing words out of his mouth the way a draft of wind almost separates a flame from its candle.

"To me, Charles Baudelaire is absolutely correct in calling Voltaire a 'sermonizer for building superintendents, *prédicateur des concierges*,'" René added gruffly a few moments later. "The passage I just quoted is the dreariest sophistry. He first advances an absurdity and then states that to God, in whom he purports to believe, at least for the moment and ad hoc, nothing is impossible. And anyone who might not believe that poppycock is arraigned in advance for 'foolish godlessness.'"

Melzer was following him. He proved it years later through an ac-count of this conversation, a recollection that tallied precisely with René Stangeler's, incidentally, for which Kajetan von S. and Sectional Councillor Geyrenhoff can be adduced as witnesses.

"In the charming, by-no-means-disarming language of psychology," René continued in a somewhat gentler tone, "which always wears a white doctor's coat and banishes demons with a faint but constantly discernible whiff of disinfectant—in that soothing terminology, what's just been said would be framed as follows: Every class of functions and every individual mechanism within those functions is assigned a spe-cific gradation of luminance in the consciousness. Should this gradation be habitually exceeded, then we are approaching the limits of normal psychology and therewith drawing closer to the area of psychopathol-ogy. Expressed in a simpler term, albeit one more accurate if also more antiquated, this whole state of affairs is fornication. It is in actuality an illness and will therefore not fail to manifest symptoms in due course. All pathology is based on the simple fact that people have become too intimate with themselves: fornication, that is. It is the fundamental sickness of our time. We live in an age of unrestricted carnal knowledge."

Melzer temporarily slipped into conventional thinking. "I wouldn't have suspected you of holding such strict views, Herr von Stangeler," he said.

"I'm not speaking in moral terms here," countered René with noticeable exasperation. "If I favor an expression like 'fornication' over the argot of the soul-fixers, it's because my chosen word does have some such undertone, however, and admittedly does come close to a purely moral evaluation. I grant you that. And that's a mistake, if for the time being only, since it's merely a question of initially determining whether a given state of affairs exists or not. But of course it can't be just left at that. So even though I just now piped up with an expression like 'insufficient degree of illumination in the consciousness,' or something else reeking of carbolic, I would nevertheless—after eliminating the actual stench of the dead dog rotting somewhere by burying it (*prope sepulchrum canis*, the captain would say!)—I would nevertheless have to revert to the word 'fornication' at the dog's graveside."

Melzer offered no opposition. He didn't establish a critical viewpoint in this case any more than he would have if some odor or sound had unexpectedly manifested itself. Deep inside him was anchored the conviction that what Stangeler was saying to him here and now was meant to penetrate, to suffuse him, at once and to the most intense degree, just as the aroma of camphor had suffused him ten days before, or the organ-grinder's tune, both like broken spots on a raised floor on which he was walking skittishly, filled with disquiet. Whether or not what Stangeler was saying really held water scientifically or logically or in keeping with any other authoritative modality didn't concern the major. It flashed across his mind for a moment that precisely these kinds of considerations were completely beside the point here and now. It seemed to him, on the other hand, as if René were speaking directly from his—that is, from Melzer's—own situation and lending it words he himself would not be capable of imparting.

"And that is how our 'signpost,' to draw on your expression, becomes dislodged," René continued, "by jostling the mechanism, which throws something off and in turn causes the needle to twitch when it should remain completely at rest because no current's being transmitted to it. But in the ferrite rods of the electric motors there's something like a residual magnetism still present when they're switched off. Self-induction. When any piece of equipment—it doesn't matter what kind —still has its indicator lights working, operating on their own, apparently independent, then something unbelievable, incongruous, and bizarre comes into being and shows tenacious force. That is when, for instance, a man loves with unconquerable passion a woman he totally rejects. The needle has gone crazy. Thanks to our corrupt nature."

He grew quiet. It had a strangely soothing effect on Melzer that René didn't keep chattering on. That he paused. Spoke slower, still curt, weighing his words all the while. There was trust here, the major felt, not primarily in what was being said but more in the legitimacy of this whole situation.

"Very well. But who has an uncorrupted nature?" Melzer now asked. He really hadn't intended to say anything. The words seemed like a reflex motion of his hand, a slight gesture of warding off something.

"After Adam and Eve, nobody. But the essential point here is gradual movement, a first tiny step away from the insanity of our time—by which I mean fornication—and back toward the solid ground of genuine existence, toward reality, from which vantage point all the machines that have been so eerily illuminated emerge once more in the light of their interrelated functions and in part vanish from sight entirely. Being able to give up false evidential criteria—that's what it comes down to, because that's what distorts the space of consciousness, drawing into it things that don't belong there and twiddling anxiously with some gadget in a way that in every instance makes no sense whatsoever, no matter how brightly it's flashing, no matter how clear the display panel, because it's not getting any current. Force and coercion make problems that don't even exist come into being. But it's immensely difficult to give up false, anxiety-driven criteria of evidence. Doing so is a heroic deed."

Melzer didn't budge. He was lying on his back on the broad, soft bearskin, to be sure, but to him it was more as if he were stretched out along a narrow edge, balanced between two possibilities, on the border of two domains, either of which, depending on the side he chose, would send him tumbling downward; it seemed he had to decide which way he would fall—and then remain and take up residence there.

"Unless that happens," continued Stangeler, but speaking slower and slower, his momentum slackening, like the keel of a boat adrift among reeds or plants growing upward from the depths, "unless that happens," he said, "exigencies emerge, questions arise, problems come about (none of this with any basis in reality); everything gets tangled together, and separate objects form into a clump. The machine, after being illuminated by the wrong source for so long a time and cited for the evidence it supposedly provides, has gone mad, along with each and every one of its working parts; they're now just dragging us along behind them. *Nolentem fata trahunt.* But these aren't really *fata*, not genuine fates; they're mirages of fates. Fata morgana. Mere matter is thinking—damned if it isn't—and this is where the *prédicateur des concierges* is right. What it's thinking is madness, nonsense, but all self-contained and in proper order; both logic and reason, joining forces with whatever necessity is prevailing—and there will always be one!— have transformed themselves into Erinyes, Furies, and they start tormenting us. A wall of gadgetry closes thick around us, and an age unchaste to its very core hacks its way—aided by its putative 'scientific methods,' wielded as if they were screwdrivers and flat-nosed pliers— into this self-created jungle, so it can thin out something that owes its existence only to an excess of thinning out in the first place. This is how the technologically oriented 'sciences' come into being, including medicine, which ought to be tossed onto the scrap heap along with economics, sociology, statistics, and all the other spawn of fornication. Everywhere you look, people are seeking to seize, by grasping them directly, those things that in conformity with life's inner mechanics can be reached only in an indirect manner; people want to take and secure for themselves that which can only be added on. Nothing is given; everything is added on instead. Sheer logic, as least as long as it hasn't turned hopelessly demonic, can teach us that inasmuch as something has been added, something has to have already been there. A shelf for setting something down or a steady surface, I want to say. But men and women of today are standing with their arms completely full while they keep being handed new educational tools, radios, machines that can produce twenty-four thousand bottles an hour, new therapies, social progress, the most up-to-date administrative methods. Sooner or later everything will have to crash to the ground and be smashed to bits. That's what will happen to all the goods we acquire in this unchaste way, goods grabbed instead of being received as added dividends, and the security everyone's been chasing leads only to naked, whimpering fear."

It seems remarkable that when he later gave an account of that evening Melzer was able to reproduce René's harangues so accurately without exhibiting the slightest reaction to them, either at the time or later. It would surely have made sense to dispute at least the manifestly absurd parts. He could have pointed out that René was arbitrarily elevating his own improvised, patchwork psychology to a model of all history and thus attempting to throw open vistas onto a realm he himself was confined in. No such thought so much as entered the major's mind, however. Though it was—we'll flatly declare this right here and now—no longer for lack of a civilian mentality. A great deal had changed for him in the past week (and René had in fact seen correctly in front of the Stein House, when Melzer's face appeared to him somehow more rugged). His not contradicting—not a whimper either then or afterward—serves to prove the inadequacy of critical faculties and of that which is generally known as dialectics. And of course Melzer, like every other human being, thought (insofar as we can speak of such a thing in his case) in dichotomies. That holds true even when we're slipping and sliding through our *trópoi*. However, this was exactly the level he'd meanwhile just put behind him. The one on which he now situated himself has as its main feature that those occupying it take away from it whatever they can make best use of at the moment— stimulants, nourishment, poisons (René had a store of those as well) to promote their own growth, though it's not as if they're trying to clarify, discern, or determine anything. The major's spirit (and a major has one too; no need to shilly-shally about it) was healthy, and it went—or rather mounted—by natural order upward by degrees and stages toward the higher realms formed by dialectic and actual thought, albeit he by no means reached the highest. Crab that he was, our Melzer was no impostor whose soul had broken false-bottomed floors with holes where people could slip through as they like, where people don't read letters out of phony discretion, even when they could, but then steal them with a grab from below. A Royal and Imperial major observes the chain of command punctiliously, however, so there are no shortcuts from the piano nobile to the attic. After zooming through the *trópoi*, the dichotomies establish themselves, and people are stretched taut between them like a drumhead, which makes them more resonant: organ-grinder, camphor, Stangeler. Thinking comes later. No discussion till after maneuvers, not before. Yes, that's how it is with these latent geniuses: Ferdinand Schachl, Nohel, Melzer, *e tutti quanti rari rarissimi*.

"It's the demon of false evidential standards," René now said. "I'm considerably fonder of that expression than of 'inadequate illumination of consciousness.' Our whole psychology is disinfected demonology. Decontaminated, scoured, sterilized. But when the devil of topsy-turviness—'the imp of the perverse' is what Edgar Allan Poe calls it—when that imp jumps onto the back of a student at the musical conservatory, so that during an all-important test recital he suddenly has to think about how the next passage goes or about fingerings that have long since been automatic and abruptly breaks off a performance that had been unfolding masterfully—then it's that demon that's been shadowing him. I marvel more and more that our entire era doesn't simply grind to a halt."

He fell silent once more, completely now, meaning for quite some time. But the silence couldn't last; that was not allowed to be, for Melzer's hour had now come. The major prepared his entry into this new territory in all the right ways, starting by brewing fresh coffee and providing newly stuffed Turkish pipes. His awakening (civilian) mentality was joined without delay by insight into its mechanical workings, which entailed gently refraining from any misplaced contradiction; to this insight was added a savvy and indeed a sassy streak, something which we who know our boy Melzer as we do are well aware was never even remotely part of his makeup. Now, however, his being so totally different from René made clear to him his friend's addictive nature, Rene's susceptibility to narcotic substances, something which for Melzer had been merely an occasional, random indulgence from his younger years in the military and could never at any point have taken such deep root in him as it did in Stangeler, with whose way of living he was here and now, for the time being, joined as in matrimony. And with the delicious but pernicious coffee and the other aromatic substance, the blue one—behind whose veils the outlines of a distant city out of the

Arabian Nights, rather than actual reality, seemed at every moment to be trying to emerge—with all this taken together came Melzer's first advance, if we may grace his fumbling with a term so resolute and military-sounding:

"But what are we supposed to do now that nature's been corrupted?"

"First of all, to realize it and accept it as a disaster without trying to turn it into something positive. Second, to follow nature anyway. To grasp what it is that has us in its grasp. To sharpen the arrow to a point when it's already in flight; that's the skill we need, that's what makes the difference. Have we taken aim? Have we fired? Do we see the target? That shot is 'indirect,' as artillerymen call it. Even more: it's likely to miss. All we can do is not disturb anything."

"And would you for that reason get married as soon you possibly can?" Melzer asked in a way that was like someone tossing a new log onto the fire.

"Yes," answered René. Into that one syllable he now gathered and bundled anything that was trying to stick out or create a snag here or there, so to say, and he picked it all up like a backpack. The major felt that if they strayed even a hand's width off to the side from the narrow path of this conversation they would be stepping into the riotous undergrowth of rather vigorous demurrals. But that wasn't what he was aiming for. When he lay back down on the bearskin, the aromas of coffee and tobacco again filling the room, he at once looked somewhere above him, up toward the ceiling, for a point from which to restore seamless continuity to this peculiar discussion such that it would hover over them like a third party, as it were, aloft there in the brightness while they lay on the dark ground, such that it would whirl and swirl and foam there on the surface, actions they could keep constantly renewing through slight and cautious movements of their own.

But René opted out.

"Incidentally, Herr Melzer, I've been asked to convey an invitation to you for Wednesday, the ninth, just after the Nativity of Our Lady, or rather, to alert you to an invitation you'll be receiving," he said.

That startled Melzer, which on the whole isn't hard to understand, even if it made little sense at first; after all, he'd been for a walk that afternoon with Editha and Eulenfeld along the Danube towpath out to Nussdorf, where the view is broadened to the wider expanse of the main river past the canal, flanked with houses and factories, and Stangeler had come from Grete Siebenschein. At this moment, however, Melzer could see the aftermath of the conversation they'd had during the hour just past; he felt as if a breach had been made, one as wide as a barn door, in the bulwark surrounding him, which he'd preserved intact all summer long with such great toil, as if he'd been guarding a treasure, a capital that—to use Stangeler's term—had been only too evident at the same time ... A memory from the war years now surfaced, a totally meaningless trifle at the time but now broad as a whale's back, dripping with freshness, sparkling and shimmering with new meaning. In Prague (his mother, who passed away in 1918, had been living there for some time instead of in Innsbruck, so he'd spent part of his leave from the front in Prague) he'd boarded an express train out of Berlin and found a place in a compartment where no one was sitting but an artillery first lieutenant. This officer was traveling back from Germany; he was a metallurgist from the War Ministry, a reservist by the way, who'd been on assignment there, most recently in Hamburg, and that seemed somehow fitting for the man, since he looked like a ship's captain, and an English one at that, Austrian uniform or no. It wouldn't have been easy to say just what made him look English, but there was more to it than his tall, blond, slender figure. Perhaps his loose-limbed, sprawling posture or the somewhat easier cut of his uniform jacket. Or his shoes. His hands. The way he smoked. This first lieutenant and engineer had been sent to Hamburg to inspect some badly damaged German ironclads towed in after the Battle of Jutland, and he had described his impressions to Melzer: gigantic openings torn into the gray behemoths by shells from the heavy English naval artillery, vast gaping holes, crumpled flanks with warped, twisted, bulging sheets of metal around the edges. A train carriage could have driven right through, in or out; that was how wide the gaping breaches were. Something of the same kind was now gaping inside Melzer as he contemplated this unbidden image inside himself. A priceless treasure of self-discipline, of unremitting self-restraint melted away, crumbled, reduced to something childish and laughable, though laughable in a whole different way from how it would have appeared to the Lieutenant Melzer of

Trnovo, who generally stayed in the Hotel Belvedere in Vienna, or on occasion—in certain cases—in the center of town.

"Who's the invitation from?" he asked, after briefly crashing through several false-bottomed floors, all very different.

"From an attractive young lady named Paula Pichler, whom I've known very well for years, in fact, since I was just a lad. Frau Pichler wants to invite you along with Thea Rokitzer, with whom she's good friends—they're even related, I think—and I'm to be a guest as well. Herr Pichler, a master mechanic and foreman at the government printing press, will be there too. They have a little house and garden in Lichtental. Thea will bring you this invitation in person."

"That's really very sweet," Melzer said. He had a feeling as if something warm, even hot, were rising up inside his body cavities. There was something red at the same time, something he thought he'd known, or perhaps dreamed, for a long time. This was coming from the earlier image, however. He'd thought of it along with the demolished ironclads—did it blaze like flames pouring out of the parts that had been hit, or gush like blood into pools and streams? "But what could have given Frau Pichler the idea," he now asked, "to invite me to her home in spite of her not knowing me at all?"

"No doubt Thea's told her a lot about you," said Stangeler. "So that would make her want to meet you in person."

"I don't really understand that," said Melzer.

"Well, let's just wait and see," replied Stangeler in passing. He was more or less half blind to whatever it was that made Paula tick and he wasn't anything more than her emissary here. But that might be exactly the reason he was handling this matter with such skill—it was totally a side issue.

"Thea will probably bring it by herself," he added. "You can ask her for more details then."

This last little barb, not in the least intended by René to be one, caught and stuck in the major's gorge. He could feel it pulling at him for the rest of that evening and even into the following morning.

And already causing a first crack in the delicate, fragile mirror of their time together and their conversation up to that point. They were dispatched to their separate ways now, dropping away and retreating to where they belonged, René Long Ears and Melzer the Crab (who had by and large held his own quite well). It really seemed to the major that the room and everything in it was moving in closer, rooted more solidly, standing more squarely, as if it had been in some sort of drifting or floating motion up to now. One last swirling ribbon of smoke drifted down to the empty coffee cups as Stangeler got up, amazingly enough without using his hands or arms but merely by uncrossing his legs, a feat of dexterity the major admired. But he didn't say anything. As René was preparing to leave, the major didn't feel very keen about staying there by himself, so he offered to go part of the way with his friend.

"I'm going to walk," Stangeler said. "Via the Steps."

That seemed practically self-evident to the major.

When they realized the time, they were more than a little astounded that it was only ten past ten. They made their way along the main gateway of the palace and onto Liechtenstein Strasse, while the slightly cooler and totally calm night air lay like a garment around their faces and limbs. As they came closer to the plashing of the fountain at the lower end of the Steps, they could see in the bright glow from the six lanterns how the whole ensemble mounted upward, two lanterns each at top and bottom and one each, entwined in green, where the ramps turned. The light was strong enough at any rate that it kept the moon, grown full this very day, from having much visible effect; only when they'd reached the top and turned around did they notice that the gleaming disc—it seemed cold, far away, and small—had risen to their right over the rooftop of one of the tall buildings on Pasteur Gasse, partly obscured by branches and leafage but glimmering through them. The Steps lay empty. Melzer could almost feel gaping into the mixture of moonlight and electric light the demolished place in that circular wall, that barricade or bulwark behind which he'd been sheltering for months. At the same time there grazed up against him, hard and from the side, his interactions and his discussions with René (even though there had been a grand total of two only, the first here on the Steps, they had by no means failed to establish a bond). The two stood side by side in silence for a while, and their lingering here together silently seemed to forge a stronger bond than any spoken word could have.

Melzer recalled springtime and how they had stood here in the same place with Editha. There was no longer any putting matters aside, shunting things off, or hoarding anything. Whatever had been hoarded, whatever treasures were weighing him down—these now had to be given away bountifully to make room for new developments. They shook hands, and the major somewhat furtively watched Stangeler as he went, slowly making his way along Strudlhof Gasse, deserted now, crossing a bright moonbeam that shone onto the sidewalk over the grounds of the Palais Liechtenstein. Then Melzer turned back and went down the Steps, ramp after ramp, and felt for the first time, now that he was alone, the presence of greenery in the night, as if that aroma had required complete silence and solitude to manifest itself. And indeed, the Steps once more contrived to be altogether deserted in spite of an hour not at all advanced.

Standing the following morning at the tea tray Frau Rak's domestic had brought in, the major was suddenly struck by the thought that René Stangeler lacked any credibility whatever, was in fact going his merry way outside the realm of credibility altogether. Melzer slipped, in a sense—had it caused physical motion, he would have spilled his tea—and turned a kind of corner that took him over the particular delicate edge along which he felt he was being led. The word "dreamer" popped into his mind. He wasn't feeling especially well as he now gulped down the self-concocted remedy meant to free him from his speculations. He continued drinking the strong, dark tea. It didn't quite want to settle, to go down smoothly, to calm him.

In addition, there was something else that had been persistently irking Melzer. At some point in the course of the previous evening—wasn't it toward the end, when they were on their way to the Strudlhof Steps?—René voiced his surprise that the major hadn't taken part in the funeral cortege of the deceased field marshal Conrad von Hötzendorf, which had taken place that afternoon. The crowds had no doubt been drenched by the downpour around three o'clock. Melzer had said nothing in return, not a word. He possessed the invaluable trait of being able to keep silent in moments of sudden inner confusion or ambivalent emotion (while others fritter away any chance of reaching clarity precisely because they're impelled to open their mouths). He was of course not aware of this important attribute of his.

In his office, around ten, a lady was announced who wished to speak with him.

Melzer was in a room off to the rear, dictating a letter. Interrupting himself was not very feasible at this point, and he made his mind up to see the job through. So he told the receptionist to ask if the lady would kindly wait for just a short time; being a good-natured Zihaloid, who had announced this unusual visit with a measure of zeal, he answered, as he always did, "Yes, Major" (never "Yes, Councillor"), and disappeared.

There was no more postponing the end of the letter, meanwhile, and while René was now undergoing a certain amount of rehabilitation in Melzer's eyes, his own situation concerning Thea now reconfigured itself as more a fatherly phenomenon and thus appeared for the time being, cocooned in this way, to be totally innocent.

He went out. The clerk, sitting in an adjoining room Melzer had to pass through, nodded to and opened one side of a double door leading to a kind of entrance hall that belonged to the records department, although nobody ever sat there. It was nothing more than a storage room for less important stacks of files, printed matter, and supplies. Editha, standing at the opposite end of the bookcases with her back to Melzer, turned around and came down the length of the room toward him, moving along the side with the shelves, since the middle part was taken up with tables pushed together to create a large surface on which a great many packages had been placed, all identically wrapped in white paper and arranged in two vertically crossed rows for some unknown reason. The sun, which shone here only in the early part of the day, wasn't quite gone and was casting white lines along the tables, in strong contrast to the dominant brown and gray in the room. Responding to this unexpected development as if throwing on a garment in a rush, before he could find the sleeve openings, Melzer moved quickly toward Editha, and because she didn't walk at a slow pace, either—lighter and faster than most women—they met halfway down the length of the narrow gap in the expanse of tables. Oddly enough, their whole manner of approaching each other like this contained for Melzer a presentiment of something decisive that would make the real situation plain when they met. Editha looked fresh and almost strange; she was wearing white, which brought out her blond hair even more. And he could see—could see very clearly and with no chance to avoid it—how her gaze was holding his, even at a distance. He sensed to a degree the "gravity of the situation," very similar to what he'd felt the evening before standing next to René Stangeler on the Strudlhof Steps, and for an inexpressibly tiny fraction of a second, that red from the evening before was also present once again, but brighter and gleaming like patent leather. Now she was with him.

But it all vanished at once when they began talking up close; the only thing remaining was the major's need to say yes to whatever she was now proposing so briskly and cheerfully, to agree at once, to deny her nothing, not to withdraw into himself. Everything inside him stood open before her, as wide as a barn door; no trace of barricades, bulwarks, circular walls, fortifications, but only the desire to hold her there for another short while, to keep her from departing right away and leaving him alone.

But she was gone after two minutes anyway. For whatever reason, she and the captain hadn't been able to reach Melzer on the phone that morning, but they wanted him to know that Eulenfeld would have an automobile at his disposal this coming Saturday afternoon and evening, lent by an acquaintance; or by a customer, if it was through a business connection; or by one of those American medical doctors he hobnobbed with—who ever knew exactly what was what with the captain?!—and they very much wanted him to come along with them on a jaunt somewhere to the outskirts of the city, so Melzer should please not make plans for Saturday or commit to any other engagement. The captain wanted this all to be arranged with Melzer as of right now.

"And last week you were gone all of a sudden," Editha had said.

He fancied that her white and gold glow was still present in the room. He looked past the bright lines on the packages. The door had just shut behind Editha. Of course Melzer had promised to go along for the ride on Saturday.

Half an hour later Thea Rokitzer was announced. She even sent in a visiting card, which Editha Schlinger hadn't considered necessary. We take note how much of a rush Paula was in to get Thea moving. In fact, she had gone to see her right after the get-together with Stangeler, taking a detour on her way home so she could stop off on Alserbach Strasse, and there Thea was, sitting in that back room opposite the well-known sideboard. What followed wasn't easy; Thea put her back up. Paula's authority soon won out, however, and the meek little lamb promised to follow her older friend's plan, though it wasn't going to be simple. Yes, the very next morning at ten! Decent manners called for delivering an invitation in plenty of time. And Paula wanted to entertain her guests on the day after the Nativity of the Blessed Virgin; that would be this coming Wednesday, September 9 (we must say she had good luck with the weather, too, though just barely! The holy day itself was cool and unpleasant, but it wouldn't have been convenient anyway because of family obligations; on Wednesday, though, her husband would be off during the day, since he was scheduled to work all through Tuesday night at the government printing press). Paula seemed to have reached a level of decisiveness in this whole matter that requires no transitional or intermediate stages or gently ascending ramps of postponement but instead sets the short boarding planks right smack-dab into the business at hand and immediately lowers the drawbridge between inside and out.

The Zihaloid proved to have a remarkable feel for delicate nuances when he informed Melzer with subdued eagerness—Melzer having resumed dictation—that he had in the meantime shown the young lady into the major's own office (inventory was going to be taken in the room used by the records department, starting at ten o'clock—that was the ostensible reason); two ladies calling on the major on a single morning, whereas he had never received visitors of any kind during business hours—that seemed to suggest extraordinary doings (and quite correctly, if we may be allowed to say so!). Be that as it may, the overriding impulse of even the Lower Zihalism when confronted with new and hitherto unanticipated contingencies will always be to cause form to triumph over content (a significant cultural impetus), which can also be brought about by amplifying the content to the dimensions of grandiose baroque drama, whereupon the incident simply stages itself. While the Zihaloid was thus weaving state secrets around door and corridor, then, Melzer went in to Thea, which is to say into his own office.

There she was. And absolutely fit to knock him over with a feather. So charmingly pretty. It's not through any definite knowledge, but rather through surmise only when we say that Paula Pichler had stood outside Thea's door that morning and inspected her from head to toe, as it were. Our surmise has quite a bit of plausibility, though, as does the further hunch that sending a visiting card in to the major had been Paula's idea. Look a little closer and you almost can't help but believe it.

The little lamb fulfilled her assignment just so, all neat and tidy. Even if she hadn't been able to bring it off, though, but had gotten stuck and merely said "baa, baa," there is no question that she would have met with success anyway. Melzer stood amazed at her transparency, at those shelves and compartments made of glass, and his failing to see just those items on display that might concern him can only be attributed to a particular optical occlusion that conveniently prevented him from noticing what was being added on for him here and leaving in dark shadow something that was as clear as daylight to Paula Pichler (a bona fide "adequate illumination of consciousness," to use Herr Nose-in-the-Air René's term). But this was the exact interval—during which they'd been silent for a little bit and he simply kept looking at her in a friendly way while keeping her hand in his—at which (according to his own later statement) he felt something close to what Paula had already discerned; and much as he knew about and could now see the disarray others had created in the glass cases, it struck him at this very moment, or split second, like a bolt of lightning, he later stated, that just then, strangely enough, he understood in a flash (a streetcar below on Porzellan Gasse had just gone over the mountain peak of its own noise, which was now subsiding but would soon cause E.P.'s study to resound with an aeolian tone)—he understood what a virgin really was. Imagine somebody discovering this in an office suite at the general headquarters of the Austrian Tobacco Administration! Besides, she wasn't one anymore, not de facto. The person who really had it sized up right, on the other hand, was the Zihaloid, the office clerk: it truly was a moment of intense baroque drama on a grand scale for Melzer, if entirely an internal one. And the staging ensued at once; he was standing in profound awe before the visitor who had called on him. This went beyond Zihalism, of course. But Melzer didn't feel it. He wasn't a Zihaloid. No, he was an infantryman instead and was now standing—not very securely at the moment, to be sure, unsteadily, in fact, as if on precariously rising ground—standing on his Greek-statue legs: and he swore to himself that he would rather die than place something inside those glass cases that couldn't be looked on with respect.

He very happily accepted the invitation.

She left.

She was gone.

She had passed along. It had an aeolian sound. It whizzed along. It echoed through all the rooms.

 Melzer slumped down at his desk. He had a hard time making his way over the peak of the mountain thrust up by the surging movement inside him. He was fighting this rearguard battle honorably so that blind panicked flight and total dispersal wouldn't ensue; he posted lookout troops.

And little by little, with difficulty, he got clear of the enemy.

The enemy.

Baa, baa!

That same afternoon, René Stangeler was on his way up to see Grete Siebenschein and could hear as he stood in front of the apartment door that it was her footstep quickly approaching through the hallway, not the maid's, not Grete's mother's. "We're totally alone, René," she said, putting her arms around him. They lingered there, embracing, just behind the door, which she'd closed.

She couldn't make any definite commitment for Sunday, Grete said, and not for the holiday on Tuesday either, because Titi would just then be back from Paris; but on Wednesday, after the Nativity of the Blessed Virgin, she would really love to get out into nature with René for the whole day, if possible; she was really craving that. She hoped the weather would be better, warmer. Her father had scheduled a completely free day for her, as compensation, so to speak, for all the strain of the day before, Wednesday. Just a long walk through lots of woods! And they could simply take something to eat with them, along with tea or coffee. All right? She was looking forward to it. How would that be? Maybe a hike through the Animal Park at Lainz. All the way to the tavern called the Hirschg'stemm.

Meanwhile, they made their way inside the apartment and wound up in Grete's room. The very moment René stepped inside, a room he was used to but that still struck him every time as being brand-new— tall black bookcase crammed full; over it a colored reproduction of Giorgione's *Sleeping Venus*; next to that, a wide, embroidered old bellpull, only a decorative touch, of course—this moment of entering the room and being greeted and surrounded by these additional garments of his beloved, so to say, brought to its conclusion for René a thought that the unexpected appearance the previous evening of Major Melzer at the entrance below had immediately quashed—it was that a flat-out decision would end up crushing equally flat anything cross-grained in him, exactly as a steamroller presses the asphalt smooth. "Good," he said. "I'll stop for you on Wednesday morning, early, and we'll stay out all day until it gets dark!" They embraced again and kept holding each other. She didn't say a word about the day before, but it was shining in her eyes just the same. Everything was happening all at once in René's mind, meanwhile: slight alarm at Grete's having chosen Wednesday, the feeling of a loose end tied up from the previous day's thought, the leap over the obstacle in his path (with slackened reins— all he would need to do was call Thea Rokitzer or the major later on and then dash off a few lines of explanation to Paula), quick agreement to Grete's suggestion.

Something else happened, something much mightier, so to speak.

Thanks to the closeness of their physical contact—Grete had sat down in a chair and René was sitting in front of her on the thick carpet, his head on her knee—he suddenly felt come over him for the first time (the first time in his life) the gigantic (yet it could make a person frantic) good fortune of being with another to have and to hold: the deeper encroachment of her body, in a sense, with its natural charms, weapons, armaments, outworks, and bastions—in engaging with which he had up to now essentially never made camp and conducted reconnaissance from any spot other than a distantly external one, always in comparatively bright light, keeping separate objects in view—encroachment past an inner boundary line that had not once been crossed up until today. His hand lay on her knee, and now he felt as if the fabric of her dress were melting away, as if the round part of her knee were growing into the hollow of his hand, even as if they were one and the same. Something about to envelop them both began slowly but forcefully descending from overhead (he was in fact picturing it as an enormously large tea cozy now settling on and covering him and Grete). He was sitting quietly on the rug in front of her but at the same time was restraining his own strength, which he knew held the charge of a live mine that would explode outward from its storehouse at the first sign, however slight—but he didn't give her one. He commanded himself not to stand up, to tower over Grete, to arch over her with his powerfully heaving chest, whose power alone, combined with no more than a quarter turn of his left arm, would suffice to squeeze the breath out of delicate, classically Hellenic, slender-throated Grete Siebenschein. He was sitting quietly on the rug and remaining quiet as he ascertained movement, across a now open border, of forces which it was not his frenzying good fortune to have and to hold: long streams of migratory hordes, clans and tribes of Aphrodite: the Tribe of Hands, gently curved and skilled in plucking the lyre, the Tribe of Shoulders, as if made of white milk glass; peaceable folk, folk who feared their gods; the Tribe of Breasts, as many as there were of the many nights of love with Grete through the many and varied years, countless, always different, here in shadow, there in light, here serene and rounded, there in rampant power when a garment dropped. The Tribe of Feet, ever on the move throughout the years, those traipsing and tripping pertly along, those doughtily, stolidly standing their ground, those unshod and foolish, those good and kind, those little heart-feet keeping pace. The inscrutable, innumerable Peoples of Loins and Thighs emerging from nights so very varied, not one of which resembles another amid this tribe, in great part almost priestly and shrouded in mystery. He was sitting quietly on the rug while the vast cohorts of the goddess went on surging and swelling; his strength lay deeply buried, under explosive pressure in the farthest corner of his storehouse, and it continued looking with wide round eyes at what kept on coming at them until they were daunted; for they were coming for the eyes, striding directly toward them.

No bow was tensed. No shot from an arrow to pierce to the marrow.

If we look at it rightly and may speak impolitely, then we would have to say that Melzer had made his way into dreadful company on that Saturday, September 5, and into chilly weather as well; just after the first of the month something close to a cold wave had set in and kept on until the Nativity of Our Lady, after which it yielded to two warmer and sunnier days.

That Thursday, for some time after Thea's departure, the Zihaloid clerk had tortured Melzer gently but cruelly, by the way, in a manner possibly reminiscent of certain extremely refined Chinese methods of execution, one of which involves causing water to fall drop by drop onto a man's shaved head at exactly the same spot and spaced by exactly the same time interval, resulting in madness and death by this unbloody means. The Zihaloid effected something similar through constant mild grumbling (not unrelated to the grousing and grumbling audible from Thea's father as she was preparing to go off to Baron von Eulenfeld's evening party on Saturday, August 20—"*anni huius*," the captain had said, or "*anni currentis*," meaning 1925). And what was spinning the gray, Zihalistic thread of anxiety inside this bureaucratic functionary? The recent incidence of calls by those two ladies, mayhap?! Not a bit of it! Quite to the contrary, for that matter; those occurrences, far outside the usual course of official business as they were, had shone out as bright spots, beams of light inside the minor bureaucrat hereunto appertaining, and had made no slight contribution—attributable to the exercise of an Old Franconian knightly *courtoisie* manifested by smiling, bowing, escorting, opening doors, stepping backward so punctiliously—to warming his heart. And making it young again! This is how far the warming effect reached: back into the distance of the years! Back to Sunday evenings on crowded platforms entwined with grape leaves, returning home from drinking the wine these grapes had made; and her warm arm in his. And he had meant something to her; her eyes were glowing a bit, looking up at him. Ah well, a young fellow! Back then a light had been shining far off, like the tips of greenery shining in spring over the wrinkly walls of small city garden patches. In between lay so many high wrinkly walls and low smooth fences thrust across our path during the stages of our lives, as they're called— all of those that we don't go ahead and live are cut off! Basically these are nothing but spiteful remarks.

The problem now was that the payroll authorization forms for the office help and the cleaning women, already signed by the major, had gone missing. The functionary had just been holding them in his hand—not the cleaning women, but the slips for the bookkeeping department—and they were still there when he had shown Editha in, but then he'd set them down somewhere, perhaps before he'd scurried off to announce the lady. Perhaps in that records room. But the flunkies now occupied in taking inventory there, vertically busy climbing up and down stepladders, horizontally busy shuffling files with dexterity, stoutly denied seeing any such documents and showed no inclination to interrupt their rituals and their calling back and forth. But the loss of the payroll slips was a stain on the man's honor somehow, no matter how often the major might say, "Enough, Kroissenbrunner. Please don't keep going on about it. Just write out the things again and report to bookkeeping that the only valid authorization is the one with today's date. Then get a receipt in duplicate, and that will take care of it." But the major had already signed the forms! So you couldn't just call them "things." They were official documents. They bore the major's signature: Melzer, Councillor. In the military, as Kroissenbrunner could still remember very well, situations like these are always made as simple as a kick in the pants. But here a mistake of this kind—*his* mistake, Kroissenbrunner's, his own incompetence—took the words "punctuality" and "meticulous performance of duty" and robbed them of the dots on the *i*'s and the crosses through the *t*'s. It made them deficient. The phrase "report to" had been repugnant to him since his days in the service as well. However, he respectfully acknowledged the major's use of the term. He had no choice but to fill out the forms (the payroll slips for the cleaning women) again. And when he was then forced to present them to the major for his signature—a second time!—("There we are; now you can calm down, Kroissenbrunner," said Melzer, quickly scrawling his name), the man felt a pang. It was one of those poor pangs a little angel at once enters with unimaginably detailed precision into a thick, snow-white book in the records department in heaven, making the entry so exact for the express purpose of offering future solace to all the Kroissenbrunners of this world (and to every latent genius of every kind and stripe), sitting as he writes not in business attire but on rosy-cheeked little buttocks.

What galled Kroissenbrunner most, when it was all said and done, what rankled him most deeply, was recalling those figures in the records room as they scuttled up and down and darted hither and yon—their impassivity, their way of barely listening, their speaking in mere scraps— in any event, their blatant unconcern, shown by their not even taking the trouble to look first: "No, nothing was lying here; we didn't see anything." Naturally he'd squeezed past the ladders, with their spidery legs; naturally he'd slithered among the horizontal shifters and shunters evenly placed around the tables (it wasn't easy; he jostled them impatiently) so he could look for himself. He didn't mind disturbing them. After all, they had made it as clear as day—and what a disgrace it was—how unfailingly someone who really needs to get something done will encounter blank stares and shrugged shoulders from those around him, their only reason for turning their attention to someone else's mishap at all being the chance it gives them to relish not being involved. And uninvolved they indeed were, these—pencil pushers, bean counters, ticket takers, since their purely menial tasks here in these entryways and storage rooms had nothing even remotely to do with preparation of records or any other kinds of documents but instead only with boxes of new pencils, pen holders, paper clips, with reams of white scrap paper, with typewriter ribbons and with miscellaneous blank forms and printed sheets; and assuming a few of these items might be missing, then they'd just be crossed off the inventory list as damaged, and that's it! No new forms, no second effort ("that will take care of it," the major had said; maybe so, in the army, anyway...), no need to obtain a second signature again.

No pang.

You can really stop going on about it now, Kroissenbrunner.

Somehow, the group was really dreadful; (the one Melzer was with on Saturday). The group, we say, not its individual elements. They were so only in part. And if, as is well known, every group is defined mainly by the lesser members present, it was very far from being obvious just who those might be. And most certainly not considering the quality and quantity of the constituent elements. Organic chemistry, a science no one could ever claim was uniformly and completely pleasant smelling, prefers for that very reason to make use of what is called structural formulas, graphic representations of the way one element has bonded to another, that is of molecular compounds apparently identical when notated as chemical formulas but revealing differences, through geometrical illustration of precisely how their atoms are arranged in three-dimensional space, that would otherwise not be manifest; only by this method can specific characteristics be accounted for. There would have been no other way to proceed in this case, either. Elements like Sectional Councillor Geyrenhoff; or Frau Camy (Camilla) von S., née Schedik; and her husband Kajetan, too, as far as I'm concerned; and Dr. Negria, while we're at it; all of them can be described as quite spruce, decent, and well turned out, in and of themselves, plus olfactorily lavendulous, potpourrious, eau-de-colognous, or labdanumous. But a sectional councillor and chronicler who with his *ad-notam*-taking beady eyes* perched on stalks minutely scrutinizes the decay of a marriage in its last phase (placing it on the record, more *zihalistico-austriaco-hispanico leviterque* grousing*ans et* grumbling*ens*); the decay between Camy and Kajetan, putrefaction in itself; the sweat lightly dripping onto Angelika Scheichs-beutel from the ceaseless groping of that handsome Negria—still the bountiful patron of the arts, but the curtain was about to come down—much though that whole affair was at the stage of drying up, now arid, thinner, compacting wet strata of beach in Kritzendorf and Greifenstein

---

*For this expression, which links to a direct oral tradition, thanks are due to the unforgettable Anton Kuh, *grand enfant terrible de la littérature*.

together like a sand rock (Sandroch), constantly evoking memories of the high summer just past and of Scheichsbeutelian gropings and grabbings, which as of the season in question had reached their zenith: considering all of this will make it easier to understand why organic chemistry must draw on structural formulas and cannot always have a pleasant odor; to understand in addition why similar configurations also need to be used in psychology or the locksmith's shop of the soul; and finally, to understand how it was that the group Melzer had joined on Saturday was somehow dreadful.

And above all—much more numerous than the major might have been expecting. If what he'd had in mind was that he'd be taking a little ride out into some greenery with Editha and Eulenfeld, *tout simplement*, to Rodaun or Kalksburg, passing through one of the gates of the Animal Park in Lainz, taking a walk and then having dinner with them at some place like the Rote Stadl, he was very sorely mistaken. What came pulling up in front of the captain's building with motors roaring, making a racket on the stairs, hooting and hollering, yelling and shouting, and then, just before they all drove off—three automobiles—one and all changing places (everything taken *ad notam* by Frau Wöss): all this must have given Melzer the impression he was joining a convoy or an expeditionary force.

He took the last car. Not took as in driving it; he was being driven instead. The captain sat up front at the wheel, somebody new next to him with hair like a firecracker going off, it was so violently yellow. Hydrogen peroxide doesn't explode, though. The captain was driving with large, thick, yellow leather gloves (not buttoned), no hat, hair (grown considerably thinner) flying, and monocle. He flung the car around corners behind the others. Melzer was sitting in the back of the sleek, narrow car with Editha. He didn't look at her from the side, nor did he keep his eyes lowered to the red patent leather of the upholstery. They were sitting half turned to each other (and falling into each other, depending on how the captain swerved and swayed).

The front car was driven by Höpfner, the jingle-monger, at that time head of propaganda for a major shipping company.

Off they went, to somewhere or another, zipping away with engines aroar. Whisked away from an intolerable situation, from painful and almost menacing feelings that rose up inside him for a girl much too young, much too beautiful. Only as he was escaping did the gateway now standing open—broken wide open, really, just a short time before—make any sense or seem to be the right thing. (The major had of course completely forgotten who had been most responsible for flinging this gateway open; he didn't link cause and effect; he didn't name him inwardly; he didn't cite René in a footnote, as we just did with Anton Kuh. If all violations of copyright law were prosecuted in life as they are in literature, all the legal systems in the world wouldn't be enough to process the resulting lawsuits, to clarify the unceasingly reciprocal networks of borrowing in the marketplace of our ideas.)

But even on the towpath along the Danube Canal that past Wednesday, as he'd been strolling back from Nussdorf with the captain and Editha, his eye following the river's rapid streaming and surging: even on that afternoon Melzer had grieved at feeling that the way he'd conducted himself all summer—behaving untowardly, in more than one sense—was beginning to bear predictable fruit. He was forced to accept that it was really and truly of his own doing. She seemed to him to have changed, as if she'd caught a chill in her soul, walking along so tight-lipped, and not beside him, either, but on the other side, next to Eulenfeld. Melzer could blame nobody but himself—his the deed, his the repercussions. He was forced to accept it. Far worse for Melzer than merely having missed something, however, was the threat of possibly losing a world of feeling that could revitalize and warm him, of losing some yearning or substance inside himself as well. So instead of turning cold and becoming free—through the withdrawal, the cessation, the receding of an allure that lay in her wish and desire to have him and only and completely him—through the receding of this allure he did not turn cold and become free but felt alarm and fear instead, because something had broken away from him and was missing; an empty place came into view…

The contents of which, charged with energy as they had once been, he would have liked to have in his possession now more than ever. While fleeing. Meek little lamb on his tail! Baa, baa!

But it was able to pass over him. This tormenting emptiness was able to close, to be filled back in, to bear his weight once more. Singling out this one isolated aspect of a larger feeling was causing Melzer to overreact, to exaggerate (and putting a single name to anything is an exaggeration, a segregation of objects from the river of life; for that matter, we're already guilty of overemphasis simply by fixing our sights more sharply onto any one given thing). In the meantime, as they were riding along, even though half turned toward each other, even though not seldom flung together (whenever the captain made his car zoom around curves to keep up with the other vehicles), that emotion Melzer had felt by the rushing water of the canal was trying to come back; it seemed as if something were forcing him and Editha apart; it was even as if he could see sticking out from whatever half-mumbled and trivial replies she gave the tip of some sharp instrument pointing right at him. And that was exactly what cooled him down quickly and totally, as if doused with cold water; his rejoinder to such tiny but perceptible jabs consisted, strangely enough (but this is no small matter!), of looking at Editha Schlinger with much greater sharpness, to the point of tarnishing the halo required to see something in its entirety, to feel its magic; whereas nothing more is needed to ruin the effect than to perceive where the tarnish has removed the varnish, uncovered an imperfection that now stands out, say on the face, like a nostril too ruddy or some other small part of the whole effect, a slightly discolored incisor next to its porcelain-white brothers or the minute little lines drawn by the years and just converging around the eyes, tracks worn smooth as they keep transporting on schedule the trains of events that are our characters.

Nonetheless, everything changed once more when they were walking side by side among the trees, and all of a sudden she spontaneously emerged from her withdrawn, frosty bearing (whose effects had perhaps not escaped her); she grew animated in her speech and asked Melzer a number of questions, which made him have to raise the lid on the whole keyboard of his memory and keep every octave, the high and the low, tuned and within reach; he played them constantly anyway, consciously or unconsciously, day in and day out—this was how it had become for our major in the course of the years, especially as of this past summer, and even more particularly since Saturday, August 22. An incredibly long time had passed from then until today, September 5, a period that it was impossible to contain within the calendar space of exactly two weeks. It assailed him now like something utterly, entirely unfathomable, like a miracle. Among other questions, she asked him (and in fact she didn't *say* anything; she just kept up a barrage of questions) about Konietzki, the "dethroned Polish king," and whether Melzer still remembered Edouard von Langl and knew what might have become of him.

"I saw them both not so very long ago," said Melzer, "on the afternoon of Friday, August 28, to be specific." She looked at him, somewhat perplexed by this exactness, which didn't fail to astonish him either. Suddenly he detected it, that tormenting light inside him he'd been starting to grow accustomed to over the past few days, and he remembered when it had commenced, but without quite putting his finger on it. It was more as if someone had brought it to him, placed it into his inner being, and then installed it permanently! Evidence! Implacable, but at the same time he was glad to be suffering under it. And an untested but entirely certain certainty arose regarding this one point—that she wasn't the wrong one, she of whom Stangeler had spoken on Wednesday. Meanwhile, the recording instrument was still running, as far as time just past was concerned:

"I think it was almost surely Konietzki, by the way, who bumped into you on the Graben on Monday morning the week before last and greeted you," he said. "You just didn't recognize him, and then you couldn't think of his name—but neither could I when you told me about it during our strange meeting on the Strudlhof Steps. Then on the Friday after that, there was a large crowd of acquaintances from the old days in the Café Pucher; we got to talking about everything under the sun, so I forgot to ask Konietzki about it."

"That could well be," she said. "But I didn't recognize him at all, so it probably wasn't just that I couldn't think of his name. It was more that he didn't look like anyone I'd ever known." She kept her eyes fixed on the path. It was wide and straight as it led with slight ups and downs through a stand of birch trees. "You see," Editha added nonchalantly, "I had nearly the same thing happen with that Budau woman at the casino in the City Park. I mean Ingrid Schmeller. I told you about it. Ancient history. You don't always remember things or get them right.

Maybe because you don't want to be forever reminded of what's past and gone." She said these last words slowly, almost dramatically, though not very loudly; instead, it sounded as if she were softly lamenting.

The tree trunks were awash in light. As Melzer and Editha looked, their gaze extended far and deep into these woods that dropped off gently from both sides of the crest along which they were walking. It seemed to Melzer that he was apprehending Editha's whole nature with its dimensions extended, as if he were entering new rooms inside her, unsure what he would find. It suddenly became clear to him in a flash how nothing in his entire previous life had ever even hinted that he would get into a situation pulling him with such incredible force in so many different directions at once, and at the same time he could feel a few minor frictions caused by it (and by practically every word Editha uttered, incidentally) without being able to name them very clearly or assign them to their proper place; it was more like sand in his shoe. When Editha invoked Ingrid Budau, however, he was overtaken by something like a dizzy spell, he thought about that lone vulture soaring high above the Treskavica, and was then grazed against for an enduring moment by that inescapable horror we might undergo in a dream when dangling over an abyss.

But it was not in ordered words (of the kind we have to use here) that he now thought about Stangeler and said to himself, "He's right. They have no memory, nothing like it. And that man can make such a determination calmly and coolly."

Melzer and Editha had drifted back a considerable distance from the others, and the rather loud noise those ahead sent echoing from time to time through the reverberant tract of woods kept growing ever weaker.

Now Editha started speaking somewhat more for the first time. "But I think back," she said, "and have vivid memories of this one or that one. That's why I asked about Konietzki and Langl. Do you remember those two weeks at the Stangelers' country house, Melzerboy?" (It did him good to hear her address him that way; he felt as if he'd been steered back to more familiar ground and now had it under his feet once more.) "Yes, I think back sometimes. I don't like to, for the most part. Except when it comes all by itself. But I have no great love of being reminded about what's past and gone. Can you still recall, Melzerboy, how we all took a walk together one time and then sat on a bench above the house at the edge of the woods? Fourteen years ago, that's quite a long time. It was in August of 1911. A beautiful day, with a clear view off into the distance." Her voice was growing more and more subdued. She came to a stop. It was almost completely quiet now; they could no longer hear the people up ahead, who had now passed over the crest and vanished from sight.

Melzer was dizzy. Moving through the changeable vistas of this afternoon was just like the way the crest rose and dipped, a roller coaster. At some time in his life there must have been a day when circumstances and mental states had risen and fallen like this; he searched for one quickly, for the length of a thought, but he didn't find any. Here she was, holding out to him what they had in common, what was past and gone, offering what he had long ago ceased claiming from her, treading ground they could both enter, but now he was wavering, suddenly apprehensive, as if he thought he'd be stepping out into thin air. He clamped himself around this emptiness; it stood inside him for a moment.

"Let's sit down a while, Melzerboy," said Editha, "and let the others just dash on ahead. They'll be sure to reserve a table and order for us. So let's go off on our own. There's a steeper downhill path over there to the left; I bet the view from there is wonderful. Shall we?"

"Yes," he said, whereupon heavy firing was directed at the emptiness from all sides and closed it. Her words, even though ringing false and parroted from somewhere—from a sense of the past and a commonality that had developed only this summer—had the power to bring that about, and so they proved stronger than anything else rising up from the depths of time, which Melzer had earlier tried in vain to activate in Editha and which she had just now been so unexpectedly willing to hold out to him; the main result, however, was to make her sudden ability and desire to remember the past come across to him as almost appallingly capricious. Meanwhile, before they reached the drop-off, as they were still walking through the pathless woods, the ground covered in part with the flat, wide leaves of wild garlic, the core began glowing, and an aura was standing around Editha. If flight was successful, it didn't look like flight anymore; the pursuing "Baa, baa!" faded and was instantly forgotten. Her voice, though, Editha's, low and soft beside him: "Beautiful; how beautiful!" And Melzer, aware— with complete certainty—that everything had now been carried through and completed, looked with eyes aglow on the spinach-green sublimity rippling out to the edge of the sky, only to have his glance rebuffed immediately, warded off, flung aside, hurled back to its point of origin. The next second they were in each other's arms, and the scent from her mouth, a blond, milky scent, knocked him flat, smashed him to smithereens; whatever force had been trying overcome the effort to drive a wedge between them now triumphed on the spot like a great hero joining in battle, while Editha's body, though pressed so tightly to his, was still scarcely able to make him aware of its power while yet breaking down and surmounting the outer fortifications.

They stood this way for a long time. And gobbled each other up— it felt like that to Melzer—all the while kissing their way through a mountain of sweet mush (amassed over a whole summer) to the gates of love's never-never land.

Editha's happiness was manifest, effervescent, almost loud:

"Dim little Melzerboy! Dimmest of all possible Melzerboys! Finally! But you and I must make a real celebration out of this! Let's not just rush in quickly! This calls for some preparation. We'll take our time, all right? And then you'll come, you'll come to me, won't you?"

"And how I'll come to you!" he said resolutely.

"It's just a bad time right now," she continued. "There's too much going on. Let's pick a day for our celebration, shall we? And then live for it. There's nothing better. What do you say? Do you agree?"

"Completely," Melzer said. "And you pick the day."

In the restaurant they'd parked their cars outside, the group was sitting cozily around a table and waiting for their food. Everybody seemed to be listening to Höpfner, including Editha and Melzer, whose separate arrival hadn't been remarked on in any way. They blended in at once. The first thing that struck people about Höpfner was that although his build was massive he spoke from a very small mouth, out of which issued the dismissive, jaded speech pattern typical of the upper social strata in Vienna, but with an undertone of efficiency, not disjoined or scatterbrained, for instance, but in complete sentences: small smoothly smiling mouth. When he spoke, Höpfner leaned his upper body over the table, hunching and slumping a bit; even so, anyone entering the room was bound to take notice of him first, his chest and shoulders powerful enough to push all those present far apart from one another, as it were. That was the image that had also struck Editha and Melzer when they entered. Höpfner was a smooth talker whose intelligence no one could doubt—but neither could anyone doubt that the things he was speaking about at the moment possessed him, that he was possessed by his topic far more than that he possessed or governed it. In short order the name Helmut Biese was voiced. The captain knew him, naturally, since he knew everybody and everything connected with that line of business. He said: "Known quantity from the Berlin days." But Biese wasn't yet at the center of Höpfner's thoughts and observations, which were now just beginning to trace lines that would meet at this future center, a development Höpfner was most likely not even very conscious of at the time. And indeed it would take forever and a day until a practical yield, harvested from these theoretical speculations and preliminary studies, would burst over the head of the ill-fated victim. Höpfner was holding forth to the effect that it was entirely possible to single out a man—provided his constitution had equipped him with extraordinary nervous strength (and here is where Biese's name had come in, Höpfner stating that strength of nerves was in no way part of Biese's makeup)—entirely possible, he was saying, to single out a man and make his life a living nightmare, even to drive him to the brink of rack and ruin, without resorting to procedures that would violate the law or come into conflict with it at all. Here is not the place to dissect Höpfner's methods, ones that called for great expense and could only be carried through as a group effort, as he pointed out. In the course of further developments, however, a campaign was cited as a kind of epitome ("All Hell Day" was what Höpfner called it), casting light backward onto all the stages that led up to it and the intensifications that culminated in nervous collapse: first the arrival of five or six telegrams—always five or six—from various cities, with instructions to be delivered at night, bearing the same message ("Requesting Information about the State of Your Health") every time; during business hours, on the other hand, special-delivery letters would be received at the office, and they were empty. Not to mention the telephone. The simultaneous delivery of several Bösendorfer concert grand pianos (ordered from the rental firms as requisite for an upcoming musicale and paid for in advance, a generous tip included) exactly coincided on this All Hell Day with instructions given in two small newspaper advertisements that had appeared the day before; the first requested that governesses with a good command of English present themselves (all at precisely the same hour) for an interview, while the second notice (once more stipulating the same time of day) solicited for immediate purchase from dog owners or breeders a male Doberman for breeding, requiring that the animal of course be brought along for inspection. All these people and objects and animals bumped into one another in front of the apartment building and in the stairwell; in the case of the pianos we have to understand this literally, for the ones that had been refused were being lugged back down with backbreaking effort just as the ones newly arriving were in the process of being hauled up. It would be altogether unnecessary and even tacky to say very much about the noise the dogs were making (in addition to the almost incessant jangling of the phone) or the distress and fear undergone by the governesses, now trapped and being shouted at by Biese. The concierge was shrieking so loud that the closest beat policeman came running, while blowing his whistle for backup. As Biese staggered out the street door, a rented limousine was just driving past at moderate speed. The four gentlemen sitting in it were wearing top hats and were dressed from head to toe in black; perhaps they were coming from a funeral. All four of them bowed with very ceremonious and measured gestures. Poor Biese simply couldn't bring out the scream that rose up when he recognized Höpfner. He tried to say something to the policeman in the entrance hall but just couldn't manage it; the officer had to hold him up. It's clear, we might add in passing, that it wouldn't have been possible to prove anything, because of the many intermediaries.

No one laughed. To be sure, the conversation had not yet dealt with fallout from All Hell Day, which still lay in the distant future, after all. Yet there's room to doubt whether the topic would have provoked much joviality anyway. The whole scheme had an undercurrent that prompted in Melzer the fleeting thought of how he wouldn't exactly want to have this Director Höpfner as an enemy. In this business something manic and even obsessive seemed to dwell; what's more, it cast a spell on the group as people quickly got swept up in the mechanics of it, in the maze of technical details and possible applications, as it were, discussing them with total seriousness. Kajetan especially got carried away. He displayed an ability to throw himself headlong into arrangements and let them take him over completely while recasting himself almost completely into this mold, so to speak, as if he thought this way and lived this way all the time. In light of his wife's disposition it would have been better to leave the whole thing alone. There was not the slightest dearth of intelligence in Camilla von S., née Schedik, though hers was of the delicate kind (insofar as a woman delicate in every other respect could also reveal delicacy here); what there was a dearth of, however, was even the faintest trace of liveliness or anything that could make her look alive. Everything about her was like fine latticework, as it were. She could become intensely engrossed in her own pursuits and for that reason wasn't equipped to take a lead from what anyone else was doing; the movements and mannerisms of others most likely reached Frau Camy only via an indirect route, that of deliberation, which made it impossible for her to realize that her husband was in a kind of inebriated state, not from wine, but from the wellspring of a soul as much a stranger to him as to her. At this moment, though, he had molded himself to its inner form with engrossment; had it been at all possible for the effect to be more long-lasting, even considering the glaring difference in their physiognomies, he would probably have begun to resemble Höpfner, albeit only to those with exceptionally keen eyesight. This was not something Frau Camy von S. was gifted with, however, even if her eyes did bulge at times. So there she sat now, the whole time looking refined but arid, her hat pulled far down her forehead, which set off her unusually beautiful blond hair to great effect. She watched her husband with slight but mounting dismay, which made her nose, too large for the rest of the face, pull the other attractive features behind it. None of this registered with Dr. Negria, however; he was revved up, engine full blast and fed by high-octane fuel. What he saw in Höpfner was the attitude of attack mode, of dynamic intervention, of breakthrough, never mind in what direction, whether into destruction or even annihilation. "But why, why all this?!" Camy exclaimed suddenly. "Where does anyone get the right to torment another human being like that? What must the person have done to have such—such machinations set in motion against him? Tell me that, if you will!" "That, dear lady, is an entirely secondary consideration," Negria said quickly, sweeping aside her objection as totally beside the point, "you simply seize on whatever opportunity comes along." "What?!" she cried. "Yes," said Kajetan, "the quality is measured by successful implementation. It has nothing to do with revenge or retaliation. They're merely a pretext." Camy exhibited real grace at this point by backing away slightly, shrugging her narrow shoulders, and saying nothing more. Höpfner studied her with affable forbearance. "It's all about taking action and nothing else!" cried Negria. "A campaign carefully prepared and ratcheted up to the limit has value; nothing else has." Because the conversation grew more scattered at this point, a sudden loud burst of laughter from the captain—one for which there was really no context—rang out much louder than he might have liked. But he simply hadn't been able to help himself. The face Angelika Scheichsbeutel made while Negria was talking had reached such intense power of expression that it would have been hailed on the stage as an outstanding achievement. She had roughly the look of a wanderer in the desert trudging deeply through sand and looking up to a mound beyond which yet another sandstorm is whirling. Eulenfeld was looking at Angelika from the side. So of course he noticed the pixie cut too, now hanging lank, drooping like a dog's ears. The whole picture could have been titled *After a Summer with Dr. Negria*. Geyrenhoff, whom Editha had ended up sitting next to, found a moment to ask her if she hadn't been in Salzburg on Monday, the twenty-fourth. (These chroniclers are all dreadful in the same exact way, whether they write anything down or not.) Melzer was chatting with Camy von S., his neighbor, half murmuring; it sounded as if he were reassuring her. "No," said Editha. "But Edouard von Langl claims he saw you there," said Geyrenhoff (perhaps he thought the discrepancy needed to be cleared up and was trying to get the matter straight before setting it down on paper). "Then it must have been my ghost," said Editha. On the way back, the cars were lined up in the same order as before, only now in the dark. A serpentine road led downhill—slowly. The lights of the city glittered as the cars turned a corner, and in no time this earthly firmament unfurled in great profusion. Editha and Melzer lay arm in arm in the leather seats, their gleaming, varnish-like red now extinguished, of course. They exchanged a quick kiss. There would have been no reason for them to rush; no one turned around, neither Eulenfeld nor the firecracker. High above the earthbound stars there suddenly appeared long, glowing streaks across the sky, two, three, many more. Editha squeezed Melzer's hand. "What should we wish for?" she whispered, close to his ear. "The same thing," he said.

On the Wednesday following the Nativity of Our Lady, Melzer came to Lichtental around four o'clock.

Editha had called him on both Sunday and Monday—short but affectionate conversations. Was he thinking about her? He was? There was "so much going on"; it would be Thursday before they could spend a short time together. She was so looking forward to it. "Are you as well?" He should expect a call from her on Thursday at five, when he'd be back from his office.

Since that past Saturday the certainty inside him had been slowed to a halt, almost like some viscous, gooey substance, like a stream of liquid now solidifying.

Yes, he was near the correct address. He crossed the narrow street, completely deserted, walked toward the wrinkly little house, and went through the archway. At first everything seemed totally quiet here. The clay-colored plaster in the low arch only seemed to strengthen that impression. To his right there was still some sunlight in the inset panes of colored glass. Now Melzer heard from the back, where the garden had to be, a weak murmur of voices through the glass door, its two panels wide open. He stopped for a moment as something quick and brightly colored came bolting through the door like a shot, launching a salvo of pattering footsteps under the echoing arch and making a beeline for Melzer, against whom it checked itself and came to rest. He looked down and felt with great distinctness through the light material of his summer suit the warmth of the bare little hands and arms now wrapped around his left leg. He looked down and she looked up. It felt for a moment like a heavy apple tumbling off a tree, rolling toward him, and now looking up at him with twinkling little eyes. Melzer bent down, set the little girl in his arm, and resumed walking. She must have felt this perch to be natural and hers by right, for she put her arm on his shoulder and leaned on it; the exquisitely downy fragrance of a cheek (not unlike sun-drenched apricots) was close. Melzer didn't resist and even ventured a kiss. He had good luck with little Therese Pichler, for she returned it instantly. This was how they both presented themselves as they walked through the glass door and into the garden.

"Would you take a look at this girl!" the foreman cried; "she just goes her merry way!"

He quickly came up to Melzer and said, "You must be Major Melzer. Alois Pichler. I'm very happy to meet you, Major! And here's my wife." She wanted to take the child, but the little girl put her arms around Melzer's neck and started giggling as she hid her face in his shoulder. "She wants to stay with me," Melzer said. He didn't turn her over but kept holding her in his arm. And later he bounced her on his knees.

Thea Rokitzer was standing in the background, near the fruit trees.

Theresa Schachl and Councillor Zihal had turned up in the meantime. "Extremely happy to meet you!" said Zihal, when Paula had brought them together. "Unfortunately I cannot introduce you to my wife today, Major; she would very much have enjoyed meeting you," Zihal went on, adding quickly, "but we had something of a domestic mishap. A jar shattered as my wife was making fruit preserves; she sustained a cut on her lower left arm."

"Nothing dangerous, I hope."

"Not to be regarded as dangerous or even serious," Zihal answered. "But she didn't want to come out right after having her arm bandaged. We went to the doctor."

So there's justice after all. It doesn't always mete out speedy punishment. The dossier often gets reshelved or filed in a different drawer and sometimes even seems itself to be delaying a resolution. Not in this case. As we see, Frau Rosa was in due course administered a good swift kick in the . . . or rather a less drastic punishment on her lower left arm, which was meaty enough anyway.

Thea Rokitzer was standing in the background, near the fruit trees.

Here once again, however, Zihal displayed his air of absolute refinement, a way of being that completely fills life's incidents and situations, even to overflowing, if one will, so that all matters attain the fullness of their true form. He was not one of those married men who just by happenstance never speak about their wives if the ladies don't happen to be present; no out of sight, out of mind for him. On the contrary. It was his duty to stand in for her. And so even though Rosa Zihal's not inconsiderable power of spatial displacement was not manifested here today, at least not on the physical plane, Zihal still tasked himself with erecting on the empty spot and then solemnly dedicating, if only by mention, a memorial to his absent wife. Considering his status as a husband, after all, it was up to the councillor (or so it might have been regarded by that gentleman) to step forth at all times as part of a couple; having in earlier years been the confirmed, dyed-in-the-wool bachelor, it was now incumbent upon him to give suitable outward expression to the transformation he had made to his newfound state of conjugal bliss. That seemed perfectly self-evident to him, as perfectly self-evident as addressing Melzer with the title "Major," thereby shunning all presumption of collegial familiarity, even though he was fully aware (through Paula) of the major's status as fellow civil servant, of his past as an officer in the Royal and Imperial army, and of his non-Zihaloid nature (by looking at him). There was a status to be upheld here as well. Not his own, but someone else's. But by that very token his own after all.

Thea Rokitzer was standing in the background, near the fruit trees. She started toward Melzer too, now that the others, the older people, had greeted the major. He was still holding little Resi Pichler in his arm. He stepped up to her quickly. Out of that viscous material, that gummy, doughy mass of the certainty inside him, Thea now leapt up like a small fountain, clear as crystal before the pale sky, open like a flower goblet, free, a last longing flung upward before the sonorous ground bass of a pain he was willing to bear as befitting—to him, his age, his life and how it had turned out. A life that had never been able or had never even attempted to take that final step into itself but was always content just to be swept up or taken in tow, on a bear hunt or a ride in an automobile with red leather upholstery shining like patent leather. So sooner or later there had to result an outcome like this, fixing everything in place and making it clear-cut, covering it with lead, as it were, but on strange terrain, not his own, which he had never reached in all the years of being passed along, say from the military to his civil service appointment. But this fountain now, this flower under a last, late-summer sky: it was his flower, his very own, but no longer his by right. Meanwhile, he could at least look at it (as the patriarch looked upon the Promised Land but would never enter it), but even that was a great deal. What he saw there: he, Melzer, could have been that, could have become that.

In these brief seconds of self-drilling below the surface of the Melzerian autobiography a minor incident occurred that practically no one took notice to (except Paula); after all, there were some egregiously old-fashioned guests here, such as Theresa Schachl, who wouldn't have found anything in the least remarkable about it.

Thea curtsied to the major. She did it by mistake, so to speak. Was it the sheer decency of these surroundings (they even gradually began taking on something of the odor of an old album) that had this effect on the girl, and that in spite of the very different social circles in which she'd been cavorting and disporting for so many months now? That's pretty much our opinion. Here something had remained whole—blithely whole, or unscathed only by chance, or surviving through its strength— whatever: it produced its aura. We won't take it upon ourselves to opine that she curtsied because Melzer suddenly struck her (it would have been for the first time) as an older gentleman.

He had to take it that way, though.

Take it in and take it on.

The sharpness with which Paula had observed this tiny little incident—Thea's inadvertent curtsy, from which her knees were simply unable to refrain; Melzer's delight at this idyllic image, combined with a wounded look of pain in his features, which he concealed by a quick bow—Paula's sharpness of discernment deserves special mention. She could read as if studying the indicator needles on an instrument panel the whole state of the amorous thrust and parry she now resolved, now more than ever, to make into her own cause. And her powers of divination proved significant—even now, a scant few minutes after making the major's acquaintance, she knew exactly where the main obstacle to her plans was located, understood with complete clarity that so unfathomable a degree of modesty signified a rampart stronger than walls many feet thick, and realized that it was impossible to take aim at the windows through which a soul like this looked out at the world and just smash them with no further ado.

At the same time, it was likewise completely clear to our Paula what an exceptionally alluring effect Thea was producing right now. The girl was at one of those peaks to which people can be raised unawares, as an unforeseen added enhancement—as the added-est enhancement imaginable—like a sudden reward for meritorious qualities about which the recipient is entirely in the dark. We cannot say, though, that Thea "is to be regarded" as one of those latent geniuses (like Lina Nohel, Ferdinand Schachl, Kroissenbrunner, *e tutti quanti rari rarissimi*); in our view—and to keep it short and sweet—she's simply too dull (just as our dear Paula is too bright), and it takes more than being a glass case to make someone a genius, much as it may be a stringent test site for becoming one (less so for old boatsmen, who are treated more leniently in general and seldom called on). One reason for Thea's heightened effect could perhaps be found in the timing of her penitential banishment, which had commenced on Sunday, August 30, nine days before ("*pænitentia nundinalis*," the captain had said, but perhaps he was quietly giving more and more thought to extending it). Thea had thus had ample opportunity to let her apricot-hued complexion, now released from reeks and fumes, regain, in sunlight and dewdrops, that subdued iridescence, that downiness, that delicate tint which the major was able to resist only because Thea Rokitzer (135 pounds) was not sitting on his arm and clinging to him like little Reserl Pichler. Nonetheless, she was inwardly holding onto the major much tighter than was the little girl. But not with her hands. And in cases like these the only meanings that count are literal, not figurative (basically these are nothing but spiteful remarks—and you, Herr Councillor, are a literary plague, just to say it right out for once). Another contributing factor to the restoration of Thea's apricot exterior might have been the collapse of her movie plans (poring over plans is what lends a person profile); what's more, weeks had gone by since that exterior had been smeared all over with synthetic tanning creams and inflamed by sunbaths taken with pure amateurishness. The Zihaloids from Saint Valentin didn't leave Thea a minute's rest to continue these indulgences. Even so, she had brought back a healthy skin color.

Something else suddenly popped up in Paula's mind however, and it now looked like an insoluble problem—now all of a sudden (never mind that up to this moment it had looked like smooth sailing), while they were taking their places at the coffee table under the fruit trees and executing the first rituals of a solemn Viennese coffee party, a Jause, holding those eighteenth-century cups, their mouths filled (not with marble cake and coffee just yet) with nineteenth-century language, the late-summer sun, the dulcet caress of faces and temples by the fruit-laden air of a day in the first third of our twentieth century . . . So there was something else our Paula saw herself confronted with, as though facing an insurmountable wall that would beyond any doubt be instantly thrust up by the major's sense of hearing if she should—not necessarily here, today; it could be at any time!—if she should say anything to him about the duplicate ladies. That had been her fixed intention ever since Stangeler (she respected his decision) had flatly refused the mission. But how?!

"Major Melzer, please forgive what might at first seem an intrusion. But you're interested in a lady named Frau Editha Schlinger. I feel it's my obligation to tell you that this lady exists in duplicate."

That would never do! Even though it was accurate.

"Major Melzer, now that I have the opportunity to speak with you in person, I would like to inform you of a fact I was able to verify with my own eyes. Namely: there are two of Frau Schlinger!"

That was utterly impossible nonsense. But true nonetheless.

"Major Melzer, on Friday, the twenty-eighth, I happened to bump into a mutual acquaintance of ours, René Stangeler, at the West Station; we were both there to meet someone. At that time we chanced to catch sight of Frau Editha Schlinger, whom you know. There were two of them, in fact."

That was pure absurdity. Even though the absolute truth. The wall in question would surely have grown many feet thick and insurmountably high.

Did it turn out in consequence, then, that she, Paula, was utterly unable to disclose this item of information to the major? She had to fight back the urge while giving the appearance of paying close attention, as was Theresa Schachl, to the exchanges taking place among Zihal, Melzer, and Alois Pichler, engaged in an animated conversation that proved not entirely uninteresting as it unfolded.

At this same time, Grete Siebenschein and René Stangeler were lying on a slope at the edge of the woods, a little under a treeless peak in the Animal Park at Lainz, as it's called, although it is no more a park than a parking lot is. Instead, it's a nature preserve (almost something similar to what the Sierscha Canyon near Dobro Pole was before the First World War, when Major Laska and Lieutenant Melzer went hunting wild boar there). A forested area and habitat for game animals directly bordering the large city. But when we say Grete and René were lying at the edge of the woods, the image might immediately arise of two people gazing off silently and thoughtfully (or thoughtlessly) into the distance, which was not the case and would not even have been possible where they were, because the woods were right in front of their noses here below the peak, whereas the treeless area lay a little above them in its rise up the slope. They were eating out of a large aluminum container, and René was drinking coffee (only as of that evening at Melzer's had he acquired a taste for coffee—wherever we look there's always something being held onto or discarded: E.P. still holding onto suspenders for a long time; Geyrenhoff introducing to a young man a fragrance that will stay with him for life). Our couple was cheerful and a little tired. Their walk that day had shown them much beauty but taken them far.

A heightened sense of caution had begun to occupy Grete Siebenschein, starting when René turned up so abruptly that previous Wednesday. In her admittedly rather indirect processes of perception, which passed every stimulus through the filter of reflection and thereby admitted of assimilation only upon reaction from within, this new and vehement impulse of Stangeler's struck her first suspicious—a sign of some infidelity he'd already committed, leading to a dramatic return to the old gods—and on second thought, as an earnest effort, one he was not about to miss, finally to regain the higher ground from which she had been more or less forced to retreat ever since her triumphs of this past summer and her own ensuing "defection" (she was still calling it that). This higher ground seemed indispensably necessary to her, however, not because she thirsted for power—such a thing was not in Grete's makeup—but because she had to reach it again as a means of protecting her weakness, or so she was imagining it as she went zooming through her *trópoi*—rapidly, trivially, just like the rest of us—between two buttered rolls here at the edge of the woods. Basically these are nothing but spiteful remarks. Any craving to stage a baroque drama on the grand scale was not in Grete's makeup, however. No such tone attempted to swell up somberly from the deep brass. What she did possess, on the other hand, was a levelheaded outlook directed unsparingly at herself but—in her opinion—insufficiently relentless in discerning and preserving her own honor. And peculiarly enough, this was not what is referred to in common parlance as "a woman's honor"; it was the honor of a man and a fighter instead—a fighter against René Stangeler. It really came down to her honor as an adversary. Holding a buttered roll in her left hand and a small piece broken off of it in her right, she successfully lengthened her neck out over the situation, and she resolved (we'll make it short and sweet) to keep René on a shorter leash in every respect from now on. Now or never. She was already regretting having practically begged René to go on this outing with her; it now seemed like a bad idea. She should have been "too busy," not had time for him, or at least have kept him waiting somewhere, somehow for a good long time. But Grete didn't know how to deploy tactics like these—ones practiced by other women everywhere and with confident ease—so it's no wonder they never worked out for her when she tried.

Her stupidity wasn't profound enough for that (this is our opinion, of course; Grete knew nothing about it). Her stupidity wasn't sturdy enough, not "anchored solid in the earth," to quote Schiller's famous ballad. That was why she then did things which, when measured against her standard of stupidity—what other one could she apply?—she was forced to deem stupid.

Another couple had escaped the city walls as well (enjoying a few additional vacation days granted by the Land Title Bank), if not those invisible walls found everywhere (all to the good, we almost want to say), and had been walking through woods and meadows. On the other side of the peak, and likewise farther down, where the trees began, E.P. and his wife were sitting in the short grass. They'd been ensconced there for quite some time. As the crow flies—or rather as the mole bores—a few hundred feet from Grete and René. Buttered rolls and anchovy paste here, too. The woman's neck shorter, though.

High up on the peak itself a striking woman was standing: striking not just because of the exposed point to which she'd climbed (passing Grete and René rather close on the way up—on the way down she would pass the other, legal couple at no great distance, in this way walking straight through those invisible walls unimpeded). She was striking because of her appearance as well. Tall, slender, and powerful, she presented itself to the observer (none present on the peak just at the moment, though) as simple, tasteful, and suitably dressed for her solitary walk in the woods. Her hat and parasol couldn't help drawing attention, on the other hand. The first item was what's known as a Florentine straw hat, abundantly trimmed with red poppies. The parasol was not meant for an adult, however; it was more for a child or a large doll. The curved bamboo handle was so tiny that it could have hung from the arm of a child no older than six. Every color of the rainbow was painted on the parasol, which the lady was carrying open over her left shoulder. It was not much greater in diameter than the hat. Neither the straw hat nor the parasol seemed to have proven at all effective, meanwhile—or had they been placed into service only later, to create this look?—for the lady's face, neck, and arms were deeply tanned. Like leather. Her wide, attractive face held two eyes, large and dark, like an animal's; it was as if two tunnels led into this face, two tunnels whose inner gleam appeared to be setting them out on display. These were the kinds of eyes, then, out of which the lady was looking far outward from her elevated standpoint, downhill and uphill into the spinach-green sublimity and, in effect, bemused because there was so much of it. This was the painter Maria Rosanka. With nary a tool of her trade. She never painted outdoors; only in her studio: large pictures, like the portrait of Civil Service Councillor Julius Zihal (a three-quarter-length rendering), but also small and repellent ones. She was twirling the parasol. She strode down the crest, making straight for E.P. and his wife (perhaps she wished to annoy these people by passing by them so closely). She was engaged in a solitary constitutional—her way of expressing it to herself through the parasol—and had crossed through a large part of the Animal Park. She was afraid of nothing and nobody, and nothing had ever happened to her. The creative result of this constitutional was a small picture painted soon thereafter, measuring about eight inches square. It depicted the crest, its peak much exaggerated. It was a pointed head, specifically that of an old man, bald on top but with a fringe of hair that on a closer view consisted of many couples painted on a minute scale, all of them contorted into the maddest and most repugnant positions. A year later, Chief Medical Councillor Schedik, Kajetan's father-in-law, spotted the small picture on a visit to Maria Rosanka's studio and immediately acquired it for a considerable sum. We can say on the whole that here, on the day following the Nativity of the Blessed Virgin Mary, in 1925, in the Lainz Animal Park, a sort of cosmos of affiliations—at least when viewed from the little garden of the Schachl house in Lichtental!—had clustered, though admittedly the parties making up this phenomenon would themselves never have looked at it in that light.

"Governmental administration," Councillor Zihal was saying, "is to be regarded as altogether one of the most difficult and delicate areas of human endeavor. When people nowadays assert that bureaucracy is growing too widespread and expanding everywhere you look, they have by that very judgment drawn the respect for administration into doubt. That respect consists of ensuring that everything remains within the modest framework of pure efficacy; the most exalted calling of public service lays claim to no more than the very smallest space, for the measurement of which, at least in the overwhelming majority of cases, there lie to hand precise guidelines, if not outright regulations. In consideration of that principle it is and remains erroneous to believe that an administrative department represents—or, as the case may be, is constrained to function as—no more than merely a means to a practical end."

"I don't quite understand, Councillor," Pichler modestly stated.

"We shall forthwith understand one another very well, Herr Pichler, if I may permit myself to remind you that every genuine manifestation of order, be it in the home or in the state, has one common characteristic, which is that it never captures anyone's attention, as it were. Our two exemplary homemakers here will testify to that" (a short but ceremonious acknowledgment in the form of a slight bow). "'Creating order is no strain; maintaining order calls for pain.' When order is being created, it approaches its hereunto appertaining objects laterally, from the side. When order is being maintained, it situates itself in the background, however. It is not possible to create order from the distorted perspective of a lateral view. Engendering order can only flow from a higher principle, one that is, if you will, sufficient unto itself: to wit, a love of order as such, and not merely of its advantageous consequences. Accordingly, Herr Pichler, not purely for the sake of functionality— albeit functionality can be served only in this way. It is altogether inappropriate for various governmental departments to pretend they are fulfilling this or that function by expanding their scope, often through arbitrary self-extension, into superfluous agendas that in some cases overstep their explicitly circumscribed areas of jurisdiction. The contrary image—the execution of absolutely indispensable necessities, and those only, while confining itself to pure functionality in its narrowest construction, is for its part a different sham, one situated at the diametrically opposite pole, but with a higher meaning, for it is only in donning such pilgrim garb, if you will permit me the expression, that the blank shield of bureaucratic prestige, of the exalted calling of public service, can be kept concealed. But what does this shield reflect? Functionality? That is to be regarded as erroneous! It reflects order in and of itself and the love for same, and by that token, for the pertinent regulations as well, those by no means to be regarded solely in consideration of their practical applicability, moreover! That shield does not simply reflect order, but automatically trains its guiding light onto one's own sphere of activity in addition. It is an attribute of order that it remains hidden, however. It is to be regarded as an official secret. The only true official secret and the most strictly reserved. The secret of officialdom's reputability. Whoever does not keep it concealed under the punctiliously parsimonious cloak of pure functionality betrays it. And thus it is that the exalted calling of public service lays claim to no more than the very smallest space. Because it is imperative that true order must remain almost completely unnoticed."

"Yes," said Pichler, "now I understand. "That's exactly how it is with us at the government publications department. But you're speaking about something you refer to as 'the exalted calling of public service,' Councillor—that used to be the phrase back in the days of the empire, if I remember correctly; at least that's how I learned it. But it's something entirely different today."

"I believe you are in error on that point, my friend," retorted Zihal good-naturedly. He lifted to his lips the small green glass in which there sparkled the pure gold of the wine that had been served. The sunlight of the waning afternoon now swelled up in the garden to a plangent splendor that seemed to dissolve all objects while at the same time punctuating itself more sharply through the sharp shadows of the fruit trees it now cast onto the gold-green of the little lawn. Pichler looked expectantly at Zihal and seemed to have forgotten the wine completely. The cigarette in his motionless hand resting on his knee was making a long strip of ash. "Because there are vacant thrones in the imperial residences, Schönbrunn and the Hofburg? It might almost be better that way, I'm tempted to say. You know I was a Royal and Imperial government official with all my heart and soul, a tiny wheel, a minute little shaving of His Imperial Majesty. He was called to his reward. Perhaps we are not meant to have any need for him at the present moment. When someone steps aside or steps down, whoever it may be, we always see more. To a certain extent the sovereign remained anonymous, if you will permit me the expression, transparent, so to speak. He does not withdraw from view, not even in the slightest, the sources of bureaucratic reputability, inasmuch as the secret of the exalted calling of public service is not to be regarded as issuing forth, not even in the slightest, from his august person, though it can conceivably be elucidated by reference to that person. If I may put it this way, the republic is possibly made of a finer, less visible fabric than the monarchy. At my age, of course, one remains fixed in earlier times with his loves and his memories. But why should I overlook those things that make me happy nowadays? I really enjoy living."

He came to a stop rather abruptly. His last words created an occasion to refill and lift their glasses as well as an occasion to propose this or that toast, which in a cordial and relaxed way (Theresa Schachl saw to that) caused any tension lingering from the topic to subside by harmonizing and uniting past and present and every other imaginable contrast. Only at this point did Melzer become aware of the amazement with which he'd been listening to Zihal, unprepared as he was to make the acquaintance of someone like that; and while his heart was making a great racket behind many walls, comparable to a thumping piston in a damaged pumping station, he found this muffling atmosphere to be a great relief, like a man whose toothache or other torture to his nerves has abated and who appears to have disappeared under a protective layer, if a thin one. This was how relieved the major felt as that scorching spurt of flame began to die down that Thea Rokitzer's devastating curtsy had sent shooting through him.

And now it was as if he were lying on a thin layer, transparent as ice, barely able to hold him up over the depths of pain and the real possibility that he could fall through it. The major didn't have much room for movement. He had to keep completely still. This fall—and his heart, pounding behind so many walls, had only a distant inkling of its true, bottomless depth—was something he was trying to avoid at all costs. A man loves everything he feels; but if the love for the feeling is more intense than the feeling itself, then he can be called sentimental; he's fixed on his own inner workings, the mechanism, the functioning "psychological stew pot" (expressions like this always originate with Kajetan, so he's another literary plague). Everyone in the world stops acting like this, however, when matters get really serious, when that squeeze around the heart comes to take the breath away, when on the inside it's a matter of life and death—whoosh! and it's gone, this charming vacillation between the main voice and the accompanying, loving observation ("and the monk rejoices..."), when we're being driven straight toward an abyss whose unplumbed waters roar past and thunder as they brutally make to engulf us. It can be said that the first is a not-yet state and the second a no-longer state of really living, although the determination of such questions is at any rate and in every case entirely irrelevant to anyone who's dreading the second state. And that was how matters now stood with the major. Under the thin layer of ice there appeared a paradoxical gleam of red (not unfamiliar to Melzer; no, indeed, very much the contrary!), and the layer itself was now in danger of melting away.

So there he sat, next to Pichler and across from Zihal, with a long face, exactly like the one he had two years before, standing at the edge of the sidewalk on Porzellan Gasse in front of the red car after the ride with—no, not with—beside Editha. (The little word "with" can be used in this context only in connection with Melzer: he was the one who'd been taken along *with* the others.)

"The major is the one you'd really have to ask," Councillor Zihal was now saying. A new conversation was just starting up. It was more trivial than quadrivial, more chatty than philosophical, and it was initiated by Zihal because he'd twice been infected by the topic: first in Saint Valentin by Thea Rokitzer, who had disturbed the orbital course of his watering routine in the garden by broaching the subject at an inopportune time and in an inappropriate manner; and then second by Paula Pichler, who'd handled herself better, namely on the occasion of her calling on Zihal and his wife in person, right after the couple had returned from their visit to the Saint Valentin Zihaloid in Upper Austria, to invite them to this very Jause (they'd returned with baskets of fruit, officially authorized ones, be it noted; and oddly enough it was while preparing these licit fruits that Frau Rosa was chastened on her lower arm!). She had not been at home, by the way, so it was then that Paula extended a feeler. Of course with no knowledge of Thea's related inquiry (baa, baa!). She didn't get anywhere either. The invitation was ceremoniously accepted on the spot, in the name of his wife as well, and the information likewise duly imparted, but it was marked by the same inscrutably Oriental impenetrability as the quondam semiofficial disquisitions at Saint Valentin concerning the same subject, specifically the acquisition of tobacco products in larger allotments by private persons. What naturally suggests itself to us is that the council-lor simply didn't know anything about it and had wriggled out of the matter with a few empty phrases. For Paula, however, as well as for Thea, no such belief suggested itself, not even faintly: a civil service councillor is a civil service councillor and therefore is one who should know better than a person representing officialdom, even if he is living in retirement, what is prohibited and what is permissible. Admittedly the two women did not comprehend—even though *Zihalismus en-demicus* was practically in their genes!—the full significance of what it meant to operate inside or outside a defined area of jurisdiction, known to bureaucrats as *Kompetenz* and spelled out by bureaucratic regulations. Meanwhile, it seems quite characteristic—of Zihal, that is—in this whole context that vis-à-vis his wife he maintained complete silence with respect to these inquiries, posed to him not once, but twice, and thus bound to stand out. And should it emerge that Frau Rosa Zihal in fact acquired any knowledge whatever of disreputable dealings related to tobacco (we don't know and therefore cannot say anything about a matter lying outside our *Kompetenz*), then it would by no means have been her husband who directed her attention to them. She may well have ended up hearing something about them, perhaps through her unmarried sister, the tobacconist—rather unlikely, though, because that lady attached practically no importance to the matter, but more likely through Frau Rokitzer and the machinations (*"ambitus,"* the captain would have said; he was party to these dealings, but fortunately for his peace of mind, he was not even aware that there existed an individual named Hedi Loiskandl, along with her hereunto appertaining fiancé)—more likely through the machinations of Hedi Loiskandl, then. Frau Rosa had in turn never asked her husband, Civil Service Councillor Zihal, anything about it. She probably considered him incompetent. All women consider the man they married incom-petent, at the very least, if not something worse. There are reasons for that. What's certain, in any case, is that Zihal told her nothing and was asked nothing in return: his report—a competent one—made to Kajetan in 1927. He was altogether openhearted and not the least Orientally inscrutable toward Dr. Döblinger.

Paula had in the meantime called on her former employer on Marc-

Aurel Strasse (we can see how diligent she'd been!). But with even less result than was had with Zihal; with none at all, in fact. Dr. Adler—perhaps a fleeting recollection of him remains from the Augarten Tennis Club—was so happy to see Paula again that all he did was bustle about her and express his sincere joy at hearing that she had a loving husband and a sweet little daughter. He wanted to see pictures, and Paula had had the presence of mind to bring some along. Adler studied the photographs with delight and then went out to the room where clients were waiting, but only to rush past them with a greeting and into the outer office, where the secretaries were sitting, one of whom he hustled off at full gallop to a florist and a pastry chef, from whom she soon returned with a gigantic bouquet of red roses and a box of chocolates fit for minor royalty. The secretaries in the outer office believed their employer to be sorely smitten, but he wasn't—though occasionally with his wife, even after all this time.

He rapidly skipped right over Paula's particular questions, however; in fact, he was hardly listening to her, and her questions became submerged in his much more numerous ones. Of course it has to be noted, too, that the subject on which Paula voiced her misgivings offered nothing to take hold of, nothing that pointed to a clear-cut legal transaction. Moreover, a Zihalistic point of view was completely alien to this lawyer. And he had more important things to read about in the newspapers than outdated stories of heists, apparently cleared up by now anyway, from various warehouses or storage facilities of the tobacco administration. There was no way of making it quite clear to Dr. Adler that this could well be a matter of some importance; he didn't have a wall inside his ear, to be sure, but something more like a curtain flapping uneasily in front of it, and it proved in the end impossible to penetrate, almost as impossible as it had proven—though only in imagination—to tell Major Melzer about the duplicate ladies. The only thing that seemed important to Dr. Adler was that his Paula Schachl, now Frau Paula Pichler, had come to visit him and that she was doing well in every respect.

And so she climbed back down the stairs with her box of chocolates (which would be a source of much joy to little Theresa for some time to come) and her bouquet of roses in her arms and walked back out onto Marc-Aurel Strasse. The old emperor, philosopher, *imperator* and *triumphator* Marcus Aurelius, whom we have several times already had occasion to mention by name, would undoubtedly have taken much joy in this *Paula amoenissima*, who was such an enhancement to his city of Vienna.

Before that, however, while she was still involved in conversation, something sprang up inside our Paula that made her completely miss any and every connection with the concerns she'd been keeping in view and the aims she'd been pursuing. She saw herself walking out the door of the building where the lawyer's office was and now looking down Marc-Aurel Strasse in the direction of the Danube Canal. The glaring intensity with which this image of seeing herself and the gray, sunlit buildings, many of them old, along the street sloping downhill far exceeded the usual way images and memories of this kind come and go; the intensity produced a kind of subdued alarm in Paula, only she couldn't figure out where it was coming from or to what place it was calling her . . . but there it was now, it came to her: visually, not with her understanding, not with insight into a specific correlation: she saw before her René's brother-in-law, at that time still his sister's fiancé; there was the café and bakery on Alserbach Strasse and the cheerful gathering of the three . . .

And the Strudlhof Steps. That scene. The old (!) man at the top and the couple in the middle. How the father had dragged the crestfallen girl along behind him! And the short young man with the large head had gone gloomily down the steps and walked away.

Of course René had explained the whole thing to her right afterward (and then again, somewhat later, when he knew more), although no explanation would really ever have been required, any more than for a play or a film at which all anyone had to do was pay attention to what was being enacted—which was exactly how she'd watched.

Now Asta's scrutinizing and not very benign glance was fixed on her. And next to Asta stood Melzer.

At just about the same time, Melzer arrived by a different and almost more erratic path of his own at the point of recognizing Paula once

more; he had previously seen her only one single time in his life, fourteen years earlier, and likewise during that scandalous incident on the
Strudlhof Steps. For him, though, that simple fact as such was much
less important than the process that brought it back into view, the wide
leap of fourteen years, one of those recent acts of seizure by his own
past that had been growing more frequent lately, firing at him from
closer and closer range, placing him under heavy barrage from his
memory, but perhaps in fact—of this he had a very deep inkling—setting up nothing more than the preparatory phase of a battle to a decisive breakthrough (since we've already started using metaphors
appropriate for a military man).

He had chosen a small spot on Thea's lower right arm as a place to
rest his eyes (her arm, suffused with soft whitish down, had a slight
natural tan from Saint Valentin), which proved to be the best way of
looking past her, of keeping the sight of her at bay without losing her
totally from his field of vision. It felt to him for moments at a stretch
as if this delicate apricot curve were moving toward him just as the
little girl's cheek had approached him under the gateway. How great
would Tantalus have been, if he had he never fallen for the trickery of
Hades, had never reached for the fruit, had never bent down toward
the receding pool, thereby making all of hell's ruses futile! Major
Melzer, on the other hand, was very nearly in command of something
like the greatness denied to Tantalus in ancient times, or perhaps denied
even now, for who can know for certain if these tricks with fruit and
water aren't still being perpetrated in this day and age? However that
may be, the arrangement now in place and hereunto appertaining was
to be regarded as ongoing. So Melzer kept looking past Thea and toward
the four fruit trees in the garden. Into the striped punctuation of green-
gold, into the gathering leaf shadows. Regarding what now seemed
mandated (and it did indeed strike him as man-dated, if only to him
and only at this moment, though he was nonetheless deeply convinced
the scales had been fairly weighted; yes, all this our major was aware of!
Who can still doubt that he really had acquired a civilian mentality as
of August 22?)—he was prepared to accept as fixed, under all circumstances and unconditionally, what seemed mandated to him, to accept
as subject to cognizance at the present moment and to assessment at

some subsequent point in time (nothing we can do—we can't help constantly feeling the tug from Councillor Zihal, especially when he's located right nearby). To accept—but not like the bent stalk of a plant in a wind that will keep blowing anyway, no, not drooping or dangling, but upright, standing tall (soldiers always place so much value on that), and not making sour grapes out of sweet ones this time (hard to do in the case of Thea!), as he'd done in the past when suddenly hit by the thought that Asta looked like Old Man Schmeller during the few seconds she spent scrutinizing the young person who'd started up from the lower end of the Strudlhof Steps with René Stangeler and Pista Grauermann, and they all ended up standing together in the middle.

And next to René stood Paula.

But neither had reached that point quite yet, neither Paula nor Major Melzer. Melzer, who had just been addressed with all due seemliness by Councillor Zihal as competent in matters of disreputable dealings pertaining to tobacco, was manifesting no very marked zeal (the passive cause being his thoroughly un-Zihaloid nature, the active being the great strain with which he was maintaining his precarious equilibrium just now) to shine as a textbook example of scrupulous professional competence; the option of giving that appearance might have been barred to him even so, for it was not at all certain that any given official of the tobacco administration would be in a position to furnish information about some particular protocol within that widely branching, hierarchical structure: such competence Councillor Zihal having seemed to imply through a question motivated entirely by politeness. Zihal did not know, moreover, in what capacity inside the structure the major functioned (and on what branch inside the structure he stood as he sang for his supper). But it might also have chanced that the major really did deal with such matters, or had in the past. In addition, it seemed to Zihal that this courteous appeal in recognition of the major's authority would be the best means of passing onto someone in the know the topic he himself had broached and, as a result, finding out something reliable at last in regard to a subject about which he'd already been quizzed in his semiofficial capacity—twice, no less.

Faced with all that, Melzer's harder struggle for the time being was aimed at maintaining the balance he felt fairly sure of by holding fast to that little patch of apricot surface; to an extent, it also stood in for little Theresa Pichler, who had soon toddled away from the grown-ups and was now playing with a beer truck, an attractive toy her father had made for her, very handsomely designed with masterfully carved little horses and twenty-four little kegs that could be taken out and put back, to that extent standing in for little Theresa Pichler and her heavenly cheek. And in cases like these, the figurative meanings are always less dangerous than the literal ones. They're not so apt to burn your fingers or, in this instance, the area under your poplin shirt closest to your heart, which has fled and entrenched itself behind many invisible walls, where it is beating somewhat irregularly and slightly damaged, as it were, behind walls immediately discerned by our steadfast Paula the minute Thea bobbed her ill-fated curtsy; for Paula, that was the main event anyway.

Councillor Zihal had not broached his subject from the angle of whether private individuals were legally entitled to purchase larger consignments of tobacco products, however—although he understood how to direct it that way—but had instead started by mentioning the thefts, larcenies, and large-scale heists that had come to light early that summer and been reported in the newspapers from time to time thereafter. That was his approach to Melzer, then. "I know almost nothing about these things," he finally said, "and my excuse is that my official capacity is in no way related to production, storage, or any other technical aspect, nor with anything involving export and transportation. I handle strictly personnel issues. But I do know for certain there was one break-in." "In connection with which no responsibility attaches to any civil servant, employee, or subordinate." "No," said Melzer, "it was a matter of breaking and entering from outside, as far as I know." "But in other instances weren't there abuses of office, defalcations, as they're generally called?" "Yes," said Melzer, "that's something I would naturally know about in my department. There wasn't any secret made of it, by the way; it was reported everywhere." "The matter is currently under investigation," said Zihal, "as I have recently been informed. That provides a basis for eventuation into access by representatives of the law and the subsequent rapid proceedings statutorily required of them, thus empowering an examining magistrate to authorize a search warrant and to initiate additional measures. Nonetheless, as I have likewise recently been informed" (hold on!—twice, no less! But here he was exaggerating a bit, our councillor!), "private purchasers of tobacco products in wholesale quantities have presented themselves over the last few months, or alternatively have made overtures at retail outlets like tobacco stores, but in unobjectionable form from the legal standpoint, inasmuch as their offer is always to remunerate at the officially fixed prices."

Melzer was trying all this time to hold fast to his little patch of apricot. But now he had to face the moment when he saw himself standing at the mailbox on Porzellan Gasse as Thea came along the street unexpectedly. Friday, July 10. (His exact recall of the date didn't surprise him in the least—it seemed almost automatic to him in anything pertaining to the past, distant as well as recent.) He'd written that letter to apologize for canceling the following day, Saturday—very clearly aware at this point, however, of feeling he'd escaped from between the two glacier crevasses that were constantly rolling him around and around as a result of his forever shrinking back!—and he'd informed Editha in the same letter, not delivered by post, after all, but directly by Thea (totally reliable, in all probability), that he would prefer to convey face to face the information she was hoping to obtain as to the proper procedure for obtaining wholesale quantities of tobacco products by private individuals. Then later there had been no further mention of the subject, even though Melzer had in fact intended to advise her against any such purchase at this point exactly because of these reports about larceny and smuggling and to let her know she'd be better off waiting for a time (it was a mystery to him what she needed these goods for, but he hadn't much worried his head about it, either). So now, as Zihal was holding forth, it all naturally popped up again: Editha and Thea and the black and yellow mailbox and his supposed cold and his agonized hesitation.

That was all history. The old agony had been replaced by a new one. And he still held on tight. To the sweet little patch of apricot.

"Looking back, it's all to the good," he thought, "that Editha put that idea about the big cigarette purchase out of her head."

He missed her at this moment, missed her inside himself; her place was empty, and he had to stand in for her, to a degree (like Zihal for Frau Rosa!). And he did so at once.

Continuing to keep his eyes fixed on that sweet stabilizing point.

It started to exhibit a change of some sort, however, a restless motion of the downy surface.

But Melzer forced his glance to hold on, attached as if by suction, and so he succeeded, just before Thea moved her arm away, changed how she was sitting, and sat up straight with a small sigh—intently following Melzer's and Zihal's conversation, especially the older man's words—he succeeded in making the leap across those fourteen years mentioned earlier and recognizing Paula once more. He now turned. He looked at her.

And they both smiled.

Melzer picked up his wineglass; she did the same.

He leaned over to her.

"Strudlhof Steps 1911?" he asked in an undertone.

"Yes," she answered in a gently melodious voice.

He now thought of the Steps exactly the way someone thinks of a person. They were right. They never disappointed.

The glass display case, completely transparent and hence entirely incapable of concealment (though we mustn't estimate a vacuum as a virtue; that would be nonsensical), was now displaying a kind of overcast, whey-like, brackish cloudiness; while listening to Zihal, pain began crossing her face, pain owing to—even if it were only through this stupid affair of the cigarettes—her being ensnared by, or even in thrall to, Eulenfeld and his circle, which in her status as a designated penitent she had not taken leave of altogether without tears but which she had by this time left far behind her, all the more with Melzer so close by. Now she felt unworthy of this closeness all of a sudden.

"It remains open to consideration notwithstanding whether or not a connection may be established between a legal transaction unproblematic in and of itself and an activity liable to prosecution," Zihal said. "It cannot be regarded as a settled question whether the officially established prices for the merchandise would in fact have been proffered and whether in this instance, as in other cases of theft or larceny with breaking and entering or peculation or diverting of property—or however we may term the defalcation—it would have turned out to be a matter of attempted deceit through cozenage. For as far as I am aware, no one followed through on any of the offers tendered, meaning that there is no instance of any of these orders having been effectuated. Very likely because of mistrust. The law-enforcement authorities would have been provided with ample opportunity, at any rate, to concern themselves with such cases in addition in the course of any investigation already in progress."

A fleeting realization (we can see it clearly) now scurried through the glass case to the effect that the captain might not have been so completely out of line when he showed anger at the way she, Thea, had presented matters to her Aunt Oplatek in Josefstadt, including how she'd blurted out his name and address.

Our civil service councillor was exaggerating wildly; everything he was saying came out as if he had access to many and varied sources of information (he was never one to have just a lone item, but always many and varied sources) allowing him to expand into the elaborate staging and lavish production values of majestic baroque political drama! How modest his actual sources were! But they grew and grew as he drew and drew—conclusions, that is. He deduced. He deduced that the one case he really had heard about could not have been just an isolated instance. Hence the plural, sources. Not entirely without justification. Not at all. So without having found out anything additional, he already knew more about it than Thea and Paula combined.

During these last comments by Zihal, Paula had pricked up her ears, a practice of hers we're already familiar with. It almost seemed to her for a moment as if he really did know more than she herself did. But she remained completely calm and unruffled. That was how her Schachlesque common sense rapidly won out over even the force of *Zihalismus endemicus*, and she became aware—something only an individual to whom bureaucracy and all its trappings are totally, absolutely alien can accomplish!—that Zihal's ever-widening trellis was covered exclusively with plants cultivated from seeds deposited by her (and Thea—but she of course didn't know about that part!). She accordingly framed three stout tenets on the spot and was able, we might add, to expend much less mental effort than would someone like Asta von Stangeler in similar situations, since the flow of energy to Paula's brain was not impeded by any frilled collar or inner tube. She was much more the one to grab hold with both hands, never hesitating for a second, moving without restraint, and so she figured it all out, just like that:

1. Civil Service Councillor Zihal isn't a rat and wouldn't go squealing to higher-ups. There's no such bone in his body.

2. Nothing can happen to Paula, no matter what.

3. I don't care what becomes of that old rogue the captain.

Done. And she was also thinking there might now be a better chance—now that she and Melzer had reestablished a totally unanticipated new old connection—to tell him about the duplicate ladies. Right away? Today? Ever? Had René not been correct after all?!

In the meantime, the last topic of conversation had faded. Before it died off entirely, Melzer said that the increased vigilance of customs officials at the borders—intended not so much to prevent exports of tobacco products as to bring stolen supplies to a halt and thus foil smugglers—would no doubt clarify the situation sooner or later, or would at least deny these criminal elements any motivation to continue operating in a sphere that now offered such bleak prospects. When Zihal posed a further question as to whether legal forms of export, that is, through official channels—inasmuch as the tobacco administration did export products in certain cases, after all—could be subjected to misuse, Melzer professed at once to know no more about the procedure or protocol involved in such cases than that it would no doubt be rather complicated, thanks to enhanced security measures, which he had just a short time before been placed into a position to learn about for himself through having been able to take a look at new forms recently drawn up for this exact purpose and then by sheer chance lying later out on a table in the records department, where an inventory of supplies was being conducted. It would be hard for him to imagine, said Melzer, that anyone, no matter how versed, would really be able to perpetrate a hoax.

Pichler listened carefully to all this and then touched wineglasses with his wife and the major, but his interest didn't seem as lively as it had been before, when Zihal was holding his discourse about the (transcendental) essence of what constituted the repute of the civil service. Paula turned to Melzer and asked if she and Thea might be permitted to call on him at home one day. (Throwing out this line of communication was her way of proceeding to direct action.) They didn't want to disturb him in his office again, she said. "I'm always back by around five o'clock at the latest," answered the major, who found himself all of a sudden flung upward by a surging wave on whose foamy crest he was balancing with some effort; "it would give me the greatest pleasure." At the same time he could sense the feebleness of these words, even if they did contain a superlative, as measured against what he was feeling but couldn't say, however much he wanted to. "It might be a good idea," Picher pointed out, "to ask the major for his home telephone number; that way you wouldn't show up at an inconvenient time." No matter how reasonable the point Alois had just made, Paula quickly and clearly sensed the solidarity behind it, how men always stick together—no doubt about it—and how male bonding made a married man quick to discern a bachelor's concerns. That pleased her, though. Now they were all standing up to say goodbye. She placed her arm in her husband's with a light pressure he then returned. The major took a card from his wallet and handed it to Paula. "Who is your landlady, Major?" Paula asked unembarrassed, while making sure there was a telephone number on the card; it was on the lower right. "You want to know everything!" said Pichler with a laugh. "A Frau Rak," Melzer answered.

Dusk was coming on. His way home was the same as Thea's; Councillor Zihal soon turned right, not before performing a ceremonious bow, returned in the same style (and with a feeling of genuine esteem) by Melzer. The brief but punctilious exchange took place on one of the narrower streets in that old part of the city, which Zihal now left.

Walking along beside Thea, who was only a little shorter, her steps not tripping along but shortened out of propriety and respect (plus:

was she in a hurry to get back to the room with the well-known side-board?!), walking through this gathering twilight of the late summer evening, Melzer now—as if he were looking back and seeing a process already completed—found that his situation had undergone a complete change within the past few days. What had developed, what had enveloped him to the point of incorporation into his entire being as if all on its own, was something he was no longer in a position to recognize, not even remotely:

He wasn't looking for a way out.

A pugilist can be great at either giving or taking.

The major took.

That his love now—as he was making his short way to Alserbach Strasse—flooded its banks and completely engulfed everything: he took that too.

Let it.

He had come late to his own life. Now it was taking him along. But in a different way from how he'd always been just taken along before.

Now something was shining above this battle (that had no fighting), just as the sky, the sun breaking through, and the edges of the hills making their play of light and shadow above an actual battlefield are unconnected with all the attacking and retreating, the encirclements and escapes being executed on the plain. But even so, anyone who really fought in the battle (and survived, of course) has brought away, perhaps unawares, impressions of the changing light; battle and light now fused in his memory as elements of an association amazingly durable and totally undeniable, no matter how little the sudden brightening of a patch of woods or a burst of emerald green in the treetops might have seemed at the time in any way related to or affected by fear and hope, daring and success, victory or despair.

At her house door he gave her his hand, of course, but he didn't kiss hers, though it was the custom. He bowed. And: as he straightened back up, she looked at him and had an open, liquid quality in her eyes, like smooth water being ruffled by a light wind. And: didn't he feel the warmth of her hand?

Yes, and a slight pressure too.

But that all stayed on the surface. It didn't have anything to say, anything to connect to, any more than did the edges of those hills gleaming in sunlight under the eye of heaven or the emerald strip of woods.

Autumn was not yet nigh. No outward sign disclosed it. Only from deep within was emerging a power that drew away, absorbed, etiolated strength, retreating to far vistas on every side, just as here the dense and the tense heart of the city gave ground in all directions as the streets thinned out into open spaces, green still, amid which one walked or stood in solitude. The sunlight was more transparent, rarefied against the buildings opposite Melzer's office as it shone on their white surfaces like fresh water. What he was soon forced to notice with astonishment—insofar as one can speak of actually noticing in matters like this—was that time was passing more quickly. Starting with the Wednesday after the Nativity of Our Lady. Somehow it was already the following evening at five o'clock, when he should be getting the phone call from Editha. The aroma of the coffee he had just drunk was still in the air. The phone rang—with deliberation. It sounded as if it meant business: at least that was how Melzer reacted to this much-anticipated signal. Her voice was affectionate. It sounded very sweet. He put on his hat and gloves at once and then reached for an accessory, a walking stick that had long been gathering dust out in the umbrella stand—for much, much longer than Melzer could call to mind right now; a short bamboo cane with a gold knob. They really did meet right on the Strudlhof Steps, not halfway between their apartments or at Editha's place along the canal walkway, which would really have been much more obvious. "I have to go look after my parents now," she said; "that takes up a great deal of time. They came back from Merano unexpectedly, much earlier than they originally intended. Papa is not doing well at all. I spend practically my whole day on Gusshaus Strasse. I have a bad conscience about this. Sad to say, I've neglected the oldsters much too much over these last years. I can't keep on like that. But then when I'm with them, they won't let me go." Melzer was happy at how confidingly she spoke to him about these family matters—as if to a husband. It had almost that effect on him. For seconds at a time he was taken by a strange and therefore noticeable feeling of ownership, like something signed, sealed, and delivered. Then it passed as he surmounted the mountain peak of noise the tension was making in his own blood. The solid, sumptuous density of summer now thinned, clearing, contours emerging, sparser sunlight here on the Steps too, standing in the slanting rays of the gold-gilding evening, but with treetops full, thick, rich green still. Their filigree went branching off into the sky above the small, ocher-yellow palace at the top right. Editha and Melzer stood on the lower ramp, above the platform with the fountain, above the babbling of the water, directly in the middle. They had to settle for just a short walk, then. As much as time allowed, though, they lingered here. And Editha now listened as Melzer portrayed for her in the most minute detail the scandal that had played itself out here on the Steps fourteen years before, an episode she'd heard about at the time (she now mentioned in passing) only from some comments made by Herr Schmeller. Melzer went full-out with his account. But the whole episode took on a chilling undertone for the major as they now stood and talked about what had once been; he was overtaken by a feeling that can come when swimming, after quickly paddling along the surface of water the sun has heated but then stopping and standing with legs down: now the relatively cooler water below the surface can be felt, and everything now seems dominated by cold. That was how the major was feeling. At this point he was very far from recalling how earnestly he had earlier hoped to be at one with Editha in sharing common memories of times past and gone. In fact, he seemed to feel as if something almost like palpable indecency were leaching out of his own narrative and its depictions and discussions of events from those days. Yet more strongly than any of this—something that rapidly threaded its way along the drawing-room floor of his soul—persisted the power of the external world, Editha's appearance as she now went up the Steps ahead of him, with that noticeable outward and sideways thrust of her hips when she walked; perhaps that was exactly what it was that made them seem wider than they really were. There was something of a mystery about her little pug nose, too; right now it looked completely straight. They walked along Strudlhof Gasse as far as Boltzmann Gasse and then followed exactly the same route Melzer had once taken with Asta von

Stangeler. It was almost totally deserted and quiet here. She spoke to Melzer with great intimacy, among other things about their upcoming celebration as a couple—especially about that, in fact—and he lent himself to this intimate tone at once, as if he were leaping to her side, helping her to support something, to carry it and keep it balanced while she complained about the heavy demands now coming at her from various quarters and their role in preventing them from setting a definite date; plus there was another reason, one Melzer could easily figure out. This was all good; they were together; it was like being married.

The major didn't really start to sense how rapidly time was flowing away until after his walk with Editha that Thursday. Stangeler, who seemed to be constantly haunting this part of the city (understandable, because of his Grete), bumped into him the following day, Friday, but it felt to the major as if this encounter were taking place immediately after his time with Editha and the rather forced narrative on the Strudlhof Steps. He happened upon his friend on Fürsten Gasse (so perhaps René had come down the Strudlhof Steps this time as well). "Hello there, Herr von Stangeler!" (René would have simply walked right past him; for some strange reason, his almond eyes were narrowed to a slit, like a cat in full daylight.) "Tell me, why didn't you mention last Wednesday, when you were at my place, that I knew or, in fact, know Frau Paula Pichler—what a delightful lady!—if not by name? You surely must have been aware of that." It never dawned on the major that he had recently begun to develop a mental acumen and accuracy going considerably, or for that matter almost dangerously, beyond the usual moderate level of illumination in his life and surroundings, all the more so the less he looked for a way out; in addition—and likewise without his finding anything remarkable about it—he was unrelentingly fixated on every matter now before him. He was living his life all around the Strudlhof Steps, so to speak, not only in space but also inside himself, the circles tightening ever smaller, almost like a vortex. Stangeler, who was probably coming from some entirely different place just now, stared at him in some confusion, indeed complete momentary perplexity. They were standing not far from the open entrance to the park of the Palais Liechtenstein. Melzer did not hold back in the least from what was on his mind. He quickly dug through whatever ballast might be keeping him and René apart at the moment. And now the dust came flying at René in the form of the year and the people present—Old Man Schmeller and all the others who just stood around on the lower ramp when it was over. "Of course!" cried René, grasping Melzer's upper arm, "what do you know! What do you know!—That is, of course you know! But I was blind. There was an invisible wall; it was inside me, and now it's been broken through from the outside! And all these years of my overlooking available evidence, just surmising Melzer and Paula had never had contact! Or I had split Melzer into two parts. Yesterday's Melzer, the lieutenant; and today's Melzer. But now they fit back together. Inside me. Do you sometimes still wear those wide white tennis shorts these days, too?" This abundantly peculiar shift of emphasis by Dr. (!!) Stangeler left Melzer unperturbed; we are the only ones judging it as odd, whereas we'll venture to say it was immediately understandable, not to say utterly self-evident, to the major. "I guess that heals the split!" he answered. As we see, he replied in the same tone and then told René all about Wednesday, about the little garden, about the Pichler couple, about blithe, dignified Theresa Schachl, about the civil service councillor (though his attempts to portray and catch the spirit of the man flopped completely; Stangeler just couldn't understand), but above all else, about the apple, the apricot-apple that had come rolling toward him under the gateway. Strangely enough, it was into none other than this piece of fruit that Stangeler greedily bit (during the rest of Melzer's report his face had shown a rather fixed rigidity, like someone set onto the wrong track). "Was it a plump apple?!" he asked with enthusiasm. "Oh yes, you can say that again!" said Melzer. "And you could feel her arms around your knee? Were they warm?!" "Indeed they were; that was so charming!" "Just imagine that!" cried René, as if he'd been given the most astonishing news ever, "I find that so cute!" It was in this lively spirit that they continued talking there on Fürsten Gasse.

Saturday and Sunday were spent with the captain; specifically, he came to visit Melzer on both days (the weather was overcast), bringing bottles, looking careworn, acting like a burden to himself, as if exposed to a climate that left him unable to act, but clever and charming, as always. Long legs outstretched. A bottle in a paper napkin. Melzer

drank only black coffee, more than was good for him. "Ah, the estimable Frau Rak," he had said in the hallway while the landlady was
standing right outside. He kissed her hand. "May she never become a
hereunto appertaining Frau Wreck! *Beati qui ambulant*, et cetera, et
cetera." She didn't understand the Latin, of course. But she liked the
baron quite a bit. Inside: "Is Pierrot being good? Not taking too great
an interest?" "There's nothing interesting on my end," replied Melzer.
He didn't ask about Editha, and the captain didn't say anything about
her, either. Instead, he said—after staring for a long time at the small
light fixture near the floor, above the bearskin and to the right of the
fireplace—"A strange excrescence. You could in all justice have another
one mounted exactly above this one, just under the ceiling. For the
sake of symmetry." (Medium-strength grunt.) While the captain was
saying these words, it struck Melzer with extraordinary vividness—
running parallel but without any connection to them, which is to say,
having overlooked available evidence, to use Herr von Stangeler's
term—that he had never told Eulenfeld anything about the former
Major and now Colonel Laska, mentioning him in passing at the most,
but never in detail. His astonishment at this realization burst open
inside him like a flashing pinwheel, glowed like a lump of brightly
burning coal. After all, there would have been plenty of opportunity
and suitable occasion years before, when he was newly acquainted with
the captain. But Melzer no longer spoke about anything military. It
was too late. At the same time, however, the major caught himself in
a congealing morass of images into which he'd waded rather deep; they
involved talking to Thea Rokitzer about Laska. But now he brought
that nonsense to an abrupt halt.

Two dates with Editha during the week that followed, the second
one on Thursday, in the center of town. They turned off the Graben
into Gerstner's (a pastry shop renowned in those days) and withdrew
into a quiet corner, chatting away intimately. On Bogner Gasse a short
time before, while he was still alone, the major had bumped into Ernst
von Marchetti, round and smooth, but very serious now: he'd just heard
that something disastrous had happened to the Grauermanns in Budapest, though he didn't know quite what. Somebody from the Foreign
Ministry had called Teddy von Honnegger on official business, and

Teddy had then come out with that news, along with the request allegedly made by Etelka that her brother, René, be called away from Vienna at once; so he was expected in Budapest or was more likely already there. Nobody had been able to find out anything further. "That can't be, though!" said Melzer. "I was just now talking with René." But when he and Marchetti went their separate ways, he realized his error. Sitting in that little corner at Gerstner's, Editha told him that she'd have to devote all of Saturday and Sunday to her parents. But if her father should improve, she would then call Melzer from Gusshaus Strasse on Sunday afternoon. "The phone is pretty much off to the side in the large front room; I hope I'll be able to talk freely," she said—so would he stay at home on Sunday afternoon as a favor to her? "That goes completely without saying," answered Melzer and quickly squeezed her hand. "And maybe I'll be able to say at that time when our celebration should happen," she added more quietly, returning the pressure, "because then I'll know if and when I can leave my parents to themselves." Melzer felt this was all good, concrete, within arm's reach, not just a mirage or some shining streak or stripe darting and flying around somewhere, only to flutter away with no grounding in reality. He felt trust and confidence. She was sitting close to him, their bodies touching, and as hard as she was trying to avoid talking about their upcoming union was also as hard as she was avoiding the touch of his arm or hand, the warm, gentle closeness of his knee. "I will do my utmost to be able to tell you on Sunday the exact day and hour I can expect you at my place," she said further, and then, after a moment, "because it's just—torture, like this. The next time will be at my place, all right?" "All right," he said, and kissed her hand energetically. That cold undercurrent he'd felt on the Strudlhof Steps was gone. He felt her desire, her manifest readiness; walls broke down, including ones that had recently run right through him; barriers burst; the ground surged up. "There's one thing I have to request," she now said; "please be on time, right to the minute. Don't keep me waiting. Waiting grinds me down and takes away my ability to function. It makes me only half human. Will you be on time?" "Totally," said Melzer. She'd hit a target just now, somehow striking the very marrow of his past, directly reaching his honor as a soldier. Punctuality, after all, was the one obligation he had never ever in his life failed to live up to. "I'm assuming you did get my letter in time, back in July, when I was sick, Editha." "Yes, I certainly did," she quickly retorted, "I'm only saying this now in general, you know, because waiting scares me so. I simply cannot wait." He had naturally asked what was wrong with her father but didn't get a very definite answer; maybe she didn't know herself; maybe they hadn't been able to reach a precise diagnosis; at any rate it appeared to have something to do with his kidneys or his gallbladder, if not both. "But he's been feeling better lately," she remarked. In between other comments, she reminded Melzer about information she'd already asked him for earlier in the summer, having to do with the possible purchase of cigarettes and Virginia cigars in rather large quantities. "For the love of heaven," Melzer said, "you're surely not going to . . ." "I don't smoke often, as you know, and then mostly when I'm alone," she replied, "but then nothing is strong enough for me." He now said to her—after first openly confessing his bureaucratic incompetence—that he thought the present time was very unfavorable for such a purchase (he thought he knew this with some certainty), for reasons that had been operable all summer long. "How do you mean?" she asked, and Melzer answered that the explanation would involve a long rigmarole best not entered into here; besides, he wanted to do some further research into the matter. For the reasons already given, however, it hadn't been possible to follow up during the height of summer (were you telling a lie or not, Melzerboy!?). She then changed the subject and talked again about her parents and the telephone call on Sunday afternoon and the upcoming "celebration," as we've already recounted.

Melzer reached home at about six o'clock. When he stepped into the hallway, the telephone was ringing shrilly. He rushed to it, knowing who was calling before he lifted the receiver. His heart bombarded him with heavy pounding as if it were ambushing, as if breaking out from behind walls that had been muffling the sound. Even as he scurried to the phone he was trying to calm himself with lightning-quick rationalizations—no reason to start getting flustered, after all!—but nothing helped; his heart kept at it while Paula Pichler was speaking and left him too short of breath to reply (she of course didn't say anything to the major about how this call was her third—it just so happened that both on Friday of the week before and again this past Monday no one had been at home; neither the major nor his landlady had answered). Would it be all right if they came to visit him on Saturday afternoon? But of course, of course! He was so happy they hadn't forgotten about him (the "they" included Thea). Now the conversation was finished. Now he was alone. Now his heart retreated to its place back behind the walls, one by one, and beat more distantly. Till Saturday.

And Saturday came in a flash. The odor of coffee was pleasant. Saturday, September 19. Pierrot had set the table like an efficient (and of course greatly interested) household manager. From the street below came the jangling and droning of a streetcar passing by rapidly and now hurrying over the mountain peak of its own noise. The sun cut a triangular plane in the top floor of the building opposite and shone with glaring brilliance on the white surface. The major wasn't meditating, wasn't lying on the bearskin, wasn't upsetting the coffee things—perish the thought! They weren't even in the room anyway; Frau Rak wanted her maid, her domestic help, to serve from an attractive coffee set. The latest dash along the *trópoi* had been fully attended to. Everything had been configured, not to say transfigured, if not yet on the outside. But whatever it was that had played out exactly four weeks before in this room was now present once more, as if on a lower floor whose ceiling had grown reassuringly sturdy a certain liveliness or stimulation had worked its way upward; everything swayed as if over a cleft or a sounding board. The light fixture down by the floor to the right of the fireplace had been covered over, incidentally, no doubt to avoid questions; Melzer had placed a chair in front of it and covered it with a small Bosnian prayer rug he owned. Now the doorbell chirped. Frau Rak remained out of sight (could she perhaps see through a crack?), but the servant girl's steps could be heard. Melzer went to his door. Thea filled the entire hallway (the gentlest but mightiest explosion of milk and blood), even though she stayed self-effacingly behind Paula, cautiously holding something longish that was wrapped in paper. Her figure struck the major as very tall and long-legged; her dress was made of some dark but patterned material, deep violet; the fabric didn't seem light, but more on the heavy side, which made it encase Thea's substantial bosom rather tightly. Melzer greeted Paula with cordiality, indeed with genuine affection, and held her hand in his for quite a few moments. "You can give your cake roll to the major now," said Paula, now carefully taking the long, paper-wrapped object out of Thea's hands. "She baked it especially for the major, in my kitchen," she explained and then asked if he might possibly have available a serving dish of that size and shape? Of course! And because the maid had just come in with the coffee, the package was handed to her; she soon brought its contents back very nicely arranged, a real showpiece of sponge cake and chocolate (which Pierrot had most certainly subjected to the expert eye of a connoisseur). While thanking them with all his heart—a heart from which the pounding and thumping had receded; it now stood, having emerged from behind its numerous walls, pale and motionless in front of them—Melzer felt threatened or at least seriously warned about the clear and present danger represented by this cake roll, this confection now gracing the coffee table; it seemed to him for some moments that this product of Thea's dainty and somewhat round hands (they were almost too small for the rest of her body) displayed an inherent kinship, though in a way not easily grasped, with a compliment or a curtsy, which made it appear to him as if their configuration was like that of an uncle with his two nieces seated together here (forgetting that the age difference between him and Paula was not significant, and between him and the little lamb not tremendous; she had, after all, reached the beginning of her trifling hereunto appertaining twenty-fourth year). The *trópoi* were making some noise on the lower floor; he heard a couple of trains whiz past; he saw a few lights blinking: but these were trains in which he was no longer sitting, everything small, like a miniature mechanical train set he could now see only from the outside. Which meant he was also on the outside and wasn't looking for a way out anymore. Meanwhile, this table where they were enjoying their Jause seemed to be rising, mounting upward after sailing away from the rest of the room along with the patch of hardwood floor it stood on, like a running board that could hold the three of them—afloat, aloft, fleet in its flight, like a gondola that never swayed. And even if it wasn't a small garden, this gondola was outfitted even so with a baldachin or an arbor distantly reminiscent of the ones that in days gone by used to adorn the brightly painted fairy-tale wed-

ding carriages on the merry-go-rounds in the Wurstlprater, the amusement park in the Prater with all the rides; they still enjoy a certain fame
in the outside world, although with a layer of patina. The gondola soared
and ascended—over the depths of the city and of time; over *trópoi*;
over the densely wooded hillside framing the Strudlhof Steps, deeply
immersed in domes of green; over dapples of sunlight and shadows of
leafage; over a bear hunt; and in miniature, as if looking into a little
case lined in red velvet, over a view from a great height of the Café
Pucher. Silvery spray and fragile foam from the wetlands unfolded
along the river above the city the higher they climbed and thus gained
a free horizon. Why try looking for a way out when every single care
had passed by, ceased even to exist, had never amounted to anything
in the first place? Paula didn't bring up her old acquaintance with
Melzer, though it was in the forefront of their minds. If you're sitting
next to a glass case, you have to be a little careful with your elbows and
with all your movements in general; you have to know what you're
doing. So Melzer let it go at that. But it animated and enlivened him
to talk a little now about the old days, especially his stint in the military
(though not about the war), however lightly he was merely brushing
against subjects and objects whose radiance he could nonetheless sense
very keenly, if at a great distance—perhaps greater than had ever been
the case before. He also told them a little about the bear hunt (Thea
listened wide-eyed), so of course he also mentioned Major Laska in
this connection. It was easy to see that the way in which Melzer spoke
about this comrade of his had a very positive effect on Paula Pichler,
that she warmly approved of this aspect of Melzer's nature (all on Thea's
behalf, always for Thea's benefit, though Melzer of course never noticed).
While he was talking about the bear hunt—the skin was lying right
there in front of them; they took a closer look; Paula even knelt down
on it for a moment and grasped the fur!—there awoke in Melzer between two breaths the joy of life he'd felt back then on the morning
after the unsuccessful night of lying in ambush and he was walking
through the beech woods with Laska, moving easily, and conscious
that every obedient muscle was relishing the exertion. "Did the shot
kill the bear at once?" Thea asked. She seemed to have sympathy for
the animal; she had lightly stroked its beautiful pelt. "Yes, definitely,"

said Melzer, giving thought to what he was saying. "There was a tremendous jolt and it leapt up as if a patch of forest ground itself had flown up in the air; then it collapsed, and that was it. Of course you have to use the right weapon. This bear weighed about four hundred and fifty pounds, which is unusually heavy for a Bosnian bear." Everything was going well, but all gondolaesque phenomena drift rapidly away, and so even though they had barely boarded their fairy-tale carriage, it turned out that their lovely ride had lasted two and a half hours already. Paula had to leave, and of course so did Thea.

Melzer walked them home. They walked along Porzellan Gasse toward Althan Platz—amid a gentle dove-gray poured out like milk and with some streetlights already beginning to shine—and then turned left; near the Palais Liechtenstein, the smaller one that housed the famous picture gallery, they crossed the street and stood by the front entrance for a time, on the same spot where ten days before, after the Nativity of Our Lady, Melzer had felt that peculiar shift of illumination inside himself, that almost explosive burst of light, but without any connection to anything happening in or around him. When Thea had said goodbye, Paula and Melzer crossed into the old neighborhood of Lichtental. Making their way down into a deeper layer of what was past and gone also meant they were descending into their personal past as well. Just before that, however, Paula had made it a point to see to the immediate future. "Will you be sure to join us if Thea and I take a walk along the towpath right by the Brigitta Bridge next Monday?" (So that got all arranged; Paula still called the bridge by its old name.) "Just to the right of the city rail station are stairs going down to the path and the riverbank. That's where we'll be. Between four and five. But can you get away from the office that early?" "I think so," said Melzer. "We'll stay until about five fifteen." "I certainly won't come much later than five," said Melzer, "probably somewhat earlier." Paula then told him that René Stangeler had given her an account, all the way back then, in 1911, of what had led up to the big scene on the Strudlhof Steps, filling her in about what had happened in the bathroom during the party and about some girlfriend of Fräulein Ingrid—the daughter of the house—who had stabbed her in the back, though she couldn't recall the girlfriend's name; "Could she have been called

Edith?" "Yes," said Melzer, "Editha Pastré." "Oh yes," exclaimed Paula; "whatever became of her later?" "She married an official in some ministry, a Herr Schlinger," said Melzer, "but she's been divorced for ages." They were now near the Blue Unicorn house, where they came to a stop. "Do you still see this Frau Schlinger?" Paula asked. "Yes, I do," Melzer answered, "and not all that seldom, either." "Then there's something I have to tell you, Major: there are two of this lady." "That's very aptly put," said Melzer; "that's something René would come out with. She really does give that impression, doesn't she? Two different people in the same body but not seamlessly joined. A gap that narrow probably never heals over completely; when two different kinds of basic elements are conjoined in the same person, there can never be a full healing, a seamless jointure." (So: our Melzer has become a civilian; such concepts can exist only inside a civilian mentality; even so, however, he was himself surprised at his using expressions that were gathering strength on their own, beyond his usual sleep-thinking, his Melzerian lethargy; indeed, it was as if the words he found were dragging him behind them and into a new life; the words were standing afloat in front of his mouth, and he was following them.) "No," said Paula. She focused her energy as if ready to dash from a starting gate: "There really are literally two of them, I mean in the flesh. I saw for myself. René drew my attention to them at the West Station." "Oh, René," said Melzer in an offhand tone, "he's one who often sees what he *thinks* ought to be there, as it were, so in this case I can easily understand his imagining something like that. Naturally he's a bit of a dreamer, too. Though his imagination isn't usually hazy or misty; it's precise and sharp, in my experience, if you can picture what I mean." "But, Major," Paula said—though her strength had left her after the initial burst—"I can't even describe how perfect the resemblance was." "Yes, I know things like that exist," said Melzer. They resumed walking. What he had now realized—always with words in the lead, as if the awareness were being imparted by his latest and most advanced organ—was illuminating his brain like a light on his forehead, like one of those small lamps with a mirror used by physicians. The truth of what Paula was saying completely obviated any question of accuracy about what she had observed and was now asserting; in fact, the whole thing appeared to Melzer in the light of a whimsically phrased formulation that had originated with Stangeler and was now being simply passed on verbatim by Paula Pichler. And she now began, on the other hand, to look on her dashes and bursts of energy as almost ridiculous, as effort expended on a totally insignificant object, one more or less passé by now. She briefly but vigorously shook hands with Melzer under the gateway: "Till Monday, then." He walked away from the little house as if from a place he knew well and felt at home in; crossing the narrow street on an angle, he now saw light in the upper story; that's where they lived, the Pichlers; and that's where the civil service councillor had once lived, he'd been told.

Home now. It had grown completely dark. The noise of the street sounded as if something like a quilt or comforter were muffling it. Melzer's hearing was closed off, plugged up. Editha's phone call tomorrow afternoon. All the assurance Melzer derived from her was enveloping him like something sweet and sticky, as if he were standing up to his neck in syrup or were full to overflowing with it on the inside. After the lavish Jause with the coffee and cake roll he wasn't very tempted to rush home and open a can of sardines with tea and bread and butter for his supper. So he passed by his front door and his empty room, where the chair with the prayer rug was still standing in front of the wall fixture near the floor to the right of the fireplace. E.P. and his wife were already seated in the Beisel, their usual restaurant, and no sooner had he entered than they waved to him. The place smelled of seasonings and tobacco. Melzer was craving a beer and something spicy to eat. He got his wish: a Serbian pilaf. "We walked down the Strudlhof Steps again today, but we didn't bump into you, Major, sad to say," E.P. started, "or are you just coming from there now?" "I always—" answered Melzer, but in order for him to cover up the truth he was about to blurt out somewhat hastily, nothing would do but to send a little white lie tripping after it. "I always—whenever I take a walk, that is—I always choose this way home. But I'm just coming from my apartment now. I had company." That was the truth, certainly. But the moment Melzer had replied with that little word "always," two syllables that characterized his current situation all too succinctly, he instantly became aware how extraordinary his situation in fact was, bent on propelling him toward a point that his words already knew but that he didn't. Putting some space between himself and the couple in this way, as if they were sitting on the riverbank and he in a boat, Melzer ate with a good appetite. Saturday, September 19. Twenty-eight days after the *trópoi*. But he didn't go to the café this time; after a cordial leave-taking in front of the Miserovsky Twins, he crossed the street instead and headed directly for home, feeling more than a little sleepy. The chair next to the fireplace had been put back, and the prayer rug was in its usual place. The light fixture was now visible. The coffee table had been cleared and put back in its normal spot. The cake roll, most of it still uneaten, was now on the mantelpiece and covered with wax paper to protect it from dust. Melzer's one wish was to go to sleep right away. The rooms here virtually invited him to do that and nothing else. As he lay in the dark on his back, the following day opened up like a hollow space surprisingly blank, devoid of intent or plan— Melzer was expecting nothing but that phone call in the afternoon. This thought, the last one he had as consciousness waned, worked its way deep into him, like an embossing stamp. No walls tilted; no barriers burst. We might say that he was merely standing in for Editha, that she was present only by proxy (like Frau Rosa Zihal in the little garden) with all that assurance of hers.

He slept deeply, without waking. When a person goes to sleep, said person wakes up, and as the person wakes up, so will the whole day be (what would ever happen to change that?!). Inside Melzer, then, this day, Sunday, harmonized perfectly with the chord, the basic triad that had been sounding when he fell asleep the night before. No taking a walk after Mass. He went directly home in spite of the relatively fair weather, as if he were observing a monastic solitude, a state he felt obligated to maintain, even this early. Moreover, Frau Rak told him he wouldn't need to go out at noon if he'd rather stay at home, because she had something nice for him, roast goose. Before that, he puttered around in his apartment and straightened the prayer rug, which hadn't been hung back up exactly right. And standing here in one corner, to the left of the fireplace, were his few books, numbering perhaps ten or twelve: a travel guide to Bosnia from the previous century, by one Boroëvič; a general staff report printed in 1879 in Vienna, titled *The*

Occupation of Bosnia and Herzegovina in 1878; one of Karl May's adventure tales; a German edition in large format of *The Three Musketeers* by Alexandre Dumas, with the illustrations by Leloir; *Drill Instructions for the Royal and Imperial Infantry*. Then a similar guide for the cavalry (once his father's property—"Melzer, Captain of Horse" was written on the flyleaf in his father's hand); a novel by Marcel Prévost, *L'automne d'une femme*, in French—somebody had somewhere at some time left it at Melzer's place, and it had occupied so many and varied rooms throughout the decades along with him; the last book that came to his hand was the one Mary Allern had once given him, not long after he'd first made her acquaintance; he opened it to the front and read: "My surroundings were filled with dangers wherever I was, and as far as that goes, every place, even now in the twentieth century, is a forest everywhere." Melzer closed the book and opened the novel by Prévost, where he read: "*Oh ténébreux et troubles, nos cœurs humains, même les plus sincères!*" This sentence was printed as a line set off by itself. Melzer could feel the absence of any connection between those words and his present state of mind. Nothing was dark or vexed inside him: he was perceiving himself as bright and neat (like the room itself), almost emptied out after a good retreat. The weather had apparently cleared up nicely. The sun was shining up to the right on the top story of the building opposite. The books had been sitting all this time in a corner, on an open shelf of a small cupboard with little columns that held them perfectly; he put them back now. We have to admit that this very modest collection—of course it hadn't been actually collected—contained nothing stuffy, nothing nasty, nothing smacking of the demimonde, or the *demi-esprit*, for that matter; we could say that all in all these books were oriented toward externals but were of more or less notable quality (in this connection we could name Doyle's *The Hound of the Baskervilles* in English as well as Stevenson's *Treasure Island*). Before they ate, Frau Rak told him (he'd knocked at her door to ask her) she wouldn't be lying down after their meal today; he should feel free to do so, however, because if a telephone call came for him, she would come and get him at once. Melzer did want to sleep a little, just for a short spell, not a kèf, but a deeper immersion, an escape from all the brightness and liveliness. He lay down on the sofa in his back room but left the door open so he could hear Frau Rak or the phone itself. His nap turned into a kèf after all, though, even without coffee or chibouk. He didn't fall sound asleep. He lay motionless on his back, to be sure, but the day remained with him as if it had come pouring in all at once; not just the bright sunlight here in the room (even though he'd reduced it by drawing the curtains), but down below in the street as well, on the square in front of the station, along the riverbank and the towpath. It wasn't his usual sleep-thinking. Melzer wasn't thinking anything. He wasn't pondering anything. He wasn't playing alternative dominoes or puzzling out his next few moves. He was simply in motion. Moving straight toward a visible wall that he knew would turn invisible but would have to allow him to pass through at the moment he stepped directly up to it; stepping up would accordingly and immediately be transformed into stepping through (remarkable notions! like a Chinese disciple of Tao!). Melzer left unconsidered any possible entrances available for him to choose from. They wouldn't be any larger than louver windows or portholes anyway. As soon as they landed in Šibenik he left the steamship without delay and headed down the gangplank, already lowered. When he woke up fully from what he thought was merely a doze, it was close to five. He sat up on the sofa, stood, moved around, and thought about nothing. The telephone rang calmly but brightly, and it sounded like serious business. No shortness of breath. Everything by proxy, although he was not standing in for Editha at this point: Melzer was standing in for Melzer. She sounded somehow inhibited as she spoke; her voice was restrained. "Can you be free tomorrow, Monday? You can? Five o'clock at my apartment. Be on time. I have to hang up now." While she was speaking, the one need he felt was to keep saying "Yes" to everything, or at least to agree and not back out. Now he was looking past the conversation, past Editha, and suddenly past Thea and Paula as well as they now went ambling along the riverbank. He could go before his date with Editha. Between four and five. This thought was a mere formality, as it were. Everything wove itself into that wall, its designated entrances now visible, indeed, but somehow not really plausible. "Thank you for listening for the phone, Frau Rak," he said to his landlady, who was just coming in from another room; "I slept for a long time. The goose was delicious, by the way. This evening I'll be going to the tavern." He quickly made coffee, very strong, too. The rooms were now filled to bursting with that sweet, sticky reassurance: almost too much so. The time vanished inside it like an underground limestone stream: it was seven before he knew it. Melzer roamed through his apartment like a scale on which nothing is weighed, which tilts from its horizontal balance with only a slight motion, as if the one doing the weighing were himself to be weighed in the balance and counted. He made a decision as he was roaming: tomorrow he would work in the office straight through until two o'clock and then call it a day; he would go to his chief, who held the high rank of Hofrat, early in the morning and ask for permission, which would be granted on the spot, and then on Wednesday or possibly Saturday afternoon make up for the time he'd missed.

Melzer was alone in the Beisel. A short stroll in the warm evening after dinner; Fürsten Gasse; along Liechtenstein Strasse; then the very quietest section of the Strudlhof Steps, at the bottom, moving toward the moss-covered urn and the stone mask from which a thin stream of water issues. The plashing of the fountain on the landing higher up could be heard. The empty stairs, the ramps and platforms illuminated by the lampposts, all struck Melzer as enormous and expansive. So now there he stands once again, and once again as if searching, like a devout pilgrim before the unbroken wall surrounding the temple precincts at Delphi. He suddenly felt somewhat oppressed by the flippancy with which he'd recounted to Editha the scene that had played itself out here in 1911. He really considered for a few moments, in all seriousness, that he had been disrespectful to the Steps. He kept standing there at the bottom for a long time without setting foot on them. There was a breath of night wind. But the genius loci, the dryad, the goddess kept silence. Not only because she was asleep by now, her small head drooping deep in the wood of a tree trunk or elsewhere, but for another reason, a very simple one—because she had long since given her answer. And the gods do not say anything twice.

Her children had left by seven thirty, the boy to school, the girl to some course, and Mary went to her bath. While she relaxed in the hot water in the tub, nonchalantly observing her body (still flawless but with its impact in abeyance here among tiled walls and nickel-plated faucets), she drifted along the moving watercourse of reveries flowing out from the previous three days, out of and behind their completion, their conclusion; she had traveled out to Rekawinkel on Thursday and stayed until the evening before, Sunday, September 20, when she returned with her daughter, who had been enjoying a short vacation of a little more than a week out there with two friends of hers, sisters, at their parents' country house. But none of them could rest easy until they talked Mary into coming out for the last three days—the phone never stopped ringing. First the two girlfriends, then right after them the parents, who hardly knew Mary; it would give them great pleasure if she came; they themselves would be very happy, and the young ladies even more so; they would love to send the car for her. So there it was on Thursday, standing by the main entrance. This or something like it was what always happened to Frau Mary when it came to all her children's friends: she was asked for, cajoled, sought after; young people gravitated to her, showed their great admiration, sat and talked with her longer than necessary and with obvious enjoyment. And the daughters, ready to enter their last year of preparatory school, were no exception; they particularly enjoyed Mary's company. And the parents stepped up right behind the children, vying as well for time with the beautiful, clever mother of their daughters' friend. That was how it was; Mary didn't sham about it, and nobody shammed with her either. People just plain liked her. She lived and moved inside the realm of popularity, which is inborn.

Of course she made every effort to act accordingly. Being considered outstanding is a slightly burdensome state every outstanding person has to carry inside, acting as a spur but at the same time creating obligations at every turn. It doesn't throw such persons back on themselves, though; instead, it drives them outward into the life around them, makes them keep proving themselves. It strengthens and energizes them in every case.

Mary, too, felt strengthened and energized. But her need for energy and strength were tapped almost without letup over the following three days, no matter where she turned, including to the bridge table (where it turned out that she was a much better player than her host, who began taking pointers from her with total delight). However, she'd left the tennis court to the young girls and their friends. When conversations were struck up, though—after dinner, for example, sitting out on a high, wide, old-fashioned wooden veranda—she was always the focal point; that seemed to come about by itself. Everyone waited for what she would say or if she would say anything in the first place. Mary naturally possessed enough self-discipline to take the best course by saying nothing at these times, or almost nothing. That didn't always work out, of course (so she thought, anyway—the truth is that it's merely a question of how calm or strong one's nerves are, because a person is almost always capable, if he or she really wants to, of saying absolutely nothing; that said, keeping silent represents quite a mental accomplishment). All in all, she'd been pushed to her utmost limit fairly often here. And now suddenly she was alone but still standing at this remote limit.

Up to now she'd hardly moved in the bathtub, to which she'd make her way directly from her bed, as it were, moving with a certain amount of caution. Now she thought about the tennis court in Rekawinkel (the wooded mountains curving freely behind it, the white balls flying back and forth, the shouts of the young people). Autumn had started to manifest itself, resonant in brightness, as isolated strips of leaves began drawing radiant, blazing streaks of color in the forest, and when the train along the western line went past, it felt as if the whistle from the locomotive just before it entered the tunnel and the faint trace of the odor from the smoke lingering in the air were opening out the far-off spaces that had gathered in the forest and were standing ready to clear the surroundings, to make them thinner and more transparent as the leaves fell. Mary could now see in front of her the tennis courts in the pale Augarten. She didn't feel in the least like going there to play: a memory was lodged in her, not in her head, but more in her arms, an organic remembering about her having played with Frau Sandroch and then, her arms made of glass but her joints feeling like wood, with Oscar against Dr. Adler and his wife. Well, that was once upon a time; she could go over there today if she cared to play! A partner could always be found, even in the morning! This thought was what caused her to make her first actual movement here in the bathtub, the first emphatic movement of the morning, for that matter. As she sat up, she accidentally bumped the soap holder so hard that its bracket flew up from the edge of the tub and dropped into the water along with the soap and the nailbrush. The soap drifted to the bottom slower than porcelain and nickel, which plummeted quickly and gave a muffled sound when they hit the bottom. She started fishing, and she caught the things. So then she began washing and grooming, but the oval cake of soap slipped out of her hands, shot down onto the ribbed bath mat, and vanished under the tub. Mary could have taken the simpler course and reached for another cake of soap already at hand lying on the broad shelf in front of the tiled wall. She could also just have given the blue silk cord with its tassel a slight tug, and her faithful Marie would have come and retrieved the escaped soap. But Mary was already out of the bathtub, kneeling down, fumbling for it with outstretched arm; and now she was sitting in the water again, but somewhat disconcerted, as if bending over an empty space that had opened up inside her—a kind of balking or small misfiring that created uncertainty, a state of being hollowed out that seemed to demand attentiveness and caution in every matter that was usually discharged automatically and smoothly. But not now; she'd just been clumsy (she'd also been clumsy when climbing back into the bathtub and had in fact nearly fallen, but she wouldn't allow that to count and completely refused to face up to her awkwardness). There came a knock. Mary called to Marie through the door that she did not want to have breakfast in the bath but at the tea table instead.

Even though Marie had just shut the window looking down the long street toward the canal so as to keep the dust from flying in and settling on the polished furniture, the warm late-summer morning outside was leaning against the panes, a friendly and soft openness of all the surroundings, lightly tinged with water vapor and still milky and misty from the early morning on the canal; weather with much space, an open cavern of expectation, and in the middle of these surroundings, which diffused into muffled form the sounds of city life, Mary was now sitting over her teacup. Between her surroundings and the interior space, however, that is the world inside the bounds of her body, she felt the presence of something like a gap separating them from each other, the outer from the inner world, thereby diminishing the reality of both realms. It felt to our Mary as if everything were at a standstill, immobile, inside as well as outside herself; that gap, so clearly marked, impeded the fluidity or commingling that ordinarily supported and bore up her approach to life. But today everything lay isolated and disconnected inside her, each separate item exacting alertness and vigilance and seeming to give advance warning, as it were, of every consequence that would unfailingly ensue if there were the slightest lapse of concentration. For the time being, she heeded that instinct, handling the tea things slowly and with scrupulous mindfulness. A fragile memory came to call, brushing against her briefly; it had to do with Lieutenant Melzer and with a statement somebody had made to the effect that even today we can find ourselves surrounded by danger in any environment, however refined or familiar, as if we were in the jungle. Mary was being slow. Today she was deploying her sense of sight, for example, with a slowness that reached into her very depths, as it were, not gliding from object to object but stopping to survey each individual stone by itself. Yet she was even now impatiently looking past the gap so sharply outlined in her person this morning (feeling hemmed in by it the whole time), looking out at surroundings into the midst of which it surely must be possible to set foot by the routine expedient of a single, simple, sensible stride.

This is where she stopped musing. The morning was devoid of plans, but its emptiness urged her to make some; they surged up in her from every side like air entering a vacuum. But these were not the kinds of plans that really animated and energized her. They weren't lively impulses; they presented themselves to her more like a list or a catalog. Mary, presently turning her gaze away from the brief survey of her inner self, had just begun running through this catalog when the telephone rang with calm, bell-like tones, a set of pearls being strung.

It was Lea Fraunholzer. Her voice sounded mellow and far away.

Only at this moment was Mary seized by a powerful and genuine impetus (the first one this morning) that pointed in a specific direction; she instantly steered her course toward it without the tiniest vestige of resistance or opposition, indeed with an eagerness to assume the liveliest of roles and to express and present the deepest of interest, not solely on Lea's behalf but on her own as well. She had a need to prove herself. More than that too. What stepped up right next to her and kept standing beside her at the phone, into which she was showing a propensity to speak with intensity now that she recognized Lea's voice, was bad conscience, which evidently had had time enough over the whole summer to grow and gather force. True, she had telephoned the Küffers about a week before, but that now struck her as nothing more than a mere formality; she'd wanted to be covered, as it were. At this moment she forgot all about Dr. Negria, who'd been the occasion of her making the call in the first place—albeit unintentionally and with no awareness of the whole background—and she reflected on the special circumstances under which she'd found out what she knew from the pediatrician and interventionist about the scenes or clashes, amounting practically to a rift, between Etelka and the consul general out in the country toward the end of August. Her bad conscience was rooted in a point in time much farther back, though; it had been troubling her since Grete Siebenschein sounded a first alarm about Mädi Küffer-Fraunholzer even before the height of summer, when Grete's eye, made especially keen by her own suffering, first noticed Etelka Grauermann's love beginning to wane. Mary hadn't concerned herself with Lea Fraunholzer since then, at least not in any actual, factual way. She hadn't written any letter at all, let alone a long one. And even if nothing that carried conviction could have been gained by sending one, what barrier might have arisen to prevent her from simply riding out to Gmunden at some point during the summer months, leaving the children to themselves in Velden or some such place? These children as good as fully grown and levelheaded. What barrier? None whatever. (Above the frilled collar. Mary couldn't see anything below it anymore. Absolutely nothing these days. With its tremendously extended diameter it looked to have grown coextensive with the wide horizon.) She perceived with almost a shock something deeply astonishing, something extraordinary: unused space, freedom not tapped, terrain unilluminated by right thinking. All that had been available, but she hadn't drawn on or entered it, had not decisively seized on a chance possibly unique. Perhaps she might have done better to bestir herself and travel out to Gmunden right after her conversation with Dr. Negria a week before.

In only a few seconds this whole train of thought sped point by point through her mind, down to the last idea, meaning right to the brink of clear-cut overstatement. On top of that, and like a sharp dot placed on the *i*, was the fact that René Stangeler had been urgently summoned to Budapest by Etelka on family business and had needed to depart swiftly. Grete Siebenschein told Mary about this development just before the older woman had set out for Rekawinkel—at the building entrance, by the car. So something had to be wrong in Budapest. Perhaps everything was topsy-turvy there. With all this in her head, Mary finally spoke, saying the same thing twice:

"I have to talk to you. I absolutely have to see you, Mädi."

These were the first words she said to her friend on the telephone.

"I certainly want to see you too, Mary," replied Lea with emphasis, insofar as any such thing could be sensed in her faraway, mellow voice. (Mary's irritation led her to blame the instrument itself or some other factor for a bad connection, although every single word could be understood easily and clearly.) "But the question is when and how. I arrived here late yesterday evening and am leaving tonight."

"Where are you going?" Mary asked.

"To Belgrade," Lea said.

"Direct?!" cried Mary (this was like a flash of inspiration).

"Yes, probably. That is, I'm not exactly certain. Maybe I'll make a stopover in—Budapest." She paused for just a split second before the last word.

"And what do you think you'll do in Budapest?!" Mary asked. She wasn't able to modulate her voice. She'd virtually lost control over it, in fact. Lea's manner of speaking, always very disengaged, was altogether familiar to her friend, but now it was generating tension and pressure inside Mary, as if she were trying to compel the other woman to abandon her normal way—just this once, just as an exception—because her way suddenly seemed to Mary to be even more out of place, less to the purpose than ever before; she started in on Lea as if she wanted to make the other woman jettison something fundamental to her. The utter futility, the outright impossibility of her exertion were evident enough, however, to thrust Mary herself into a state of impatience it was just barely possible for her to contain.

"Perhaps I'll talk to Etelka Grauermann," came the answer, gentle and almost dreamy (like deep, soft shadows in coves or inlets).

"No, you mustn't do that, Lea!" (Suddenly she was saying "Lea" instead of "Mädi.") "That would be the worst course of action you could possibly take. What's more, I hear a hornet's nest of some kind has just now been stirred up at the Grauermanns'. Etelka sent for her brother from Vienna, and he had to depart quickly. I happen to know his fiancée; that's how I found out all this on Thursday. Does Robert know that you want to go to him in Belgrade?"

"Yes. He sent for me."

Mary at first paused and said nothing. Then: "So Robert is definitely not in Budapest?"

"No. Robert's waiting for me in Belgrade. He handed in his telegram on Friday morning, but I didn't receive it until Saturday and started out yesterday."

"Oh if only you'd set out on Saturday! Then we would have had more time," Mary cried.

"I wanted to. But Kitty" (this was the Fraunholzers' daughter) "was just home from her studies over the weekend and was so glad to be with me. I just couldn't bring myself to leave her in the lurch. And on Sunday I couldn't have taken care of getting the things Robert needed or anything else anyway."

"When did Robert leave Gmunden?"

"On the tenth."

"And how long was he with you?"

"More than a week. From August thirty-first, to be exact."

"And how was it?"

"I can't really tell you over the phone the way I'd like to," answered Lea Fraunholzer after a brief, silent pause. "I might still—be happy again. But only under certain conditions."

"Conditions! My sweet, good Mädi . . ." All of a sudden the driving force inside Mary now discovered gentleness as its best means; it struck her as the best way to obtain entry at last into the mellow, faraway world that never quite unfurled but before which she'd always beaten her wings (and had them beaten), humming and buzzing like a bumble-bee trying to find the right hole. "Conditions! It's up to you to create those conditions, but not to dictate them ... and in Belgrade, not Budapest; trust me on that ... But we can't talk about this on the phone, Mädi dear. I have to see you. Urgently; no two ways about it. No matter how much you have to do in Vienna over this one single day. I can only imagine. So any time you like. Even if it's just for half an hour. That's enough time."

"But they've booked me solid with errands and business of all kinds," said Lea, although not in a tone of complaint or opposition, but more with a tinge of kindhearted regret. "Robert too. His telegram went on and on. There was so much about important matters that are personal and business-related at the same time and about how he has to wait in Belgrade to see how they turn out. Can you picture it? And on top of all that, he's scheduled a certain discussion for which he thinks I'm more appropriate than he. I hope he's not wrong."

For a long moment Mary's hopes—raised quite high—were summarily dashed; they had sprung up on learning that Fraunholzer had asked his wife (is that what she was again?! is that what she could once more become?) to journey to Belgrade. What now popped into her mind, quick as lightning and with no words (à la *trópoi*, as for all of us) could have been rendered with grammatical truncation roughly as follows: "Men; put nothing past them. He needs her now, simple as that." But her anxiety that mere pragmatic issues could loom substantial enough to outweigh, let alone rule out, the reconciliation of man and wife couldn't survive more than a very short spell in Mary's mind. She had too deep a belief in her nights with Oscar. This quashing of her hopes had passed by in a flash, the way telegraph wires running alongside the train tracks appear to drop back down at each pole, interrupting their renewed ascent each time—or the way a light bulb sometimes blinks. It was over that soon. Her initial outlook was restored that soon. She was confident that the business end could be settled, but confident of so much more as well (who would be inclined to hold the opposite opinion, by the way?). Even so, Mary's own weakest point was bound to become apparent to her sooner or later during this telephone conversation, the one point that quite significantly diminished the clarity and value of her judgment in regard to the present situation: she didn't know Fraunholzer, not more than slightly, at any rate, or not really at all, considering everything—a handsome man, energetic. Years before. That was it. A gap here. Here she was out of her depth with Lea. Grete Siebenschein's observations about Fraunholzer couldn't balance out Mary's deficiency, which realization again brought her bad conscience to the fore, inducing in her a feeling almost like that of a schoolgirl who hadn't prepared and then is unexpectedly called on. She could long before have sought out opportunities to study Fraunholzer from closer up, as it were. Right after early summer, for example. But he was in Belgrade all the time. Still. Before then. Years before, in fact. She didn't understand her own self at this point. Yet didn't look for excuses. Her attitude really deserves to be pointed out.

"On top of everything else are all the errands I'm supposed to take care of for mother and Lily out in Wolkersdorf" (Lea meant her younger sister, the one Mary's children were friends with), "all waiting for me in Vienna. You know how totally helpless Lily is with so many day-to-day concerns, like understanding a letter from the bank and how to answer it what directions to give—all those kinds of things. Yes, she's still out there" (answering a question Mary had tossed in), "because the weather is still so fine; the children are already back, though, because of school, but then she wasn't feeling very well, either, and neither was Mama; Walter's out there as well" (that was Lily's husband—incidentally, the Küffer sisters didn't bear the slightest resemblance to each other; Lily was wheat-blond and slender, a very stylish type), "and he doesn't know how to do anything, either; 'I'm not a businessman,' he always says. And the whole lot of them are too lazy ever to come up to Vienna—just a short hop away—to take care of whatever needs seeing to. They pile everything onto the housekeeper's shoulders as 'urgent business for when the Frau Consul returns from Gmunden.' They knew what I'd be facing, of course, but not that I'd be able to stay in Vienna for no more than a single day. It's too bad I really couldn't get away from Gmunden any sooner; the boy wasn't feeling well" (the Fraunholzers' younger son). "And now all of a sudden Robert sends a telegram about some appointment I'm supposed to keep for him here, at the Sacher Hotel, of all places, and with some geriatric Frenchman."

"And with everything in such a rush, how are you supposed to get visas for Hungary or Belgrade?"

"Robert arranged the whole thing by telephone from Belgrade. All I have to do is go there with my passport, and I'll have it in ten minutes."

Mary thought with lightning speed and remarkable precision for a woman: "If she really wants to, she can also use her connections to get a proper visa for Hungary right away, which will let her spend time in Budapest." Mary didn't know whether a transit visa for the trip to Belgrade was even required, nor whether Mädi was also going to have to call at the Hungarian consulate general in any event. The question was already on her lips when it appeared to be getting too far ahead of things, too nigglingly concerned with petty details, too close to the sensitive spot. Instead she said:

"So what you'll do, then, is speak your beautiful French at the Sacher and manage things beautifully. I know you, Mädi!" Mary's voice was now unusually gentle. "But now tell me, dear heart, when and where can I see you, no matter for how short a time?" (As she was speaking, Mary resolved as quick as lightning to maintain a uniformly gentle approach during their upcoming conversation and in this spirit simply to ask as a favor of Lea not to leave the train in Budapest under any circumstances or to confront her husband with an either-or choice or to make any of the other serious mistakes to which it seemed her friend had lately been inclining.)

"I'm not going to be at home for more than an hour all day," Lea said. "From five thirty to six thirty at the latest. Then I'll take off with my little traveling case, though I'm not going directly to the station. Before that I have to stop off and see a friend of my mother's who's invited me to supper. She lives near the Belvedere Palace, which works out well, because I'm leaving late in the evening from the State Station." (She wasn't yet calling it the East Station, the name just now coming to be standard.) "I already had my luggage sent there from the West Station. But I really need at least that one short hour at home to take a little breather, smarten up a bit, and drink a cup of tea. Come to me then. But please, no later than six. I really want to talk to you."

Mary solemnly promised.

She stepped away from the phone.

Now she was alone once more.

All that spirited, strenuous talking had left Mary's mouth dry; she sat back down at the breakfast table and poured more tea. As she was setting the cup back down, she was confronted in a strange way—as if it were approaching her in total silence from every side at once, fully shaped and formed—with an inward attitude, one she understood completely, though it remained behind glass, so that it could have no grasp on her (the double sense being obvious: Mary could neither actively and effectively grasp what was being presented to her from outside, nor could she in turn come within its grasp—it remained encased in crystal, behind a purely transparent wall, as if the air had turned solid, become an invisible wall). What she ought to do—and she felt it very distinctly—was change places at once with all that was occupying her now, to push it off to the edge and place herself in the center. Everything was in reverse placement at the moment, however. Even so, she felt called upon to stand up, walk over to the window, and look along the street. Were the taxis quietly and slowly rolling across it in uniform order? She got up. Not quickly, but with deliberate slowness instead, heedful, first looking down at herself. Even without the sun beaming in directly, light fell onto her from the tall, broad window. An astute woman, beautifully poised, her features—those of an ancient race—now grown quite august, her copper-gleaming thick hair around temples whose skin shimmered like the inside of a pearl oyster; and all these qualities—her limbs, covered now, her tunnel-deep eyes instinctive with spirit, her small hands, her slender but strong legs, on which she stood so firmly, her tiny feet, so steadfast and sturdy in supporting her—all of these were aspects of a perfection mounting to fullness when their total effect was contemplated as they blended into a true womanly splendor seldom achieved until about age forty, with most women not attaining to that fulfillment, if at all, until they're around fifty. Daughter, granddaughter, great-granddaughter! Budding and blossoming worlds away from me, yet within her there moved the identical mechanism of spirit as in you, in me, in the reader. She who sensed the summons from the window; who intuited the concentric onslaught of the silence; who felt the readiness of the spangled, spectral battle ranks, battalions of strength, in the emptiness; alert to the rightness, the rescuing force of the command to change locations lightning fast, which would have made room for the right positions to be rearranged immediately.

But there was no Mary there.

She began at once to link pieces together. Her thoughts did not just flee from the admonition to change places; they packed it down tight, crammed it in, squeezed it hard, and tied it together.

First and foremost, she had not yet found out anything about how exactly long Lea had in mind to stay in Belgrade with her husband (which is what he needed to turn back into, *had* to become once again, in spite of everything!). Besides, if some kind of scandal had suddenly broken out in Budapest, wasn't it within the realm of possibility that Lea wouldn't even find him in Belgrade but would be received instead upon her arrival by a housekeeper or some retainer of that kind acting on instructions? Mary now deeply regretted that she hardly knew Fraunholzer! And at some point she really ought to have observed Etelka Stangeler and Grauermann, once at least, which would have been easy to arrange through Grete here in Vienna at some time before the height of summer! She had the same feeling a farmer might have who suddenly discovers among his fields whole expanses he'd never seen before, tracts never turned over by a plow, never planted, never harvested. A farmer would be able to make such an appalling discovery only in sleep and dreams, which would be dire enough, whereas in this case it was almost as if she had either never lived at all in regard to all these matters or lived only behind invisible walls.

She started walking back and forth in the room. Not pacing leisurely, though. Something was impelling her.

Very well: it was what it was. And she'd see what she'd see in the afternoon. She held fast to her decision about pursuing a gentle course.

But just then it occurred to her that she'd already made another appointment for the late afternoon. Her next rapid footsteps, then, hushed by the carpet, were back to the telephone. She listened. The room was silent; the bright furniture was gleaming. The instrument chirped, hummed, and then went dead. Mary dialed again; she was trying to reach her dentist. The line was busy. Everywhere in the room small invisible eddies were whirling. Past the street outside—the taxis protruding left and right—past and beyond the street, across the canal, the trees were aglow, green still in the sunlight, their leaves hardly turned, or better yet, not at all. A short whistle from the railroad, more a little snort.

She finally reached the office and postponed her appointment.

There was no more thought of tennis in the afternoon. Just now she had several telephone calls to make. Everything had to be rescheduled! Well, what of it! After all, quite a good bit more rescheduling was about to take place, and once and for all, at that—for Lea.

Without taking time to ponder in much detail, Mary was attempting to clear her afternoon and leave it completely blank, odd as that might seem; but you couldn't rely for certain on anyone's being punctual, besides which, having to wait in this or that case (at the dentist's, for example) appeared almost unavoidable, which meant it would be best not to take on any obligations that might hamper her ability to arrive on time at Lea's home in Döbling. While Mary was doing all she could to move forward into the morning most of the appointments and activities scheduled for the afternoon, the earlier time of day naturally grew more and more crowded as she kept busy at the phone, talking, waiting when a connection couldn't be made right away, which of course happened repeatedly today. Her arms drooped; she stayed slightly bent over the little telephone table, and an almost sad look came into her face; nowhere to call home in the emerging emptiness. Finally, after a considerable time, all these calls—most of which interlocked and thus had to be made in a certain order—were over, and everything had fallen into place (for example, it would have made no sense to go to her milliner's without bringing the materials and samples promised her by a certain shop in the center of town if she could come at three o'clock, but if what she needed had in turn been delivered to the shop already, then her appointment at the hatmaker's could be rescheduled over the phone for earlier instead of having to be canceled outright for today; Mary wasn't fond of showing up anywhere unexpectedly, because that usually resulted in having to wait longer; every one of her calls and visits was arranged for a fixed time, and she would hold to the appointed time precisely). She was able to step away from the telephone table now that everything was finally taken care of, even if not exactly as she would have preferred. But whatever could be changed had been changed. At just that moment, however, she suddenly caught sight of the list she'd been making, quickly and mechanically, to fill the vacuum of a morning that seemed completely free at that point, right up to the moment before Lea Frauholzer's call had come to fill it to the brim from an unexpected quarter. But Mary wanted to have that list, to recall it: she seemed even to need it, reacting with a certain amount of apprehensiveness. It had been easy to make, but now it was only with effort that she succeeded in focusing on it again after the agitation of her talk with Lea. She did manage to retrieve it from that earlier void, though, the crucial point of which she herself had initially fixed on at the breakfast table, and added the lesser items to the initial vacuum by following a kind of gravitational pull. The item with highest priority was undoubtedly the Estudiantina (a large musical organization of Spanish students), whose general secretary was staying in Vienna at the moment and could be consulted during a sort of office hour he was holding at the Grand Hotel this morning. So Mary went swiftly to her bedroom and put on her hat, whereupon Marie came hurrying in—she never missed when Mary was about to go out, and now she needed a pod of vanilla, and could her employer perhaps bring one back from town? As for the Estudiantina, Mary was active in her role as a mother; the Spanish students had organized a kind of exchange, which included secondary students as well. Along with English and French, her boy had been pursuing Spanish out of sheer interest and had developed his ability to a remarkable extent (according to his teacher not long before). Mary went darting down the steps all fresh and fit. But at one point she tripped over a runner which was kinked and not lying flat. At least that was how it felt to her, so she told herself she'd stumbled. But that wasn't necessarily how it really was; perhaps she hadn't even made contact with that spot but had set her foot down awkwardly instead, not with elasticity and lifting power, but more in such a way as to bring about a kind of rebound and slight bump.

There's no reason for us to dog Mary's every footstep while she went about her errands in town.

She wasn't able to take care of them all anyway.

She arrived at the Grand Hotel too late, for example.
The general secretary had already gone out.

Around four o'clock on that Monday, September 21, 1925, Melzer left
his apartment carrying the bamboo walking stick with the gold knob.
As soon as he stepped onto the landing and closed the door behind
him—with utmost care, avoiding all unnecessary noise, the model and
archetype of the "quiet tenant"—he detected a change in the atmosphere
of the stairwell, whose airy odor of clean whitewash was blunted today
by a moldy or clammy smell that reeked of damp basement. As Melzer
had expected, this odor grew stronger as he went down the stairs, just
as he knew the little door by the porter's lodge would be standing open,
so that as he went past he could see into the small storeroom where
two old bicycles and other discarded items were standing; this time
Melzer caught sight of a carpenter's bench besides. The association
triggered by this open room and its marked odor, detectable even at
the top of the stairs, arose in Melzer's mind so concretely that he didn't
have to search it out for even a split second: the mute, green-shaded
inwardness of the room below the large glassed-in wooden veranda at
his mother's house in Neulengbach, the mugginess of rotting leaves,
his bicycle there, a few old chairs and garden tools leaning in a corner—all these objects presented themselves again, to be called up and
called upon as readily as Asta's tiny room in the underwater light behind
the jalousie blinds or the walk he'd taken out in the country between
the herb gardens and the rose gardens three weeks earlier, down toward
the stream and across the little bridge, where he'd then waited for Asta.
The colored glass balls were sparkling.

Still, if Melzer felt no real shock of recognition or pressing need to
begin ruminating (totally unnecessary in any case), this brush with
memory somehow turned Melzer away from his direction or toward
a different direction—had he fixed on a definite one to start with when
he left his apartment in the domain of "interested Pierrot"? Having
just leapt inwardly across a long period of time with such agility, he
felt this sense of expanded dimensions now carrying over to the external realm and releasing him a little from the clamp of circumstance,

from the alternatives that seemed to arise from such constriction, from wristwatch and pocket watch, from intents and purposes, from doling and parceling out the day. He turned right from the house door. A detour, then. But one can speak of a detour in the strict sense only when a specific goal has already been set.

In a way entirely divorced from rational thought or sense, Melzer ended up carrying the teetering scale to the place where he intuited its suspension point and indicator would be.

The weather felt warm to him. He stopped at the quietest part of Strudlhof Gasse, down below, before the Steps, and looked at the occasional passersby going up or down, forced into a stately walk diagonally along the ramps, compelled to readjust when tracing a course, pressed for that matter into being ambulatory emblems of the structure imaged here while yet deflected from leaping in a flat-out, frenetic, frog-like jump from intent to purpose, barred from a mad dash along some featureless path toward a goal or an ending point any closer examination of would in the majority of cases only ratify the same absence of any feature. Frog leaps, mad dashes—any such hasty, heedless hurry straight down the chicken ladder was successfully impeded here.

The major didn't recognize who was coming toward him until René had reached the platform in front of the fountain.

Melzer called to him and started making his way to the stairs.

René had stopped and was now leaning against the balustrade and looking down at Melzer.

Oddly enough, they just stayed where they were. As if something were about to descend upon them that could longer be buttressed or shored up, as if there were now falling away a certain nervous timidity and schoolboy embarrassment that invariably prevents two people from taking one another's measure when they happen to meet—so they just stood there, the major below and the full-fledged but ridiculous PhD above. Perhaps it was the import of the moment hanging over them that now imparted something of its momentous importance to them and held the power to release them from abiding in and hiding behind petty purpose. René started down as the major went up to meet him. They met halfway up to the fountain level, Stangeler a little higher, Melzer a little lower, and stopped on the stairs once more.

"I heard you were in Budapest, Herr von Stangeler?"

"Yes. I got back to Vienna this morning."

"And how is your sister?"

"Etelka is dead."

It happened that no one was coming past. The silence stood as if a block of metal had plummeted into the empty street. Only now for the first time did Melzer genuinely notice (though he would have had plenty of time and opportunity to do so before Stangeler's arrival!) that the treetops to the left and right of the ramps and above them were now showing spots and patches of autumn colors.

He guessed. Not for nothing had he watched the last legions of Pompeius subside and perish three weeks before. Very briefly, then: "her doing?," a nod from Stangeler, and they'd said all they needed to. Not until then did Melzer ask about particulars. When he started to apprise René of what he'd witnessed with his own eyes in the country at the end of August, it turned out that Stangeler already knew all about it. Through Asta. Based on the alarming if not very specific information that the good man her husband, Government Building Inspector Haupt, had had no choice but to pass on to her, she had returned to Vienna right before René's departure. But it was only on his return from Budapest, however, that René first talked with Asta and Haupt. In addition, a kind of family conference had been convened in which various relatives took part; the main point under discussion was how they should tell old Herr Stangeler out at the country house—but above all, *what* they should tell him. Only Haupt and René advocated for telling the full, unvarnished truth, even at the cost of sparing the old man. René's statement (which he now repeated to Melzer)—"You can't conceal from someone who has lost a child that it was a suicide; that would mean stealing from the man a piece of his own individual fate"—that statement was passed over, not heard or not taken to cognizance, which was usually the case with statements René made within the family circle; from the very start they were considered beside the point, muddled, and immaterial (for which judgment there was admittedly ample reason). So they all came to an agreement about a cover-up and made up some story about a sudden catastrophic bout of influenza or something along that line; it was probably nonsense from the medical standpoint (they imagined they could fob off this absurdity onto the father, though when the time came he made no reply at all, merely dilating his nostrils a bit as if sniffing out the humbug; he grasped the whole truth at once but never said anything; mostly for his wife's sake—it was easy to sugarcoat things with her, and she preferred it that way—he joined in singing the same tune instead). Asta let herself be talked into this cover-up. What won out was the deep tenderness for the old man that was at all times alive inside her; she wanted above anything else for him not to be hurt. And so Herr Stangeler's elder sisters, who lived somewhere in distant countries, were also notified to the same effect. After the family conference, which had lasted until about three thirty, René was now on his way to Grete; all he'd said to her over the phone was that he was back from Budapest, since he'd found himself simply unequal to conveying to her at all adequately through the crackling and buzzing of the phone line the impact of the real news he needed to tell her. He answered her pressing questions only by saying that he would tell her everything later in the afternoon but that it was impossible for him to do so now, by telephone. And because René foresaw all the back and forth in the family and the difficulty of reaching a decision, he fixed on five o'clock at the earliest as the time he would show up at Grete's (though the debate had been resolved and the gathering dissolved well before then); for that matter, he asked the favor of being released from punctuality this time, since the meeting could run even later.

So now here he stood out on the street at three thirty, after the first flood was over.

In no hurry to rush off to Grete right away.

In fact, he was delaying, and very much so at that. He was delaying deep inside, on a profoundly interior level, we might say. His state of mind was such that he wouldn't have been able to stomach even the stairwell of Grete's building, with its silly tassels and festoons and brass rings, with its elevator in the middle. He felt what amounted to an absolute, utter incapability of facing it at the moment, in a manner not unlike Melzer's in the wetlands by Greifenstein some time before, when he'd realized it was totally and absolutely out of the question to tell Editha Schlinger anything about Colonel Laska.

And so, the scale inside him teetering as he delayed and hesitated, Stangeler ended up at the place where—in a way divorced from rational sense—he intuited the nexus of events to lie. Where, himself having just reached the spatter and chatter of the fountain from the opposite direction, he caught sight of the major standing on the lower, shorter, quieter part of Strudlhof Gasse.

What Melzer was hoping to find out first and foremost was what had happened in Budapest, especially anything about the final segment of Etelka's journey along the path to her destruction. That couldn't be discussed while they were here on their feet, though, especially as people were now constantly passing up or down. They walked away from the Steps. Melzer felt himself in a peculiar sense released from duty to his pocket watch, as it were, given time off, now placed under a whole different set of laws. They looked for some secluded place to untie and open this package from fate's post office, and they finally found it on a bench in the grounds of the Palais Liechtenstein, its widespread green spaces still open in those days to anyone from the district seeking a moment's relaxation.

"Every single time a case like this arises, all people can think of is how to proclaim yet again some supposedly watertight exception to the Ten Commandments!" René commented regarding the outcome of the rapidly assembled family gathering as Melzer and he were taking a seat. "It's like living in some goddamned carnival. All of a sudden a hurdy-gurdy pipes up because somebody's hit a bull's-eye; the clown doll falls over, the cuckoo pops out, the rooster crows. There's a big hubbub; something's happened. All parties involved turn themselves inside out. The burst of panic quickly swamps all sense of proportion. People just take whatever slams into them from wherever and then pride themselves on rolling with the punches, but only because it all comes tumbling down when things grow really serious; you can't talk about holding on or holding out. Life bares its teeth; people draw in their tails. Then all the hustle and bustle die down, at least for now. That would be the right moment for something, anything, everything to change that would prevent more of the same contemptible posturing in the future, but what happens? Exactly nothing; the restored calm is not taken as an admonition to prepare oneself thoroughly for a possible next explosion; the space now opened up will not be occupied by reflection; the opportunity presented by the expanding silence and emptiness will not be seized on, though putting it to good use could perhaps even lead to averting a repetition of the calamity."

That last word sat on his tongue like an airborne seed that had flown into his mouth from somewhere, perhaps from the park grounds; aside from its meaning, it even had a pleasant taste. It surprised him, and he fell silent. Since his departure from Budapest, Stangeler had elected to handle the pain of his grief through anger; he kept pounding it back and forth like a punching bag. Which didn't make anything better. But René thought of this pugnacious pose his egoism struck as a spirited act and believed he was guarding against maudlin reactions by this means. At the same time (and he would probably have reacted quite rudely if anyone had said it to him) he was putting himself through all this to prepare for seeing Grete Siebenschein again.

Now he finally resumed his account:

"On Wednesday evening—I'd just come from seeing Grete—my brother-in-law Haupt (you don't know him, do you?)—I'm living with Asta and him for the time being on the third floor of my parents' house—my brother-in-law greeted me right when I came through the door with a message that I was to travel to Etelka in Budapest that very night. Grauermann had called on the phone, but no one was at home here, and he was tied up in his office. So what Pista did then was get in touch with one of his former colleagues at the Hungarian consulate general on Bank Gasse, which was how the message got delivered to the house just fifteen minutes before I got home; it also said I would be issued a visa at the consulate immediately. My passport itself was in good order, fortunately, still valid from this spring and summer (a horror to look back on). Haupt and I were not able to find out or piece together exactly what had happened or might still be going on in Budapest. Plus my brother-in-law wasn't saying much anyway. He looked pretty glum; I think he already had his suspicions. Enough—the way we understood it, Etelka was urgently asking for me, so I had to take off at once. Office hours were long since over on Bank Gasse, of course, but I simply gave my card to the doorman, and they stamped a visa into my passport without delay; then some functionary vanished for a few minutes to get a signature. I never got to see the particular colleague with whom Pista had spoken over the phone and didn't even know his name. On instructions from my brother-in-law I was handed an envelope after signing a receipt—there was money in it, Austrian, and Hungarian as well, more than enough. I was well provided for anyway, since I'd just received a payment in a decent amount. I packed a small bag at home and called Grete: she asked lots of questions, but of course I couldn't answer a single one. So I was able to catch the night train from the East Station without having to rush too much . . . Now listen to this, Major, because I want to tell you what was unusual about my trip to Budapest. It wasn't my first. But in a certain respect it was nonetheless very similar to my first trip—this past spring, sometime after my exams at the university—at least as far as my inner disposition is concerned, but not the least bit like my second trip to Budapest in July, which came right after I'd had another rift with Grete. I was desperately unhappy at the time. But on this last trip, even while the train went gliding out of the station, I could clearly understand the basis for my current mood, so very different, so much better despite the anxiety the situation was causing. It had to do, strangely enough, with my being in a position to depart immediately and smoothly, with my not leaving any loose ends in Vienna, nothing left undone, no unfinished business forever postponed 'even unto the end of time,' (you know our old turn of phrase based on Matthew's Gospel), tasks waiting to be performed with pain and strain, with moaning and groaning. I was in a fluid state, all ready to go. It was deeply satisfying to me that the kind of well-ordered empty space was present inside me that's an indispensable requirement for allowing anything to enter in, to penetrate in any true and effective way. It struck me that I'd just now attained to this state for the first time in my life; to be sure, though, it would need to become grounded much more solidly, develop into a habitual, normal state of affairs. Nothing can step to the forefront, take on plasticity, be clearly seen from outside in its full impact while being distinctly recognized on the inside for what it truly is, unless it is surrounded by empty space and thereby becomes a singular object or even a unique entity. There can't be any authentic life when we're in the midst of the madding crowd. One clown doll falls over, another one pops right up to take its place. There I was, though, sitting back in the seat cushion, deeply apprehensive and yet cool, calm, and collected as the train pulled out and started along the track. That is how a man sets out to confront fate. I was never able to reach this insight before, which is a proof of how delayed my development is, because I'm well over thirty; it's also a proof that I was treated to either no real upbringing at all or at best a woeful one that totally failed even to attempt instilling into me at any time the rudiments of mental and emotional discipline or the faintest idea of how to begin approaching it. Incidentally, today is the Feast of Saint Matthew the Evangelist." After this abrupt addendum René caught his breath.

Surely it would be legitimate to conjecture at this point that Melzer's patience—he was expecting a narrative of events, after all—was more than slightly strained by René's long excursus (we're tempted to speak of excesses), his foray into the purely subjective realm, all the more in that the major's limited time was passing by as Stangeler rambled on. But that was absolutely not how Melzer took it, as he later assured people repeatedly. His calm reinforced by looking around the park grounds, he realized, and not without amazement, that right here and now—and especially since the previous day, Sunday!—he was totally, completely imbued with the state of mind Stangeler considered it necessary to harangue him about with such verbosity as a major demand posed by life. Much later on (Kursk, 1942), the major expressed himself to the effect that he had felt not even a twinge of impatience or pressure as he sat there on a bench next to Stangeler in Liechtenstein Park but instead had serenely looked over the grounds and at the old trees—their branching boughs against the brilliant, faraway sky, against which departing summer (seeming to stay "even unto the end of time") and oncoming autumn lay peaceably together as if reconciled, embracing, suffusing each other while patiently grounding the highest, most delicate, intricately filigreed twinings and now setting it all out on display for the first time while yet holding it all together as a sonorous organ-pedal point. And even though time was passing and conflicting appointments were parting ways like a fork in the road, calling out for a decision—that all remained as if behind the curtain of some all-encompassing but still invisible plan, remained as if rolled up into the folds of the curtain, lost and hidden. In the meantime, Stangeler was continuing his narrative:

"The train I had taken arrived in Budapest at some totally ungodly hour. I didn't wake up until Kelenföld Station; you have to travel through half the city to get from there to the East Station, Keleti. It was still dark. It didn't seem likely that I'd be able to take the streetcar, so I decided to get a taxi at Keleti Station and have it take me to Vilma királynö út. But somebody called my name as I was going through the barrier at the end of the platform. It was a Herr Ladislaus von P.—called Lala in Hungarian—a relative of my brother-in-law Grauermann, chief physician at the largest spa for medical treatment in Budapest, the Saint Lukács Thermal Baths. A very remarkable man, by the way: a Hungarian baron from an old family, he originally studied theology and became a Calvinist minister. But even after he'd obtained an appointment as pastor he threw over the whole thing to resume his studies, this time of medicine, going through all the coursework and the clinical years, partly in Vienna and partly in various other countries. It wasn't long before he began having success in his new career as a physician. That must have been his genuine and true gift. I knew Lala quite well from my stay in Budapest in the spring. I always envied him, by the way. He seemed to live life with an easy touch, as it were, in spite of a complicated biography caused by finishing doctorates in two different disciplines and changing professions like that. Lala also married very early, as a young pastor. He seemed to have that light touch—at least, that's how it looks to me. It can often strike people that way when dealing with gifted Hungarians. They're built to be adaptable, well able to cope. They have a kind of cheerfulness that's in the exact place where it belongs but where the rest of us are able to see it only as an abstract philosophical aim, so to speak. That said, this cheerfulness by no means precludes conscientious and strenuous effort. What I mean is that nature has placed their center of gravity exactly right. I might add that Lala bears a certain physiognomic resemblance to Teleki, the famous equestrian; he was our riding instructor at the officers' training school, and we really loved and respected him. Anyway, Lala called out to me at the barrier; he'd come on his motorcycle to pick me up and perhaps to prepare me as well. He looked serious, almost somber (a Hungarian face can look very somber indeed). Somewhat stiffly and with a bit of trouble I crawled into the torpedo-shaped sidecar. It was warm in Budapest even though it was early morning. Lala drove at breakneck speed but with total calm. We turned right and stopped in front of the Saint Lukács Baths."

A clock struck somewhere, but Melzer didn't look at his watch. Two strokes. Perhaps from the church tower in Lichtental. Half past four.

"I washed and shaved at his place there, and we had breakfast in his office; he took special care to make sure I ate enough. Bacon and eggs. His friendly attention wasn't just out of sheer hospitality. The physician in him was on the alert. I could sense that, and it was a little off-putting. We barely spoke a word. I didn't ask any questions. I can honestly say it wasn't faintheartedness that make me hold my tongue; I just wanted to keep from breaking off in advance any piece from the outline of events as I was about to hear them. Full daylight had emerged while we were sitting there. The room, hardly even medium in size, formed a kind of cozy, thick shell or husk around us, crammed with a whole array of objects, as if a library had been blended with the den in a hunting lodge: there were light and heavy weapons, mounted antlers, an exotic buffalo head, fishing gear, and leather pouches. The room smelled like leather too. We could look onto the spa grounds through the window on the first floor. Behind the grounds a train from the electric rail system went past. The sun had come up just a few minutes before, and it sent a warm, glowing reflection onto two bandoliers hanging from a stag's antlers.

"Lala offered me a cigarette and then very calmly told me everything.

"First, that I would find my sister unconscious and that she was wasn't really expected to regain consciousness. There was no doubting, he said, that the quantity of narcotics Etelka had taken—an immense number of different sleeping pills, all very strong—could only have been hoarded over years, which now threw a whole new light on the constantly reiterated complaints she'd long been voicing about her intermittently recurring total insomnia. It was precisely the great variety of substances that had by now been wreaking havoc on her body for over thirty hours that was making simultaneous efforts at counteracting them so difficult and to some extent impossible. As to that, Etelka had seemingly gone to great lengths—it could only have been on purpose—to guarantee the longest possible time span between ingesting the pills and her condition being discovered. This past Tuesday, around midnight, she feigned something like healthy sleepiness in front of her husband and her maid, voicing in an apparently good mood the hope that after such a long time she might be in store for a night of real sleep—so she hoped everybody would please be extra quiet in the morning and not even think of disturbing her before ten o'clock. Then she vanished into her room and must have 'swallowed the whole lot of devil's poison' (which was how Lala expressed it) while lying in bed. He said it was an almost unbelievable amount; she must have needed a good ten or even fifteen minutes just to ingest it all. They found the empty containers on her night table. She must have swallowed everything directly, followed with sips of water, instead of dissolving the tablets in the glass, which showed no residue or other traces. The large crystal carafe of water was now two-thirds empty, even though it had been full to the brim. When she hadn't stirred by eleven the following morning, the maid opened the door a crack and cautiously peered in; she was looking straight at the headboard and at Etelka, who had foam around her nose and mouth and was breathing in quick, shallow gasps. Right away the maid began screaming and crying. 'But the cook kept her head,' Lala told me, 'called Pista on the phone at once, and then got hold of me. It goes without saying that we immediately started applying all possible measures and doing everything imaginable for Etelka. I called in a number of specialists, one of whom had been my pharmacology professor in medical school. I have to tell you, though, René, that if you emptied the containers of everything your poor sister took, you would soon have two heaping handfuls.'

"'Nonetheless,' Lala finished, 'her constitution is very strong, and it's continuing to fight. But in vain. You need to be fully aware that there's no hope left, René. Of course we're still trying various treatments, the most recent one today. She'll last until tomorrow or—much less likely—the day after. But then the end will definitely come.'

"He added this: Etelka's suicide presented exactly the opposite picture of the way a woman usually kills herself. Almost all such cases represent more of a cry for help, but with consequences far beyond what was intended. Etelka acted with total premeditation, however. That was the most striking aspect of her case, but the most horrifying at the same time. 'Not least from the theological standpoint,' he concluded.

"On her nightstand she left a note for her husband. Just a few lines in pencil—a farewell and a plea for forgiveness. At the end (very hard to make out—was the poison already beginning to take effect?)—these words: 'Find yourself a woman who's like you.'"

René came to a stop. Melzer looked up into the treetops. Into a more spacious vista, as it were. Inside him was an absolute certainty (self-evident, and for that reason untested), one he hardly even noticed, that this chance encounter with Stangeler and the news it brought was only a kind of beginning, just as no one living in the mountains hears the ominous rumble of an avalanche reverberating distantly in the fragile quiet of early spring without unconsciously waiting for more, and just as no one hears the first rifle salvos hailing Easter morning without inwardly anticipating the many answering volleys from farmsteads near and far.

In spite of the street noise, distant but still able to make its way into the grounds, a fragile quiet prevailed here as well. Fragile quiet had prevailed since Sunday, the day before. In it, set off clearly and surrounded by space and emptiness, stood an image of Etelka as Melzer had last seen her: in front of the post office with Asta, both in their colorful regional garb, waving while the bus started in motion and began making its rapid way downward through the valley. The image was deep and sharp; it was filled with color, especially red, as if against a deep red background.

Melzer asked Stangeler no questions, just as René had refrained from pouncing on Baron P., Lala, after arriving in Budapest. He felt he knew enough. No "why?" crossed his lips, nor any other sign of nervous embarrassment in place of sincere condolence. His silence was Melzer's condolence. He thought he knew all he needed to. Enough light had been shed—red light. Only small details could follow now. Let them follow. He understood the art of waiting.

"We drove to the hospital. Again at a mad dash but also totally calm. The city was very busy by this time of day. At first we went the same way we'd come from the station; on Margaret Bridge the eye takes in an enormous, dazzling expanse; dazzling in its magnificence, that is. The city cleft by the mighty river. The morning sun was gleaming by this time. Budapest has broad, splendid streets. We drove right down the middle of them. I was seeing the city in a way that made me think it was just now precipitating out of thin air, not solidly *there*, not fixed and aglow in the sun but instead aflow, on the run, everything swirling and reeling inside me as we banked and leaned into the curves, one vista and view flung up against the next, one backdrop thrust in front of another in a mad jumble but then pulled back and hidden once again. Then it started turning bleak and barren. Out on the outskirts. Tenements. Railroad switchyards. These are the grim, dreary parts of a city. You see them in wartime or if something happens to you. We were now driving pretty fast in a straight line up a long street that climbed somewhat, then we curved off to the left and stopped in front of a large building located higher up. To my right I could see the lines of railroad tracks, but they weren't part of any route; this was an extensive side yard, set deep back, with tracks after tracks, all side by side, carriages of all sorts parked on them, handsome sleeping cars and dining cars as far as the eye could see. Life, but now brought to a standstill; the life of more fluid highways and byways now halted in their turnings and twinings. This whole yard full of rolling stock swung around to the left, underneath the roadway but following its bend. I could see down onto the gray roofs of coaches stretching on endlessly, on and on to the horizon. But enough. I'm mentioning all this only because I'm unable to separate it—will never be able to separate it—from what was about to follow. The hospital was ultramodern, as they say; airy, roomy, with wide corridors. Deadly quiet, by the way. Grauermann was standing in front of the door to Etelka's room. We hugged.

"What came next was a great deal less awful than those moments after breakfast with Lala, when every word he spoke brought a block of irrevocable reality dropping down from the ceiling, as it were. Less awful, too, I should say, for the simple reason that it was external. External the way war is external, or a burning village, the bellowing of close combat with bludgeons and bayonets, an epidemic of typhoid fever in Siberia. It was external. It was a horror, but the narrow confines of our conscious mind can grasp only a small fragment of it; and because it's external, purely external, there always remains a gap, a tiny bit of breathing room between us and the utmost that external reality can confront us with. Etelka looked exactly as Lala had described. She was lying on a bed in the middle of a very bright, large room, flat on her back, covered with a linen sheet up to her neck and shoulders. I was struck by how flat and sunken in her body was, like a board. Her breathing was regular but short and shallow. When she exhaled, a kind of foam or spittle appeared around her nostrils and the corner of her mouth; the nurse wiped it away from time to time. Two doctors had just left the room. Lala and Pista came in with me. I then noticed that Lala was praying as he stood at the foot of the bed; as he did, his upper body kept performing a kind of wrestling motion.

"Enough, though—more than enough. Teddy von Honnegger came later. He didn't say a single word. But later I heard from him about what you might call the last part of the lead-up—I'll get to that in a moment; not that there's much to tell, but at least it's from an absolutely reliable source. So now there were four men standing around Etelka's bed; that was pretty appropriate, I thought. She herself looked almost like a man, like a talented, gifted man at that. Her hair was back from her forehead, which stood out too prominently. The lower part of her face usually looked too weak, too round, and too soft whenever she would brush back that front thatch. Now her chin was thrust up somewhat, powerful, like a small bastion. 'The fifth one will have to come soon,' I thought, but I considered it possible that Grauermann hadn't even informed Consul General Fraunholzer. That's how the situation looked to me.

"I found out more about that, but later. I spent this time in the hospital room as if I were sitting at an unmoving midpoint, an axle or fulcrum of a disc rotating uniformly. I watched the sun advance toward the window and retreat from it. I stepped aside, moving to the wall or out to the corridor when the doctors were occupied with Etelka. The nurse patiently held aloft a large glass vessel from which hung two thin tubes or hoses whose metal nozzles had been inserted left and right underneath Etelka's skin, above her breasts; they went deep in, or at least that's how it seemed to me. I didn't understand anything about what that was for. Her chest was swelling out, probably because of the fluid. There was quite a distant view from this window, not of a landscape, but of another building similar to the one we were in. The sun was gleaming on its pale walls as well. This wasn't the real Hungarian sun, not the sun of this wheat-blond country as I knew it, its strength, the source of its pleasantness but also of its power and its greatness. The outermost district of Budapest is the greatest horror of any city district anywhere. It's all just cardboard; wouldn't it be possible to pull out the *puszta* from underneath it or from the wetland woods of the meandering river all of a sudden?! Etelka had been so fortunate as to live in this wonderful country, which had always and from every side enveloped her—full of love, I might say—so it could make her its daughter. Hadn't she had a Hungarian name from the time of her birth? And now she was ending her days in a grim, dreary place. Foaming at the mouth. Pale sunlight on the walls outside. Deathly quiet in the corridors. At noon we went to a small tavern to eat. Honnegger went with us too. The lined-up, curving rows of railroad cars went swinging past again, following the bend in the road. I noticed a kind of overgrown park with no fence or grating, small trees, shrubs with many paths between them. The greenery quite dusty. Maybe it was an old cemetery. I came back to it from time to time, leaving the deathbed and the hospital behind. I sat on a small stone bench worn smooth and I smoked. This garden was my place of urgently needed solitude, a cell I had settled into, as it were. On the following day, Friday—it was September eighteenth—I finally persuaded Grauermann to send Fraunholzer a telegram in the morning. I didn't want to do it without his knowing. Etelka died at three o'clock that afternoon."

He paused. The city, its noise muffled by the park's wide expanse, was honking, rumbling, beeping, and bellowing its "tutti" after the "solo."

"Fraunholzer arrived on Saturday morning. They'd washed and groomed Etelka by then. No more foam or spittle; no more breath to produce them. She lay with her head a little more elevated, I thought. Her forehead was still uncovered, but her hair had been combed and brushed smooth. Now there were five of us! I saw Robert collapse at the foot of the bed, crumple as if someone had emptied a sack of logs. A messy bundle all disarrayed, from which came weeping and wailing, literally a case of head over heels, limbs all tangled up. Behind his tears the full, stored-up force of his whole life's energy had gathered to a point; I couldn't help feeling even at the moment that this was what made his pain so terrible. He pulled himself together and bolted from the room. I remember thinking, too, that it was a good thing he had seen Etelka cleaned up and at peace, that he could carry this image with him and not the picture of her intense but futile struggle as she lay unconscious with her shallow gasping and her hair in disarray. Now she looked dignified. She hadn't mastered her troubles, but they were at least all behind her, and her face testified to that now. If we'd sent a telegram on Thursday, she would have presented a different appearance to Fraunholzer on Friday. And even with her still alive he would have seen little more than I or anyone else did. She was beyond answering any questions. She'd been set free of all motives and means. She had taken her course of action. It was up to us to come to terms with it. Robert left that same evening. I went to the station with him; he'd asked me to. Now here's something I have to tell you, Herr Melzer: What I wanted most was to stay with him that evening, to travel with him. I could only imagine that traveling by himself would be a horror. I was afraid for him in his situation, afraid of the loneliness waiting for him in Belgrade, where he lived more or less as a bachelor but where it would be borne in on him that Etelka was no longer there for him in Budapest—even if things between them hadn't lately been quite as they were at one time—his knowing that she was gone, transmuted, retreated to the constantly receding horizon of what was already past and gone. But even as we were still standing on the platform, Fraunholzer took this weight off my heart just before they started calling "All aboard"; his words made me happy, and with no second-guessing. He said to me: 'My wife is expected in Belgrade on Tuesday. Two hours before the news about Etelka arrived I had sent her a telegram asking if she could take care of some business matters for me in Vienna and then come to me as soon as possible, which means that she'll travel from Vienna as early as Monday evening if she can. I'll have her with me. That's a good thing.' It was as if he were talking to himself, not addressing me or directing information to me. In his eyes I could see everything with certainty, and I mean everything: he was traveling to a place of solace, perhaps even to a place of happiness. I knew this even though I had no inkling at the time of what had played out just around the time you were out there in the country, Herr Melzer; I hadn't heard anything about it until Asta told me the story this morning."

René was quiet for a few moments. Then:

"I'm aware you'd been informed, too. She told me you know the whole history quite well; she gave you full reports in the country, at the end of August."

"Yes," said Melzer. "Briefly, but masterfully, too, encapsulating the entire situation with a single deft swirl of the compass." He marveled at his own words even as he was speaking them, at how they didn't disconcert him in the least; they weren't being quoted from somewhere, hadn't popped up out of some unknown source. They had risen up from somewhere deep inside himself instead, something substantively new coming out of his mouth, seemingly independent of that network of nervous impulses, different from the sapwood of the immediate moment, cut, rather, from the heartwood of his own situation; he was again feeling how he had sat next to Asta on the bench in Pastor's Woods against a landscape that didn't remain silent or self-contained, didn't rebuff or turn away anyone, but that instead had risen up, sunk back down, breathed, and taken great strides with him.

"Asta's heart is just where it should be, and so are her lips," René answered, "and she's a master at keeping things simple. Anyone who's calmed by that simplifying way of hers is inclined to package the subject and reduce it to the simplistic, so that the subject itself can shrink to right size. But what Honnegger told me was that Etelka, the moment she got back to Budapest at the beginning of September, immediately resumed the rather frenzied way of living (let's just leave it at that) she'd been pursuing in July, even doubling the tempo, for that matter. She stopped paying attention to her child almost entirely. She'd brought him with her because he had to go to school. Pista was prudent enough to have the boy brought to the older generation in Bratislava on the day of the disaster. Lala's wife made the arrangements. Etelka carried on this way in Budapest for a good week. Then Pista was the first to catch on. The second one was the wife of that Imre, who saw what was going on with her own husband—did Asta tell you about him?"

(Melzer nodded.) "In a moment I'll ask you to read a letter she wrote to Etelka. It didn't arrive until my sister was dying, and I took it with my brother-in-law's permission. There's one damaging circumstance I have to mention just in passing now. The whole correspondence between Fraunholzer and Etelka—letters covering several years—was in the hands of a woman very close to Grauermann at exactly this critical time. How that's possible and how it came about is something I can't think about, at least not now, for it would lead me too far astray. I have the impression that Etelka's death severed this connection, incidentally; that is, they're not at all close anymore. Besides the open scandal Etelka had bred and fed in Budapest, the matter took on an official aspect, one that would have destroyed her standing in the case of a divorce and would have led to the brink of her having custody of her child legally taken from her and turned over to the father as the sole responsible party, even though we can't say that would definitely have come about. If only she'd tried to fight it, though. But she didn't have any fight left in her. Even so, she was terrified of losing the boy, Honnegger told me."

Stangeler grew silent. Melzer ventured a pointed comment:

"So she ended up taking the mother entirely away from the child."

"You're absolutely right," René answered, reaching into the breast pocket of his jacket. "Here's something else, Herr Melzer: when I got home from the station this morning and stepped into my room—I confess openly that it was like safe ground and home turf after journeying through a storm!—I found a letter from Etelka waiting for me on my desk. I felt a real shock. The deceased was speaking to me once more. Etelka sent me this letter on the afternoon of the day she committed suicide, late that evening. Notice the date, Herr Melzer," added René; "it's only on the postmark; there's none on the letter itself." He passed Etelka's letter to Melzer but held on to a second one he'd taken out of his pocket at the same time.

As the major reached for the envelope, his glance fell onto René's watch. It was easy to read; he saw the hands pointing to eleven after five. The bells chiming the hour had apparently been drowned out by the street noise that had happened to swell up just then; besides, the story René was telling had absorbed all his attention. The hour was far advanced, but that fact was somehow incidental to Melzer, something quite marginal or peripheral. Placed in the gravitational field of events, he felt their weight to be so much heavier as to excuse him completely from anything else, taking it for granted that an excuse this weighty would be totally understandable to anyone else anywhere. He took the letter out of the envelope. There were two sheets of paper covered with round handwriting, the lines spaced widely apart. He read:

"Dear René,
Your loving words did me so much good!"

"Oh you'd written to her before?" Melzer asked.
"Yes," answered Stangeler. "About a week or so earlier."
"That's a good thing," the major said, "a very good thing. And look, Etelka was thinking about you on her last day." He went on reading:

"Give Grete a kiss from me. I've been so happy all along to have her in Vienna, but now I don't know what's going to happen. Some gross, vulgar crusaders have put their paws on a delicate, complicated life situation—and are trampling me underfoot.

"Imre is unhappy and defenseless; he just doesn't have the brute force he needs. He has a gentle artistic nature, so he's been crushed. But I spent thirty-nine years waiting for him ..."

"How old was your sister?" Melzer asked.
"Thirty-nine," said René.

"... and I was completely happy for the first time in my life. I'd finally found my true soulmate. He was already half-crazy over our having to say goodbye; Lala says his state was pathological. So he sent me away one afternoon, went to his petty-minded wife, and told her everything. A major scandal ensued—the mother, brother, and brother-in-law were all mobilized by telephone; he was fenced in by this solid vigilante group; the children woke up and started to cry; the wife wanted to leave him, so he buckled and gave his word of honor.

"Now he writes to me: 'I'm walking along the edge of a

precipice with tottering footsteps.' Well I am too, René! And I can't stand it that Pista's willing to have me stay with him out of the goodness of his heart.

"I'll say to you what Imre just wrote to me: 'Everything that surrounds me is bleak, alien, cold, and deep as an abyss.' It isn't right that my life is shattered like this—and it's so hard to bear as well.

A big hug to you and Grete. Don't hurt yourselves needlessly, kids; that's insane. Be happy as long as you love one another! Etelka."

"There's no doubt she's right about the last part," Melzer commented after a few seconds. "No 'epoch-making resolves' there, René."

"I know," Stangeler said.

"I don't believe, incidentally, that this letter was written on the same day your sister—took that action. It's just that it was sent on Tuesday. She could easily have written it earlier, though."

"Yes, I was thinking the same thing. After all, her breakup with Imre had already taken place the previous week. Lala told me that."

"Would you have taken off for Budapest right away if you'd received this letter a few days earlier, René?"

"No," said René somewhat firmly, "I wouldn't have. Even though my affairs were in good order here. Yet there is one passage in the letter that would have struck me as somewhat alarming. Not 'walking along the edge of a precipice…' (he was quoting from memory, without taking the letter back from Melzer) or 'everything is bleak, alien, cold, and deep as an abyss.' I mean the part that says 'it isn't right that my life is shattered like this…'"

"That makes sense," the major said, handing the letter back to him.

Stangeler gave him the other one. It was just five fifteen now. The sun, shining ever more at an angle, slanted everything it touched, as it were, threading it all together, brushing the treetops, the grass, and the pathways with strands of light gleaming ever brighter. Melzer looked at the long violet envelope adorned on the back with a monogram and a crown, the Hungarian manner of writing the address ("Nagys. Grauermann Istvànné úrnönek"), the eight-fillér stamp with the Crown of Saint Stephen, and finally, the handwriting itself, about which there was nothing at all special. It was evident from the postmark that the letter had been sent on Wednesday, September 16, at around eleven in the morning, more or less at the exact time Etelka had been found when her maid, peeking through the crack in the door of her bedroom, discovered her condition. Now the major took the two sheets of paper out of the envelope. As he began reading, his unanticipated state of extreme receptivity just then made him keenly aware of every mistake in grammar or spelling the Hungarian lady could not have helped making, even though her German was remarkably lucid and fluent, considering the degree of pain and upheaval that must have had her in their grip as she was writing—the letter itself gave ample testimony to her state. But these slight mistakes were more than just that in Melzer's eyes, not merely errors but somehow small markers, as it were, just as clearly integral and intrinsic to the tonal center, the key in which these events happened to be playing now, along with the secluded spot here amid the greenery, the sun shining ever more slantwise, the muffled street noise, and René's outstretched watch. Only now, a bit belatedly, did Melzer look at the date at the top of the letter before turning the page: Budapest, September 15, 1925. So the letter had been kept overnight before it was sent off. It had "been slept on," as they say.

Esteemable Madam,

I believe the devil is guiding my hand and whispering these words to me, I don't know if I'm doing the rite thing or the wrong—no matter, these words must be written. I would have come to see you but fear only of doing something stupid, you see I'm most volatile. Hear me calmly and collectedly, for my letter is a denunciation.

My life was filled with sunlight, I was a woman pampered by one and all, energetic, who saw her path in life clearly. A beautiful love, mutual devotedness filled my life to the brim, a total harmony irradiated it; my husband was my one and all, from my 15th year onward. You entered my life like a demon, an outlaw, selfish and ruthless. You dragged my husband down into your world of lies, you lured him into deceiving on me.

(Melzer began reading faster, because he'd become familiar with the handwriting and could tell where this was going too.)

> . . . me, to whom he had spoken no lies eleven years long. Was it some absolute evilness that led you to select none other than him? It made no matter to you who it might be—as long as it was a man—I have good reasons for saying such—who could help fill in your empty afternoons. Did it never dawn upon you that while he was with you a miserable woman was struggling terribly for her life and yearning for her husband to be to home? And that this man could only have been far away from you in spirit even whilst in your arms? You must possess an enormous fund of energy, esteemable lady . . .

It got a lot stronger than that. Among other things, she wrote:

> Your wiles have met with success—I suffer unspeakably. If you look deeply inside yourself, you will have to confess that it was a perverted thinking on your part to have chosen a model husband and father, a man only too good, for your entertainment.

The signature consisted only of initials. Melzer, who'd read faster and faster and had dashed through the last part, handed the letter back to Stangeler. René put it, along with Etelka's, back in his left-hand breast pocket and stood up. "I assume," Stangeler said, standing in front of the major—he could speak with no restrictions, because they'd remained alone on this bench the whole time, no one occupying a seat or a bench anywhere near them—"I assume," he said, "you're thinking the same thing I am."

"What would that be?"

"That this woman is completely right." (Melzer nodded.) "Her outbursts referring to demonic machinations or absolute evilness that led Etelka to 'select' Imre as a victim or to 'perverted thinking' in her deepest self—I think we have to grant her all that. She had to make the object of her hatred even more hateful so she could hate all the better. That's commonly known in dialectical thinking as a polemical construction. And so Imre's wife ascribes to poor Etelka a diabolical dimension she would never have had the slightest idea of. For the rest, though, this letter falls like a hammer, and there's no ifs, ands, or buts to cushion the blow." He shook Melzer's hand and raised his hat as he made his way deftly, even almost hurriedly, through the palace grounds.

The major looked after him and then did *not* consult his watch. Had René stayed, Melzer would have been the one to stand up and make off; that was how elemental, how imperatively directing him to push everything aside, his one single need was—to be alone. He quickly took out his cigarette case and drew smoke greedily into his lungs as he sat leaning forward. Those letters stayed persistently fixed in his mind. But what about them? Their content? Very much not so. It was the language they used instead. And it was the same, whether in the last letter the deceased woman had written or in the one addressed to her but arriving too late; it was the same tonality or mode, even though author of the other one had been a foreigner; what was wrong about it wasn't the mistakes, because Etelka's struck the same false note—it was virtually her last hour and yet she'd presumed to express herself in such language! But a third element pressed in on him now, and with it a three-dimensional space was created from a flat, plane surface with no meaning in and of itself; a third element, far more appalling, rose up and moved toward him. He could hear as clearly now as if it had been recorded on a wax disc some four weeks before:

> … Etelka—that's René's sister—was just crazy about Grete, and they understood one another very well, but the Grauermanns got exactly nowhere with her, and so they had to be the bearers of bad tidings when they went back to René. And while we're on the topic—they say things haven't been at all on the up-and-up with the Grauermanns for a long time now, either; something's seriously wrong, I hear. Supposedly she loves another man …

He was listening to himself, Melzer, Major Melzer. The missing third dimension about the two women and their letters. It was as if he were staring at his own words, but not so much at these in themselves as at the astounding feat of memory dredging them up now, cruel and implacable, from the shifting sands of days past and gone. This most recent and most highly developed faculty of his was clashing with the part of him that had progressed the least. He immediately grasped, as if a single blow had struck him, that this kind of language—he'd had it completely in common with Etelka Grauermann or Frau von G.—was responsible for creating a space in which all these problems and conflicts, even up to and including adultery and suicide, became possible. He too had spoken this language, had dwelt inside that space and animated it, even though he'd already been preparing to leave it, albeit in the opposite direction—toward a dead person.

Outside him, at the edge of the space around Melzer, it struck twice: five thirty.

He was still in the grip of the idea that he'd later be able to explain everything to Editha or Thea.

Even so, he considered the decisive aspects of this day (and we'll see that a day isn't over till it's over!) to be signed, sealed, and delivered; it was his opinion, in fact, that he was purely and simply holding the outcome of the past several weeks in his hand. That was what was causing the major to remain sitting there for a few more minutes, until five thirty-eight—as a glance at his pocket watch finally told him, when he took it out—utterly unaware, however, that in precisely two-and-one-half minutes, counting from that very second, a mighty blow would strike him. Much later, nonetheless, when everything was long since over and done and the carnival dolls and other contraptions had stopped twisting and turning and were again at rest, he came back (as he said himself) to his initial opinion, strangely enough, with regard to what had actually been decisive, for him—Melzer, that is—on this September 21 of the year 1925.

From the palace grounds Stangeler went directly to the square in front of the station. Right past the Stein House, where his Grete lived, without a second's hesitation.

The sun at his back. As if it were sweeping him along. The stairwell with its festoons and mirrors and elevator: none of this felt "indigestible" to him any longer. No, what he needed now was to have it out in his mind with Melzer. With Melzer, this obnoxious toad hopping back onto the self-justification of whatever he was feeling, disallowing anything that wouldn't reinforce that feeling: "epoch-making resolves," the major had quoted, not without delicate malice (polemical construction!?). And now he bitterly regretted having had such an intimate conversation with Melzer that time on the bearskin, or even having had anything whatever to do with him in the first place. This was how he dismissed the major, Melzer now in truth cast as the Moor in Schiller's play, who had discharged his duty—in part, at least—and was still standing at the ready to finish doing so. Had anybody tried making clear to Herr Nose-in-the-Air René, here and now, that this all was not part of his indwelling character but only a contingent character element, that said someone would have gotten somewhere, just as had once happened in a certain familial configuration making the rounds of the Animal Park at Lainz, which had resulted in a frightening picture by the painter Maria Rosanka; first evoked and then executed, it ended up turning itself into a separate entity (in the possession of the Schedik family still today).

And he, René, had flatly capitulated on the spot and said, "I know."

He reexamined his words, probed them, listened to them once more. Now they didn't seem quite so stupid to him. If you gave a noncommittal, oh-by-all-means "I don't know" or something like it in answer to everything; if you never told anybody anything whatever (and not a single word had been breathed to that malicious backstabber Melzer on the crucial matter of the duplicate ladies!—what a wellspring of comfort, what a soothing balm of satisfaction poured out onto his polemical breast as the thought came to him!); if, in addition, lying flat on any bearskin anywhere—he bored a certain party to distraction and, under given conditions, allowed himself with utmost patience to be bored in return—wasn't he thereby placing himself in the most favorable position to accomplish down to the last detail everything it was really vital to arrange, without being accosted by someone who'd encroached via the Strudlhof Steps and, without a word of warning, being injected with some poison that would render all efforts fruitless and counteract all energizing tension?

With perspectives opened this wide and thinking at this height, the polemical construction flipped over as he came near the bridge. Stangeler began making his way more smoothly, so the racket soon stopped. The machinery was now running evenly and quietly, the screws—no longer whirring in empty air, the rear lifted up in the storm—gripped the water again and found resistance, the craft glided along, headway had been gained.

O ship drifting so smoothly!

Just then an actual steamship was indeed passing downstream under the bridge, its smokestack lowered to a horizontal position. Stangeler came to a stop. People soon began lining both bridge railings, first on the left side and then, a bit later, on the right; they all stopped to look down at the deck of the ship drifting past below them. It was the small gathering that had first caught René's attention, and only then what was causing it. Wanting to see the ship better and more closely, he spontaneously turned right and began walking down one of the ramps that led down from the bridge to the green dockside along the bank. Only now, after leaving the wide street, did he become fully aware of how heavy the traffic was; appropriate for the time of day, what a swirling hubbub of people and honking of vehicles dominated, passing by overhead to the other side of the Danube Canal.

The steamer was now passing under the bridge, cleaving the water with its stem post; René took a few more hurried footsteps as it emerged in all its breadth and continued along the dockside. Thea Rokitzer, by contrast, was just making her way very slowly up the steps from the riverbank next to the station on the other side of the bridge. René wouldn't have been interested even if he'd seen her, and he would hardly have noticed her facial expression or construed its meaning, if we can even speak of an expression in the first place. Her face was rigid with pain and sorrow, totally wide open for all to see. She walked past the station and turned right once more, away from the teeming street.

René remained standing down there for not much more than five minutes. The steamer, small and crunched up when seen from behind, was approaching the bend in the stream. Opposite, past the water again flowing emptily along, there stood rows of windows in the white glare of the sun's reflection, having reddened here and there by now.

He had another short but intense bout of grappling with Melzer.

Then all of a sudden he felt love for him again.

Here, as if banished, standing far off to the side, on this empty, unexpected patch of grass, near the embankment and the water.

Of course there were no "epoch-making resolves."

Everything remained constant and unchangeable.

And now his task was to live up to that state with all his heart and soul.

At this point the marksman stepped slightly back from the target. The bow drew tense. Now the red ring leapt into an abyss of blackness, its center glowing brightly.

Our Stangeler might have lingered here for longer than those five minutes except that a changing current of air now suddenly brought a cold, cellar-like miasma, one that was literally, not figuratively, issuing forth from underneath the city itself. As he stood there, René suddenly saw—really observed, that is— where his few absent footsteps had led him: he was at the wide mouth, or discharge point, of a main sewer, the paved-over underground bed of the stream that had been known for well over five hundred years as the Als, now dry and empty. The water, long since diverted, poured into the river from a point farther upstream. But this very clean and capacious entrance point, a vast, beckoning, accessible gateway into the mysterious underbelly of the city—you could see a good way into it, as into a hall—emitted such a cold, depleting, disheartening odor, however, as to make whatever poison Melzer in all his evilness might have injected (at least to Stangeler's mind) appear to be a bracing tonic by comparison.

René looked into the wide opening of a world unknown to him but apparently in good order; strangely enough, he welcomed this sobering reek, because he had the feeling for several seconds of being equal to this counterbalancing force that was effortlessly able to subdue a mere illusion. Enough, though! He stood there for about as long as it takes to count to ten. Then he started away from this embankment, if not with the bounding steps of earlier, and quickly walked up the ramp.

To the hustle and bustle of the street. A glance at his watch told him it was five thirty-seven. Moving along as fast as he wanted to wasn't so easy; he had to bob and weave a little to cleave a way among all the other pedestrians on the busy sidewalk. As he approached the Stein House, someone emerged through its wide front portal, moving quickly in the same direction as René; a woman in a dark-blue suit, whose way of walking had something in common with Grete's. He looked after her for a few seconds, was then seized with thoughts of Grete, and hastily entered the building.

Around quarter to five, Paula Pichler set in motion her scheme whereby the major, when he came down to the embankment here after work (she didn't doubt in the least his doing this), would find Thea by herself.

She explained to the little lamb that she, Paula, needed to go home, or else her little girl would be all alone. Aunt Theresa, who was minding the child, had somewhere to go at five o'clock and had asked Paula to be back just before then to pick up her daughter. Paula said she hadn't thought of it on Saturday or hadn't even really known it at the time.

At once, Thea wanted to go with her.

Or Paula could stay here and Thea would babysit the child at home.

Gently but firmly Paula drove her little lamb onto that strip of pasture she'd yearned for so keenly in her heart. By virtue of her authority she in fact simply tethered the poor thing to the spot and could hear from some distance the dear animal bleating "baa, baa," but she kept calmly on her way until she was gone.

O meek lamb in the meadow! On the green grass by the bank! On the opposite side, farther from the river, a merry-go-round had been set up, the kind of carousel whose turning central shaft was surrounded by small swing seats suspended by cables or chains from the circular roof surmounting the shaft; as it spins faster and faster, the centrifugal force of the whirling seats lifts the riders, safely buckled in, higher and higher over the heads of the spectators until they're practically horizontal. As the movement starts to slow toward the end, the riders drop back at an even rate, lower and lower, until their seats are hanging vertical again and they can step onto the circular floor, with the shaft at a standstill. Then new riders come scurrying at once.

Up there, the carousel kept on spinning, over and over; the little points of color flew around and around, went whirling higher and higher, gradually came dropping back, and it all came to a stop once more. It was quiet. The shifting breezes sent over faint snatches of mechanical music, but only in scattered bursts. Now it was turning again. Now it was standing still again. The rides and the pauses were almost exactly the same in length. Now that it was quitting time, there was an uninterrupted stream of riders, so a continuous need was forever being satisfied by constantly repeated circular flight.

It was only on looking more closely that the eye could make out this action of the boatlike swings amid the not insubstantial crowd of people. Now and then it was even possible to see the bottom of a seat as it flew ever higher.

Thea saw all this.

Now it was turning again.

Now it was standing still.

Along the embankment, made of paving stones, with steps at intervals, individual people were sitting here and there.

The whole time she stood looking at the whirling and the stopping in such even alternation, there kept flowing inside Thea a persistent calculation, and it squeezed together the outcome of her whole situation, as it were, compacting it into a space that went on growing narrower and become no more than a function of it: the only way Melzer could come down to the embankment here would be via the stairs next to the station. Here, and for a long stretch ahead, the climbing roadbed offered no way to cross over or pass through.

She didn't have the nerve to venture a full, direct look at these stairs (as if she were afraid she'd no longer be able to turn him aside, afraid a trap could snap shut that would catch him and hold him fast).

Even while she and Paula were watching the workers along the tracks—this stretch was just then being electrified and would be reopened not much later—she'd realized that the street was completely separated from this landing place by the viaduct leading up to the platform.

So Melzer had to come by way of the steps.

But Thea did not turn toward them; she preferred to stay here, where she was, a considerable distance away from them, facing the water, her glance directed at the uniform alternation of stopping and starting on the other side. Then she took a few steps down some stone stairs. She saw water swirling and strongly rushing below. A powerfully compressed stream came gushing into the river out of a tunnel. It made white foam.

She went back up and now moved toward the station and the stairs. The five strokes of the clock that had rung a while before from one or another of the church towers hadn't caused Thea any concern; she hadn't even looked at her own little watch. Now, however, a greater tension began to arise between that fixed point and the onward-striding now.

She looked over at the steps, which usually had nobody on them. She took fright a few times when a pedestrian left the sidewalk and came down. But the steps remained empty for the most part.

The fact was she had pinned all her hopes on them. But then with great suddenness it struck her as most unlikely, pitilessly unlikely, that this gray stone would simply be enlivened in the way she was so yearning and hoping for. No, that wasn't going to be. What was she doing wishing for such things anyway?

But she remained where she was, as though frozen to the spot or as though she'd sunk into the ground a little. For a long time. Her waiting had ceased being gentle and sweet, flowing and fleeting at the same time, as joyful waiting can be if it doesn't last too long or threaten to be futile. She stood there as if tethered. Her waiting had become dreary and weary. She tried moving under this heavy pall, at first to no avail. The weight of her own body seemed to be drifting ever farther downward, immuring her foot.

Finally, because she saw so many people standing at the bridge landings and looking at the river, she turned around. A steamship was coming downriver slowly, small, wide, foreshortened. She watched as it approached and saw beyond the river the three ripples the mountains formed on the horizon. A building many stories tall, standing alone to the left and cutting into the forested hills. Two factory smokestacks. The ship came closer and seemed to stretch out now. Thea walked along with it. She almost felt for a moment as if she had loaded her own freight onto the ship, now carrying her weariness and pain beyond the bridge and away—but it refused them and left her what was hers. Now she could see the broad white stern. Reaching the top of the stairs—and now, having set herself in motion, she took a look at her watch—Thea turned away, exhausted and numb, from the hubbub and excitement of all the people constantly streaming onto the bridge. She left the wide street as well, followed the roadbed for a bit, and then turned left into the empty space between buildings—into her own emptiness, guided, as if following a last thread that had not yet snapped, by the remembrance of a walk, almost despondent, she'd taken earlier here, in the same neighborhood.

At almost the same time that Paula Pichler had tied up her little lamb at the green landing place and gone on her merry way, Grete Siebenschein was standing at the door of her parents' apartment, which was empty at the moment (her father had closed the office a little early today and everybody else had gone out as well). She was looking at a note she'd pinned to it with two thumbtacks. It said, "Dear R.! If no one answers, please wait here. I'll be right back." Grete had the distinct feeling that the present time and place were basically unconducive for following through on certain objectives which had germinated inside her in the familial cosmos of the Lainz Animal Park. She even admitted later, for that matter (to Frau Mary), that the way she was conducting herself—strictly on the inside, let it be noted, a mere matter of planning, scheming, and contriving—before seeing René again after his return from Budapest seemed even to herself to be quite tedious or even shallow. And simply not appropriate at the moment, either. So she'd appropriated a scrap of paper for something inappropriate. Be that as it may, her newly won insights needed to be put into action sooner or later, even if new reasons, or just new excuses, arose constantly to make it seem as if the occasion were presenting itself at just the wrong time!

That was what made her keep looking for a brief minute at the note she'd attached to the door, and only after that (pleased somehow, in spite of everything) to start up to the next floor, upstanding and honest in her mind, to ring Mary K.'s doorbell.

Frau Mary, who had taken a nap after lunch today—obeying an

absolutely imperative need for relief from everything, she'd plummeted like a sinking stone, deep and fast, as if enclosed in a narrow chamber—Mary had woken up only half an hour ago and was bustling about to get ready for her expedition to Döbling-Nussdorf. (Or to be more exact: Lower Döbling—that was where the Küffers' villa was; Mary would be taking the streetcar to Nussdorf, though not to the end of the line; she would have to transfer before that.) Just now, after what we might call the second morning, the one her afternoon sleep had thrust squarely into the course of her day, Mary thought, smoothing her wrinkles, how little probability there was that Lea would really follow up on the idea of interrupting her trip to Belgrade by getting off the train in Budapest and seeking a confrontation or final settlement of some kind with Etelka Grauermann about matters at hand, a conclusive clearing of the air between them that would proclaim the beginning of a new era in her marriage to Robert: Mädi's naiveté really did surpass all bounds, so you couldn't put anything past her when it came to these things, not even the possibility that she'd rather sweep a teetering scale right off the table, as it were, than watch it very carefully and then place on it exactly the right amount of weight where it was lacking! These upstanding and honest women! These righteous men of honor in women's garb! Grete was another one! And of course wastrels and ne'er-do-wells could do anything they wanted with them. No, Lea would not make a stop in Budapest. In the first place, the night train was bound to pull in at some impossible hour, and that alone would keep Mädi in her sleeper, which was all to the good; pitch darkness, a strange city (did Lea even know the address of the Grauermanns in Budapest? —though of course there was always the telephone book!). In addition, and above all, she'd informed Lea that conditions in the Grauermann household were chaotic just now; some kind of a scandal had arisen, and the situation there was like a hornet's nest. That was exactly how she'd put it to Lea on the phone, naming her source and giving the point special emphasis; and she was now feeling the utmost satisfaction at having done so. Surely that would help to make everything work out.

During the short time—as she paced back and forth between open wardrobe doors, took out her blue suit and just the right hat to go with it (a tiny little toque with a small feather; it looked fantastic on her!)—during these few moments of bustling about, a hollow space of some kind seemed to open beneath her feet, and into it everything she was now engaged in felt as it were dropping away from her. Her trip to Döbling to have half an hour's conversation with Lea now struck her at bottom (the bottom of that hollow space or fissure beneath her) as pointless. She couldn't improve on what she'd already done for Mädi and might in fact even make matters worse by provoking resistance on the part of this overgrown schoolgirl, who apparently thought it was still possible at her age to gulp down the gluey mush of adult life—thick but also dangerously explosive—with the little baby spoon from her childhood years. Mary came to a stop. By the linen cupboard. A scent wafted to her—heliotrope, old, living in this wardrobe for heaven only knew how many years!

No! She rationalized at once, the opportunity to talk with Lea once more had to be seized. It would be unforgivable of her not to!

But another thought now flashed across her mind like a meteor. (It had escaped her notice the whole time, but she grew aware of it now at once! She'd somehow been thinking it all along anyway; it's what had been behind everything the whole time!) She needed to know if Stangeler was back from Budapest and what exactly was going on there! This was what she had to find out, this, and nothing else—and of course, before she talked with Lea.

She immediately took three steps over to the telephone by the bed, switched it on to make an outgoing call (which meant she was switching off the other one, in the breakfast room) and began dialing the Siebenscheins' number.

Grete was almost always at home around this hour.

There was a knock at the door.

An upstanding, honest face with classical features surrounded by ebony-black hair looked through the crack.

They hugged and kissed each other.

"How was it in Rekawinkel?"

"Really wonderful—they did nothing but pamper me. How did you get in, by the way? I didn't hear the bell ring."

"Marie was just looking out the door."

"Well, how are you, Grete? Is your René back from Budapest yet?"

This didn't sound as if it were jumping out, as anything more pointed than just a routine question that would be asked about whatever the other person considered most important. The long-standing solid foundation of utterly impregnable discretion concerning anything that connected Mary with Stangeler's sister, however indirectly, held without shaking, long since anchored in habit and its automatic responses. In addition, a deliberate veil of mindfulness was spread across it now. But it really was just a veil after all, barely covering the foundation.

"I expect him after five o'clock."

"And what's going on in Budapest?"

"I don't know. All he said to me on the phone was that he would tell me everything in person."

"Yes," answered Mary, "these things are really too complicated for a telephone conversation; he's right about that."

Mary was thinking the whole time—and her train of thought ran so smoothly, with such fleetness, that it seemed like something outside her, not coming from herself but hovering above her, as it were, like the pure essence of the best possible solution—she was thinking that she should have René Stangeler come up to her apartment so she could sit with him and Grete here, at the tea table in the front room. Whatever she might find out she could then immediately convey to Lea over the phone in her bedroom without being disturbed, if any of it was substantive. So then she might not have to travel out to Döbling after all—what was most important under any circumstances was to pass on any news René might bring; anything Mädi knew in advance could have crucial significance for her right after her arrival in Belgrade. Admittedly she didn't know René Stangeler personally, so now it was proving a hindrance that she had never given Grete an opportunity to bring him along when she visited, although that had always been Grete's wish, not at all hard to feel and discern. But Mary had never allowed that wish to be voiced but instead had always changed the subject whenever it seemed about to arise, in this way creating a distance that would guard against her setting in her own home, so to speak, her seal of approval on a relationship she considered unhappy and mistaken.

It was just past quarter to five.

So now.

"It's getting close to five o'clock," she said to Grete, taking her last steps back and forth in the room.

"Are you going out?" Grete asked.

"Yes, later," answered Mary, slipping off her nightgown. "But I'm getting ready now. Why don't you stay for a while, and we'll have tea. Somebody's got to be at home in your apartment who can let René in. Do they know you're up here?"

"Nobody's at home," Grete said. "But I put a note on the door for René to wait for me."

"On the door?"

"Why not?"

"Is René usually on time?" Mary asked.

"Yes," said Grete. "Almost always. But he told me earlier he wouldn't be able to show up on the dot this time. Something or other about a talk with his family, something like that; I don't know what's going on, but in any case, his time frame depends on other people today."

Wouldn't you know it, Mary thought, and then said out loud, "Well, don't let the poor fellow just stand there at your door when he comes by. Go put up a note saying he should ring the bell up here. I'll ask him to tea and then he can give full report. Or do you think he won't want to if I'm here? He knows I'm your friend, of course, even if he doesn't really know me, or just knows who I am. But I have to say I'm curious myself about what happened in Budapest."

"He'll tell us everything if I say it's all right."

"Then go downstairs and write a new note. Wait a second!"

She handed Grete a tablet and a pen.

Grete wrote, "Dear R., please ring at the K.'s apartment one floor up." She left. She was truly happy. But yet:

She was standing at the door of her own apartment and reading what she'd written just fifteen minutes before.

Strange: it can be made impossible for someone to put a reasonable intention into effect!

Upstairs Mary K. finished getting ready, meanwhile, and instructed Marie to prepare the tea table for three. It fit in perfectly that neither of the children was expected home: the boy was at his Spanish course and the girl was being picked up from her business school and would hardly be back before eight o'clock. Grete's presence in Frau Mary's bedroom as the older woman was preparing to go out had felt to her like an annoyance, if the truth were told; Mary really didn't like anyone to talk to her or stand in her way while she paced from the linen closet to the wardrobe to the hatboxes. Today, however, her feeling of annoyance had been covered over by the effort to seize this important opportunity by the forelock; it was the very last chance. Yet she had needed to do so delicately, as if with tweezers.

Now Grete came back in.

Mary was ready.

As was the tea.

They went to the table.

It was five minutes past five by now.

She was going to have to decide quite soon, of course, whether to remain here or to ride out to Döbling.

Right away she led the conversation away from René and Budapest. "I went into the center of town this morning," she said, "and wasn't able to get anything accomplished: I was either early or late for everything. I got some hat mock-ups sooner than I expected, but then the milliner was sick all of a sudden and her shop was closed. And I didn't catch the gentleman from the Estudiantina in time. My son was very disappointed at noon."

"There are days like that," Grete said. "All thumbs, from head to toe. How's the piano coming along, Mary? I seldom hear you playing these days."

"Unfortunately," she answered.

A lull set in and lasted for quite some time, as if all Mary was not saying were now spreading out wider and wider without being named, pushing everything else back to the walls. The silence kept expanding; the water climbed up to her neck, to her ears, where there now was a buzzing sound while she sat there. The heliotrope from the deep, cool, clean linen closet came back. It might be a good idea to call Lea immediately, no matter what, just to let her know about a possible delay and its cause, which was that she, Mary, had to wait for someone. It didn't make any sense to look at the clock. The silence of her home, the gleaming polished surfaces of the furniture, the clean scent of meticulous care reigning in every nook and cranny—all this produced in Mary a kind of sorrow not entirely unrelated to the sorrow of farewell that precedes a separation. She simply couldn't stay here. She felt utterly incapable of it.

"I will say, though," she said, "that if things didn't work out, it couldn't have been through any clumsiness of mine; it was purely outside circumstance. What did my two left feet have to do with the milliner's sudden sickness or the decision by the executive secretary of that organization for students of Spanish to cut short his office hours just that morning and leave his hotel earlier than usual? There's nothing you can do about those things. But what you can do something about is your own left feet—there, you can take decisive action, and that's not a bad thing! Left feet, indeed—for the most part these are just fancies people talk themselves into. All you have to do is step out firmly with your right foot."

"René says the opposite," Grete remarked.

"And that's not just some excuse of his?"

"For what?" asked Grete, in a notably soft tone. Her voice could sometimes take on a deep sound, like a viola or cello.

Mary struck a gentler note at once:

"Well no—all I mean is . . . if I were really of that opinion, then there would be a constant danger, for me at least, of giving up whenever things grew tough and simply yielding to my own laziness."

"Oh, come on, Mary!" said Grete with a laugh, "lazy is the absolutely last thing you are!"

"Every person is lazy," Mary retorted agreeably. Her tone and facial expression were irresistibly engaging as she spoke—intelligent and openhearted. She was really and truly the extreme opposite of a silly little goose, too, and not just Grete Siebenschein, whose even face had only a few minutes before been under slight tension (a simple, genuine feeling, not polemically heightened in any way, not thirsting for a resolution) from those disparities that had been passing through her whole world for years on each floor, the upper as well as the lower; and it was just during René's absent times that she acted like a proxy for him on all different levels, occasionally recognizing with something close to shock how totally she'd grown to be his. It even went so far that she could at times be heard uttering statements that would have met with her vehement contradiction if they had been voiced by René himself. So she could occasionally grow alarmed when she caught herself in this act of deputizing for him. And it had almost been like that a moment before, even though she'd quoted that opinion as René's; yet it wasn't a rarity for his ideas to issue from her lips.

"Grete, how about if you take a seat at the piano?" Mary asked after a while.

Grete did so, with her usual modesty. She never pointed out her skill, by no means negligible and in fact, of professional quality. Although she guarded this depository, she never fell back on it internally—or externally, either, since her time in Norway. Mary heard Grete lift the lid in the next room. She stood up, obeying a sort of compulsion, and stepped over to the window. The piano remained silent all this time. Off at the end of the street a taxi rolled slowly and noiselessly across; a second; a third, at brief, even intervals. Across the canal, above the treetops, rows of windows were gleaming in the white glare of the sun's reflection, having reddened here and there by now.

The piano resounded with clear and correct intonation.

Mary smelled the scent of heliotrope again. It was coming from her lingerie and stood out, even though she'd been using a different perfume for some time.

The doorbell rang.

Mary looked at her watch; it was five twenty-two.

The piano stopped.

They heard a bright voice. Not Marie's. Mary's daughter came in, followed by the maid, who was bringing a fourth teacup. Grete came in from the next room.

It's a testimony to Mary's fair-mindedness and good nature, not to mention the affectionate feeling she was always disposed to, that her first reaction was happiness at seeing the girl, no matter that this unexpected appearance by her daughter only served to heighten the urgency and muddle of a situation growing more tangled by the minute. If Stangeler should arrive now, it would be out of the question for Mary to pull him aside and start him talking—at least not without revealing her own vested interest in the matter. It wouldn't have been hard to alert her daughter by a small sign. But the three had already taken seats at the tea table, so if Stangeler should come walking in now it would be hard to signal quickly and inconspicuously enough. He would have to be introduced to two women he'd never met and might then prefer to postpone communicating his news to Grete until later and on the floor below. All these deliberations of Mary's were being intruded on by the conversation around her, the topic just now concerning what had caused the young lady to return home so early and unexpectedly: a whole crowd had been planning to attend a film premiere, but some misunderstanding had arisen, because the movie everyone else wanted to see held no interest whatever for Mary's daughter (a film jam-packed with prehistoric dragons, based on a book by the English writer Conan Doyle). So she'd simply made her way home. Grete observed this young girl with friendliness, even with admiration, for that matter. The life of this child, not yet even fifteen but acting at least eighteen, seemed to be structured around a balanced center, which hinted at— no, outright proclaimed—a self-confident poise almost unimaginable at her age. Grete could almost have wished a little of it might rub off on her.

No Stangeler.

The doorbell did not fire the expected shooting stars into the empty space.

Mary began clearing a field that had become too complex. And in the greatest hurry, at that.

"I really have to leave now, Grete; there's nothing I can do about it," she said as she stood up. "Why don't the two of you just stay here? Don't let me break this up."

But Grete now stood as well.

"I hope you'll excuse me, but I'm expecting someone downstairs," she said cordially to the young girl, who had likewise stood. In the dark eyes below her reddish hair there gleamed a far more perfect knowledge of other people than many full-grown, if not full-blown, adults ever reached at their peak. "Of course," she answered gently. Mary had disappeared into the bedroom. She'd beaten a retreat, we have to say. While she was putting on her hat in front of the mirror—that charming little toque! and what a delightful effect the slight swell of her flesh-colored blouse with its ruffles made under the blue fabric of her suit jacket—while she was putting her hat on, then, she felt the great soothing effect, the sheer relief that consisted simply of being alone. Being alone so you could get your thoughts in order, think things over when you're in such a hurry, when you're darting from one open wardrobe to another or busy putting your hat on. She won back lost territory in these few seconds. She was right on the verge of just letting her arms drop, of breathing deeper, even of just yielding and—sitting down? There was a chair right by the bed. The last rays of the evening sun were receding from the room. Surely she could grant herself a minute or two. But Frau Mary did not brook such behavior, or at least very rarely did. She was a sensible woman. It had happened only now and then over the years that she had balked, as it were, that she had broken free. Just now, nonetheless, as she was setting her hat to rights, something as fine as gossamer was in her hands, covering them like a sheath or a coating that was hindering her from handling objects easily and securely. For no longer than a second, like a sudden cave-in or collapse, there opened up in her the prospect of being gripped by panic, of losing control—and while it lasted, she saw this prospect as being far more advanced, having made much deeper inroads, than she'd had any idea of. Her hands were filled with something alien and fixed, something remotely comparable to hurtling along at top speed with the reins flying loose. Now she was ready, trim and spruce, and she left the bedroom. Grete was waiting for her. What she'd just experienced had done her good, but now it was once again too much—the presence of other people, that is. Marie now came in as well. "I'll be back home at seven," Mary said. Grete had already opened the door to the landing and stepped through. Mary followed but stopped for a second to gather her energy, and then she looked at her wristwatch. It was always accurate, and now it showed that the time was nearly twenty to six. While she was walking quickly toward the stairs, followed by Grete, she thought about that slight bulge in the carpet runner that she'd tripped over in the morning, so she was a little more cautious as she approached the spot, between her floor and the Siebenscheins'. But the caretaker had smoothed out the bump in the meantime, perhaps as a result of someone's complaint. She shook hands cheerfully when they got to Grete's landing. Now she increased her pace, moving more fleetly, quickly scampering down the steps to the rather ostentatious, tacky entrance hall. And she'd soon stepped past the small glass door set into the wrought-iron grille of the tall portal, featuring just as many flourishes and curlicues as all the rest. Mary made her way quickly on a diagonal across the sidewalk, here as wide as a boulevard. She was facing into the evening sun at this hour. She squinted, looking toward the center of the square would have to cross, whether it were to get to her streetcar stop or to hail a taxi on the opposite side, by the station, which she was now considering.

It wasn't just the foot traffic on the sidewalks that had swelled to a major hustle and bustle; the nearness of the train station did its part as well. Mary stood on the shore of this sea of traffic, in which the red and white streetcars were the most unassuming vehicles and the profusion of delivery trucks drew the most attention. She felt the strong constraint of needing to proceed painstakingly, with all her wits about her, following the traffic regulations here to the letter. But somehow she didn't seem to be comprehending or grasping them clearly enough. Something gently pushed her back onto the sidewalk, while immediately after that, like a movement not decided by her head, but one running up her body like an ascending ripple, a totally unanticipated arbitrary act on the part of her knees and legs, she started across, moving just as she had down the staircase, one foot in front of the other. Now she was in the middle, already joined in battle, so to speak. Back now, step out here, now stop. Someone yelled something from a truck. Just keep moving along. A streetcar was making toward Alserbach Strasse; it had a rear car attached that was swaying sharply from side to side. (Captain Eulenfeld called them rattletraps.) Looking out from, and even hanging over, the rear platform appeared a passenger whose resplendent figure, in a dapper light-beige suit no less, didn't stand in the right relation to this very plain conveyance, seemingly built to hold only shriveled-up little occupants. He was looking out with an eagle eye that ranged across the sky without seeming to have any reason to fix on anything. It was Dr. Negria. "And where in heaven's name might he be headed?" Mary asked herself, looking after the vehicle, which turned the back of the rear car to face in her direction as it went quickly trundling on. But there would have been just as little reason for interesting speculations as there had been earlier for the purposeful, alert traversal of the skies, for Dr. Negria was on his way, all dutifully and responsibly, to the children's hospital, where he had night duty later. Perhaps he was coming from the Augarten Tennis Club.

Grete Siebenschein had stopped on the landing. She went to the apartment door and looked for a moment at the slip of paper, the second one, the replacement that got her nowhere. She could still hear Mary's rapid footsteps down in the entrance hall. Then the street door shutting. During these few seconds, Grete was thinking she might take the note down from the door and put the first one back up with the same two thumbtacks; she'd put it in one of her dress pockets. And then just go off somewhere. Perhaps back up to the fourth floor to sit at the tea table with that perceptive young girl? As her alert ear was listening to her own emptiness, meanwhile, she caught the sound of the small street door below as it opened and then was shut again by the automatic door lock. She recognized René's walk right away; he would have given himself away even without dashing up the steps, which nobody in the building besides him ever did.

Grete tore up the second note and left the first one in her pocket. She opened the apartment door and was now standing in the doorway even before Stangeler appeared on the landing.

He came up the last few steps and darted toward her. She drew him to herself, and the door clicked shut.

Even in the foyer it was somehow easy to tell the apartment was empty at the moment.

He put his arms around her. Grete grew slack as he held her, and quickly, too. Everything grew slack.

Then he told her what there was to tell and had her read Etelka's last letter.

They went into Grete's room. The force of the blow sent them into a tight embrace, as if it had been ordained.

Mary's daughter remained sitting at the tea table.

A curtain of silence had fallen behind the departing women. Smooth and quick. No folds that could furl. A *courtine*. A fire curtain.

Oh young girl, not little lamb!

Daughter, granddaughter, great-granddaughter—writing your biography would be the most fascinating of all the alluring tasks I'm not charged with. Where are you today? Who was your lord and master? Who could ever have even dared presume you were his?

You are the midpoint of these moments here, during which unspeakable pain was inflicted on you in the surrounding area, in the world outside. Pain of which you have not the slightest inkling, and it is the absence of any foreboding that makes your beauty possible at the present moment.

"Well, it will soon be time, Editha darling," the captain said around quarter to five (just as Paula Pichler was tethering her little lamb and Grete Siebenschein was pinning her—first—note to the apartment door).

"What business is it of yours?!" Editha retorted.

"Friendly concern," said Eulenfeld. "And that includes Melzer."

"How sweet of you," she remarked; nothing more.

"What do you hear from Wedderkopp?" he asked.

She placed back into her purse a letter she'd skimmed through once again.

"Well, he thinks it's all stupid. He's on a rampage, in fact. He wants me just to keep everything stored here."

"What's he mean, 'everything'?"

"The government-issue cigarettes."

"Ah! Her tobacco romance. Listen, didn't you tell me Wedderkopp doesn't know a thing about it, and you're eager to surprise him, and so on and so on?"

"I told him in the meantime," she said casually.

Full-strength grunt. Then:

"What further is being imparted in the Wedderkoppian epistle?"

"That if I'm not with him in two weeks or haven't at least set a date for my arrival by then, he'll come to Vienna. Then he's saying we'll get married here, with the German consul general as officiating authority—can such a thing even happen?—and then he'll take me away with him."

"Not at all stupid, our Gustav," said Eulenfeld. "In short: Wedderkopp *ante portas*."

She stood up and began getting ready in front of the mirror on Eulenfeld's wall, her hands raised to her hat. Mimi didn't budge on the sofa. She lay propped up on her elbows with her knees drawn up, just staring into empty space in front of her. "Essentially just as opaque a creature as her Enrique," thought Eulenfeld, looking Mimi over, "they're a good fit." Then out loud: "You'd probably be most pleased if our boy Melzer never put in an appearance. Am I right, Editha dear?"

She didn't reply. She was tired. Her impulse to contradict now extinguished or at least very restrained, it was only too clear to Editha how accurately Eulenfeld was able to look into the abrupt and volatile mechanism of her being, into what could be called the dilettantism of anything and everything she pursued, no matter how clever and cunning it looked at the outset; she could never see it through. But it wasn't just the way she pursued her chosen goals that was dilettantish; it was the goals themselves, which of course always fizzled out. She was by no means stupid enough, our Editha Schlinger (Editha Schlinger, she of the Pastrés and now of the Wedderkopps, in a matter of days), not to find a modicum of self-recognition at the basis of her fatigue or depression. The thought of simply being bowled over by Wedderkopp did her good in the depths of her soul; in fact, it was what gave her the main support she needed just at present.

Suddenly she turned around and was soon kneeling by the sofa in front of Mimi, covering her with kisses:

"So please come right away if I call you. I'm going to wait twenty minutes at the absolute longest for Melzer. If he doesn't show up, I'll call right away, and you set out at once. Please, Mimi, sweetheart? For my sake? And if you do come, how about if we make this tormentor, this prison warden, happy, shall we? Because that will release us from our confinement! We'll have to celebrate! Don't you think?! How about if you change right away in the next room? So we're both wearing the same thing! Isn't this fun, Mimi?"

"Well, I guess," Mimi answered. "What did you have in mind?"

"A tea gown. Very glamorous. Beige touched with gold."

And in fact Editha had carried things so far lately that she'd had two of everything made in advance.

Mimi promised her whatever she asked. Now Editha jumped up and adjusted her clothes. It was six minutes to five. The captain reached for a bottle on the table and filled a blue-tinted glass halfway. He held it out to Editha and muttered:

"A stirrup cup?"

She swallowed it obediently.

"You don't seem worried about injuring your swain with a fierce burst of flame."

Editha said nothing and left.

Silence now spread throughout the captain's room. In the corner of the sofa—where Melzer and Thea had once sat so cozily—Mimi Scarlez had bunched herself up even tighter, her expression utterly inscrutable, though now without the broad backdrop of mountain and castle. In what twilight reveries of memory was she engrossed, what rainbow-hued streaks and stripes were drifting and swirling? The Lagos with its boat trips, swans, an excursion farther away, to Tigre, or, close to her apartment, the Recoleta Cemetery with its godly, poignant burial vaults, all aboveground? The Madeleine in Paris or the twelve columns in front of the cathedral at home, each reminiscent of the other? The Calle Cerrito, the drive leading to the Teatro Colón. Right across from the office of Cassullo, her dentist. The two buildings next to it were lower, and the fourth, past a cross street, had a dome. All of it exactly as ghastly as in Paris or Vienna. But she loved it all. She could smell it. Enrique knew hundreds of lines from the Spanish classics by heart, and she always made him recite them to her, even before she really understood the language and could only speak to him in French or English. But his mouth, when he pronounced Spanish in this pure and lofty tone, took on changing shapes, which would cause Mimi to fall head over heels in love, again and again, with utter abandon (insofar as any such thing can be spoken of in her case). But come to think of it, she did act with abandon side sometimes. When she was desperate. Then she was even capable of slapping and flailing out at anyone who might be in her presence at the wrong time, as one will perhaps be pleased to call back to memory.

The captain kept silent as well and was in fact very serious. It seemed there might open up not just to the twins, but to himself as well, when this absurd comedy was finally over, some kind of windup that would bind up the situation. It was during these cogitations, by the way, that the captain decided to send Scarlez a cable; the man's letters had been demonstrating considerable impatience, if not in the form of an ultimatum, like our good old Gustav's missives issued. Eulenfeld would tell Mimi's husband to see to it that he come to Vienna and settle matters with his in-laws in person. So then they would both, the two hereunto appertaining sons-in-law, appear on the hereunto appertaining scene at the same time. Prior to that, both daughters were to be presented, in duplicate and in a trice, to their parents. What he had in mind was to wind up and wrap up and make short work of things after the charade was over. During old Herr Pastré's illness, especially after his return from Merano, Eulenfeld had undergone his share of fear and trembling on behalf of Mimi and her interests, both as to reconciling with her parents and as to the inheritance; because what if Editha should get married in the meantime; because who could tell what kind of a stunt good old Gustav might pull if the will hadn't been changed? And so on. He couldn't wrest away from Mimi her statutorily mandated share, but to be left only that would be enough of a calamity for her and Enrique. Luckily Old Man Pastré was doing significantly better. But how could anybody be sure? The man was seventy-nine. *Aetatis suae septuagesimo nono.* Thusly and accordingly, to wit: as soon as possible: the whole family: get them cantering in a circle! Assemble them for a proper mustering, make short work of the lot, happiness for all and sundry to be arranged forthwith—or forcibly imposed, if need be. "This could be a case for that activist idiot Negria!"

This last thought pulled the captain out of his reflections and at the same time tore Mimi away from the streaks and stripes of her dreams, whatever name they had.

"Five o'clock. We'll be needing to get ready."

"For what?" asked Mimi in a somewhat whining tone. "We don't even know…"

"Oh yes we certainly do know. Melzer's definitely not going to show up at Editha's."

"What makes you think that?"

"Paradoxical but simple: because he would have come long before now. To you, that is—understand, dear heart? So now please be so good as to *te lever*, meaning get off your fanny, so we can head over now. Editha seems to be in great need of considerable assistance today."

She obeyed. It was the easiest course of action. And in fact the captain brought matters to the point where they were finished dressing to go out by five fifteen and were standing in the entrance by the telephone, Mimi with a resigned look on her face.

The phone rang at five seventeen.

Mimi looked wide-eyed at Eulenfeld.

Yes, it was Editha. "Come over, and make it fast. I don't want to be alone. Hand the receiver to Mimi for a minute."

"Yes, ma'am," said the captain. "Listen, Editha dear, we'll be there in two minutes. If Melzer still hasn't come by that time, leave the apartment door open just a little; I mean the door to the stairwell, opened only a crack. But if it's shut, we'll know you're not alone, so we won't even ring; we'll just turn around and go. Are you understanding me, little friend?"

"Yes, Otto," she said, "but the door will certainly be open."

Now the two sisters spoke for a moment in an affectionate whisper. Mimi was lovingly warding off some comments, as if inordinately intense words of praise or protestations of love were coming from the other end of the line.

The captain looked at his watch in the meantime (not quite eighteen past five) and then through the apartment to make sure everything was right—gas tap, light switches, ashtrays. Out in the corridor with Mimi, he shut the door carefully, not before making certain his keys were in his pocket. The manner in which Mimi waited for him to move through these rapid but concentrated checks was very much how a well-behaved child would act while an adult is taking care of whatever is necessary. She looked like a child, for that matter. His accurate prediction that Editha would call, and then her actually doing so, had yet again given rise to one of those moments—and there was no scant number of them—that constituted the basis of Eulenfeld's authority over the twins, and on a molecular level, as it were.

The door to Editha's apartment was open, wide open, in fact, inviting them to come in, and she greeted them as tenderly as she did tempestuously. The captain stood there patiently and was soon on his own in the white salon with the distant view (where the tea table was set for two), for Mimi had been dragged off at once through one of the door panels with the grapevines and angels above them; it was the right-hand door as you entered (the opposite side led into Mimi's large bedroom—"this way to the gondola"—while Editha had made do with the smaller one behind the hidden door). The room situated to the right, which the twins hardly ever used—it had originally been planned and furnished as a dining room—now held several large, handsome clothing wardrobes Editha had procured, and it was in these that the Schlinger treasures—some of them in duplicate—were stored. While the twins were now slipping into their gold-trimmed beige dresses, the captain hauled his flask from his pocket (well, what was he supposed to do?) and was just about to unscrew the silver cap when the apartment doorbell rang: in truth, a shooting star leaping to the eye.

One of the twins looked out from the dressing room (and the captain himself—by the very devil!—really couldn't tell for a second which one it was, because each of them was nearly finished putting on the same dress), and called in a quiet voice:

"Go take a look, Otto. See if it's Melzer and then tell us. But don't open the door!"

Eulenfeld went—slowly, even circumspectly. They could hear him in the entrance calling through the door, "Just a second, please, I'm coming right away." Then he came back and said:

"It's Thea Rokitzer."

"All right!" Editha said quietly. "Is she in for a jolt! Let's give her something to look at! Take her quietly into the small bedroom. Let her stay there until we're ready; Mimi has to quick put on different stockings. Tell her there's a big surprise waiting for her! And she's not to come out until you call her. Mimi will go into the other room, then you have Thea come out, clap your hands, and we'll come in through the large doors, left and right, and walk straight up to her. What do you think? Yes?"

"Yes," said Mimi and nodded, even showing a certain amount of excitement. That seemed to make Editha happy, for she suddenly gave her twin sister a hug and a kiss.

"So be it, then!" said the captain, not without a flourish, "finish preparing and then go to your places! *Denique comoedia finita erit.*" And he vanished into the entrance.

Thea had an absent air, but it would have been hard to say what she was absent from—because being absent from a perfect vacuum is yet more paradoxical than not showing up because you haven't already shown up.

She sat down on a small armchair standing next to the bed placed in front of a stand with nickel trim, its writing surface covered with glass piled with a jumble of books and even more so with letters and boxes of writing paper.

She made out the name "Melzer," but it was devoid of any association, the name itself being the total contents of her whole existence, the universally inclusive designation of her own vacuum, so to speak, simply written down there on a piece of paper in ink or pencil. At its lower edge. It was note-size and typed. Thea opened her leather purse and dropped the name into it (oh, and of course the paper it was written on).

But there it was again. In ink this time, the same handwriting, at the lower edge of a large piece of paper this time, one that had small printing on it here and there but mostly showing lines, divisions, headings of some kind.

Thea helped herself to this "Melzer" too.

But then there it was yet again. Twice this time. Then came more papers of the same kind, but with no "Melzer" on them. Thea took these as well. Underneath was now only the shiny glass surface. Thea clasped her purse shut. The captain was calling her from the next room.

Thea did not react to the spectacle staged before her now in any way that could have been anticipated.

When the captain clapped (just as Thea was stepping through the hidden door) and the two ladies appeared left and right in their gold-beige dresses in the white salon and started toward her, the young woman let out a short scream—not shrill or piercing, but deep instead, as if from an innermost chamber, almost reminiscent of a roar from a wild animal—and bolted right down the middle with loping footsteps before they could even reach her. She was too quick for the captain to stand in her path and keep her there. Thea had slammed the apartment door by now and was off.

She went clattering down the steps faster and faster, her purse clutched under her arm. She turned left at the street door. Three men were coming along the sidewalk, two of them in short topcoats and leather spats, conversing with a uniformed policeman, the third. They all smiled vaguely at Thea, and they may even have called something out to her, something flattering. But she was no longer capable of establishing any connection between herself and the outside world. The line had been cut. Nothing had anything to do with her. Just past the next corner, a small, open two-seater automobile was standing. It was coming her way. Thea recognized Oki Leucht, the captain's friend. Next to him were some large boxes; now the car turned left at the corner, toward the Danube. Thea hurried along the arrival side of the station, but she slowed her pace when she reached the spot where she was now planning to cross the square. But that wasn't possible there: traffic was approaching first from the right, then from the left, and the evening sun was blinding her. The face of the clock that told the official time up on the post looked hostile and even vicious, the hands scrunched at a sharp angle. It was twenty to six. She leaned forward slightly and started out into the sea of traffic.

Melzer had to laugh. The sight of Dr. Negria, looking like a giant dressed in light-colored clothes as he emerged or surged out of the preposterously small trailer attached to the streetcar—Negria's head seemed just about to graze the roof of the platform, and his arms were lifted, moreover, so he could hold on with both hands to the overhead leather straps, which in turn made his upper body look even more massive, since his elbows were spread far apart—the sight was irresistible not least because of the gaze, the eagle eye with which our pediatrician and activist was ranging through the skies. That was the panorama that went driving past after the major had left the park, almost covered the distance (about one hundred sixty paces) to the station square, and was only steps away from it as he passed the wine bar on the corner. Also steps away from keeping his date with Editha Schlinger and without delay explaining both the unforeseen situation and the lateness it had forced on him. His appointment with Paula Pichler and Thea, however, was definitely no longer on; it couldn't be kept now. The regret that came over Melzer grew until it was a sharp pang: but a pang for this one absence and this one only, not for any kind of decisive or final break. No, it surely wasn't that. The major realized as much, beyond any doubt.

As he was standing at the corner, he saw Mary. Her face was turned toward Alserbach Strasse, looking after the streetcar just then driving away. She was standing still. Then she began walking again, still looking back in the same direction. The streetcars in Vienna drove on the left-hand track in those days. Mary was standing in the middle of the track on which Negria's car, which she was still following with her eyes, had driven past her and Melzer; so she still had to cross the second track, along which at this point, emerging to Melzer's view behind the conveyance driving away, another streetcar was coming from Alserbach Strasse in the opposite direction, with Mary now making for it from off to the side. She walked straight into its path. Even before the brakes were pulled so hard that the vehicle shook, even before onlookers who'd witnessed the accident began screaming, Melzer turned left and raced toward the middle of the square.

Exactly like charging full on in battle: hurtling fully into it as if one's own will were a gigantic hairy fist whose force a man has been trained all his life, however small and insignificant it has been, to receive.

At her side. With blood spurting red everywhere, spattering the man's knees. But the man was a professional soldier, a soldier who'd weathered many different battles. He pulled off his belt and moved her shredded and bloody clothing aside. He felt around the wound, calmly and clearly realizing within mere seconds that the leg had been severed almost completely above the knee, and he saw where the dead-white, uninjured flesh began: that's where he applied a tourniquet. He skillfully thrust his walking stick (along with its gold knob) through his belt as he was tightening it, and now he gave it a twist. The blood that had been gushing out at even intervals now stopped; the pool by his knee grew no larger. Someone was helping the whole time, moving things aside, making sure the walking stick was inserted properly and then holding it steadily in place so that Melzer could let go and catch his breath. He turned to this helper—and kneeling next to him in the pool of blood, spattered and sullied all over, just like he was, he saw Thea Rokitzer.

The very fact of their kneeling side by side in blood meant that after the stunning blow of the catastrophe a relatively stable situation (in more than one respect) had now set in. The blow had been struck; the arrow stuck fast. This occurrence represented a new configuration, and they were going to have to figure out how to deal with it. These were some of those seconds during which a fact only now turns into one before our eyes even though it is already accomplished, but the simple phenomenon alone of its meteor-like incursion out of what might be called a realm beyond our world (which is where they all come from, and where they seem to be in plentiful supply) still keeps us disconnected from it. Here is what else must be added if a fact is to become a fact: duration, at least a certain amount of duration. Sometimes minutes or even halves of minutes have wrought wondrous works of weal. So it was here. Life's innumerable fine feelers and feeders, setting to work forthwith, flickering in rapid motion, begin assimilating the new nourishment their insatiable maw has already begun absorbing, begin smoothing out moment by moment the bulge, its original shape protruding, made by occurrences.

This ring-shaped bulge, usually made of earth disturbed by the impact of a grenade or a bomb from a fighter plane, was made of human beings in this case.

Having been formed by a sudden blow, given its nature, it was already changing shape, even starting to crumble here and there.

What had happened during those seconds when Melzer was bolting headlong into the battle of his life, leaping from the corner by the wine bar with a real tiger spring, was that they had hauled Mary out from under the streetcar and its front-mounted safety guard and moved her to the side, at which point the major reached her. They'd been able to free her without much difficulty because she hadn't been pinned under; the safety guard had been off the ground slightly, whether because of the shaking caused when the streetcar braked or because of Mary's body itself—perhaps both. But that was exactly what had enabled the left front wheel to amputate. Several policemen now cleared some space and calmed the crowd, moving away from the tracks the people who were still crowding in, and after they'd taken information from the eyewitnesses—especially after they'd questioned the driver of the vehicle involved in the disaster—a rather long string of streetcars that had arrived at the scene and been forced to stop now began moving again across Althan Platz toward the Danube. Looking out from their coaches, the passengers—passersby in the truest possible meaning of the term, since they'd been bypassed—watched the bulge receding.

Toward its epicenter there proceeded apace the absorption of the occurrence, its rounding down, its leveling off and realignment with the surface contour of the given facts, which those present had in fact now attained. Bandaging material was brought from the train station. Melzer himself applied the first emergency bandage but wisely left the belt and stick where they were; the stick was now firmly secured, so

Thea could finally let go of it. She was helping Melzer while at the same time a young policeman, tall and handsome, kept directing the same request to the onlookers still crowded around; in an appealing tone he asked them to make more room and then to go on their way: "Ladies and gentlemen, there's nothing more to see with this poor woman"; and this covert appeal to their humane feeling, as it were—though he was not far from calling their ghoulish curiosity by its name—had some effect. The actual point of transition from the catastrophe to a world of newly created facts—at least that's what it was for Melzer and Thea, since Mary lay deeply unconscious—was made manifest when the couple stood up from their kneeling position, out of the pool of blood, which was by now sending runnels in several directions, some of them continuing to ooze along, almost reaching the feet of the bystanders, but in other places combining and flowing together. They now lifted Mary, very slightly and with the greatest caution, removing her from the tracks entirely and bringing her to the edge of one of those "safety islands," the name of which, ordinarily more figurative, in this case became filled, packed to capacity with meaning, having been caught up with by blood-soaked reality. Melzer, with no more reason whatever to be careful of his clothes, sat down on the curb and had Thea and the young policeman set Mary down such that her head was resting on his thighs; he was leaning slightly to the left, supporting himself with his left arm on the ground. Thea, who—only now—had tears in her eyes, arranged Mary's arms. Melzer had stabilized her leg as well as he could with some of the bandaging; the limb was almost completely severed but still attached. He and Thea were drenched up past their elbows in blood. The policeman asked Melzer and Thea for their names and addresses. Was Melzer a doctor? No, an army major, he said, his eyes on Mary all the while; he had gently removed her hat, half torn off anyway, smoothed her hair, and set the little toque on top of Mary's handbag, which the policeman had secured when the crowd first came rushing in and had now set down on the curbstone. Had Melzer witnessed the accident himself? Yes, said the major, and there could be no question but that the injured woman had walked straight into the streetcar, meaning that the driver could in no way be held responsible, and he, Melzer, as eyewitness, would testify to that effect.

Thea was sitting to his right on the curb as well. Practically all the onlookers were dispersing by now. Mary's identity was established by the police; her purse contained her membership card for the Augarten Tennis Club, among other items. Just as one of the men was leaving to inform the relatives immediately—she lived in the immediate vicinity, after all—an ambulance arrived at effectively the same time as a doctor from the area whom someone had called to the scene.

Throughout all this detailed unfolding of events, which took a goodly amount of time, Melzer essentially had eyes for nothing, took nothing to cognizance, except for Mary's head; turned to the right, her pale profile was framed by her loose hair; it was frighteningly but not fatally pale; did not show the pallor which had suddenly come over the dying colonel's face even while he was speaking to his friend. Besides, Mary's breathing was comparatively strong; her face still had color—to Melzer it was appealing and patrician, even dignified, and there was no sign of that fearsome caving-in of the flesh between cheekbones and skin, as though the skin were receding inward and causing the structure of the skull to show, that can sometimes be observed in people who have just died, and not just ones with haggard faces, either. What Melzer was seeing here was not death—Melzer knew death. What was hovering around this delicate head, rather, was the whole burden of a life that would go on.

And while he observed her, he knew with utter certainty, beyond any doubt, that she would triumph. This wasn't just anybody. This was Mary.

The church bells rang unceasingly; that was the second phenomenon Melzer kept absorbing all this while, the first through his eyes, the second with his ears. The sound must have been coming from Lichtental, from the Church of the Fourteen Holy Helpers.

The third stimulus was not confined to an individual sense but instead was borne in on all of them at once, the inner and the outer, the visible and the invisible, the tingling cells, the open portals of body and soul—what flimsy barriers would not have been smashed to smithereens by a blow this mighty; what walls could still remain standing intact? Thea was sitting here next to him, at this very hour, here and now, today.

The ambulance arrived. The sound of its siren brought other vehicles to a stop and turned the heads of those pedestrians who had not taken notice of the accident. After hopping out of the ambulance and checking the whole situation, the doctor asked Melzer, taking a look at his blood-drenched clothes, if he had been the person to provide emergency aid. "A good thing you did," he said, and Melzer nodded. A small crowd had once more congregated. The stretcher slid into the ambulance. "Your handsome walking stick," said the doctor, who was exchanging a few words with a colleague from the area who turned up just when the medics were finishing (perhaps the two doctors knew each other), "your handsome walking stick, I say," turning to Melzer, "you're going to have to retrieve it from the admissions desk at the accident ward on Lazarett Gasse. Do you know this unfortunate lady?" "Yes," answered Melzer. "Can you please tell me, Doctor, if there's any danger of death?" he added quickly and emphatically. Oddly enough, however, he himself felt as if the question were no more than a mere formality. "I can't be sure yet," the doctor answered as he got into the ambulance, "but thanks to your skillful first aid, perhaps not." The young policeman quickly handed Mary's purse and hat to the medics. The ambulance drove off, siren wailing.

So they were left standing out on the street, their clothes soaked in blood for no apparent reason now, since the reason had been cleared away, vanished.

Just now, in fact, the last traces were indeed disappearing: an older police inspector on the scene had promptly turned to the car washers who worked near the taxi stand at the station; they came and emptied a few wooden buckets of water over the surface where the blood had spilled. The red vanished. A clean sweep. Somehow it brought up thoughts of closing time at a tavern. Even though the talk between the officer and the men he had fetched couldn't be made out in detail, it sounded easygoing and jovial.

Melzer, now seeing himself, along with Thea, increasingly abandoned on every side, as it were, and thus confronted more and more urgently with his own external, extremely conspicuous appearance, turned to the young policeman still standing nearby and asked him to flag down or call a taxi—"since we can't possibly walk the street in this condition," he said. "Of course, Major," the young man answered, coming to attention for a moment. He stepped off the island onto the square and raised his arm just as a cab was approaching. One look at Melzer and Thea and the driver immediately grasped the situation, all the more since the address Melzer gave was hardly more than a hundred paces from where they were. The driver tossed his linen dustcover over the upholstery to protect against bloodstains. Now they were seated. The policeman saluted. During the short drive, everything—no differently for Melzer than for Thea—was clear and present. Seated next to him, she was unceasingly occurring; an eruption, a crater, a place in life where said life was flinging up its inmost and achieving its utmost. He heard the question she asked during the short trip—"Major, do you know the lady who suffered the accident?"—but heard it as if blurred and from a distance, tamped down and covered over by the din that was Thea. "Yes," he said, talking as if half asleep, "the last time I saw her was fifteen years ago." They reached the door of his building. "Come in with me, Fräulein Thea; let my landlady take care of you. You can't go home to your parents like this; they'd be frightened out of their wits." Thea stepped into the entrance as Melzer held the door open. "Thanks very much, sir!" the taxi driver called across the sidewalk. Melzer had paid his fare with a large bill but then waved aside the man's attempt to give him change.

It was important not to alarm Frau Rak (they hoped she was at home). Pierrot was not the most robust of women. But the concierge, Frau Gruber, was. Melzer rang her bell. He became aware just at this moment that the usual clean smell of whitewash was prevalent again, not that musty odor of rubber. The door to the little storeroom or workroom was closed. Frau Gruber, a buxom young woman, who answered in slippers and without stockings, was quick to grasp what Melzer was telling her (especially since she was able to look at Thea the whole time).

In addition, she'd already heard about the accident on Althan Platz (news like this does travel fast through the neighboring streets). Now she ran up the steps to prepare Frau Rak, followed slowly by Melzer and Thea Rokitzer.

Thea was immediately taken in hand by Pierrot (whose dark eyes were gleaming like jet buttons in light of a sensation like this). Melzer asked only that someone should knock at his door when the bathroom became free so he could come out to the hallway. Then he vanished into his own rooms. It suddenly came to him that he was more than overdue to be by himself with all the turmoil that had filled him to bursting, and he flung himself with deep breaths onto the bearskin, just as he was. He simply stayed still there for the moment. It didn't sicken him that he had Mary's blood on his clothing. But dread now had him in its grip, pouncing instantly at full tilt, in full force, feverish and final: his common lot with Thea. They were now a "we," irrevocably so, and it was on that silent understanding that he had entered his apartment with her. Now that she was separated from him, however, and was being looked after by Frau Rak, so to say, the whole matter tormented him with doubt and came close, in fact, to effecting the total collapse of what had just a few minutes before seemed self-evident; the change was no greater and no less than this. Melzer heard footsteps and voices. He leapt up in terrible fear and clutched at his heart as if feeling the first emptiness of an unimaginable loss. Then it grew still in the corridor. He listened; his knees were shaking. Now he took a deep breath. His fear ebbed, its menacing surge receded. He turned the key in the lock and threw into the bedroom everything he was wearing. His body itself was caked with blood too, especially around his knees, where the fabric of his suit had pressed directly against his skin and had been completely drenched by the pool of blood. Likewise all the rest of him—his arms up to the elbows, his thighs up to the groin. His underwear, brownish red, had clung to his body. It was Mary's blood. It had held him fixed to the spot, to the place to which Thea had come too. He snatched up from the floor the silk shirt he'd been wearing that day, pressed the bloody spots to his face, and kissed them. Then he walked over to the small table between the windows, where among other grooming items there lay a pair of scissors. Melzer cut a narrow strip, about as long as his hand, from the blood-soaked bottom part of the shirt. Some of the blood Mary had shed that day was to remain with him forever. What to do with it, though, where to keep it? He walked through both rooms as he was. The books in the small niche with the columns! He took out a volume. He opened it. He read: *"Oh ténébreux et troubles, nos cœurs humains, même les plus sincères!"* That was where he placed the strip of silk, brown-red with dried blood, like a bookmark. There came a knock at the door. And not until that very instant did he understand the sentence he had just read—and only too well now.

When Melzer was coming back from the bathroom, Frau Rak's maid stepped out of his apartment carrying over her arm all the things he'd dropped. She was also holding his brown shoes in her right hand, the tips pointed toward him, and he noticed that they were bloodstained as well. She asked if she could bring tea in a few minutes and added, with a slight, modest smile: "The young lady is ready now." "Yes," said Melzer, "but I have to get dressed first. I'll ring twice when I'm finished, all right?"

He was quick and dexterous when getting dressed (it all went very smoothly—no button poked at him, no shoelace missed an eyelet), but he was very attentive to detail as well. Why don't we just say it outright?—this was not at all stupid of him. You don't have to be called Gustav Wedderkopp in order to be "not at all stupid." That's not a prerogative reserved exclusively for the Wedderkopps of this world. Rather, and in a word: like all the rest of us. Melzer looked into the mirror. He was now wearing a violet shirt à la Konietzki. His hand hesitated before the buzzer. A whirlpool whipped up around the buzzer, a small cyclone, as though time were twisting in turmoil over his tarrying. He pressed the buzzer twice and looked around the room. The mantel over the fireplace held an ashtray at the left end and another at the right, but nothing else. No clock (very soon now there would be no hour for it to strike anyway). Down close to the bearskin on the floor, with no chair or prayer rug in the way, the little wall bracket was fully open to view. Let it be! Just now Melzer liked the thing very much. Thea might ask him about it, and then he could explain what it was meant for. This thought suddenly filled him with great warmth. He would soon have to introduce Thea to E.P. and his wife, in any case. A thrust forward—stop! Now he was once more beyond the edge of reality; the gap between him and it was just about to open out into an abyss of fear again. But Thea was no longer in Frau Rak's hands, as it were; she was standing at his door and knocking instead.

The little lamb's getup nearly beggared description—more than a little comical (to us), ravishingly enchanting (to Melzer). Frau Rak, not as fully proportioned as Thea, had searched her wardrobe with her sparkling little eyes for quite a while and finally taken out a summer dress patterned white and blue that might have come from a time when she was a bit more solid and that had never been altered. Fortunately, Frau Rak had not followed fashion in every regard, particularly not as to hemlines, which women wore quite short in those days, although its constant shrinkage would not reach its low point—or rather we should say its high point—until about 1927. Had Frau Rak been standing at the height of fashion in her time, the skirt of the borrowed dress Thea was wearing when she stepped into the major's apartment would have come up at least a handsbreadth past her knees at a conservative guess. But that was not how it was. Pierrot was in all likelihood bowlegged, so she couldn't show her knees, meaning that the creation doing service for Thea was just this side of presentable. She was buttoned or crammed into this summer dress as if into a sausage casing full to bursting. Under her arm she was carrying her leather purse, much too large for what the fashion of that time dictated (whenever the author of this narrative caught sight of her purse, it reminded him of Editha Schlinger's arrival in Buenos Aires years earlier: she went ashore with a similar handbag under her elbow—if not quite a satchel with handles, at least a larger model fashionable in Vienna back then, a long rectangle in sturdy crocodile leather with a heavy metal clasp. In very short order, though, as Editha became aware of what was in vogue there, she took herself off to Harrod's on the Calle Florida and immediately adapted to the local customs—and in several other respects as well). Of course there was a story behind this unusually large leather purse of Thea's: it was in a certain sense a relic of her aspiration to filmdom, which didn't lie very far back in time, after all. But while it lasted, she always carried photographs of numerous greats from that world, men as well as women, along with a collection of articles with pictures and features about them cut out of the newspapers, plus some studio photographs of her own attractive face so she would have them right on hand should occasion arise to present them. But none ever did. And today her purse held a more than slight surprise for Melzer. So this was how she entered; on the whole her face and figure had the effect in this getup of some precious object someone had stolen and quickly covered in cheap wrapping—that was how Melzer thought of it: the power of beauty blooming naturally with no makeup was what was borne in on him; for that matter, it even seemed to him for a few brief seconds as if Thea were entering almost naked. Behind her, the maid with the tea tray. She set it down on the table opposite the fireplace in the other corner of the large room (it was the same table that had been set for the festive Jause the previous Saturday, two days before), laid everything out, and arranged two chairs. Apparently she thought they should drink tea here, in this corner, and it was just snug enough for two. The servant wasn't allowed to place table, chairs, or anything else on the bearskin in front of the fireplace. Now she was finished and gone.

Both Melzer and Thea were somewhat hungry, and the strong, dark tea was very welcome, for it started bringing about a relaxation of the nervous tension they could each feel deep down: though the tension that remained was like the force that keeps a bridge suspended. Everything flowed back and forth smoothly. Melzer could have been compared on the inside to a room in which someone had flung open all the doors and wardrobes and bureaus and the windows to boot. No flimsy barriers were smashed. Because there weren't any. Hardly any walls either. Melzer surrendered, by now unconditionally. The great upheaval was upon him. Everything was standing upright in the open breaches of his being, ready to tumble and topple, to fall through and fall down, to stream and gush in torrents; and only the paper-thin, tightly stretched surface of the situation prevailing just now (that they still weren't in each other's arms) presented, on a strictly temporary basis and merely as a last gasp of decorum, what might be called the final stage of damming up, if only to honor the claim reality was making for the very short duration of this climactic phase: for a minute or two, at least. During that interval he told her all about Mary, past and present. He told her with the tip of his tongue, so to say, his words hardly touching on the situation, just as the two of them seemed to touch everything on the table with extreme caution, using the absolute tips of their fingers only, since the tension from one hand to the other was tremendous. There was no more holding back. Especially not for her. She could just barely keep hiding her confusion; dropping her hands into her lap, smiling, her bosom heaving, tears coming to her eyes. He saw all this, even though twilight was falling like smoke as time passed faster and faster. They reached the edge. Thea's helplessness grew totally obvious, and just then Melzer stood up and flung himself on his knees before her, without their ever having come anywhere close to touching each other before, not even with their fingertips. They toppled into each other, into each other's arms. Thea, sobbing loudly, was utterly beside herself. "You, you, you . . ." she kept gurgling. She pressed herself against him, and he was able to feel how much strength was in this young woman; she squeezed the breath out of him. From on high, however, there now issued the final decision on their case, and it set its indelible seal. Some few moments after they had been entwined in their embrace and during their first kiss the god appeared, standing right in the middle of the mantel: at first he might have been mistaken for a sizable porcelain figure shining a little in the fading light. However, the eyes were flashing, glowing, and now they were beaming. He draws an arrow, extends his rosy, lustrous hip. The bow grows taut. The wasplike, menacingly solemn sound of the arrow whizzing in flight only sounds to the lovers, though, like a tone sent from heaven, on top of which they believe, in their utter benightedness, that it's coming from themselves, of their own volition. The shot penetrated Melzer's chest cavity on a left slant from the back, then burst Thea's bonds below her billowing left breast. They were still holding each other tight, pinned like butterflies, but feeling a sweetness in their wounds compared with which the tone of the syrinx or the taste of honey would have to be called wormwood and gall. Now there was nothing more on the mantel: just for a few remaining moments that whitish glow (almost like the bright gleam from a dying ember when fanned with the bellows one last time) always left behind by deities vanishing, whether from the field of battle or, as here, from official transactions in matters of the heart. This glow, however, seems more real and solid than the surrounding objects it leaves behind.

Starting from the very hour, we would say, if it weren't really more starting from the minute Melzer knelt down in front of Thea, the major began exhibiting something we can't call haste, exactly, which would indicate merely a passing condition; instead, it was nothing less than a fundamental trait: velocity (*gradus ad Parnassum*?!). During minute three after their first kiss he asked her if she would be his wife. Oh! Oh! Baa, baa! Melzer struggled for breath as he asked, because Thea's arms seemed to be growing stronger all the time, and she was not about to let him go, no, no! ("Always tie up large objects, and tight, too.") During minute ten he was already calling for her to speak to her parents, and yes, that very day; he wanted to see her home in any case and explain to them what had happened, why she had been at his apartment, and how it was that she was coming home in a dress different from the one in which she had left. Thea wasn't grasping much of this, so there wasn't any real protest on her part, as a result of which Melzer had already reached fulfillment of his plan only half an hour later (a genuine activist, practically a Negrian!) and was sitting with Thea's parents by the art nouveau sideboard while she slipped out of Frau Rak's sausage skin in her own room. It would be logical to think at this point that Herr Rokitzer was exuding a thread—thin, to be sure, but in unbroken continuity—a thread of apprehension. Such was not the case, however. The parents had noted with gratification and relief a change in Thea's spirit since her return from Saint Valentin. Admittedly they didn't know very much about the collapse on Saturday, August 29, of her plans for movie stardom and the penitential banishment imposed by Eulenfeld effective as of Sunday the thirtieth, but they were struck nonetheless by certain adjustments in her daily life, such as appearing promptly at dinner and staying home when it ended.

And now, not long after these changes, the major had turned up out of the blue. No wonder they connected them with him. He somehow seemed, then, like the personification of Thea's improved ways. In addition, he was displaying great self-assurance throughout, and the display was all the more assured by his not being in the least aware of it. At the end of his report about the accident and before Thea appeared, he requested of Herr Rokitzer the favor of an interview on the following day—"regarding a matter of concern to me as well"—and was asked to come sometime after six o'clock. It already seemed quite obvious which way the wind was blowing. Melzer didn't stay much longer. He waited only for Thea to come back and then took his leave. She walked him into the vestibule and to the door. There he told her he would be coming to call on her father the next evening: could she be home after six? He kissed her hand with strong pressure. When Thea went back into the dining room, she found the atmosphere so charged that she felt compelled to tell her parents everything right then and there.

Starting with exactly who Melzer was. That had an activating, even galvanizing effect on her father, which manifested itself the next morning. He asked his wife to mind the store for an hour and took himself to the headquarters of the tobacco administration on Porzellan Gasse, which wasn't very far. He found out from the doorman what department Melzer was assigned to and the name of the division chief and then he went directly to the latter's office. Rokitzer's stationery store also dealt in business cards, and so he had a supply of his own. It all fell together. The chief, with the rank of Hofrat, was a humanist in every sense of the word (that goes without saying when the Higher Zihalism is operative), so he perceived at his very first glance the nature, the background, and almost the exact occupation of the decent but worried man who had taken a seat next to his desk. "Herr Rokitzer, sir"—after the caller had stated his business as if it were an official matter, one surely not treated in any service manual but just as surely very close to his heart—"Herr Rokitzer, sir, if your daughter has become engaged to the major, all I can do is congratulate you and her. Regarding Major Melzer, we are dealing with a gentleman of the highest repute, be it as an officer—decorated with the Order of Leopold—as a government-service official, or as a human being pure and simple. I knew his father; that is, I was under his command at officers' training school—which was in Wels—yes, the very same man was our major's father. His mother was the daughter of a Royal and Imperial consul general. I'm telling you all this, Herr Rokitzer, only so I can place this whole matter into its proper light for you, so to speak. And how old is your daughter, if I may ask?" "She'll be twenty-four," answered the nervous shopkeeper. He reached into his briefcase, which allows us to see that he always carried a picture of Thea with him. This he laid down on the desk. "Very charming!" cried the Hofrat, who had leaned over to have a closer look and then thought to himself: "Wouldya look at Melzer! Quite the rascal!" We can skip the rest, because of course it goes without saying that the major stayed for dinner at the Rokitzers' that evening. Thea had gone to the hospital before noon. Melzer had asked her the day before to make inquiries the next morning, although he was unable to tell her what Mary's married name was. They'd both seen the wedding ring on her hand, but that was all they knew. The effect of Melzer's limited knowledge on Thea cannot—it's incumbent on us to be truthful—be described as detrimental. What she found out was that there was no danger of death but that the patient was not permitted visitors for the time being. Starting then, Melzer and Thea set up a kind of duty schedule. Thea would go for updates in the morning, and in the afternoon, when Melzer's working day was finished, they both walked over to Lazarett Gasse, preferably by way of the Strudlhof Steps, which was their meeting point. The newly activated major went to great lengths to observe scrupulous propriety, by the way. He informed Frau Rak of his engagement (Pierrot turned somersaults for joy) and after that would not allow Thea to put in an appearance at his apartment any longer, except for once, when she brought back Frau Rak's things and expressed her thanks: Melzer was in the office at the time. Frau Rak also received a handsome thank-you gift on this occasion, incidentally, a token of gratitude from Rokitzer Stationers, as it were, tendered by Thea with warmest regards; a large gift box of the most sumptuous, deluxe ivory-colored writing paper with our Pierrot's monogram. What would she ever have written on it, though, if anything? And to whom? Colombine? Ridiculous. Basically these are nothing but spiteful remarks.

They would mostly sit side by side in Liechtenstein Park now. That spot was a new discovery for Melzer, one could say, even though its extensive grounds and gardens lay just behind the building where he worked; his rooms had all their windows facing the other way, though, onto Porzellan Gasse. It was along these paths here, now surrounded by autumn in its fullness; on these benches, where a tranquil, faraway spirit welled in on every side in the midst of this walled enclosure among the clamor of the city; it was here that a memory rose up inside Melzer, grew as vivid and complete as an object in the outside world, a memory that since 1910 had dwelt inside him in hazy, fragmented form only: that walk through the forest with Laska after the first, futile time of lying in wait for the bear. Now Melzer felt once again untethered from the stake of his own self, and he was in command of every movement of his body, even the slightest, as never before, all the while taking in everything around him with particular clarity and sharpness, as when the image of a garden falls into a sunny room through a freshly washed window. Since one result of Mary's reappearance and her disaster, her bursting in upon his life, was that a pillar immense in strength had been set into that life, far to the back, a pylon into his own past, which he was struggling to assimilate, he could for the first time look much farther back and with much more surety through this gateway into a new realm lying far deeper back in time than, say, Asta's tiny room in the green underwater light or the dappled, haze-filled dreaminess below the veranda of the house in Neulengenbach, the twining strands of wild grapes or ivy, his bicycle, the faint smell of rubber. He sensed a field lying far back, the one he'd come from, a place he was able to speak about, however, in a language that had grown within him only there, but not here. During these days Melzer found himself looking every now and then at moments in his own life as if in a cupped hand. All of this affixed itself to Thea, beleaguered her, took aim at her, kept her in its sights, fusing with her indissolubly, nay, uniting them as one.

The first of their explanations on both sides took place here in the park as well, in greater detail than had been possible up to now, the god's feathered shaft practically still quivering in their chests and backs. When they were together on the first days after the Feast of Saint Matthew, the day of the accident, they lacked, as it were, both enough breath to elaborate and that minimum distance required to utter speech instead of dissolving into a face not standing opposite ours but penetrating ours instead, penetrating like a tone, the tone of the syrinx. Melzer explained what had made him late and why as a result he hadn't turned up at the landing place on the Danube. As he talked he felt strange; he felt as he did when walking here in the park or on the street or even in his apartment: in the same way as he could feel how every compliant muscle took pleasure in movement, so now the main particulars lined up on their own with the smooth tiles of the tale in the telling, which didn't have to labor at chopping and chiseling pieces of background information—Thea knew nothing at all about Etelka Stangeler, for instance, and hardly anything about René—but that instead pieced themselves together effortlessly and yielded a sustained, articulate account. He spoke with brevity and as if he were walking. His most advanced organ was moving in the same way his body had lately been doing, with even steps, conducive to steady progress, and it's hard to decide here whether a new infantryman was finally producing language of his own or whether it in turn was producing a brand-new infantryman. Thea understood. It seems worth noting that she would now sit up very straight sometimes, arch the small of her back, and take deep breaths, as if she were allowing to enter her bosom, without even knowing she was doing it, forces that had before now cramped and stifled her, had beleaguered and oppressed her. When she sat with Melzer and held his hand now, her left in his right, here on a park bench (meaning it couldn't be considered indecorous), then Thea acquired something like dignity along the lines of a simple, almost feral person who has become caught up in a complicated set of living conditions but comes through them well, guided by the worthy core in the storehouse of the heart.

She of course explained what had brought her to the station square just at the decisive moment and told the story leading up to it, not leaving out the twins. If Melzer had had his walking stick he would have been drawing pensively in the sand with it. No surprise; no exclamation; what broke in on him now as a news item in the sapwood of this hour in the park had slowly been growing for some time in the heartwood of his awareness. Now, sitting where he was, a last paper-thin dividing wall between inner and outer fell away; no, it wasn't so much the falling of a wall as the bursting of a delicate membrane or some kind of separator or divider, such as we feel happening in our nose and ears when a cold is breaking up, enabling us once more to enter the world of hearing and smell on the level of assimilation we'd been used to and had previously taken for granted. If the major was keeping silent now and looking quietly down at the sand (during which Thea didn't disturb him), it wasn't dismay but keen concentration directed toward some process inside himself that his full being was allowing to play itself through as something completely autonomous; all he knew about it, though with great certainty, was that there were things he could learn from it, that truth was enacting itself here (similar to its compelling manifestation on August 22 by way of the odor of camphor and the sound of a military march). Specifically, Editha Schlinger split into two separate components, like a cloudy suspension when it has precipitated out and two distinct layers, each a different color, are standing one over the other, clearly contrasted and demarcated. He also knew when and where. Until his short stay with the Stangelers in the country at the end of August, it had been the other one, the woman whose unwontedly gentle tone of voice had faded away after that; there had been only one further echo of it. That much Melzer clearly knew, but when, but where? He didn't chase it; he didn't parse it; all he did was wait, looking down at the sand on the path. Then it came washing up to him on the next wave: again there were green trees and sand, there was the bank of the Danube Canal, the bridge in the distance, teeming with life, the bend in the river as it went under the bridge. A merry-go-round on the opposite bank, turning from time to time. The three of them were walking along, the captain, Editha, and himself; Stangeler had been with him that evening, and that was how he remembered the exact date, Wednesday, September 2. Here, at the canal, she had again been present—though ebbing away and taking

her farewell even then, barely speaking to him, walking along on Eulenfeld's other side—a summer sweetheart (that's how he now thought
of her, without shying away from her but also as though from a great
distance, as if she had died!), and from the vantage point of his involvement with her it nevertheless appeared impossible to construct a connection, working backward, to Editha Pastré, that Editha Pastré who,
as she made her way along the tennis court, alongside the surface with
the white stripe, was once again headed directly toward him, locking
eyes, not smiling, only to walk right past him at the net. From then
on, however, from the time they walked along the canal, there had been
only the one; she was the one who had called on him in his office, and
between her and the Editha Pastré from fourteen years before at the
Stangelers' country house there was no dichotomy; instead, one of
them could be slid inside the other like the separate parts of a stereo-
scopic image, one accommodating the other smoothly and with total
overlap, all the while that the first one, the stranger, was delicately
fading away like an aureole encircling Editha for a time, bestowing on
her the radiance of color, of all the colors of the rainbow, though now
growing more pale. He saw her lying in the boat under the resounding
arch of trees spread out high above the river branch dense with reeds,
over which a waterbird with a broad yellow beak now skittered with a
cry. One oar was jammed against the green bank of the smooth, clear
water: it was she herself, the distracted and abstracted one, appearing
to be Editha in the flesh; the ephemeral and delicate one, who hadn't
known what was even meant by "Strudlhof Steps" and who was all of
a sudden baffled by the name Frau von Budau: half-present twin sisters
from a different though palpably present world: the resounding tone
of this summer. Did she even exist any longer? Wouldn't she be bound
to wane, pale, and almost entirely fade away, like the moon in daytime,
if she were placed here and now opposite Editha's nontransparent
physical solidity? Melzer did not doubt that he would now be able to
tell the sisters apart. But they both dimmed and receded, flew off to
the horizon, one shining and one shone upon; and they slipped free of
all obligations, annulled all debts and duties: duplicate, and therefore
not actually real. Which one had he spoken with, after all, with which
one had he made a date (though on second thought it came to him:

most recently with Editha Schlinger-Pastré!); but never mind, because it could be pertinent equally to both, could be claimed by either as pertinent, which made any fixed point dwindle to invisibility along with almost every promise made earlier! Now he thought about Paula Pichler, who not long before, on the previous Saturday, had tried to tell him what he already knew down deep but had whizzed past his outer ear so quickly that on Monday, sitting on the bench with Stangeler, it had never entered his mind, not even remotely, to question René about this wild fancy to which he was supposed to have been an eyewitness. Of course it wasn't so fanciful anymore: not now, at least, but was very much so at the time. Whatever stays purely external has as little real existence as anything purely internal.

At this point Thea's large handbag was opened, and out of it came, to Melzer's amazement, the papers—this isn't to say that we've gotten to the bottom of this purse, though!—she had taken from Editha's room behind the hidden door. She filled in that part of the story and handed the papers to Melzer. The first one—he recognized it immediately—was the note-size sheet his office assistant Kroissenbrunner had so expansively and so agonizingly (to the extent that even an angel working in the office of the records department in heaven would quickly have had to flop down on his rosy-cheeked little behind) bewailed having misplaced. The connection with Editha's visit was almost too clear and obvious. This remained a purely external circumstance, however, merely a technicality (but granted, the thought processes and the *trópoi* of intelligent men, à la Stangeler senior, Robby Fraunholzer, or Cornel Lasch, always end up in such technicalities, but ones they've mastered to perfection!). For Melzer it was more that the difference between the sisters now emerged in its final, full dimensions: what he was holding in his hand here—the stolen papers and a signature forged so brilliantly, as on the note, he could almost have mistaken it for his own—was essentially the dark, impenetrable core of that Editha from 1911, from 1923 on the Graben, from 1925 in the reception room or entrance hall of the records department as she made her way toward him alongside the tables pushed together, down the surface of which white stripes made by packages lined up in a row had stretched. That had been the one shone upon, but now without any reflected light, without all the soaring rainbow colors within which these kinds of maneuverings, these chicaneries and artful dodges, all these gyrations (even if it was no more than a dilettantish botheration, for how could she possibly have put to any use papers incomplete for lack of a stamp, no matter how many signatures they bore!)—within which, we say, all these mighty efforts by Editha Pastré could never have found a place to take root any more than could a flier in the flutter of the spring breezes. He recalled now that the other one, the earlier one, whose name he didn't even know, this midsummer day's dream had on some occasion asked him something pertinent, but in a trailing voice, absentmindedly, and without ever coming back to the subject. And perhaps—or probably—as instigated by her sister. In short, it was along these lines of the official forms that the Pastré twins came apart with a final clean tear, just as once the circle of the Zihal kith and kin had been split asunder, with Frau Rosa's clandestine fruit as the line of division.

On the Thursday after the Feast of Saint Matthew they had gone to see Paula, who could never in her wildest dreams have anticipated that her clever and successful machinations from the previous Saturday as well as the unsuccessful, yet successful, ones from Monday would have led so quickly to such a happy outcome. They told her everything, more or less, and here it was Melzer who kept the essence of the events contained within a swirl of the compass; he reported on Thea's part of it as well. Paula, however, wrinkling her nose a bit, suspected at once, thanks to some instinct not readily understandable, that the major had indeed been expected by Editha Schlinger: hardly did the thought cross her mind than the major mentioned it, and—he realized only now—for the first time. What he quite reasonably left unsaid, however, was that he had been meant to meet Editha alone. "They might have played the same trick on you, Major, as they did on Thea," said Paula. Her husband, Alois, listened to all of this attentively and seriously; he'd long since known about the accident on Althan Platz, but not who the victim and the other involved parties were. "I'll probably have to go and see the duplicate ladies and the captain again," the major said, "at first if only to apologize for my failing to show up. Maybe in a week; I don't feel much like it just now. In the second place, I'm quite curious myself. And third, there are a few things that still need to be discussed." He looked at Thea. Neither she nor he had uttered a word about the papers. He took her right hand and kissed it briefly. This seemed to touch Herr Pichler somehow; he looked at Melzer for a few seconds with special warmth. Theresa Schachl made an unexpected appearance in the garden with coffee for all. She reacted to the news about the engagement in a way that suggested she considered what she'd just been told the merest formality; she took the conviviality of the gathering on the Nativity of Our Lady as proof that the matter had been clinched even then. When that little get-together—it lay over two weeks in the past—was touched on, it gave Paula reason enough to launch into what was really in her heart, a proposal that had probably started piecing itself together in her mind little by little: "We'll celebrate the engagement here, right here in the garden! What do you think?" "Absolutely; of course we will," commented Alois, making this the first time today he'd opened his mouth, but going directly to the heart of the matter. So now they talked over the details: when, and who should be invited. There was no getting around key family members (Melzer didn't have any, though). That meant: Thea's parents; the two aunts, Frau Zihal and Frau Oplatek (everyone of course thought of the councillor himself as a kind of resplendent display piece, like a baroque centerpiece); Paula's mother and her husband too, but without the younger generation of Loiskandls—both Paula and Alois Pichler vetoed Hedwig Loiskandl as if speaking from a single mouth. They left the date open. "Perhaps after the major had paid his visit to the duplicate ladies," Paula said, "because then we'll get to hear all about it. That visit will clear up a good many points. It's nobody else's business, though." Not long after that, Melzer and Thea would vividly recall these words of Paula's, at which point they would appear downright prophetic to both of them. Nobody thought of René Stangeler, not even Paula. In planning the engagement party they were working from the image that had presented itself here in the garden on September 9, and René hadn't been part of that picture. Nobody here knew that after the many fluctuations from one extreme to the other between intrafamilial and extrafamilial concerns he had made a decision to travel back out to the country, where his parents were planning to keep the house open through October. So toward the end of the same week that had begun with Mary's catastrophic accident (which of course he heard about from Grete), Stangeler set out, journeying toward an overpowering need to breathe deeply, in and out, and to feel the silence of the almost empty house, where only the old people were now staying, while outdoors the trees were shedding more and more of their many-colored garb and everything was growing more open to view, more expansive, little by little, while the air spun Chinese silk over the distant, furry forests and the ticking of an old clock in the entry sounded louder. Even on cliff walls and crags the light had turned milky-mild. Elelka's remains had reached Vienna on Tuesday, September 22, for interment in the family vault. The presence of the parents at the ceremony did not even come up for consideration, in light of the old gentleman's physical immobility, because of which his wife would not, and did not, leave him. It all took place very quietly; only a few people followed Etelka's casket, among them Grete Siebenschein (greeted cordially but silently by Asta, incidentally). Melzer was present as well. He'd telephoned Asta from his office that morning. This funeral service was the last place that he would last see René for a long time.

He'd no sooner been introduced to Asta's husband, Building Surveyor Haupt, in the funeral chapel at the cemetery, where the few mourners had gathered, than he recognized him from before. But not the other way around. Only on their way home to Asta's—she brought him back from the cemetery for a cup of tea—did the major bring up the point and lead him down the path of memory.

Now, meantime, after the concluding words of a Lutheran pastor—who in simple and heartfelt terms advocated for his true and rightful lord, underneath whose picture he was standing—as they walked along wider and then narrower paths on this half-sunny, half-overcast autumn day, behind the casket, Melzer's state was such that a new pillar rising up in his past almost supplanted any thought of the deceased, whom he had last seen alive on Sunday, August 30, standing in front of the village post office next to Asta in their colorful regional garb, both of them waving while Melzer began quickly (and thoughtfully) journeying down through the valley and toward the city. But walking ahead of him now, tall and dressed in black, with Asta on his arm—her unusual attractiveness shone forth from her mourning dress like a jewel set deeper into a new mounting—was an English ship's captain in the uniform of an Austrian artillery lieutenant, who had at one time, about ten years before, told him during a train trip between Prague and Vienna about how the damaged German ironclads had looked after the Battle of Jutland. Could it be any wonder, then, in view of such a change in setting and costume, that Mary had promptly turned up at the crucial moment? That veil that blurs all contours was now torn to shreds, the veil leading us to imagine over and over again that occurrences past have receded backward, been erased, could even be negated or denied as convenience dictated. That was not so with Melzer. For more than a few seconds he felt to the point of irrefutable evidence and undeniable presence how all the teeming throngs of those past and gone are all densely crowded behind the backdrops—and in the passageways between them—of the scene now being played out, ready to burst forth and flood the stage, taking over all the action. They were all neither more nor less real than those now present and visible. The others were invisible, to be sure, but close at hand nonetheless. They counted too. Mary had always been nearby, just a few paces distant, ready to step forth.

Less astonishing than Haupt was Grauermann; Melzer had last seen him all of fourteen years earlier. The consul struck the major as a being utterly perfect and highly polished, as though Grauermann had borne himself in the flow of time gone by like a clean pebble in a stream: above him a depth almost completely transparent, a depth that vanished, indeed, when someone bent over it; it turned into a nearness you could touch, almost without any refraction of the light; the eye was unable to prove its wonderful powers. Grauermann's impeccable bearing affected Melzer almost like the self-contained and fulfilled quality of a work of art no longer subject to flux or change. Grauermann vanished, along with Stangeler and Grete Siebenschein, immediately after the burial. Perhaps the three just wanted to be by themselves.

Grete was in a bad way.

Here at the cemetery she'd done everything in her power to remain in control (the effort made her nose turn white, as if she were cold), because no one else was crying and thus it had seemed to her that it would be out of place if she were to cry, someone not a relative; she did make an effort, even so, to push through the visible pain to a place close to the deceased; that would even have been her due, but it was denied her, since her position was still not clear, though at the moment it was genuinely hard for her to stand her ground, wherever that was. So we see what Grete, our righteous man of honor in the garb of a woman, was a victim of—essentially the very same sickness she'd always had, even back in the distant days of Norway. In addition, the blows had come thick and fast. Monday: news of the death from Budapest and then Mary's dreadful accident, which she'd heard about from the daughter not long after. It was as if horrors were suddenly bursting in from all sides. On Tuesday morning, Grauermann had no sooner arrived from Budapest, where he had made arrangements for transfer of the remains, than he called Grete on the phone—the hearse with the casket was expected at the cemetery in Simmering at three o'clock, and his presence was required. Would she and René be willing to go there with him and support him? They were out there half an hour ahead of time; open space; they could see far along the road. The grass was still green, but faded, ready to turn prairie brown; the distant view opened up now was in turn closed off by fog. It was the east, or rather the southeast, into which they were now looking, a place at the edge of the city that no one (except for the local residents) ever visited if they didn't have business there, such as burying the dead. No hills or vineyards. A grim, dreary part of the city. The hearse (Grauermann said *"fourgon"*) could be seen from a distance, still no more than a dot, with a little cloud of dust running along to its right, the way the wind was blowing. (It felt to them as if Etelka were coming not from a relatively nearby city but from somewhere far off in the East, from steppes, from Central Asia.) They weren't wrong; it was indeed the box-shaped hearse with the casket, its chassis outfitted in proper funereal display, black and with four columns and garlands. On time practically to the minute. When Grauermann then exchanged some words in Hungarian with the staff, Grete shuddered at the sound of the foreign language (though it really couldn't have been as foreign as all that to a Viennese), as though Etelka had been destroyed by it and by the immensity stretching out steppe-like to the East, from which this language appeared to have come just now.

Mary was permitted to have a brief visit for the first time on Saturday. Melzer and Thea went together. Even entering by the high portal on Lazarett Gasse was daunting. The world of the hospital buildings and pavilions that surrounded them on all sides, extending however far they looked, presented to view just a single one—complete in every detail as it was—of the innumerable prisms of life; consciousness kept incessantly declaring that this one prism was the reverse side, though at least every bit as valid as all of the others we see as a rule and take as the norm, a view that makes all those others appear suspect, and on its own, at that, without our ever having to formulate anything relating to it in our thoughts. Entering this realm was vaguely akin to a fleet putting out to the high seas while the base itself is left unsecured or might possibly even be destroyed. Before they were allowed to enter Mary's room, they were cautioned to be very quiet and not to stay long; furthermore, the patient had been informed of the impending visit and told who the callers were. Then the nurse opened the double door. The light in the room was subdued. Mary was lying such that the visitors could at once see her head on the pillow when they entered. Melzer and Thea remained by the door for a moment; then they took a few quiet, discreet steps closer and knelt down side by side next to the bed. Melzer kissed Mary's hand; it lay along the edge. The little lamb also touched it with her milky mouth. Mary laid her hand on Melzer's head. They stayed like that for a little. Then the visitors took their leave. In the corridor the nurse gave Melzer his walking stick and belt. Both had been cleaned.

On the next day, Sunday, at the decent hour of eleven in the morning (after having set the date over the phone), Melzer took Thea to visit Herr and Frau E.P.; he was eager to introduce his fiancée to the couple. From the moment they met, the P.s made something of a cult of Thea, and it wouldn't be far off the mark to say that they classified her among their most beautiful puppets. On this basis a remarkable portrait of Frau Major Melzer came into existence later, for Herr E.P., his expert eye in matters artistic always busily on the lookout in every direction, had long since taken note of the painter Maria Rosanka, whose occasionally rather strange canvases undeniably spoke to his whimsical, squirrel-like self-containment. It was he, then, who arranged for both his own wife and Thea to have their portraits painted a year after Melzer got married, so it is thanks to him that two pictures, excellent in every respect, came to exist; later on, both were displayed at an exhibit in Stuttgart that featured a rather large collection of Rosanka's work, for which occasion Melzer had placed the portrait of his wife at the disposal of the artist, who had requested the loan. The picture was his property; he had purchased it upon completion and did not then reject it (unlike Councillor Zihal at one time), even though careful scrutiny would also have disclosed in Frau Melzer's portrait no lack of a decidedly exaggerated sharpness, which an observer lacking in understanding might well have construed as bordering on caricature. It was around the eyes. They more or less leapt out of the picture—wonderfully rendered in their beautiful deep blue!—toward the observer. It was only by a hair, a hint—too much of a good thing. Rosanka was simply unable to hold back. Looking at this painting, classically educated people (such as Captain Eulenfeld) would probably have been reminded of the expression Homer uses to describe the eyes of the goddess Hera, whom he calls "cow-eyed" (βοῶπις πότνια δεά). The most striking aspect of it all, however, was the title under which the piece was listed in the catalogue of the show in Stuttgart: *Exterior of Heavenly Fruit* (and not something like *Portrait of Frau Th. M.*). When that came to Melzer's attention—through Herr E.P., since the portrait of his own wife was likewise on display in Stuttgart, but titled in the normal way—the major just shook his head and was almost peeved. That was in 1927. Twenty-one years later, when Rosanka had been living in Paris for a long time, one of her paintings was hung in a large international art exhibit in Vienna, a picture she called *Interior of Fruit*. It was of a pumpkin, split open. Rosanka called the two pictures companion pieces, which no one could understand (or was there nevertheless not really a connection, in fact?). At that point the whole thing got lost in the realm of the arcane.

It was only eleven days after the accident on Althan Platz that Melzer placed a phone call to Frau Editha Schlinger, largely at Thea's urging, behind which, of course, lurked Paula Pichler with her curiosity, enabling her as it did to pick up scents, one could say, her nostrils sometimes flaring causing many small wrinkles (which could remind us of old Herr von Stangeler). She seemed to be anticipating something, some decisive development, before which the engagement party in the garden could not take place. She was adamant about it.

The early days of that October 1925 were marked by unusual warmth; it was a true Indian summer with stifling heat and brilliant sunlight. Temperatures as high as 90 degrees had been measured.

The captain answered the phone. The major, his tone of voice totally guileless, asked about Editha Schlinger; he needed to come and apologize, especially since he'd not been heard from for such a long time.

"Then drop everything, Melzer, old boy!" Eulenfeld cried. "And make it snappy! What? Half an hour? What do you want to drink? *Ginum* or *vinum cognaci*? *In gino veritas.* Let me look around and see what's on hand: a complete *omelette surprise.* Special occasion."

Once Melzer arrived—acting the total innocent, of course—he was treated to the same spectacle as Thea.

The captain welcomed him, guided him at once with an air of mystery through the hidden door into the bedroom at the rear, and told him to wait there until he was called: just be patient for a few minutes!

And it took no longer than that. In this brief span of time, though, something became obvious to Melzer—he was examining the trim secretary desk with its brass fittings from which Thea had removed those papers (he now had them on him)—something he'd realized as Thea had told her story became absolutely certain and altogether unmistakable: that this was the bedroom of the real Editha Schlinger, and she was the one who'd purloined the papers in the waiting area of the records department; he wasn't in the room of the other one, she of this summer's radiance and rainbow stripes. There was no further specific inference or implication needed for the space to declare it plainly: this was not a room inhabited by his peculiar companion in the Danube wetlands who had fluttered in the wind like a brightly colored curtain in front of a past from which she'd been torn. Here everything was impenetrable, more solidly fixed. Now the captain was calling, and he clapped as Melzer emerged.

The twins appeared at once, entering left and right through the double doors and stopping in front of them; white against the white doors of this bright room, whose broad window framed the wooded mountain and the distant castle. Editha didn't choose gold-trimmed beige this time but had fixed instead on white, even selecting a fabric that wasn't the most becoming and that moreover was entirely out of fashion at the time: they were wearing piqué dresses. Perhaps a reminder of the days of their youth. Everything remained completely still for the moment. Then Melzer, rooted to his spot right before the hidden door, bowed slightly to the left and then to the right. He sensed very vividly in these moments the presence of the white-streaked sky looking in and the sunlight lying on the nearby houses, on a stretch of the river visible from here, and on the distant mountains. The captain had stepped off to the side.

"Dear lady," Melzer said facing left, to Editha, "I'm very behindhand in coming to apologize to you for failing to show up on Monday, September 21, when you were expecting me to tea. However, I was prevented from calling on you by two catastrophes that transpired that day—the death of René Stangeler's sister, Frau Consul Grauermann, who put an end to her own life, and a terrible accident here on Althan Platz involving a lady I know, which happened at the time we were to meet. Perhaps you've heard something about it."

Nobody had any reply to his somber words. It was altogether as if Melzer were reshaping a situation arranged by others into a form that suited him better or adjusting a completed picture, straightening its frame. Editha had taken a step away from the door and toward Melzer. But he now turned to his right.

"And on August 28, dear lady, you entrusted your fountain pen to me," said the major, taking a longish case in brick-red leather out of his jacket pocket, "to have the nib repaired. Here it is, and it's in good working order. I tested it." He held the case out to her.

She didn't reach for it, even though she took two steps toward him. "Now I see the real you, Melzer dear, my soldier boy, everything neat and squared away," she said, standing in front of him with her arms hanging down straight. Past her enigmatic head the patch of sky, restless with its high-scudding streaks of white cloud, was heaving like a giant swath of bunting, the faraway forested mountain with its castle, its fortress that looks out to the eastern plains, summer in and summer out, and into the lonely longing, deep as an abyss, that could at every moment swallow us up if we didn't fend it off. "I don't know if you're aware, Melzer," she added, with a freedom as complete as it was unfamiliar, "that I was in love with you." The major, from this point in command of a rapidly matured capacity for discernment and discretion, set his civilian self onto the legs of the infantryman with irreproachable skill. And—although really not trained in the art of speaking—he did not sidestep the situation but instead spoke well-chosen words worthy of a self-effacing but cultivated gentleman. "If that was ever the case," he said, taking her hand and kissing it with a bow—one that for all its lack of affectation yet adumbrated at its core the ceremonial quality of a majestic, stately baroque drama—"if that was ever the case," he repeated, "then please forgive me. I once did you an injustice. It was in surmising that you had merely forgotten things a person would never forget but that you never knew anything about in the first place. Your sister can explain that to you in regard to Frau von Budau, née Schmeller. And I thank you. For many charming hours."

"Well, knock me over with a feather!" cried the captain, achieving a breakthrough with his exclamation so that the picture, changed and rearranged as it was anyway, almost broke loose from its frame and moved on its own. "So our boy Melzer can tell the double-dealing dollies apart! Glasses raised on high! This instant!" He reached for a bottle and glasses. "Am I forgiven?" asked Melzer, stepping over to Editha and kissing her hand as well, the usual practice in Vienna at that time. "You are, Major," she responded a bit sheepishly and in an almost weepy undertone. "And myself—?" This last question got lost in the ensuing movement. The captain had passed around the glasses while Mimi brought in the tea tray. They drank the gin before they sat down, though Melzer hardly even sipped it. Inside him, ready for use, if one will, the shape, frame, and trimmings were on hand that would allow for renewed control over a situation showing signs of beginning to unravel.

Now, in the meantime, the captain stretched out his legs and told Melzer what there was to tell (but of course not all there might have been to tell). He told his story in an easygoing but nonetheless concise way; through the altogether casual manner in which he narrated the previous history of the twins, delivering it with virtuosity but suggesting the mere flick of a wrist, a critical ear would have identified unmistakably the sounding board of the instrument now being played by a German captain of horse, a genuine hussar, opting on this occasion for a more judicious requisition of baroque and classical drolleries but proving as if merely in passing that the formal periodicities of the German language, or perhaps of all the Western languages in general, can be mastered only by one in whom the clear and ordering radiance of Latin prose has been mounting upward for at least a few generations, enabling this light to break through now and cast its luster on the present discourse. "The two baby dolls sitting here before us," he said, "were separated in their tender youth. The one fled her dismal family home and found, across the seas, a more pleasant milieu and gladsome conjugal companionship. She is now seated to your right, Melzer, and her name is Mimi Scarlez." (Melzer bowed slightly to Mimi as this ex post facto introduction was being made.) "And now, having returned after many years, she will finally be reconciled with her parents here in Vienna. The other fair creature, the one situated to your left, is abundantly familiar from the more felicitous days of her bygone youth, although she has been dwelling once more in our hereunto appertaining midst only since the end of last month." This was how he went on.

The major had of course been subjected to questioning before this point, about Stangeler's sister Etelka, known to the captain only by name (he also hadn't seen anything of René himself for more than two weeks), and about the Althan Platz accident victim, whom Melzer had just mentioned he knew; Melzer's concise, summary answers had formed a sort of prelude to the captain's ensuing speech. Apparently the situation as it now stood, meaning in the form into which Melzer had been molding it from the start, was not going to undergo significant alteration. It was as though the autumn clarity suffusing the room were keeping its outlines distinct and in that way implacably bringing forth all these developments under the aspect of their transitoriness and movement toward finality.

Melzer, who had been observing Editha inconspicuously but very carefully while Eulenfeld was talking, was able to notice in her features fleeting signs of dejection deepening into despondency and even outright misery. Not while Eulenfeld was dashing through the story of the twins' appearance in front of Thea (which really didn't need to be told in detail at any rate, since Melzer had just been treated to the same display, though it of course had elicited a substantially different reaction). Now, however, the captain was describing the unexpected visit by the police, which had occurred only about a minute after Thea's headlong departure: not that the latter action had had any causal connection with the former, as Editha (but only she), by her own later admission, had for a moment suspected—which was exactly like her, added the captain. "To your no doubt considerable astonishment, you would have had a face-to-face encounter with the flatfoots, or with the fuzz, as they say here in Vienna, had the hereunto appertaining mishap in front of the station not detained you." Then, he continued, the police officers had—in the politest of terms ("as is generally the procedure with you people here")—produced a search warrant, duly signed by a judge, and of course their official identification as well. (Legal stability was still very strong in Austria in 1925, practically absolute by today's standards.) One was "a certain Herr Zacher, as he styled himself"; Eulenfeld clearly relished bringing out his rather antiquated turns of phrase; he hadn't caught the other name. They had two "house-search orders" (the captain didn't say "search warrants," which was the usual term here). One of them was issued for Eulenfeld's apartment, the other for Editha Schlinger's; they had already been to Eulenfeld's and had come from there, as it later emerged. Eulenfeld found out that the police had turned up at his apartment immediately after he'd left with Mimi. He knew the exact minute, because he'd happened to look at the clock just as they were going: twenty minutes past five. "Editha called us to come over here, because you hadn't showed up, Melzer. We were supposed to help her pass the time. There was no sign of life at my place, so of course the bulls turned to the concierge—wait a minute, just hold on!" he exclaimed, since Melzer wanted to know (which he didn't, yet) what the gist of this whole story was and why the police had come in the first place. Now, however, Eulenfeld began to bring Frau Oplatek, the tobacco-store proprietor, into his narrative and to mention Thea's innocence and utter naïveté (a kind of instinctive sensitivity he was barely aware of checked him from saying anything openly ill-disposed toward Thea). The search of Eulenfeld's apartment had taken barely twenty minutes, thanks to the uncluttered state of his tidy bachelor establishment, thrown open with alacrity by Frau Wöss. What the authorities were looking for primarily were the kinds of sizable crates and cartons which could have escaped their notice only with difficulty. Of course the concierge had brought to their notice Editha's apartment, the one they were now in, as well as the presumed presence there of the missing occupant, Eulenfeld said; Frau Wöss had seen him leave the house with Mimi, after all; but then how did they come to have a search warrant, all duly drawn up and signed, for this apartment as well? "Unusual time of day for official transactions of this kind, I might add," said the captain. "They ordinarily start such business in the early morning." (It slipped out, so to say.) But long story short! He now mentioned in passing the connection between the Hawelkas here and the Wösses there and his little falling out with the concierge in August ("which almost turned into a literal falling down—her flung headfirst down the steps, I mean"). Long story short—the police had obviously intended from the start to conduct a search at Editha's, too. Clearly the source of such detailed knowledge by the police lay with Eulenfeld's concierge. It even seemed Frau Wöss had been called on earlier by one of Vienna's Finest. (It was really only Hedi Loiskandl, though, as we have managed to find out; she had approached the Wöss-Hawelka contingent in the Café Franz Josef Station, where the men of both families like to play cards, as Dolly Storch had observed. But in the end, Hedi was enough for the purpose.) So then everything had likewise proceeded quickly here at Editha's. Only those large wardrobes in the next room were given more thorough scrutiny. (Two minute-long searches of premises, one right after the other, with totally negative results in both cases, had probably contributed to changing the examining officers' picture of the situation. Said officers were not regaled with all that much of the twin-sister phenomenon: the captain—conducting himself with great dignity and impeccable bearing during all these proceedings—did everything in his power to prevent from coming to their sight this odd game on nature's part by shunting Mimi first to the kitchen and then to the bathroom; all the rooms were examined without exception. There can be no doubt, however, that Frau Wöss would have told the police all about the twins; ever since Editha's return in August, after all, they'd constituted the chief topic of general conversation with Frau Hawelka, with whom Frau Wöss was on friendly terms.) What the captain found most amusing about the elaborate formalities of the process, almost ceremonially baroque, was something he very naturally did not pass along: it was the matter-of-fact, cool-handed way Oki Leucht, turning his little car around, immediately betook himself from the scene of the action, along with the materials he'd procured—from Scheichsbeutel, at the legally fixed price and therefore entirely without risk, through the agency of two hotel managers—for Editha. Scheichsbeutel had merely nodded his hard head. He had taken to providing such favors without any questions asked or advantage to himself: smoothly, promptly, punctually. Leucht had meanwhile taken it as a given that he should not immediately pull in front of Editha's building without further ado but would be better off stopping on a side street and reconnoitering. So it was then that he saw the two gumshoes in civilian clothes—not eluding recognition as ones of their type by experienced observers—walking in the company of a uniformed officer toward the street door (which Thea Rokitzer had just before exited, though that interested Herr Leucht much less). The uniformed policeman might have just happened to be walking partway with his nonuniformed colleagues; he did not turn up at Editha's apartment, anyway, although the sight of him had been enough to put Oki Leucht on a more heightened alert. Scheichsbeutel supposedly did no more than shake his head afterward and return the goods to their source. Dilettante that she was, Editha didn't lose money.

Now the captain came to the aftermath.

There was one phenomenon here that could not have escaped the attention of the police officers: the striking amount of correspondence piled up everywhere, but in what could be called two different general conditions: on Mimi's secretary (she was incapable of ever parting with any missive she'd ever received, even the silliest and most trivial little note), as methodically ordered as if by a librarian, filling all the open small compartments in packets and rows, even with protruding little slips of paper at intervals, ones that recorded the month in which they were received (mostly from Scarlez and Editha); in the small bedroom, by contrast, on Editha's stand with its glass surface next to the bed, a much less encompassing conglomeration of letters and cards, jumbled up with boxes of stationery and books, all of it in a chaotic disarray that seemed to be just a random heap. After the police officers had talked briefly and quietly among themselves, they explained to Frau Schlinger that they were unfortunately duty bound to impound temporarily these numerous postal materials for purposes of careful perusal. All the letters were counted on the spot. Editha received an official receipt which would authorize her to retrieve her letters if and as soon as their irrelevance to the ongoing investigation could be ascertained. The whole kit and caboodle then vanished into two black attaché cases, to the captain's no small delight, as he now flatly confessed.

Melzer looked over for a quick moment at Mimi's little white secretary—its compartments dark in their emptiness, though they had also appeared very organized when chock-full—but then directed his glance back to Editha and, paying ever closer attention during the last part of Eulenfeld's account, his intense concentration, now entirely unconcealed, increasingly trained on Editha like a light growing brighter and brighter as it shone on her. The effect on Editha soon became overpowering. She kept looking down at the floor as if under extreme strain. While the captain was telling them in a casual way about how he'd been given to understand at the police station, where he'd called earlier, that as far as it looked now Frau Schlinger would probably be able to retrieve her letters quite soon and that there didn't seem to be anything more to this whole affair—in addition to which a notice had appeared in all the papers today (Melzer knew nothing about it) to the effect that an official investigation had tracked down the murky source of the smuggled cigarettes, the notice being what had prompted Eulenfeld to go and make inquiries—while the captain held forth with this reassuring addendum to his main story, Melzer reached into his jacket pocket and laid the purloined papers and forms onto the tea table in front of Editha.

As she bent far down over these items, her head hanging low as well, Editha's face took on a geometry we can observe in certain kinds of glass that are sometimes made into small objects for everyday use, such as salt shakers and the like—it was crisscrossed with innumerable tiny cracks. She was being torn between extreme contradictions, feeling abrupt relief at being rescued, but at the same time, and in diametrical opposition, anguish at such a glaring exposure of behavior as humiliating as it was ridiculous—this conflict left her no other option than to capitulate fully on the spot, her innate and ready impudence for once unable to suggest and put into motion any other. She sat up, looked into space, and as she started crying, laid her hand onto Melzer's knee and kept saying: "Melzer, Melzer." A hard gray knot of anxiety dissolved inside her. But through all the chambers of her being there now came sweeping the forceful gale of her full disgrace, banging and slamming all the doors. In her present windswept condition there no doubt resided significant possibilities for development and renewal, but it cannot be our task to pursue them here; that touches more directly on Herr Wedderkopp's sphere of influence, and he was beyond all question endowed with the gift of ignoring Editha's little ways and wiles, pressing her to the wall instead, and in a manner very agreeable to his partner, nay, very much yearned for by her. So have at it! Full steam ahead! Let's get it moving! Wedderkopp *ante portas*. It would surely be of benefit to him, too, that he would be entering into this new phase and starting afresh with an Editha Schlinger-Pastré whose rambunctious personality had been undeniably chastened or at least toned down. And Gustav would in fact soon achieve a breakthrough here in Vienna. The first contact is always important. If only Gustav could have bowled over our Editha in 1911! To be sure, however, Wedderkopp could not have been as crucially helpful to her then as René, that forlorn scamp, when it came to mountain climbing, because he wasn't from an Alpine region (all told, though, his marriage with Editha turned out to be splendidly happy and blessed with many children).

Meanwhile, she was crying. Casting a glance over at Mimi, Melzer realized that she had withdrawn far away and once and for all from this whole state of affairs, which had been obliterated without trace when she spoke her final words, totally free now, to Melzer. She was sitting comfortably in her chair, which she'd pulled back from the tea table in such a way that the broad window with its distant view stood just behind her head. During these moments, Melzer took his leave of her, and the parting was hard. (*Oh ténébreux et troubles, nos cœurs humains, même les plus sincères!*) It was as if her face were fleeing into the background, as if it were dissolving in it, as if were by that means going home whence it had come. It was certain that this face would never appear again. Unique it surely was—did I at all do justice to it, he asked himself (if only hazily). And for the space of a breath he was grazed by the same feeling from fifteen years before, after he'd taken leave of Mary and was sitting in the train with Major Laska—the feeling of an irreplaceable loss.

Even at that, however, this voice was growing fainter. What was astonishing to him now was his certain knowledge that Mimi—whom he'd never seen in tears—would have cried in an entirely different way, in all likelihood like rain gently falling on a mild spring day, her eyes open, tears flowing softly without gulping and gasping and baby-like wrinkling and crinkling of her face. That is assuredly how she would have cried. Not like Editha, who was crying in fits and starts, the way a chicken drinks in sips and darts. Her way of crying made an open disgrace of her selfhood in its utter emptiness and insignificance, as it were. The profound difference between the two sisters could never have been made more overtly manifest than now, in these few fleeting moments, Melzer felt; and that was how he knew it was all over.

The captain had suddenly picked up the papers lying in front of Editha; she hadn't managed to snatch at them and keep them in her grasp. Editha dropped back into her chair. Out came Eulenfeld's monocle. Full-strength grunt. Melzer watched him very carefully. What the major had been assuming all the while was now confirmed before his eyes: it was that Eulenfeld was looking for the very first time at something totally new to him (never mind that Editha had left these papers lying around on the stand with the glass shelves, among all the rest of the clutter, for a full eighteen days!—was the logical conclusion that the captain's dealings with the twins had grown less intimate or frequent?).

Editha didn't look at Eulenfeld. She looked off to the side, at a spot on the floor near her chair.

The captain's facial expression had meanwhile changed in such a way as to cause Melzer apprehension about a volcanic outburst of bellowing.

"Eulenfeld," he said with determination, "I need to ask you a favor."

"What might it be?" Eulenfeld asked in a totally formal tone: this was the only thing the captain could present to the outside world at the moment, so to speak, for he was keeping himself under control with the most concentrated effort of his entire person; this was evident to Melzer.

"I'm asking you to promise me that this business with these wretched papers" (what if Kroissenbrunner had heard that!) "will not lead you to continue castigating or upbraiding Frau Editha in any way. Not after I'm gone from here, either."

"That will be difficult for me," the captain said loudly and emphatically. "For we are confronted here, at the point at which we are now stopped, with nothing less than the birth of mean-spiritedness out of simplemindedness. Contemplation of this appalling sight urges me to be more vigilant henceforth regarding my own self, however, instead of now lending expression to my contempt. And in this consideration let your favor be granted. You have my word of honor as an officer and a gentleman that Editha will hear not a whisper of rebuke from me in this matter, as little in future as at present."

He stretched his right arm across the table, and he and the major shook hands.

"Melzer, Melzer," whimpered Editha.

Mimi Scarlez remained sitting there all this while as if she were a mere backdrop. She muttered nothing, she uttered nothing. She did not look at the papers, now lying beside Eulenfeld's teacup. She was completely absent, departed, far away on her journey. She might have been riding in a boat with Scarlez and feeding the white and black swans that swam all around. To the rear, among the densely arching treetops, there stood a blue-gray pavilion with an onion roof on tall, thin columns.

A mighty red wave surged up high inside Melzer. Only now did he begin to apprehend how deliverance and protection had come surging in on him from every side. In that red, Thea and Mary fused for some moments as if into a single undivided person.

"It would appear, dear lady," he said to Editha, who now sat up as he addressed her, "that you have no adequate conception of the unrelentingly rigorous attitude governing certain official dealings in our country. Had I chanced to encounter the police here on September twenty-first, for example, and thus been confronted with the need to present identification, then my very presence on the scene would in itself and beyond all doubt have entailed serious consequences in light of the position I occupy; this is to say nothing about what would have ensued had the police found the paperwork originating from my department and subsequently pilfered by you. My lack of any involvement in this whole affair would certainly have emerged in full clarity during the course of further investigation, but most assuredly not without my having been suspended from my post beforehand and undergoing a disciplinary hearing (not to mention further questioning by the police and possibly by the judicial authorities as well), any one element of which would have meant for me, under the special circumstances of my life at present, a calamity of almost immeasurable proportions."

"Precluded only thanks to action on the part of Thea Rokitzer, it would seem," said the captain, "inasmuch as the said Thea filched the whole accursed lot from Editha's hereunto appertaining bedroom next door on the twenty-first of the month gone by, about five thirty-five in the afternoon. That is how the matter presents itself to me through a simple process of logical deduction."

"And you're correct," said Melzer.

"It would appear that full knowledge of the duplicate individuals now sitting here was imparted to you by a subsequent and hereunto appertaining preliminary situation report tendered by Thea Rokitzer and that you were accordingly surprised not a whit today."

"All your surmises are accurate," noted Melzer.

"As is, unfortunately, the lesson to be derived therefrom, which is that without adequate supervision, scrutiny, and surveillance, duplicitous and duplicate specimens of their ilk will ceaselessly continue to venture upon ever new and ever hair-raising foolishness, world without end. I'm giving consideration, incidentally, to freeing myself in the near future of such duties, in the fulfillment of which, I readily concede, I have fallen markedly short. In addition, attempts to push this old hussar off to the side within the past few weeks, and for that matter even to give him, on repeated occasions, the hereunto appertaining heave-ho, have met with success, as you see." Full-strength grunt. Then he fell silent. Melzer turned to Editha once more.

"As for yourself, dear lady, I implore you from the bottom of my heart for your own sake to keep clear of such trickery once and for all. One has to be ignoble to bring it off, and you are far from being that! But precisely for that reason—fancy your letting the corpora delicti simply lie around for weeks on your desk!—this business would by no means have allowed you to walk away without serious consequences as well."

"I promise you, major," said Editha bowing; she looked at him and her hand reached out falteringly for his.

"All right! Over and done!" cried Eulenfeld. "Danger past and gone! Wedderkopp *ante portas*. In the immediate future, you know, Melzer, old boy, the human entity in question here will once more be blushing under the bridal veil. Yoked with one named Gustav. Gustav Wedderkopp from Wiesbaden."

Melzer had briefly but firmly taken hold of Editha's hand. "Please accept my best wishes, dear lady," he said, and then, "completely and with all my heart" (she had almost inaudibly whispered her question as to whether he forgave her). Now he picked up the papers from the tea table and stood up. "These need to be destroyed," he said, walking over to the stove. Mimi at once handed him a small silver cigarette lighter. At the last moment Melzer pulled out of the pile the one item his office assistant Kroissenbrunner had so sorely missed: he intended to give it back with a casual comment about how he had accidentally put it into his attaché case at the time. That's where he deposited it

PART FOUR · 819

now. The whole stack of paper started burning in the empty stove; the flames leapt up, at moments glowing white like all the brightness here, as though it were striving to move outward, where everything lay glowing in a similar shine. The others had stood up too, and were standing around the stove, whose mouth was now black and empty again; Mimi plied the poker a little, making sure the papers were completely reduced to ash. Melzer stepped back.

After the mouth of the stove had been closed, the others changed places too, restoring unawares the same order as at the beginning, when the major had come through the hidden door: Editha to the left and Mimi to the right of the broad window, the captain off to the side. No one spoke. After all that had just occurred they had gained enough freedom to be able to accept the expanding silence and to keep the emptiness complete, like a serving tray for whatever might arise. The silence wasn't burdensome or thick. It was more thin and alert instead. It was connected to the silence outside, on the slopes, on the edges of the forest, along which the trees and bushes were slowly shedding their first leaves and letting them sway to the ground. It was autumn. Autumn (on this Friday, October 2) in the room here as well, with its white double doors and the panels over them with grapevines and angels. Melzer's glance kept alternating between the two women. Finally he spoke and said:

"You were one and now you are two. With me, matters are almost exactly the opposite. So things have held together."

He stepped closer and said goodbye, first to Editha, then to Mimi, whose hand he held onto for a moment after he'd kissed it. Then he turned to leave. His look now fell onto Eulenfeld, who was standing by the door between the two women, as identical as two pillars framing a gateway. Melzer stopped and spoke then to him, too.

"Eulenfeld, friend, I must tell you that I've been engaged to Fräulein Thea Rokitzer since September twenty-first."

No sound behind him. Touched, Eulenfeld stepped toward the major. "The best news I could hear, Melzer. My good Melzer. This crown yours. This wreath yours. Will we be seeing you again?" He shook Melzer's hand. "Not very soon," Melzer said as he was leaving and after he had bowed to the two uncanny ladies once again. They were standing (in their white piqué dresses) as motionless as wax figures in the middle of the room, which now, seen from the threshold of the entry, looked extremely bright, like an operating room.

Then the apartment door clicked shut and Melzer went down the empty stairs.

Even before he'd reached the halfway point, the bright, orderly stairwell seemed to him to turn gray for a moment; then inside himself everything was suddenly engulfed in darkness, as if massive amounts of black ink had been spilled. A single detail, far off in the distance amid all the goings-on just past, and occupying only a point in space like the head of a pin, now began looming larger and larger and then burst open, in doing so unexpectedly taking on a name and a shape: among the letters to Mimi sequestered by the police there would have to be, or at least almost certainly would have to be, the note he had handed to Thea on the street in July, the one in which he had promised to provide Frau Scarlez—who he thought at the time was Editha Schlinger—with face-to-face information "concerning the procurement of tobacco products in wholesale quantities." His words flashed before him like a bolt of lightning from nearly three months earlier. He wanted—he badly wanted—to stop, go back, and ask about it directly. He kept going down the stairs, though, and was soon on the street. As the day began coming to an end, it now dropped upon him like a heavy burden. It pressed down, it lay still, it weighed oppressively.

Along the edges and the outer ring of the place where the blow had landed, there commenced a murmuring sound made by gently flooding, cleansing, eroding springs in search of new pathways, streams, and sources whose water had remained in abeyance for only a short moment, just as a prattling jet of water in a fountain will stop flowing into the basin for a few seconds if there's an earthquake.

They swirled around the object that had suddenly become a rock-solid entity born of a threat to Melzer's identity, attempting to make it emerge in greater detail, to heighten its contours, to penetrate into its hard, smooth structure and create rivulets or grooves. The fissures opened ever faster. But the sum total of the weight now breaking up remained the same, which was the exact point Melzer had to acknowl-edge while continuing to walk on and reaching the station square, all the while in his thoughts feeling around the place where the blow had struck until the following went through his mind: he could go and confide this entire matter (but how much of it?!) to his superior, the Hofrat, which would mean not being faced with grave consequences. That last thought had a relieving effect for only about half a breath, however. A deeper distrust crept up on our major as a cold undercurrent does on a swimmer: were the deliverance and protection, so abundantly proffered from every side as if through doors abruptly flung open, new doors in walls unbroken and seamless up to now, all of it set in motion and making its way toward him—was all of this only some elaborate mechanism (he even thought now of Stangeler, whom he'd otherwise completely forgotten, who, by stopping in the park, had made him, Melzer, come to a stop too!), some elaborate mechanism designed to steer him, Melzer, to this one point, where the jaws of fateful decision gaped wide? At the same time, however, he felt that what was sticking in him now like a missile, like the shaft of an arrow protruding from him and hampering his movements, in no way rescinded or canceled out anything that had happened, or rather *hadn't* happened, that noth-ing was being mitigated or annulled through the safeguard of circum-stances understandable as separate, individual items but incomprehensible in their total effect. He was suddenly assailed by disgust with himself, with his own anxiety, his near panic; this disgust shook his attitude back into right shape and tore through the cobwebs of petty apprehen-sion over picayune concerns.

Now he was supposed to stop by Thea's parents' apartment to pick her up for one of their dates in the park; at this point, though, the arrow still lodged in him, as it were, prevented him from following up. So when he found himself standing by a public telephone booth after crossing the square, he stepped into it immediately so he could ask Thea if she would please come and meet him right away in the grounds of the Palais Liechtenstein.

Even before he heard her voice in the receiver, Melzer knew he was going to tell her everything; as they sat on a bench in the park, he would tell her not only what had happened at Frau Schlinger's—she was awaiting his report with eager curiosity, not just her own but Paula Pichler's too—but also all the latest developments, including this last slight but painful snag he was caught on now; she should know all about it anyway, because she was destined to live with him (this thought was not without its harsh clarity). Immediately before the intimate sound of Thea's voice reached his ear, two feelings leapt up inside Melzer like crossed searchlights: he sensed for the first time that he had a mainstay in her, one he could feel and touch and hold onto. The second feeling was hope: no hairsplitting or worldly wisdom could touch it.

Time enough for that later; meanwhile, they were sitting together. Thea realized immediately from Melzer's features that something new had happened. She was holding his left hand in her right, still with all due propriety but more firmly than usual. He was once more able to tell the story skillfully; one thing flowed briefly and clearly into another. And this easy saunter through language took all the weight off every point he raised; it was mainly this adeptness that brought Melzer even more peace in the depths of his heart than the chance just to "unburden himself" (to use an expression which means nothing other than the wish to set down casks growing too heavy). No, it was his ability to express matters in orderly sequence—not excluding his note of July 10 to Frau Schlinger—that relieved his mind.

The moment had now come for that handbag, that stupid oversized purse, finally to disgorge its deepest contents, the secret concealed in its remotest compartment on the side. Even as it was being opened, Melzer felt strangely relieved.

The little lamb turned as red as the flowers in the garden around her and, with her head facing away, handed him the note in question, slit open by Paula Pichler, using her nail scissors, along the Danube landing place quite some time before.

"I was so jealous," she said, but almost inaudibly.

Melzer took the sheet of paper out of the envelope and read what he'd written earlier, the dubious nature of which was now only too evident when considering the whole set of (literally) surrounding circumstances, especially what significance this quick note might have taken on in connection with the papers Thea had removed at (literally) the last minute from the glass stand in Editha's little room.

He held the note in his left hand, took her right, and merely said her name. Finally she turned to face him. Her eyelashes were wet with tears. She said his name too. Not "Melzer," to be sure, but his first name instead, which she'd of course known for a long while now.

So what did she say?

Sorry, but we don't know Melzer's first name.

That's right, the author does not know his character's first name, really and truly does not (any more than Melzer knew Thea's address when he wanted to write her a postcard on Saturday, August 29, at the landing place while having coffee outside). He was always just "Melzer." What did he need a first name for? That said, he certainly required one now, so that Thea Rokitzer could say it, so that this membrane of two or three syllables could swell and expand under the pressure of a whole second life trying to enter that space. She will say his name as no other human being will ever be able to say it, for she will flow into this name. In this way Melzer will finally receive his just and true name, the same one that's been on his baptismal certificate all this time but that the author doesn't know. This is how Melzer will now become a person, indeed fully human, for the first time. That is a great deal, and the way from a Bosnian trooper to a real human being is far. What else could come after this; what higher stakes are there; who would need a greater redemption? For us this man now ceases to be a character in a novel. He could accordingly become at best an author himself, the author of his life story, perhaps. But we've already taken care of that for him. You may go whenever you're ready! And you'll always be just Melzer to me. This is it, then, Melzer; so long!

They stayed sitting there in the park and now, released from pressure, everything floated off into all sorts of giddy, effervescent silliness, as the bubbles in an open bottle of soda water fizz and rise to the surface. What they did first was burn Melzer's note to Frau Schlinger; Thea held it by one corner, and the major set the lighter to it, finally dropping the bright flame onto the gravel in front of their bench, where it burned intensely in the last glow of evening, took on the shape of a heart for a moment (at least that's what our major imagined), and fell to ashes.

Melzer ground it to powder with his shoe. Mimi popped into his mind, for she had done the same with the poker earlier that afternoon, while outside the sun had been beating down strongly on the mountains.

Amid the rest of their innocent silliness they now entertained themselves with counting the days until the wedding (which had been set for a date much too far off, in the opinion of our major, reactivated in a whole new sense). Looking through Thea's little pocket calendar, they noticed that this very day, October 2, was the Feast of the Guardian Angels; we can hardly think ill of Melzer for believing he had found his very own one. He said that to her, too. Amid such charming but not exactly sharp-witted comments, they left the park as evening was obscuring the shrubbery, the gray was welling forth, and the streets, deepening in the twilight amid the first lights, swelled to greater sound. Melzer brought Thea to her front door.

He went to eat in his usual tavern-restaurant, his Beisel, remained sitting a long time, and drank some wine. He thought nothing. He managed not to think about any of the things we generally think about; in this very blankness, and of course without having an inkling of it, Melzer brought off the second substantial inner achievement in his life (after the first one in Liechtenstein Park) by realizing, though unawares, the corrupt nature—in its deepest essence in fact the immoral nature—of the language he had shared with two women, one dead and the other living. Now, however, after the clanking of the machinery had stopped and the clown doll was standing still, along with all the other carnival figures, his whole previous life stood before him like a fully rounded-off body, oval and self-enclosed, looking into an emptiness no longer filled with red but with the blue-violet of silent dawn and morning shadow; on this cushion reposed all that had been, from the Treskavica to Porzellan Gasse.

He left around half past nine. Headed to the Steps, of course, as if to the navel of a world from which he was in the process of parting: that was something else Melzer realized (and indeed the married couple would move to an apartment out in Döbling). Somewhat deliberately, with restrained footsteps, yes, even with reverence, he crossed Liechtenstein Strasse.

The Steps were almost deserted. The moon, again at its full today, was still rising behind the tall buildings on Pasteur Gasse, where the sky glowed in milky brightness. Above and behind him, however, as Melzer slowly made his approach to the pirouetting Steps, began climbing and looking up, he caught sight of individual stars shimmering softly. The night wasn't cool; indeed, the day's warmth seemed to be gathered under the bushes and wafting outward at the turns in the stairs as they swept into the terrain so dense with trees. Melzer came to a stop on the second ramp. He looked up, first at the small mansion to his right, rising over the treetops not in ocher gold now, to be sure, but more cutting into the night as a dark cube; now into the sky; and at the same time as if into himself, though not into his own hollow hand alone but into a larger hollow, a more expansive space instead. The few points of his fundamental life story that were now glistening inside it, he finally realized, had always been joined one to another somehow. Now, however, having risen, they were standing above his inner as well as his outer horizon, softly lustrous, a constellation that could be read, that took on shape, connected from star to star by fine silver spider threads.

That recent imbroglio with Melzer and the twins had placed the captain very much in the ascendant, especially with regard to Editha, against whom he had of late been practically in league with Mimi; Editha's appalling humiliation had started a downward slide and in effect marked a natural tipping point. What's more, Wedderkopp had recently been heard from again, and even more insistently this time. His breakthrough was imminent (absolutely no question that he was a Negrian!); he was heralding his arrival here in Vienna within a few days.

Because Eulenfeld was holding his strongest card, the trump, very close to his chest, he didn't play it until Friday, a few minutes after Melzer's final departure: a cable had been delivered to him from Enrique Scarlez (Eulenfeld had specifically requested that any message be delivered to his address). Whether it was that that the journey now fit conveniently into the South American cigar wholesaler's business arrangements or that he was at leisure and had a free hand, he too announced his arrival in the near future, naming the specific date of his departure, from which it was clear that they would have Scarlez in Vienna before the middle of November. He didn't seem to be afraid of the cold weather—or at least less of it than of the danger to Mimi's inheritance. The captain's telegram (he'd spent quite a tidy sum!) had in fact been as exhaustive as it was unambiguous.

Thusly and accordingly, the captain mustered the hereunto appertaining Pastré family, all its members included, for a high-stepping canter on Monday.

He drove the twins before him like two sacrificial nanny goats into the family home on Gusshaus Strasse after forcing Editha to telephone her parents and tell them she was coming to visit; then he set up his headquarters and battle station in a nearby café. He immediately dispatched Editha as the advance party and kept Mimi back for the time being as reserve staff. Editha had been provided with a sheet of paper on which was noted the telephone number of the post now being occupied. After contact with the enemy and initial outpost action—this was how the captain was referring to the gradual, gentle preparatory measures directed toward the older people before Mimi's appearance—a situation report was to help determine whether the chief action could proceed. Everything had been painstakingly organized, and the old waiter had also been informed that a telephone call to Baron von Eulenfeld was expected within no more than an hour. The advance guard moved out. Eulenfeld had no doubt of its success. Editha had been placed under pressure, after all—Weddenkopp at the gates, to say nothing of Scarlez. Moreover, the captain knew these elders of his quite well from many an exchange of letters.

So he remained duly calm for the time being and entered into closer execution of the particulars in the form of a four-story cognac. What the old reliable headwaiter had initially brought in response to the captain's order had been examined by the astonished guest through the monocle, removed from his eye and now used like a magnifying glass. And indeed, the vessel consisted of a tiny, thick-walled glass, in the remote depths of which all that glittered was indeed gold, but a tiny glint only, no more than would have fit into a thimble (in those days any guest who ordered cognac in a coffeehouse was thought to have come down with something). "Dear friend," the captain said, "it will be necessary to ply the multiplication tables here—by a minimum of four times, shall we say." "What does the gentleman mean?" asked the waiter with old-school ceremonious politeness. "Well," responded the captain affably, as he held up the relatively heavy but tiny glass, "it would be desirable to reverse the present proportion between glass and liquid. Be so good as to pour a quadruple quantity of the latter into the hereunto appertaining container, my good man, and then we'll see where we are." "Of course, Baron," said the waiter, now translating Eulenfeld's elaborate mode of expression into a phrase that meant business: "Four shots of cognac in one glass." He didn't shake his head until he'd turned the corner. What he brought back was stylistically debatable: one of those wider, shallower glasses in which cocktails are usually served but filled halfway with Eulenfeld's cordial. He gave a low-strength grunt. Mimi sat resignedly with her soft drink in front of her.

What she was imminently facing, the use to which they were putting her, floated toward her from the outside in only a vague, feeble way, even though she did by and large apprehend very well the need for taking the action now being set in motion. Even so, this whole matter and all of its mechanisms and processes struck her as a side issue. Her inner being was filled with a joy growing steadily greater at the impending arrival of her husband in the near future, after which she would fix her return journey—with him—to her real home, which is what it had long since become for her; and it was this that remained real, the one genuine, ripened fruit of this summer (and indeed, it was only in the following years that Mimi Scarlez would become to the fullest extent what is called a happy woman). Right here and now she cared nothing about being reconciled with her parents. She was simply being held in *durance vile* by Eulenfeld. And yet everything depended on what was coming, though she wasn't able to recognize that just then. Let us note at this juncture, however, that Mimi came to this realization later on.

Editha called after forty minutes; Mimi should come now.

The chief staff officer mustered the troop to execute the main maneuver (mild grunt). We could say that he provided it with an escort, for Eulenfeld not only went to the street door with Mimi but climbed the steps with her as well. Here in the stairwell, the hygienic scent of the penates' impeccable order had been carried to such an extreme that it assailed the nostrils: excruciating cleanliness. No tassels or festoons, everything sleek and smooth. Brass was twinkling in the sunbeams as if the metal had just been alloyed and manufactured for the first time: the full effect of every mounting and fixture along the stair landings came into its own only now. The same for the plaque on the door painted in high-gloss red brown: Pastré. Nothing else visible. Mimi had turned pale as she mounted upward toward the family guillotine. She'd managed through her dreams to keep distant and aloof, somewhere in the beyond, with Enrique, beyond the water; now, however, the demons of the house came howling and roaring in swarms toward her, all up and down the immaculate stairwell, squatted on her shoulders like monkeys, took her by the neck, and jabbered in her ears; there no longer existed any rainbow-colored salon with a view of the water, no little park in the Palermo district, not a trace of black and white swans, not one single line of Spanish verse being shaped by the mouth that is shaping it. Nothing but brass, excruciatingly clean, much more present and real by far than the whole colorful, surging background into which Mimi was only too willing to disappear. But first she had to get down to brass tacks. She was almost nauseated.

The captain pressed the doorbell without a word and immediately turned to go down the stairs. Descending slowly, he heard footsteps coming nearer, probably a chambermaid's—rapid, impersonal, undifferentiated, and seemingly indifferent—through what was apparently an extensive entry. The door opened as Eulenfeld was just at the turn of the stairs. White apron and cap—then something like a soft cry or exclamation (the twins had continued dressing identically even up to now). Now the door closed once more. Silence. The brass plaque gleamed: Pastré. And nothing else.

The captain went slowly down the stairs.

The decisive quality of this day for his life now emerged with absolute clarity. He needed to call a halt here; he needed to bring things to a close here. And it was time to take up something that had been lying on the ground for years, sunk halfway in mud that had bogged him down in the slow lane, and was now showing its snaky tracks. He left this building in a very different frame of mind from the one in which he had entered it, in general more upright and with the small of his back arched. He needed to reinforce this new posture here; he needed to stop disdaining and rejecting the outside help previously offered, since he now proposed to venture onto new ground in his way of living. He knew a Herr von Leiningen, who had once been a major in the Third Dragoon Regiment here. Among other tasks, this gentleman looked after a stable of horses that needed exercise; he was on the board of a large equestrian club, and in its stalls were housed some fine horse-flesh. Even as Eulenfeld was stepping onto the street, he was leaving behind this house, its stairs, the brass plaque, the domain of sterile penates, and above all, the Pastré twins themselves, much more quickly and conclusively than Mimi, say, had been able to escape all of that through her dreams and flee to her true home. The street now saw him as a free man in possession of his own energies, his own time, his own advancing years. It must have been getting on toward five o'clock (for purposes of providing military escort the captain had even taken the afternoon off from the office!). Probably nobody would still be present at the offices of the Campagne Equestrian Society. Nonetheless, Eulenfeld made his way toward the Ring Strasse by the opera. And found Herr von Leiningen right there on the spot.

Even before the maid was able to announce Mimi, Editha had rushed out to meet her sister in the foyer of the apartment; now she took tight hold of Mimi's wrist (not her hand) and dragged her along.

Walking through a small salon with a few genuine engravings in the late style of the French Revolution—no improper etchings to be seen here, though!—they stepped into a flight of four long rooms; Mimi still didn't notice that her father was sitting at the other end, as if framed by the double door. Editha seemed resolved on getting everything over and done with in a rush, taking advantage of what was apparently numbness on Mimi's part. As they drew closer, their mother came toward them. (She was beautiful: all the deep-set, dark, burnished beauty of the woman who had been Mademoiselle Meriot was now laid open to view like an ebony shrine, shining out once more as she came to meet the child who'd been restored to her.) It happened at the very moment when she caught sight of her father—now the actual manifestation of a very old man, which is what she had always felt him to be—while he was raising his arms, all of a tremble from this doubled apparition, though he stayed seated in his chair, it happened that his mouth fell wide open, silently, and wouldn't close; his chin had dropped, and he was incapable just then, for whatever reason, of activating his facial muscles and restoring his gaping and gawking look to normalcy.

Still the length of a large room away, Mimi balked; Editha realized why, but not the mother, who was coming toward them with outstretched arms. Still holding Mimi by the wrist, Editha could tell from this contact with Mimi's body that her sister might turn on her heel at any second and dash back through the flight of rooms, bolting headlong into a flight of her own, tearing everything here to pieces and forging a whole new chain of complications. That was what now lent Editha a burst of decisive, rapid energy. Holding Mimi's wrist in an iron grip the whole time, she gave her sister such a powerful shove in the back that the movement propelled her straight toward their father and past the wide-open but still empty arms of the mother; that push placed her directly in front of the armchair in which the old gentleman was sitting. There Mimi collapsed, crying piteously, for no other reason than exhaustion, but also because she'd been subjected to mistreatment so recently. Herr Pastré naturally interpreted his daughter's kneeling and weeping at his feet altogether differently (while his wife gently placed her hand under his chin and helped him close his mouth). Of course he blessed his prodigal daughter and tried to lift her up. The fact is, however, that by these actions he was actually bypassing these present moments, with their almost fortunate misunderstandings, and entering into genuine reality and its heartwood, just now still overlaid with the sapwood of the immediate moment and the network of nervous impulses; for her own part, Mimi would—much later on and having long since returned to Buenos Aires—catch up inside herself with this prostration before her father and thus in retrospect come to discern the meaning, one that was anything but demeaning, of a gesture she had executed out of utter emptiness, as it were. For the time being, though, she at least managed to stand back up and come to rest in her father's arms; then, finally, in those of her mother as well, who, because those arms had been empty for seventeen years, didn't end up considering the delay of a few minutes as amounting to much.

At six the following morning someone was leading a brown, lightweight Hungarian mare out of its stall in the Prater, not far from the tree-lined promenade called the Hauptallee. It wasn't exactly a thoroughbred, but its lines were good, its stance firm, and its hindquarters powerful. A good-looking animal, carefully groomed. There was an old hussar, too, and he looked quiet pleasant and charming in his civilian riding outfit. Eulenfeld laid his arm across the mare's withers and began whispering into its left ear things a person wouldn't understand but the horse certainly did; then Ilonka tossed her head high and whinnied with a bright sound into the sunny October morning. "Well now!" said the captain. Without using the stirrup he leapt up into the seat and came to rest in the saddle, fitting his feet into the stirrups only when he was ready to ride off.

"Melzer, my boy," he thought, "valiant infantryman brave and true, but what is that, *par comparaison*, against the gallant arts of horsemanship?"

Rising from the ground was the haze from fields and meadows; it was in its morning freshness now, but in the evening, oversaturated with all the scents the vegetation pours out by day, it can induce in us lonely longing. This early, however, everything lay as in a bracing, unseen smoke, but without mist or fog, gleaming in cleanliness and sharply etched, freshly washed in a dewy moisture whose delicate vapors bring out more strongly the aureole surrounding every object. The horse stepped off, and its confident pace was enough to tell Eulenfeld everything about Ilonka before he'd scarcely even tapped her flank. Now, on the long, straight bridle path, he and the mare came into full rapport; she snorted and began prancing with the shortest trot he could sit, drawing her hind legs in fully. With almost no marked quickening of her pace, the captain gave a signal for the mare to begin galloping, as though they were exercising in an indoor manège, and Ilonka picked up speed at once; it was easy to see that the man seated on this horse was a person in whom expert horsemanship was deep-seated. And the one seeing it was Herr von Leiningen himself. As they flew along yet faster, Eulenfeld sank down into the mare until they'd reached a delightful centaur-like fusion, as if her hindquarters were growing into his own body from below. Even at this early hour, an old white-haired gentleman, straight as a ramrod, was taking a walk along the promenade beside the bridle path. He planted his silver walking stick in the ground, followed horse and rider with his eyes, and nodded slightly.

Melzer, my boy, valiant infantryman. If a certain old hussar, a Captain of Horse, hadn't intercepted a certain letter, the infantry would now be in a scrape, considering all the bad luck it had been having (mild grunting sound). Now it's high time to start something else, though, specifically to enter into a closer affinity with the worthy Suetonio Tranquillo and said author's twelve first Roman emperors, *duodecim Caesaribus*. Those old Romans had a bee in their bonnet—about keeping it brief. Calling Sallust the greatest master of terseness, *subtilissimum magistrum brevitatis*; wrote us a biography of Horace that takes up all of two printed pages. Would've liked to know a smidgen more. But the Caesars are going to be translated the way they should be. Today, quitting time, is when we'll start. Listen up, Ilonka, you're quite a proud filly.

A German hussar, a Captain of Horse. A humanistic hussar. Bar set damn high. School satchel jam-packed.

The long, straight bridle path, continuing as far as the eye could see, kept drawing him on. The captain slowed to a trot. Ilonka stretched her legs under him and gave a soft grunt. "I can grunt too," he said, did it, and proceeded briskly along the rest of his way.

Don't we all? Don't they all? Even if on only one leg instead of four, which the captain had made provision for this morning. After all, he *is* the Master of Horse. Only the dead don't (*exceptis mortuis*). Dr. Negria went flying past us up Alserbach Strasse in an old rattletrap. The rest of *his* way we could have more or less have ended up predicting. Semski had simply retreated with a shake of his head at the time, whereupon Negria downright closed in on Frau Sandroch. Exactly that—considering the dry, bone-brittle material she was made of anyway—was what led to her complete undoing, however. She got caught between activistic millstones and came out on the other side as powder ground extremely fine (*poudre impalpable*). This is one of the few cases, by the way, in which every last bit of a woman was used up by a man, similar to those Russian-style cigarettes of which not even the most minute stump or butt is left (no *mégot*, as they say in Paris; no *Tschik*, to speak Viennese; no *Kippe*, as they call it in Berlin), so that someone looking to pick up such precious morsels finds nothing but sullenness on the sidewalk after stooping over the white mouthpieces. That was how it was with Frau Sandroch.

There was one respect in which the Negrianism of our major, despite his new status of reactivation manifested as of September 21, 1925, had not been able to effect a breakthrough, as has already been intimated: it was concerning the date of the wedding. If Melzer had had his way, they would have set out on the morning after Mary's accident, at the very crack of dawn, if not even earlier, with all due or undue haste, and would have kept ringing the bell at the rectory of the parish church in Lichtental without letup to roust out the pastor and make him post the banns that minute on the door of the Church of the Fourteen Holy Helpers, to use its full name. (What we saw on that day instead was Rokitzer betaking himself at a decent hour to the administrative headquarters of the Austrian Tobacco Administration, with Thea's picture next to his heart in his billfold—as well as deep inside that father's heart of his—and his visiting card in the same place.) Negrianism with the brakes on, then. Whether the Rokitzer parents thought there might be more to it (basically these are nothing but . . . Councillor Zihal, please—you're going to have the last word in this book as it is, so I'm asking you, don't make life any harder for me right now!)—long story short, we don't know. If so, the thread of any suspicion along those lines must have spun out thinner and thinner until it just broke off.

The wedding took place before winter set in, and on a very mild day at that. It was a noteworthy event for Lichtental. Fourteen carriages were standing in front of the church, down the aisle of which the bride walked on the arm of Councillor Zihal through the swelling surge of the organ as if through a heavy curtain parting before her; anyone seeing this picture would have had to realize, with a greater or lesser degree of conscious understanding, that well-nigh perfect aesthetic configurations can sometimes unexpectedly and as if on their own crystallize amid the hustle and bustle, the tumble and jumble of life; to be sure, they then dissolve and break apart just as quickly, though. Here, however, content and form, so often at odds, attained to rare unity, the setting assumed its right proportions, what was proper and fitting took on a glow; everything was located in its natural place and occupied it to the full—the young girl, innocent as a rose in the garden, the dignified gentleman at her side, gently propelled by centuries of a culture that had formed him and brought him to this point. Little Theresa Pichler carried the bride's train. It's rumored that while the bridal party was quickly putting itself to rights in front of the church, Sectional Councillor Geyrenhoff, who was in attendance, was unable to refrain from lightly pinching the trainbearer's cheek, which seems quite pardonable when considering the degree of sheer sweetness life can sometimes exhibit, to the point of being absolutely irresistible. The wedding ceremony also created one of those assemblages that allows us to view in the nave not only the couple now entering into union, but also, by surveying the congregation, to see which friends and acquaintances remain interconnected by some direct or indirect affiliation with the couple now being conjoined. Among others caught sight of, aside from Thea's parents and relatives, were Herr and Frau Gustav Wedderkopp (Wiesbaden), Herr and Frau Enrique Scarlez (Buenos Aires), Herr and Frau Alois Pichler (Vienna), Sectional Councillors Langl and Geyrenhoff—we've already made mention of the latter—retired Captain of Horse Baron von Eulenfeld, Herr Ernst von Marchetti, the former His Majesty the King of Poland (Vienna), a department chief with the rank of Hofrat from the general directorate of the Austrian Tobacco Administration whose name we don't know (Geyrenhoff knew him), and additionally Herr Kroissenbrunner, plus, last but not least, Fräulein Theresa Schachl. The Stangeler family was not represented; they were in mourning. The majority of those named here were also guests at a luncheon given later in the dining room of an eminent old hotel on the Mehlmarkt. A smaller group was observed on this occasion by none other than the Hofrat from Porzellan Gasse, who may have had an especially sharp eye for caucuses of this kind. It was a conventicle that forgathered in one of the smoking rooms after the wedding banquet and the speeches and that gained significance in retrospect for having unexpectedly taken up matters that pointed almost directly into the future; such groups will sometimes happen upon more meaningful topics, purposely or by chance, in the midst of talking about banalities, especially when being observed by people disposed to see such portents anyway. This conventicle consisted of three persons—Sectional Councillor Geyrenhoff, Civil Service Councillor Zihal, and Alois Pichler, master mechanic and foreman (in his chronicle, Geyrenhoff would later describe this gathering almost exactly as the Hofrat remembered and verified it). The three gentlemen held a very lively conversation, which they seemed to be enjoying immensely; Herr von Geyrenhoff did not address the civil service councillor by his official title, of course, but used the more companionable expression "Herr Kollege." The newlyweds joined the gathering later on, as did Frau Rosa Zihal and Frau Paula Pichler. The only person really missing was River Master Schachl, but if we're now going to sketch in the future here as well as the past (this circle of family and friends didn't seem at that time to be as cohesive and self-evident as it does today), then Thea Melzer's children were missing as well.

The bride and groom showed up slightly late for the luncheon, incidentally, after everyone was seated and had been waiting for a good while. After the ceremony, Melzer and Thea left in tuxedo and wedding gown—not headed to the photographer's, where newly married couples tend to go (and even if they'd gone to that neighbor of the tobacco-store proprietor, it wouldn't have meant anything to present company, because Fräulein Oplatek was a guest at the luncheon as well!), but directly to the hospital to visit Frau Mary. They'd been to see her quite often and had stayed for somewhat longer visits a few times. What they talked about on these occasions is something else we don't know. It also doesn't matter in the long run, though, whether or not the unconnected connection between Etelka Stangeler's demise on the one hand and Mary's accident in front of the station on the other, standing as close as they did side by side but yet not linked, ever ended up getting resolved in

Melzer's brain. It's hardly a matter for doubt, however, that in later dealings between the Melzers and Frau Mary all these matters were talked over and filled out in greater detail on both sides. Mary was not spared a certain amount of bitterness concerning the entirely pointless aspect of her hasty and disastrous rush away from home on September 21, only a few yards away from Stangeler's arrival, if one will. (It never did come out that before then he had been dallying by the bridge instead of rallying; events that occur with such minute exactness are never revisited with anything like that same exactness; the captain was undeniably right in his conversation with the twins.) This time the couple's visit with Frau Mary was only a brief one, naturally; in addition, it was very similar to the first call they had paid here; right after they entered Mary's room, Thea and Melzer went to her bedside and knelt down. Mary laid her hands on each of their heads, and Thea placed her bouquet on the blanket. They left quite soon after that. Mary closed her eyes. Her state of mind on that day was not good. Even so, she would later on recall with great precision some rather strange words that went through her head after Melzer and Thea had left. (She told this to Kajetan von S. years later.) As she was falling asleep, she thought: "So Melzer's beaten me in singles after all." But he had never been her tennis partner. Not in Ischl, either.

Many are of the opinion that matrimony will not only consolidate or solidify a love affair (albeit there had not been any such thing, at least not in the usual sense of the term, between Thea and Melzer) but will also relieve it by this means alone of any and all problems—at least in certain areas. At any rate, they expect that the couple will have put something behind them upon marrying. That may be true. But man and wife have placed a great deal more in front of them by tying the knot. The essential point remains that marriage can never create a solution but can only reconfigure the problem instead, to whose adjusted proportions the couple in question must now orient itself: that's something that could surely be said of René Stangeler and Grete Siebenschein, among others. Put differently: nothing that has even the remotest connection with that heaven-sent scalawag who appeared on the mantelpiece that time will ever solve or even sort out any problem, but will only ever lead the way deeper into it. So it is that the organic fluidity of our physical existence will always detour around schemes hatched by every conclusive, now-and-forever organizer or visionary, implementation-to-the-last-detail politico, whose ambitions would long since, well before the beginning of our own era, have brought the world to a standstill. Considering the points just laid out, it is in my humble opinion (at least in regard to circumstances presently under discussion) astonishing that so many better novels, when they end well, close with the relevant parties hitched. People seem to consider such a wrap-up an ending and not a beginning (of the novel, that is, or of "the ordeal," if we were to translate it into Paula Pichler's terms). The truth is, however, that such an ending furnishes nothing but an unusually good opportunity—a splendid one, for that matter—to reinstate emptiness by way of fulfillment, removal of suspense, and, if you like, by condign satisfaction of justice and fairness in some form; at any rate, that state of affairs promising the greatest happiness for all involved parties will be brought to fruition (silence in the carnival booth after the bull's-eye, when the twitching and the clattering of the dolls and puppets has stopped along with the squawking of the hurdy-gurdies and jukeboxes), the state of affairs making it possible to unfurl and stretch out behind our lives that restful undercoat required for us to make out anything clearly in the first place, providing us in turn, given this more nuanced view, with opportunities to forestall any further shenanigans or even to eliminate them in the spirit of Zihalism at its most highly developed; not, to be sure, by rigidly determining all matters either this way or that, like those implementation-to-the-last-detail politicos, but rather by just simply waiting for them to unfold, never seeking out that which can only seek us, never grasping what can only be added on, never trying to bludgeon things that leave on their own without dudgeon. Here, then, a legitimate reason becomes discernible for closing novels at the point of "happily ever after"—to leave our dear readers with the precious legacy of emptiness, even though it may last for only a brief, ideal moment, to leave them in their virginal state, as it were; and that is why the author will now slip away at this point and insist to the publisher that his manuscript is finished. Basically these are nothing but spiteful remarks.

With that, however, we're where we're supposed to be—not at

Melzer's wedding luncheon (after all, one can only be an awkward guest at such events), but in the garden of the Schachls' little house on October 7. It was the Feast of the Holy Rosary. This was the date on which the festive engagement party took place; and we're watching that charming little gondola, this wedding carriage on the merry-go-round in the Wurstlprater, Vienna's amusement park—the garden seems to us to be transformed into something like that—floating merrily with cheery music through the depth of the years, even soaring upward like a hot-air balloon into the October sky, in which there was standing a burnished gold like the gleam of wine. Here everything was at its peak of ripeness, and crystal sparkled here more brightly than in any exclusive store. Our civil service councillor lifted his glass and made a speech. He had at his command the solid underpinning and the grave momentum given to the language of the Royal and Imperial Finance Ministry as it had been brought to the fullness of its ripening by centuries of use in official manuals and publications. He commanded it, and it commanded him (as in a good marriage). Civil Service Councillor Julius Zihal had undertaken to discourse on a topic of no slight import, specifically to define the concept of happiness. He led up to his main rhetorical question and its rhetorical reply through a kind of reverse snowball system, meaning that he started with a waggish indirection, talking around the subject—pertinent quotations from Ferdinand Raimund's play *Der Verschwender* (*The Spendthrift*) and a few rather grumpy side comments delivered in a style we're abundantly familiar with—but ended up leaving all that aside. Finally the definition came rolling forth, round and right, like a billiard ball on the green felt. It was more than just a definition, in a certain sense, because it pointed very clearly to the one way in which an entire tribe of people with its peculiar characteristics can achieve happiness, the single means by which it can be secured. "Happiness does not come" (this was Zihal's concluding summary) "when you forget your stress, and that is something I do not profess; such a thing can only happen in an operetta. Any approach or attitude of that sort would signify nothing less than an omission of necessary evidence or would at least have to be regarded as such. No, happiness is much more likely to occupy the domain of a person the extent of whose own demands remains so far behind the decisions reaching said person from a higher quarter that a considerable residue of contentment naturally ensues." What else can we say? Isn't that the major to perfection?

AFTERWORD

"The Precious Legacy of Emptiness":
Heimito von Doderer's Anti-historical Art of the Novel

I

The true beginning of this novel does not come at the outset but rather after a good hundred and fifty pages. A young man named René Stangeler, the author's alter ego and the most intelligent character in the book, is roaming the woods near his parents' country house in summer. We're at the beginning of part two. Until now most readers have probably found the novel confusing more than anything else: A host of characters has appeared, some only possessing a last name, others designated by their first name, and still others only by their initials, according to no discernible system; we're caught in a thicket of flashbacks and flash-forwards, which seem neither particularly significant nor easy to follow. But then, suddenly, we are accompanying the young René into the woods.

Heimito von Doderer's *The Strudlhof Steps* occupies a paradoxical position in German literature: that of a classic, which, however, is not part of the canon. The novel's status is undisputed, but even the well-read often know little about it. A surprise awaits those who read it: Doderer is so much better than most other twentieth-century authors—and not only the German-speaking ones—that from the heights of his prose the reader regards many of them with amused bewilderment. He is as zany as Thomas Pynchon, he is an artist of the German language on a par with Thomas Mann, he is a psychologist like Arthur Schnitzler, his gift for metaphor rivals Nabokov's, and he is, in his own incomparable way, mad. His decisions remain unpredictable, and in light of his fiendishly intricate compositional technique, the reader is never quite sure whether his books offer wild chaos or artistry of the highest level.

René's walk in the woods—the moment when *The Strudlhof Steps* truly comes to life and after a long run-up finally begins—is one of the most perfect encounters with nature that German-language literature has produced. Unexpectedly, the dreamy boy is confronted with a gigantic grass snake:

> René felt every one of the snake's motions as if he himself were the one executing them, only turned inward, to the inside of him, as it were: encountering an obstacle—a branch or a rock—when crawling, the head hesitating while the long body remained in motion, bunching strongly in tighter coils behind it; the suddenly resumed forward slithering of the neck, now stretched out from the resulting cluster, which was resolving, flex by flex, into ever shallower curves; the continuous writhing and weaving of the gray body, which might have been well over three fingers thick at its widest part. Only now, as the snake went creeping past close to him, was its full powerfulness apparent to René.
>
> And he felt love for it.

Where there's a great serpent—Doderer doesn't avoid the biblical association—the fall into sin is, of course, not far off. And sin gives rise to knowledge:

> Whatever it was that stole over him and crept up on him here—the mountain forest glowing in the back of his thoughts the whole time—was accompanied by the deepest uneasiness. And all of a sudden it hit him, as though plummeting vertically into him, and as though it had been the remotest of all possibilities—that here, for the first time, he was feeling repugnance when looking at a snake. Perhaps because it was so large. But there the repugnance was, and he knew now—knew with pain, as with the sweet sorrow of parting—that it would never go away again.

Thus the woods of Lower Austria become a prehistoric wilderness, and the Arcadian beauty of nature is suddenly afflicted with the growth of a diffuse sexuality shadowed by disgust. At that very moment René encounters another alter ego of Doderer's, Sectional Councillor Geyrenhoff (the narrator of Doderer's novel *The Demons*), who describes the young man—who, after all, in another dimension, he himself is—in an unsparingly disparaging manner. Autofiction, then, but raised to the second power: "René's face struck me as unattractive, and I became clearly conscious of how brutality and gentleness were converging there with a strangely glutinous apathy, all at the same time."

As a writer, Doderer is a master of self-loathing—for good reasons to be elaborated below. This storyteller has understanding and sympathy for all his characters except for those that are masks of himself: "Our young friend was struggling," he proclaims of René in the woods, "toward a goal he wasn't all that numb to feel, either. But now, the question is, how shall we describe it? Was it the unity and integrity of his personhood, meaning the process of becoming a person and attendantly for the first time (we'll go ahead and risk saying it) truly becoming a human being, which is what a young troglodyte would have yearned for as he looked out from his gloomy cave, where all his talents and abilities must surely have been shackled in heavy chains?" Becoming a human being—the central concept in Doderer's mental universe. For Doderer no one is simply born a true human being; rather we become human only by casting off ideologies, false convictions, all forms of obsession, blindness, and passion. In the case of René, the process of becoming a thinking individual begins at that moment in the woods:

> Wasn't he essentially agonizing over ways to force disparate phenomena, circumstances, or internal and external spaces having no basis for comparison onto some common ground so they could be subjected after all to the magical power of comparison, the one power able to master objects through the ordering thread of memory, which would otherwise come apart all over again every time it's drawn on? Memory, then, remembrance—that's what it was about for René, and it didn't matter how young he was!

The chaos of life, then, which otherwise defies mastery, is to be grasped by "the ordering thread of memory." This is the path René takes from that point on: he becomes a chronicler of himself, setting him on the course of becoming a human being. Much later along the way, he will learn to tell the story of his own life, leading one day to the writing of the novel we are holding in our hands. All this remains implied. *The Strudlhof Steps* is not a self-creating book like Proust's *In Search of Lost Time*, which ends with its own composition, but in this passage the novel subtly demonstrates its own preconditions. This huge book about a group of people in Vienna during the period before and after the First World War interprets itself as resulting from the work of remembrance—as the product of an ordering look back into the jumbled contents of memory.

2

Doderer's own paths to becoming a human being were full of twists and turns. Born near Vienna in 1896, into a well-to-do bourgeois family, he was a soldier in the First World War, was taken prisoner by the Russians, and after the war lived as an unsuccessful writer in Vienna. In 1933 he joined the Nazi Party, which was banned in Austria at the time, doing so in part out of opportunism and the hope that under the Third Reich he would have the writing career that had so far eluded him, but also in part (hard to say which motivation is less inexcusable) out of genuine, deeply felt anti-Semitism. The years that followed brought great disenchantment. Doderer distanced himself from National Socialism—without, however, leaving the party—spoke in his diary of his "barbaric error," and became a writer of profound self-disgust: "My actual work consists, in all seriousness, not of prose or verse," he later wrote in his only autobiographical text, "but of recognizing my stupidity."

After the Second World War, due to his party membership, Doderer was initially required to perform labor service and banned from publishing. *The Strudlhof Steps*, written in the last years of the war, was impossible to publish under these circumstances. Only in 1951, with the help of Jewish writers like Hans Weigel and Hilde Spiel, could the book appear, and it proved a great success. From then on Doderer lived as a peculiar literary grand seigneur, gave sly interviews, delivered lectures to large audiences, and died—controversial, despised, highly honored, and showered with awards—in 1966.

As to whether or not Doderer ever reckoned with his political error, which was also a moral and intellectual lapse of the first order, the answer is complicated. He never apologized, nor did he write an auto-biography revealing how such a thing could happen. At a time when every artist is judged in moral terms, this makes him difficult to place: these days someone can be labeled a Nazi for various lapses, but Doderer was a Nazi in the proper meaning of the word, an admirer of Hitler and a card-carrying member of the Nazi Party.

Instead of a reckoning, he offers something else: starting in the 1940s, the motif of "becoming a human being" enters his work—again and again he tells of how people become entangled in senselessness and stupidity, how they make the stupidest mistakes, and how some of them, and not others, gradually extricate themselves from this thicket of their errors. At the same time, Doderer almost never writes in that way about the Third Reich (except in a single enigmatic story with the telling title "Under Black Stars"), and yet with his help it's possible to understand on a deeper level than in the work of many other authors how this world-shaking catastrophe of stupidity and cruelty could come to pass—a catastrophe that is indeed always present to him, though he doesn't speak about it.

The concepts of a second reality, of self-inflicted blindness, and of "becoming a human being," of release from obsession and error, lie at the heart of Doderer's novels and stories. *The Strudlhof Steps* is the long tale of the growing clarity within Lieutenant Melzer, tracing a young man's emergence from the good, stupid military way of life into a "civil-ian mentality" and intellectual freedom. In the end Melzer is even ca-pable of seizing his good fortune before it escapes him, of intervening in an accident to save the life of the victim, and of light-handedly tear-ing away the webs of intrigue that have been spun around him.

3

The Strudlhof Steps attempts nothing less than to reproduce the perpetual undulation of everyday life: People meet, part, meet again in different and yet always similar constellations, and throughout the novel it's less a matter of what happens during the meetings than of this movement itself, the unending round dance. Motifs are introduced and only taken up again hundreds of pages later; foreshadowed events transpire and flashbacks fill in narrative gaps only after a long time. Not until very late in the book do elements of an almost pulpy narrative mechanics come into play—an intrigue involving twins, a never-realized smuggling plan—all of which are so tangential that the reader is tempted to take them either as deliberate parody or as a mocking concession to a convention that Doderer didn't want to fully relinquish even if he actually disdained it.

In an essay, the writer Martin Mosebach compared the experience of reading Doderer to attending a party: Many things happen, you have numerous encounters, but afterward you can remember only a little, and in retrospect at once a great deal and nothing at all has occurred. In some respects, *The Strudlhof Steps* is a realistic novel. Perhaps nothing better has ever been written about Vienna; there are hundreds of downright overpowering descriptions of the city and its environs. At the same time, however, it's always summer here, always fine weather. The years pass, but this novel seems to take place in a timeless parallel universe where wars, crises, and catastrophes of history, just like rain clouds and storms, are registered only as a distant echo.

Behind all this, deeply embedded in the structure of the novel, is a theory of the insubstantiality of history. This becomes clearest in the downright disconcerting way *The Strudlhof Steps* leaps over the First World War, as if it had no meaning. For Doderer, between the old Austria of the Kaiser and the new republican Austria nothing seems to have changed—all the circumstances of life remain intact; the supposedly great historical caesura turns out to be sheer illusion. Doderer doesn't deny that war can be deadly, but he won't admit that it's also of consequence:

From 1914 to 1918, Melzer was in on the action just about wherever there was any action to be in on—Gorlice, Col di Lana, Flitsch-Tolmein . . . names never to be forgotten! Anyone living through a war, though, acquires again and again a sense, not of himself, but of everybody else. Inside the world of legally organized terror, the harvest is not gathered into the core of the individual person but is instead redistributed throughout the collective. That's why, incidentally, there's such a special fondness for storytelling in almost all soldiers.

Doderer must be taken literally: Whoever tells stories of the war (and that's almost everyone) has in his opinion not actually experienced it; indeed the essence of war defies experience as much as memory and remains as bloody as it is insubstantial—afterward, for those who are still here, life goes on as if nothing had happened. The true substance of life lies not in the drastic but in the everyday and the flux of little things. This idea recurs toward the end of the novel when René, now himself a former soldier and war veteran, must hurry to Budapest, where his sister Etelka has just committed suicide. René reports coolly on his visit to the hospital on the desolate outskirts of the city: "Then it started turning bleak and barren. Out on the outskirts. Tenements. Railroad switchyards. These are the grim, dreary parts of a city. You see them in wartime or if something happens to you."

With this brusque report, however, he does not intend to underscore the intolerability of the event—on the contrary, the worse an event is, the more it withdraws from experience, the more banal it becomes:

> [I]t was external. External the way war is external, or a burning village, the bellowing of close combat with bludgeons and bayonets, an epidemic of typhoid fever in Siberia. It was external. It was a horror, but the narrow confines of our conscious mind can grasp only a small fragment of it; and because it's external, purely external, there always remains a gap, a tiny bit of breathing room between us and the utmost that external reality can confront us with.

The horrible, according to Doderer, cannot be taken in by consciousness; it doesn't penetrate the psyche, which is why in this novel even the trauma of the front-line soldier returned from the trenches is only a further form of second reality, from which he can free himself through attention, thought, and inner clarity. Even this somewhat restorative attitude contributed considerably to the success of the novel in the 1950s—when Doderer wrote *The Strudlhof Steps* in inner retreat from the Third Reich, such denial of fate, drama, and historic greatness was at odds with all the fashionable tendencies; when the book appeared, however, it was precisely what the public wanted to hear: If the First World War had not been so important after all, then perhaps the Second World War wasn't either, and the crimes that they themselves had just committed were more a regrettable confusion than a rupture of civilization for all time.

On closer examination, however, the war has left a deeper mark on at least one main character of *The Strudlhof Steps* than he himself and perhaps even his author would like to acknowledge. The former lieutenant Melzer is repeatedly assailed by flashes of memory having to do with a fatherly friend, Major Laska—short scenes, isolated images, disturbing snapshots, which never cohere into a consistent whole; the interplay of trauma and repression has perhaps never been portrayed in a more concentrated and subtle way. Only late in the novel does it dawn on the reader that Laska bled to death in Melzer's arms. And must we not interpret that inner rigidity, that lack of flexibility and human openness from which Melzer can break free only by "becoming a human being," as the mental devastation of war?

4

The Strudlhof Steps takes place in two strictly separate social realms. On one side lies the grand bourgeois world of the Stangeler family, of Dr. Negria, Mary K., and the Pastré twins. On the other side is the petty bourgeois milieu of the married couples Schachl and Zihal, as well as Thea Rokitzer. Melzer stands between the milieus, and precisely because in the end he attaches himself not to the rich but to the petty bourgeois his narrative strand leads to an almost conventional happy ending, while the grand bourgeois strand runs a tragic course: René's relationship with his fiancée Grete fails in the most tormenting way, his father succumbs to dementia, and René's sister Etelka resorts to senseless suicide. Yet Doderer immediately feels inclined to distance himself from the idyll of the petty bourgeois engagement on the other side, as cheerfully and vibrantly as it is depicted: "Here, then, a legitimate reason becomes discernible for closing novels at the point of 'happily ever after'—to leave our dear readers with the precious legacy of emptiness, even though it may last for only a brief, ideal moment, to leave them in their virginal state, as it were; and that is why the author will now slip away at this point and insist to the publisher that his manuscript is finished."

Doderer mocks conventions of any kind without restraint—even the narrative conventions of his own work. If only due to his humor, which frequently veers into sheer anarchism, Doderer resists any unequivocal classification as a traditionalist. Very late in this novel that over long stretches is almost devoid of plot, there's suddenly a lot of action—but it's so convoluted and improbable that the reader can't escape the feeling that this is simply Doderer's way of making fun of the principle of action itself.

For he grows serious whenever nothing at all is happening. "The precious legacy of emptiness"—here, for once, Doderer may be taken literally. This emptiness is the truth behind the constant bustle of our lives spent in the nightmare of world history. Consciousness of the ahistorical truth of things, however, is something we must acquire—by working on ourselves, by discipline and attention, sometimes even by reading a literary work of art. Whether we speak of Zen or of *nunc stans*, which according to the medieval Scholastics is the actual truth behind the illusion of temporality, it amounts to the same thing: the movement of a story that is actually aiming at standstill—a novel about "the depth of the years" that in our memory assumes the form of a single endless summer day.

Whoever finds Heimito von Doderer—who by his own account sought to make art out of his stupidity—abhorrent as a human being would probably have met with Doderer's wholehearted approval; this writer is the opposite of a narcissist: he dislikes himself, and his imagination strikes the strangest sparks off his self-repudiation and his disgust with his own life. Whether Doderer ought to be called a representative of traditional narrative, the last figure of Viennese modernism, or one of the first practitioners of postmodern play can hardly be definitively decided. From any of these perspectives, however, *The Strudlhof Steps* stands out among German-language novels of the previous century as one of the most significant and at the same time strangest, one of the most imposingly elegant and at the same time maddest.

—DANIEL KEHLMANN
Translated by Ross Benjamin

TITLES IN SERIES

For a complete list of titles, visit www.nyrb.com.

GABRIEL GARCÍA MÁRQUEZ Clandestine in Chile: The Adventures of Miguel Littín

LEONARD GARDNER Fat City

WILLIAM H. GASS In the Heart of the Heart of the Country and Other Stories

WILLIAM H. GASS On Being Blue: A Philosophical Inquiry

THÉOPHILE GAUTIER My Fantoms

GE FEI The Invisibility Cloak

GE FEI Peach Blossom Paradise

JEAN GENET The Criminal Child: Selected Essays

JEAN GENET Prisoner of Love

ANDRÉ GIDE Marshlands

ÉLISABETH GILLE The Mirador: Dreamed Memories of Irène Némirovsky by Her Daughter

FRANÇOISE GILOT Life with Picasso

NATALIA GINZBURG Family *and* Borghesia

NATALIA GINZBURG Family Lexicon

NATALIA GINZBURG Valentino *and* Sagittarius

JEAN GIONO Hill

JEAN GIONO A King Alone

JEAN GIONO Melville: A Novel

JEAN GIONO The Open Road

JOHN GLASSCO Memoirs of Montparnasse

P.V. GLOB The Bog People: Iron-Age Man Preserved

ROBERT GLÜCK Margery Kempe

NIKOLAI GOGOL Dead Souls

EDMOND AND JULES DE GONCOURT Pages from the Goncourt Journals

ALICE GOODMAN History Is Our Mother: Three Libretti

PAUL GOODMAN Growing Up Absurd: Problems of Youth in the Organized Society

EDWARD GOREY (EDITOR) The Haunted Looking Glass

JEREMIAS GOTTHELF The Black Spider

JULIEN GRACQ Balcony in the Forest

A.C. GRAHAM Poems of the Late T'ang

HENRY GREEN Back

HENRY GREEN Blindness

HENRY GREEN Caught

HENRY GREEN Doting

HENRY GREEN Living

HENRY GREEN Loving

HENRY GREEN Nothing

HENRY GREEN Party Going

HENRY GREEN Surviving

WILLIAM LINDSAY GRESHAM Nightmare Alley

HANS HERBERT GRIMM Schlump

EMMETT GROGAN Ringolevio: A Life Played for Keeps

VASILY GROSSMAN An Armenian Sketchbook

VASILY GROSSMAN Everything Flows

VASILY GROSSMAN Life and Fate

VASILY GROSSMAN The Road

VASILY GROSSMAN Stalingrad

LOUIS GUILLOUX Blood Dark

OAKLEY HALL Warlock

PATRICK HAMILTON The Slaves of Solitude

PATRICK HAMILTON Twenty Thousand Streets Under the Sky

PETER HANDKE Short Letter, Long Farewell

PETER HANDKE Slow Homecoming